Free Included: Get the PDF and EPUB editions of this book NOW as well - included in your purchase of this title.

Read your book on any tablet, eReader, desktop, laptop or smartphone simultaneous - **Get it NOW.**

How?

Simply send an email with a blank subject and empty content to:

MORE@EMEREO.NET

Follow the easy directions in the reply email and you will have access to your title in EPUB and PDF format to read on any tablet, eReader, desktop, laptop or smartphone simultaneous - Get it NOW.

Note: Images of the original pages are available through /American Libraries. See /details/systemidwifer00rigb

Lea & Blanchard have lately published.

NEW REMEDIES,
The Method of Preparing and Administering them;
THEIR EFFECTS
UPON THE
HEALTHY AND DISEASED ECONOMY, &c. &c.
BY ROBLEY DUNGLISON, M. D.
Professor of the Institutes of Medicine and Materia Medica in
Jefferson Medical College of Philadelphia; Attending
Physician to the Philadelphia Hospital, &c.

THIRD EDITION BROUGHT UP TO 1841.
IN ONE VOLUME.

A NEW EDITION
Completely Revised, with Numerous Additions and Improvements,
OF
DUNGLISON'S DICTIONARY
OF
MEDICAL SCIENCE AND LITERATURE:

CONTAINING

A concise account of the various Subjects and Terms, with a vocabulary of Synonymes in different languages, and formulæ for various officinal and empirical preparations, &c.

IN ONE ROYAL 8vo. VOLUME.

A Fourth Edition Improved and Modified, of
DUNGLISON'S
HUMAN PHYSIOLOGY:
ILLUSTRATED WITH NUMEROUS ENGRAVINGS.
IN TWO VOLUMES, OCTAVO.
Brought up to the present day.

A PRACTICAL TREATISE
ON THE
HUMAN TEETH:

Showing the causes of their destruction and the means of their preservation. By Wm. Robertson: with plates. First American, from the second London edition. In one volume.

OUTLINES
OF A
COURSE OF LECTURES, ON MEDICAL JURISPRUDENCE.
BY THOMAS STEWART TRAILL, M. D.
From the Second Edinburgh Edition,
WITH AMERICAN NOTES AND ADDITIONS.

ARNOTT'S ELEMENTS OF PHYSICS.
Complete in One Volume.

A new edition of Elements of Physics, or Natural Philosophy, general and medical, written for universal use, in plain or non-technical language, and containing New Disquisitions and Practical Suggestions, comprised in five parts: 1st. Somatology, Statics and Dynamics. 2d. Mechanics. 3d. Pneumatics, Hydraulics, and Acoustics. 4th. Heat and Light. 5th. Animal and Medical Physics. Complete in one volume. By Neil Arnott, M. D., of the Royal College of Physicians. A new edition, revised and corrected from the last English edition, with additions, by Isaac Hays, M. D.

THE NINTH BRIDGEWATER TREATISE.
A FRAGMENT,
BY
CHARLES BABBAGE, ESQ.
From the Second London Edition.
IN ONE VOLUME, 8vo.

A New Edition with Supplementary Notes, and Additional Plates; of BUCKLAND'S GEOLOGY AND MINERALOGY, considered with reference to Natural Theology; from the last London Edition with nearly one hundred Maps and Plates.

PROFESSOR GIBSON'S RAMBLES IN EUROPE, in 1839:—Containing Sketches of Prominent Surgeons, Physicians, Medical Schools, Hospitals, &c. &c. In One Volume.

AN ATLAS OF PLATES, illustrative of the Principles and Practice of Obstetric Medicine and Surgery, with descriptive Letter Press, by Francis H. Ramsbotham. This will form a large super royal volume, with over One Hundred lithographic plates—to be ready in November.

THE PRINCIPLES AND PRACTICE of MEDICINE, By Professor Dunglison in 2 vols. 8vo. This work will be ready the approaching fall.

THE LIBRARY OF PRACTICAL MEDICINE. Edited by Tweedie, is now complete in five volumes, royal octavo, handsomely bound in leather, to match. The different volumes may be had separate, bound in extra cloth.

A SYSTEM OF MIDWIFERY.

BY
EDWARD RIGBY, M. D.,
PHYSICIAN TO THE GENERAL LYING-IN HOSPITAL, LECTURER ON MIDWIFERY,
AT ST. BARTHOLOMEW'S HOSPITAL, ETC. ETC.

A

SYSTEM

OF

MIDWIFERY.

WITH NUMEROUS WOOD CUTS.

BY
EDWARD RIGBY, M. D.,
PHYSICIAN TO THE GENERAL LYING-IN HOSPITAL, LECTURER ON MIDWIFERY,
AT ST. BARTHOLOMEW'S HOSPITAL, ETC. ETC.

WITH NOTES AND ADDITIONAL ILLUSTRATIONS.

Philadelphia:
LEA & BLANCHARD.
1841.

GRIGGS & CO., PRINTERS.

[Pg 4]

THE EDITOR'S PREFACE.

This System of Midwifery, complete in itself, was published in London, as a part of Dr. Tweedie's "Library of Medicine." The first series of the Library, that on "Practical Medicine," recently completed, has been received with extraordinary favour on both sides of the Atlantic, and the character of the publication is fully sustained in the present contribution by Dr. Rigby, and will secure for it additional patronage.

The late Professor Dewees, into whose hands this volume was placed, a few weeks before his death, in returning it, expressed the most favourable opinion of its merits; and the judgment of such high authority renders it supererogatory to add a word farther of commendation.

It is only necessary for the editor to say that the production of the author is so complete as to have rendered his labour a light one. He has restricted himself mainly to such additions and references as he conceived would render the work more useful to American practitioners. The object of the publication being to present the most condensed view of each subject, he believed it to be inexpedient to depart from the plan by making extensive additions, and entering into the discussion of controversial points, most of which are of minor practical importance.

[Pg 5]

CONTENTS.

7

expulsion.—Malposition complicated with deformed pelvis or spasmodically contracted uterus.—Embryulcia.—The prolapsed arm not to be put back or amputated.—Presentation of the arm and head.—Presentation of the hand and feet.—Presentation of the head and feet.—Rupture of the uterus.—Usual seat of laceration.—Causes.—Premonitory symptoms.—Symptoms.—Treatment.—Gastrotomy.—Rupture in the early months of pregnancy, 264

[Pg 12]

[Pg 13]

A SYSTEM OF MIDWIFERY.

INTRODUCTION.

By the term Midwifery is understood the knowledge and art of treating a woman and her child during her pregnancy, labour, and the puerperal state. We employ it in this extended sense, because most systematic writers of later times have adopted this arrangement. The terms, Art des Accouchemens of the French, the Ostetricia, and Arte della Parteria, of the Italians and Spaniards, and the Geburtshülfe of the Germans, are restricted to the process of parturition, although they have been and continue to be, used in the same extended sense as that in which we propose to use the term Midwifery.

Although pregnancy and parturition, strictly speaking, are perfectly natural functions, yet they involve such a complication and variety of other processes, and also changes of such extent, that the whole system is rendered more or less subservient to them during the periods of their existence: hence, therefore, their number and variety must ever render them more or less liable to deviations and irregularities of action, which will necessarily be aggravated by the effects of civilized life, and in many instances are productive of derangement in the general economy of the system. Under such circumstances the irritability of the system increases at the expense of its strength and vigour, and not only increases its liability to these derangements, but diminishes its power of resisting their effects.

In order that we may render the nature and treatment of the changes and phenomena, which take place in the human system during the periods above alluded to, more intelligible, we shall take a short anatomico-physiological view of the structure, form, arrangement, and function of the parts and organs which are[Pg 14] more or less directly concerned in these important processes. This will embrace the subject of embryology, a department of physiological knowledge, which, though it has lately been much enriched by valuable discoveries, still affords a rich field of investigation and research.

The diagnosis and course of healthy pregnancy, and its various diseases, terminating with the subject of healthy parturition and its treatment will form the subject of the succeeding part.

Parturition properly speaking, will come under two separate heads eutocia and dystocia; the one signifying natural or favourable labour, the other, unnatural, faulty, or unfavourable labour.

The concluding part will contain a short account of some of the more important diseases which occur to the female during the first month after parturition.

[Pg 15]

PART I.

THE ANATOMY AND PHYSIOLOGY OF UTERO-GESTATION.

CHAPTER I.

THE PELVIS.

Ossa innominata.—Sacrum.—Coccyx.—Distinction between the male and female pelvis.—Diameters of the pelvis.—Pelvis before puberty.—Axes.—Inclination.

The Pelvis, as the frame-work which, in great measure, contains, supports, and protects, the complicated apparatus of the generative organs, first claims our attention; since an accurate knowledge of the form, size, and uses, of its different parts is indispensably necessary, not only to understand the situation of the viscera it contains, but also to form a correct view of the mechanism upon which the process of parturition depends.

This osseous canal or circular archway, consists essentially of three bones, the right and left os innominatum, which form the sides of the arch, with the sacrum between them, acting as a keystone, and supporting the whole weight of the trunk above.

Ossa innominata. The ossa innominata in early life consists of three distinct bones, the iliac or hip bones at the sides, the ischia or lower portion upon which we sit, and the ossa pubis which meet each other anteriorly to form the front part of the pelvis. In the adult these are consolidated into one bone, merely leaving irregular lines and ridges here and there to mark their previous existence.

These bones present several striking points of resemblance with those which belong to the upper extremities, viz. the scapula and clavicle; and in the early stages of development, this similarity is much more distinctly seen: it is remarkable, that although the ischia and ossa pubis are formed later than the ilia, yet they unite with each other much sooner than with the ilia, so that the two consolidated bones bear the same relation to the ilium which is separated from them, that the clavicle does to the scapula: many other points of resemblance between the bones of the shoulder and[Pg 16] pelvis might be noticed if necessary. (Meckel, Anat. vol. ii. p. 239.) The ossa innominata meet each other in front, forming the symphysis pubis, having layers of fibro-cartilage interposed between their extremities, and bound together by ligamentous fibres constituting the ligamentum arcuatum, or annulare ossium pubis, and by which a more rounded appearance is given to the pubic arch. They are united to the sacrum posteriorly, one on each side of it, forming the right and left sacro-iliac symphysis or synchondrosis; this differs in many respects from the symphysis pubis, the cartilaginous coverings of the opposing bones being much thinner, especially those of the ossa innominata; the surfaces are extremely uneven from the deep indentations which each bone presents at this part, locking, as it were, into each other, and thus contributing greatly to increase the firmness of the joint, which is also still farther strengthened by the support of powerful ligaments.

Between the ligamento-and cartilaginous layers which cover the surfaces of the bones at the pubic and sacro-iliac symphyses, a minute collection of synovial fluid may be detected, like that found in the fibro-cartilages between the vertebræ; it serves to lubricate their surfaces, and separates them more or less, thereby increasing the thickness of the intervening cartilaginous structure; and separating also the edges of the bones, to a certain extent, more especially at the symphysis pubis. (Portal, Anat. Méd.) These laminæ of intervening fibro-cartilage are thicker in the female than in the male, although of smaller extent; and this is still more remarkable during pregnancy, this ligamento-cartilaginous structure becoming now more cushiony and elastic, while in the latter months we can easily distinguish blood-vessels ramifying through it, which are branches of the pudic arteries and veins.

Sacrum. The sacrum, which forms the upper and posterior portion of the pelvis, contributes greatly to the general solidity of the whole bony circle. From its wedge-like shape, it is admirably adapted to support the entire weight of the trunk, and acts, as we have before observed, as a kind of keystone to the arch which is formed by the ossa innominata. It is of a triangular shape, being concave before and convex behind. In the fœtus it consists of five distinct pieces of bone separated by intervening layers of cartilage, like the vertebræ of the spinal column, and from their resemblance to those bones they have been called false vertebræ. These cartilages, after a time, gradually disappear; bony matter is deposited in their place; so that by the period of puberty the five sacral vertebræ become united into one solid bone, although they may be distinguished, until an advanced period of life, by the ridges which their edges form.

The upper surface of the sacrum, having to sustain the whole weight of the spinal column, is broad and flat, and corresponds to the lower surface of the last lumbar vertebra. Its anterior surface forms with that of the other mentioned bone a considerable angle,[Pg 17] which projects forwards and more or less downwards towards the symphysis pubis, and is called the promontory of the sacrum. Beneath this point, the sacrum takes a considerable sweep backwards as it descends, gradually advancing again forwards, as we approach its inferior extremity, forming an extensive concavity upon its anterior surface: this is termed the hollow of the sacrum.

Coccyx. The lower end is prolonged by a small bone, called Coccyx or os Coccygis, from its supposed resemblance to a cuckoo's beak. It usually consists of four, and sometimes (especially in women) of five portions; they are much smaller than the bones of the sacrum, and are very imperfect rudiments of vertebral formation; like these, they are at an early period little else than cartilage, and even when the bones are fully formed, they are united by intermediate cartilage, and thus retain so much mobility upon each other, as well as upon the lower end of the sacrum, as to admit of being forced backwards to the extent of a full inch, thus contributing greatly to increase the capacity of the outlet.

The sacrum not only serves to form the posterior parietes of the pelvis, but by the curve which its lower portion takes forwards, together with the coccyx, it gives a powerful support to the pelvic viscera.

When we take a general view of the bones which collectively form the pelvis, we find that it is evidently divided into two portions—an upper and a lower one. On the Continent these have been called the large and the small pelvis; in Britain we merely speak of the pelvis above or below the brim, the line of demarcation being the linea ilio-pectinea at the sides, the crista of the os pubis in front, and the promontory of the sacrum behind. The alæ of the ilia form a prominent feature in the upper pelvis, and not only afford an attachment for numerous muscles, but furnish a powerful and ample means of protection and support to the pelvic and lower abdominal viscera. In the female pelvis this is remarkably the case, the cavitas iliaca being well expanded and of greater extent than in the male, the crista of the ilium thrown more outwards; hence the distance between the antero-superior processes is much more considerable.

Distinction between the male and female pelvis. At the brim, the female pelvis presents several well-marked points of distinction from that of the male. The male pelvis has a contracted brim of a rounded or rather triangular form, with the promontory of the sacrum considerably projecting; whereas, that of the female is spacious, of an oval shape, and with a slightly prominent sacrum, thus affording more room for the passage of the child through the brim. The cavity of the male pelvis is deep, while in the female pelvis it is shallow, a circumstance which is very strikingly seen in comparing the length of the symphysis pubis in each, that of the male pelvis being nearly double the length of the female. This is an important point of difference as regards parturition, [Pg 18]because in a shallow pelvis, the extent of surface exposed to the pressure of the head will be much less than where it is deep, and hence the resistance to the passage of the child will be proportionably diminished: in confirmation of this, we find that tall women, in whom the pelvis is usually deep, do not, on the whole, bear children so easily as women of middling stature in whom the pelvis is more shallow. The capacious hollow of the sacrum in the female pelvis adds also greatly to the extent of its cavity, and peculiarly adapts it for parturition, the injurious pressure of the head upon the soft linings of the pelvis being thus prevented, and every facility afforded for its quick and easy transit through the cavity. This applies especially to the neck of the bladder, which would almost inevitably suffer in every labour, were it not for the ample hollow of the sacrum relieving the pressure of the head against the anterior portions of the pelvis. The bones of the female pelvis being more slender and delicately formed, the foramina ovalia and sacro-ischiatic notches are wider, and thus add still farther to the capacity of the cavity.

In no part of the pelvis is the difference between the sexes more strongly marked than at the outlet. The spacious and well-rounded arch of the pubes in the female of the slender rami, is a striking contrast to the contracted angular arch of the male pelvis; and the tuberosities of the ischium being much wider apart, the head is enabled to pass under the arch with greater facility, and thus still farther to relieve the anterior of the pelvis from its pressure. The length of the sacro-sciatic ligaments, and the mobility of the coccyx upon the sacrum, by which it can be forced backwards to the extent of an inch by the pressure of the head during labour, not merely serve to distinguish it from the male pelvis, but afford a beautiful instance of design and adaptation.

The greater width of the pubic arch in the female pelvis is seen by comparing its angle with that of the arch in the male pelvis. In the female it has been estimated to form an angle varying between 90° and 100°, whereas in the male it is not more than between 70° and 80°. (Osiander, Handbuch der Embindungs-kunst, cap. iv. p. 58.)

From the greater width of the female pelvis, the acetabula are farther apart, and the great trochanters of the thigh-bones more projecting; hence the greater motion of the hips in the female when she walks, which is still more visible when she runs, for the motion is communicated to the whole trunk, so that each shoulder is turned more or less forwards as the corresponding foot is advanced. The thigh-bones, which are so far apart at their upper extremities, approach each other at the knees, contributing to produce that unsteady gait which is peculiar to the sex. "The woman," says Mr. John Bell, "even of the most beautiful form, walks with a delicacy and feebleness which we come to acknowledge as a beauty in the weaker sex." (Bell's Anat. vol. i.)

[Pg 19]These characteristic marks of the female figure, upon which its beauty in great measure depends, are well seen in all great works of art, whether of sculpture or painting. "The ancients," as Mr. Abernethy has observed, "who had a clear and strong perception of whatever is beautiful or useful in the human figure, and who, perhaps, delicately exaggerated beauty to render it more striking, have represented Venus as measuring one-third more across the hips than the shoulders, whilst, in Apollo, they have reversed these measurements." (Physiological Lectures.)

Diameters of the pelvis. It is of the utmost importance to the obstetrician, that he should be thoroughly acquainted with the various dimensions of the female pelvis, for, without this, he can form no correct idea of the manner in which the presenting part of the child passes through its brim, cavity and outlet during labour; indeed, unless he be thoroughly versed in this necessary point of obstetric knowledge, he will remain in almost total ignorance of the whole mechanism of parturition, which must, in great measure, be looked upon as the basis of practical midwifery. The dimensions of the brim cavity and outlet of the pelvis may be given with sufficient correctness for all practical purposes, by measuring three of their diameters,—1. the straight, antero-posterior, or conjugate; 2. the transverse; and 3. the oblique. At the brim they are as follow:—the straight diameter, drawn from the middle of the promontorium sacri to the upper edge of the symphisis pubis, 4·3 inches; the transverse diameter, from the middle of the linea-ilio-pectinea of one ilium to that of the other, 5·4 inches; and the oblique diameter, from one sacro-iliac synchondrosis to the opposite acetabulum, 4·8 inches. The oblique diameters are called right and left, according to the sacro-iliac symphysis from which they are drawn.

Fig. 1. Fig. 2.

In the annexed representations of the superior and inferior aspects of the female pelvis are shown the three diameters of its brim and outlet; those of the former in fig. 1., and those of the latter in fig. 2. The same letters of reference are used in each figure to indicate the several diameters; thus a p refers to the antero-posterior, t t to the transverse, o o to the right oblique, and o' o' to the left oblique diameters.

In fig. 2. the coccyx is represented in situ.

In the cavity these dimensions vary more or less. The straight diameter, measured from the centre of the hollow of the sacrum to that of the symphysis pubis, is 4·8 inches; the transverse, from[Pg 20] the point corresponding to the lower margin of the acetabulum on one side to that of the other, 4·3; and the oblique, drawn from the centre of the free space formed by the sacro-ischiatic notch and ligaments on one side of the foramen ovale of the other, 5·2.

At the inferior aperture or outlet the alteration is still more remarkable. The straight diameter, from the point of the coccyx to the lower edge of the symphysis pubis, measures only 3·8 inches; but from the mobility of the coccyx enabling it to be pushed back during labour to the extent of a whole inch, it is capable of being extended to 4·8 inches. The transverse diameter from one tuberosity of the ischium to the other, measures 4·3 inches: and the oblique, from the middle of the lower edge of the sacro-sciatic ligament of one side, to the point of union between the ischium and descending ramus of the pubes on the other 4·8 inches.

Although these are the proportions of the brim cavity and outlet of the female pelvis in the skeleton state, their real dimensions during life, when the pelvis is thickly lined with muscular and other structures, are very different. The large masses of the psoas magnus and iliacus internus, besides other muscles of inferior size, contribute to alter materially the relations of the pelvic diameters to each other; hence we find that, so far from being the longest, the transverse diameter is one of the shortest, being little more than the antero-posterior. This holds good, especially during labour, because these muscles being thrown into powerful contraction, their bellies swell, and thus tend still farther to diminish its length. The oblique diameters are, in fact, the longest during life, because not only are the parietes of the pelvis at the brim covered by a very thin layer of soft tissues in these directions; but as the extremities of these diameters, in the cavity and outlet, correspond to free spaces which are merely filled up with soft yielding structure, it follows that their length can be somewhat increased when pressure is applied in these directions; the antero-posterior diameter of the outlet can alone be compared with the oblique diameters in this respect, and then only when the coccyx is forced backwards to its full extent by the pressure of the head.

Pelvis before puberty. The proportions of the adult female pelvis are no longer what they were during childhood; before the age of puberty they resemble those of the male pelvis, the brim being contracted and more or less triangular, and the antero-posterior diameter equalling or even exceeding the transverse. Indeed, at a still earlier period, it presents many points of resemblance even to the pelvis of animals; as, however, growth and development advance, and the various changes which constitute puberty take place, the transverse diameters of the brim, cavity,[Pg 21] and outlet increase at the expense of the antero-posterior, until at length, it has assumed the proper proportions of the adult female pelvis.

Axes. Of not less importance is it that the obstetrician should be thoroughly acquainted with the direction which the central line or axis of the entrance and outlet of the pelvis takes. The axis of the superior aperture has been considered to form with the horizon an angle varying between 50° and 60°; this was noticed long ago by Dr. Smellie: "when the body of a woman," says this valuable author, "is reclined backwards, or half sitting half lying, the brim of the pelvis is horizontal; and an imaginary straight line, descending from the navel, would pass through the middle of the cavity; but in the last month of pregnancy such a line must take its rise from the middle space between the navel and scrobiculus cordis in order to pass through the same point of the pelvis." (Treatise of Midwifery, book i. chap. i. sect. 2.)

Inclination of the pelvis. The angle which the axis of the superior aperture of the pelvis forms with the horizon, when a woman is in the upright posture, necessarily marks what has been called the inclination of her pelvis, and varies, of course, in proportion to the angle which the above mentioned axis forms. In a tall woman of slender figure, where the different curves of the spinal columns are slight, the inclination of the pelvis is much less than in a short thick set woman, where the spine is much more strongly curved. Where the inclination is slight, the hollow of the sacrum is generally small, and the vulva directed more forwards; where, on the other hand, the pelvis is much inclined, the

13

hollow of the sacrum is generally observed to be deep, and the vulva directed more or less backwards. The axis of the lower aperture or outlet appears to depend, in great measure, on the curve which the lower part of the sacrum takes downwards and forwards; but, as a general rule, we think it will be found to form, more or less, a right angle with the axis of the brim. The greater the angle which the axis of the brim forms with the horizon, the less will be that which the axis of the outlet forms, and vice versâ; or, in other words, the angle with the horizon which the axis of the one forms is inversely to that of the other.

The consideration of the various deviations, as to size and form, from the natural proportions which the female pelvis occasionally presents, belongs, more strictly speaking, to that species of faulty labour which arises from these conditions. We, therefore, refer to the fourth species of dystocia, viz. Dystocia Pelvica, where the different pelvic anormalities are described.

[Pg 22]

CHAPTER II.

FEMALE ORGANS OF GENERATION.

Internal and external.—Ovaria.—Ovum.—Corpus luteum.—Fallopian tubes.—Uterus.—Vagina.—Hymen.—Clitoris.—Nymphæ.—Labia.

The female organs of generation have been usually classed by the English authors under the two heads of internal and external; a similar arrangement has also been followed by the Continental writers, but with the advantage of using distinctive terms which are more expressive of their peculiar functions, viz. the formative and copulative organs. Under the first are included the ovaria, Fallopian tubes, and uterus: under the second, the vagina and external parts. We propose to give a short description of these in the unimpregnated state, and then to describe the changes which they present during pregnancy, labour, and the puerperal condition. In point of situation and arrangement they bear a considerable resemblance to the generative organs in the male, being situated at the lower portion of the trunk, and arranged in symmetrical order, so that they either occur in pairs, one on each side the median line of the body, or singly, being equally divided by it throughout their whole length. Although there is in many points considerable difference between the male and female organs, still there is sufficient resemblance to entitle them to be considered as being formed upon the same fundamental type, a resemblance which is seen still more strikingly in the early periods of foetal life. They differ essentially from all the other organs of the system, being in activity during a portion of a woman's life only, and then only at intervals.

Ovaria. The ovaries are situated in the upper part of the cavity of the pelvis, one on each side, near to the uterus, to which they are merely attached by a ligament (the ligamentum ovarii) which is a portion of that duplicature of the peritoneum which connects the uterus to the pelvis, and is known by the name of ligamentum latum, or broad ligament.

They are of an oval figure; their anterior and posterior surface is convex, the superior margin is also convex, while their lower edge is straight or somewhat concave: towards their inner and outer extremities they become thinner.

Their external surface in the virgin state is usually smooth, but in[Pg 23] advanced age they become uneven and shrivelled; when fully developed they are about an inch and a half in length: their greatest breadth, which is at that portion of the ovary which is farthest from the uterus, is half an inch; their thickness is somewhat less.

Convoluted arteries of the ovary,
crossing it in nearly parallel lines.
The ovaries are supplied with blood by the spermatic arteries, which are of course considerably shorter in the female; they pass between the two layers of the broad ligament to the ovarium, assuming there a beautifully convoluted arrangement, very similar to the convoluted arteries of the testis. These vessels traverse the ovary nearly in parallel lines, forming numerous minute twigs, which have an irregular knotty appearance from their tortuous

condition, and appear to be chiefly distributed to the Graafian vesicles. The external covering of the ovaries is formed by peritoneum, which here receives the name of Inducium; it envelopes the parenchymatous tissue of the gland called stroma, which is a dense laminar cellular tissue of a reddish colour; its external portion which is in contact with and firmly adherent to the indusium, is condensed into a species of covering of a firm structure and whitish colour, and is called the tunica albuginea of the ovary. In the substance of the stroma are embedded a number of vesicles of various sizes, which, although previously described by Vesalius and Fallopius, have been called Graafian vesicles, after De Graaf. These do not commonly become visible until the seventh year, from which period they gradually enlarge until puberty, when the ovaries increase in size, become softer and more vascular, and one or two of these vesicles may be observed to be larger, more developed, and projecting considerably from the surface of the gland.

The proper capsule of the Graafian vesicle is composed of two layers. The outer is formed of dense cellular tissue, in which are ramified many blood vessels; the inner layer is thicker, softer, and more opaque than the preceding, to which it is closely united, and from which it receives vascular twigs.

Ovum. The contained part or nucleus of the vesicle of De Graaf consists of, first, a granulary membrane, enclosing, secondly, a coagulable granular fluid; thirdly, connected with the granulary membrane on one side is a circular mass or disc of granulary matter, in the centre of which is embedded, fourthly, the ovum.

This disc, called by Baer the proligerous disc, presents in its centre on the side towards the interior of the vesicle, a small rounded prominence, called the cumulus, and on the opposite[Pg 24] side a small cup-like cavity hollowed out in the cumulus. The cavity is for the reception of the ovum.[1]

Diagram of a section of the Graafian Vesicle and its contents, showing the situation of the Ovum.

a The granulary membrane. b The proligerous disc. c Ovum. d The inner and outer walls of the Graafian vesicle. e Indusium of the ovary. From T. W. Jones.

From the very minute size of the human ovum, and the difficulty of detecting it, the existence of this little corpuscule was not satisfactorily ascertained until modern times. Although De Graaf had observed ova in the Fallopian tube so early as 1668, which fact had been confirmed by the researches of Dr. Haighton and Mr. Cruickshank, still, as no traces of such ova had been discovered in the Graafian vesicle, and as it was evident that the Graafian vesicle, from its size, &c. could not pass along the Fallopian tube, it was concluded that the inner surface of the vesicle was a species of glandular structure which secreted the fluid with which it was filled, and which was analogous to the semen of the male testicle; hence, in former times, the ovaries were known by the name of testes muliebres. The celebrated anatomist Steno[2] first pointed out the analogy between these organs and the ovaries of the fish tribe: this view was afterwards supported by De Graaf,[3] and they have since continued to retain the name of ovaries.

To Professor von Baer, now of St. Petersburg, is due the merit of having first pointed out the distance of the ovum in the Graafian vesicle, and of thus putting beyond all doubt the accuracy of De Graaf's observations, as well as those of Dr. Haighton and Mr. Cruickshank.

Corpus luteum. Upon impregnation taking place, one or more[Pg 25] of the most prominent Graafian vesicles begins to show marks of considerable vascularity, both in its external capsule and in the surrounding stroma of the ovary. The vesicle swells, and at length bursts, discharging its contents into the funnel-shaped extremity of the Fallopian tube, which firmly grasps the ovary at this point by means of its fimbriæ.

These changes begin to take place immediately after impregnation; the inner lining of the vesicle, which Professor von Baer considers to be a mucous membrane, appears to undergo a rapid development, much more so than the external capsule which contains it. It is, therefore, thrown into a number of corrugations by which the cavity of the vesicle is greatly diminished; it becomes much thicker, and assumes a yellow colour. As its growth proceeds, the cavity of the vesicle becomes still farther contracted, until being unable longer to retain its contents, it bursts and discharges them as above described.

Corrugation of the lining membrane of the
Graafian capsule after impregnation.
From Baer.

The remains of the ruptured vesicle form a round glandular yellow coloured body, called corpus luteum: it projects considerably from the surface of the ovary, attaining the size of a small mulberry. In the middle of this projection there is a little irregular and generally triangular depression or indentation, which is the opening through which the ovum was discharged from the Graafian vesicle: this after a short time closes, forming a little cicatrix on the surface of the ovary.

Corpus luteum in the third month.
From Dr. Montgomery.

"Upon slitting the ovarium at this part, the corpus luteum appears a round body, of a very distinct nature from the rest of the ovarium. Sometimes it is oblong or oval, but more generally round. Its centre is white, with some degree of transparency; the rest of its substance has a yellowish cast, is very vascular, tender and friable, like glandular flesh. Its larger vessels cling round its circumference, and these send their smaller branches inwards through its substance: a few of these larger vessels are situated at the cicatrix or indentation on the outer surface of the ovarium, and are there so little covered as to give that part the appearance of being bloody when seen at a little distance."[4] Upon making a section[Pg 26] of a corpus luteum, we observe that its cavity has an angular form, from which, as from a centre, white lines radiate to the circumference of the vesicle; an appearance which is evidently the corrugation of the inner membrane of the vesicle, as above alluded to. To a similar cause we may also attribute the lobular appearance, which the structure of the corpus luteum presents when a section is made of it. The number of these corpora lutea corresponds exactly with the number of newly formed ova. Meckel, after having examined no less than two hundred pregnant animals of the class mammalia, found that the number of corpora lutea corresponded exactly with that of the young produced. "When there is only one child," says Dr. W. Hunter, "there is only one corpus luteum, and two in the case of twins. I have had opportunities of examining the ovaria with care in several cases of twins, and always found two corpora lutea. In some of these cases there were two distinct corpora lutea in one ovarium, in others there was a distinct corpus luteum in each ovarium."

A Graafian vesicle cannot be converted into a corpus luteum except by actual and effective sexual intercourse; and the strange and discrepant accounts which have every now and then been published, even by authors of considerable repute, of corpora lutea having been found in the ovaries of virgin and even newly-born animals merely prove that the true characteristics of the corpus luteum were not sufficiently known. The irregular cysts, cavities, or deposites of whitish or yellowish structure which are frequently found in the ovary, independent of impregnation, and which have been improperly enough called virgin corpora lutea, present points of difference so marked that they can scarcely be mistaken by an experienced eye. The angular cavity opening externally, the stellated, radiated, cicatrix-like appearance, which a section of the corpus luteum presents, its soft and delicate structure as described by Dr. Hunter, and above all its vascularity, and the facility with which its vessels can be injected from the general tissue of the ovary, are characters only found in a true corpus luteum. Virgin corpora lutea frequently occur under circumstances of disease, especially those of a tubercular character. They frequently appear as distinct cysts, the walls of which are semi-cartilagenous; at other times they seem to be nothing more than a coagulum of blood: they seldom project much from the ovary, and in no instance have they the peculiar structure of the corpus luteum, nor the external cicatrix, nor are they capable of being injected.

After awhile the cavity of the corpus luteum contracts, and the opening into it closes. The surrounding stroma loses its vascularity, the prominence at this part of the ovary gradually subsides, and the ovary returns to its former size. The periods[Pg 27] at which these changes take place vary, but with the exception of those first mentioned they proceed slowly whilst pregnancy lasts, after which time, now that the increased activity of the pelvic circulation peculiar to that period has ceased, they advance more rapidly.

Corpus luteum at the end of the ninth
month. From Dr. Montgomery.

"If an examination be made within the first three or four months after conception, we shall, I believe, always find the cavity still existing, and of such a size as to be capable of containing a grain of wheat at least, and very often of much greater dimensions: this cavity is surrounded by a strong white cyst (the inner coat of the Graafian vesicle,) and as gestation proceeds the opposite parts of this approximate, and at length close together, by which the cavity is completely obliterated, and in its place there remains an irregular white line, whose form is best expressed by calling it radiated or stelliform."[5] Dr. Montgomery adds, "I am unable to state exactly at what period the central cavity disappears, or closes up to form the stellated line. I think I have invariably found it existing up to the end of the fourth month. I have one specimen in which it was closed in the fifth month, and another in which it was open in the sixth: later than this I never found it."

When pregnancy is over, the corpus luteum gradually diminishes and disappears. Dr. Montgomery states that "the exact period of its total disappearance I am unable to state, but I have found it distinctly visible so late as at the end of five months after delivery at the full time, but not beyond this period." Hence it will be seen that in a few months after the termination of pregnancy, all traces of the corpus luteum are lost, and that, therefore, it will be impossible to decide as to how frequently impregnation has taken place, merely by examining the ovaries, as has been supposed. There is also another point to which Dr. Montgomery has alluded, which is well worthy of notice: in mentioning the fact that a vesicle may contain two ova, and thus a woman be delivered of twins, and yet there be but one corpus luteum, he observes that "the presence of a corpus luteum does not prove that a woman has borne a child, although it would be a decided proof that she has been impregnated, and had conceived, because it is quite obvious that the ovum, after its vivification, may be, from a great variety of causes, blighted and destroyed, long before the fœtus has acquired any distinct form.[Pg 28] It may have been converted into a mole or hydatids: thus, however paradoxical it may at first sight appear, it is nevertheless obviously true, that a woman may conceive and yet not become truly with child, a fact already alluded to, as noticed by Harvey; but the converse will not hold good. I believe no one ever found a fœtus in utero without a corpus luteum in the ovary; and that the truth of Haller's carollary, 'nullus unquam conceptus est absque corpore luteo' remains undisputed."

During childhood, the ovaries present a perfectly smooth surface, and their structure appears to be homogeneous, consisting of a dense cellular tissue. About the seventh year, the first traces of the Graafian vesicles make their appearance; as the period of puberty approaches, the whole gland enlarges, becomes softer and more vascular; the Graafian vesicles are more numerous, and generally one or two will be found larger and more prominent than the rest. After repeated impregnations, and especially towards that time of life when the catamenia are about to disappear, the ovary becomes more or less flabby and corrugated, and at a still more advanced age presents a shrivelled appearance.

The ovaries are liable to inflammation and its consequences, more especially abscess, general enlargement, and induration: the malignant changes of structure, viz. cephaloma, hæmatoma, and cancer, rarely have their origin in the ovaries, but extend to these organs from the adjacent parts. Lipomatous or fatty tumours are occasionally met with, containing hair, rudiments of teeth, &c. Cysts not unfrequently occur in the ovaries, and attain a very considerable size; they are simple or compound, sometimes consisting of several cysts one within the other, and distended with fluids, which vary considerably in their character. These tumours come under the general head of Ovarian Dropsy. The ovaries are also liable to many remarkable morbid changes in the puerperal state, such as softening and complete disorganization, the natural structure of the organ being entirely broken down and converted into a bloody pulpy mass; in some cases the whole gland is apparently dissolved away, so as scarcely to leave a trace of its previous existence.

Fallopian tubes. The Fallopian tubes, which act as excretory ducts to the ovaries, take their course through the upper portion of the broad ligaments, running from without inwards, towards the superior margin of the uterus, the ovaries being situated behind and somewhat above them. They are somewhat contorted, and are considerably more dilated at their abdominal extremity where they are unattached, than where they are connected to the uterus, being as much as from three to four lines at the former point; whereas, at the latter, they are not more than half a line.

Their abdominal extremity, which is like the mouth of a funnel,[Pg 29] has its edge strongly fimbriated, and has hence been called the morsus diaboli. Their other extremity opens into the cavity of the uterus at the angle which the fundus forms with its sides, and the whole of the tube is about five inches.

The Fallopian tubes receive their external covering from the peritoneum, which becomes connected at their open extremity with the membrane which lines them. Between the external and internal membrane is the proper tissue of the tubes, and which, except in very muscular subjects, seldom display the fibrous structure; still, nevertheless, two layers of fibres have been observed—an outer or longitudinal, and an inner or circular layer. The Fallopian tubes are lined with mucous membrane, forming numerous longitudinal rugæ. The canal is not pervious during the early months of fœtal life, the abdominal extremity being closed and rounded; this appears to open about the fourth month. The canal is relatively larger, the younger the embryo is, and may, therefore, be easily demonstrated at this time.

At the period of impregnation, the Fallopian tubes implant themselves by means of their fimbriated extremity upon that part of the ovary where the Graafian vesicle is about to burst; they become remarkably engorged with blood, assuming a deep purple colour, and are now much thicker; the canal enlarges, so that a tolerably-sized probe can be introduced, whereas, at other periods it will scarcely admit a large bristle. The uterine extremity of the tube is closed by a continuation of that pulpy coagulable lymph-like secretion which now lines the cavity of the uterus, forming the membrana decidua of Hunter, and which, especially on the side where the corpus luteum is found, extends into the tube to nearly the distance of an inch. The tubes are now observed to be in a state of distinct peristaltic motion, "like writhing worms," as Mr. Cruickshank has well expressed it; "the fimbriæ were also black and embraced the ovaria (like fingers laying hold of an object) so closely and so firmly, as to require some force and even slight laceration to disengage them."[6] From the great degree of vascularity which is observed in the Fallopian tubes at this period, some anatomists have been induced to consider that their proper tissue was vascular, analogous to the corpora cavernosa penis. Besides the peristaltic motion already mentioned, other movements called ciliary have been observed in the Fallopian tubes at this period, consisting of minute portions of mucous membrane moving briskly and whirling round their axis, apparently for the purpose of propelling the ovum.[7]

As pregnancy advances, the Fallopian tubes undergo other changes as respects their situation, which are worthy of notice.[Pg 30] The broad ligaments, in the upper parts of which the Fallopian tubes take their course, are well known to be merely expansions of peritoneum from each side of the uterus, and therefore become gradually unfolded and shorter as the uterus increases in size. "In proportion as the fundus uteri rises upwards and increases in size, the upper part of the broad ligament is so stretched that it clings close to the side of the uterus, so that in reality the broad ligament disappears, no more of it remaining than its very root, viz. its upper and outer corner, where the group of spermatic vessels pass over the iliacs immediately to the side of the uterus. In this state, though the small end of the tube opens in the same part of the uterus as before impregnation, yet the tube has a very different direction. Instead of running outwards in the horizontal direction, it runs downwards, clinging to the side of the uterus. And behind the fimbriæ lies the ovarium, for the same reason clinging close to the side of the uterus."[8]

Uterus. The uterus is a hollow fibrous viscus situated in the hypogastric region between the bladder and the rectum, below the intestinum ileum and above the vagina, and is by far the largest of the generative organs. It is of a pyriform figure: its upper portion which is the largest is triangular, becoming gradually smaller inferiorly; that portion of it which is above the spot where the Fallopian tubes enter is called the fundus uteri; the lower and cylindrical portion receives the name of cervix; that between the cervix and fundus is called the body of the uterus.

The parietes of the adult uterus are nearly half an inch in their greatest thickness, which is about the middle of the body, the body being slightly thicker than the cervix, which is of a somewhat harder structure. Near the point at which the Fallopian tubes enter the uterus the parietes become thinner, gradually diminishing from four or five to only one line in thickness.

The cavity of the uterus is triangular, its base being directed upwards, the superior angles corresponding to the points where the Fallopian tubes enter it. The cavity of the uterus is so small, owing to the thickness of its parietes, that they are nearly in contact: it is only four lines in breadth; the fundus, which forms the base of the triangle, is convex both internally as well as externally; whereas, the sides which form the body are convex internally, but somewhat concave externally.

The cavity of the uterus is most contracted at the point where the cervix is united to the body, which here forms the os uteri internum; from this point the cervix gradually dilates as far as its middle portion, when it again contracts; its lower extremity terminates in the upper part of the vagina by an anterior and posterior cushion-like projection, of which the posterior is usually[Pg 31] the longest, although from the direction of the uterine axis the anterior is commonly felt lowest in the pelvis. Between these there is a transverse fissure known by the name of os tincæ or os uteri externum, the lips or labia of which are formed by the two above-mentioned prominences. The internal surface of the body of the uterus is smooth, whereas that of the cervix is uneven, forming upon its anterior and posterior wall a number of delicate rugæ diverging obliquely in an arborescent form, and hence called the arbor vitæ. The lips of the os uteri are smooth, except when slight lacerations have taken place during labour.

In the virgin state the uterus is about two inches long, of which the cervix occupies the smaller half: the greatest breadth of the body is sixteen lines; that of the cervix from nine to ten. The uterus which has been impregnated, especially when this has been frequently the case, scarcely ever regains its original dimensions, and the fissure which the os tincæ forms becomes broader from before backwards. The weight of an adult virgin uterus is from seven to eight drachms, but the uterus which has been once impregnated is seldom less than an ounce and a half. It lies between the bladder and rectum, its upper half being covered by peritoneum, which closely adheres to it. In the adult state it is situated entirely in the cavity of the pelvis; the fundus, which is below the upper edge of the symphysis pubis, is turned forwards and upwards, while its mouth is directed downwards and backwards, so that its long axis is nearly parallel to the axis of the superior aperture of the pelvis.

The uterus is connected to the neighbouring parts by several duplicatures of peritoneum, which are continuous with that portion of it which covers the fundus. The most considerable are the broad or lateral ligaments: these arise from the sides of the uterus, which is enclosed between their anterior and posterior layers or laminæ; they proceed transversely outwards towards the sides of the pelvic cavity, which is thus divided into two portions, and are then continued into that portion of the peritoneum which lines the cavity.

The round ligaments arise from the sides of the uterus close beneath and a little anterior to the uterine extremity of the Fallopian tubes. They pass between the two layers of the broad ligaments, behind the umbilical arteries, and before the iliac vessels, in a direction upwards and outwards to the external opening of the inguinal canal; they then make a turn round the epigastric artery downwards, inwards, and forwards, and pass through the abdominal ring, and dividing into numerous fasciculi and fibres are gradually lost in the cellular substance of the mons Veneris and upper portion of the labia. Besides consisting of cellular substance and blood-vessels, the round ligaments contain some very distinct bundles of muscular fibres, of which the upper arise from the external layer of uterine fibres, and the[Pg 32] lower from the inferior edge of the internal oblique muscle, and pass upwards.

Upon a superficial examination, the structure of the uterus would almost seem to be homogeneous, nevertheless a number of reddish yellow strata interspersed with whitish streaks running from behind forwards may be perceived even in the unimpregnated state; between these strata the vessels of the uterus take their course, forming numerous anastomoses.

There is much difference of opinion among anatomists as to the fibrous structure of the uterus. The majority however agree as to the presence of muscular fibres,[9] some considering that they always exist, while others, and by far the greater number, consider them as appearances peculiar to pregnancy: they are, it is true, extremely indistinct in the unimpregnated state, but they are far from being peculiar to pregnancy, as they are frequently developed by any circumstances by which the formative powers of the uterus are excited. Thus in cases where the uterus has been much distended by some anormal growth, its fibres become much developed and distinctly fasciculated. Lobstein observed them very distinctly in a uterus which had been distended to the size of a seven months' pregnancy by a fatty tumour.

The uterine fibres have been usually considered as fleshy, but they differ from the red fibres of voluntary muscles, in being of a paler colour, flatter, and remarkably interwoven with each other: nevertheless they appear to be really muscular fibres from the powerful contraction with which they expel the fœtus and placenta, and nearly obliterate the cavity of the uterus. In the unimpregnated state they resemble the fibrous coat of an artery, whereas, those of the gravid uterus are more like the fibres of muscle. Most anatomists agree in describing two sets of fibres, viz. longitudinal and transverse. The external layer of fibres appears to form the round ligaments, which seem to have the same relation with them as tendon and muscle. "The fibres arise from the round ligaments, and regularly diverging spread over the fundus until they unite and form the outmost stratum of the muscular substance of the uterus. The round ligaments of the womb have been considered as useful in directing the ascent of the uterus during gestation, so as to throw it before the floating viscera of the abdomen: but in truth it could not ascend differently; and on looking to the connexion of this cord with the fibres of the uterus, we may be led to consider it as performing rather the office of a tendon than that of a ligament."[10] "On the outer surface and lateral part of the womb, the [Pg 33]muscular fibres run with an appearance of irregularity among the larger blood-vessels, but they are well calculated to constringe the vessels, whenever they are excited to contraction. The substance of the gravid uterus is powerfully and distinctly muscular, but the course of the fibres is less easily described than might be imagined: this is owing to the intricate interweaving of the fibres with each other—an intermixture however which greatly increases the extent of their power in diminishing the cavity of the uterus. After making sections of the substance of the womb in different directions, we have no hesitation in stating that towards the fundus the circular fibres prevail, that towards the orifice the longitudinal fibres are most apparent, and that on the whole, the most general course of the fibres is from the fundus towards the orifice.

"This prevalence of longitudinal fibres is undoubtedly a provision for diminishing the length of the organ, or for drawing the fundus towards the orifice. At the same time these longitudinal fibres must dilate the orifice and draw the lower part of the uterus over the head of the child.

"In making sections of the uterus while it retained its natural muscular contraction, I have been much struck in observing how entirely the blood-vessels were closed and invisible, and how open and distinct the mouths of the cut blood-vessels became when the same portions of the uterus were distended or relaxed. This fact of the natural contraction of the substance of the uterus closing the smallest pore of the vessels, so that no vessels are to be seen, where we nevertheless know that they are large and numerous, demonstrates that a very principal effect of the muscular action of the womb is the constringing of the numerous vessels which supply the placenta, and which must be ruptured when the placenta is separated from the womb."

"Upon inverting the uterus, and brushing off the decidua, the muscular structure is very distinctly seen: the inner surface of the fundus consists of two sets of fibres, running in concentric circles round the orifices of the Fallopian tubes; these circles at their circumference unite and mingle, making an intricate tissue. Ruysch, I am inclined to believe, saw the circular fibres of one side only; and not adverting to the circumstance of the Fallopian tube opening in the centre of these fibres, which would have proved their lateral position, he described the muscle as seated in the centre of the fundus uteri. This structure of the inner surface of the fundus of the uterus is still adapted to the explanation of Ruysch, which was that they produced contraction and corrugation of the surface of the uterus, which, the placenta, not partaking of, the cohesion of the surface was necessarily broken. Farther, I have observed a set of fibres on the inner surface of the uterus, which are not described: they commence at the centre of the last described muscle, and having a course in some degree[Pg 34] vortiginous, they descend in a broad irregular band towards the orifice of the uterus: these fibres co-operating with the external muscle of the uterus, and with the general mass of fibres in the substance of it, must tend to draw down the fundus in the expulsion of the fœtus, and to draw the orifice and lower segment of the uterus over the child's head." (C. Bell, op. cit.)

There are other circumstances which prove the muscularity of the uterus, beyond the mere evidence of its fibres, as seen during pregnancy. "In the quadruped," as Dr. Hunter observes, "the cat particularly and the rabbit, the muscular action or peristaltic motion of the uterus is as evidently seen as that of the intestines, when the animal is opened immediately after death." It is also proved by the powerful contraction which it exerts during labour, and "by the thickness of the fibres corresponding with their degree of contraction." (Ibid.)

The inner surface of the uterus is lined by a smooth or somewhat flocculent membrane of a reddish colour, which is continued superiorly into the Fallopian tubes; inferiorly it becomes the lining membrane of the vagina.

Mucous follicles are only found in the cervix, especially at its lower part: when by chance these become inflamed, the orifice closes, and the follicle becomes more or less distended by a collection of thin fluid. The mucous casts of these follicles have been known by the name of ovula Nabothi, having been mistaken by an old anatomist for Graafian vesicles, which had been detached from the ovary, and conveyed into the cavity of the uterus.

The mucous membrane which lines the cervix uteri is corrugated into a number of rugæ, between which the mucous follicles are chiefly found.

Uterus duplex.
Before quitting this subject, it will be necessary to point out the changes which the uterus presents at different periods of fœtal life, and the great resemblance it has at these periods to the uterus, as it appears in the lower classes of the mammalia. We may, however, observe in the first place, that the uterus is not found to exist as a separate organ until we come to the class mammalia; and even in the lower genera of this class it bears a strong resemblance to the tubular character of the generative organs in the inferior classes of animal life. The nearest to the tubular uterus, and where the transition from the oviduct in birds, &c. to the uterus in mammalia is least distinctly marked, is in the uterus duplex. Although the uterus is double, there is but one vagina into which the two ora uteri open; its low grade of development is marked by the resemblance which each uterus bears to an intestinal tube: there are as yet no traces of a cervix, each os uteri merely forming a simple[Pg 35] opening at the lower end of what is little more than a cylindrical canal. We do not find that thickening at the lower extremity of the uterus which distinguishes the cervix in the higher mammalia. This species of uterus is found among a large portion of the rodentia, and is also occasionally met with as an abnormal formation in the human subject. The next grade of uterine development appears under the form of the uterus bicollis. The double os uteri here ceases to exist, and the division

begins a little higher up, so that the two cavities of the uterus communicate for a short space: the ova, however, do not reach the common cavity, but remain each in its separate cornu. In this form of uterus, the os uteri is not only single, but the lower portion is thickened, although it has not yet formed a distinct neck or cervix; it is met with among some of the rodentia, and also certain carnivora.

Uterus bicollis.
Uterus bicorporeus.
In the uterus bicorporeus, the union of the cornua is higher up, so that the lower portion is single, while the upper part alone is double, consisting of two strongly curved cornua. This conformation is peculiar to ruminating animals. If two ova be present they are separate from each other, each being contained in its own distinct body or cornu, but a portion of the membranes extends along the common cervix, from one body to the other.

Uterus bifundalis.
A still higher grade is the uterus bifundalis, where the fundus alone is double, the cornu being formed only by this portion. This formation is observed in the horse, ass, &c.: the common cavity is here the receptacle of the ovum, so that in the unimpregnated state, the cornua appear only as appendices, into which a portion of the membranes extend.

In the uterus biangularis, the double formation has nearly disappeared, except at the fundus, where the uterus imperceptibly passes into the tubes: this is the case among the edentata, and some of the monkey tribes.

The highest grade is the uterus simplex: every trace here of the double form is lost; the fundus no longer forms an acute angle, where it bifurcates into two cornua; but is convex. We now for the first time see the divisions of the uterus into body and cervix distinctly marked.

Uterus biangularis.
The human uterus presents a similar variety of forms, as it[Pg 36] gradually rises in the scale of development during the different periods of utero-gestation. It is at first divided into two cornua, and usually continues so to the end of the third month, or even later; the younger the embryo the longer are the cornua, and the more acute the angle which they form; but even after this angle has disappeared, the cornua continue for some time longer.

Uterus simplex.
The uterus is at first of an equal width throughout; it is perfectly smooth and not distinguished from the vagina either internally or externally by any prominence whatever. This change is first observed when the cornua disappear and leave the uterus with a simple cavity. The upper portion is proportionably smaller, the younger the embryo is. The body of the uterus gradually increases, until at the period of puberty it is no longer cylindrical, but pyriform: even in the full-grown fœtus the length of the body is not more than a fourth part of the whole uterus; from the seventh even to the thirteenth year it has only a third, nor does it reach a half until puberty has been fully attained. The os tincæ or os uteri externum first appears as a scarcely perceptible prominence projecting into the vagina; it increases gradually, in size until the latter months of gestation, when the portio vaginalis is relatively much larger than afterwards.

The parietes of the uterus are thin in proportion to the age of the embryo. They are of an equal thickness throughout at first: at the fifth month, the cervix becomes thicker than the upper parts; between five or six years of age, the uterine parietes are nearly of an equal thickness, and remain so until the period of puberty, when the body becomes somewhat thicker than the cervix.

As the function of menstruation with its various derangements will be considered among the diseases of the unimpregnated state, we proceed to consider these changes which the uterus undergoes during pregnancy as well as during and after labour: these are very remarkable both as regards its structure, form, and size.

Shortly after conception, and before we can perceive any traces of the embryo, the uterus becomes softer and somewhat larger, its blood-vessels increased in size, and the fibrous layers of which its parietes are composed looser and more or less separated. The internal surface when minutely examined has a flocculent appearance, and very quickly after conception becomes covered with a whitish paste-like substance, which is secreted from the vessels opening upon it; this pulpy effusion soon becomes firmer and more[Pg 37] dense; it bears a strong analogy to coagulable lymph, and forms a membrane which lines the whole cavity of the uterus, and which in the course of a few weeks (from changes to be mentioned hereafter) crosses the os uteri and thus closes it. The uterine cavity in a short time becomes still farther closed by the canal of the cervix being completely sealed, as it were, by a tough plug of gelatinous matter which is secreted by the glandules of that part.

The structure of the uterus becomes remarkably altered; its fibrous structure is much more apparent; in fact, it is only during pregnancy, or when the uterus has been distended by some anormal growth, that we are able to detect the uterine fibres with any degree of certainty. This has led some anatomists to consider that they are only formed at such periods, a supposition which is not very probable; at any rate they now become very distinct: hence the uterus does not owe its increasing size to mere extension, but it evidently acquires a considerable increase of substance, a fact which is not only proved by examining the contracted uterus after labour at the full period, but also by comparing its weight with that of the unimpregnated organ. The adult virgin uterus weighs about one ounce, whereas the gravid uterus at the full term of pregnancy, when emptied of its contents, weighs at least twenty-four ounces, showing that there has been an actual increment of substance in the proportion of one to twenty-four. Having ascertained this point, it next becomes a question, whether the parietes of the gravid uterus increase in thickness during pregnancy, or whether they become thinner. Meckel, who is one of the greatest modern authorities on these subjects, states that from careful admeasurement of sixteen gravid uteri at different periods of gestation, he finds the parietes become thicker during the first, second, or third months, but after this period they become gradually thinner up to the full time: they are thicker in the upper parts of the uterus, whereas inferiorly they are a third or nearly a half less.

Nothing proves the actual increase of bulk and substance in the uterus more than its appearance when contracted immediately after labour at the full term; it forms a fleshy mass as large as the head of a new-born child, the parietes of which are at least an inch in thickness.

"The spongy or cellular tissue (says M. Leroux) becomes considerably developed during pregnancy, and its porous cells increase in proportion as the uterus dilates, more especially at the fundus and the spot where the placenta is attached, where they become so large as to admit a goosequill. The internal membrane is pierced with numerous orifices, of which some are the mouths of arteries, and others communicate with the cells already mentioned. This membrane also during pregnancy forms those[Pg 38] irregular tufted rugæ, which serve to give a more intimate connexion between the uterus and the placenta. In the unimpregnated uterus and in the intervals between the menstrual periods the little orifices which are observed in the lining membrane of the uterus contain only a transparent lymph, which lubricates the interior of the uterus; during the appearance of the menses they contain blood, and during pregnancy they are connected with the vessels of the placenta and chorion."[11]

There is no circumstance in which the gravid uterus differs more from the unimpregnated than in the size and termination of its blood-vessels. The arteries, both spermatic and hypogastric, are very much enlarged. The hypogastric is commonly considerably larger than the spermatic, and we very often find them of unequal sizes in the different sides. They form a large trunk of communication all along the side of the uterus, and from this the branches are sent across the body of the uterus both before and behind. The cervix uteri has branches only from the hypogastrics, and the fundus only from the spermatics; or, in other words, the hypogastric artery gives a number of branches to the cervix, besides sending up the great anastomosing branch, and the spermatic artery supplies the tube and fundus uteri before it gives down the anastomosing branch on the lateral parts of the uterus. All through the substance of the uterus there are infinite numbers of arteries large and small, so that the whole arterial system makes a general network, and the arteries are convoluted or serpentine in their course.[12] Hardly any of the larger arteries are seen for any length of way upon the outside of the uterus. As they branch from the sides where they first approach the uterus, they disappear by plunging deeper and deeper into its substance.

The arterial branches which are most enlarged are those which run towards the placenta, so that wherever the placenta adheres, that part appears evidently to receive by much the greatest quantity of blood, and the greatest number both of the large and small arteries at that part pass through to the placenta, and are necessarily always torn through upon its separation. The veins of the uterus would appear to be still more enlarged in proportion than the arteries. The spermatic and hypogastric veins in general follow the course of the arteries, and like them anastomose on the side of the uterus. From thence they ramify through the substance of the uterus, running deeper and deeper as they go on, and without following precisely the course of the arterial branches.[Pg 39] They form a plexus of the largest and most frequent communications which we know of in the vessels of the human body, and this they have in common with the arteries that their larger branches go to, or rather come from, that part of the uterus to which the placenta adheres: so that when the venous system of the uterus is well injected, it is evident that that part is the chief source of returning blood. Here, too, both the large and small veins are continued from the placenta to the uterus, and are always necessarily broken, upon the separation of these two parts. As I know no reason for calling the veins of the uterus sinuses, and as that expression has probably occasioned much confusion among the writers upon this subject, I have industriously avoided it.[13]

The form of the uterus changes considerably during pregnancy: the upper part appears to increase in greater proportion than the lower, a fact which appears to be proved from the alteration which takes place in the relative position of the Fallopian tubes, which are situated much lower down the sides of the uterus at full term than in the unimpregnated state, nor do they entirely regain their former position after labour, until the female has attained an advanced age; hence as the cervix diminishes in length during the latter half of pregnancy, it follows that the difference in point of size between the fundus and the body of the uterus, and this part will be continually increasing.

As the uterus increases, the fundus of course rises and can be felt through the distended abdominal parietes: its anterior surface, especially in the latter month of pregnancy, lies immediately behind the anterior wall of the abdominal cavity, and pushes the small intestines upwards, backwards, and to the sides.

The form of the gravid uterus differs also from that in the unimpregnated state in other respects, and this difference appears to depend in great measure upon its increase of size, and upon the form of the cavities which it occupies. Thus in the unimpregnated state when it occupies the cavity of the pelvis, its anterior surface which corresponds to the bladder is flattened; whereas its posterior surface, which is turned towards the hollow of the sacrum, is convex; it is however the reverse during the latter half of pregnancy. The anterior surface is now strongly convex, being merely covered by the yielding anterior wall of the abdomen; whereas posteriorly the uterus is nearly concave, corresponding to the solid convexity of the lumbar vertebræ, a fact which may be easily ascertained by examining the abdomen of a patient in the last month of pregnancy while lying down. The situation and position of the uterus are also changed in the unimpregnated state; the fundus is inclined somewhat backwards,[Pg 40] the os uteri being nearly in the centre of the pelvic cavity, but the gravid uterus during the latter half of pregnancy has its fundus strongly inclined forwards and the os uteri directed backwards towards the upper part of the hollow of the sacrum.[14]

A minute and intimate knowledge of the changes and appearances which the uterus presents at every period of pregnancy, is essential to the diagnosis and treatment of the various derangements to which this process is subject. The numerous and important questions in medical jurisprudence connected with pregnancy can alone be determined by its means; and it is only by more close and attentive observation of every step in the gradual development of the uterus up to the full term of gestation, that we can expect to increase our means of forming a correct and certain diagnosis in those cases of doubtful pregnancy, where not merely professional reputation is more or less at stake, but the character, happiness, and even life of the individual upon whose case we are required to decide.

During the first month of pregnancy the changes are not very appreciable upon examination during life. The uterus has become larger, softer, and more vascular, much as it does during a menstrual period. The portio vaginalis of the cervix, which in the unimpregnated state is hard and almost cartilaginous to the feel, becomes softer and larger:[15] the transverse fissure which the os uteri forms is more oval.

In the second month, the abdomen becomes somewhat flat: the portio vaginalis can be now reached by the finger with greater ease than at any time of pregnancy, which is not from the uterus itself being lower in the pelvis, but from not yet having altered its position; any increase of its size therefore will cause its inferior extremity to be felt lower down and nearer to the os externum. The os uteri has undergone a considerable change, inasmuch as its edges have lost their lip-like figure; they now form a ring or rather dimple-like concavity at the lower end of the cervix, its canal being closed by the gelatinous plug already mentioned.

In primiparæ, or women pregnant for the first time, the [Pg 41]margin of the os uteri thus closed is not only circular but perfectly smooth; whereas in multiparæ, not only is the cervix usually larger in every direction, but the os uteri itself is larger, thicker, and of an irregular shape; it is also knotty here and there from little callous cicatrices, where its edge has been torn in former labours.

In the third month of pregnancy the uterus rises above the brim of the pelvis. A slight protrusion of the abdomen may be sometimes observed above the pubes; the os uteri is not reached so easily as in the preceding month. The alteration which takes place in the situation of the uterus during the third month appears to result from gradual shortening of the broad ligament as it increases in size. As the uterus rises it pushes up that portion of the small intestines which rests upon it; these however being confined by the mesentery to the spine, and therefore prevented ascending before the uterus, at length slip down behind it, and the fundus being freed from the superincumbent pressure rises in a direction upwards and forwards into the cavity of the abdomen. The direction of the uterus becomes much altered; the os uteri is no longer in the middle of the pelvic cavity, but inclines towards the upper part of the hollow of the sacrum, whereas the fundus approaches more and more to the anterior parietes of the abdomen.

In the fourth month, the fundus uteri has risen about two or three fingers' breadth above the symphysis pubis; this is not very easily ascertained even in a thin person, still less where the patient is stout and the parietes of the abdomen therefore thick. The directions which the celebrated Rœderer has given for making an examination of the abdomen during the early months of pregnancy, are well worthy of notice. Having evacuated the bladder and rectum, the patient should be placed in a half-sitting posture with the knees drawn up, so as to relax the abdominal parietes as much as possible: she must then breathe slowly and deeply; and if the hand be suddenly pressed against the abdomen a little above the symphysis pubis, at the moment of her making a full expiration, we shall in all probability feel the hard globe of the uterus.

In the fifth month, the fundus will be felt half way, or a little more, between the symphysis pubis and umbilicus. The increased size of the abdomen cannot be concealed by the dress; the portio vaginalis has become distinctly shorter, and the os uteri is situated higher in the pelvis and more posteriorly.

In the sixth month, the fundus has risen as high as the umbilicus; the irregular folds of the skin which form the fovia umbilici or navel depression begin to disappear; the first perceptible movements of the child may occasionally be felt; the portio vaginalis has lost half its length, being scarcely half an inch in length.

[Pg 42]

Cervix uteri about the sixth
or seventh month.
In the seventh month, the fundus rises an inch or so above the umbilicus, the folds of which have nearly disappeared. In some cases it begins to protrude, forming a species of umbilical hernia: this varies a good deal in different individuals, being more marked in primiparæ; whereas in women, whose abdomen has been distended in previous pregnancies, little or no convexity of the navel is produced until a later period, and not always even then, the umbilical depression being merely diminished in point of depth, and its folds not so strongly marked. The movements of the child are now perfectly distinct; the portio vaginalis is still shorter, and approaches more and more to the upper part of the hollow of the sacrum. The anterior portion of the inferior segment of the uterus, or that part which extends from the os uteri towards the symphysis pubis, is now considerably developed and convex, and on pressing the point of the finger against it, the presenting part of the child will be felt. When this is the head as is usually the case, it will feel like a light ball which rises when pushed by the finger, but which, if the finger be held still, in a few moments descends and may again be felt.

Cervix uteri in the eighth month.
In the eighth month, the fundus has risen half way between the umbilicus and the scrobiculus cordis. The abdomen has increased considerably in size, and has become more convex; the umbilical depression in primiparæ has entirely disappeared. The portio vaginalis is still shorter, being barely a quarter of an inch in length. The os uteri is so high up as not to be reached without difficulty; the presenting part of the child can be distinctly felt.

Cervix uteri in the ninth month.
In the ninth month, the fundus has reached nearly to the scrobiculus cordis, and by the end of the month is quite in it; this is more especially the case with primiparæ: the anterior parietes of the abdomen not allowing the fundis to incline so strongly forwards, the oppression of breathing is therefore more marked in them than in multiparæ, for the fundus uteri rising so high prevents in great measure the action[Pg 43] of the diaphragm, so that the chest is expanded by other muscles; hence the shortness of breath and inability of moving, so frequently complained of at this period of utero-gestation. The portio vaginalis is still shorter, and in the primipara forms little more than a soft cushiony ring which marks the os uteri. The inferior part of the uterus is becoming more spherical, and is usually occupied by the presenting part of the child: this latter is no longer so moveable as before, its size as also its weight being evidently increased. That portion of the uterus which extends between the symphysis pubis and os uteri is

now not only more convex but lower in the pelvis than the os uteri itself.

During the last four weeks of pregnancy a considerable change is observed. The fundus is now lower than it was in the preceding month, being about half way between the scrobiculus cordis and umbilicus; the abdomen has, as it is called, fallen; and from the diaphragm being now able to resume its functions the breathing becomes more easy, and the female feels more comfortable and capable of moving about. On examination per vaginam the anterior portion of the inferior segment of the uterus will be felt still deeper in the pelvis: if the head presents it distends this part of the uterus, so that, in many cases, we have to pass the finger round it before we can reach the os uteri, which is now in the upper part of the hollow of the sacrum. All traces of the cervix have now disappeared, it having been required to complete the full development of the uterus; the situation of the os uteri itself is marked merely by a small depression or dimple; there is no longer any distinction between the os uteri internum and externum; the edges of the opening are so thin as to be nearly membranous, but remain closed in primiparæ until the commencement of labour.[16]

In women who have had several children, a considerable difference is observed as regards the state of the cervix and os uteri: the cervix does not undergo that shortening during the latter half of pregnancy, which is the case in a primipara, a portion of it at least remaining up to the full term of utero-gestation: in many cases, especially where the female has had a large family, it is nearly an inch long at this period; nor is the lower portion of the uterus so spherical as in the primipara; to this circumstance may probably be attributed the fact of the head not descending so deep into the pelvis just before labour. In multiparæ the os uteri is also very different: instead of being perfectly round with its edges smooth, it is irregular and uneven, and seldom loses altogether the lip-like shape of the unimpregnated state in consequence of the greater thickness and elongation of its lips from former labours; its edges here and there is uneven and knotty, from little callous[Pg 44] cicatrices, where it has been torn; moreover it does not remain closed till the commencement of labour, but the os uteri externum (commonly called os tincæ,) and sometimes even the os uteri internum will be more or less open during the last three or four weeks of pregnancy. These peculiarities are of great importance in coming to a conclusion as to whether a patient be in her first pregnancy or not: although not invariable in the utmost sense of the word, still their occurrence, even after a single labour, is sufficiently frequent to make them worthy of careful observation. Indeed, on more than one occasion, we have known them occur even after a miscarriage, a circumstance on the strength of which the patient had ventured to deny that she was pregnant. On the other hand, we sometimes meet with the os uteri in a second pregnancy so little altered by the effects of the previous labour, that it would be extremely difficult to come to a decision.

When labour is over, the uterus contracts very considerably, and, in a few days after, its parietes will be found at least an inch in thickness. It now gradually diminishes in size, and continues to do so for some weeks; the blood-vessels contract, and losing the peculiarly loose spongy structure of pregnancy it becomes harder, firmer, and more compact. It nevertheless remains softer and larger than in the virgin state, and does not attain its original size and hardness until an advanced period of life.

The os uteri, which in the latter months of pregnancy had formed a circular opening, resumes its former shape, except that its lips, especially the posterior one, which are more or less irregular and uneven, are thicker and longer than in the virgin state. For the first weeks after labour, the os uteri is high in the pelvis, soft, and easily admits the tip of the finger; at the end of the second week it is much lower in the pelvis, and no longer permits the finger to pass. Immediately after labour, the contracted uterus forms a hard solid ball, the size of a new-born child's head; this state of contraction is not, however, of long continuance: in the course of half an hour, or even less, it begins to increase in size, becoming softer and larger, and continuing to increase slowly for some hours, when it again gradually diminishes, until, as before observed, it approaches its original size in the unimpregnated state. The state of powerful contraction in which the uterus is felt immediately after labour, after a time gradually relaxes; its spongy texture, from which the blood had been forcibly expelled by the violent action of its fibres, becomes again filled with blood; the organ swells and becomes softer and more bulky, and the orifices of the vessels which open into the cavity of the uterus are again partly pervious, and emit a sanious fluid called the lochia. This state lasts for two or more days after delivery, when the vessels begin to recover their former caliber, and lose[Pg 45] that degree of dilatation peculiar to the gravid state. The lochia become less and less coloured, and now, and not before the uterus undergoes that gradual diminution of size and bulk which we have just alluded to.

The copulative or external organs of generation are the vagina, hymen, clitoris, nymphæ, and labia, the three last being known by the term vulva.

Vagina. The vagina is a canal of about four inches in length and one in breadth, broader above than below; its parietes are thin and are immediately connected with the uterus. It envelopes the portio vaginalis of the uterus at its upper or blind extremity (fundus vaginæ,) and is continuous with its substance; inferiorly, where it is narrowest, it passes into the vulva. It is situated between the bladder and rectum, and attached to each by loose cellular tissue. Its direction differs from that of the uterus, for its axis corresponds very nearly with that of the pelvic outlet, running downwards and forwards. Posteriorly it is somewhat convex, anteriorly concave.

The vagina consists of two layers; the external, which is very thin, firm, of a reddish-white colour, and continuous with the fibrous tissue of the uterus; and a lining mucous membrane which is closely united to it. This latter is much corrugated, especially in the virgin state, the rugæ running transversely in an oblique direction, and gathered together on its anterior and posterior surface, forming the columna rugarum anterior and posterior, which appear to be a continuation of the corrugations which form the arbor vitæ of the cervix.

In the upper part of the vagina there are considerable mucous follicles, which moisten the canal with their secretion, and which during sexual intercourse, and particularly during the first stage of labour, pour forth an abundant supply of colourless mucus for the purpose of lubricating the vagina, and rendering it more dilatable. Near its orifice, especially at the upper part, the veins of the vagina form the plexus retiformis, a congeries of vessels which has almost a cellular appearance, and from this reason has been called the corpus cavernosum of the vagina; it appears to be capable of considerable swelling from distension with blood, like the corpus cavernosum penis, and by this means serves to contract still farther the os externum during the presence of venereal excitement. A similar disposition to form plexuses of vessels is seen in the venous circulation of the nymphæ, bladder, and rectum.

Hymen. The lining membrane of the vagina is of a reddish-gray colour, interspersed here and there, especially at its upper part, with livid spots like extravasation. At the os externum it forms a fold or duplicature called hymen, running across the sides of the posterior part of the opening, and usually of a crescentic figure, the cavity looking upwards. The duplicatures of [Pg 46]membrane are united by cellular tissue. In some instances, the hymen arises from the whole circumference of the os externum, having a small orifice in the centre for the escape of the menses and vaginal secretions: in some rare cases it is cribriform; and in others it completely closes the vaginal entrance. When torn in the act of sexual intercourse, it generally forms three or four little triangular appendages, called carunculæ myrtiformes, arising from the posterior and lateral portions of the os externum.

From the identity of its fibrous coat with that of the uterus, the vagina possesses considerable powers of contraction, when excited by the presence of any body which distends it; hence it is a valuable assistance to the uterus during labour: it also stands in the same relation to the abdominal muscles that the rectum does, so that as soon as it is distended by the head, &c. it calls them into the strong involuntary action, which characterizes the bearing down pains of the second stage of labour. The orifice of the vagina (os externum) is surrounded by a thin layer of muscular fibres, which arise from the anterior edge of the sphincter ani; they enclose the outer margin of the vagina, cover its corpus cavernosum, and are inserted into the crura clitoridis at their union. It has been called the sphincter or constrictor vaginæ, and assists the corpus cavernosum still farther in contracting the os externum.

Clitoris. The clitoris is an oblong cylindrical body, situated beneath the symphysis pubis, arising from the upper and inner surface of the ascending rami of the ischium, by means of two crura of about an inch long, and uniting with each other at an obtuse angle. It terminates anteriorly in a slight enlargement, called the glans clitoridis, which is covered with a thin membrane or a loose fold of skin, viz. the preputium clitoridis. It is a highly nervous and vascular organ, and like the penis of the male, is composed of two crura and corpora cavernosa, which are capable of being distended with blood; they are contained in a ligamentous sheath, and have a septum between them. The clitoris is also provided with a suspensory ligament, by which it is connected to the ossa pubis. Like that of the penis, the glans clitoridis is extremely sensible, but has no perforation. Upon minute examination, it will be found that the gland is not a continuation of the posterior portion of the clitoris, but merely connected with it by cellular tissue, vessels, and nerves; the posterior portion terminates on its anterior surface in a concavity which receives the glans. In the glans itself there is no trace of the septum, which separates the corpora cavernosa. On the dorsum of the clitoris several large vessels and nerves take their course, and are distributed upon the glans, and upon its prepuce are situated a number of mucus and sebaceous follicles.

The crura clitoridis at their lower portion are surrounded by two considerable muscles, called the erectores clitoridis, arising[Pg 47] by short tendons close beneath them from the inner surface of the ascending ramus of the ischium, and extending nearly to their extremity.

Nymphæ. The nymphæ or labia pudendi interna, are two long corrugated folds, resembling somewhat the comb of a cock, arising from the prepuce and glans clitoridis, and remaining obliquely downwards and outwards along the inner edge of the labia, increasing in breadth, but suddenly diminishing in size. At their lower extremity they consist of a spongy tissue, which is more delicate than that of the clitoris, but resembles considerably that of the glans, of which it appears to be a direct continuation. It has been called the corpus cavernosum nympharum, and is capable of considerable increase in size when distended with blood. The two crura of the prepuce terminate in their upper and anterior extremities; they are of a florid colour, and in their natural state they are contiguous to, and cover the orifice of the urethra. The skin which covers them is very thin and delicate, bearing a considerable resemblance to mucous membrane, especially on their inner surface, where it is continuous with the vagina; externally it passes into the labia.

The space between the nymphæ and edge of the hymen is smooth, without corrugation, and is called vestibulum.

Close behind the clitoris, and a little below it, is the orifice of the urethra, lying between the two nymphæ: it is surrounded by several lacunæ or follicles of considerable depth, secreting a viscid mucus; its lower or posterior edge is, like the lower portion of the urethra, covered by a thick layer of cellular tissue, and a plexus of veins, which occasionally become dilated and produce much inconvenience; it is this which gives the urethra the feel of a soft cylindrical roll at the upper part of the vagina; and in employing the catheter, by tracing the finger along it, the orifice will be easily found.

Labia. The labia extend from the pubes to within an inch of the anus, the space between the vulva and anus receiving the name of perineum.

The opening between the labia is called the fossa magna: it increases a little in size and depth, as it descends, forming a scaphoid or boat-like cavity, viz. the fossa navicularis.

The labia are thicker above, becoming thinner below, and terminate in a transverse fold of skin, called the frænulum perinei, or fourchette, the edge of which is almost always slightly lacerated in first labours. They are composed of skin cushioned out by cellular and fatty substance, and lined by a very vascular membrane, which is thin, tender, and red, like the inside of the lips; they are also provided with numerous sebaceous follicles, by which the parts are kept smooth and moist.

[Pg 48]

CHAPTER III.

DEVELOPMENT OF THE OVUM.

Membrana decidua.—Chorion.—Amnion.—Placenta.—Umbilical cord.—Embryo.—Fœtal circulation.

Membrana decidua. The earliest trace of impregnation which is to be observed in the cavity of the uterus, and even before the ovum has reached it, is the presence of a soft humid paste-like secretion, with which the cavity of the uterus is covered, and which is furnished by the secreting vessels of its lining membrane. This is the membrana decidua of Hunter: properly speaking, it should be called the maternal membrane, in contra-distinction to the chorion and amnion, which, as belonging peculiarly to the fœtus, are called the fœtal membranes.[17]

Although at first in a semi-liquid state, it soon becomes firmer and more compact, assuming the character of a membrane: it appears to be nothing else than an effusion of coagulable lymph on the internal surface of the uterus, having "scarcely a more firm consistence than curd of milk or coagulum of blood." (Hunter, op. cit. p. 54.) Hence, although much thicker than the other membranes, it is weaker; it is also much less transparent.

It is not of an equal thickness, being considerably thicker in the neighbourhood of the placenta than elsewhere; inferiorily, and especially near the os uteri, it becomes thinner: during the first weeks of pregnancy it is much thicker than afterwards, becoming gradually thinner as pregnancy advances, until it is[Pg 49] not half a line in thickness. In the earlier months its external surface is rough and flocculent, but afterwards it becomes smoother as its inner surface was at an earlier period.

It is much more loosely connected with the uterus during the first months of pregnancy than afterwards, and this is one reason why premature expulsion of the ovum is more liable to take place at this period than during the middle and latter part of utero-gestation. It is more firmly attached to the uterus in the vicinity of the placenta than any where else, which is owing to the greater number of blood-vessels it receives from the uterus at this point; whereas commonly "it has no perceptible blood-vessels at that part which is situated near the cervix uteri," (Ibid.,) this portion being much more loosely connected with the uterus. The course which the decidual vessels take on coming from the inner surface of the uterus is admirably adapted to render the attachment of this membrane to it as firm as possible.

Vascularity of the
decidua. From Baer.
Upon examining the lining membrane of the uterus at a very early period, when the decidua was still in a pulpy state, Professor v. Baer observed[18] that its villi, which in an unimpregnated state are very short, were remarkably elongated: between these villi, and passing over them, was a substance, not organized but merely effused, and evidently the membrana decidua at an extremely early age. The uterine vessels were continued into this substance, and formed a number of little loops round the villi, thus anastomosing with each other. On account of this reticular distribution it was impossible to distinguish arteries from veins; there is evidently the same relation between the uterus and the decidua as between an inflamed surface and the coagulable lymph effused upon it.

Professor v. Baer considers that at a later period the connexion between the decidua and mucous membrane becomes so intimate, that it is impossible to separate the former without also separating the latter from the fibrous tissue of the uterus. This, we apprehend, is the stratum which, as Dr. Hunter observes, "is always left upon the uterus after delivery, most of which dissolves and comes away with the lochia." He does not appear to have been fully aware of the close connexion between the decidua and lining membrane of the uterus, although he evidently observed the fact from the following sentence: "in separating the membranes from the uterus we observe that the adhesion of the decidua to the chorion, and likewise its adhesion to the muscular fibres of the uterus, is rather stronger than the adhesion between its external and internal stratum, which, we may [Pg 50]presume, is the reason that in labour it so commonly leaves a stratum upon the inside of the uterus." According to the observations of Dr. Montgomery, a great number of small cup-like elevations may be seen upon the external surface of the decidua vera, "having the appearance of little bags, the bottoms of which are attached to, or embedded in, its substance; they then expand or belly out a little, and again grow smaller towards their outer or uterine end, which, in by far the greater number of them, is an open mouth when separated from the uterus: how it may be while they are adherent, I cannot at present say. Some of them which I have found more deeply embedded in the decidua were completely closed sacs. They are best seen about the second or third month, and are not to be found at the advanced periods of gestation."[19]

Decidual cotyledons. From Dr. Montgomery.

a Uterus. d Decidua reflexa.
b Fallopian tube. e Ovum. c Decidua.
The membrana decidua does not envelope the ovum with a single covering, but forms a double membrane upon it, somewhat like a serous membrane; in fact, the descent of the ovum through the Fallopian tube is very similar to that of the testicle through the inguinal canal into the scrotum. The ovum pushes before it that portion of the decidua which covers the uterine extremity of the Fallopian tube, and enters the cavity of the uterus, which is already lined with decidua, covered by the protruded portion which forms the decidua reflexa. It must not be supposed that this reflexion of the decidua is completed as soon as the ovum enters the uterine cavity; the ovum usually remains at the mouth of the Fallopian tube, from which it has emerged, covered by the plastic mass of soft decidua, and the reflexion of this membrane will take place in proportion as the[Pg 51] ovum gradually increases in size. The external layer of decidua is called decidua vera; the internal or reflected portion is called the decidua reflexa, having received this appellation from its discoverer, Dr. Hunter. These membranes would, as Dr. Baillie has correctly observed, be

more correctly named the decidua uteri and decidua chorii: the decidua chorii or reflexa is reflected inwardly from above downwards; it is connected on its inner surface with the chorion: externally it is unattached, whereas, the decidua uteri or vera is unconnected on its inner surface, but attached to the uterus externally.

The membrana decidua differs in its arrangement from that of a serous membrane, inasmuch, as it is not only reflected so as to cover the chorion, but at the point of reflexion it is continued over the chorion externally, where it forms the placenta, so that the chorion is enclosed in all directions by the decidua: this latter portion, however, is not formed till about the middle of pregnancy. The decidua uteri or vera does not extend farther than the os uteri internum, which is filled up by the plug of tough gelatinous substance above described; the decidua chorii or reflexa, from its forming the outer covering of the chorion, of course passes over the os uteri.

Membrana decidua.

The lower orifice corresponds to the os uteri,
the two upper ones to the Fallopian tubes.
From Dr. Hunter.

According to Mr. John Hunter, the decidua vera is continued some little way into the Fallopian tubes, more especially, on that side where the corpus luteum has been formed; it is perforated at the points where the Fallopian tubes enter, as well as at the os uteri, a fact which is beautifully shown in Dr. Hunter's last plate: but this does not continue long, for, as Mr. John Hunter observes, the inferiour opening becomes closed in the first month, and, according to Lobstein's observations, the openings of the Fallopian tubes are closed after the second month. "Where the decidua reflexa is beginning to pass over the chorion, there is, at an early period of pregnancy, an angle formed between it and the decidua, which lines the uterus; and here the decidua is often extremely thin and perforated with small openings so as to look like a piece of lace.

"In proportion as pregnancy advances, the decidua reflexa becomes gradually thinner and thinner, so that at the fourth month it forms an extremely fine layer covering the chorion; it comes at the same time more and more closely in contact with the decidua, which lines that part of the uterus to which the placenta is not fixed, till at length they[Pg 52] adhere together."[20] That portion of the decidua which passes between the placenta and uterus during the latter half of gestation, is called the placental decidua, the description of which will be given with that of the placenta.

To Dr. W. Hunter are we indebted for the first correct description of the decidua; indeed, so excellent is it, that the membrane has been called after him, the decidua of Hunter. Although he was the undoubted discoverer of the reflexa, the existence of the decidua was distinctly noticed by Burton, in 1751. In stating the post mortem examination of a woman, who died undelivered at the full time of pregnancy, he says, "Upon wiping the inside of the uterus very gently with a sponge, there seemed to be pieces of a very tender thin transparent membrane adhering to it in such parts of the uterus where the placenta did not stick to it; but as the womb was somewhat corrupted, and the membrane so very tender, we could not raise any bulk of it so as to be certain what it was." (Burton's Midwifery.)

The decidua seems chiefly intended to form the maternal part of the placenta: (see Placenta:) hence in all those quadrupeds when the maternal part of the placenta is permanently appended to the internal surface of the uterus, no decidua is found.

Having described the maternal membranes of the ovum, we come now to the membranes which form the parietes of the ovum. These are called the fœtal membranes, for they are essentially connected with the origin of the fœtus itself. They are the chorion and the amnion; besides which, there are two others that require notice, viz. the vesicula umbilicalis and allantois.

Chorion. The chorion is the proper covering of the ovum, and corresponds to the membrane lining the shell of an egg, in oviparous animals. It is a thin and transparent membrane, and presents on its external surface a ragged tufted appearance, being covered externally with groups of arborescent villous processes, which after a time unite into trunks to form the umbilical vessels, which, according to Lobstein's observations, are merely veins during the early period of gestation. These loose tufts of venous radicles appear to absorb nourishment for the ovum, much in the same manner as the roots of a plant. Although the chorion is so thin and transparent, it consists nevertheless of two laminæ or layers, between which the villi, which produce this shaggy appearance, take their course. Although the chorion on its external surface is nothing but a net-work of villi, which in process of time become vascular, anatomists have[Pg 53] been unable to detect blood-vessels in the structure of the membrane itself. Its vascularity, however, has been asserted chiefly on the ground of the known vascularity of the decidua, it being supposed that the vessels of the decidua penetrate into the chorion. The chorion, however, belongs so essentially and exclusively to the fœtus, that it appears extremely improbable that any maternal vessels should ramify in its structure for the purposes of its nourishment and growth, and the more so when we reflect that the nutrition of the fœtus itself at this early period is obtained in so different a manner. It is, moreover, extremely difficult to distinguish between the venous absorbing radicles of the chorion, which form the early rudiments of the umbilical vessels, and any vessels which may take their course in the structure of the membrane itself; and the more we consider the relation between the chorion and the decidua, the less are we inclined to accept Meckel's explanation of the vascularity of the chorion, viz. that the vessels of the decidua have the same relation to those of the chorion as the blood-vessels of the maternal part of the placenta have to those of the fœtal part.

Neither nerves nor lymphatics have been discovered in the structure of the chorion, unless, indeed, those white filaments, which are observed here and there about the edge of the placenta, perform the office of lymphatics. This has been hinted at by Dr. Hunter, where he says, "these are the remains of those shaggy vessels which shoot out from the chorion in a young conception, and give the appearance of the ovum being altogether surrounded by the placenta at that time. With a magnifying glass, they appear to be transparent ramifying vessels, which run in corresponding furrows upon the internal surface of the decidua, and a good deal resemble lymphatics." (W. Hunter, op. cit. p. 53.)

The chorion undergoes various changes during the different periods of pregnancy, and forms a very important part of the physiology of utero-gestation. Its thickness, which in the earlier months of pregnancy is more considerable than afterwards, at this period is uniform in every part of the ovum: its external surface covered with those villous prolongations which have already been alluded to. In the second month of pregnancy these become larger, and much more arborescent; after the third month a considerable portion of them gradually disappears, generally from below upwards, so that the greater part of its external surface becomes nearly smooth, except at that point where the umbilical cord has its origin, at which spot the villous prolongations become more developed, and unite to form the umbilical vessels. This part of the chorion, together with the corresponding portion of the membrana decidua, forms a flat circular mass, which at the end of pregnancy covers nearly one-third of the surface of the ovum, and constitutes the placenta or after-birth.[Pg 54] At this point the chorion, which forms its inner surface, is considerably thicker than elsewhere.

At the commencement of pregnancy the chorion is but loosely connected with the decidua, but by degrees it becomes so closely connected by fibres, which are the remains of the little vascular prolongations, especially where these two membranes combine to form the placenta, that in the latter months of pregnancy, they can scarcely, if at all, be separated.

For the more minute consideration of the formation, development, and functions of the chorion, we must refer to the description of the placenta and fœtus.

Amnion. The amnion is the inner membrane of the ovum. It is transparent, and of great tenuity, "yet its texture is firm, so as to resist laceration much more than the other membranes." (W. Hunter, op. cit. p. 50.) It is loosely connected with the chorion on its external surface, except when this membrane unites with the decidua to form the placenta at which spot it adheres to the chorion much more firmly. Its inner surface, which is in immediate contact with the liquor amnii, is very smooth; whereas externally, from being connected with the chorion by an exceedingly fine layer of cellular tissue, its surface is not so smooth. Dr. W. Hunter considers that this intervening tissue, is a gelatinous substance: it seems, however, to possess too much elasticity for such a structure; and, from the reticular appear-ance which it generally presents upon the membranes to which it adheres, we are inclined to adopt the opinion of Meckel in considering it cellular. "In the very early state of an ovum the amnium forms a bag, which is a good deal smaller than the chorion, and, therefore, is not in contact with it." (Ibid. p. 75:) hence, therefore, a space is formed between the two membranes which is filled with a fluid called the liquor amnii spurius, or more correctly the liquor allantoidis. "In the course of some weeks, however, it comes nearly into contact with the chorion, and through the greater part of pregnancy the two membranes are pretty closely applied to each other." (Ibid.) Lobstein, in his admirable Essai sur la Nutrition du Fœtus, observes, that the membranes continues separate from each other so late as the third and fourth month. Cases every now and then occur where a considerable quantity of fluid is found between the chorion and amnion in labour at the full period of pregnancy.

We shall defer the minute description of the amnion and its relations, during the very early periods of utero-gestation, until we describe the embryo. The amnion is reflected upon the umbilical cord at its insertion into the placenta, envelopes the umbilical vessels, the external covering of which it forms, and is continued to the anterior surface of the child's abdomen, passing into that projecting portion of the skin which forms the future navel.

Blood-vessels and nerves have not as yet been discovered in the[Pg 55] structure of the amnion, but Meckel considers it extremely probable that the fine layer of cellular tissue by which it is connected with the chorion contains vessels for its nutrition.

Liquor amnii. The amnion contains a fluid known by the name of liquor amnii. In the earlier months of pregnancy it is nearly, if not quite transparent; as pregnancy advances it becomes turbid, containing more or less of what appears to resemble mucus: it has a distinctly saline taste; its specific gravity is rather more than that of water. Its relative and absolute quantity vary considerably at different periods of pregnancy: thus the relative weight of liquor amnii to that of the fœtus is very considerable at the beginning of pregnancy, at the middle they are nearly equal, but towards the end, the weight of fluid to that of the child, diminishes considerably, so that during the last weeks of pregnancy it scarcely equals a pound, and seldom more than eight ounces, whereas the medium weight of the child is usually between six and seven pounds: the quantity, however, varies considerably, sometimes amounting to several quarts. In the early months the absolute quantity increases, so that between the third and fourth months it sometimes equals as much as thirty-six ounces. Chemically it consists chiefly of water, a small quantity of albumen and gelatine, a peculiar acid called amniotic, with a little muriate of soda and ammonia, and a trace of phosphate of lime.

The source of the liquor amnii is still unknown. Dr. Burns asserts that "it is secreted from the inner surface of the membrane by pellucid vessels," but as he confesses that "these have never been injected or traced to their source (Principles of Midwifery, by J. Burns, M. D. p. 222.,) little weight can be attached to such a view." Meckel considers (Handbuch der Menschlichen Anatomie, vol. iv. p. 707,) that the greater part of it, especially in the early months, is a secretion from the maternal vessels, but that afterwards, as pregnancy advances, it becomes mingled with the excretions of the fœtus. It appears to be a means of nourishment to the fœtus during the first part of pregnancy, from the fact that it contains more nutritious matter in the early than in the latter months, since at that time a considerable coagulation is alcohol, &c. The disappearance of this coagulable matter of the liquor amnii, towards the end of pregnancy, may be attributed to its having been absorbed at an earlier period, and to the process of nutrition being now carried on by other means. Besides being a source of nourishment to the fœtus, it serves many useful purposes; it secures the fœtus against external pressure or violence, and supports the regular distension of the uterus; on the other hand it diminishes and equalises the pressure of the fœtus upon the uterus; during labour by distending the membranes into an elastic cone, it materially assists to dilate the os uteri; it also serves to lubricate and moisten the external passages.

Placenta. The placenta is formed essentially by the chorion[Pg 56] and decidua; it is a flat, circular, or more or less oval mass, soft, but becoming firmer towards its edge. It is the most vascular part of the ovum, and by which it is connected most intimately with the uterus. Its longest diameter is generally about eight, its shortest about six inches; its greatest thickness is at that spot where the umbilical cord is inserted, which is usually about the middle of the placenta, although it occasionally varies considerably in this respect, the cord coming off sometimes at the edge. The placenta, as ordinarily seen after labour, is barely an inch in its thickest part, but when filled with blood or injection it swells very considerably, and is then little short of two inches. It is generally attached to the upper part of the uterus in the neighbourhood of one of the Fallopian tubes, and more frequently on the left side than on the right; its inner or fœtal surface is smooth, being covered by the chorion, which at this part is much thicker.

The placenta cannot be distinguished from the other parts of the ovum until the end of the second month, at which period it covers nearly half the surface of the ovum, gradually diminishing in relative size, but increasing in thickness and absolute bulk up to the full period of utero-gestation. It forms a spongy vascular mass, its uterine surface being divided unequally into irregular lobes called cotyledons.

The uterine surface of a full-grown placenta is covered by a pulpy membrane, resembling in structure the decidua which covers the chorion, and of which it seems to be a continuation. This is always found present at the end of pregnancy: it covers the lobes of the uterine surface of the placenta, descending into the sulci which runs between them: in some parts it is thicker than in others, especially where it is connected with, or in fact becomes, the decidua of the chorion or decidua reflexa. This membrane, which has been called the placenta decidua, is pretty firmly attached to the vessels of the placenta, so as not to be separated without rupture; but by maceration, its texture is more or less destroyed, so that we may easily distinguish the extremities of these vessels. "This decidua, or uterine portion of the placenta," says Dr. Hunter, "is not a simple thin membrane expanded over the surface of the part: it produces a thousand irregular processes, which pervade the substance of the placenta as deep as the chorion or inner surface; and are every where so blended and entangled with the ramifications of the umbilical system, that no anatomist will perhaps be able to discover the nature of their union. While these two parts are combined, the placenta makes a pretty firm mass, no part of it is loose or floating; but when they are carefully separated, the umbilical system is evidently nothing but loose floating ramifications of the umbilical vessels, like that vascular portion of the chorion, which makes part of the placentula in a calf; and the uterine part is seen shooting out into innumerable floating processes and rugæ, with the most irregular[Pg 57] and minutely subdivided cavities between them that can be conceived. This part answers to the uterine fungus in the quadrupeds: it receives no vessels demonstrable by the finest injection from those of the navel string; yet it is full of both large and small arteries and veins: these are all branches of the uterine vessels, and are readily filled by injecting the arteries and veins of the uterus, and they all break through in separating the placenta from the uterus, leaving corresponding orifices on the two parted surfaces." (Hunter, op. cit. p. 42.)

According to Lobstein's observations, although this membrane appears to be a continuation of the decidua which covers the chorion, it nevertheless does not exist during the earlier months. During the first months of pregnancy the placenta does not present a solid mass, with its uterine surface covered with projecting lobuli, as it does at the full term of pregnancy; but the vessels of which it is composed (fœtal) are loose and floating, as if it had been subjected to maceration. It has been supposed, that this irregular lobulated appearance of the uterine surface of the placenta was produced at the moment of its separation from the uterus during labour; this, however, is not the case, for Lobstein having opened the uterus of a woman who died in the fifth month of pregnancy, and separated the placenta with great care, found these lobular prominences, although not yet covered by the membrane of which we have just spoken. Wrisberg, professor of anatomy at Göttingen, considered that this membrane was distinct from the decidua reflexa, since with care the two membranes can be easily separated.

Uterine surface of the Placenta.

In examining the uterine surface of a full grown placenta it is necessary to place it upon something convex, in order that it may resemble, as nearly as possible, the form which it had when attached to the concave surface of the uterus; the cotyledons are thus rendered prominent and separated from each other; the sulci, which run between them, are wide and gaping: whereas, when the placenta is laid upon a flat surface, its cotyledons are closely pressed together, and the sulci more or less completely concealed. On minute examination of these sulci a number of openings may be observed, varying in size and shape, but usually[Pg 58] more or less oval, their edges distinct, smooth, and thin; on directing a strong light into some of the larger ones a number of smaller apertures may be observed opening into them, in much the same way as is observed when looking down a large vein. Some of these canals do not immediately lead to smaller orifices as above described, but open at once into an irregular-shaped cell or cavity, in the parietes of which numerous small apertures may be observed, through which blood oozes when the adjacent parts of the placenta are slightly pressed upon. Besides these openings at the bottom of the interlobular sulci, others may be seen here and there upon the cotyledons; these are generally smaller, their edges thicker, and in most instances they are round; but they are not so invariably met with as the openings between the cotyledons, these lobular projections being sometimes very thickly covered with placental decidua. The openings observed on the uterine surface of the placenta correspond to the mouths of the uterine veins and arteries, which, in the unim-pregnated state, open into the cavity of the uterus, but which now, by means of the decidua, convey maternal blood to and from the placenta. "Any anatomist," says Dr. W. Hunter, "who has once seen and understood them, can readily discover them upon the surface of any fresh placenta; the veins, indeed, he will find have an indistinct appearance from their tenderness and frequent anastomoses, so as to look a good deal like irregular interstitial void spaces: the arteries which generally make a snake-like convolution or two, on the surface of the placenta, and give off no anastomosing branches, are more distinct." (Hunter, op. cit. p. 46.) From the observations of Messrs. Mayo and Stanley, and from their examination of the original preparations in the Hunterian museum at the College of Surgeons, London, illustrating this subject, it appears that, in all probability, most of the large thin-edged apertures at the bottom of the interlobular sulci are connected with the uterine veins; whereas, the smaller orifices, the margins of which are thicker, and which are chiefly observed upon the cotyledons, are continuations of the uterine arteries.

These openings were also pointed out by the late Dr. Hugh Ley, in describing the post mortem examination of a woman who had died at the full term undelivered (Med. Gaz. June 1, 1833:) "The uterine surface (of the placenta) thus detached from the uterus, exhibited its lobules with their intersecting sulci, even more distinctly than they are seen in the uninjected placenta; and in several parts there could be perceived, with the naked eye, small apertures of an oval form, with edges perfectly smooth, regularly defined, and thicker, as well as more opaque, than the contiguous parts which they penetrated." The communication between the openings of the placental cells, and the mouths of the uterine veins and arteries, which convey their[Pg 59] blood to the placenta, as before observed, is effected by means of the placental decidua. The connecting portion of canal is of a flattened shape, runs obliquely between the uterus and placenta, and appears to be formed entirely of decidua. The manner in which the arteries pass to the placenta is very different to that of the veins: "the arteries," as Dr. W. Hunter observes, "are all much convoluted and serpentine; the larger, when injected, are almost of the size of crow-quills: the veins have frequent anastomoses." Mr. J. Hunter has described this point more minutely, and gives still more precise notions of the manner in which the arteries pass to the placenta. "The arteries of the uterus which are not immediately employed in conveying nourishment to it, go on towards the placenta, and, proceeding obliquely between it and the uterus, pass through the decidua without ramifying: just before they enter the placenta, making two or three close spiral turns upon themselves, they open at once into its spongy substance, without any diminution of size, and without passing beyond the surface as above described.

The intention of these spiral turns would appear to be that of diminishing the force of the circulation as it approaches the spongy substance of the placenta, and is a structure which must lessen the quick motion of the blood in a part where a quick motion of this fluid was not wanted. The size of these curling arteries at this termination is about that of a crow's quill. The veins of the uterus appropriated to bring back the blood from the placenta, commence from this spongy substance by such wide beginnings as are more than equal to the size of the veins themselves. These veins pass obliquely through the decidua to the uterus, enter its substance obliquely, and immediately communicate with the proper veins of the uterus; the area of those veins bear no proportion to their circumference, the veins being very much flattened."[21]

On examining these vessels in an injected uterus to which the placenta is attached, we shall therefore find that all traces of a regular canal or tube are suddenly lost upon their entering the placenta; each vessel (whether artery or vein) abruptly terminating in a spongy cellular tissue. If a blow-pipe be introduced into a piece of sponge, we shall have a very simple but correct illustration of the manner in which the uterine blood circulates through the placenta. The cell into which each vessel immediately opens is usually much larger than the rest, so that when the cellular structure of the placenta is filled with wax, a number of irregular nodules[22] are found continuous with these vessels[Pg 60] and passing into an infinity of minute granules, which are merely so many casts of smaller cells. That this cellular tissue pervades the whole mass of the placenta, and communicates freely with the uterine vessels by which it is filled with blood, is proved by repeating a very simple experiment of Dr. Hunter, viz. "if a blow-pipe be thrust into the substance of the placenta any where, the air which is blown into the cellular part opens, and rushes out readily by, the open mouths both of the arteries and veins." (Hunter, op. cit. p. 46.) That it also envelopes the umbilical vessels of the cord is shown by the fact, that if a pipe be inserted beneath the outer covering of the cord near to its insertion into the placenta, we shall be able to "fill the whole placenta uniformly in its cellular part, and likewise all the venous system of the uterus and decidua, as readily and fully as if we had fixed the pipe in the spermatic or hypogastric vein; so ready a passage is there reciprocally between the cells of the placenta and the uterine vessels." (Ibid. p. 47.)

The maternal portion of the placenta therefore consists of a spongy cellular tissue, which is filled by the uterine vessels, and also of those trunks which pass through the decidua, and which form the communication between these vessels and the placental cells.

Fœtal surface of the placenta.

The fœtal surface of the placenta is smooth and glossy, being covered by the amnion and chorion; it is much harder than the uterine surface, and is streaked over by the larger branches of the umbilical vein and arteries, which radiate irregularly from the point where the cord is inserted; and which pass beneath the amnion, and between the two layers of which the chorion is composed, to which they are intimately connected. These vessels supply the various lobuli of which the placenta is composed, so that each lobulus receives at least one of these branches; for, although the umbilical cord consists of two arteries and one vein, this arrangement does not continue into the body of the placenta. "Every branch of an artery," as Dr. Hunter observes, "is attended with a branch of a vein: these cling to one another, and[Pg 61] frequently in the substance of the placenta entwine round one another, as in the navel string." (Ibid. p. 40.) Each cotyledon receives its own vessels, so that the vessels of one cotyledon have no direct communication with those of the adjacent ones, as proved by Wrisberg's examinations; for if we inject the vessel or vessels of one of these lobuli, the injection will not pass into those of the others. When the vessels have reached the cotyledons, they are divided and subdivided ad infinitum; they are connected together by a fine cellular membrane, which may be very easily removed by maceration, and then they may be seen ramifying in the most beautiful and delicate manner possible; the main branches having no communication or anastomosis with each other.

The umbilical arteries anastomose freely with each other upon the fœtal surface of the placenta, before dividing into the branches above-mentioned; hence, if an injection be thrown into one umbilical artery it will return almost immediately by the other; but if this be tied also, the injection, after a time, will return by the umbilical vein, but not until all the vessels of the placenta have been filled, proving that there is a free passage of blood from the arteries into the veins.

From these remarks, founded chiefly on the admirable observations of the Hunters, and repeated examinations of the placenta, which we have made with the greatest care and impartiality, it may be stated with confidence, that the placenta consists of two portions—a maternal and a fœtal. The maternal portion consists, as we have before observed, of a spongy cellular tissue; and also of those trunks which pass through the decidua, and which form the communication between the uterine vessels and the placental cells. The fœtal part is formed by the ramifications of the umbilical vessels: "that each of those parts has its peculiar system of arteries and veins, and its peculiar circulation, receiving blood by its arteries, and returning it by its veins; that the circulation through these parts of the placenta differs in the following manner: in the umbilical portion the arteries terminate in the veins by a continuity of canal; whereas, in the uterine portion there are intermediate cells into which the arteries terminate, and from which the veins begin." (Hunter, op. cit. p. 48.)

Although various observations and anatomical injections show that to a certain degree, there is a communication between the uterus and the placenta, inasmuch as the blood of the former is received into the sinuses or cells of the latter, we possess no proof that the blood can pass from these sinuses into the umbilical vessels: on the contrary, every thing combines to prove that the circulation of the fœtus is altogether independent of that of the mother. We know from daily experience that in labour at the full term of pregnancy, the placenta is easily expelled[Pg 62] from the uterus: that, upon examining the surface which had been attached to the uterus we find no laceration, and that a discharge of more or less blood takes place for some days afterwards. We know, also, that when the placenta becomes detached from the uterus during the progress of gestation, it is followed by a considerable hemorrhage, which greatly endangers the life of the mother. These facts prove that there is a circulation of uterine blood in the placenta, which is destroyed upon its being separated from the uterus. That this uterine circulation in the placenta is unconnected with the circulation of fœtal vessels in the placenta is proved by the fact first pointed out by Wrisberg, viz. that, where the mother has died from loss of blood, and the maternal vessels therefore drained of their contents, those of the fœtus have been full of blood. Still farther to illustrate this fact, he killed several cows big with calf, by a large wound through the heart or great vessels, so as to ensure the most profuse and sudden loss of blood possible, and never found that the vessels of the calf were deprived of blood, although those of the mother were perfectly empty; moreover, no anatomist has ever yet succeeded in making injections pass from the fœtal into the uterine vessels, or vice versâ. Lobstein has mentioned a mode of illustrating this fact (Essai sur la Nutrition du Fœtus,) which is both simple and striking. Upon examining the uterine surface of a placenta which has been expelled at the full term, it presents the appearance of a spongy mass gorged with blood, which may be removed by washing or maceration, and if a placenta thus prepared be injected, the fluids will pass with the greatest facility from the umbilical arteries into the umbilical vein, but not one drop into its cellular structure; it is evident, therefore, that the blood which had filled the intervals between the vessels, and which had been removed by washing and maceration, could not have belonged to the fœtus, but must have come from the mother; for if any of the vessels had been ruptured the injection would not have succeeded.

In concluding these observations upon the placenta, we may briefly state, that there is the same relation between the umbilical vessels and the maternal blood, which fills the placental cells, as there is between the branches of the pulmonary artery, and the air which fills the bronchial cell.[23]

[Pg 63]Umbilical cord. The umbilical cord, funis, or navel string, is a vascular rope extending between the fœtus and placenta, by which they are connected together. It usually arises, as we have before observed, from about the middle of the placenta, and terminates at the umbilical ring of the fœtus; it consists of two umbilical arteries and one umbilical vein; the former conveying the blood from the common iliac arteries of the fœtus to the cotyledons of the placenta; the latter formed by the union of the collected umbilical veins, on the inner surface of the placenta, and returning this blood to the fœtus. In the early periods of pregnancy it also consists of the duct and vessels of the vesicula umbilicalis, the urachus, and more or less of the intestinal canal. The umbilical cord does not present the same form or appearance at every period of gestation; the younger the embryo, the shorter and thicker is the cord; in fact, there are no traces whatever of a cord at first, the embryo adhering, by its lower or caudal extremity, directly to the membranes. By the fifth or sixth week it becomes visible; at this early period the vessels of which it is composed pass from the fœtus in a straight direction, but as pregnancy advances they become more or less spiral, winding round each other, and usually from left to right: according to Meckel, they take the opposite direction much less frequently, viz. in the proportion of one to nine.

The vessels of the umbilical cord are imbedded in a thick viscid substance; upon minute examination, it will be found to consist of a very fine cellular tissue, containing an albuminous matter which slowly exudes, when pressed between the fingers. This cellular tissue itself may be demonstrated by the inflation of air or injection with mercury: it seems to accompany the umbilical vessels as far as the posterior surface of the peritoneum; and Lobstein is of opinion that it is a continuation of the cellular tissue, which covers this membrane. (Lobstein, sur la Nutrition du Fœtus. § 75.)

Externally, the umbilical cord is covered by a continuation of the amnion, which, although it be the inner membrane of the ovum, is the outer covering of the cord: in some places it is very thick and strong, and not easily ruptured. From repeated observations, the weakest part of the cord seems to be at about three or four inches distant from the umbilicus, this being the spot where it has invariably given way in every case we have seen, where the cord has been broken at the moment of the child's birth.

From the time of the commencement to the full time of utero-gestation, the cord becomes gradually longer, so that it attains an average length of from eighteen to twenty inches; this, however,[Pg 64] varies remarkably. We have known the cord exceed forty inches; and a case is described by Baudelocque, where it was actually fifty-seven inches long: on the other hand, it is sometimes not more than four or five inches in length.

It is remarkable that the cord, which at the end of pregnancy is usually of about the same length as the fœtus, is relatively much longer during the sixth month; hence we may conclude, that in those cases where knots have been found upon the cord, the knot must have been formed at this period when the fœtus was small enough to pass through a coil of it.

Neither blood-vessels nor lymphatics have as yet been found in the structure of the cord itself. A filament of nerve from the solar plexus has been occasionally seen passing through the umbilical ring, and extending to a distance down the cord.

The vesicula umbilicalis and allantois, being essentially connected with the earliest grades of fœtal development, will be considered under that head.

Embryo. There is, perhaps, no department of physiology which has been so remarkably enriched by recent discoveries, as that which relates to the primitive development of the ovum and its embryo. The researches of Baer, Rathke, Purkinje, Valentin, &c. in Germany; of Dutrochet, Prevost, Dumas, and Coste, &c. in France; and of Owen, Sharpey, Allen Thomson, Jones, and Martin Barry in England, but more especially those of the celebrated Baer, have greatly advanced our knowledge of these subjects, and led us deeply into those mysterious processes of Nature which relate to our first origin and formation.

These researches have all tended to establish one great law, connected with the early development of the human embryo, and that of other mammiferous animals, viz, that it at first possesses a structure and arrangement analogous to that of animals in a much lower scale of formation: this observation also applies of course to the ovum itself, since a variety of changes take place in it after impregnation, before a trace of the embryo can be detected.

At the earliest periods, the human ovum bears a perfect analogy to the eggs of fishes, amphibia, and birds; and it is only by carefully examining the changes impregnation in the ova of these lower classes of animals, that we have been enabled to discover them in the mammalia and human subject.

As the bird's egg, from its size, best affords us the means of investigating these changes, and as in all essential respects they are the same in the human ovum, it will be necessary for us to lay before our readers a short account of its structure and contents, and also of the changes which they undergo, after impregnation. In doing this we shall merely confine ourselves to the description of what is applicable to the human ovum.

Section of a hen's egg
within the ovary.

a The granulary membrane forming
the periphery of the yelk. b Vesicle
of Purkinje imbedded in the cumulus.
c Vitellary membrane. d Inner and
outer layers of the capsule of the
ovum. e Indusium of the ovary.
The egg is known to consist of two distinct parts, the vitellus or yelk surrounded by its albumen or white; to the former of[Pg 65] these we now more particularly refer. The yelk is a granular albuminous fluid, contained in a granular membranous sac (the blastodermic membrane) which is covered by an investing membrane called the vitelline membrane or yelk-bag. The impregnated vitellus is retained in its capsule in the ovary, precisely as the ovum of the mammifera is in the Graafian vesicle. The whole ovary in this case has a clustered appearance, like a bunch of grapes, each capsule being suspended by a short pedicle of indusium.

a Vitelline membrane b Blastoderma.
From T. W. Jones.
In those ova which are considerably developed before impregnation, the granular blastermodic membrane is observed to be thicker, and the granules more aggregated at that part which corresponds to the pedicle, forming a slight elevation with a depression in its centre, like the cumulus in the proligerous disc of a Graafian vesicle. This little disc is the blastoderma, germinial membrane or cicatricula; in the central depression just mentioned is an exceedingly minute vesicle first noticed by Professor Purkinje of Breslau, and named after him: in more correct language it is the germinal vesicle.

According to Wagner, the germinal vesicle is not surrounded by a disc before impregnation; and it is only after this process that the above-mentioned disc of granules is formed. By the time the ovum is about to quit the ovary the vesicle itself has disappeared, so that an ovum has never been found in the oviduct containing a germinal vesicle, nothing remaining of it beyond the little depression in the cumulus of the cicatricula.

The rupture of the Purkinjean or germinal vesicle has been supposed by Mr. T. W. Jones to take place before impregnation; but the observations of Professor Valentin seem to lead to the inference that it is a result of that process, and must be therefore looked upon as one of the earliest changes which take place in the ovum or yelk-bag upon quitting the ovary.[24]

During its passing through the oviduct (what in mammalia is called the Fallopian tube,) the ovum receives a thick covering of albumen, and as it descends still farther along the canal the membrane of the shell is formed.

[Pg 66]On examining the appearance of the ovum in mammiferous animals, and especially the human ovum, it will be found that it presents a form and structure very analogous to the ova just described, more especially those of birds. It is a minute spherical sac, filled with an albuminous fluid, lined with its blastodermic or germinal membrane, in which is seated the germinal vesicle or vesicle of Purkinje. When the ovum has quitted the ovary the germinal vesicle disappears, and on its entering the Fallopian tube it becomes covered with a gelatinous, or rather albuminous covering. This was inferred by Valentin, who considered that "the enormous swelling of the ova, and their passage through the Fallopian tubes," tended to prove the circumstance. (Edin. Med. and Surg. Journ. April, 1836.) It has since been demonstrated by Mr. T. W. Jones in a rabbit seven days after impregnation. The vitellary membrane seems, at this time, to give way, leaving the vitellus of the ovum merely covered by its spherical blastoderma, and encased by the layer of albuminous matter which surrounds it.

From what we have now stated, a close analogy will appear between the ova of the mammalia and those of the lower classes, more especially birds, which from their size afford us the best opportunities of investigating this difficult subject.

In birds, the covering of the vitellus is called yelk-bag; whereas, in mammalia and man it receives the name of vesicula umbilicalis. Its albuminous covering, which corresponds to the white and membrane of the shell in birds, is called chorion: by the time that the ovum has reached the uterus, this outer membrane has undergone a considerable change; it becomes covered with a complete down of little absorbing fibrillæ, which rapidly increase in size as development advances, until it presents that tufted vascular appearance, which we have already mentioned when describing this membrane.

The first or primitive trace of the embryo is in the cicatricula or germinal membrane, which contained the germinal vesicle before its disappearance. In the centre of this, upon its upper surface, may be discovered a small dark line;[25] "this line or primitive trace is swollen at one extremity, and is placed in the direction of the transverse axis of the egg."

a Transparent area. b Primitive trace.

As development advances, the cicatricula expands. "We are indebted to Pander,"[26] says Dr. Allen Thomson in his admirable essay above quoted, "for the important discovery, that towards the twelfth or fourteenth hour, in the hen's egg the germinal membrane becomes divided into two layers of granules, the serous and mucous layers of the cicatricula; and that the [Pg 67]rudimentary trace of the embryo, which has at this time become evident, is placed in the substance of the upper-most or serous layer." "According to this observer, and according to Baer, the part of this layer which surrounds the primitive trace soon becomes thicker; and on examining this part with care, towards the eighteenth hour, we observe that a long furrow has been formed in it, in the bottom of which the primitive trace is situated; about the twentieth hour this furrow is converted into a canal open at both ends, by the junction of its margins (the plicæ primitivæ of Pander, the laminæ dorsales of Baer:) the canal soon becomes closed at the cephalic or swollen extremity of the primitive trace, at which part it is of a pyriform shape, being wider here than at any other part. According to Baer and Serres, some time after the canal begins to close, a semi-fluid matter is deposited in it, which on its acquiring greater consistence, becomes the rudiment of the spinal cord; the pyriform extremity or head is soon after this seen to be partially subdivided into three vesicles, which being also filled with a semi-fluid matter, gives rise to the rudimentary state of the encephalon." "As the formation of the spinal canal proceeds, the parts of the serous layer which surrounds it, especially towards the head, become thicker and more solid, and before the twenty-fourth hour we observe on each side of this canal four or five small round opaque bodies, these bodies indicate the first formation of the dorsal vertebræ.

a Transparent area. b Laminæ dorsales. c Cephalic end. d Rudiments of dorsal vertebræ. e Serous layer. f Lateral portion of the primitive trace. g Mucous layer. h Vascular layer. k Laminæ dorsales united to form the spinal canal.

"About the same time, or from the twentieth to the [Pg 68]twenty-fourth hour, the inner layer of the germinal membrane undergoes a farther division, and by a peculiar change is converted into the vascular mucous layers." (A. Thomson, op. cit.) It will thus be seen, that the germinal membrane is that part of the ovum in which the first changes impregnation are observed. The rudiments of the osseous and nervous systems are formed by the outer or serous layers; the outer covering of the fœtus or integuments, including the amnois, are also furnished by it. "The layer next in order has been called vascular, because in it the development of the principal parts of the vascular system appears to take place. The third, called the mucous layer, situated next the substance of the yelk, is generally in intimate connexion with the vascular layer, and it is to the changes which these combined layers undergo, that the intestinal, the respiratory, and probably also the glandular systems owe their origin." (A. Thomson, op. cit. p. 298.)

a Serous layer. b c Vascular layer. d Mucous layer. e Heart.

The embryo is therefore formed in the layers of the germinal membrane, and becomes, as it were, spread out upon the surface of the ovum: the changes which the ovum of mammalia undergoes appear from actual observation, to be precisely analogous to those in the inferior animals. (Baer, Prevost and Dumas.) From the primitive trace, which was at first merely a line crossing the cicatricula, and which now begins rapidly to exhibit the characters of the spinal column, the parietes of the head and trunk gradually approach farther and farther towards the anterior surface of the abdomen and head until they unite; in this way the sides of the jaws close in the median line of the face, occasionally leaving the union incomplete, and thus appearing to produce in some cases the congenital defects of hare-lip and cleft palate. In some way the ribs meet at the sternum; and it may be supposed that sometimes this bone is left deficient, and thus may become one of the causes of those rare cases of malformation, where the child has been born with the heart external to the parietes of the thorax. In like manner the parietes of the abdomen and pelvis close in the linea alba and symphysis pubis, occasionally leaving the integuments of the navel deficient, or, in other words, producing congenital umbilical hernia, or at the pubes a non-union of its symphysis with a species of inversion of the bladder, the anterior wall of that viscus being nearly or entirely wanting.

The cavity of the abdomen is therefore at first open to the vesicula umbilicalis or yelk, but this changes as the abdominal [Pg 69]parietes begin to close in; in man and the mammalia merely a part of it, as above mentioned, forms the intestinal canal, whereas, in oviparous animals the whole of the yelk-bag enters the abdominal cavity, and serves for an early nutriment to the young animal. Another change connected with the serous or outer layer of the germinal membrane is the formation of the amnion. The fœtal rudiment which from its shape has been called carina, now begins to be enveloped by a membrane of exceeding tenuity, forming a double covering upon it; the one which immediately invests the fœtus is considered to form the future epidermis; the other, or outer fold, forms a loose sac around it, containing the liquor amnii. Whilst these changes are taking place in the serous layer of the germinal membrane, and whilst the intestinal canal, &c. are forming on the anterior surface of the embryo, which is turned towards the ovum, by means of the inner or mucous layer, equally important changes are now observed in the middle or vascular layer. "In forming this fold," says Dr. A. Thomson, "the mucous layer is reflected farthest inwards; the serous layer advances least, and the space between them, occupied by the vascular layer, is filled up by a dilated part of this layer, the rudiment of the heart." (Op. cit. p. 301.)

Whilst this rudimentary trace of the vascular system is making its appearance, minute vessels are seen ramifying over the vesicula umbilicalis, forming, according to Baer's observations, a reticular anastomosis, which unites into two vessels the vasa omphalo-meseraica. (British and Foreign Med. Rev. No. 1.) These may be demonstrated with great ease in the chick: the cicatricula increases in extent; it becomes vascular, and at length forms a heart-shaped net-work of delicate vessels, which unite into two trunks, terminating one on each side of the abdomen.

b Is a portion of the convexity of the amnion, upon which, at a is the fundus of the diminutive human allantois.

c The duct of the vesicula umbilicalis, dividing into two intestinal portions; and besides this duct are two vessels which are distributed upon the vesicula umbilicalis, and form a reticular anastomosis with each other. From Baer.

The umbilical vesicle now begins to separate itself more and more from the abdomen of the fœtus, merely a duct of communication passing to that portion of it which forms the intestinal canal. The first rudiment of the cord will be found at this separation; its fœtal extremity remains for a long time funnel-shaped, containing, besides a portion of intestine, the duct of the vesicula umbilicalis, the vasa omphalo-meseraica (the future vena portæ,) the umbilical vein from the collected venous radicles of the chorion, and the early trace of the umbilical arteries. These last-named vessels ramify on a delicate membranous sac of an [Pg 70]elongated form which rises from the inferior or caudal extremity of the embryo, viz. the allantois; whether this is formed by a portion of the mucous layer of the germinal vesicle, in common with the other abdominal viscera, appears to be still uncertain: in birds this may be very easily demonstrated as a vascular vesicle, arising from the extremity of the intestinal canal; and in mammalia, connected with the bladder by means of a canal called urachus: from its sausage-like shape, it has received the name of allantois.

The existence of an allantois in the human embryo has been long inferred from the presence of a ligamentous cord extending from the fundus of the bladder to the umbilicus, like the urachus in animals. But from the extreme delicacy of the allantois, and from its function ceasing at a very early period, it had defied all research, until lately when it has been satisfactorily demonstrated in the human embryo by Baer and Rathke. It occupies the space between the chorion and amnion, and gives rise occasionally to a collection of fluid between these membranes, familiarly known by the name of the liquor amnii spurius, which, strictly speaking is the liquor allantoidis.

The function of the allantois is still in a great measure unknown. In animals it evidently acts as a species of receptaculum urinæ during the latter periods of gestation; but it is very doubtful if this be its use during the earlier periods. It does not seem directly connected with the process of nutrition, which at this time is proceeding so rapidly, first by means of the albuminous contents of the vitellus, or vesicula umbilicalis, and afterwards by the absorbing radicles of the chorion; but, from analogy with the structure of the lower classes of animals, it would appear that it is intended to produce certain changes in the rudimentary circulation of the embryo, similar to those which, at a later period of pregnancy, are effected by means of the placenta, and after birth by the lungs, constituting the great functions of respiration.

In many of the lower classes of animals, respiration (or at least the functions analogous to it) is performed by organs situated at the inferior or caudal extremity of the animal: thus for instance, certain insect tribes, as in hymenoptera, or insects with a sting, as wasps, bees, &c.; in diptera, or insects with two wings, as the common fly; and also the spider tribe, have their respiratory organs situated in the lower part of the abdomen. In some of the crustacea, as, for instance, the shrimp, the organs of respiration lie under the tail between the fins, and floating loosely in the water. Again, some of the molusca, viz. the cuttle-fish, have the respiratory organs in the abdomen. We also know that many animals, during the first periods of their lives, respire by a different set of organs to what they do in the adult state: the most familiar illustration of this is the frog, which, during its tadpole state, lives entirely in the water.

[Pg 71]

a Bronchial processes. b Vesicula umbilicalis. c Vitellus. d Allantois. e Amnion. From Baer.

As the growth of the embryo advances, other organs whose function is as temporary as that of the allantois, make their appearance: these also correspond to the respiratory organs of a lower class of animals, although higher than those to which we have just alluded,—we mean bronchial processes or gills. It is to Professor Rathke (Acta Naturæ Curios. vol. xiv,) that we are indebted for pointing out the interesting fact, that several transverse slit-like apertures may be detected on each side the neck of the embryo, at a very early stage of development. In the chick, in which he first observed it, it takes place about the fourth day of incubation: at this period the neck is remarkably thick, and contains a cavity which communicates inferiorly with the œsophagus and stomach, and opens externally on each side by means of the above-mentioned apertures, precisely as is observed in fishes, more especially the shark tribe; these apertures are separated from each other by lobular septa, of exceedingly soft and delicate structure. Rathke observed the same structure in the embryo of the pig and other mammalia; and Baer has since shown it distinctly in the human embryo. It is curious to see how the vascular system corresponds to the grade of development then present: the heart is single, consisting of one auricle and one ventricle; the aorta gives off four delicate, but perfectly simple branches, two of which go to the right, and two to the left side; each of these little arteries passes to one of the lobules or septa at the side of the neck, which correspond to gills, and having again united with the three others, close to what is the first rudiment of the vertebral column, they form a single trunk which afterwards becomes the abdominal aorta. In a short time these slit-like openings begin to close; the bronchial processes or septa become obliterated, and indistinguishable from the adjacent parts; the heart loses the form of a single heart; a crescentic fold begins to mark the future division into two ventricles, and gradually extends until the septum between them is completed. It is also continued along the bulb of the aorta, dividing it into two trunks, the aorta proper and pulmonary artery; at the upper part the division is left incomplete, so that there is an opening from one vessel to the other, which forms the ductus arteriosus.[27] A similar[Pg 72] process takes place in the auricles, the foramen ovale being apparently formed in the same manner as the ductus arteriosus; these changes commence in the human embryo about the fourth week, and are completed about the seventh.

At first the body of the embryo has a more elongated form than afterwards, and the part which is first developed is the trunk, at the upper extremity of which a small prominence less thick than the middle part, and separated from the rest of the body by an indentation, distinguishes the head. There are as yet no traces whatever of extremities, or of any other prominent parts; it is straight, or nearly so, the posterior surface slightly convex, the anterior slightly concave, and rests with its inferior extremity directly upon the membranes, or by means of an extremely short umbilical cord.

The head now increases considerably in proportion to the rest of the body, so much so, that at the beginning of the second month, it equals nearly half the size of the whole body: previous to, and after this period, it is usually smaller. The body of the embryo becomes considerably curved, both at its upper as well as its lower extremity, although the trunk itself still continues straight. The head joins the body at a right angle, so that the part of it which corresponds to the chin is fixed directly upon the upper part of the breast; nor can any traces of neck be discerned, until nearly the end of the second month.

The inferior extremity of the vertical column, which at first resembles the rudiment of a tail becomes shorter towards the middle of the third month, and takes a curviture forwards under the rectum, in the fifth week the extremities become visible, the upper usually somewhat sooner than the lower, in the form of small blunt prominences. The upper close under the head, the lower near the caudal extremity of the vertebral column. Both are turned somewhat outwards, on account of the size of the abdomen; the upper are usually directed somewhat downwards, the lower ones somewhat upwards.

Diagram of the fœtus and membranes about the fourth week.

a Vesicula umbilicalis already passing into the ventricular and rectum intestine at g. b Vena and arteria omphalo-meseraica. c Allantois springing from the pelvis with the umbilical arteries. d Embryo. e Amnion. f Chorion. From Carus.

The vesicula umbilicalis may still be distinguished in the second month as a small vesicle, not larger than a pea, near the insertion of the cord, at the navel, and external to the amnion. From[Pg 73] the trunk, which is almost entirely occupied by the abdominal cavity, arises a short thick umbilical cord, in which some of the convolutions of the intestines may still be traced. Besides these it usually contains, as already observed, the two umbilical arteries and the umbilical vein, the urachus, the vasa omphalo-meseraica, or vein and artery of the vesicula umbilicalis, and perhaps, even at this period, the duct of communication between the intestinal canal and vesicula umbilicalis, the fœtal extremity of which, according to Professor Oken's views, forms the processus vermiformis.

Diagram of the fœtus and membranes about the sixth week.

a Chorion. b The larger absorbent extremities, the site of the placenta. c Allantois. d Amnion. e Urachus. é Bladder. f Vesicula umbilicalis. g Communicating canal between the vesicula umbilicalis and intestine. h Vena umbilicalis. i i Arteriæ umbilicales. I Vena omphalo-meseraica. k Arteria omphalo-meseraica. n Heart. o Rudiment of superior extremity. p Rudiment of lower extremity. From Carus.

The hands seem to be fixed to the shoulders without arms, and the feet to adhere to the ossa illi; the liver seems to fill the whole abdomen; the ossa innominata, the ribs, and scapulæ are cartilaginous.

In a short time the little stump-like prominences of the extremities become longer, and are now divided into two parts, the superior into the hand and the fore arm, the inferior into the foot and leg; in one or two weeks later, the arms and thighs are visible. These parts of the extremities which are formed later than the others, are at first smaller, but as they are gradually developed they become larger. When the limbs begin to separate[Pg 74] into an upper and lower part, their extremities become rounder and broader, and divided into the fingers and toes, which at first are disproportionately thick, and until the end of the third month are connected by a membranous substance analogous to the webbed feet of water birds; this membrane gradually disappears, beginning at the extremities of the fingers and toes, and continuing the division up to their insertion. The external parts of generation, the nose, ears, and mouth appear after the development of the extremities. The insertion of the umbilical cord changes its situation to a certain degree; instead of being nearly at the inferior extremity of the fœtus as at first, it is now situated higher up on the anterior surface of the abdomen. The comparative distance between the umbilicus and pubis continues to increase, not only to the full period of gestation, when it occupies the middle point of the length of the child's body, as pointed out by Chaussier, but even to the age of puberty, from the relative size of the liver becoming smaller.

Though the head appears large at first, and for a long time continues so, yet its contents are tardy in their development, and until the sixth month the parietes of the skull are in great measure membranous or cartilaginous. Ossification commences in the base of the cranium, and the bones under the scalp are those in which this process is last completed.

The contents of the scull are at first gelatinous, and no distinct traces of the natural structure of the brain can be identified until the close of the second month; even then it requires to have been sometimes previously immersed in alcohol to harden its texture. There are many parts of it not properly developed until the seventh month. In the medulla spinalis no fibres can be distinguished until the fourth month. The thalami nervorum opticorum, the corpora striata, and tubercula quadrigemina, are seen in the second month; in the third, the lateral and longitudinal sinuses can be traced, and contain blood. In the fifth we can distinguish the corpus callosum; but the cerebral mass has yet acquired very little solidity, for until the sixth month it is almost semi-fluid. (Campbell's System of Midwifery.)

About the end of the third, during the fourth, and the beginning of the fifth months, the mother begins to be sensible of the movements of the fœtus. These motions are felt sooner or later, according to the bulk of the child, the size and shape of the pelvis, and the quantity of fluid contained in the amnion, the waters being in larger proportionate quantity the younger the fœtus.

The secretion of bile, like that of the fat, seems to begin towards the middle of pregnancy, and tinges the meconium, a mucous secretion of the intestinal tube which had hitherto been colourless, of a yellow colour. Shortly after this the hair begins to grow, and the nails are formed about the sixth or seventh[Pg 75] month. A very delicate membrane (membrana pupillaris,) by which the pupil has been hitherto closed, now ruptures, and the pupil becomes visible. The kidneys, which at first were composed of numerous glandular lobules (seventeen or eighteen in number,) now unite, and form a separate viscus on each side of the spine; sometimes they unite into one large mass, an intermediate portion extending across the spine, forming the horse-shoe kidney.

Lastly, the testes, which at first were placed on each of the lumbar vertebræ, near the origin of the spermatic vessels, now descend along the iliac vessels towards the inguinal rings, directed by a cellular cord, which Hunter has called Gubernaculum testis: they then pass through the openings carrying before them that portion of the peritoneum which is to form their tunica vaginalis.

The length of a full-grown fœtus is generally about eighteen or nineteen inches; its weight between six and seven pounds. The different parts are well developed and rounded; the body is generally covered with the vernix caseosa;[28] the nails are horny, and project beyond the tips of the fingers, which is not the case with the toes; the head has attained its proper size and hardness; the ears have the firmness of cartilage; the scrotum is rugous, not peculiarly red, and usually containing the testes. In female children the nymphæ are generally covered entirely by the labia, the breasts project, and in both sexes frequently contain a milky fluid. As soon as a child is born, which has been carried the full time, it usually cries loudly, opens its eyes, and moves its arms and legs briskly; it soon passes urine and fæces, and greedily takes the nipple. (Naegelé's Hebammenbuch.)

Thus, then, in the space of forty weeks, or ten lunar months, from an inappreciable point, the fœtus attains a medium length of about eighteen or nineteen inches, and a medium weight of between six and seven pounds. As these observations on the development of the ovum show that the structural arrangement of the embryo undergoes a succession of changes, by which it gradually rises from the lowest to the highest scale of formation, so we shall find it furnished with a succession of means for its nutrition, each corresponding more or less to the particular grade of development which it may have attained. Its earliest source of nourishment is doubtless the vitellus, or albuminous contents of the vesicula umbilicalis. The radicle or primitive trace, in this respect, bears a strong analogy to the seed of a plant; it brings with it its own supply of nourishment for its first stage of[Pg 76] growth; in the latter, the cotyledons afford nourishment to the little plumula, until, by the formation of roots and absorption of moisture from the surrounding soil, it is enabled to support the early rudiment of the future plant. The early function of the chorion is very analogous to that of roots; it is an absorbing apparatus, collecting nourishment by means of its numerous absorbing fibrillæ: hence, according to Lobstein, the umbilical vein exists for some time previous to the umbilical arteries, and seems to perform an office in the fœtus similar to that of the thoracic duct at a later period; its radicles or absorbing extremities seem to absorb a milky fluid, which after the first two months is found in the placenta, and which must be looked upon as a means of nourishment which does not exist in the latter months. This milky fluid was noticed by Leroux, who even then expressed his doubts, whether the radicles of the umbilical vein receive blood from the mother, or whether they only serve to absorb a white fluid which resembles chyle. In some manuscript notes of Dr. Young's lectures, which were taken by the late Dr. Parry, of Bath, when a student at Edinburgh, we find the following observation: "There is evidently in the placenta, besides blood-vessels, some other substance, which serves to absorb juices from the uterus, and to convert these into a chylous matter proper to nourish the fœtus, and this matter is absorbed by the umbilical veins. This seems to be proved from the consideration of the placenta of animals which have cotyledons; for, on squeezing these glandular substances, we force out a sort of chylous liquor, and these are surrounded by the placenta, which absorb their liquor and convey it to the fœtus."

The absorbing power of the umbilical vein continues till the fifth month; during the second or third, the fœtus receives a good deal of nourishment from the liquor amnii, which at this period contains a considerable quantity of albuminous matter; this diminishes in the latter months of pregnancy. Moreover the body of the fœtus begins to be covered with the vernix caseosa towards the seventh month, so that in the eighth and ninth months the absorption of liquor amnii by the skin is considerably impeded.

How far the full formed placenta, as seen after the fifth month, serves as a means of nutrition to the fœtus, may still be a matter of doubt; its chief use after this period is, as we have already shown, for the purpose of producing certain changes in the blood of the fœtus analogous to those of respiration;[29] still, however,[Pg 77] it would seem that its function of nutrition is not entirely at an end, even at a late period of pregnancy. The numerous little granules of phosphate of lime, which are frequently found on the uterine surface of a full-grown placenta at a time when ossification is rapidly advancing in the fœtal skeleton, would surely lead us to infer that the placenta in some way or other supplies the materials for this process.

Fœtal circulation. We have already shown, that, in the early stages of development, the heart of the embryo is single, consisting of one auricle and one ventricle; that a septum gradually divides these into two parts until the double heart is formed, leaving two openings of communication between the right and left sides, the one between the auricles called the foramen ovale, the other between the pulmonary artery and aorta, viz. the ductus arteriosus.

From these and other peculiarities it will be seen that the fœtal circulation differs essentially from that of a child after birth; and, in order to comprehend the nature and mechanism of the changes which take place in it when respiration first commences, it will be necessary that these peculiarities should be thoroughly understood. The condition of the fœtus must also be remembered: surrounded by the liquor amnii, the fœtus does not respire; its lungs have as yet been unemployed; they are therefore small and collapsed, and present a firm solid mass, nearly resembling liver in appearance. In this state but little blood from the pulmonary arteries can circulate through them; for, as the extreme ramifications of these vessels are distributed upon the mucous membrane lining the bronchi and air-cells, the free passage of blood through them will in great measure depend upon a previous condition of the air-cells. The pulmonary arteries in the fœtal state are therefore small, and transmit but a small quantity of blood into their numerous ramifications, just sufficient to keep pervious these vessels which after birth are to be so greatly distended: in this state the lungs when thrown into water sink.

Hence, as the pulmonary arteries do not afford a sufficiently free exit to the contents of the right side of the fœtal heart, nature has provided it with a peculiar means for carrying off the overplus quantity of blood, which is poured into the right auricle from the vena cava. This is attained first by the foramen ovale, an oval-shaped opening in the septum between the right and left auricles, and furnished with a semilunar valvular flap, so constructed, as to allow a free passage for the blood from the right to the left auricle, but none in the contrary direction. By this means a considerable quantity of blood is transmitted at once from the right to the left auricle, and, consequently, much less into the right ventricle and pulmonary artery. Still, however, more blood passes into the right ventricle than the pulmonary artery, in the collapsed state of the fœtal lungs, is capable of conveying away.[Pg 78] The pulmonary artery is therefore continued beyond its bifurcation into the aorta at its curvature, by means of the ductus arteriosus, which, in the full-grown fœtus, forms a short thick passage between these two vessels; and in this manner is the right ventricle enabled to get rid of its surplus quantity of blood. Thus we see that the fœtal heart although consisting of two auricles and two ventricles, continues to perform the functions only of a single heart, both ventricles assisting simultaneously to propel the same column of blood, viz. that of the aorta, and thus enabling the heart to act with considerable power.

The chief part of the blood, which flows through the iliac arteries, instead of being sent to the inferior extremities, is carried into the umbilical arteries, which passing up along the sides of the bladder meet the umbilical vein at the navel, and thus form the vessels of the umbilical cord. These arteries convey the blood of the fœtus to the placenta, where, having undergone changes to which we have already alluded, it is returned by the umbilical vein. This vessel, which afterwards forms the round ligament of the liver, passes through the umbilicus along the anterior edge of the suspensory ligament; it supplies the left lobe with blood, and having given off a communicating branch to the vena portæ, which supplies the right lobe, it passes at once by a short passage, called canalis venosus, into the vena cava.

Thus, then, the peculiarities of the fœtal circulation may be considered as four, viz. the foramen ovale, or passage from the right to the left auricle; the ductus arteriosus, or communication from the bifurcation of the pulmonary artery into the arch of the aorta; the umbilical arteries arising from the iliac arteries, and carrying the blood along the cord into the placenta; and, lastly, the canalis venosus, or passage between the umbilical vein and vena cava.

Let us now examine the changes which take place in the fœtal circulation at the moment of the child's birth. The child, which had hitherto been immersed in the bland and warm medium of the liquor amnii, is at once exposed to the action of the external air. By means of the sympathy existing between the skin and respiratory muscles, sudden and convulsive efforts at inspiration take place; the air-cells of the lungs become partially inflated, and, after a short time as the respiration increases in power and activity, become distended throughout their whole extent. The thorax rises; the flaccid diaphragm, which hitherto had been pushed up by the large fœtal liver, now contracts, pressing down the liver into its natural situation. The lungs, from being a hard solid heavy substance, resembling liver, at once become inflated, elastic, and crepitous, light and permeable to air in every part.

The capillary terminations of the pulmonary artery, which ramify in the mucous membrane, forming the parietes of the [Pg 79]air-cells, and which hitherto had been firmly compressed by the collapsed state of the fœtal lungs, are suddenly rendered pervious throughout their whole extent. By this means, a vacuum, as it were, is formed in the ramifications of the pulmonary artery; each inspiration is accompanied by a rush of blood from the right ventricle into the newly-inflated structure. The pulmonary artery, at its bifurcation, swells and becomes turgid: the blood is carried off into its numerous ramifications as fast as the right ventricle can supply it; this may be easily understood from the law, in anatomy, viz. that the area of two arteries is greater than that of the trunk from which they bifurcate. From this state of distension, the distance between the pulmonary artery and the aorta is increased; the ductus arteriosus, which has now become empty, is stretched, and thus partially closed; the right auricle, which, but for the foramen ovale, could not have cleared itself of the whole quantity of blood which was poured into it from the vena cava, is now enabled to transmit its entire contents into the right ventricle; the left auricle, which before birth was supplied only by the foramen ovale from the right auricle, is now rapidly filled by the blood brought into it by the four pulmonary veins;—the equilibrium between the two auricles becomes altered;—the right, which hitherto had been somewhat gorged with blood, is now able to clear itself with facility; whereas, the left, which was but partially supplied, is now distended with a much greater quantity: there is now rather a disposition for the blood to regurgitate from the left to the right auricle; this, however, is prevented by the semilunar fold of the foramen ovale, which now acts as a valve, and generally becomes firmly attached to the septum. The obliteration of the canalis venosus at the posterior margin of the liver, and of the umbilical vein at the anterior edge, may, we think, be explained by the changes which necessarily follow the inflation of the lungs: the diaphragm, when it contracts, pulls down the liver into its natural situation; the distance, therefore, between the liver and the heart is increased, and the canalis venosus is consequently stretched, and considerably pressed upon, and precisely the same results follow with the umbilical vein.

PART II

NATURAL PREGNANCY AND ITS DEVIATIONS.

CHAPTER I.

SIGNS OF PREGNANCY.

Difficulty and importance of the subject.—Diagnosis in the early months.—Auscultation.—Changes in the vascular and nervous systems.—Morning sickness.—Changes in the appearance of the skin.—Cessation of the menses.—Areola.—Sensation of the child's movements.—"Quickening."—Ausculation.—Uterine souffle.—Sound of the fœtal heart.—Funic souffle.—Sound the movements of the fœtus.—Ballottement.—State of the uterine.—Violet appearance of the mucous membrane of the vagina.—Cases of doubtful pregnancy.—Diagnosis of twin pregnancy.

There is, perhaps, no subject connected with midwifery, which is of such importance, or which, from its difficulty and the serious questions it involves, demands such attentive consideration, and requires so familiar an acquaintance with every part of it, as the diagnosis of pregnancy. The responsibility which a medical man incurs in deciding cases of doubtful pregnancy, and in thus giving an opinion which may not only affect the fortune, happiness, character, but even life itself of the individual concerned, is rendered more painful by the perplexing obscurity of the circumstances under which these cases sometimes occur, being not unfrequently complicated with diseases which add still farther to the difficulty of coming at the truth, and occasionally rendered peculiarly obscure by wilful and determined falsehood and duplicity.

[Pg 81]To render this subject more intelligible to our readers, we propose first to consider the general effects which pregnancy produces upon the system, and then to describe those changes and phenomena which are peculiar to this state, and which may therefore be taken as so many means of diagnosis.

Under all circumstances, the diagnosis of pregnancy must ever be difficult and obscure during the early months; the development of the uterus is still inconsiderable, and the effects which it may have produced upon the system, although appreciable and even distinct, are nevertheless too capable of being also other causes, to warrant our drawing any decided conclusion from them.

The effects over the whole animal economy, which result from the presence and advance of this great process, are very remarkable, and show themselves in every portion of it.

The vascular system undergoes a considerable change; the actual quantity of blood in the circulation appears to be increased; the pulse is harder, stronger, and more full; in many instances the blood, when drawn, exhibits the buffy coat, as in cases of inflammation; the vagina is more vascular, it is warmer, and the secretion of mucus considerably increased; there is a disposition to headach, and occasional flushing of the face; the animal heat over the whole body is increased. In the nervous system we also observe distinct evidences of a change having taken place: the irritability is increased; there is weariness, lassitude, and a peculiar alteration of taste and disposition; women, who otherwise are of a cheerful disposition, are now gloomy and reserved, and vice versâ; in some the temper becomes fretful and hasty, and in those who are naturally so, a most agreeable change for the better is sometimes observed. [30] Some are liable to spasmodic affections, palpitations, spasmodic cough, vomiting, fainting, headach, toothach, &c.: under this head will come the "morning sickness," which is so commonly observed during the first weeks; the nature and treatment of which will be considered under the Diseases of Pregnancy; on the other hand, women who are constantly suffering from spasmodic affections, for instance, asthma, &c. are now entirely free from them, and appear to be insensible to causes which, in the unimpregnated state, would induce an attack. To changes in the nervous system must we, in great measure, attribute not only the sickness just mentioned, but also those extraordinary longings or antipathies for certain articles of food or drink, and in some cases, as in chlorosis, for substances which, under[Pg 82] other circumstances, would excite disgust. In many, the changes in the function of the digestive apparatus does not amount to actual disease, the stomach merely refusing to digest articles of food which before had agreed with it: but in others, producing severe cardialgia, acidity, or even vomiting. Hence, we not unfrequently observe that women who had hitherto enjoyed a good digestion, now suffer from dyspepsia, and are obliged to be exceedingly careful in their diet; whereas those, in whom the digestion had been previously weak, are now able to digest almost any thing. The secretions of the whole alimentary canal are altered both in quality and quantity; the saliva frequently becomes tenacious, white, and frothy (Dewees,) and at times is so much increased in quantity as to amount to actual salivation; the secretions of the stomach are remarkably altered, as shown by the copious formation of acid in some cases during pregnancy; the mucus is ropy, and frequently vomited up in considerable quantities. The bowels are in some cases much relaxed; in others, constipated. This latter condition, however, may in part be attributed to the pressure of the gravid uterus obstructing the peristaltic motion.

The changes in the appearance of the skin during pregnancy are also worthy of notice. Women, who are naturally pale and of a delicate complexion, have frequently a high colour, and vice versâ; in some the skin assumes a sallow or cadaverous hue; copper-coloured blotches appear on the face and forehead: in others the skin appears loose and wrinkled, giving the patient an aged haggard expression, and destroying her good looks. Mole spots become darker and larger, and these, with a dark ring beneath the eyes and the changes already mentioned, combine to alter the whole appearance of the face. In some women a considerable quantity of hair appears in those parts of the face where the beard is seen in the other sex; it disappears after labour, when the skin resumes its natural functions, but returns on every succeeding pregnancy. In others a similar appearance takes place upon the breasts. The secretions of the skin are more or less altered; women who perspire freely have now a dry, rough skin; whereas those who at other times have seldom or never a moist skin, have copious perspiration, which is not unfrequently of a peculiarly strong odour. Cutaneous affections, also, which have been very obstinate, or had even become habitual, sometimes disappear, or at least are suspended during the period of utero-gestation. Similarly favourable changes are observed for a time in severe structural diseases of certain organs: the fact of well-marked phthisis apparently disappearing whilst pregnancy lasts, is well known.

The breasts become larger, blue veins are seen ramifying beneath the skin, and the circular disc of rose-coloured skin which surrounds the nipples becomes remarkably changed in colour, &c.;[Pg 83] appearances, the description of which we shall defer until we come to the consideration of those phenomena pregnancy, which may be looked upon as diagnostic.

The urine undergoes various changes; it is sometimes considerably increased, at others it is very high-coloured, or shows a peculiar milky sediment. A case has been quoted by Dr. Montgomery from Professor Osann's Clin. Rep. for 1833, p. 27., where the patient in three successive pregnancies was affected with diabetus mellitus, which each time completely ceased on delivery, and again returned when she became pregnant. None of the changes above enumerated excepting of those of the breasts, whether taken separately or conjointly, will enable us to form a correct diagnosis as to the existence of pregnancy. The appearance and feel of the abdomen during the early months afford no sure data: in fact, there is not a single symptom of pregnancy at this period, upon which we can rely with any degree of certainty.

Cessation of the menses. One of the most remarkable changes pregnancy, and one which most constantly appears, is the cessation of the menstrual discharge. From its occurring so uniformly and so soon after conception, it is generally used by women as the best means of reckoning the duration of their pregnancy: still, however, it is very far from being a certain sign, and never can be depended upon by itself in forming our diagnosis. It is well known how many causes produce suppression of the catamenia, independent of pregnancy; and, on the other hand, ample experience has shown that suppressed catamenia are by no means a necessary consequence of pregnancy.

Although the fact has been contradicted by men of experience, still the regular appearance of the menses for the first few months of pregnancy is of such frequent occurrence as to place the matter beyond all doubt: in stating this, we do not allude to occasional discharges of blood from the vagina, but to regular periodical appearances of fluid distinctly bearing all the characters and peculiarities of the catamenia. This fact has been noticed so long ago, as by Mauriceau, who says, "I know a woman who had four or five living children, and who had with every child her menses from month to month, as at other times, only in a little less quantity, and was so till the sixth month, yet notwithstanding she was always brought to bed at her full time."[31]

It is rare, however, to meet with the catamenia at so late a period, although cases do now and then occur where it lasts throughout pregnancy; more frequently it does not continue beyond the third or fourth month. The source of this discharge[Pg 84] appears to be from the vessels of the upper part of the vagina[32] and from the cervix uteri;[33] the gradually shortening of the latter as pregnancy advances may be considered as the reason why, in the majority of instances, the discharge diminishes after the second or third month, and usually ceases by the fifth or sixth. Dr. Dewees supports the same opinion with some excellent observations which are worthy of attention. "We are" says he "acquainted with a number of women who habitually menstruate during pregnancy until a certain period, but when that time arrives it ceases: several of these menstruated until the second or third months, others longer, and two until the seventh month; the last two were mother and daughter. We are certain there was no mistake in all the cases to which we now make reference. First, they (the menses) were regular in their returns, not suffering the slightest derangement from the impregnated condition of the uterus; 2. they employ from two to five days for their completion; 3. that the evacuation differed in no respect from the discharge in ordinary, except that they did not think it so abundant; 4. there were no coagula in any one of these discharges, consequently it could not be common blood of hæmorrhage; 5. in the two protracted cases, the quantity discharged regularly diminished after the fourth month, a circumstance perhaps not difficult of explanation." (Compendious System of Midwifery, § 235.)

It occasionally happens that the first appearance of the catamenia after conception is more abundant than usual, a circumstance which had been noticed by Dr. W. Johnson in 1769, and confirmed by Dr. Montgomery in his admirable work on the signs of pregnancy, who also confirms the general fact of the menses occasionally appearing during pregnancy by his own experience, and by very ample references. (Op. cit. p. 46.)

The rarest and most extraordinary deviation of this kind from the usual course of things is the appearance of the menses only during pregnancy. Cases of this sort have been recorded by authors of the highest respectability, so that there can be no doubt as to the correctness of their statements. Thus, for instance, Baudelocque says, "I have met with several women, who assured me that they had not had their menses periodically except during their pregnancies; their testimony appeared to me to deserve more credit, because they only applied for an explanation of this extraordinary phenomenon."[34]

By far the most interesting and detailed case of this nature is[Pg 85] one described by Dr. Dewees. "A woman applied for advice for a long standing suppression of the menses; indeed she never had menstruated but twice. She had been married a number of months, and complained of a good deal of derangement of stomach, &c. We prescribed some rhubarb and steel pills; about six months after this she called to say that the medicine had brought down her courses, but that she was more unwell than before. The sickness and vomiting had increased, besides swelling very much in her belly; we saw this pretty much distended and immediately examined it, as we suspected dropsy; but from the feel of the abdomen, the want of fluctuation and the solidity of the tumour, we began to think it might be pregnancy, and told the woman our opinion. On mentioning our impression she submitted to an examination per vaginam; this proved her to be six months advanced in pregnancy. After this she had the regular returns of the catamenial period, until the full time had expired; during suckling she was free from the discharge. She was a nurse for more than twelve months; she weaned her child, and shortly after was again surprised by an eruption of the menses, which as on a former occasion proved to be a sign of pregnancy." (Op. cit. § 237.)

There are other circumstances also connected with the catamenia, which warn us against placing too much confidence in its disappearance as a sign of pregnancy: a woman may become pregnant who has never menstruated, a fact which has been noticed by several authors, and which has been explained as well as confirmed by Levret in his Art des Accouchemens, § 230:—"A woman," says he, "may conceive, although she has not yet menstruated, provided menstruation would otherwise have made its appearance shortly."[35]

Another circumstance, of much more frequent occurrence, is the fact that a woman may become pregnant without having had a return of the menses since her last confinement; hence we occasionally meet with cases where, from a rapid succession of pregnancies, the menstruation has not appeared for several years. From what has now been said, it will be seen, beyond all doubt, that[Pg 86] the non-appearance of the menses cannot be looked upon by itself as a diagnostic of pregnancy, or vice versâ: this is more particularly the case when any morbid condition of the system is also present; under such circumstances, little or no confidence can be placed upon it as a guide in forming our diagnosis. In cases where it is an object to conceal pregnancy, the appearance of the menstrual fluid upon the clothes has been imitated in order to deceive. (Montgomery, op. cit. p. 50.) Although, therefore, the cessation of the menses, when taken in connexion with other symptoms, will prove useful in assisting us to a correct opinion, nevertheless, when taken by itself, it will scarcely ever enable us to decide with certainty.

Areola. Among the earliest of those symptoms which must be considered as diagnostic are the changes observed in the appearance of the breasts; "they increase, become full; they are occasionally painful and grow hard: the veins in them are rendered conspicuous from their blue colour; the nipple becomes more bulky and appears inflated, its colour becomes darker, the surrounding disc undergoes a similar change, increases in extent, and is covered with little prominences like so many diminutive nipples."[36] "The several circumstances (says Dr. Montgomery, p. 59,) here enumerated at least ought in all cases to form distinct subjects of consideration, when we propose to avail ourselves of this part as an indication of the existence or absence of pregnancy. One other, also, equally constant and deserving of particular notice, is a soft and moist state of the integument, which appears raised and in a state of turgescence, giving one the idea that if touched by the point of the finger it would be found emphysematous. This state appears, however, to be caused by infiltration of the subjacent cellular tissue, which together with its altered colour, gives us the idea of a part in which a greater degree of vital action is going forward than is in operation round it, and we not unfrequently find that the little glandular follicles, or tubercles, as they are called by Morgagni, are bedewed with a secretion sufficient to damp and colour the woman's inner dress.

These changes do not take place immediately after conception, but occur in different persons after uncertain intervals. We must therefore consider, in the first place, the period of pregnancy at which we may expect to gain any useful information from the condition of the areola. I cannot say positively what may be the[Pg 87] earliest period at which this change can be observed, but I have recognised it fully at the end of the second month, at which time the alteration in colour is by no means the circumstance most observable; but the puffy turgescence, though as yet slight, not alone of the nipple, but of the whole surrounding disc, and the development of the little glandular follicles, are the objects to which we should principally direct our attention, the colour at this period being in general little more than a deeper shade of rose or flesh colour, slightly tinged occasionally with a yellowish or light brownish hue. During the progress of the next two months the changes in the areola are in general perfected, or nearly so, and then it presents the following characters: a circle around the nipple, whose colour varies in intensity according to the particular complexion of the individual, being usually much darker in persons with black hair, dark eyes, and sallow skin, than in those of fair hair, light-coloured eyes, and delicate complexion.[37] The extent of this circle varies in diameter from an inch to an inch and a half, and increases in most persons as pregnancy advances, as does also the depth of the colour."[38]

"In the centre of the coloured circle the nipple is observed partaking of the altered colour of the part, and appearing turgid and prominent, while the surface of the areola, especially that part of it which lies more immediately around the base of the nipple, is studded over, and rendered unequal by the prominence of the glandular follicles, which, varying in number from twelve to twenty, project from the sixteenth to the eighth of an inch; and lastly the integument covering the part appears turgescent, softer, and more moist than that which surrounds it; while on both there are to be observed at this period, especially in women of dark hair and eyes, numerous round spots, or small mottled patches of a whitish colour, scattered over the outer part of the areola, and for about an inch or more all round, presenting an appearance as if the colour had been discharged by a shower of drops falling on the part. I have not seen this appearance earlier than the fifth month, but towards the end of pregnancy it is very remarkable, and constitutes a strikingly distinctive character exclusively resulting from pregnancy. The breasts themselves are[Pg 88] at the same time generally full and firm, at least more so than was natural to the person previously, and venous trunks of considerable size are perceived ramifying over their surface, and sending branches towards the disc of the areola, which several of them traverse along with these vessels. The breasts not unfrequently exhibit about the sixth month, and afterwards, a number of shining, whitish, almost silvery lines like cracks; these are most perceptible in women, who, having had before conception very little mammary development, have the breasts much and quickly enlarged after becoming pregnant."

In enumerating these various changes which are observed in the breasts, we fully agree with Dr. Montgomery in saying, that the alteration in the colour of the areola is by no means that upon which we can depend with most certainty: in the first place, we frequently meet with so little discolouration during the earlier months as to be altogether inappreciable; we have also already shown that if the patient be a brunette, and has already had children, the colour of the areola cannot be trusted to, as it never entirely disappears after her first pregnancy. On the other hand, we occasionally meet with a considerable change of colour in the unimpregnated state, arising from uterine irritation, as in dysmenorrhœa, &c. Where, however, this is accompanied by the other changes above enumerated, there can be, we apprehend, no doubt as to the existence of the pregnancy. Dr. Smellie, and also Dr. W. Hunter both considered the areola as proof positive of pregnancy. The latter one decided upon a case of pregnancy under very extraordinary circumstances; the body of a young female was brought into the dissecting room, which at the first glance he pronounced to be pregnant, but the accuracy of his diagnosis was not a little doubted when it was ascertained that a perfect hymen was present: to decide the point he had the abdomen opened when the uterus was found to contain a small fœtus.

Movements of the fœtus. The sensation to the mother of the child moving in the uterus, cannot be looked upon as a certain sign of pregnancy, for even women who have had large families of children are frequently deceived in this respect by the movement of flatus in the intestines, by occasional spasmodic twitchings of the abdominal muscles, &c.; but when the motion of the child can be distinctly felt by the hand of an experienced practitioner, it will no longer admit of any doubt: this, however, is a symptom which can seldom be made use of before the middle of the sixth or seventh month.

Quickening. This leads us to the subject of quickening as a symptom of pregnancy. The very vagueness of the term quickening is of itself a sufficient objection to its use as a source of information on these points. Strictly speaking, it refers to that moment of pregnancy when the woman is supposed to have become quick with child, or in other words, when the fœtus becomes[Pg 89] endued with life, "an error," as Dr. Montgomery observes, "which the continued use of the term was obviously calculated to foster and to prolong" (p. 75.) As far as we can understand, the word "quickening" at the present day refers to two different events during pregnancy: the one is when the motion of the child first becomes perceptible to the mother; the other consists of those effects which are frequently observed when the uterus quits the pelvis, and rises into the abdominal cavity, viz. fainting, sickness, &c.; in either case it will be evident that no correct conclusion can be formed by this means. It may safely be asserted that until the last twenty years we possessed only three diagnostic marks of pregnancy, viz. the appearance of the areola, a series of changes but little understood; the being able to feel the movements of the child through the abdominal parietes, and the head of it per vaginam. Hence Dr. W. Hunter in describing the uncertainty of the signs of pregnancy says, "I find I cannot determine at four months, I am afraid of myself at five months, but when six or seven months are over, I urge an examination."

In the primipara, the changes which pregnancy produces upon the os and cervix uteri are generally sufficient to lead to an accurate conclusion. The round dimple-like depression which the os uteri forms, the soft cushiony state of the cervix, are changes which we consider as peculiarly the effects of pregnancy, but their distinctness and certainty ceases when the patient has had several children; the irregular shape of the os uteri, its thickened edges, hard here and there, and the os tincæ, itself more or less open, the cervix scarcely, if at all, shortened, even at a late period of gestation, tend not a little to perplex the diagnosis furnished by this mode of examination; and where disease is complicated with pregnancy, the difficulty is greatly increased, and not unfrequently so much, that scarcely a single satisfactory point will be obtained.

Auscultation. Of late years, an immense advance has been made in the diagnosis of pregnancy, by means of the stethoscope. M. Major of Geneva,[39] in 1819, observed the interesting fact that he could hear the pulsations of the fœtal heart through the parietes of the mother's uterus and abdomen: he appears, however, to have carried his researches no farther; and little attention was excited to the circumstance until three years afterwards, when a masterly essay on the subject was read before the Académie Royale de Médecine of Paris, by Lejumeau de Kergaradec.[40] In this interesting memoir, the author has described two sounds, which are perfectly distinct from each other in point of [Pg 90]character. One of them consists of single pulsations, synchronous with those of the mother's heart, accompanied with the deep whizzing rushing sound, which may be heard over a large portion of the uterus at once; the other of sharp, distinct, double pulsations, producing a ticking sound, and following a rythm, which is not synchronous with that of the maternal circulation. Kergaradec supposed that the former sound was the circulation of the blood in the spongy structure of the placenta, and hence called it the souffle placentaire; later observations[41] have, however, shown that it is not connected with the placenta, but depends upon the increased vascularity and peculiar arrangement of the uterine vessels during the gravid state. The other sound is the pulsations of the fœtal heart.

Uterine souffle. The uterine sound, or souffle, may invariably be heard in one or other of the inguinal regions, and usually over a considerable portion of the uterus, extending anteriorly or along the sides of the organ; and according to the observations of Professor Naegelé jun.,[42] there is no part of the uterus, capable of being osculted, in which this sound may not be heard. He considers that the souffle, which is so uniformly heard in the lower parts of the uterus, especially in the inguinal regions, seems to be the uterine arteries before they enter the uterus; these vessels, as soon as they arrive at the broad ligament, assume a different character, become larger than they were on branching off from their original trunk, and are much contorted before entering the parietes of the uterus. Dubois first pointed out the similarity which exists between the sound heard in the gravid uterus, and that of aneurismal varix, where there is a direct passage of blood from an artery into a vein: the sound in this latter condition is the current of blood rapidly issuing from the dilated artery, and mixing with the slower flowing stream of the dilated vein. The circulation of blood in the dilated arteries of the uterus present a considerable resemblance, in many respects, to that of the above-mentioned disease.

That the uterine sound is not confined to that part of the uterus where the placenta is attached, as was supposed by Professor Hohl,[43] is proved by the fact that we can frequently hear it in two different and sometimes opposite parts of the uterus at the same time, which, if his opinion be correct, would indicate the presence of twins; and yet the result of labour has proved that the uterus has contained but one child, and that the placenta had neither been attached in the one or other of these situations. The very circumstance which we have already mentioned, of this sound being invariably heard in one, if not in both, of the inguinal regions, shows that it is independent of the vicinity of the[Pg 91] placenta; nevertheless, it must be allowed, that as the uterine vessels undergo the greatest degree of development at this part, the sound will usually be at least as distinct here as in any other portion of the uterus.

The uterine souffle is the first sound which auscultation detects during pregnancy; it may be heard as early as the fifteenth or sixteenth week, but cases now and then occur where it has been even distinguished in the thirteenth or fourteenth week, and Dr. Evory Kennedy, has given some very interesting examples where he was able to hear it with certainty at the twelfth, eleventh, and even in one instance, at the tenth week. (Kennedy, op. cit. p. 80.) During these earlier periods, the sound is weaker, but extends over the whole uterus, from the diminutive size of which it can be heard most readily immediately above the symphysis pubis; in fact, there is every reason to suppose, that the uterine souffle might be detected at a still earlier period, if the uterus were at this time within reach of the stethoscope. As pregnancy advances, it becomes more distinct and powerful, and is occasionally so to a remarkably degree. During the latter periods of pregnancy, it frequently presents considerable modifications of tone, especially where there is general or local vascular excitement, as in cases of fever, or dispositions to hæmorrhage, where the vessels are usually distended, or where (Naegelé, op. cit. p. 86,) the placenta is situated near the os uteri, it assumes a piping, twanging sound of considerable resonance: the same is also observed where, either from the weight of the gravid uterus or any other cause, pressure has been exerted on any of the main arterial trunks: hence, as we shall show more fully when speaking of labour, a remarkable change is produced in the tone of the uterine souffle by the first contractions of that process. The causes of these modifications are not always very easily explained; we sometimes observe the souffle on the same side of the uterus vary rapidly in its degree of intensity, and occasionally even disappear for awhile without our being able to assign any satisfactory reason for such changes.

The uterine souffle taken by itself, although a very valuable sign of pregnancy, can scarcely be looked upon as one which is perfectly certain and diagnostic, since a similar sound may be aneurism of the abdominal aorta and its large branches: there is much reason to think that the uterus, enlarged from other causes than that of pregnancy, and pressing upon the iliac arteries, will produce a similar sound. Professor Naegelé, jun., has also shown that the sounds of the patient's heart may sometimes be heard very low in the abdomen, even as far as the ossa ilii, a circumstance which seems to have depended upon the sound being transmitted through the intestines distended with flatus. Where any of these causes of abdominal souffle have existed in connexion with suppressed catamenia, swelling of the[Pg 92] breasts, &c., we might be liable to be deceived if we allowed ourselves to be entirely guided by this sound.

With regard to the fœtal pulsations, we find them generally beating at the rate of from 130 to 150 double strokes in a minute, and the age of the fœtus appears to have no effect upon their rapidity, for even at the earliest periods at which we can detect these sounds the rate of the pulsation is the same as at the full term of pregnancy.

Although Dr. Kennedy has in a few cases detected this sound even before the expiration of the fourth month, it will not in the majority be possible until a later period. "At the fourth month it frequently requires not only close attention, but considerable perseverence to detect the fœtal heart; and at this period it has occurred to us to examine patients whom there was strong reason to suppose pregnant, and after spending a considerable time in endeavouring to detect this sound, we have been on the point of giving up the search as hopeless, when it has been suddenly discovered in the identical spot that had before perhaps been explored without success." (Kennedy, op. cit. p. 101.)

The sound of the fœtal heart is usually heard at about the middle point between the scrobiculus cordis and symphysis pubis, usually to one side, and that, generally speaking, the left. The extent of surface over which the sound may be heard varies a good deal, and depends, in great measure, on the distance which intervenes between the fœtus and stethoscope; hence, when the uterus is distended with a large quantity of liquor amnii, or when the uterine and abdominal parietes are very thick, it is heard over a much larger space, although with diminished intensity; on the other hand, when there is but little liquor amnii in the uterus, it is audible over a small portion only, but is remarkably distinct: this is peculiarly the case during labour after rupture of the membranes. The rapidity and strength of the fœtal pulsations appear to be entirely independent of the mother's circulation; violent exercise, spirituous liquors, &c., which will raise her pulse to a considerable degree, have no influence whatever on the fœtal pulse. In cases of fever, where the mother's pulse has ranged between 110° and 120°, and even higher, not the slightest change was observable in the sound of the fœtal heart; even in acute inflammatory affections, in pneumonia, pleurisy, where there was severe dyspnœa, and also in tubercular phthisis; in cases where the patient has been bled; in cases of menstruation during pregnancy; and even in severe flooding, and when the mother's pulse has been greatly reduced, no perceptible change has been observed in that of the fœtus. (Naegelé, op. cit. p. 39.) Dr. Kennedy has observed some remarkable cases where the fœtal pulse appeared to vary in accordance with that of the mother (op. cit. p. 91;) but when we bear in mind the frequent changes in point of rapidity, &c., to which the fœtal[Pg 93] heart is subject, independent of any thing of the kind in the mother's pulse, and that similar changes are constantly observed in the child shortly after birth; and, moreover, that very considerable acceleration of the maternal pulse has decidedly no effect upon that of the fœtus in many well-marked instances, we cannot agree with him in supposing that a connexion of the sort to which he has alluded exists. The double pulsations of the fœtal heart can only be heard at one point of the uterus at a time, provided there be but one child; but if there be twins, then the sound is heard in two places at once. It has been supposed by some authors (Dubois) that the heart of the second child could not be distinctly heard until labour, when the membranes of the first child had ruptured. Generally speaking, both sounds can be heard pretty distinctly during the last weeks of pregnancy, one of them being low down on one side, and the other high up in an opposite direction. Although in some twin cases there is an evident difference of rhythm between the two fœtal hearts, still in many others they are so nearly synchronous as to be scarcely if at all distinguishable in this respect. Hence, therefore, from the known variable character of the fœtal pulse, it will be necessary that the sound of each heart should be ausculted at the same moment, minute for minute, by two observers, and thus the slightest appreciable difference between them determined.

Funic souffle. Dr. Kennedy has shown that, where a portion of the umbilical cord passes between the child's body and the anterior wall of the uterus, or crosses any of its limbs or other projections, pulsations are heard synchronous with those of the fœtal heart; although not possessing the same characters. "In some cases where the uterus and parietes of the abdomen were extremely thin, I have been able," says Dr. K., "to distinguish the funis by the touch externally, and felt it rolling distinctly under my finger, and then, on applying the stethoscope, its pulsations have been discoverable remarkably strong; and, on making pressure with the finger for a moment on that part of the funis which passed towards the umbilicus of the child, I have been able to render the pulsations less and less distinct, and even, on making the pressure sufficiently strong, to stop it altogether." (Op. cit. p. 121.) In many cases where the umbilical arteries, by their convolutions round a limb, or by any other cause, are subjected to slight pressure, a distinct whizzing sound is produced, which is called by Dr. Kennedy the funic souffle.

The sound of the fœtal heart must be looked upon as a sign of the highest value in the diagnosis of pregnancy, since, however complicated and obscure the other symptoms may be, whether from co-existing disease, wilful deception, &c. if this sound be once heard unequivocally, the real nature of the case is satisfactorily established beyond all possibility of doubt.

[Pg 94]Another sound in the gravid uterus has been lately noticed by Professor Naegelé, junior, which promises to equal that of the fœtal heart, as a certain diagnostic of pregnancy, and must be looked upon as a valuable addition to our means of ascertaining the truth in cases of this sort. The movements of the fœtus may be distinguished by the stethoscope at a very early period of pregnancy, long before they are perceptible to the hand of the accoucheur, and in many cases before the patient has been aware of them herself. According to Professor Naegelé's observations, these sounds may usually be heard some little time before the fœtal heart is audible, and are sounds which can neither be feigned nor concealed: they can only be heard in the gravid uterus, and under no other circumstances.

Although the sounds of the heart and movements of the fœtus are unequivocal proofs of pregnancy, which may be heard at a very early period, still it must, in some degree, remain uncertain at this time, how far their absence can be looked upon as a proof of its non-existence. Under such circumstances, the examinations require to be conducted with the greatest possible care, and to be repeated at favourable opportunities, until no doubt as to the correctness of their results can any longer exist.

The soft cushiony feel of the cervix uteri is a change pregnancy, which, in our opinion, has not received that attention which it deserves; as far as we are able to judge, this condition of the cervix is peculiar to pregnancy, and exists very shortly after conception. We occasionally meet with a soft flaccid state of the os and cervix uteri in certain diseases; but the feel which this communicates to the finger is very different to that above-mentioned, which resembles more the elastic inflated condition of the nipple during pregnancy, than any thing to which we can compare it.

Ballottement. At the beginning of the seventh month we shall be able to feel the head of the fœtus upon examination per vaginam. If we direct our finger against the uterus, midway between the os uteri and symphysis pubis, and suddenly exert a slight degree of pressure, we shall become sensible of having struck against something hard within the cavity of the uterus; upon repeating the experiment immediately, we shall probably not feel it, the fœtus having risen in the liquor amnii to the upper parts of the uterus; but if hold our finger still for a few moments, it will, by this time, have again descended, and we shall again feel it; at other times, when the fœtus is larger and heavier, the head will rest like a light ball, on the tip of the finger, from which circumstance it has received the name of ballottement by the French authors.

Motion of the child. The sensation of the child's movements to the mother is a symptom of very little value, and is liable to mislead the practitioner if he place much reliance upon it; for[Pg 95] the passage of the flatus along the bowels, or little spasmodic flickerings of the abdominal muscles, will produce a very similar sensation, and will even completely deceive a patient who has been the mother of several children; but when they become perceptible to the experienced hand of the practitioner, this may also be looked upon as a certain indication that pregnancy exists. The fœtal movements can seldom be felt distinctly until the beginning of the seventh month, and even then it requires some caution before we can venture upon a positive opinion. Their activity varies considerably in different cases; in some their nature is almost immediately evident; whereas, in others they are so few and feeble, as to make it very difficult to decide. It has been recommended to put the head in cold water previous to applying it upon the abdomen, as, by this means, a considerable shock is produced which excites these movements more distinctly. We cannot say that we have found this proceeding of any use, since, by this means, the abdominal muscles are rendered so irritable as frequently to obstruct the examination considerably: it is rather desirable to have them in as perfect a state of repose as possible, in order that no movement of the fœtus, however slight, should escape our notice. It is in cases of abdominal enlargement from disease; that this means of diagnosis is occasionally very difficult, and where men, even of great experience, have been led to form a very erroneous opinion. The celebrated Peter Franck has related a case of this sort which occurred to himself, where the patient was supposed pregnant, and where he imagined that he had felt the motions of the child: she died shortly afterwards, and the examination of the body showed it to have been a case of ascites complicated with hydatids. Dr. Dewees has given a still more remarkable case of a similar error having occurred to himself. A young lady had her menses suppressed for several months; the abdomen swelled very much, the breasts became enlarged, she had nausea and vomiting in the morning, and other indications of pregnancy; "examining the abdomen carefully, I found it," says Dr. Dewees, "considerably distended; there was a circumscribed tumour within it, which I was very certain was an enlarged uterus. While conducting this examination I thought I distinctly perceived the motions of a fœtus. The case proved to be one of accumulation of menstrual fluid in the uterus." (Dewees's Essays on several Subjects connected with Midwifery, p. 337-8.)

In reviewing what has now been stated respecting the diagnosis of pregnancy, it will be observed that we have enumerated four symptoms, which must be looked upon as perfectly diagnostic of this condition, and in the accuracy and certainty of which we may place the fullest confidence: two may be recognised at an early period by means of auscultation, viz. the sounds the movements of the fœtus and by the pulsations of[Pg 96] its heart; the two others are not appreciable until a later period, and are afforded by manual examination, viz. the being able to feel the head of the fœtus per vaginam, and its movements through the abdominal parietes. The next in point of value after these are the changes in the os and cervix uteri, those connected with the formation of the areola in the breasts, and, at a somewhat later period, the sound of the uterine circulation, changes, which, although they cannot separately be entirely depended upon, are nevertheless symptoms of very great importance in the diagnosis of pregnancy.

Two other signs of pregnancy have also been mentioned, viz. the appearance of a peculiar deposite in the urine as described by M. Nauche, or rather by Savonarola (Montgomery, op. cit. p. 157.,) and the purple or violet appearance of the mucous membrane lining the vagina and os externum, as described by Professor Kluge of the Charité at Berlin, and by M. M. Jacquemin, Parent Duchatelet, &c. of Paris. With regard to the first, which is an old popular symptom of pregnancy, there is too much variety in the appearances of the urine, depending on general health, diet, temperature, &c., to enable us to place much confidence in any change of this sort. "I have myself tried it," says Dr. Montgomery, "in several instances, and the result of my trials has been this:—In some instances no opinion could be formed as to whether the peculiar deposite existed or not, on account of the deep colour and turbid condition of the urine; but in the cases in which the fluid was clear, and pregnancy existing, the peculiar deposite was observed in every instance. Its appearance would be best described by saying that it looks as if a little milk had been thrown into the urine, and having sunk through it had partly reached the bottom, while a part remained suspended and floating through the lower part of the fluid in the form of a whitish semi-transparent filmy cloud." (Op cit. p. 157.)[44]

[Pg 97]The purple colour of the vaginal entrance appears, from the extensive experience of the above-mentioned authors, to be a pretty constant change the state of pregnancy; it probably occurs at a very early period. How far a similar tinge is the state of uterine congestion immediately before a menstrual period, we are unable to say; at any rate, the character of the examination itself must ever be sufficient to preclude its being practised in this country.

The diagnosis of pregnancy is a subject well worthy of the student's most serious attention; for he will of course be liable, when in practice, to be called upon to give his evidence before a court of justice under circumstances when the responsibility must ever be of the most serious and not unfrequently of the most fearful nature, the more so as the old custom of impanelling a jury of "twelve discreet matrons" to determine whether the woman be quick with child has fallen deservedly into disrepute. He should lose no opportunity of making himself familiar with the various symptoms of pregnancy above enumerated, and of so practising the different senses of hearing, touch, and sight, as instantly and certainly to detect their presence.

Numerous cases are on record, where a false diagnosis in women convicted of capital offences, has led to most lamentable results, and where dissection of the body after death has shown that she was pregnant. Dr. Evory Kennedy has recorded an interesting case of this sort which occurred at Norwich in 1833, when[Pg 98] a pregnant woman was on the point of being executed through the ignorance of a female jury. (E. Kennedy's Observations on Obstetric Auscultation, &c., p. 197.) We may also mention a dreadful case of this nature which occurred to the celebrated Baudelocque at Paris, during the horrors of the French revolution.[45] A young French countess was imprisoned during the revolution, being suspected of carrying on a treasonable correspondence with her husband, an emigrant. She was condemned, but declared herself pregnant; two of the best midwives in Paris were ordered to examine her, and they declared that she was not pregnant. She was accordingly guillotined, and her body taken to the school of anatomy, where it was opened by Baudelocque, who found twins in the fifth month of pregnancy.

Equally important is it (and perhaps in some respects even more so) to determine the absence of pregnancy in cases where it has been supposed to exist. In many instances the character and happiness of the individual must depend upon the judgment which the practitioner pronounces; and, painful as will be the task of communicating an opinion which implies guilt and loss of honour, how infinitely revolting and inexcusable must that step be considered, which turns out to have been founded upon an incorrect diagnosis. Hence the importance of separating those symptoms of pregnancy which may be considered certain, and therefore trustworthy, from the crowd of others, which, although collectively they may warrant a suspicion, yet never can justify a decision that pregnancy exists, more especially in cases where so much is at stake. No two symptoms have led more frequently to this cruel error, and therefore to the most unjust suspicions, than the cessation of the menses with swelling of the abdomen, and yet from how many different causes may they arise besides that of pregnancy? Putting even the impulse of common feeling aside, we would ask how a practitioner can dare recklessly to incur the responsibility of injuring a woman's character by hazarding an opinion which involves so much, and is based upon symptoms which, by themselves, prove so little? Whether he exercise his profession in town or country, cases of doubtful pregnancy will constantly come under his notice. We cannot, therefore, too strongly urge the importance of ascertaining how many of the certain symptoms are present, before we allow ourselves to be influenced by those which are uncertain. In speaking of the enlargement of the abdomen as a sign of pregnancy which is extremely equivocal, Dr. Dewees well observes, "But little reliance can be placed upon this circumstance alone, or even when combined with several others; for I have had the pleasure in several instances of doing away an injurious and[Pg 99] cruel suspicion, to which this enlargement had given rise. Within a short time, I relieved an anxious and tender mother from an almost heart-breaking apprehension for the condition of an only and beautiful daughter on whom suspicion had fallen, though not quite fifteen years of age: this case, it must be confessed, combined several circumstances which rendered it one of great doubt, and, without having had recourse to the most careful and minute examination, might readily have embarrassed a young practitioner. This lady's case was submitted to a medical gentleman, who, from its history and the feel of the abdomen, pronounced it to be a case of pregnancy, and advised the sorrow-stricken mother to send her daughter immediately to the country as the best mode of concealing her shame. Not willing to yield to the opinion of her physician (a young man,) and moved by the positive denials of her agonized child, the mother consulted me in this case. The menses had ceased, the abdomen had gradually swelled, the stomach was much affected, especially in the morning, and the breasts were a little enlarged. On examination it proved to be a case of enlarged spleen." (Dewees, on the Diseases of Females, p. 178.)

We occasionally, also, meet with cases of self-deception, as to the existence of pregnancy, to an extent which would scarcely seem credible. Women who have been the mothers of several children, will, upon some very slight founda-tion, suppose themselves with child. Knowing from previous experience many of the symptoms of this state, they will frequently enumerate them most accurately to the practitioner, who, if he rest satisfied with general appearances, may easily be led into a wrong diagnosis. A case of this kind we published in our midwifery reports, where the patient, the mother of two children, came into the General Lying-in Hospital, not only under the supposition that she was pregnant, but that labour had actually commenced; the catamenia had ceased about nine months previously, and the abdomen was considerably enlarged. Examination proved that she was not pregnant. (Med. Gaz. June, 1834.)

In a work solely devoted to cases of doubtful pregnancy by the late W. J. Schmitt, of Vienna, these cases have been very fully discussed. "We occasionally observe certain conditions of the female system, which put on a most striking resemblance to pregnancy, both functionally as well as organically, without at all depending on the actual presence of pregnancy. The abdomen begins to swell from the pubic region exactly in the same gradual manner as in pregnancy; the breasts become painful, swell, and secrete a lymphatic fluid, frequently resembling milk; the digestive organs become disordered; there is irregular appetite, nausea, and inclination to vomit; constipation, muscular debility, change in the colour of the skin, and frequently of the whole condition of the body; the nervous system suffers, and even the mind[Pg 100] itself frequently sympathizes; the patient is sensible of movements in the abdomen like those of a living fœtus, then bearing down pains running from the loins to the pubes; at last actual labour-pains come on as with a woman in labour, and if by chance her former labours have been attended by any peculiar symptoms, these, as it were, to complete the illusion, appear likewise." (W. J. Schmitt, Zweifelhafte Schwangerschafts-fälle.) A most extraordinary case of the self-deception with regard to pregnancy, has been published by the celebrated Klein of Stuttgardt: it has been quoted in the work of W. J. Schmitt above alluded to, and a brief sketch of it has been given by Dr. Montgomery in his Expositions of the Signs and Symptoms of Pregnancy, p. 172, to which we must refer the reader for much valuable information on this and all other subjects connected with the diagnosis of pregnancy.

Diagnosis of twin pregnancy. Before concluding this chapter, we shall offer a few observations on the diagnosis of twins. A variety of symptoms have been enumerated as indicating the presence of two fœtuses in utero, such as the great size of the abdomen, its flat square shape, the movements of a child at different parts of it, &c. The size of the abdomen can never be admitted as a diagnostic mark of twin pregnancy; first, because it equally indicates the presence of an unusual quantity of liquor amnii, or of a very large child; and secondly, because women pregnant with twins are not always remarkable for their size: the flatness, &c., of the abdomen is, we presume, a symptom based on the supposition that there is a fœtus in each side of the uterus: this is very far from being correct, as it is well known that the children usually lie obliquely, the one being, perhaps, downwards and backwards, while the other is situated upwards and forwards. The sensation of the child's movements in different or opposite parts of the uterus is no proof whatever that there are twins, because it is constantly observed where there is but one child—a circumstance which is very easy of explanation.

The stethoscope affords us the only certain diagnosis of twin pregnancy; and even here it is limited to the sounds of the fœtal hearts; the increased extent and power of the uterine souffle, as remarked by Hohl, arising, as he supposed, from the large mass of the double placenta, is not a proof which can be depended upon. In cases of suspected twin pregnancy the auscultation must be conducted with the greatest possible care, and, generally speaking, a certain diagnosis can only be obtained by two observers ausculting the two hearts at one and the same moment; for, otherwise, the difference between their rhythm is frequently so small as to be inappreciable. The sounds are seldom or never heard at the same level, one being generally heard high up on one side, the other in a contrary direction.

[Pg 101]

CHAPTER II.

TREATMENT OF PREGNANCY.

Sympathetic affections of the stomach during pregnancy.—Morning sickness.—Constipation.—Flatulence.—Colicky pains.—Headach.—Spasmodic cough.—Palpitation.—Toothach.—Diarrhœa.—Pruritus pudendi.—Salivation.

In the preceding chapter we have enumerated those changes and phenomena which are observed to take place in the system during pregnancy: many of these amount to actual derangements of function, and will, therefore, as such, demand our attention in a practical point of view, for the purpose of alleviating or removing them. Many of these changes are the altered distribution of blood, as well as by the actual increase of quantity which now exists in the circulation; the nervous and also the vascular system of the uterus are now in a state of high excitement and activity—a condition which must necessarily communicate itself to those organs which are supplied by the same nerves; viz. the sympathetic, and by the same portion of the circulation, viz. the branches of the abdominal aorta.

No organ, except the stomach, possesses sympathetic connexions so widely extended over the rest of the system as the uterus; and, we may add, that no two organs are so intimately and reciprocally united as the uterus and the stomach. In the unimpregnated state, we see this manifested in a remarkable degree; if the stomach becomes deranged the uterus sympathizes; thus the states of gastric disturbance, known under the general term of dyspepsia, are frequently followed by leucorrhœa, or some derangement of the menstrual function: on the other hand, uterine disease is invariably accompanied by symptoms of gastric disturbance, and, in many cases, to such an extent as to conceal the real seat of the evil, and mislead the attention of the patient and her medical attendant. In like manner we find that during pregnancy, especially in the early stages of it, the patient is annoyed with a great variety of symptoms more or less indicative of derangement in the functions of the primæ viæ.

Morning sickness. One of the most troublesome, and by no means the least frequent, is vomiting, which, from coming on[Pg 102] usually in the morning, is commonly called morning sickness; in some cases the female merely rejects what food or mucus may be present in the stomach, after which she feels relieved; in others she continues to strain violently and ineffectually for some time. In the former case it resembles the common vomiting from a deranged stomach, and cannot be considered as the direct result of sympathy with the uterus: the tone of the stomach has become impaired, and vomiting has followed as a consequence of its being loaded with undigested food and depraved secretions. Hence, in these cases, it is generally preceded by nausea and the other common precursory symptoms of this act: in the latter, however, it appears to be the immediate result of irritation transmitted from the uterus, and assumes rather a spasmodic character; the patient is suddenly seized with involuntary efforts to vomit, which are not preceded by nausea or oppression, and come on independently of the stomach being full or empty.

Morning sickness usually appears during the first few weeks after conception, and continues until the third or fourth month; in some cases it continues throughout pregnancy; in a few it does not begin till much later, and in many it does not appear at all. It scarcely deserves to be called a disease of pregnancy, for it frequently appears as a salutary effort of nature to relieve a cause of much gastric irritation, and, unless it proceeds to a very exhausting degree, must rather be looked upon as a favourable symptom, as it tends to prevent the formation of too much blood, which is so frequent a cause of abortion during the early months. (Hamilton, on Female Complaints.) Hence, therefore, experience verifies the correctness of the old proverb, that a "sick pregnancy is a safe one."

The ejected matter on these occasions, when there is but little or no food upon the stomach, consists of a glairy ropy mucus, sometimes mixed with a considerable quantity of intensely sour fluid, containing a large proportion of muriatic and acetic acid: in some cases more or less bile is vomited.

The treatment of morning sickness will depend in great measure on the severity of the attack: where it is slight, the patient may assist its operation with a little warm water, or chamomile tea: after which the bowels should be briskly opened by a saline laxative, as for instance, a seidlitz powder, sulphate and carbonate of magnesia, &c.: small doses do more harm than good, as, from their slow and ineffective action, they rather tend to increase the irritation and aggravate the symptoms. In severe cases, especially where the pulse is excited, a small bleeding may be used with much advantage, but in most instances the usual treatment of gastric derangement, as it occurs in the unimpregnated state, produces most relief. The bowels should be first opened in the way already mentioned, after which a [Pg 103]combination of Pil. Hydrarg. and Extr. Hyosc. or Extr. Humuli, is to be given at night, and a vegetable tonic during the day.

Acids, more especially the mineral, have been very judiciously recommended by Dr. Dewees, and, when combined with any bitter infusion, will be found of great service. Where the constant secretion of acid is very distressing, the nitric acid will be found particularly useful; it allays the irritability of the stomach, and produces a healthy state of its secretion. Opiates are by no means desirable remedies, and rather tend to aggravate the disease by still farther injuring the tone of the stomach and producing constipation. We have known them given in considerable doses and in very powerful forms, but without relief. Hydrocyanic acid, creosote, &c., have also been tried, but with no permanent success; in such cases Dr. Burns has found the application of leeches useful, "especially if accompanied with pain or tension in the epigastric region." On the same principle, we presume, have we found a sinapism of great service. Where the vomiting, in spite of all the above modes of treatment, still goes on unabated, there is nothing which, in our experience, is so useful as covering the epigastrium with a hot flannel, upon which a mixture of camphorated spirits of wine and laudanum has been sprinkled. "We have," says Dr. Dewees, "in several instances, confined patients for days together, upon lemon juice and water with the most decided advantage. We have repeatedly found much benefit from the use of the spirit of turpentine three or four times a day, in doses of twenty drops: this medicine is very easily taken, if it be mixed in cold sweetened water. When the system is not excited to febrile action, and where the stomach rejects every thing almost as soon as swallowed, we have often known a table-spoonful of clove-tea act most promptly and successfully." (Compendious System of Midwifery.)

Heartburn is another form of gastric derangement which frequently occurs to a very distressing degree, and must be looked upon as a modification of morning sickness; in many cases it arises from the presence of acid in the stomach, but in others it is merely a sympathetic result of gastric irritation, without any proof of acidity being present. The treatment of heartburn is much the same as that just described for morning sickness, the main object being to restore the stomach and bowels to a healthy condition. Besides the mineral acids, small quantities of iced water will be found very grateful, relieving the sense of burning in the back of the pharynx, and diminishing, in great measure, that gastric irritability of which it is a symptom.

The frequent, and sometimes almost unlimited, use of antacid absorbents, viz. magnesia or chalk, in this disease, is a practice much to be deprecated: compounds are thus formed in the stomach which are positively injurious, and, beyond the temporary relief procured by removing the acid, they tend to aggravate[Pg 104] these symptoms, by increasing the state of gastric derangement. The only chemical antacid which should be given in these cases is the carbonate of soda; by this means a compound is formed (the common muriate of soda,) which of all others is most grateful to the stomach, and which, from its gently laxative effects, is well adapted to keep up a healthy action of the bowels. It is scarcely credible to what extent the use of antacids may be carried to relieve the cardialgia of pregnancy. Dr. Dewees mentions having attended a lady with several children, "who was in the constant habit of eating chalk during the whole term of pregnancy; she used it in such excessive quantities as almost rendered the bowels useless. We have known her many times not to have an evacuation for ten or twelve days together, and then only procured by enemata, and the stools were literally nothing but chalk. Her calculation, we well remember, was three half pecks for each pregnancy. She became as white nearly as the substance itself, and it eventually destroyed her, by deranging her stomach so much that it would retain nothing whatever upon it." (System of Midwifery, § 275.)

The constipation, flatulence, colicky pains, and headach, the spasmodic cough, palpitation, toothach, &c. are symptoms arising from the same cause, a knowledge of which circumstance will influence our treatment of them more or less. Still, however, the indications are the same, viz. to restore and keep up a healthy action of the stomach and bowels. Thus, we frequently find that a severe headach, obstinate cough, or attacks of palpitation, are relieved by aperient medicines; that toothach may be relieved, or even removed, by occasional doses of carbonate of soda, or by blue pill and aperient tonics. Indeed, it is a question in many cases, whether it is proper to extract a carious tooth under these circumstances, for the shock which it produces is sometimes so great as to run the risk of exciting abortion; and in many instances we might extract every tooth on the painful side, and yet not relieve the suffering which arises from nervous pain induced by gastric irritation, and, if carefully examined, the pain will be found to be not confined to a single tooth but to spread over the whole side of the face, darting from the edge of the ear, and extending even to the forehead. The breath is usually sour, and the acid state of the saliva is indicated by the instantaneous reddening of litmus paper laid upon the tongue; in many cases there is at the same time a considerable deposit of lithic acid observed in the urine.

Spasmodic cough, or palpitation, if allowed to continue, may ultimately bring on abortion. The treatment just detailed is equally applicable here, and if the circulation be at all excited blood-letting will prove useful. In bleeding women at this early stage of pregnancy it is not desirable, or even safe, to draw a large quantity suddenly from the system, as it may greatly endanger the life[Pg 105] of the fœtus, and from the state of the nervous irritability, may even run the risk of bringing on convulsions; syncope is always more or less hazardous to a pregnant woman, and should if possible be avoided. Some caution will be also necessary in our choice of aperient medicines; drastic purgatives, as aloes, colocynth, scammony, &c. are not suited to the state of pregnancy, as they irritate the lower bowels, and thus excite a disposition to uterine contraction; mild, but effectual laxatives, such as castor oil, confectio sennæ, a seidlitz powder, are better adapted; the latter, especially will be found useful, as, from its being taken during effervescence, it is better calculated to quiet the stomach.

Diarrhœa is sometimes an exceedingly troublesome symptom during pregnancy. It not only weakens the patient and thus tends indirectly to induce abortion by destroying the life of the fœtus, but it acts also in a more direct manner by exciting uterine contractions, particularly when accompanied, as is frequently the case, with tenesmus. The diarrhœa which is met with in pregnant women is not so frequently, as has been supposed, the result of irritation from the uterus, producing simply an increased peristaltic action of the bowels without any considerable derangement of their functions; by far the most usual form is connected with a very deranged state of the alimentary canal; the evacuations are offensive and generally very acrid; the liver is torbid or secretes an unhealthy bile, so that at length a state approaching to dysentery is produced. Even if the patient go to the full term of utero-gestation, she is much reduced, and is ill able to make those exertions which will be required during labour. If the motions, though frequent, are scanty in proportion to the ingesta, or if scybala are occasionally expelled, one or two doses of castor oil will be required; a few drops of Liq. Opii Sedativ. may be added with advantage to allay the irritability of the bowels, after which, equal parts of blue pill, or Hydr. c. Cretâ, and Dover's powder, will excite the liver to a healthier action, and still farther control their inordinate activity. If the disposition to tenesmus be troublesome, a small injection of starch and opium will afford relief. If the stomach will bear it, a rice-milk diet for a day or two is desirable; it is a gentle demulcent to the irritable intestines, and has a slightly constipating effect.

Pruritus pudendi to a very distressing degree occasionally comes on during pregnancy, and though in most instances a very manageable form of disease, yet if its nature be not properly understood it proves exceedingly obstinate, and much suffering is the result. It appears to be essentially different from the common prurigo, being an aphthous state of the lining membrane of the vagina and skin which covers the perineum and external organs. There is great heat and redness of the parts, which are more or less swollen, and from the scratching which the intense itching demands, the cuticle, where it has been raised by the pustules,[Pg 106] becomes abraided, so that severe excoriations, and, where there has not been sufficient attention to cleanliness, even ulcerations may be produced. The pustules on the external parts frequently attain a considerable size, being more distinct than in the vagina, which is usually incrusted with one confluent mass of aphthæ; whereas, on the perineum and margins of the labia we have seen them as large as peas. These cases for the most part yield to the tepid Goulard lotion, or solution of borax.

Where the patient is plethoric, and the system in a state of considerable excitement from the irritation, blood-letting will be necessary, followed by cooling saline laxatives; and if there be much inflammation of the parts, leeches will prove of great service. In every case the bowels ought to be attended to, for constipation will greatly increase the inflammation, and the obstinacy of the disease. It is to Dr. Dewees that we are indebted for first pointing out the real cause and nature of this troublesome affection.[46]

Aphthæ of the vagina are not unfrequently met with in cases of uterine disease, where the discharge is extremely acrid, but the prominent symptom, viz. the intense pruritus, is absent. The aphthous vagina of pregnancy is not a common affection.

Salivation is another affection which is occasionally, though rarely, met with in pregnancy. It is usually attended with morning sickness, constant nausea, and deranged bowels, and may reduce the patient excessively: attention to the state of the bowels, followed by gentle alteratives and tonics, generally gives relief.

[Pg 107]

CHAPTER III.

SIGNS OF THE DEATH OF THE FŒTUS.

Difficulty of the subject.—Signs before labour.—Motion of the Fœtus.—Sound of the fœtal heart.—Uterus souffle.—Signs during labour where the head presents—where the face, the nates, the arm, or the cord, present.—Fetid liquor amnii.—Discharge of meconium.

Well has the celebrated Mauriceau observed, "S'il y a occasion où le chirurgien doive faire plus grande reflexion, et apporter plus de précaution aux choses qui concernent son art, c'est en celle où il s'agit de juger si l'enfant qui est dans la matrice est vivant, ou bien s'il est mort." There are few circumstances more painful to the feelings of an accoucheur, than the uncertainty as to whether the child be alive or dead, in a labour where the passage of the head is rendered unusually difficult or dangerous for the mother, even with the aid of the forceps; whether the difficulty be want of proportion between the head and pelvis, unusual rigidity of the os uteri, &c. Could he assure himself that it was alive, he would feel justified in either trusting still longer to the efforts of nature, or in applying the forceps, even although he knows that the delivery cannot be effected without considerable difficulty and suffering: whereas, if he could once feel satisfied that the child had ceased to exist, he would have recourse to perforation, for the purpose of diminishing the size of the head, and thus releasing the mother from the dangers of her situation.

The increasing success which has attended the Cæsarean operation of late years, adds still more to the importance of having the signs of the child's life or death in utero carefully investigated and understood; for, under such circumstances, it becomes a most serious question whether we are always justified in destroying the life of the fœtus by perforation, when we might in all probability have saved it by resorting to another means of delivery, which, formidable as it is, is now infinitely less so than it was in former times. It becomes a question whether we ought not, in certain cases to adopt the same indications for performing the Cæsarian operation, as are used upon the Continent, and apply it not only[Pg 108] to those cases where the child cannot be delivered par vias naturales, but also in those cases of minor pelvic obstruction, where, if we could feel sure of the child's death, we should have recourse to perforation. Under circumstances of this nature, the question becomes one of fearful responsibility, the painfulness of which is not a little increased by the uncertainty as to whether the child be alive or not. Mauriceau was the first author who devoted a chapter expressly to the consideration of this subject, and those few who have done the same since his time, have borrowed largely from his observations.

A great number of symptoms have been enumerated as indicating the child's death in utero, but for the most part they are deserving of very little confidence, frequently occurring where the result of labour has shown the child to be alive and strong, or vice versâ. The most practical arrangement of these symptoms will, we think, be under the two following heads: those which occur before labour, and those which occur during labour.

The symptoms of the child's death, which are usually enumerated as occurring before labour, are, cessation of the child's movements; the abdomen undergoes no farther increase of size, but rather diminishes; the uterus has no longer the tense elastic feel of pregnancy, but becomes flaccid and moveable; the patient has a sensation of coldness and weight in the abdomen, so that when she turns from one side to the other, she feels as if a heavy weight rolled over to that part of the abdomen which is lowest; the breasts are flabby, and sometimes there is a fetid slimy discharge from the vagina. These changes are accompanied by some or all of the following symptoms: the patient is seized with a sudden shivering, languor, and debility; she loses her appetite and spirits; the stomach and bowels become disordered; the breath is fetid, and the face pale, sallow, and of a dark leaden colour under the eyes. All these symptoms taken collectively will enable us to decide, with a tolerable degree of certainty, that the child is dead: but scarcely any of them alone can be trusted to. The most trust-worthy is the sensation of a heavy weight rolling about the abdomen: when the female turns in bed, rises from her chair, or in any way alters her position, this weight is felt as it were tumbling down to that side which is lowest. A woman who is pregnant with a living child, feels nothing of the sort; she may even dance or jump, and yet she feels no more of a living fœtus than she does of her own liver or spleen. The living fœtus obeys the laws of organic life; the dead fœtus those of gravity. When once the child has ceased to exist, it acts like any other mass of inanimate matter, and pushes the uterus down to that side which is lowest.

In most instances this symptom will be sufficient to make us suspect that the child is dead, but it now and then occurs where the result of labour proves the child to be alive; this must rather[Pg 109] be looked upon as an exception to the rule, for it is not of frequent occurrence. We have observed it in two or three cases: it has been also noticed by Dr. E. Kennedy, (op. cit.;) and, therefore, cannot invariably be looked upon as a certain sign of the child's death. We have observed it frequently in cases threatening abortion at an early period: in many it has been followed by premature expulsion, but in others the symptom has gradually disappeared as the health improves, and the patient has eventually been delivered of a living child at the full period.

In these cases, we should rather attribute the source of this symptom to a loss of the firmness and tone peculiar to the uterine parietes during pregnancy, and which depends upon the increased activity of the circulation in them at this period: when this is considerably diminished, the uterine parietes will necessarily become more flaccid, and, therefore, less able to withstand the influence of gravity, or sustain the uterus in its proper situation. The embryo itself during the first two or three months is too small and too light to produce this symptom itself.

The sensation (to the mother) of the child's movements is as fallacious an indication of the child's life as it is of pregnancy; nor can the absence of this sensation be looked upon as a proof of its death. Women are very liable to be misled in this respect; so much so, that it will be much safer for the practitioner never to allow his diagnosis to be at all influenced by their statements; the more so, as it applies equally to mothers of large families as to primiparæ. Thus cases every now and then occur where the patient declares her conviction that the child is dead; that she has not felt it move for several days before labour; that she feels altogether differently to what she did in any of her former pregnancies, and yet she is delivered of a healthy living child. On the other hand, we as frequently meet with cases where, up to the very commencement of labour, the patient asserts that she has distinctly felt the motion of the child, and yet she brings forth a child in such a state of decomposition as proves beyond all doubt that it must have been dead some eight, ten, or more days.

As the sound of the fœtal heart is the surest sign of pregnancy, so it is an equally certain proof of the child's life: but is the absence of this sound, a certain symptom of its death? at the best it is a negative evidence, and the value of it must entirely depend upon the skill of the ausculator and the care with which he makes his examination. If, after repeated and careful auscultation of the abdomen, the well-practised ear can no where detect a trace of the fœtal pulsations, it may be asserted on very safe grounds that the fœtus has ceased to live. This is more particularly the case during the last weeks of pregnancy, when the pulsations are stronger, and the bulk of the child, in proportion to that of the liquor amnii being absolutely, as well as [Pg 110]relatively, greater. The distance between the heart and surface of the abdomen is less during the last weeks of pregnancy also; the child's movements are not so free as at an earlier period; and hence, if the fœtal heart is beating, it will be more easily discovered.

The uterine souffle affords us little aid in the diagnosis of the child's death: it is frequently very distinct when the child is evidently alive; and where it has been heard previous to its death, it will continue for some hours afterwards, although with diminished strength and over a smaller space.

During labour there are a variety of symptoms, by the aid of which we can pronounce, with a very tolerable degree of certainty, whether the child is alive or not; if alive, the fœtal heart can invariably be detected; and, for the reasons above stated, will be heard more distinctly than in the earlier months of pregnancy. If, from the violence or duration of the labour, or any other cause, the child is becoming exhausted, the pulsations become weaker and slower until they stop; so that by the aid of auscultation we possess distinct evidence of the child's life being endangered, and of its complete extinction.

If the head presents during labour, a firm elastic swelling (caput succedaneum) will rise on that portion of it which first enters the vagina: this is the circulation in the presenting part of the scalp being obstructed by the pressure which the os uteri and vagina exert upon it, an effect which can only be produced upon the head of a living child: where, on the other hand, the child is dead, the scalp will be felt to be soft, flabby, and without swelling. This may be looked upon as a very certain proof of the child's death in primiparæ, where the head is advancing slowly, and where it is tightly encircled by the distended vagina. But in multiparæ, where the soft passages have been dilated by repeated labours, the pressure upon the head is so slight, and its passage through them so rapid, that little or no swelling is produced: even in these cases the finger of the accoucheur will easily distinguish the head of a dead child by the loose yielding flabby feel of its integuments; the cranial bones are more moveable, and overlap each other at the sutures more than usual; their edges feel sharp, as if no longer covered by the scalp; and frequently communicate a grating sensation when they rub against each other. The great fontanelle is flaccid and loose; the bones, which form it, appear falling together, from a want of sufficient contents to keep them asunder, a circumstance which probably arises from the circulation in the brain having ceased; and in those cases where the child has already been dead some time, a crackling or crepitous sensation is communicated to the finger from emphysema, the result of decomposition.

The only case in which the swelling of the head is capable of misleading us, is in lingering difficult labours, where the child[Pg 111] has been alive at the beginning, the swelling has formed, but from the duration and severity of the labour the child has died: wider such circumstances, a dead child may be born with the usual swelling of the cranial integuments which is observed in a living child. This can only happen where it has been expelled almost immediately after its death, for in two or three hours the swelling loses its former firm tense feel, and becomes so soft and flaccid, as not to be easily mistaken.

If the face presents during labour, the flabby state of the lips will instantly lead us to suspect that the child is dead: the tongue is also flaccid and motionless. Whereas, in a living child the lips are firm and full; if the face be approaching the os externum, a considerable swelling will be felt on that side which presents; the tongue is firm, and frequently moves upon the finger.

If the nates present, the state of the sphincter ani will be a sure guide in ascertaining whether the child be alive or not. If it be alive, it will be found closed, and will contract distinctly upon the finger; whereas, if dead, it will be relaxed, and insensible to the stimulus of the finger.

In an arm presentation, where the child is alive, the arm will swell, and grow livid or nearly black; but if it be dead, no swelling will be observed, the arm will be very flabby, and where it has been dead some time, the epidermis will peel off. In this case, as in head presentations, the date of the child's death will more or less modify these appearances; if it has not taken place until some time after the commencement of labour, a dead child may be born exhibiting the swelling and discolouration above-mentioned. The pulse in the wrist of the prolapsed arm is no guide, as the very degree of pressure, which produces these changes in its appearance, will be generally sufficient to render it imperceptible.

In cases where the cord has prolapsed, we have certain evidence with respect to the child's life: if alive the cord is firm, turgid, and distinctly pulsating; if dead, it is flaccid, empty, and without pulsation.

Fetid liquor amnii, and the discharge of the meconium, have also been enumerated as signs of the child's death, which occur during labour. The first affords no proof whatever, as cases not unfrequently occur in which the liquor amnii is excessively fetid, and of a thick slimy consistence, and yet the child is born alive and healthy.

The appearance of meconium during labour is a suspicious sign where the nates do not present, and will at any rate justify the supposition, that if the child be not actually dead, it is very weakly; in nates presentations, however, this will not hold good, for the meconium is constantly discharged during labour, where the child is in this position, and yet it will be born alive and well.

[Pg 112]

CHAPTER IV.

MOLE PREGNANCY.

Nature and origin. — Varieties. — Diagnostic Symptoms. — Treatment.

When any cause has occurred to destroy the life of the embryo during the early weeks of pregnancy, one of two results follows, either that expulsion takes place sooner or later, or the membranes of the ovum become remarkably changed, and continue to grow for some time longer, until at length they form a fleshy fibrous mass, called mole, or false conception.[47]

It is well known that the venous absorbing radicles of the chorion, which give it that shaggy appearance during the first months of pregnancy are the means by which the embryo is furnished with a due supply of nourishment at this period: if the embryo should die from any cause, and the uterus show no disposition to expel the ovum, the nourishment which has been collected by the absorbing power of the chorion appears now to be directed to the chorion itself, which therefore puts on a fleshy growth and increases very rapidly in size. (Rœderer, Elementa Artis Obstetricæ, p. 738.)

In other instances, the thick fleshy character of the ovum is not a growth of substance, but is the result of hæmorrhage from rupture of some of the vessels which run between the uterus and the ovum. In this case, if the placental cells be already formed, they become distended with the blood of the hæmorrhage which solidifies by coagulation; and not only render the chorion or incipient placenta much thicker and more solid, but give it also a lobulated tuberculated appearance: from the same reason, the little funis, which is probably not an inch long, is greatly distended, being in some cases as thick as the body of the embryo itself, the blood having penetrated from the placental cells into the cellular tissue of the chord. This is by no means an uncommon form of mole; externally it is covered by the decidua, which appears to be in a natural condition, and the inner surface of the cavity is lined by a fine membrane, having all the[Pg 113] usual characters of the amnion. The lobulated appearance is chiefly seen from within, the amnion being raised by a number of irregular convexities.

"When the blood is poured out from its containing vessels into the substance or cells of the placenta, or between the membranes, gradually coagulates, and assumes a very dark purple, and sometimes almost a melanotic black colour: after a time, however, it begins to lose this tint, the colouring matter gradually becomes removed, and the coagulum successively assumes a chocolate brown, a reddish or brownish yellow hue; and latterly, if time sufficient be allowed, it presents a pale yellowish white or straw-coloured substance, the fibrinous portion of the coagulum being then left alone."[48] This form of mole, as far as our own observation goes, seldom attains any considerable size, rarely exceeding four inches in length, and is usually expelled between the eighth and twelfth week. The size and condition of the fœtus varies a good deal; in some cases it appears nearly healthy, although the cord is much thickened and distended; this is probably owing to its having been expelled shortly after its death, or to its having gone on to live a short time after the injury which had caused hæmorrhage: in this way alone can we explain why we occasionally meet with cases where the parietes of the ovum are much thickened and solidified, and yet the embryo is in such a state of integrity as to prove that its death must have been very recent. The extravasation of blood between the ovum and uterus does not appear to be sufficient to annihilate immediately the nutrition of the embryo, so that the blood has had sufficient time to solidify before the ovum was expelled. At other times the embryo exhibits evident marks of having been dead some time: it is much smaller and younger in proportion to the size of the ovum; sometimes it has disappeared entirely, a short rudiment of the funis merely remaining to mark its previous existence.

"Should the embryo die (suppose in the first or second month) some days before the ovum is discharged, it will sometimes be entirely dissolved, so that when the secundines are delivered, there is nothing to be seen. In the first month the embryo is so small and tender, that this dissolution will be performed in twelve hours; in the second month, two, three, or four days will suffice for this purpose." (Smellie.)

Where the growth of the ovum proceeds after the destruction of the embryo, it increases very rapidly in size, much more so than would be the case in natural pregnancy, so that the uterus, when filled with a mole of this sort, is as large at the third month as it would be in pregnancy at the fifth.

Another form of mole is where the uterus is filled with a large mass of vesicles of irregular size and shape like hydatids, which[Pg 114] appear to be the absorbing extremities of the veins of the chorion distended with a serous fluid; it is difficult to distinguish these from real hydatids; the more so, as Bremser asserts that he has occasionally met with real hydatids among them. Perhaps the mode of their attachment will in some degree assist the diagnosis: these vessicles, or hydatids of the placenta, as they have been called, are attached over a large portion of the uterus,—an arrangement we believe, not generally seen in real hydatids, which are mostly attached to a single stalk or pedicle. Indeed, it may be doubted if the masses of vesicles which are occasionally expelled from the uterus are ever true acephalocysts, as they are invariably connected with a blighted ovum, and are, therefore, formed as before observed, by a dropsical state of the venous radicles of the chorion.

A variety of other molar growths have also been enumerated by authors; in fact, "the term mole has been rather vaguely applied to almost every shapeless mass which issued from the uterus, whether this proved to be coagulated blood, detached tumours, or a blighted conception." (Churchill, on the Principal Diseases of Females, p. 153.) Thus a fibrinous cast of the uterus, which has been formed by a coagulum of blood, from which the colouring matter has been drained, has been called a fibrous mole: these, however, may easily be distinguished from real moles, which are invariably the product of conception: from inattention also to this circumstance, fungoid, bony, and calcareous tumours have been described as so many species of moles.[49]

Diagnostic symptoms. The diagnosis of a mole pregnancy is exceedingly obscure; in fact, for the first eight or ten weeks we know of no symptom by which we can distinguish it from natural pregnancy. As the death of the embryo is intimately connected with the first morbid changes in the condition of the ovum, and in most cases precedes them, the earliest symptoms which can excite our suspicions are those which indicate this event: thus we shall find that the face becomes pale and chlorotic, the digestion deranged, the breasts flaccid, with unusual lassitude, debility, and depression of spirits; many of the sympathetic affections which belong to early pregnancy, such as the morning sickness, nausea, &c. cease suddenly; in some cases, an attack of hæmorrhage comes on, and may be repeated several times, causing much loss of strength and exhaustion, and attended with a good deal of pain, more especially if the uterus be about to throw off its contents. In that form of mole where the parietes of the ovum have been thickened[Pg 115] and lobulated by masses of coagulated blood, the uterus undergoes little or no more increase of size, but the mole, especially the hydatic, continues to grow rapidly; and the unusual increase in the size of the abdomen, as already mentioned, will be an additional reason for suspicion. In all cases, hæmorrhage sooner or later makes its appearance, the patient's health still farther declines, leucorrhœa comes on, followed by œdema of the feet, general breaking up of the health, and even incipient cachexia. Occasionally the discharge is excessively putrid and offensive. Where it is of the hydatic species, we can frequently ascertain its character by the expulsion of two or three hydatids which have separated from the main mass, or by the escape of some limpid colourless water resulting from the rupture of one or more of them. The expulsion of the mole itself clears up all doubts.

The amount of hæmorrhage will chiefly depend upon the extent of surface by which the mole is attached to the uterus: hence it is observed to be greatest in cases of hydatic mole, from the large size of the mass to be expelled:

indeed, under these circumstances, it is frequently more profuse than hæmorrhage from detachment of the placenta. The process of the expulsion itself resembles that of an abortion: pain in the back, groins, and lower part of the abdomen comes on, with more or less discharge of blood; at length bearing down pains succeed, and the mass is expelled.

We cannot better describe the symptoms the presence of a hydatic mole, and the mode of its expulsion, than by quoting a case from the work of Dr. Gooch, on some of the most Important Diseases peculiar to Women.

"I was sent for to — —, a few miles from London, to see a lady, who, having ceased to menstruate for one month, and becoming very sick, concluded that she was pregnant. The next month she had a slow hæmorrhage from the uterus, which had continued incessantly a month when I saw her: she kept nothing on her stomach. On examining the uterus through the vagina, its body felt considerably enlarged, and there was a round circumscribed tumour in the front of the abdomen, reaching from the brim of the pelvis nearly to the umbilicus. I saw her several times at intervals of a fortnight, during which the hæmorrhage and the vomiting continued unrelieved: the peculiarity about the case was the bulk of the uterus, which was greater than it ought to be at this period of pregnancy; it felt also less firm than the pregnant uterus, more like a thick bladder full of fluid. Eleven weeks from the omission of the menstruation, she was seized with profuse hæmorrhage; towards evening there came on strong expelling pains, during which she discharged a vast quantity of something which puzzled her attendants. The next morning I found her quite well—her pain, hæmorrhage, and vomiting, having ceased. I was then taken into her dressing-room, and[Pg 116] shown a large wash-hand basin full of what looked like myriads of little white currants floating in red-currant juice. They were hydatids floating in bloody water."

The treatment previous to the expulsion of the mole should be gently alterative and tonic; the chylopoietic functions should be kept in regular action, and the strength sustained. When hæmorrhage comes on, we must be guided a good deal by the quantity lost, and by the effect which it has upon the pulse. Generally speaking, when the pulse has been a good deal reduced in strength and volume, we shall find the os uteri relaxed and dilated, and in all probability a portion of the mass protruding into the vagina, which may be hooked down by the fingers, and thus the expulsion of the whole mass facilitated. For farther details regarding the management of such cases, we must refer to the chapter on premature expulsion of the ovum, between the symptoms and treatment of which, and of mole pregnancy, there is a close analogy. The after treatment will always be a matter of considerable importance, and will, in a great measure resemble that in abortion or mis-carriage.

Patients who have suffered from a mole pregnancy generally have their strength seriously reduced and their health much broken: hence, they are liable to leucorrhœa, menorrhagia, or dysmenorrhœa, which entail a long series of troublesome and even dangerous affections, the recovery from which will be slow and difficult, requiring a long course of tonic medicines, and removal to the sea-coast or some watering-place where there are chalybeate springs.

[Pg 117]

CHAPTER V.

EXTRA-UTERINE PREGNANCY.

Tubarian, ovarian, and ventral pregnancy.—Pregnancy in the substance of the uterus.

The ovum when impregnated does not always quit the ovary and pass along the Fallopian tube into the uterus. It may remain in the ovary and become here developed; it may pass into the Fallopian tube and remain there; or from some defect in the action of the fimbriated extremity of this canal, it may escape into the cavity of the abdomen, and become attached to some of the viscera. Hence, extra-uterine pregnancy has been divided into three species, viz. graviditas tuberia, ovaria, and ventralis, according to the situation which the ovum takes. A fourth has been also described by M. Breschet, which he has called graviditas in substantia uteri, a modification probably of tubarian pregnancy.

a The uterus, its cavity laid open. b Its parietes thickened, as in natural pregnancy. c A portion of decidua separated from its inner surface. d Bristles to show the direction of the Fallopian tubes. e Right Fallopian tube distended into a sac which has burst, containing the extra-uterine ovum. f The fœtus. g The chorion. h The ovaries; in the right one is a well marked corpus luteum. i The round ligament.

[Pg 118]This singular deviation from the usual course of conception is fortunately of rare occurrence, for few cases terminate favourably. If it be in the Fallopian tube or ovary, these become immensely distended into a species of sac or cyst, to the sides of which the placenta adheres: as the ovum increases, this at length gives way from excessive distension, and the patient usually dies from internal hæmorrhage. In ventral pregnancy, the sac is attached to the abdominal viscera, and is usually imbedded among the convolutions of the intestines: hence the duration of extra-uterine pregnancy will depend upon its situation; thus, if it be in the Fallopian tube, it rarely lasts beyond two months; whereas, ovarian pregnancy will continue for five or six months; on the other hand, in ventral pregnancy the fœtus will not only be carried to the full term, but far beyond that period, amounting to several years.[50]

Although the uterus does not receive the ovum into its cavity as it does in natural conception, it nevertheless undergoes many of those changes which are known to take place in regular pregnancy. The layer of coagulable lymph, which is effused upon its internal surface, and which forms the membrana decidua of Hunter, is present, and the uterus undergoes a slight increase of volume. As the ovum increases, excruciating pains are felt in the lower part of the abdomen, coming on at irregular intervals, and of irregular duration; in some cases lasting for a short time, in others continuing for twenty-four hours. These attacks of pain are generally accompanied with very painful forcing and tenesmus, and not unfrequently with a discharge of bloody mucus from the vagina. In tubarian pregnancy, however, the case generally follows a much shorter course: the patient is suddenly seized with an acute pain in the lower part of the abdomen, followed by nausea and vomiting; she becomes faint and weak; the abdomen evidently increases in size (from effusion of blood into the cavity;) the debility becomes more alarming, and death quickly follows.

In ovarian pregnancy the fatal termination is merely postponed till a later period, during which the patient has to undergo attacks of most terrible suffering: at length, after a paroxysm more than usually severe, and frequently attended with the sensation of something giving way in the abdomen, faintings come on, speedily followed by death. During the attacks there is obstinate constipation, which is attended with painful and fruitless efforts to evacuate the bladder and rectum; the face is pale, and expressive not only of the most acute suffering, but of great anxiety and[Pg 119] mental depression; nevertheless, in the intervals of the attacks she feels easy, and appears well and cheerful.

The termination of a ventral pregnancy is very different; after a time the fœtus dies, and may either remain enclosed in the cyst for life, or it may be discharged in portions by means of an abscess, either through the intestines, uterus, vagina, or abdominal parietes. Cases have occurred where it has come away by the bladder; in the former case, where it is retained, it diminishes more or less in size, becomes hard and closely packed together, and, in some instances, encrusted with a layer of calcareous matter.

It is to our venerable friend, the late Dr. Heim, of Berlin, that we are indebted for much curious and interesting knowledge respecting extra-uterine pregnancy. Although the symptoms in the very early stages are so obscure as to render it nearly impossible to detect its presence, he has nevertheless observed some facts connected with it, which are peculiar, and deserve to be noticed. No morning sickness has been observed in cases of extra-uterine pregnancy, a circumstance which can easily be accounted for, if we bear in mind the causes of morning sickness in natural pregnancy: the patient could only lie on the affected side, and the abdomen was observed to swell irregularly, not in the same manner as in regular pregnancy.

In tubarian and ovarian pregnancy, the pain was in the pelvis, but in ventral pregnancy it occupied more or less the whole abdomen, the parietes of which were very tender upon pressure. In cases where the fœtus died at an early period, the symptoms gradually disappeared after a time, especially when followed by the bursting of an abscess through the rectum or any other part. One of the most remarkable facts which Dr. Heim observed, was a peculiar whining tone of voice, with which the patient expressed her sufferings during a paroxysm of pain; so peculiar, that when once heard, the sound can never be mistaken. On several occasions Dr. Heim was enabled by means of this symptom alone to decide confidently as to the nature of the case the moment he entered the room, a fact which would appear scarcely credible had not the results of the cases proved the correctness of his assertion. A most interesting case of this sort occurred, which he pronounced to be ventral pregnancy, and when it had gone the full term gastrotomy was performed, a living child was extracted but the unfortunate mother perished: she could not be induced to submit to the operation until inflammation had come on, and she died in two days after.

It must always remain a matter of great obscurity as to the immediate causes of extra-uterine pregnancy, more especially of the ovarian and ventral species; and the more so as we are still ignorant of the mechanism by which the fimbriated extremity of the Fallopian tube grasps the ovary immediately over the impregnated[Pg 120] vesicle of de Graaf at the moment of conception. In many cases we are inclined to think that this function of the Fallopian tube is destroyed by adhesions between it and the ovary, a circumstance of not uncommon occurrence; but from the alteration in the shape and size of these parts, as also from the extensive adhesions which are usually found after death, in such cases it will ever be difficult, and perhaps impossible, to prove it.

The treatment of extra-uterine pregnancy must be chiefly guided by the prevailing symptoms: where any portion of the abdomen is very tender to the touch, leeches and warm fomentations will be required; the pain during the attacks can only be alleviated by frequently repeated opiates; and constipation must be carefully guarded against by laxatives and enemata between the paroxysms. Where an effort is made by nature to discharge the fœtus by means of an abcess, the case will require all our care to sustain the powers of the system through a long protracted struggle. Portions of the fœtus come away from time to time, and if the exit afforded them be by way of the intestine, the suffering produced is very great, particularly when any of the larger bones are passing. The presence of such a mass of semi-decomposed animal matter in the abdomen is of itself sufficient to injure the general health materially: hence it is that patients, during the process of expulsion, suffer greatly from severe attacks of fever, which recur from time to time. Where the abscess opens through the abdominal parietes, the whole is completed with much greater ease and safety to the patient: in some instances the tumour has been opened, and a fœtus with a large quantity of putrid pus has been removed. (Medical Obs. and Inquiries, vol. ii. p. 369.)

A case of ventral pregnancy has recently come under our care, a short account of which will enable the reader to understand the subject better than a mere enumeration of symptoms; the more so as we believe it to have been the first case of extra-uterine pregnancy in which the stethoscope has been used.

The patient, æt. 32, and the mother of four children, was admitted, May 26, 1837, into St. Bartholomew's Hospital, under Dr. Latham, who kindly consigned her to our charge. She considers herself to be six months advanced in pregnancy; is continually suffering from attacks of acute pain in the lower part of the abdomen, both at the sides and front, causing her to moan from its great severity; this is accompanied with a constant dragging pain on the right side, and in the loins: the attacks of abdominal pain go off at intervals, leaving her comparatively easy. She is pale, with an anxious expression of face. Pulse 120, and firm. Tongue moist. Bowels very constipated.

The abdomen is as large as in common pregnancy at the sixth month, but does not present the same uniform distension, being irregularly shaped. At the left hypogastrium is a soft tympanitic[Pg 121] prominence of considerable extent, and appears, from its feel and also from auscultation, to consist of a large portion of the intestines pushed over to that side: at the inner edge of this tumour a solid mass, as large as the head of a six months' fœtus, can be felt. Between this and the median line of the abdomen, and half way between the pubes and umbilicus, a small hard knob-like and moveable prominence is felt immediately beneath the abdominal parietes, and intensely painful to the touch. From this point, quite to the right side, the abdomen has a solid irregular feel; below this to the symphysis pubis, a very loud souffle is heard, synchronous with the mother's pulse, having all the characters of the uterine souffle in common pregnancy except its extraordinary loudness. Its limits, superiorly, are remarkably defined; below a transverse line, drawn half way between the umbilicus and pubes, it is heard in full strength, whereas, immediately above it the sound ceases: it is also heard some way to the right side. At the upper part of the right iliac region two ridge-like prominences, like the extremities of a child, may be felt close beneath the abdominal parietes. No trace of fœtal pulsation can be heard over any part of the abdomen, although it has been carefully ausculted round to the loins: it was however distinctly heard the day before we saw her, by two gentlemen who are proficients in the use of the stethoscope, and whom we consider fully capable of judging in such a case.

On examining per vaginam, the os uteri is found high up and backwards, barely within reach. Its edges are thick, soft, and closed; the cervix is short, and seems less than half an inch. The anterior portion of the inferior segment of the uterus feels somewhat firm and full, as if there was something in the uterus. We were confirmed in this respect by our friend, Dr. Nebel, jun., of Heidelberg, who was on a visit to this country at the time, and who examined the case with us. He was at first induced to suppose that it was the head. We considered that it was the uterus more or less anteverted, the fundus being pressed forwards and downwards, and the os uteri backwards, by the extra-uterine cyst above; farther examinations tended to confirm this view.

She states that the catamenia appeared last in November, during the middle of which month she was attacked with inflammation of the bowels, for which she was treated, and soon afterwards began to have the violent attacks of pain of which she now complains. She felt the child move at the usual time; it evidently formed the mass which occupies the lower part of the abdomen, and its movements appeared unusually close to the surface. During the last few days they have ceased altogether. The above-mentioned attacks of pain have continued to recur ever since at short intervals and with increasing severity.

As leeches had been applied without relief, and as the pulse[Pg 122] was quick and hard, she was ordered to be bled to eight ounces, and to take half a grain of morphia immediately.

June 2.—Has been in constant suffering, in spite of leeches and morphia; bowels obstinately constipated, but moved at length by repeated injections and doses of house medicine. Has not felt the motions of the child since the intestines have become tympanitic: still, however, the mass can be felt lying across the abdomen, half-way between the pubes and umbilicus, commencing from about three inches to the left of the median line, and extending to about four inches on the opposite side. On the left side it feels firm and rounded, and so superficial, that it can almost be grasped through the abdominal integuments. Face very pale and anxious. Pulse 120.

June 10.—Was easy and free from pain when we first saw her: the souffle is heard over a smaller extent; in the centre of the space where it is heard it is as remarkably loud as ever, but it gradually becomes indistinct towards the circumference. As she was able to rise we examined her standing: the os uteri is exceedingly high up to the left sacro-iliac symphysis, so that it can scarcely be reached; the cervix is short, the lips somewhat larger than usual, and the whole very firm and immoveable. The anterior portion of the uterus, to be felt through the vaginal parietes, is somewhat firmer and larger than usual: on pressing the tumour in the left hypogastrium, this appeared to lie altogether anterior to the uterus. Little motion is communicated to the os uteri when this is moved.

June 20.—Has been in much suffering since last report; much emaciated; complains of a fetid taste in the mouth; bowels inclined to be purged; stools of a whitish purulent appearance; tongue clean; pulse tolerably natural; has continued to pass portions of fibrinous matter from the vagina, mixed with bloody mucus, since last report. The hard globular swelling at the left side of the abdomen is more distinct at times: the hand can almost pass round it: it has the precise feeling of the head; the mass which lies across the abdomen is also more distinct: the souffle is heard over a much smaller space and is diminished in strength.

June 27.—Much the same, except that, after severe bearing down and tenesmus, she has passed a considerable quantity of blood from the rectum and vagina. The little prominences on the right side, presumed to be the extremities, are remarkably distinct, like two heels or knees.

July 18.—No material change has taken place since last report; she has suffered from irregular attacks of pain, and has had repeated discharges of blood from the vagina, which always give relief; is weaker than usual, and feels exhausted from the continued character of the pain; abdomen less swollen; the globular mass on the left side is lower and much nearer to the median line;[Pg 123] the little prominences on the right are also lower, and nearer the median line; the whole mass appears much more compressed together and nearer to the pubes; it is extremely painful on the left side, and at the most painful spot the skin is red and inflamed; the bowels, appetite, &c. are natural; pulse feeble, but regular; scarcely any trace of souffle to be heard.

Shortly after this she left the hospital, and for some time continued to enjoy tolerable health, occasionally suffering from severe paroxysms of abdominal pain; the abdomen diminished considerably in size, and the various prominences became indistinct.

In May, 1839, she was again admitted in a state of great exhaustion from constant severe pain. The abdomen had diminished still more, and a portion of the mass had descended between the uterus and rectum; the constipated bowels were moved with great difficulty, but with much relief. The symptoms gradually diminished, and she was discharged in the first week of the following August.

In January, 1840, she returned to the hospital, all her former sufferings being greatly aggravated. The abdomen had subsided still farther; early in February she passed a quantity of putrid purulent matter from the rectum, after which the abdomen diminished considerably. The pain appeared to be chiefly situated in the upper part of the rectum, accompanied with severe bearing down, and on examining per vaginam the mass was felt deep at the posterior part of the pelvic brim: the debility and emaciation increased, and she died early in February. Our notes of the post mortem examination were as follows:—

Much emaciated, abdomen concave, but on pressing it the tumour can be felt at the brim of the pelvis. On opening the abdominal cavity, the mass was found adhering firmly to the neighbouring intestines, and on the right side to the soft linings of the pelvis: it was of an irregular form, with spots of livid vascularity in different parts: on the upper and left side of it, fetid purulent matter was seen exuding from a small orifice. The uterus was below, its fundus pushed over to the left side. On separating its adhesions, and attempting to raise the sac from the pelvis, the half-softened parietes gave way, and the decomposed putty-like mass of the foetus became visible; the cranial bones were at the left side; the feet were still distinct on the right side; the whole was immersed in a quantity of thick fetid pus, and there were no traces either of umbilical cord or placenta.

Cases of ventral pregnancy have been recorded where the child has remained in the mother's abdomen without producing any dangerous symptoms, and where she has again become pregnant in the natural way. The earliest instance of this sort was recorded so long ago as by Albucasis. A very interesting case of this nature is described by Dr. Bard of New York. (Med. Obs. and Inquiries, vol. ii. p. 369.) It was the patient's second [Pg 124]pregnancy; at the end of nine months she had pains, which after a time went off; the tumour gradually diminished somewhat, and in about five months after she conceived again, and in due time was delivered, after an easy labour, of a healthy child. "Five days after delivery she was seized with a violent fever, a purging, suppression, pain in the tumour, and profuse fetid sweats:" an abscess formed in the abdomen, which was opened, and a vast quantity of extremely fetid matter was discharged; the opening was enlarged, and a foetus of the full size was extracted. Dr. Bard "imagined the placenta and funis umbilicalis were dissolved in the pus, of which there was a great quantity."

It becomes a question of deep interest whether it be really possible to save the patient and the child in cases of ventral pregnancy, by performing gastrotomy. The separation of the placenta from the walls of the cyst can only be effected with much difficulty and hazard; indeed, we are at a loss to conceive how it can be removed with any degree of safety, where the child has been found alive. The attachment in these cases was more than usually firm, and it has been left to undergo that process of solution which has been described in Dr. Bard's case. In all the cases where gastrotomy has been performed some time after the child's death, little or no trace of the placenta has been found, but in its place a quantity of ill-conditioned purulent matter, which was excessively fetid.

The fourth species of extra-uterine pregnancy, which M. Breschet has described as taking place in the substance of the uterus, is of very rare occurrence, four cases only having been recorded by him. (Med. Chir. Trans. vol. xiii.) M. Breschet has attempted a variety of explanations of this singular anomaly, but without success; and from the circumstance of the cyst having always been found situated in the fundus to one side, the Fallopian tube of which was closed at its uterine extremity, we think that there can be little doubt of its having been a modification of tubarian pregnancy, where the ovum had been obstructed at that portion of the Fallopian tube where it passes obliquely through the wall of the uterus: in one case the tube appears to have given way at this part, and the ovum to have insinuated itself between the uterus and peritoneum. In these cases the sac ruptured at about the same period as in tubarian pregnancy, except in one instance, where she went five months. A rather inexplicable case of extra-uterine pregnancy has been recorded by Mr. Hay, of Leeds (Med. Obs. and Inquiries, vol. iii.,) where a full grown foetus was found enclosed in a large sac, which filled the abdominal cavity, and which communicated inferiorly with the uterus. On tracing the umbilical cord, "we were led," says Mr. Hay, "to a large aperture in the right side of the inferior globular sac already mentioned, from which that which contained the foetus seemed to have its origin. This inferior sac we now[Pg 125] found to be the uterus, containing a very thick placenta, which adhered very firmly to about three-fourths of its internal surface, having the navel string attached to its centre, and this centre corresponded nearly with the centre of the fundus uteri. The placenta filled up the greatest part of the aperture of communication between the uterus and sac. The Fallopian tube on the left side was very small; the place of that on the right was occupied by the beginning or orifice of the sac." (Op. cit.)

This would seem to have been a case of pregnancy in the substance of the uterus, and where a portion of the ovum had burst its way into the cavity of the uterus lined with decidua, to which it adhered; the other portion, containing the embryo, distended the uterine parietes in a contrary direction, and thus formed the large sac which communicated with the cavity of the uterus.

CHAPTER VI.

RETROVERSION OF THE UTERUS.

History.—Causes.—Symptoms.—Diagnosis.—Treatment.—Spontaneous terminations.

During the earlier months of pregnancy the uterus is liable, although rarely, to a peculiar species of displacement, called retroversion, in which the fundus is forced downwards and backwards into the hollow of the sacrum, between the rectum and posterior wall of the vagina, and its os and cervix are carried forwards and upwards behind the symphysis pubis.

a a Half the bladder on each side turned over the spine of the os ilium. b Anterior extremity of the vertical incision by which the bladder was opened. c One turn of the rectum, which was seen at the posterior end of the same incision. W. Hunter.

Retroversion of the uterus appears to have been known to the ancients, as we find it alluded to by Hippocrates (De Nat. Mulieb. sect. 5.) and Philumenus (Histoire de la Chirurg. par Dujardin and Peyrhille, t. ii. p. 280.) Œtius, who has quoted the works of the celebrated Aspasia, describes this displacement of the uterus very exactly, and gives rules for introducing two fingers into the rectum, in order to remedy it. Rod. a Castro, who wrote in the sixteenth century, in his work on the diseases of women, quotes what Hippocrates had written on the subject of this displace-ment; and it is astonishing that no farther notice was taken of it until the eighteenth century, when it excited consider-able attention among accoucheurs. (Martin le Jeune, p. 137.) Gregoire appears to have been the first who gave a good description of it; his pupil, Mr. W. Wall, on his return to England, met with what he considered to be a case of this displacement, and not being able to restore the uterus to its natural position, requested the advice of Dr. W. Hunter. On passing his finger between the os uteri and symphysis pubis, and thus removing, in some degree, the pressure upon the neck of the bladder, a considerable quantity of urine was discharged, but he was unable to return the uterus to its natural situation, and the patient gradually sunk. The bladder was found immensely distended; the lower part of it, "which is united with the vagina and cervix uteri, and[Pg 127] into which the ureters are inserted, was raised up as high as the brim of the pelvis by a large round tumour, (viz. the uterus,) which entirely filled up the whole cavity of the pelvis. The os uteri made the summit of the tumour upon which the bladder rested, and the fundus uteri was turned down towards the os coccygis and anus." (Medical Obs. and Inquiries, vol. iv. 404.)

Causes. This displacement may also occur in the unimpregnated state, either from the fundus being pushed into that position by some morbid growth, or where this effect has been the violent pressure of the abdominal muscles in lifting heavy weights, under circumstances where the uterus has been larger and heavier than usual;[51] but it is in the early months of pregnancy that it is most likely to happen, because now the fundus is both larger and heavier than before, and, therefore, more liable to be affected by the pressure of the intestines and abdominal muscles, and has not yet attained a sufficient size to prevent its undergoing this displacement in the pelvis: this period is about the third or fourth month, often before it, but never after it. (Burns's Anatomy of the Gravid Uterus, p. 17.)

It has been supposed by many authors, especially Dr. Burns, that distension of the bladder is, in many instances, the immediate cause of retroversion, owing to the intimate connexion which exists between the lower part of the uterus and this organ, inasmuch, "that whenever the bladder rises by distension, the uterus must rise also." In the later editions of his work on the principles of midwifery, he has considerably modified this opinion, and from careful examination of the parts in situ, in the third month, is not disposed to consider the distension of the bladder as the cause, but the effect of retroversion. In every case which has come under our own observation, the bladder has not been distended until the retroversion had taken place, in consequence of which the os and cervix uteri had been tilted up behind the symphysis pubis, and having thus compressed its neck had caused the difficulty in passing water.[52] Whenever any force is applied to the fundus uteri at this period of pregnancy, either from external violence, or the action of the abdominal muscles pressing the intestines and bladder against it, it will be pushed against the rectum, in which case the rectum will be flattened at that part against which the fundus rests; and if any mass of fæculent matter be passing along the intestine, its course will be obstructed at this point, and the rectum quickly[Pg 128] become distended with an accumulation of fæces above, by which means the fundus will not only be prevented from rising, but in all probability be forced still lower down. If the force which has originally pushed the fundus backwards be of sufficient degree and duration to carry it past the promontory of the sacrum, the increase of space which it will meet with in the hollow of the sacrum, and the straining efforts which are induced by the displacement itself, contribute powerfully to complete the mischief, and to bring the fundus so low into the pelvic cavity as at length to turn it nearly upside down.

As soon as the fundus of the uterus is pressed with any degree of force against the posterior parietes of the pelvis, its os and cervix will be directed forwards and upwards against the symphysis pubis, and from the pressure which they exert against the neck of the bladder, the patient either experiences complete retention of urine, or, at any rate, considerable difficulty in passing it; hence, therefore, we find, that where retroversion has come on suddenly, the patient is generally sensible of the pain the displacement, before she has experienced any difficulty in evacuating the bladder.

A modern French author of great experience, (Martin le Jeune, p. 178,) in enumerating the causes of retroversion, appears to take a similar view of the subject, and places retention of urine very far down in his list. "Sudden and violent contractions of the abdominal muscles and diaphragm in attempting to vomit, to evacuate the bowels or bladder, or to lift heavy weights; the throes during an abortion at an early period of pregnancy; strong mental emotions; retention of urine; tumours in the neighbourhood of the fundus, which by their weight or pressure force it backwards towards the sacrum, are the causes which may produce a retroversion of the uterus."

Retroversion may also come on gradually, from "the uterus remaining too long in that situation which is natural to it when unimpregnated, namely, with its fundus inclined backwards. This may depend on various causes; such as too great width of the pelvis, or the pressure of the ileum full of fæces on the fore part of the uterus. In this case the weight of the fundus must gradually produce a retroversion, and she will be sensible of its progress from day to day." (Burns's Anat. of the Gravid Uterus. p. 18.)

It will thus be seen how peculiarly liable the uterus is to retroversion during the early months of pregnancy. At this time, the fundus is not yet free from the weight of the superincumbent coils of intestine; and if from any cause its ascent out of the pelvis be delayed beyond the usual time, its liability to retroversion is still farther increased; for, not only does the size of the fundus press it still farther backward, but any sudden contractions of the abdominal muscles, or external violence, act upon it with increased effect.

[Pg 129]The symptoms of this displacement are as follow:—the patient is seized with violent pain, bearing down, and sense of distension about the hollow of the sacrum, with a feeling of dragging and even tearing about the groins, the violent stretching of the broad and round ligaments; the bearing down is sometimes so severe and involuntary as to resemble labour pains, and cases have occurred where it has been mistaken for labour. With all this she finds herself unable to pass fæces or urine, from the pressure of the fundus upon the rectum and of the os uteri upon the neck of the bladder. Upon examination per vaginam, the altered position and form of this canal instantly excite our suspicion: instead of running nearly in a straight direction backwards and somewhat upwards, it now takes a curved direction upwards and forwards behind the symphysis pubis; the hollow of the sacrum is occupied with the globular and nearly solid mass, (the fundus uteri,) which is evidently behind the vagina, the posterior wall of this canal being felt between it and the finger; behind the symphysis pubis, the vagina is more or less flattened, and its anterior wall put violently upon the stretch, so much so that, according to Richter, the orifice of the urethra is sometimes dragged up above the pubic bones, (Anfangsgründe der Wundarztneikunst, vol. ii. p. 45:) the os uteri is found high up behind the symphysis pubis, and in most cases can be reached, although with much difficulty; sometimes we shall be able to reach the posterior lip only, which is now the lowest: but "if the retension of urine has been of some duration, it will be impossible to reach the os uteri above the pubic bones with the finger. On examining per rectum, we shall feel the same tumour pressing firmly upon it, and preventing the farther passage of the finger, thus proving that the tumour is situated between the rectum and the vagina; for, in such cases, the bladder forms a considerable swelling below it, and prevents the finger from passing up." (Op. cit.)

"The uterus being situated in the centre of the pelvis, between the rectum and bladder, its retroversion cannot take place without deranging the functions of these organs: the symptoms thus produced come on rapidly when the displacement is sudden, slowly when it is gradual. Their severity is in proportion to the size of the uterus, the degree of retroversion, its duration, and the various circumstances which increase the impaction of the uterus in the cavity of the pelvis: they also determine the degree of inflammation and gangrene of this organ and the neighbouring parts." (Martin le Jeune, p. 178.) Hence we frequently observe in the earlier stages of retroversion, before the displacement has become complete, that the patient is able to relieve the bladder to a certain extent, although very imperfectly, and that with some difficulty; a slight dribbling of urine continues to a very advanced stage, when the bladder is enormously distended, and upon the[Pg 130] point of bursting: this is not so much the case with the rectum, the passage of fæces being generally completely obstructed at an early period, partly from the pressure of the fundus against it, and partly from the solid nature of its contents. "When such suppressions once begin they aggravate the evil, not merely by causing pain, but by occasioning a load of accumulated fæces in the abdomen above the uterus, which presses it still lower into the cavity of the pelvis, at the same time that the distension of the bladder in this state draws up that part of the vagina and cervix uteri with which it is connected, so as to throw the fundus uteri still more directly downwards." (Dr. W. Hunter, Med. Obs. and Inquiries, vol. iv. p. 406.) These conditions of the bladder and rectum, and the retroversion of the uterus, act reciprocally as cause and effect; for the continuance of the distension of the bladder and the descent of the fæces from the part of the intestine above the obstruction, must elevate still more the os uteri, and depress to a still greater degree the fundus. The retroversion, on the other hand, increases the affection of the bladder and rectum, from which the principal danger of the disease arises. (Burns's Anat. of the Gravid Uterus.)

The diagnosis of retroversion is, generally speaking, not very difficult, the os uteri tilted up behind the symphysis pubis, and the fundus forced downwards and backwards between the vagina and rectum, are sufficiently characteristic of this displacement. We cannot agree with Dr. Dewees that it can easily be mistaken for prolapsus uteri; in cases of sudden prolapsus which has been caused by great violence, there will be, it is true, intense pain in the pelvis, with sensation of forcing and tearing in the direction of the broad and round ligaments; there will also, probably, be inability to evacuate the rectum and bladder; but then the examination, per vaginam, will present such a totally different condition of parts as to preclude all possibility of mistake: the vagina merely shortened, neither altered in direction or form; the os uteri at the lower part of the tumour, which is in the vagina; the mobility of the tumour itself, all conspire to show that the case is one of prolapsus not retroversion.

We occasionally meet with cases of retroversion where the os uteri, although carried more or less upwards and forwards, is not forced, to that extreme height behind the symphysis pubis as is usually observed. Instead of looking towards, or rather above, the symphysis, the os uteri itself looks downwards, the neck or lower part of the body of the uterus being bent upon the fundus like the neck of a retort.[53] If, under such circumstances, we[Pg 131] cannot satisfy ourselves as to the existence of pregnancy, we might easily be led to form an erroneous diagnosis, and to conclude that some tumour had forced itself down into the hollow of the sacrum, between the rectum and vagina, and had thus pushed the uterus upwards and forwards, above the brim of the pelvis. An extra-uterine ovum of the ventral species may occupy this situation, but its slow and gradual growth, its greater softness and elasticity, and the slight degree of uterine displacement produced in its early stages, would enable us to ascertain its real character. The same would hold good to a certain extent with an ovarian tumour, although in all probability this would produce more or less displacement of the uterus to one side.

The danger in retroversion of the uterus chiefly arises from the distension or rupture of the bladder, and from the gangrenous inflammation which may then take place, not only in it, but also in the uterus and neighbouring parts. The very displacement itself is sometimes immediately attended by alarming symptoms, such as faintness, vomiting, cold sweats, weak irregular pulse, as seen in cases of inversion or strangulated hernia. In some cases the suffering at first is but trifling, and only increases in proportion to the degree with which the bladder is distended.

Retroversion not reduced may experience a spontaneous termination in two ways, either by abortion being excited, after which the uterus, now diminished in size, returns to its natural situation, or it may go on to increase in this position until a more advanced period of pregnancy, when if it be not capable of being replaced by the action of the pains, sloughing takes place in the fundus, and the fœtus is discharged, either by the rectum or vagina, as in a case of ventral pregnancy.

In the treatment of retroversion of the uterus, our object should be, first, to remove the accumulated contents of the bladder and rectum, and secondly, to endeavour to restore the uterus to its natural position. The relief of the bladder must be our first aim, for here is the greatest source of danger. The elastic catheter should always be used in these cases, and greatly facilitates the operation of drawing off the water. The altered direction of the urethra must be borne in mind; in many cases we must pass the catheter nearly perpendicularly behind the symphysis pubis: by pressing the uterus backwards, we shall diminish its pressure upon the urethra, and thus enable the catheter to pass with great ease.[54]

"The catheter should be employed occasionally, and the bowels emptied daily, either by medicines of a mild kind, or by injections:[Pg 132] if this plan do not succeed in restoring the fundus, we should then consider the propriety of mechanically replacing it. To aid us in our judgment, we should consider, first, the period of gestation; secondly, the degree of development the uterus has undergone; thirdly, the nature and severity of existing symptoms. The period of gestation ought almost always to influence our conduct in this complaint, and we may lay it down as a general rule, the nearer that period approaches four months, the greater will be the necessity to act promptly in procuring the restoration of the fundus: the reason for this is obvious, every day after this only increases the difficulty of the restoration from the continually augmenting size of the ovum. The degree of development should also be taken into consideration, as some uteri are much more expanded at three months, than others are at four. The extent or severity of symptoms must ever be kept in view; as, for instance, where the suppression of urine is complete, and not to be relieved by the catheter, in consequence of the extreme difficulty and impossibility to pass it: here we must not temporize too long, lest the bladder become inflamed, gangrenous, or burst; for the bladder, from its very organization, cannot bear distension beyond a certain degree, or beyond a certain time, without suffering serious mischief." (Dewees, Compend. Syst. of Midwifery, 6th Ed. § 276.) Our next step should be to relieve the rectum of its contents by emollient enemata; this is not always very practicable, owing to the flattened state of it: hence a glyster pipe of the ordinary sort is too large, and meets with much resistance; in such cases it will be desirable to use a common elastic catheter, or thin elastic tube without an ivory nozzle, which will, therefore, better adapt itself to the form of the bowel. A few doses of a saline laxative should be given to render the contents of the bowels more fluid, and the enemata repeated until a sufficient evacuation has been effected. Where the retroversion is not of long standing, and the patient not far advanced in her pregnancy, these means are generally sufficient; and the uterus, in the course of a few hours, will return to its natural position, either spontaneously or with very slight assistance. Where, however, the uterus is large and firmly impacted, where it has already been displaced more than twenty-four hours, where the suffering from the very beginning has been acute, independently of that the distended bladder, we cannot expect that the spontaneous replacement will follow the mere removal of the accumulated urine and fæces; nor must the uterus be suffered to remain in the state of retroversion, as not only will its pressure on the neighbouring parts produce serious mischief, but from the increasing growth of the ovum, every day will add to the difficulty of moving it out of the pelvis. In determining upon the artificial reposition of the uterus, it must be borne in mind that the chief difficulty is[Pg 133] to raise the fundus above the promontory of the sacrum, for if we can once succeed in gaining this point, the rest will follow of itself; our object, therefore, will be to raise the fundus upwards and forwards, in a direction towards the umbilicus of the patient. To effect this purpose various methods have been proposed: some have recommended that, with a finger in the vagina, we should hook down the os uteri, while with one or two fingers of the other hand passed into the rectum, we endeavour to push the fundus out of the hollow of the sacrum. Some object to any attempt being made through the rectum. (Naegelé, Erfahrungen und Abhandlungen, p. 346.) We agree with Richter in the utter inutility of attempting to bring down the os uteri; in most instances we can barely reach it with the tip of the finger, and even were we able to lay hold of it, we should run little or no chance of moving it so long as the fundus is impacted in the hollow of the sacrum. The fingers which are in the vagina must endeavour to raise the fundus, and in doing so may be assisted by one or two fingers in the rectum according to circumstances; the very effort to press per vaginam against the fundus, necessarily puts the anterior wall of the vagina upon the stretch, and thus tends of itself to bring the os uteri downward.[55] In all cases where the reposition of the uterus is at all difficult, Professor Naegelé recommends the introduction of the whole hand into the vagina, by which we gain much greater power. Under such circumstances it is desirable to place the patient upon her knees and elbows, as in a difficult case of turning, because now the very weight of the fundus will dispose it to quit the pelvis. The only difficulty which we shall meet with in thus using the whole hand, is the violent straining and efforts to bear down, which the patient is involuntarily compelled to make, from the presence of the hand in the vagina. Dr. Dewees in such cases very judiciously recommends bleeding to fainting, not only to obviate these efforts which would have prevented our raising the fundus, but also to relax the soft parts as much as possible. In our attempts to replace the uterus we must not be discouraged by finding that at first no impression is made upon it; by degrees it will begin to yield, and with a little more perseverance we shall be enabled to push the fundus above the promontory of the sacrum. (See Mr. Hooper's Case, Med. Obs. and Inquiries, vol. v. p. 104.)

Where the pain in the pelvis indicates considerable pressure of the uterus upon the surrounding parts, arising probably from[Pg 134] swelling and engorgement with blood, the result of vascular excitement, a smart bleeding will afford great relief; the size and firmness of the tumour are diminished, the soft parts in which it is imbedded are relaxed, the general turgor and sensibility are alleviated, and if the moment of temporary prostration which it has produced be seized upon by the practitioner, he will find that the reposition of the uterus, which was before nearly impracticable, is now comparatively easy.

Where, however, the circumstances of the case are so unfavourable, and the fundus so firmly impacted in the hollow of the sacrum as to resist the above-mentioned means, Dr. Hunter proposed, "Whether it would not be advisable, in such a case, to perforate the uterus with a small trocar or any other proper instrument, in order to discharge the liquor amnii, and thereby render the uterus so small and so lax as to admit of reduction." (Med. Obs. and Inq. vol. iv. p. 406.) Dr. Hunter did not live to see this plan carried into execution. In latter years, several cases of otherwise irreducible retroversion have thus been successfully relieved: the remedy, it is true, necessarily brings on premature expulsion of the fœtus sooner or later. Under such circumstances, this result cannot be made a ground of objection. In cases of such severity as to require paracentesis uteri, there can be little or no chance of the fœtus being alive; and even if it were, of what avail would this be, when almost certain death is staring the mother in the face, unless relieved by this operation?[56] Puncture of the bladder has also been tried where the urine could not be drawn off. [57]

Cases have now and then been met with where the retroversion of the uterus has continued to an advanced period of pregnancy without producing serious injury to the patient: Dr. Merriman has even recorded some, where the uterus has continued in this state up to the full term. Some of these had been actually published as cases of ventral pregnancy; but for their history he has shown that they evidently were cases of retroversion: the patient had been subject to occasional suppressions of urine and difficulty in passing fæces; these symptoms had gradually diminished as pregnancy advanced; the os uteri could not be felt,[Pg 135] or, if it were capable of being reached, was found high up behind the pubes, the head of the child forming a large hard tumour between the rectum and vagina. The condition of the vagina afforded strong evidences of the nature of the complaint: on introducing the finger in the usual direction, it was stopped, as if in a cul-de-sac: but on passing it forwards, the vagina was found pulled up behind the symphysis pubis. In some of these cases the uterine contractions gradually restored the fundus to its natural position: the os uteri descended from behind the symphysis, and the child was born after long protracted suffering; in others, which have been mistaken for ventral pregnancy, the fundus has inflamed and ulcerated, and the child has been gradually discharged by piecemeal.

[Pg 136]

CHAPTER VII.

DURATION OF PREGNANCY.

There are few questions of great importance and interest respecting a subject under our daily observation, about which such uncertainty and so much diversity of opinion exists, as the duration of human pregnancy; and yet, as is the case with the diagnosis of pregnancy, upon a correct decision frequently depend happiness, character, legitimacy, and fortune. In like manner it frequently happens, that the data upon which we have to found our opinion are exceedingly doubtful and obscure; and to increase the difficulties of the investigation still farther, we have not uncommonly to contend with wilful deception and determined concealment.

The duration of pregnancy must ever remain a question of considerable uncertainty so long as the data and modes of calculation vary so exceedingly. "Some persons date from the time at which the monthly period intermits; others begin to calculate from a fortnight after the intermission; some reckon from the day on which the succeeding appearance ought to have become manifest; some are inclined to include in their calculation the entire last period of being regular; and others only date from the day at which they were first sensible of the motions of the infant."[58]

"A good deal of the confusion on this point seems to have arisen from considering forty weeks and nine calendar months as one and the same quantity of time, whereas, in fact, they differ by from five to eight days. Nine calendar months make 275 days, or if February be included, only 272 or 273 days, that is thirty-nine weeks only instead of forty. Yet we constantly find in books on law, and on medical jurisprudence, the expression "nine months or forty weeks." Another source of confusion has evidently had its origin in the indiscriminate use of lunar and solar months, as the basis of computation in certain writings of authority."[59]

It is owing to this uncertainty that a considerable latitude has been allowed by the codes of law in different countries for the duration of pregnancy, in order to prevent the risk of deciding where the data are so uncertain.

[Pg 137]Experience has shown that the ordinary term of human pregnancy, wherever it has been capable of being determined with any degree of accuracy, is 280 days or forty weeks; and this period seems to have been generally allowed even from the remotest ages. As, however, it is so difficult to fix the precise moment of conception, it has been customary in different countries to allow a certain number of days beyond the usual time; thus the Code Napoléon ordains 300 days as the extreme duration of pregnancy, allowing twenty days over to make up for inaccuracy of reckoning. In Prussia it is 301 days, or three weeks beyond the usual time. In this country the limit of gestation is not so accurately determined by law, and therefore gives rise occasionally to much discrepancy of opinion.

The grand question which this subject involves, is, whether a woman can really go beyond the common period of gestation. A great number of authors have considered that the partus serotinus, or over-term pregnancy, is perfectly possible; but by far the majority use such an uncertain mode of reckoning that little confidence can be placed in them.

Two questions here arise, the determining of which will greatly assist us in forming a correct view of this intricate subject, viz. first, what has been the duration of those cases of pregnancy where the moment of conception has been satisfactorily ascertained? secondly, what are the causes which determine the period at which labour usually comes on?

The circumstances under which it happens that we are able to ascertain the precise date of impregnation occur so rarely, that it is nearly impossible to collect any considerable number of such cases. Three have occurred under our own notice, in which there could be little doubt as to the accuracy of the information given, and in each of these the patient went a few days short of the full period. One, a case of rape, was delivered on the 260th day; in the two others, sexual intercourse had only occurred once; in one case she went 264, in the other, 276 days. We could have mentioned several others, but where even the slightest shadow of doubt as to their accuracy has existed, we have rejected them as inconclusive.

The mode of calculating the duration of pregnancy, which is ordinarily adopted, viz. by reckoning from the last appearance of the catamenia, although the chief means which is afforded us for so doing, is nevertheless much too vague and uncertain to ensure a decided result; for although it is a well-known fact, that conception very frequently takes place shortly after a menstrual period, there can be no doubt that it is liable to occur at any part of the catamenial interval, and particularly so shortly before the next appearance: hence, by this mode of reckoning, we are not more justified in expecting labour in nine months time from the[Pg 138] last appearance of the catamenia, than at any part of the interval between this and what would have been the next appearance.

Dr. Merriman, who has devoted much attention to this intricate but important subject, says, "When I have been requested to calculate the time at which the accession of labour might be expected, I have been very exact in ascertaining the last day on which any appearance of the catamenia was distinguishable, and having reckoned 40 weeks from this day, assuming that the two hundred and eightieth day from the last period was to be considered as the legitimate day of parturition" (Synopsis of Difficult Parturition, p. xxiii. ed. 1838;) and gives a valuable table of "one hundred and fifty mature children, calculated from, but not including, the day on which the catamenia were last distinguishable." Of these,

5	were born	in the 37th week,
16	——	in the 38th,
21	——	in the 39th,
46	——	in the 40th,
28	——	in the 41st,
18	——	in the 42nd,
11	——	in the 43rd;

so that about one-third were born three weeks after the 280 days from the last appearance of the catamenia; a circumstance which is perfectly easy of explanation, from what we have just observed, without the pregnancy having overstepped its usual duration: in other words, it would appear that 28 of these cases had conceived one week, 18 two weeks, and 11 three weeks after the last appearance of the catamenia.

The question therefore of the partus serotinus; as far as these data are concerned, remains still undecided: of 10 cases which have occurred under our own immediate notice, where the patients determined the commencement of their pregnancy from other data than the last appearance of the catamenia, a similar variation was observed, viz. that nearly one-third went beyond 280 days, six of these individuals reckoned from their marriage, and four from peculiar sensations connected with sexual intercourse, which convinced them that impregnation had taken place: of these, seven did not go beyond the 280th day, two having been delivered upon that day, and three went beyond it, viz. to the 285th, 288th, and 291st days: the two former reckoned from their respective marriages; the latter, who went 291 days, from her peculiar sensations.

The calculation from the date of marriage is liable to the same objections as that taken from the last appearance of the catamenia; for if it had been solemnized (as is usually the case where it is possible) shortly after a menstrual period, and if conception did[Pg 139] not take place until a fortnight or three weeks afterwards, the patient's pregnancy would thus have appeared to have lasted so much longer than the natural term. The case, however, which is stated to have gone 291 days, does not come under this head, for here the pregnancy really appears to have lasted 10 or 11 days beyond the full period, which cannot be accounted for in the way above mentioned: we should not have ventured to quote this, if a similar instance had not been recorded by Dr. Dewees. "The husband of a lady, who was obliged to absent himself many months, in consequence of the embarrassment of his affairs, returned, however, one night clandestinely, and his visit was only known to his wife, her mother, and ourselves. The consequence of this visit was the impregnation of his wife; and she was delivered of a healthy child in 9 months and 13 days after this nocternal visit. The lady was within a week of her menstrual period, which was not interrupted, and which led her to hope she had suffered nothing from her intercourse; but the interruption of the succeeding period gave rise to the suspicion she was not safe, and which was afterwards realized by the birth of a child."[60]

Although it is to be regretted that this case has been calculated in the ordinary vague manner of calendar months, yet it is perfectly evident that the pregnancy was longer than the ordinary duration. We shall, therefore, endeavour to investigate the possibility of over-term pregnancy still more closely by a consideration of the second question, viz. what are the causes which determine the period at which labour usually comes on?

It is now ten years ago since we first surmised that "the reason why labour usually terminates pregnancy at the 40th week is from the recurrence of a menstrual period at a time during pregnancy when the uterus, from its distension and weight of contents, is no longer able to bear that increase of irritability which accompanies these periods without being excited to throw off the ovum."

Under the head of Premature Expulsion, we shall have occasion to notice the disposition to abortion which the uterus evinces at what, in the unimpregnated state, would have been a menstrual period: for some months after the commencement of pregnancy, a careful observer may distinctly trace the periodical symptoms of uterine excitement coming on at certain intervals, and it may be easily supposed that many causes for abortion act with increased effect at these times. Where the patient has suffered from dysmenorrhœa before pregnancy, these periods continue to be marked with such an increase of uterine irritability as to render them for some time exceedingly dangerous to the safety of the ovum. Even to a late period of gestation, the uterus continues[Pg 140] to indicate a slight increase of irritability at these periods, although much more indistinctly; thus, in cases of hæmorrhage before labour, especially where it arises from the attachment of the placenta to the os uteri, it is usually observed to come on, and to return, at what in the unimpregnated state would have been a menstrual period. We mention these facts as illustrating what we presume are the laws on which the duration of pregnancy depends, and also as being capable of affording a satisfactory explanation of those seeming over-term cases which are occasionally met with.

From this view of the subject it will be evident, that the period of the menstrual interval at which conception takes place, will in great measure influence the duration of the pregnancy afterwards; that where it has occurred immediately after an appearance of the menses, the uterus will have attained such a dilatation and weight of contents by the time the ninth period has arrived, that it will not be able to pass through this state of catamenial excitement without contraction, or, in other words, labour coming on: hence it is that we find a considerable number of labours fall short of the usual time, so much so that some authors have even considered the natural term of human gestation to be 273 days or 39 weeks: for a somewhat similar reason we can explain why primiparæ seldom go quite to the full term of gestation, the uterus being less capable of undergoing the necessary increase of volume in a first pregnancy than it is in succeeding ones.

On the other hand, where impregnation has taken place shortly before a menstrual period, the uterus, especially if the patient has already had several children, will probably not have attained such a volume and development as to prevent its passing the ninth period without expelling its contents, but may even go on to the next before this process takes place: it is in this way that we would explain the cases related by Dr. Dewees and Dr. Montgomery. We are aware that, under such a view of the subject, the duration of time between the catamenial periods of each individual should be taken into account, some women menstruating at very short, and others at very long, intervals; but although this will affect the number of periods during which the pregnancy will last, it will not influence the actual duration of time, as this will more immediately depend upon the size and weight of contents which the uterus has attained.

The valuable facts collected by M. Tessier respecting the variable duration of pregnancy in animals, which have been quoted by some authors in proof of the partus serotinus, are scarcely applicable to this question in the human subject; the absence of menstruation, and the different structure of the uterus, prevent our making any close comparison.

CHAPTER VIII.

PREMATURE EXPULSION OF THE FŒTUS.

Abortion.—Miscarriage.—Premature labour.—Causes.—Symptoms.—Prophylactic measures.—Effects of repeated abortion.—Treatment.

The uterus does not always carry the ovum to the full term of pregnancy, but expels it prematurely. This expulsion of its contents may occur at different periods, and is characterized accordingly: thus, among most of the Continental authors, it has been divided under three heads; those cases which occur during the first sixteen weeks coming under the head of abortion; those which occur between this period and the twenty-eighth week are called miscarriages; and when they take place at the latter period, until the full term of utero-gestation, they receive the name of premature labours.

It is perhaps useful to distinguish those cases of premature expulsion which occur before from those which occur after the fourth month, inasmuch as they seldom prove dangerous before that time, from the diminutive size of the ovum and from the slight degree of development which the uterine vessels have undergone; whereas, after this period the hæmorrhage is more severe, and the general disturbance to the system greater. In other respects it will be more simple to divide premature expulsion of the ovum under two heads only; those cases which happen before the twenty-eighth week, or seventh month, being termed abortions, and after this period (as before) premature labours. This division is highly important in a practical point of view, since it marks the period before which the child has little chance of being born alive; whereas, after this date it may with care be reared.[61] A fœtus may be expelled, at a very early stage of pregnancy, not only alive but capable of moving its limbs briskly for a short time afterwards, but it is unable to prolong its existence separate from the mother beyond a few hours. Cases do occur now and then[Pg 142] where a child is born in the sixth month, and where it manages to struggle through, but these are rare, and must rather be looked upon as exceptions to the general rule.

Abortions usually occur from the eighth to the twelfth week, a period which is decidedly the least dangerous for such accidents. "The liability to abortion is greater in the early than in the later periods of pregnancy; for as the union between the chorion and decidua is not well confirmed, as the attachment of the latter to the internal face of the uterus is proportionably slight, and as the extent of surface which the ovum now presents is very small to that which it offers in the more advanced state of pregnancy, and as it can of course be affected by smaller causes, it will be seen that a separation will be more easily induced, and prove much more injurious to the well-being of the embryo, than a larger one at another stage." (Dewees, Compendious System of Midwifery, § 929.) Abortions coming on at a later period, viz. from the sixteenth to the twenty-eighth week, which corresponds to the second division, or miscarriages, of the continental authors, are not only more dangerous than abortions at an early stage, for the reasons above-mentioned, but also than premature labours, as in this last division the uterus has attained such a size as to make the process rather resemble that of natural labour at the full term.

Causes. Premature expulsion may be induced by a great variety of causes, which may be brought under the two following heads: those which act indirectly, by destroying the life of the embryo, and those which act directly on the uterus itself. These various causes may be general or local; the process of nutrition for the growth and development of the embryo may be defective and scanty, from general debility or disease: hence, whatever depresses the tone of the patient's health renders her liable to abortion by causing the death of the embryo. Thus, dyspepsia and derangement of the chylopoietic viscera; debilitating evacuations; depressing passions of the mind; bad or insufficient nourishment; intense pain, as in toothach; severe suffering from existing disease, especially where the health is much broken down by some chronic affection; syphilis, and febrile attacks, all act as indirect causes of abortion.[62] Salivation from mercury not unfrequently has a similar effect; in some instances, however, febrile affections appear to act much more directly, stimulating the uterus to powerful contractions and rapid expulsion of its contents. The symptoms which indicate the death of the child have already been detailed in the chapter upon that subject.

The period which may elapse between the death and the expulsion of the embryo varies exceedingly: in the early months the one usually follows the other pretty quickly, owing probably[Pg 143] to the slight attachment of the ovum to the uterus; during the middle third of pregnancy the interval may be of considerable duration, and cases every now and then occur where the fœtus is retained, not only several weeks, but even some months after its death; whereas, during the latter third of pregnancy, expulsion follows the death of the child after a short interval, seldom exceeding two or three days; for now the weight of the dead fœtus speedily irritates the uterus to contraction, and, as has been observed by Smellie, the membranes, running gradually into putrefaction, and being now unable to bear the weight of the liquor amnii, burst, and expulsion soon follows.

Among the causes which act locally in inducing premature expulsion by first destroying the child, may be enumerated external violence applied to the abdomen, such as blows, falls, and other violent concussions; these act indirectly by producing separation of the ovum from the uterus, and thus destroying the life of the child. Under the same head may be classed all violent exertions, as lifting heavy weights, straining to reach something high above the head, &c. The mere act of walking, when carried to such an extent as to induce exhaustion, will suffice, in weakly delicate females, to bring on expulsion; sudden and violent action of the abdominal muscles, when excited by a half-involuntary effort to save herself from falling, or receiving any other injury, may produce a similar effect: if the fœtus be so young that its movements cannot be felt by the mother, she feels from this moment more or less pain in the pelvis, with a sensation of weight and bearing down; and this, in all probability, will be followed by a discharge of blood from the vagina: where pregnancy has sufficiently advanced for the motions of the fœtus to be perceptible, the mother will frequently feel them in an unusually violent degree for a short time immediately after the injury, and then they cease entirely.

Premature expulsion may also be induced immediately without the previous death of the child, by causes which directly excite the uterus to action: thus, various violent mental emotions, as rage, joy, horror, may act in this manner, although they may also act more indirectly; sudden exposure to cold, as sudden immersion in cold water, will occasionally produce it instantly. Irritation in the intestinal canal will directly excite uterine contraction; hence an attack of dysentery is frequently a cause of abortion, and we not unfrequently meet with patients who are liable to this affection in every pregnancy: a similar effect may be the improper use of drastic purgatives, which irritate the lower bowels, viz. aloes, scammony, savin, &c.; or the uterus may, in some cases, be excited to contract from the peculiar action of secale cornutum. On the other hand, a loaded state of the bowels equally predisposes to abortion, by impeding the free return of blood from the pelvis. A state of[Pg 144] general plethora acts in the same manner; and this is more particularly the case if it takes place at what would, in the unimpregnated state, have been a menstrual period; for, occurring in conjunction with the increased vascular action which prevails at these periods in the uterine system, it produces, as it were, an apoplectic state of the uterine sinuses, which form the maternal portion of the placenta; blood is extravasated between the ovum and uterus; their connexion is more or less destroyed, and the death of the fœtus becomes unavoidable: hence, in these cases the expulsion may result either from this latter circumstance, or from the uterus being irritated to contract by the effused blood between itself and the membranes.

In patients who have suffered from attacks of dysmenorrhœa in the unimpregnated state, the irritable uterus, when pregnant, is very apt to contract upon its contents and expel them. This usually happens at what would have been a menstrual period, and not unfrequently takes place so soon after impregnation as merely to be looked upon as an unusually severe attack, the little ovum having been imperceptibly expelled among the discharges. Under this head must be brought those cases of spasmodic affection of the uterus, which Dr. Burns has described, and where, from the diminutive size of the ovum, the case has rather resembled one of menorrhagia. Cases of abortion are also mentioned by authors where the uterus is stated to be incapable of undergoing the necessary dilatation and increase of size which pregnancy requires; but we are strongly disposed to refer them to the above head of great uterine irritability, as we neither know of any diagnostic marks which will enable us to detect this condition during life, nor are we aware of any physical condition of the uterus short of actual disease, to be detected after death, which can produce this inability.

The uterus may be also excited to expel the fœtus, without its previous death by local causes, as acute leucorrhœa, or other inflammatory affections of the vagina, by inflammation and other affections of the bladder, as calculus, &c. Too frequent sexual intercourse during the early months of pregnancy is peculiarly liable to excite abortion: this is especially observed among primiparæ of the better ranks, where, from luxurious living, &c., there is but little physical strength in proportion to the great irritability of the system: hence we find that a fifth, or even a fourth, of these females abort in their first pregnancies. In conclusion we may briefly state that the same circumstances which in the unimpregnated condition produce menstrual derangement and other disorders of the uterine system, now act as so many causes of abortion.

The sudden cessation of the breeding symptoms, with sense of weight and coldness in the lower part of the belly, flaccid breasts, pain in the back and loins, and discharge of blood from the[Pg 145] uterus, are pretty sure signs of abortion: they are those which are " separation of the ovum and contraction of the uterus," (Burns;) the one is attended by hæmorrhage, the other by pain. Although these are two chief symptoms which characterize a case of threatened abortion, and although they must necessarily be present more or less in every instance where premature expulsion actually happens, still neither of them, either separately or conjointly, can be considered as a certain proof that the uterus will carry its contents no longer. Cases not unfrequently happen where patients have repeated attacks of hæmorrhage during the early months of pregnancy, and sometimes to a considerable amount, without any apparent disturbance to the process of gestation, and are delivered of a living healthy child at the full term: on the other hand, we have known instances where the pain of the back was severe, and where, on assuming the erect posture even for a minute, the sense of weight and bearing down in the lower part of the abdomen was so great as to make the patient fear that the ovum was on the point of coming away; still even these threatening symptoms have gradually subsided, and the pregnancy has continued its natural period. Puzos considered that neither pain nor hæmorrhage were necessarily followed by expulsion. (Mém. de l'Acad. de Chir. vol. i. p. 203.) When, however, both occur together, and to a considerable extent, the case must be looked upon as one of at least doubtful if not unfavourable termination. Where pain comes on at regular intervals, with hardness of the uterus, and dilatation of its mouth, this is a serious symptom, for it shows that the uterus will no longer retain its contents, but is evidently preparing to expel them.

The part of the ovum at which the separation of it from the uterus has taken place, not only determines which of the above symptoms will appear first, but also the probability of expulsion. "When a considerable separation takes place, as must be the case when it commences at the upper parts of the uterus, pain will more likely occur than when it happens near the neck; hence we sometimes have pain before the blood issues externally. The uterus in this instance suffers irritation from partial distension from the blood insinuating itself behind the ovum; contraction ensues; the blood is thus forced downwards, and is made to separate the attachment between the ovum and the uterus in its course, until it finally gains an outlet at the os tincæ. In consequence of the uterus being excited to contraction, the friendly coagula which may have formed from time to time are driven away, and the bleeding each time is renewed and accompanied most probably with increased separation of the ovum, until at last from its extent the ovum becomes almost an extraneous body, and is finally cast off. Hence a separation at or near the os uteri will not be so dangerous, and in all probability[Pg 146] there will be hæmorrhage without pain, which is the contrary when it takes place near the fundus." (Dewees, Compend. System of Midwifery, § 981, 982.) The pain during the abortion is sometimes exceedingly severe, and not unlike that of dysmenorrhœa: this is probably owing to the violent contractions of the uterus, which are required to dilate the os and cervix before the ovum can pass: they are frequently attended with nausea, vomiting, and fainting, and sometimes with more or less general fever and local inflammatory action; the pain is generally attended with much irritability of the bladder, and frequent desire to pass water; the pulse is mostly quick and small, and where there is arterial excitement, it is sharp and resists the finger.

Treatment. The treatment of premature expulsion consists in, 1, that which is intended to guard the patient against its occurrence, or prophylactic; and 2, in that which is required during an attack.

A knowledge of the various causes of premature expulsion will materially assist us in the prophylactic treatment; under all circumstances, even where there is not the remotest fear of such an accident coming on, it is nevertheless highly important to pay strict attention to the state of the stomach and bowels, for these are almost always more or less influenced by the presence of pregnancy; the vomiting and sickness must be relieved in the manner already pointed out under the chapter on the Treatment of Pregnancy; the bowels, if constipated, must be moved by the mildest laxatives, such as castor oil, Confect. sennæ, or a Seidlitz powder; and thus all sources of irritation in the primæ viæ prevented as far as possible. The patient must carefully avoid every thing which may excite the circulation, such as violent affections of the mind, rich indigestible and stimulating food, violent exertion, &c. The diet should be light, nourishing, and moderate; heavy meals must be forbidden, and especially suppers; she should keep early hours, take gentle and regular exercise, and in fact, endeavour by every means in her power to raise her health to a full degree of tone and regularity. In those patients who have already miscarried in their previous pregnancies, these precautions must be enforced with double vigilence; for the system becomes exceedingly irritable, and the uterus soon acquires, as it were, a habit of retaining its contents only to a certain period, and then prematurely expelling them. When this is the case, it becomes exceedingly difficult, and is often actually impossible, to make it carry the ovum to the full term of utero-gestation, and, despite of the greatest care, the symptoms of premature expulsion will come on at about the same time at which they occurred in former pregnancies, and sometimes to the very same week.

In the treatment of such cases, where there is so much liability to abortion, we must first examine the precise condition of the circulation,[Pg 147] and ascertain whether it be above or below the natural standard of strength; for as abortion may arise from very opposite conditions of the circulation, our treatment must consequently vary. If there be signs of arterial excitement, a small bleeding may be necessary; it unloads the congested vessels, diminishes the force of the circulation, and therefore also the chance of an extravasation of blood between the uterus and ovum; the bowels must be kept open by cooling saline laxatives, and the circulation may be still farther controlled, by the use of nitre two or three times a day. The diet must be spare; she must take regular exercise in the open air, wear light clothing, dress loosely, and sleep upon a hard mattress.

In these cases we are often warned that congestion of the uterine vessels is present, by pain and throbbing, and sense of fulness in the groins; leeches applied to these parts give much relief, and frequently render venesection unnecessary. Tight lacing ought to be strictly prohibited in all cases of pregnancy, particularly where there is a disposition to plethora: among other bad effects, it prevents the proper development of the breasts, the nipples are pressed so flat as to be nearly useless, the child being unable to get sufficient hold of them: this may in some degree be avoided, by putting thick ivory rings upon the breasts, and thus shielding the nipples from injurious pressure. It will, however, be much better to have the dress made loosely, to allow for the development of the breasts, which takes place during pregnancy; for there can be little doubt, that irritation of these glands is very liable to be followed by a corresponding state in the uterus.

The common but erroneous notion that it is necessary to take an extra quantity of nourishment for the support of the child as well as of the mother must be strenuously opposed. Nature contradicts it in the most striking manner; for, by the nausea and sickness which most women experience during the first half of their pregnancy, she raises an effectual obstacle to any error of this kind. "It certainly cannot be intended for any other purpose, since it is not only almost universal, but highly important when it occurs, as it would seem to add much to the security of the fœtus; for it is a remark as familiar as it is well grounded, that very sick women rarely miscarry; while on the contrary, women of very full habits are disposed to abortion, if exempt from this severe, but as it would seem, important process." (Dewees, on Children, § 45.)

Where the case has become one of habitual abortion, the patient's only chance will be by living separate from her husband for twelve or more months: the uterus, not being exposed to any sexual excitement during this period, becomes less irritable, and it gradually loses the disposition which it has acquired of expelling its contents prematurely. In such a case, when pregnancy[Pg 148] has again commenced, it requires to be watched most narrowly; every possible source of irritation must be removed by the strictest attention to diet and regimen, and the patient must make up her mind to be entirely subservient to the rules laid down by her medical attendant. Although the chances are against her escaping without premature expulsion, still we are not to despair, experience showing that cases every now and then occur where the patient has gone the full term of pregnancy in safety, in spite of repeated previous abortions. Dr. Young of Edinburgh, in his lectures on midwifery, describes a case where the patient actually miscarried thirteen times, and yet bore a living child the fourteenth time.

On the other hand, where the condition of the patient evinces a state of strength considerably below the natural standard, we find a very different set of symptoms to those which have been just described, requiring opposite treatment: the face is pale and even sallow; the pulse is soft, small, and irritable; the tongue pale and flabby; the digestion impaired; the bowels torpid; and the extremities cold: fatigue, or rather a sense of exhaustion, is induced by the slightest exertion, and this is attended with dull, heavy, dragging pain about the pelvis and loins, and a feeling as if the contents of the abdomen required more support, and were disposed to prolapse either by the rectum or vagina, on her maintaining an upright posture for any length of time.

Even at a very early period of pregnancy, there is the sensation of a weight in the lower part of the abdomen, falling over to that side which is lowest, as we described among the signs of the death of the fœtus at a later period, resulting in all probability from a loss of tone and firmness in the uterus. In this state, if nothing be done to restore the mother's strength, the embryo will inevitably perish, and expulsion follow, sooner or later, as a necessary result.

In all cases where pregnancy occurs, in a weakly delicate woman, measures should be taken to increase the general tone of health, in order to fit her for going through this process safely, by removing her to the country, or to the sea-side, or to some watering place, where she will have the opportunity of drinking a mild chalybeate, and enjoying a purer air. Where it is even hazardous to move her, she should be put upon a course of mild chalybeates. The food should be light and nourishing, and a glass or two of wine or mild ale, may generally be taken with advantage. Where she can bear it, tepid salt-water bathing, or sponging, will have the best effects.

"For a number of years, (says Mr. White of Manchester,) I have been convinced of the good effects of cold bathing, not only in preventing miscarriages when every other method has been likely to fail, but other disorders which are incident to pregnant women, and generally attendant upon a weak lax fibre. I[Pg 149] don't mean the cold bath in the greatest extreme, but such as that of Buxton or Matlock, or sea-bathing, or bathing in a tub in the patient's house, with the water a little warmed. I have frequently advised my patients to bathe every other day, at a time when the stomach is not overloaded, and not to stay at all in the water; to begin this process as early as possible, even before they have conceived, as there will be then no danger from the surprise, and continue it during the whole term of pregnancy; and several have bathed till within a few days of their delivery." (White, on Lying-in Women, p. 70.) Where exercise can be taken without fear, it should be done regularly but cautiously, so as not to induce fatigue or exhaustion, which is the very effect we must be so careful to avoid; in fact, every means and opportunity should be used of recruiting the powers and the vigour of the system. In proportion as the strength increases, so does the irritability diminish; the uterus becomes less sensitive to external impressions, and can, therefore, bear its gradual development without being excited to contraction; the fœtus receives its due supply of nourishment; the feeling of relaxation and deficient support of weight, and bearing down, go off as health returns; and by thus keeping up the powers of the system to the proper standard, it will be enabled to continue the process of pregnancy to the full term.

Although some women recover very quickly after an abortion, and appear for the time to suffer but little from its effects, they seldom escape with impunity, more especially if it has been repeated more than once: anæmia, with its varied train of anomalous symptoms and concomitant gastric and cerebral disturbance, profuse leucorrhœa, menorrhagia, and dismenorrhœa, are some of the more direct results of repeated abortion; we may also enumerate prolapsus uteri, inflammation of the cervix, with induration and scirrhus, as the more remote effects.

In the treatment of a case where expulsion is threatened, our object will be either to stop that process in time to save the life of the fœtus, or if this cannot be attained, to carry it through, in such a manner, as to expose the mother to as little danger and injury as possible.[63] In the first instance, we must be guided nearly by the same rules as in the prophylactic treatment: if there be considerable arterial excitement, and evidence of general plethora, a small bleeding will be useful in restoring a calm to the circulation; the most perfect quiet of body and mind must be insisted upon; the patient should lie upon a hard mattress, and be covered with as little clothing as is consistent with safety; she must refrain from all exertion, and strictly maintaining the [Pg 150]horizontal posture for a considerable time. The indications for our treatment will be, 1. to remove every thing which may, in any degree excite the circulation, and, 2. to prevent the contraction of the uterus. Stimulants of every description, and animal food must be forbidden; the bowels must be opened by gentle saline laxatives; and if the pulse still betrays any sharp or resisting feel to the finger, small doses of nitre may be taken as already recommended. When the circulation has become perfectly calm, and every trace of excitement allayed, opiates will prove of inestimable value: they stop any disposition to uterine contraction, and remove the pain in the back and loins which this will cause. The form which we prefer is the Liquor Opii Sedativus, as being more sure in producing a sedative effect than common laudanum, while at the same time, it produces less irritation and derangement in the stomach and bowels.

A moderate discharge of blood from the vagina, although showing that a separation has taken place between the ovum and the uterus, cannot be looked upon as an unfavourable sign, for it relieves the pelvic vessels, diminishes the pain in the back, and makes the patient feel more light and comfortable; but if it be at all brisk, and continues so after the employment of the above remedies, if also there be heat and throbbing in the region of the uterus, it will be necessary to apply cloths wrung out of cold water to the lower part of the abdomen and vulva, and to the groins and sacrum; and this treatment must be continued in full force until the symptoms of congestion have abated, and the discharge lessened or stopped.

If the hæmorrhage be really profuse, it shows that the separation of the ovum from the uterus must be of considerable extent; and as there will be no chance of preserving the life of the fœtus under such circumstances, the expulsion of the ovum is no longer to be avoided, but rather to be promoted; our attention therefore must now be directed to assist the uterus in the evacuation of its contents, with as little injury and danger to the mother as possible. It is, however, no easy matter to decide with certainty when we must give up all hope of preserving the ovum, for a large quantity of blood may be lost without expulsion being a necessary consequence. Uterine contractions may have even taken place, and yet by careful management the mischief may be sometimes averted, and the patient be enabled to go her full time. Even where they have been of sufficient force and duration to dilate the os uteri, we are not justified in discontinuing remedial measures unless the flooding has seriously affected the patient's strength, and the ovum be actually projecting through the os uteri. "We might often prevent abortion (says Baudelocque) if we were perfectly acquainted with its cause, even when the labour is already begun. A very plethoric woman felt the pains of childbirth towards the seventh month of her pregnancy, and the labour[Pg 151] was very far advanced when I was called to her assistance, since the os uteri was then larger than half a crown; two little bleedings restored a calm, so much that the next day the orifice in question was closed again, and the woman went the usual time. Food of easy digestion prudently administered quieted a labour not less advanced in another woman, where it was suspected to be the consequence of a total privation of every species of nourishment for several successive days. Delivery did not take place till two months and a half afterwards, and at the full time. Emollient glysters and a very gentle cathartic procured the same advantage to a third woman, in whom labour pains came on between the sixth and seventh months of pregnancy, after a colic of several days' continuance, accompanied with diarrhœa and tenesmus." (Baudelocque,) § 2232. Nor is it always easy to decide whether it be the ovum or not which we feel protruding through the os uteri. "When the abortion is in the second or third month, the practitioner must bear in mind that it may have been retention of the menses, and, therefore, what he feels in the os uteri may either be an ovum or a coagulum of blood. To decide this point he must keep his finger in contact with the substance lying in the os uteri, and wait for the accession of a pain (for where clots come away, pains like those of labour are present,) and ascertain whether the presenting mass becomes tense, advances lower, and increases somewhat in size; this will be the case where it is the ovum pressing through the os uteri. On the other hand, if it be a coagulum, which it is well known assumes a fibrous structure, it will neither become tense nor descend lower, but be rather compressed. Generally speaking, the ovum feels like a soft bladder, and at its lower end is rather round than pointed, whereas, a plug of coagulum feels harder, more solid, and less compressible, and is more or less pointed at its lower end, becoming broader higher up, so that we generally find that the coagulum has taken a complete cast of the uterine cavity. If we try to move the uterus by pressing against this part, it will instantly yield to the pressure of the finger, if it be the ovum; whereas, the extremity of a coagulum under these circumstances is so firmly fixed, that when pressed against by the finger the uterus will move also. When abortion happens at a later period of pregnancy, we shall be able to feel the different parts of the child as the os uteri generally dilates, viz. the feet, or perhaps the sharp edges of bones, although we cannot distinguish the form of the head from the cranial bones being so compressed and strongly overlapping each other." (Hohl, on Obstetric Exploration.)

Although expulsion must be looked upon as the only means of placing the patient in a state of safety, where the symptoms have advanced so far as to preclude all hopes of preserving the life of[Pg 152] the fœtus, there are so many steps of this process to be gone through before it can be entirely completed, that more or less time must necessarily be required for that purpose. The ovum must be completely separated from its attachments to the uterus, and the contractions of that organ must have been of sufficient strength and duration to produce such a degree of dilatation of its mouth and neck as to allow the ovum to pass; but before this can be effected, such a quantity of blood may have been lost as greatly to endanger the life of the patient. Hence we must use such means as shall enable us to control the hæmorrhage, whilst we give the os uteri time to dilate sufficiently: this object will be gained most effectually by plugging the vagina. The best mode of performing this operation is that recommended by Dr. Dewees of Philadelphia: a piece of soft sponge, of sufficient size to fill the vagina without producing uneasiness, must be wrung out of pretty sharp vinegar, and introduced into the passage up to the os uteri; the blood, in filling the cells of the sponge, coagulates rapidly, and forms a firm clot, which completely seals up the vagina without producing any of those unpleasant effects which are the insertion of a napkin rolled up for the purpose. A hard unyielding mass of this nature frequently produces so much tension, pain of back, and irresistible efforts to bear down, as to render it incapable of being borne for any length of time. The sponge plug may be borne for hours without inconvenience; we may either leave it to be expelled with the ovum, or after awhile remove it for the purpose of ascertaining what progress has been made. If the os uteri be still undilated, and the hæmorrhage going on, the plug must be returned. It is however by no means a remedy to be used in every case of hæmorrhage, for in most instances the treatment already mentioned will be sufficient to keep it within safe bounds. Where, however, the flooding has become very alarming, and the os uteri still remains firm and but little dilated, the plug will prove an invaluable remedy; and so long as the os uteri remains in this condition, and the uterus itself shows no disposition to contract, we may safely trust to perfect rest, cold applications, and the plug. Opium, which in the early stages of the attack is so useful in keeping off contractions of the uterus, will now for this very reason be contra-indicated; it will diminish the power of the uterus, and interfere with the process of expulsion.

The acetate of lead has been extolled as a powerful remedy for stopping hæmorrhage, more especially by Dr. Dewees, who states that "in many cases it seems to exert a control over the bleeding vessels as prompt as the ergot of rye does upon the uterine fibre." (System of Midwifery, § 1045.) We have never tried this remedy in premature expulsion, having found the means of treatment above mentioned sufficient; the authority however[Pg 153] of such an author demands respect, the more so as it is known to be a valuable remedy in certain forms of menorrhagia.

Where a considerable quantity of blood has been lost, and the patient is much reduced, we must endeavour not only to excite the contractile power of the uterus, but also to assist this organ in the expulsion of its contents: syncope in these cases is a dangerous symptom, because, as the patient is in the horizontal posture, it will seldom be induced except by a serious loss of blood; although we must not therefore allow her to flood until she faints, still, however, when the pulse has become considerably affected, the os uteri dilates more readily, and in this way facilitates the expulsion; we must no longer trust to the plug, for the whole system is beginning to sympathize and grow irritable, the pulse grows quicker and smaller, and the stomach rejects its contents. Although vomiting as well as syncope are symptoms which we cannot safely wait for, they are nevertheless means which nature adopts to relieve herself from the impending danger: by syncope she not only produces greater dilatability of the os uteri, but also, by causing a temporary cessation of the heart's action, she favours the coagulation of blood, and thus checks the discharge; whereas, by the involuntary effort of muscles which she excites by the action of vomiting, the ovum is more speedily separated and expelled.

Where it becomes evident that expulsion cannot be prevented, it is our duty to promote this process before nature has had recourse to the means just mentioned. The ergot of rye is here a valuable remedy, for by inducing or increasing the contractions of the uterus we shorten the process and diminish the danger: the powder given in cold water is decidedly the best form in which it can be given; in infusion its powers seem to be injured by the heat of the water, and in tincture by the action of the spirit: the addition of about half its quantity of borax renders its action more powerful and certain. Borax has been long considered in Germany to possess a specific power in exciting uterine contraction, but it was first recommended for that purpose in this country by Dr. Copland. (Dict. Pract. Med. art Abortion.) A scruple or half a drachm of ergot powder with ten grains of borax may be given in cinnamon water, and this repeated every hour for several times.

In all cases threatening premature expulsion, wherever there has been much pain and discharge, the napkins which come from the patient should be carefully examined by her medical attendant, for otherwise the ovum may escape among the coagula and not be perceived. Where the separation is nearly complete, a portion of it protrudes at the os uteri; and this we can sometimes hook down with one or two fingers, and bring away: a still better mode is recommended by Levret, viz. of throwing up a pretty powerful stream of warm water by means of a syringe. Dr.[Pg 154] Dewees has recommended a wire crotchet, which he has used with very good effect. (Op. cit. § 1011.)[64] We ought not, however, to be in a hurry to bring away the ovum, for when the uterine contractions have been of sufficient strength to dilate the os uteri, it will generally come away of itself. One objection to the wire crotchet is, that it tears the membranes, and lets out the liquor amnii, and perhaps the embryo.[65] This is by all means to be avoided; the larger the body which is to be expelled, the more powerfully and effectually does the uterus contract upon it: hence, therefore, if the membranes of a three or four months' ovum be imprudently pierced with a view to hastening the expulsion, the liquor amnii and embryo escape, but the secundines remain and require protracted efforts of the uterus to expel them, during which time the sufferings of the patient are prolonged, and the hæmorrhage kept up; whereas, if the ovum had remained whole, it would have been expelled more easily and quickly. On the other hand, where the fœtus has already attained a considerable size (fifth month,) the plan recommended by Puzos of rupturing the membranes is very desirable; by this means the size[Pg 155] of the uterus is reduced by the escape of liquor amnii, and thus the hæmorrhage checked; and the fœtus remaining in the uterus is of sufficient weight and bulk to excite contractions to expel itself and the membranes.

The treatment after abortion varies considerably: in many cases it will be merely necessary for the patient to remain in bed for a few days afterwards; but where she has been much reduced, a mild course of tonics will be necessary, in order to prevent that disposition to leucorrhœa and menstrual derangement which is so common a result: this, where it is possible, should be combined with removal into the country, or to the sea-side, or, what is still better to a watering place, where there are mineral springs of chalybeate character. For the treatment of anæmia we must refer our readers to the chapter on Hæmorrhage.

[Pg 156]

PART III.

EUTOCIA, OR NATURAL PARTURITION.

CHAPTER I.

STAGES OF LABOUR.

Preparatory stage.—Precursory symptoms.—First contractions.—Action of the pains.—Auscultation during the pains.—Effect of the pains upon the pulse.—Symptoms to be observed during and between the pains.—Character of a true pain.—Formation of the bag of liquor amnii.—Rigour at the end of the first stage.—Show.—Duration of the first stage.—Description of the second stage.—Straining pains.—Dilatation of the perineum.—Expulsion of the child.—Third stage.—Expulsion of the placenta.—Twins.

Parturition may be divided into two great orders, Eutocia and Dystocia, the one signifying natural labour which follows a favourable course both for the mother and her child; the other signifying faulty or irregular labour, the course of which is unfavourable.

We may define eutocia to be the safe expulsion of the mature fœtus and its secundines by the natural powers destined for that purpose. No function exhibits such infinite varieties, within the limits of health and safety to the mother and her offspring, as that of parturition; no two labours, even in the same individual are exactly alike; still, however, the great objects of the process will be the same, viz. 1st. the preparation of the passages and the fœtus for its expulsion; 2dly, the expulsion of the fœtus; and 3dly, the expulsion of the placenta and membranes.

That we may form a clearer and more comprehensive view of this process, labour has usually been divided into stages or periods, marked by the changes just now alluded to: hence it is generally said to consist of three stages; the first, or preparatory[Pg 157] stage, commencing with the first perceptible contractions of the uterus, and terminating in the full dilatation of the os uteri; the second, or stage of expulsion, terminating with the birth of the child; and the third, consisting of the expulsion of the placenta.

Preparatory stage.—Precursory symptoms. For some time before the commencement of actual labour, a variety of changes are taking place which must be looked upon as the precursors of this process: during the last weeks of pregnancy, nature appears, as it were, to be preparing for the great change which is at hand, and to be making such arrangements as shall enable it to be completed with the least possible danger both for the mother and her child.

One of the earliest warnings which we have of approaching labour is an alteration in the form of the abdominal tumour; the cervix uteri has by this time (especially in primiparæ) entirely disappeared; the presenting part of the child has therefore descended to the lowest part of the uterus; the fundus has sunk lower and more forwards; and from the diaphragm being enabled to act with greater freedom, the respiration is performed with more ease and comfort to the patient; she therefore feels more capable of moving about, and is in better health and spirits than for some time previously. Upon examination per vaginam, the head will be found deep in the cavity of the pelvis, covered by the lower and anterior segment of the uterus; the os uteri is still closed, and situated in the upper part of the hollow of the sacrum, forming merely a small circular depression. In women who have already had children, a portion of the cervix uteri is still remaining; it is thick and bulky; and in some cases, where the uterus has been greatly distended in several successive pregnancies, it is nearly as long as in the unimpregnated state; the os tincæ or os uteri externum is open, its edge irregular from former labours; the upper extremity of the canal of the cervix is contracted, and forms the os uteri internum; it has been closed during the greater part of pregnancy, but usually is now sufficiently open to admit the finger; the os uteri is neither so high up nor so far backwards in the pelvis as in primiparæ, and is reached with greater ease; whereas, the head of the child, instead of being felt in the cavity of the pelvis, generally remains at the brim until labour is more advanced.

First contractions. The first contractions of the uterus (in a state of health) are so slight as scarcely to be noticed by the patient: they create a sensation of equable pressure and general tightness round the abdomen, and during the contraction the uterus feels somewhat firmer, but they are neither attended with pain, nor do they appear at first to have any effect upon the os uteri; these precursory contractions generally come on a day or two before actual labour commences, and sometimes are felt at[Pg 158] intervals for one or two weeks. Where the uterus has been exposed to any source of irritation, and especially where there is a disposition to rheumatic affection of this organ, they may produce much suffering and give rise to one form of what are called false pains, hereafter to be described. "The first contractions, says M. Leroux (Sur les Pertes de Sang, § 41.,) are feeble, and communicate no sensation to the patient; in order to discover them we must hold our hand upon the abdomen, and if we feel the globe of the uterus raise itself and become hard, this is a true contraction. These contractions gradually increase until they excite pain: but pain is not essential to a contraction; it depends on the distension and compression of the nerves the resistance of the body upon which the uterus acts, and increases in severity in proportion to the degree of resistance and contraction."

In proportion as the lower part of the uterus descends into the cavity of the pelvis, so does it exert a degree of pressure on the neighbouring parts; the capacity of the bladder and rectum is diminished; and being therefore unable to contain the usual quantity of urine and fæces, and being probably rendered more irritable by the pressure above-mentioned, the patient experiences frequent calls to pass water and evacuate the bowels, which is some-times effected with considerable difficulty: in some instances she is obliged to lean forward, or support the abdomen, in order to take the weight of the child off the neck of the bladder before she can empty it: the same cause occasion-ally requires the use of the catheter, and sometimes renders the introduction of it a matter of considerable difficulty.

As these various changes make their appearance, the patient becomes restless and anxious; she cannot remain long in the same posture; the slight precursory contractions which have been just described, are becoming stronger, and begin to produce a sensation of pain; the os uteri (in primiparæ) opens somewhat, its edge at first is exceedingly thin, and feels almost membranous; by degrees however it swells, grows thick and cushiony, and is now more dilatable.

Action of the pains. The os uteri does not dilate merely by the mechanical stretching which the pressure of the membranes and presenting part exert upon it; it dilates in consequence of its circular fibres being no longer able to maintain that state of contraction which they had preserved during pregnancy; they are overpowered by the longitu-dinal fibres of the uterus, which, by their contractions, pull open the os uteri equally in every direction.

The vagina also swells and grows more cushiony, and this is followed by a copious secretion of colourless and nearly inodorous mucus. "The more albuminous it is the better, and it is always a good sign when lumps of albumi-nous matter come away[Pg 159] from time to time; the thicker, softer, and more cushiony the os uteri is, the more mucus does it secrete." (Wigand, Geburt des Menschen, vol. ii. p. 292.) The thin hard os uteri does not dilate, its fibres are all in close contact, and like a well-twisted cord will not yield; whereas, when they are separated from each other by the swelling of the os uteri, they easily yield to the dilating force which is applied to them. Besides serving the purpose of lubricating the passage, the secretion of mucus is of great importance as a topical depletion, for, by thus unloading the congested vessels, they diminish the vascularity and heat of the part, and render it more capable of dilatation. "If, on the other hand, the entrance of the vagina is small, the neighbouring parts cool, dry, inelastic, and as if tightly stretched over the bones; if the finger, in spite of being well oiled and carefully introduced, produces pain upon the gentlest attempt to examine, we may expect a tedious and difficult labour." (Op. cit. p. 190.)

The patient is now no longer able to conceal her pains when they come on. If she be in the act of conversing she stops short, and remains silent until the severity of the pain is over; if she be walking about her room she is obliged to stand still for the time, and rest against or hold by something until the pain has gone off. The true labour pains are situated in the back and loins; they come on at regular intervals, rise gradually up to a certain pitch of intensity, and abate as gradually; it is a dull, heavy, deep sort of pain, producing occasionally a low moan from the patient: not sharp or twinging, which would elicit a very different expression of suffering from her.

Auscultation during the pains. "If we direct our attention to the changes of tone which the uterine pulsations present during auscultation, we shall find them generally stronger, more distinct and varied in tone during labour; and this is especially the case just before a pain comes on. Even if the patient wished to conceal her pains, this phenomenon, and more especially the rapidity of the beats, would enable us to ascertain the truth. The moment a pain begins, and even before the patient herself is aware of it, we hear a sudden short rushing sound, which appears to proceed from the liquor amnii, and to be partly the movement of the child, which seems to anticipate the coming on of the contraction: nearly at the same moment all the tones of the uterine pulsations become stronger; other tones, which have not been heard before, and which are of a piping resonant character, now become audible, and seem to vibrate through the stethoscope, like the sound of a string which has been struck and drawn tighter while in the act of vibrating. The whole tone of the uterine circulation rises in point of pitch. Shortly after this, viz. as the pain becomes stronger and more general, the uterine sound seems as it were to become more and more distant, until at length it becomes very dull, or altogether inaudible. But as[Pg 160] soon as the pain has reached its height and gradually declines, the sound is again heard as full as at the beginning of the pain, and resumes its former tone, which in the intervals between the pains is as it was during pregnancy, except somewhat louder. This is the course of things if the pain be a true one, and attain its full intensity: where the pains are false or irregular it is very different; the uterine sound either remains unaltered, or increases only for an instant, or its seeming increase of distance, as above mentioned, is not observed." (Die Geburtshülfliche Exploration, von Dr. A. T. Hohl, erster theil, s. 105.)

Effect of the pains upon the pulse. It is curious to observe the effect which a regular pain has upon the rapidity of the mother's pulse; as the former comes on and goes off, so does the other increase or diminish. "The increasing rapidity of the pulse announces the commencement of the pain; it rises and attains its summum with it; and as the pain subsides so does the pulse gradually resume the rate which it had during the intervals; a similar ebb and flow may be heard in the uterine souffle. The more regular the pain is, and the more distinctly it rises to its full extent, the more marked, regular, and distinct, is this change in it. We may also invert the order of things, and say, the more distinctly the rapidity of the pulse comes on and announces the pain, the more regularly it rises and attains a certain height, which it maintains, and then gradually subsides; in like proportion will the pain be more perfect, attain its full extent more completely, and act more efficaciously upon the regular progress of the labour. Where however the rapidity of the beats subsides before it had scarcely begun to increase, the pain is too weak; or where the rapidity rises by sudden starts, the pain is a hurried one; and in either case its effect will be imperfect." (Hohl, op. cit. vol. i. p. 108.) In order that we may ascertain these changes correctly, we ought to note the rapidity of the pulse during each successive quarter of a minute as directed by M. Hohl; thus, in a pain which lasts two minutes, the increase and diminution in the rapidity of the pulse may be as follows, 18. 18. 20. 22.; 24. 24. 22. 18. As labour advances it increases, so that shortly before the birth of the child we shall find that what was the rate of the pulse during the height of the pains at the beginning is now the rate of it during the intervals.

Symptoms to be observed during and between the pains. When a pain comes on, the uterus grows hard and tense; if the fundus be somewhat to one side, as is not unfrequently the case, it now gradually moves, so that the median line of the uterus corresponds with that of the patient's body; the various prominences of the child are no longer to be felt, the whole is now firm and unyielding; the os uteri is put tightly upon the stretch, the membranes which were loose become tense and are firmly pressed against it, and the presenting part is rendered indistinct: as the[Pg 161] pain gradually subsides, the uterus becomes softer, and yields to the pressure of the hand; the different parts of the child which project, as also its movements, can now be felt more distinctly; the patient is free from pain, and feels herself in an agreeable state of tranquillity, which is frequently attended by a short refreshing doze; the os uteri, which has become somewhat more dilated during the last pain, is now soft and loose, so that we can hook the finger into it and move it about; the tight bladder of membranes becomes relaxed and flaccid, and retracts more or less into the uterus, so that we shall now be able to introduce the finger into the os uteri and feel the presenting part through the membranes; while the presenting part of the child, which during the pain was fixed, can be moved somewhat by the finger.

Characters of a true pain. In examining the course of a true pain we shall find that the contractions of the uterus do not begin in the fundus, but in the os uteri, and pass from the one to the other. (Wigand, op. cit. vol. ii. p. 197.) Every pain which commences in the fundus is abnormal, and either arises from some derangement in the uterine action, or is sympathetic with some irritation not immediately connected with the uterus, as from colic, constipation, &c. We very seldom find that a contraction of the uterus, which has commenced in the fundus, passes into the cervix and os uteri, and becomes a genuine effective pain; usually speaking, the contraction is confined to the circumference of the fundus, without detruding the fœtus at all. When a genuine pain comes on, so far from the head being pressed against the os uteri, it at first rises upwards, and sometimes gets even out of reach of the finger, whilst the os uteri itself is filled with the bladder of membranes: if it had commenced in the fundus instead of the inferior segment of the uterus, so far from the head being drawn up at the first coming on of the pain, it would have been forcibly pushed down against the os uteri. In the course of a few seconds the contraction gradually spreads over the whole uterus, and is felt especially in the fundus; the head which had been raised somewhat from the os uteri is now again pushed downwards to it, and seems to act as a wedge for the purpose of dilating it; it is not until the whole uterus is beginning to contract that the patient has a sensation of pain. We may, therefore, consider that a genuine uterine contraction consists of certain phenomena which occur in the following order: first, the os uteri grows tight, and the presenting part rises somewhat from it; then the rest of the uterus, especially the fundus, becoming hard, the patient has a sensation of pain, and the presenting part of the child advances. The period of time necessary for all these changes varies not only in different individuals, but in the same individual in different labours, and in different stages of the same labour.

"The more completely the os uteri is opposite the fundus, and[Pg 162] the more the axis of the uterus corresponds with that of the pelvis, the sooner are the pains, cæteris paribus, capable of dilating the os uteri." (Wigand, vol. ii. p. 273.) The cushiony state of the vagina and os uteri, and the free secretion of thick albuminous mucus from these parts, as already mentioned, will be of great importance in ensuring their easy dilatation. Where this secretion is either absent, or very scanty, the passages become dry, hot, and tender, from no relief being afforded to the congested vessels by its effusion; and vice versâ, where there is a febrile state of the circulation and considerable topical excitement, the secretion is sparing, or, perhaps, stops entirely. This state may arise from a variety of causes, such as from general plethora, too warm clothing, bad ventilation, derangement and irritation of the primæ viæ, and abuse of spirituous and other stimulating liquors: it may arise from constipation, or may be induced by rough and too frequent examination. The patient becomes flushed, excited, and feverish, with a hot skin, dry tongue, thirst, and headach; the uterine contractions become irregular, they produce much suffering, and but very little advance in the progress of the labour; the passages are in a state of inflammation, and more especially the os uteri, which is much swollen and excessively tender. The process of labour is completely interrupted, and can only be restored to a healthy condition by bleeding, warm bath, laxatives, and enemata.

Formation of the bag of the liquor amnii. When the os uteri has dilated more or less, a quantity of liquor amnii begins to collect between the head and the membranes, so that when a pain comes on they form a tense, elastic, and conical bag, which presses firmly against the os uteri, and protrudes through it into the vagina, and from its form and elastic nature greatly facilitates the speedy dilatation of it. If the edge of the os uteri be still thin, it will become so tense during the pain, and the bag of membranes will press so firmly against it, that we shall have some difficulty for the moment in distinguishing the one from the other. As the labour advances, the intervals between the pains become shorter, whereas the pains themselves are of longer duration and more effective. In this way pain succeeds pain until the os uteri, at length, attains its full degree of dilatation; if the membranes have not yet ruptured, we may now expect them to burst with every succeeding pain.

Rigour at the end of the first stage. At this moment the patient is occasionally seized with a sudden and violent fit of shivering, so much so as to make the teeth chatter, and even communicate a tremulous motion to the bed itself; this is not the result of cold, nor is it relieved by the application of external warmth; and, in many cases, the patient will express her surprise that she should shiver thus violently, and yet not feel cold. It appears to be a modification of convulsive action, excited by sympathy between[Pg 163] the os uteri on its becoming fully dilated, and certain muscles in other parts of the body.

Show. On examination at this stage of the process, streaks of blood will be found in the mucus which soils the finger, and sometimes it amounts to a slight discharge of blood: this appearance is called by midwives "a show," as it usually indicates that the os uteri is nearly or fully dilated. It is a separation of the membranes from the vicinity of the os uteri, and consequent rupture of any little vascular twigs which may have passed from the uterus to them.

The full dilatation of the os uteri terminates the first stage of labour. During this stage, the action of the pains does not appear to have been so much for the expulsion of the child, as for preparing it as well as the passages for this purpose, viz. by so arranging and regulating the different forces of the uterus, and at the same time by giving the child such a position (i. e. with its long axis parallel to that of the uterus,) and the os uteri such a degree of dilatation, as shall ensure its expulsion with the greatest possible ease and safety.

Duration of the first stage. The duration of the first stage of labour varies exceedingly, both in primiparæ and those who have had several children; nor is it at all easy to determine with precision the exact moment when labour commences. The sensation of pain to the patient is no guide whatever, for what is attended with much suffering in one patient is scarcely sufficient to excite the notice of another. The dilatation of the os uteri as marking its commencement, must also be taken with some caution: in primiparæ, where it generally remains closed until the contractions are becoming painful, it would obviously be wrong to date the commencement of labour from the moment that the os uteri opens, as regular uterine contractions have been evidently present for some hours previously, although not of sufficient force to produce actual pain. On the other hand, in women who have already had several children, the os uteri is found open some days and even weeks before labour comes on. As a general rule, we may state that regular and genuine contractions of the uterus, sufficiently powerful to produce pain, seldom require more than six hours to effect the full dilatation of the os uteri; in many cases a much shorter time will be sufficient; whereas, in others, the first stage of labour may last for more than quadruple this period before it is completed: in neither can it be considered as abnormal; and we usually find that where the pains of the first stage have been slow and lingering, they become remarkably quick and active during the second stage. This agrees with the experience of Dr. Churchill, in his report of the Western Lying-in Hospital at Dublin, viz. that, "no evil consequences resulted, and they (the labours where the first stage[Pg 164] was so protracted) were amongst those in whom the remaining stages of labour were shortest."

The first stage terminates with the full dilatation of the os uteri; the rupture of the membranes is a change which is necessarily more or less uncertain, as to the precise period of labour at which it takes place. Thus, in primiparæ, it frequently occurs before the first stage is completed; whereas in other cases the membranes sometimes do not give way until the head approaches or has even passed through the os externum; generally speaking, however, they burst at this period of the labour, and usually effect a remarkable change in the whole process. The pains are now of longer duration and more powerful, the intervals between them are shorter, and yet, although the suffering is actually more severe, it is more tolerable to the patient than that of the first stage. During the first stage they are chiefly confined to one spot in the loins; and as they must necessarily continue for some hours without any distinct evidence of the labour being advanced by them, the patient feels discouraged and gets a little impatient at the endurance of so much apparently useless suffering: but as soon as the gush of liquor amnii takes place, she feels that a great alteration has been produced; the abdomen becomes smaller: the pains assume a very different character, and every thing combines to assure her that she has made progress, and encourages her to patience and resolution.

Description of second stage. The os uteri has now disappeared entirely, so that the vagina and uterus form one continuous canal, and is thus admirably adapted for the easy passage of the head: the anterior lip, however, dilates much more slowly than the other parts of it, and this is especially the case in primiparæ, for, being pressed between the head and pelvis it becomes œdematous, and swells to a considerable size: if the pains be strong, it is pushed down more or less before the head, and may be frequently felt beneath the symphysis pubis, and occasionally it is detruded so far as to be visible between the labia. According to Wigand, the swelling of the anterior lip sometimes attains such a size as makes it liable to be mistaken for the bladder of the membranes (op. cit. vol. ii. p. 308;) it seldom produces much obstacle to the advance of the head, and with a little patience gradually disappears of itself. All attempts to push it up above the head are objectionable, because, in the first place, the finger cannot reach sufficiently high to effect this object, and therefore the swelling descends again to its former situation; and, secondly, the efforts to push it up only tend to inflame it and increase the swelling. Those who imagine that they can push up the anterior lip of the os uteri above the head deceive themselves; and even if they do succeed, it merely shows that had they let it alone, it would have gone up very shortly of itself.

[Pg 165]Straining pains. As the head enters the vagina, not only do the contractions of the uterus become much more powerful, but now another set of forces are called into action, and the half involuntary efforts of the abdominal and other muscles come to aid the uterus in expelling its contents. The sole object of this stage is the expulsion of the child, and even the vagina by its contractions contributes to effect it. The head is therefore subjected to considerable pressure; hence we may now feel the cranial bones overlapping each other at the sutures, and the fontanelles diminished in size; and, from the tightness with which the head is embraced by the vagina, the circulation in the scalp is more or less impeded, and a large œdematous swelling, called caput succedaneum, forms on that part of the head which presents.

Each pain is attended with a violent and irresistible impulse to bear down, and every muscle which can assist in effecting this object is now brought into play. The tone of the patient's voice, the expression of her face, the hurried breathing and sudden inspiration, stopping short the moment a pain comes on, in order that she may add still greater power to the efforts which she is about to make, all betoken a very different process to that of the first stage, and one which requires a powerful struggle of muscular strength and energy for its completion. Hence it is that the sound of the patient's voice during the pain is frequently of itself sufficient to inform us how far labour is advanced, for "we never see the really powerful straining pains come on (the head may be never so low in the pelvis,) so long as the os uteri is not fully dilated." (Wigand, op. cit. vol. ii. p. 310.) This is a wise provision of Nature, for by this means it prevents the danger of laceration to which the os uteri would be otherwise exposed, and shows the importance of not permitting a patient to strain and bear down until the os uteri be fully dilated. In those cases where a patient has been induced to exert herself prematurely, the efforts being voluntary are never so powerful, and soon produce much fatigue.

Several reasons have been assigned why the straining pains should come on at this stage. It cannot be owing to the pressure of the head upon the parts of the pelvis, as has been supposed and especially the rectum, thus producing the sensation of a violent desire to evacuate the bowels, because, in almost every case of first labour, the head for several days before the actual commencement of labour is sufficiently deep in the pelvis to produce these effects. It evidently arises from a sympathetic connexion "between the os uteri and vagina on the one hand, and the abdominal and other muscles on the other. We see this connexion most distinctly in those difficult labours where the head is pushed down deeply in the pelvis even to the very outlet, and where the os uteri which is but little dilated is protrud-ed before it. In such cases we never see the really powerful and continued[Pg 166] action of the abdominal muscles excited, let the head press never so forcibly upon the rectum; but as soon as the os uteri (perhaps after much suffering) has retracted over the head, the whole auxiliary action of the abdominal muscles commences." (Ibid. vol. ii. p. 467.)

There is the same relation between these muscles and the vagina, as there is between them and the rectum: the moment the vagina becomes distended, it begins to contract upon the distending body, and like the rectum excites them to strong and involuntary action. The tenesmus of dysentery is a sympathetic action of the same nature; the rectum is highly irritated by the acrid nature of its contents, and excites an irresistible disposition to bear down. The patient wishes for the next pain and yet she dreads it, from the suffering it creates, and the tremendous effort which it compels her to make; the pulse is quicker, and is not only so during the intervals, but undergoes a greater increase of rapidity during the pains themselves than in the first stage; the face becomes red, swollen, and bathed in perspira-tion; the breath is hurried; the lips are apart; the eyes are wild; every thing betokens a state of the highest excite-ment. When a pain comes on, she catches hold of whatever she can reach, plants her feet upon any thing which is firm, and, by thus fixing her extremities, she is enabled to bear down with greater power and effect. During the struggle the face often changes its expression surprisingly, so much so, that even her own attendants would scarcely recognise her.

Dilatation of the perineum. As pain succeeds pain, gradually increasing both in force as well as duration, the head descends along the vagina, and begins to press against the perineum; the rectum becomes flattened; the sphincter ani dilated, and therefore any fæcal matter which may have been lodging there is unavoidably expelled; the anterior wall of the rectum is pressed close against the anus, and where the pressure is very great, even protrudes some-what through it; the hæmorrhoidal veins are frequently much distended, and form a roll of cushiony swelling around the anus. A small quantity of liquor amnii dribbles away from time to time, but is neither during a pain, nor during the absence of a pain, for in the former case the pressure of the head acts as a plug and prevents its escape, and in the latter there is no uterine contraction present to expel it: the liquor amnii dribbles away only at the moment when a pain is coming on or going off.

Expulsion of the child. As the head descends farther it begins to press more powerfully on the perineum, and during each pain pushes it out like a large ball; and then, as a contraction goes off, and the resiliency of the soft parts regain their superiority, it retires again. The breadth of the perineum (viz. from the anus to the vulva) increases, whilst it diminishes considerably in thickness, especially towards its anterior margin. Whilst passing[Pg 167] through the inferior aperture or outlet of the pelvis, the head advances more or less forwards under the pubic arch, and begins to distend the os externum; during a pain it separates the labia, and protrudes between them, and again retires as the pain goes off; a larger and larger portion of the head gradually forces itself through the os externum as this dilates; the perineum becomes still thinner, so that at length it is scarcely thicker than parchment. When more of the head has passed through, it does not now recede when the pain goes off; the os externum and perineum are at their greatest distension, for the largest diameter of the head, which is presented to the os externum is now encircled by it; the next pain brings the head into the world.

This is the moment of greatest pain, and the patient is frequently quite wild and frantic with suffering; it approaches to a species of insanity, and shows itself in the most quiet and gentle dispositions. The laws in Germany have made great allowances for any act of violence committed during these moments of phrenzy, and wisely and mercifully consider that the patient at the time was labouring under a species of temporary insanity. Even the act of child-mur-der, when satisfactorily proved to have taken place at this moment, is treated with considerable leniency. This state of mind is sometimes manifested in a slighter degree by actions and words so contrary to the general habit and nature of the patient, as to prove that she could not have been under the proper control of her reason at the moment. It is a question how far this state of mind may arise from intense suffering, or how far the circulation of the brain may be affected by the pressure which is exerted upon the abdominal viscera.

A short cessation of pain succeeds the birth of the head. The violent distension of the os externum has ceased for a time, and the patient feels comparatively easy; but in the course of a few minutes the pains return as before, although not quite so severe: first, the shoulder, which is turned forwards, passes under the pubic arch, followed by the other which sweeps over the perineum. The rest of the child is expelled with comparative ease, and as soon as its pelvis has passed through the os externum, a gush of the remaining liquor amnii, which had been retained in the upper portions of the uterus, follows; the whole abdomen instantly sinks and becomes flaccid, while the uterus contracts into a firm globe upon the placenta, which is shortly to be expelled. A most delightful and perfect calm succeeds, and the sense of freedom from suffering, and joy for the termination of her trial, are expressed in the liveliest terms of gratitude.

Third stage.—Expulsion of the placenta. The period between the birth of the child and expulsion of the placenta varies considerably. Sometimes it follows the child very rapidly, so that, apparently, they are both expelled by the same effort of uterine action; at others, the interval is more considerable. There is[Pg 168] generally an interval of ten or fifteen minutes, and then pains of a totally different character make their appearance: these are supposed to denote the separation of the placenta from the uterus, and, from their being usually attended with discharge of more or less blood, have been termed dolores cruenti by many of the foreign writers. The expulsion of the placenta is attended with little or no suffering; it descends into the vagina inverted, i. e. with its fœtal or amniotic surface turned outwards: whether or not this is pulling at the cord is perhaps a question.

Twins. If there be twins, the placenta of the first child is seldom expelled until after the birth of the second child. The membranes of the second ovum become distended with liquor amnii, project into the vagina and burst as in a common single labour; the passages have been sufficiently dilated and prepared by the birth of the first child, so that, when the uterus begins to contract, the expulsion of the second will be readily and easily effected. The uterus may resume its efforts for this purpose in twenty minutes after the birth of the first child, or it may remain quiescent for several hours without at all disturbing the regular and natural course of the process which will be precisely the same as in the previous case.

The placentæ of twins are usually expelled together, forming one large placentary mass; their vessels, however, are distinct from each other, so that with care one placenta can be peeled away from the other. In other cases, they are separated from each other by an intervening space of membranes; and in one rare instance of triplet placentæ the umbilical arteries of two placentæ anastomosed with each other, before dividing into smaller branches.

Upon the expulsion of the placenta, the uterus, being now emptied of its contents, contracts into a firm hard ball, which may be felt behind the symphysis pubes, or sometimes a little to one side, of about the size of a full grown fœtal head. This state of hard contraction gradually disappears, and a discharge of blood called lochia follows, which having continued for a few days becomes colourless, and at length ceases altogether. For a description of the changes which the uterus and passages undergo in returning to their former condition as in the unimpregnated state, we refer to the chapter on the Female Organs of Generation.

[Pg 169]

CHAPTER II.

TREATMENT OF NATURAL LABOUR.

State of the bowels.—Form and size of the uterus.—True and spurious pains.—Treatment of spurious pains.—Management of the first stage.—Examination.—Position of patient during labour.—Prognosis as to the duration of labour.—Diet during labour.—Supporting the perineum.—Treatment of perineal laceration.—Cord round the child's neck.—Birth of the child, and ligature of the cord.—Importance of ascertaining that the uterus is contracted after labour.—Management of the placenta.—Twins.—Treatment after labour.—Lactation.—Milk-fever and abscess.—Excoriated nipples. — Diet during lactation. — Management of lochia. — After-pains.

This is a subject of great extent as well as importance, because it comprehends the whole mass of rules for the management of a woman, not only just previous to and during, but also after, her confinement. On nothing does the course of a natural labour depend so much, as upon the careful removal of every source of irritation which may tend in any way to derange or interrupt the regular progress of that series of changes or phenomena which constitutes the great process of normal parturition. It will be necessary that the reader should have made himself thoroughly master of the subjects discussed in the last chapter, before commencing those of the present one. With each change there mentioned, the state of the system and its functions should be carefully watched, and every slight deviation from the natural course of things checked by appropriate dietetic or medical treatment. Hence, therefore, the more a woman can follow her usual avocations, and take that degree of exercise to which she has been accustomed at other times, the better; for by so doing the circulation is equalized, the digestion is kept in full activity, and the tone and general strength of the system maintained.

It would almost seem, by rendering a woman more capable of moving about during the last weeks of pregnancy (which has already been shown to be the sinking of the fundus, enabling the respiration to act more freely,) that Nature intended she should use exercise at this period, and thus prepare her, by[Pg 170] increased health and strength, for a process which requires so much suffering and exertion.

Her hours should be regular and early, her meals light and moderate, and by agreeable and cheerful occupation she should fit herself, both in body and mind, to meet the coming trial.

State of the bowels. Attention to the state of the bowels is of first importance, and must never be neglected. It is a subject nevertheless upon which women are remarkably careless, and they will frequently, when not attended to, allow labour to come on with their bowels in a very loaded and highly improper condition.

There is, perhaps, no one circumstance which is found to exert such a prejudicial influence on the course of a natural labour, in so many different ways, as deranged and constipated bowels. Where the contents are of an unhealthy character, the irritation which they produce in the intestinal canal is quickly transmitted to the uterus, and tends not a little to pervert and derange the due and healthy action of this organ: hence arises one of the most fertile sources of spurious pains, a subject which will shortly come under our consideration. Where the bowels are loaded, in consequence of the pressure upon the ascending cava, considerable obstruction to the free return of blood from the pelvic viscera is produced, the vessels of which become considerably engorged. No organ feels these effects more than the uterus: from the immensely dilated condition of its veins, a state of local plethora is engendered, which, from the congested state of the uterine parietes, considerably interferes with the free and regular action of its fibres, and not unfrequently predisposes to hæmorrhage.

Moreover, the rectum being distended with fæces, diminishes proportionally the capacity of the pelvis, and prevents the ready descent of the head into it; occasionally it forms, at the beginning of labour, a solid cylinder of indurated fæces, so hard, as, at the first touch, almost to induce the suspicion of a projecting sacrum. As a measure of common cleanliness, the bowels ought always to be attended to before labour, for, besides the more serious effects now enumerated, the labour may be rendered exceedingly filthy for the patient, and not less disgusting for the practitioner; for, as the sphincter ani loses all power of contraction when the head advances deeper into the pelvis, it follows that whatever fæcal matter may have been lodging in the rectum will now be unconsciously pressed out.

Hence, therefore, for the last few days of pregnancy, the bowels should be regularly opened (unless they are so spontaneously, which is seldom the case) by castor oil or other mild laxatives: and if labour has already commenced before this measure has been taken, and if, therefore, there is not sufficient time for[Pg 171] the operation of the medicine, an enema should be given.[66] In Germany it is a rule to throw up some chamomile infusion at the commencement of every labour, by which means the process is rendered more cleanly than is frequently the case in this country; and also, for the reasons already given, the early stage is less apt to be tedious from spurious and ineffective pains.

Form and size of the uterus. The more regular the first precursory pains are, the more symmetrical and uniform will be the shape of the uterus; and again, on the other hand, the more uniform its shape, the more regularly and effectively will it act.

It is these slight but early contractions, which, although they produce little or no effect upon the os uteri, exert a very important influence over the first half of labour; for it is by their action, in great measure, that the form of the uterus is determined, as also the correct position of the child. Hence, therefore, some practitioners lay considerable stress on ascertaining the precise form of the abdomen as a means of determining what sort of labour the patient will have.

In a woman pregnant for the first time, and in a state of perfect health, the uterus is of an oval or rather elliptical form at the beginning of labour: when seen in profile, the abdomen presents nearly a uniform degree of convexity. In this state the child lies with its long axis parallel to that of the uterus, that is, with its head or inferior extremity turned towards the brim of the pelvis; and if the fundus has already sunk in the manner above-mentioned, the practitioner may very confidently prognosticate that the head presents, even before making an examination per vaginam.

In a perfectly healthy primipara there is scarcely any inclination of the uterus either to one side or forwards, its median line corresponding with that of the abdomen: whereas, in the multipara, the axis of the uterus is seldom straight, inclining more or less to one side, or, from the greater relaxation of the abdominal parietes, being somewhat pendulous. The size of the uterus should also be taken into consideration, especially in first pregnancies; a large uterus shows that either its parietes are gorged with too much blood, or that its cavity is distended with an unusual quantity of liquor amnii, or that the child is very large, or that there are twins. Whatever may be the cause of the distension, it interferes with the regular and effective contractions of the uterus, and tends to make the labour (at least the first part of it) tedious. A moderate sized uterus is much more capable of active exertion, for its fibres not being put so much upon the stretch are enabled to contract better.

[Pg 172]True and false pains. If the patient is already beginning to suffer pains, it is of great importance to ascertain whether they be genuine or spurious; upon the correct diagnosis of which, the favourable or unfavourable course of the labour not unfrequently in great measure depends.

A genuine labour pain comes on at tolerably regular intervals, rises gradually to a certain degree of intensity, remains at that point for a few seconds, and then subsides as gradually; the body and the fundus of the uterus increase in hardness, and the os uteri in tenseness, in proportion as the pain rises, and vice versâ; the pain is seated in the back and loins, and is of a dull aching character: but with the spurious pains it is quite the reverse; they come on and go off suddenly and irregularly, the pain is in the abdomen, and produces a sharp twinging sensation, and the hardness of the uterus and tenseness of its mouth bear no proportion to the pain.

Spurious labour pains are the early contractions of the uterus perverted and rendered irregular, spasmodic, and painful by irritation, congestion, or inflammatory action; they sometimes come on several days before actual labour commences, and if not recognised and removed, may expose the patient to considerable suffering and exhaustion. Derangement of the stomach and bowels is one of the most frequent causes of spurious pains, for by the irritation which is thus produced, the uterus is almost sure to sympathize, and to have its action more or less disordered. This may arise from unhealthy irritating contents of the bowels producing spasmodic, griping, and colicky pains, or from diarrhœa with tenesmus arising from exposure to cold, or from irritation caused by the pressure of the gravid womb. Spurious labour pains of this character also frequently occur in patients who are accustomed to indulge in the luxuries of the table, or in the lower classes, who are addicted to the use of spirituous liquors. Constipation has been already mentioned as a cause of this condition. The state of plethora, congestion, or inflammation, acting as a cause of spurious pains, may arise from various sources: it is frequently observed in strong healthy young women, especially those pregnant for the first time; the pains do not assume the proper character of genuine labour pains, and exhaust the patient by continued but useless suffering. The os uteri probably dilates somewhat, but its edge remains thin and tense, and the pains appear to have no effect in dilating it any farther. The mucous secretion of the vagina is not of the character described at the beginning of labour in the preceding chapter. The pulse is strong and more or less excited, and the flushed face, and generally increased heat of skin indicate the condition upon which those symptoms depend. The inflammatory form of spurious labour pains is not unfrequently of the rheumatic character, a condition which has not been much noticed in this country, but[Pg 173] which is capable of exerting a very considerable influence upon the course and progress of the labour. It is usually exposure to cold and the other common causes of rheumatism in other parts of the body, and is generally accompanied with more or less derangement of the stomach and bowels. In this state each contraction of the uterine fibres is attended with much suffering, although the contraction itself may be so slight as to produce little or no effect upon the os uteri. Most of these conditions, in a severe degree, form that species of dystocia which arises from a faulty state of the expelling powers, for the farther consideration of which we must refer to our chapter upon that subject. In a minor degree they produce these slight derangements of uterine action, which we are now considering under the name of spurious pains.

Treatment of spurious pains. The indications of treatment depend in great measure upon the cause; and we cannot impress it too strongly on the young practitioner, as a rule never to be lost sight of, that, whatever is wrong in the state of the circulation or of the bowels must be first rectified before having recourse to opiates. Where the stomach is much deranged at the beginning of labour, nature frequently induces spontaneous vomiting, with considerable relief to the patient, and mitigation of the pains; if not a gentle emetic may be administered. Where the bowels are loaded, the treatment already mentioned must be put into practice, after which ☐ xx of Liquor Opii Sedativus and of antimonial wine in peppermint water, or gr x of Dover's powder may be given. When there is diarrhœa with a good deal of griping and tenesmus, a dose of castor oil with Liquor Opii Sedativus in any aromatic water may be administered; and if the labour be not yet commenced, gr v of Pil. Hydr. and Dover's powder may be also given at night. If there be a plethoric or even inflammatory condition, the lancet will be of the greatest service; it reduces the temperature of the body, relaxes the soft parts, brings on copious secretion of mucus, and by relieving the congested state of the uterine parietes, enables the fibres to contract with more regularity and effect. In the rheumatic form, laxatives followed by diaphoretics, the warm bath, and even venesection will be necessary.

By thus treating the spurious pains according to their cause, they will usually subside readily enough, and be either followed immediately by pains of a more genuine and effective character, or leave the patient perfectly free for several hours, or perhaps even days. It is by inattention to, or ignorance of, these conditions, that patients have been allowed to remain for several days in suffering, during which they have been treated as if they had been in natural labour, until at length they have become so exhausted that, when labour really made its appearance, they were incapable of undergoing the exertions which this process demands.

[Pg 174]Management of the first stage. The preparatory pains of labour, which form the first stage, do not require that the patient should take to her bed at this early period; and this is especially the case in primiparæ, where the first stage is usually somewhat tedious. Until nearly the end of the first stage, she ought rather to be induced to suppose that actual labour has scarcely yet commenced, and that she may still sit up or walk about the room as best suits her feelings, taking care at the same time that every thing is in readiness against the moment when it shall become necessary for her to lie down. A nurse who understands her business will of course duly arrange all these matters, but it behoves the accoucheur, nevertheless, to pay attention to these little details, and to see that every thing is properly prepared: that the bed is ready, and guarded either by several folds of sheeting, or by a leather for the purpose, to prevent the blood and other discharges during labour from soaking into the bedding beneath; this must be done either on the right side or at the foot of the bed, in order that the patient may be better within the reach of the accoucheur: that the patient should be partially undressed, and covered with her dressing-gown: that all the linen should be well aired: that there should be towels, napkins, hot and cold water in readiness, and also a bottle of vinegar, and one of spirit in the room, in case of hemorrhage, suspended animation in the child, &c. &c. These and many other arrangements of less importance are by no means beneath his attention, and require but a moment's glance to assure him that every thing is properly prepared.

By encouraging the patient to sit up as long as she can, or even to move about occasionally, the pains are rendered more tolerable as well as more effective; the time passes more agreeably and quickly; and by the time that it has become necessary for her to lie down, the labour has made so much progress that the rest of its course seems to be much quicker than was at first expected. On the contrary, where the practitioner at an early period of the first stage, informs her that she must stay up no longer, that she must go to bed and remain lying on her left side, her mind is solely occupied with her pains, which become wearying and irksome; the time passes heavily away; she becomes impatient and therefore dispirited; and is much disappointed, that, after remaining in this state for some time, the termination of the labour appears to be as far off as ever. Nothing eases the pains of the first stage, or increases their effect, so much as frequent change of position and moving about; when, however, they are severe or of long continuance, and the patient becomes fatigued, she will require rest, and this opportunity, afforded by her lying down, should be seized for the purpose of making an examination.

Examination. The manner in which this operation should be[Pg 175] proposed to the patient cannot be too delicate: it should, as Dr. Dewees has justly observed, always if possible be done by means of a third person, such as the nurse or any elderly female friend who happens to be present. If the accoucheur has proposed it with that degree of gentleness and good feeling which it ought to behove every one to show under such circumstances, he will rarely, if ever, experience the slightest unwillingness to accede to his request: the better the patient's rank in life is, the more docile will she prove at these times, and the more resolute to undergo whatever she is told it is necessary to submit to. The object of an examination is to determine whether the child presents rightly, whether the labour is far advanced, and to form some degree of prognosis as to its course and duration, &c.: these are points which are of such importance as well as interest to ascertain, that the dread which a patient feels at undergoing an operation so repugnant to her feelings is generally merged more or less in the intense anxiety to know if all is right.

An examination at an early period of labour is important in many respects. We ascertain the condition of the vagina, whether it be soft, cool, relaxed, and well lubricated with mucus, as described at the beginning of the last chapter; whether the os uteri be dilated; whether its edge be thin and tense, or already becoming soft, cushiony, and yielding; whether the membranes are ruptured; whether the presentation be a natural one, and whether the pelvis be rightly formed. In cases where the umbilical cord is prolapsed, it is particularly desirable to ascertain the existence of this displacement as early in labour as possible.

It is usually directed to examine during a pain, because at this moment we feel the os uteri tense, and therefore more distinct to the finger; but it is far better to examine during the interval between the pain: the os uteri being now relaxed, admits the finger more easily; the membranes being loose are not so liable to be ruptured; and, from their not being distended, we shall feel the presenting part more distinctly.

Wherever the os uteri is nearly or fully dilated, or from its condition and the effect which the pains have upon it shows a disposition to dilate with rapidity, the patient should go to bed, as we cannot be sure when the membranes may rupture, more especially in primiparæ, in whom this usually takes place early. It is equally desirable, also, in those who have already had children, that the patient should be upon her bed at this moment; because, if the pains be strong, and the os uteri yielding, the head is apt to follow the discharge of the liquor amnii, and sudden expulsion of the child might result at a moment when the patient is unprepared for such an occurrence.

The accoucheur should always examine when the membranes give way, because not only will he be able to feel the presenting part now more distinctly, but if the cord has prolapsed, a coil of[Pg 176] it will come down into the vagina and cannot escape his notice; in fact, if there is any thing unusual about the presentation, he will be now able to distinguish it with greater certainty. In women who have had large families, the head remains very high in the pelvis until this moment, so that it is frequently extremely difficult to reach it and to ascertain its position: the same is observed with presentations of the nates and of the shoulder, which seldom descend into the pelvis until the liquor amnii escapes.

Position of the patient during labour. The position which the patient should take during the actual process of labour has been a subject of considerable discussion, and even at the present day varies exceedingly in different countries. In the earliest periods of history, women appear to have been delivered in a sitting posture, as is described in the first chapter of Exodus: this mode was revived in comparatively modern times; thus Ambrose Paré, in 1573, speaks of a labour chair with an inclined back, which he preferred to a common bed. Labour chairs were brought into very general use upon the Continent in the beginning of the last century by Hendrick van Deventer of Dort in Holland, and although they have been in great measure discontinued in modern times, there are still some districts of Germany where they continue to be used. It is a species of chaise percée furnished with straps, cushions, &c. by which the patient can fix her extremities, and thus enable the abdominal muscles to act with the greatest power. This is the very reason which renders labour chairs objectionable. The presenting part of the child is forced through the soft passage with great violence, before they have had time to yield and to dilate sufficiently; hence it has been noticed that lacerations of the perineum are of very frequent occurrence in those countries where labour chairs have been in general use. In some remote parts of Ireland, and also of Germany, the patient sits upon the knees of another person, and this office of substitute for a labour chair is usually performed by her husband. Labour chairs, as far as we are acquainted with their history, were never used in this country, nor have they been used for the last century in France, where the patients are usually delivered in the supine posture, on a small bed upon the floor, which has not inaptly been termed lit de misére. A modification of the labour chair is the labour cushion first used by Nuger, and afterwards by the late Professor von Siebold of Berlin and Professor Carus of Dresden; it is a species of mattress, with a hollow beneath the nates of the patient for receiving the discharges which take place during the labour. The patient is compelled to lie upon her back during the greater part of labour, and thus maintain the same posture for some time, which must necessarily become irksome and even painful to her. In this country and in Germany the patient is delivered upon a common bed, prepared for the purpose as above mentioned: in England she is placed upon her left side, the nates[Pg 177] projecting to the edge of the bed, for the greater convenience of the accoucheur: in Germany, except in Vienna and Heidelberg, where the English midwifery has in great measure been introduced by Boer and Naegelé, the patient is delivered upon her back.[67] In former times the supine posture was also used in this country, but for about a century the position on the left side has been preferred; the patient lies more comfortably to her own feelings; her face is turned from the practitioner who sits behind her, and who, from this posture, is able to examine or to perform any other necessary manipulation without her feelings being annoyed by seeing what is going forward. It is decidedly the easiest position during the last moments of tremendous suffering and exertion; when the presenting part is passing she is not able to exert an undue degree of violence, and from the knees being kept together, there is less danger of the perineum being torn. The left side seems moreover to be the natural position for a woman at the moment of parturition, for if accidental circumstances have occurred, such as sudden labour, &c. by which she is deprived of all assistance at this moment, she will almost invariably be found upon the ground lying on her side supporting herself with one hand. In some cases she will remain during these moments upon her knees, into which posture she has gradually dropped from that of standing: in by far the majority of cases she will take the position upon her side, as above mentioned.

So long as the os uteri is not fully dilated, the patient is not involuntarily compelled to strain and bear down: hence it is important to caution patients, more especially primiparæ, not to be induced by an ignorant nurse or friend to exert themselves improperly during the first stage of labour, for not only is the process of dilatation considerably impeded, and much exhaustion produced, but frequently severe febrile or inflammatory action excited, which may lead to serious results after labour. All attempts to accelerate the course of a natural labour, especially the first stage, either on the part of the patient by premature straining, or on the part of the practitioner by attempts to dilate the os uteri and passages, or by giving her stimuli, &c. cannot be too strictly forbidden. It is a mode of practice which has long since been strongly condemned by the highest authorities in midwifery, except in Scotland, and which may very easily lead to most mischievous results. Quick rapid labours are by no means desirable, for they are seldom safe; nor is it possible to limit this or that stage (especially the first) to any given duration of time.

[Pg 178]No conscientious practitioner, who has clear and enlarged views of the process and mechanism of natural labour, would feel himself justified in interfering with its course, merely because some portion of it has extended beyond a certain fixed period; but would rather guide his conduct by the habit and strength of the individual, and by the effects which the labour has upon her. We have before stated, that no two labours are alike; we may also add, that no two individuals are similarly affected by the same degree and duration of labour, nor indeed are any two labours exactly alike in the same person: hence it will be evident, that what to one patient would prove a protracted and exhausting labour, to another would be nothing more than a perfectly regular labour, natural both in its character and progress. Among other injurious effects which premature efforts on the part of the patient will have, is, that the membranes are liable to give way too soon—this is by all means to be avoided, for nothing is so likely to render the first stage protracted as the occurrence of this accident; the course of the labour frequently undergoes an immediate change; the pains lose their regular and effective character; the os uteri remains thin, tense, and unyielding, and the process of dilatation is greatly retarded.

Prognosis as to the duration of labour. There are few subjects upon which an accoucheur is so frequently importuned, or about which it is so difficult to give a decided opinion, as the probable duration of labour. It is natural enough that both she and her friends should be anxious to know how long this process of suffering is likely to last: nothing, however, is more hazardous than a prognosis in these cases; and we would warn our junior brethren to be cautious how they commit themselves by venturing an opinion, which the result of the labour may prove to have been founded upon guess-work or ignorance. The character of the labour during the second stage, is frequently very different to that of the first, so that the mode in which the labour commences is by no means a criterion for its latter part. A labour which has commenced briskly and regularly, and with every promise of a rapid progress and termination, frequently becomes exceedingly lingering during the second stage, so that the expelling powers may, perhaps, even fail altogether in making the head pass through the os externum; whereas, on the other hand, a labour, the first stage of which has been slow and protracted, frequently experiences a complete alteration of character, and advances with a degree of quickness and energy, which could scarcely have been anticipated from the manner in which it commenced. In primiparæ, especially, it is particularly difficult to foretell, with any thing like certainty, the duration of labour: hence it is, that unguarded assertions in this respect are not only liable to disappoint the patient, but destroy her confidence in the practitioner.

Wigand's views. The celebrated Wigand of Hamburgh [Pg 179]considered that the form of the vagina would frequently furnish the means of a pretty certain prognosis, as to the duration of labour: thus, if it were wide and yielding throughout its whole length, the labour would be quick, both at its beginning and termination; if, on the other hand, it were small, rigid, and contracted throughout, the labour might be expected to be of a very opposite character. If on examination the vagina is found roomy and well dilated at its upper part, but contracted and rigid near the os externum, the labour will be probably quick and easy during the first half, but slow and difficult afterwards; on the contrary, where the os externum is yielding and wide, but the upper portion of the vagina narrow, the labour may be expected to be slow at first, but to be brisk and active afterwards. We have already stated, that the course of labour varies in every possible way; in some cases the same peculiar character of labour shows itself through two or three successive generations: hence it has been observed, that very tedious or very violent and rapid labours sometimes seems to be hereditary; the mother, daughters, and grand-daughters, being all remarkable for their lingering or rapid labours.

Diet during labour. The diet of the patient during labour should be simple and unirritating; if every thing is going on naturally and briskly, some gruel or tea, with or without a little biscuit or bread and butter, will be quite sufficient; but if the process is becoming tedious and exhausting, some beef-tea, broth, or any other mild nourishment of this sort will be required to support the strength.

During the first stage of labour there is no need for the practitioner to be constantly in the room, nor even during the early part of the second, unless the pains are very violent and protrusive; for, by taking frequent opportunities of quitting the patient for a few minutes, she is left more free from restraint, and the presence of the practitioner becomes less irksome when it is really necessary; whereas, if he continues at the bed-side, she is justified in expecting that the labour must be advancing rapidly to demand so unremitting an attendance, and, therefore, becomes disappointed and impatient to find that his presence has been of so little use to her. The conversation should be light and cheerful, and every means taken to encourage her and keep up her spirits.

Supporting the perineum. As the head approaches the os externum our attention must be directed to giving the perineum such a degree of support, as shall secure it from any serious degree of laceration during its passage. The greatest danger of ruptured perineum is in primiparæ, for the soft parts never having been subjected to such a degree of dilatation before, do not yield so readily as in multiparæ. The anterior margin of the perineum, called frænulum, is, we believe almost invariably ruptured in every first case; but the laceration ought not to extend[Pg 180] farther. The more gradual the advance of the head is through the os externum, the better will be the dilatation of the soft parts: hence therefore, when the pains are violent, and the head is thrust with great force against the perineum, it will be desirable to restrain it in some degree, until the parts shall have had sufficient time to yield; on the other hand, where the pains are more gradual, the perineum and os externum may receive the whole dilating force of the head, and every succeeding pain will show that a progressive advance is taking place.

The increasing thinness of the perineum itself, and the frænulum becoming tense during the height of a pain, may be looked upon as warnings that the expulsion of the head is not far distant, and now the support of the hand will be needed to prevent laceration; for this purpose the position on the left side is peculiarly convenient, besides having the additional advantage of relaxing the external parts more completely. If the pains be violent, and the impulse to strain very considerable, we must desire the patient to lie as passive as she can, and do her best not to bear down, for otherwise the head is sometimes driven through the os externum with a single effort, and the mischief done in spite of all our care.

The support of the perineum has been variously directed by different authors; we prefer using the left hand, because then we have the right at liberty for any manipulations which may be necessary, such as examining if the cord be round the child's neck, &c. &c. It is awkward at first, because it requires the hand to be considerably twisted, and makes the wrist ache a good deal; but a very little practice soon conquers this slight difficulty, and the superiority of the mode will then be apparent. As our object is not merely to support the perineum, but to direct the head as much forwards under the pubic arch as possible, in order that the anterior portions of the os externum should undergo their share of dilatation, and thus in some measure spare the perineum, the chief pressure should be applied near to the sphincter ani, gradually diminishing it up to the frænulum perinei in front: for this purpose the left hand protected by a napkin (partly for the sake of cleanliness and partly for the purpose of having a firmer hold upon the parts, and preventing it slipping) should now be applied with the palm in the vicinity of the sphincter ani, so that the tips of the fingers should project somewhat beyond the frænulum; the whole should be laid as flat and close to the part as possible. In order that we may be sure of the hand being applied exactly along the raphe of the perineum, we should guide it by the examining finger of the right hand, bearing in mind, that when we place this against the posterior margin of the os externum, and bring the middle finger of the left hand in contact with it, we shall hold the left hand in the desired direction.

[Pg 181]It is desirable also to hold the examining finger of the right hand against the frænulum perinei when a pain comes on, because then we know exactly when the tension of the perineum is becoming such as to endanger its integrity, and when the head is about to pass out. Until this moment the frænulum is seldom on the stretch, although the rest of the perineum is: hence we need not apply our support until now, and thus give the parts the full benefit of the dilating force, which the head exerts upon them, until the very last instant. To relax them still farther, the patient's knees ought not to be separated by a pillow or cushion placed between them, as is usually done, although it must be confessed that in some cases she is relieved by it.

In applying the left hand to support the perineum, it should be placed somewhat more backward than the spot which we intend to support: for by this means we are enabled to push the soft parts somewhat forwards, and thus relax them. By this means, also, we not only direct the head against the other parts of the os externum but avoid the danger of its perforating the perineum. When the moment of greatest distension arrives, the process cannot be too slow; we must therefore desire the patient not to bear down, and endeavour, if possible, to make the head remain in the state of crowning until the next pain comes on: the os externum having been held for some moments at its utmost dilatation, permits the head to pass with greater ease and safety. As the globe of the head passes forwards and emerges through the os externum, we feel the posterior portions of the perineum become soft and lax, while the forehead, followed by the face, and lastly the chin glide over the anterior margin of it.

The passage of the head is not the only moment of danger to the perineum, for laceration is even still more liable to be produced during the expulsion of the shoulders; any slight rupture of the anterior edge is now apt to be converted into a considerable laceration, unless the support be continued until the thorax be expelled. We have already stated that the frænulum perinei is generally torn through in the first labour; but the laceration ought not, if possible, to extend farther, because serious injury may be produced either to the vagina, or even to the sphincter rectum. To say, however, that laceration of the perineum need never happen, would be preposterous; because cases every now and then occur, where, from the contracted and unyielding state of the os externum, and from the size of the child, it is nearly impossible that the perineum can escape without injury; fortunately, although considerable lacerations are by no means uncommon, they are seldom observed to extend into the sphincter ani, the direction of the rent being usually to one side. Under the ordinary circumstances of perineal laceration, little more than mere attention to cleanliness is required; for the parts contract so astonishingly after labour, that what was a wide rent of an inch and a[Pg 182] half long, in a couple of days will be scarcely more than two or three lines in length. Rest, great cleanliness, and gentle-relaxed bowels, constitute the chief treatment.

Treatment of perineal laceration. Where, however, the laceration extends into the rectum, the case becomes exceedingly troublesome and difficult to cure, and the patient is liable to be rendered a miserable object for life; for the action of the sphincter being entirely destroyed, she is unable to retain fæces or flatus in the rectum; besides which, from the injury to the posterior wall of the vagina, prolapsus uteri is an almost certain consequence. In these cases the slightest movement of the thighs upon each other alters the position of the lips of the wound, and thus tears it open afresh, so that at length the edges of the wound become callous and refuse to heal. A great deal in these cases depends upon the patience and good conduct of the patient herself; for if she have the resolution to lie perfectly still for at least a week, she will have every chance of a perfect cure. If there be much swelling of the edges, and a disposition to slough, a warm poultice of chamomile flowers should be applied, and the bowels kept in a nearly liquid state by gentle and repeated doses of salines, in order to prevent distension of the rectum when the evacuation is passing; she should preserve the supine posture, and have her knees confined together by a piece of tape, as is done with patients after the operation of lithotomy. Straps of adhesive plaster are seldom or never of any use, but if the rent be very severe a suture or two may be required. The great fault in applying these means for bringing the edges of the wound together is the attempting to unite them throughout their whole length; for by so doing the tension of the parts is increased, and therefore there is less disposition to unite; and even if we succeed in effecting complete union of the whole wound, the perineum is so contracted and unyielding from the cicatrisation, that it can scarcely escape a repetition of the injury in succeeding labours. It is, therefore, much better that we should content ourselves with uniting merely the posterior half of the laceration; the parts heal much more readily, and the os externum is left of a sufficient size to escape all danger of laceration on future occasions.

Where the edges have become callous and refused to unite, they require to be pared and brought together again; this, however, does not always succeed, and the case becomes very difficult and protracted: under these circumstances, the treatment adopted by Dr. Dieffenbach, of Berlin, is well worthy of attention. Having pared off the callous edges of the wound, he brings them into the closest opposition by transfixing them with needles in several places, as is done for the operation of hare-lip; and in order to isolate the wound as much as possible from the surrounding parts, and prevent any tension, he makes a free incision through the integuments, parallel with the wound, at a little [Pg 183]distance from it, and nearly of the same length; by this means, every cause which might tend to separate the edges is removed; whilst the parallel cuts, being fresh incised wounds, soon close by granulation.[68]

It sometimes, although rarely, happens that the perineum, instead of being torn from before backwards, is perforated through its centre by the head, so that the child is not born through the os externum, but through a lacerated opening in the body of the perineum. This accident may arise from a variety of circumstances: the direction of the pelvic outlet may be faulty, or the inclined plane formed by the lower part of the sacrum, by the sacro-sciatic ligaments, &c. may be insufficient to guide the head forwards under the pubic arch; or the perineum may be unusually broad; in which cases the power of the uterus being directed against the centre of it, the head becomes enveloped in a bag of protruded perineum; and if the pains are violent, and the head not properly supported, it at length bursts its way through the centre without even injuring the frænulum. The treatment of this form of ruptured perineum is the same as that of the more common species; the bowels must be kept open, and a fomentation of chamomile flowers applied to the wound, which, from the gradual contraction of the surrounding parts after labour, diminishes remarkably, so that in the course of a short time it will have entirely or nearly closed.[69]

Besides the above-mentioned advantages in supporting the perineum, we may mention another which is not generally noticed, and which is sometimes of considerable service. In cases where the head has completely descended upon the perineum, and begins to protrude somewhat through the os externum, the pains occasionally fail at this moment, the labour becomes very lingering, while the advance of the head and state of the parts show that two or three active pains would bring the child into the world; firm pressure applied at the lower end of the sacrum, in a direction forwards, materially adds to the effect of each pain in bringing the head through the os externum, and seems also to excite the patient to make a more powerful effort with the abdominal muscles. On several occasions we have thus assisted the expulsion of the head, when otherwise the labour would have been very protracted, or would have even required the forceps to disengage it. Madame La Chappelle is the only authority in midwifery, as far as we know, that has noticed this fact.

Cord round the child's neck. As soon as the head is born, we must examine whether the cord be twisted round the child's neck; and here the advantage of supporting the perineum with the left[Pg 184] hand becomes evident: it is ready to support the shoulders when they begin to pass, while the right hand is at liberty to perform any manipulations which may be necessary. If it be important to support the head during its passage over the perineum, still more so will it be to support the shoulders; for if a small laceration has already been produced, it is invariably converted into a wide rent at this moment, if great care be not taken: indeed, we are justified in saying that most of the cases of severe perineal rupture are the shoulders, not by the head.

Passage of the shoulders. If the pains cease for a time, or the child be large, the shoulders do not pass immediately: in this position the face swells and grows purple from the pressure upon the neck, although it does not necessarily result from the cord being round it; if, however, we find that this is the case, we can in most instances loosen it somewhat by the finger, and as the shoulders advance, slip it first over one and then the other: we must recollect that the shoulder, which is forwards, passes out first, and that, therefore, we must slip the cord over it first.

It is seldom necessary to assist the shoulders by applying any extractive force to the head, for in the course of a minute or two the uterus generally resumes its activity and expels it: on the other hand, when the shoulders pass through the os externum, the right hand should be in readiness to prevent the body of the child from being born too rapidly: the uterus can scarcely be emptied of its contents too gradually, for by this means it contracts equably, powerfully, and permanently, and throws off the placenta without difficulty; whereas, if suddenly evacuated, it frequently becomes powerless for a time, or if contraction does take place, it is so irregular and incomplete as to endanger partial separation, retention of the placenta, and hæmorrhage.[70] If, however, the cord be twisted exceedingly tight round the child's neck, and imbedded so deeply into the skin, as to render it impossible to push the coil over the shoulder, it may become necessary to divide it in order to let the child pass, in which case the practitioner must seize the divided ends as well as he can, and apply a ligature the instant the child is born. We believe that this is rarely, if ever, necessary; for in proportion as the child advances, so does the fundus descend, and thus relieves, in some measure, the tension to which the cord is exposed. This subject, however, belongs rather to the third species of dystocia, to which we must therefore refer.

Birth of the child and ligature of the cord. As soon as the child is born, we must place it in such a position as will enable it to breathe with ease. The sudden exposure to the[Pg 185] external air is generally sufficient to excite respiration; if not, a gentle pat on the nates, or blowing suddenly in the face, will usually succeed: if, however, the child still remains insensible, recourse must be had to those means which are recommended under the head of Asphyxia neonatorum. The cord should not be tied until it has ceased to beat, for unless the circulation be well established in its new course, the breathing is apt to stop, and the child relapse into insensibility: the cord should be tied about three inches distant from the umbilicus; it should be applied tightly, because otherwise it is apt to become loose, as the cord grows flaccid. In tying the ligature, one hand should be supported against the other to prevent giving the cord any jerk in case the ligature breaks; we are able also by this means to tie it more firmly.

The cord should be divided at some little distance from the ligature, so as to prevent all chance of its slipping off, and it should be done with a pair of blunt scissors, by which means the vessels of the cord are so bruised as to be rendered nearly impervious. There is no need to apply two ligatures; in fact it is better not, for, as Dr. Dewees justly observes, "the evacuation from the open extremity of the cord will yield two or three ounces of blood, which favours the contraction of the uterus and expulsion of the placenta." It has been recommended, in case of twins, to apply a second ligature, to prevent all chance of the second child bleeding through the cord of the first. There is, however, no connexion between the two placentæ, although they usually form what appears to be one mass. We only know of one case where the umbilical arteries of one cord anastomosed with those of the other, an anormality of very rare occurrence: still, however, it is better to apply a second ligature upon the cord, where we find that twins are present, as a precaution: and also to prevent it being said, in case the second child is still-born, that it had died from no ligature having been applied upon the placental extremity of the cord. It has been questioned whether it was really necessary to tie the cord before separating the child from the mother, from the well known fact that nothing of the sort is required in animals; and that, in cases of rapid labour, where the child has been unexpectedly dashed upon the floor and the cord broken, no hæmorrhage has resulted. This arises from the bruised and lacerated condition of the cord under these circumstances: animals not only bite the cord, but also draw it through their teeth several times, so as to contuse the vessels for a considerable extent; whereas, if it was merely divided with a sharp instrument, there is no doubt but that the new-born animal would quickly bleed to death.[71]

[Pg 186]Importance of ascertaining that the uterus is contracted. As soon as the child is separated from its mother and removed, or even sooner, if this process has gone on slowly, we ascertain if the uterus has contracted: this we shall know by its feeling like a large hard ball behind the symphysis pubis: if there be one rule more important than another, it is this, for without it we cannot be certain of the patient's safety for a single minute: so long as we feel the fundus to be hard, we know that the uterus is contracting, and that it will expel the placenta quickly, and ensure the patient against hæmorrhage; but if it be soft and relaxed, she cannot be considered safe even if their be no hæmorrhage; for the placenta may have been separated, and may be lying across the os uteri, or the os uteri itself may be contracted, or blocked up with coagula, so as to prevent the blood from escaping; it therefore collects in the cavity of the uterus in large quantities, to the imminent danger of the patient. Even where the uterus has contracted, the patient is not permanently safe, for it may again relax and grow soft, and hæmorrhage come on.

Management of the placenta. The placenta sometimes follows the child immediately, and occasionally is expelled by the same pain; usually, however, a few minutes intervene, during which time the uterus remains more or less in a state of inaction; it then begins to contract, and the dull and peculiar pains which characterize the separation of the placenta are now felt. The interval after the birth of the child varies considerably, and depends in many cases on the degree of rapidity with which the uterus has been emptied: hence in some cases we feel the fundus hard almost immediately, whereas, in others some considerable period elapses before it resumes its state of activity, a period which, if any separation of the placenta has already taken place, will be attended with the greatest danger. The occurrence of pains indicates fresh contractions, and therefore we should now examine to ascertain if the placenta has been detached. As a general rule it may be stated, that if we can reach the insertion of the cord with our finger we may presume that the placenta is ready to be expelled; if not, that it is still partially or wholly attached to the[Pg 187] uterus. So long as this latter is the case, the less we meddle with the cord the better, for by pulling at it we only excite the os uteri to contract, and thus seriously impede its removal.

Where some time has elapsed without any symptoms of contraction coming on, we may excite the uterus by circular friction of the abdomen, fanning the face, or by sprinkling a little water upon it, &c.: if, however, the uterus is hard and yet the placenta not within reach, we may pull slightly at the cord, pressing it at the same time back with the fore-finger into the hollow of the sacrum; we thus bring it down in the direction of the pelvic axis, and generally succeed in moving it into the vagina. No violent effort should be made, as this would probably tear it off from its insertion into the placenta, but, by keeping a gentle pressure upon it, the placenta will slowly pass through the os uteri, and then come away without farther difficulty. Following the axis of the vagina, we now guide it downwards and forwards; and when it approaches the os externum, it should be seized with the finger and thumb, and rotated several times: the membranes are thus twisted into a rope, and are less liable to be torn in separating from the uterus. The uterus being now completely emptied, contracts into a hard ball of about the size of a child's head. If, however (whether before or after the expulsion of the placenta) the uterus grows soft and swells, if the patient becomes pale and restless, and complains of faintness, sickness, load at the præcordia, darkness before the eyes, &c. we may be sure that hæmorrhage is going on. We refer to the chapter upon uterine hæmorrhage for the measures to be adopted.

Twins. Where there are twins, the above rules for ensuring the safe expulsion of the placenta require to be still more strictly observed: the uterus has been more distended, the mass of placenta is larger, and is attached to a much greater extent of surface than where there has been only one child: hence there is not only a greater liability to hæmorrhage, but if it does take place, will probably be much more dangerous. We cannot be too cautious how we extract the placentæ of twins: from the size of the mass, the uterus remains larger, and therefore less contracted: hence, if we venture to pull at the cord before being able to reach the placenta with our finger, we shall feel it yield; but this is not from the placentæ being detached and coming away, but from the fundus itself being pulled down with it—a state which would rapidly pass into inversion if the force were continued. In order to detach the mass more equally, we should twist the two cords together; by so doing there is less danger of their giving way. The same rotating movement should be used when the placentæ approach the os externum; the two bags of membranes are thus twisted together, and come away entire: if this be not attended to, the membranes are torn, portions of them are left adherent to the uterus, and come away some days afterwards in a half putrid[Pg 188] state producing a fetid discharge, and sometimes considerable fever.

Treatment after labour. As soon as the placenta is expelled, the soiled and wetted sheet should be removed and a warm napkin applied to the external parts: the patient should remain thus for half an hour or more, and enjoy a little rest, or even a short sleep: by this time the nurse will have washed and dressed the child, and be ready to attend to the mother. The external parts should be sponged with warm water, her linen changed, and a broad bandage pinned firmly round the abdomen to give it the necessary degree of support. Where there has been great abdominal distension and more than one child, it is sometimes advisable to apply the bandage immediately after the birth of the first, in order to assist the uterus in expelling the second, and in contracting afterwards. The bandage, therefore, should be gradually tightened as the abdomen diminishes in size: without this precaution the removal of so much pressure from the abdominal circulation will be sometimes attended with alarming faintings. A similar effect may be the patient incautiously sitting up in bed to take any refreshment which may be offered to her at this moment; she should be warned, more especially if she be a primipara, not to raise herself from the horizontal posture for a few hours after labour; at any rate, not until the bandage has been properly applied: from inattention to this point, cases have occurred where, on the patient's sitting up immediately after labour, she has fallen back in a faint from which she never recovered; in other cases it has been attended by profuse hæmorrhage, which has instantly proved fatal. "The influence of position," says Dr. Meigs, "in determining the momentum of blood in the vessels is well known to the Profession, but there are few cases where it is of more consequence to pay a profound regard to this influence than in the parturient woman. A uterus may be a good deal relaxed or atonic, and yet not bleed, if the woman lie still with the head low; whereas, upon sitting up suddenly, such is the rush of blood down the column of the aorta, the hypogastric and the uterine and spermatic arteries, that the resistance afforded by a feeble contraction is instantly overthrown, and volumes of blood escape with an almost unrestrained impetuosity: the vessels of the brain under such circumstances become rapidly drained, and the patient falls back in a state of syncope, which now and then proves immediately fatal." (Philadelphia Practice of Midwifery, by Charles D. Meigs, M. D. p. 192.) Even if all these directions have been strictly obeyed, if every thing has gone well, and the uterus is firmly contracted, we are not sure of its remaining so: after the lapse of many hours it may again relax, and flooding come on, its power of contraction being impaired either by the exhaustion of the previous labour, the warmth of the bed, &c. It will, therefore, be desirable to adopt such[Pg 189] measures, as will ensure the patient against this occurrence: in most cases it will be sufficient to keep the room moderately cool, and ensure a due degree of ventilation; but where the uterus has shown a disposition to relax, we know of nothing which guards the patient so effectually against hæmorrhage after labour, and enables us to leave her with so much confidence, as putting the child to her breast. The sympathetic connexion between the breast and the uterus is now well known; nor are there any means so certain of producing permanent uterine contraction as this natural act: it is a duty which nature instinctively prompts the mother to perform, not only for the preservation of her child, but for the safety of herself. We, therefore, make it a rule, whenever the patient intends to suckle her child (a duty which is performed more frequently now than it was a few years ago,) to have it put to the breast before quitting the house: the first excitement of the mother's feelings towards her offspring is a favourable moment for the performance of this act, the erectile tissue of the nipple becomes turgid, the child takes the breast with ease, and the effect upon the uterus is not less certain than complete; even if the child sucks fairly well for only five minutes we feel satisfied, for we cannot call to mind a single case of hæmorrhage after the effects of this operation.

Lactation. When the wet clothing has been removed, and fresh linen substituted, the patient should be left to enjoy perfect quiet both of body and mind, in order that she may have some sleep, for "the refreshment of sleep seems to be the most powerful natural means of inducing full contraction of the uterus."[72] After this, the child should be placed at her side, in order that it may enjoy the warmth of her body, and make another trial of taking the breast. That new-born animals are not able to maintain a sufficient degree of warmth, is seen by the care with which a bird shelters her young beneath her wings, and by the manner in which kittens, puppies, &c. crawl close to the mother's abdomen to enjoy that degree of heat which of themselves they are unable to produce. Dr. Edwards has shown that the animal heat of a new-born infant is several degrees below that of the adult: the mother's breast is, therefore, the natural place for it, where it can not only enjoy the necessary warmth, but take that nourishment which has been destined for its support at this early period. A child is capable of sucking the moment it is born; indeed, we would say, better at this moment than later, for the power of instinct in it is fully as great as in other animals; whereas, if not put to the breast soon after birth, but fed instead, it quickly loses it. A vigorous healthy child immediately seeks its mother's[Pg 190] breast, and if it does not find it, sucks at every thing which touches its mouth, even its own little hand or finger when presented to it: so strong is this instinct, that, on more than one occasion, we have known the child suck at the finger of the medical attendant when the head had only just cleared the os externum.

It has been, and even still is, a very general practice not to apply the child to the breast until the second or third day, upon the plea that there is no milk: a more erroneous and mischievous plan of treatment could not be devised, for it is a fruitful source of much injury as well of suffering both to the mother and her child. The child should be put to the breast, "whether there be signs of milk or not." (White, on Lying-in Women.) There is always more or less thin watery fluid called colostrum which is admirably adapted to form the first nourishment of the infant; it is slightly purgative, and, therefore, well fitted to unload the bowels of the viscid green mucus, called meconium, which fills them. The colostrum has been variously described by authors; some speak of it as a thin watery fluid, others as a thick creamy milk: this difference depends in great measure upon the interval between the birth of the child and its application to the breast: where this has taken place early, as we have just recommended, the colostrum has almost always the thin watery appearance above mentioned; whereas, if some period of time has been allowed to pass before the child is applied, the breast begins to secrete a fluid containing a larger proportion of caseous matter, or, in other words a more perfect milk, which not being drawn off, the watery part of it is absorbed, leaving the thicker portion to be removed by the process of sucking. Instead of giving the child this bland and natural fluid when in a state best fitted for its delicate digestive organs, it is but too frequently the practice to make it swallow some soft sugar, or a tea-spoonful of castor oil, and follow this up with a little gruel. The effects of such treatment upon a stomach which has never yet received food may be easily imagined; the digestive function becomes deranged, pain is excited, acid is secreted, gas is disengaged, flatulence, diarrhœa, &c. are the result, with all those manifestations of gastric irritation, such as strophulus, aphthæ, colic, &c. from which new-born children are made to suffer so severely.

Besides the above advantages in applying the child thus early to the breast, there are others of even greater importance which require to be mentioned. The breast is not yet distended; it is soft and conical, and therefore in a most favourable condition for being drawn; the child can seize the nipple and draw it out with ease, and by thus straightening the lactiferous tubes it commands a ready flow of their contents. By the gentle irritation of sucking, an earlier secretion of milk is excited, and being drawn off as fast as it is formed, the breast is never distended[Pg 191] by an accumulation of milk. On the other hand, where some time has elapsed before putting the child to the breast, it will have in great measure lost the instinctive desire to suck; the breasts have become distended and painful; instead of being soft and conical, they are now hard and flattened, the nipple is shortened, or even sunken in; and if the child does succeed in drawing it out, it is at the expense of severe suffering to the mother. The process of sucking in this state of the breast is very difficult; a considerable effort is required to elongate the nipple, and the thin delicate skin which covers it is abraded; excoriations and deep fissures round the base of it are produced, and each application of the child is one of absolute torture. In many cases, partly from having been fed, and partly from the difficulty it meets with, the child refuses the breast altogether; in others, the suffering is so severe as to oblige the mother to discontinue the attempt. The breasts now increase in size and hardness, producing great pain from their weight and tension; hard painful knots from the distended tubes and vessels are felt in different parts, and the pain and dragging extends to the axillæ, the glands of which are also swollen and painful.

Milk fever and abscess. By this time, or even earlier, the patient will in all probability have been attacked with a smart shivering fit followed by a hot and then a sweating stage, and accompanied with headach and febrile excitement of the circulation. This is the febris lactea, or milk fever, an affection which, at one time, was very generally supposed to be necessary for establishing the secretion of milk: experience, however, has shown that it chiefly results from neglect in not putting the child to the breast sufficiently early; the secreted milk has been in part absorbed into the system, fever has been induced, and the patient has been relieved by the natural crisis of a sweating stage. The febrile excitement will be considerably moderated, and the tension of the breasts relieved, by the action of saline laxatives: the shoulders which are usually kept warm for the purpose of promoting the secretion of milk, should now be clothed more lightly; the relief, however, is but too frequently partial, the breasts still remain large and painful; the process of suckling is just as difficult as before, and the indurated spots increase in hardness, sensibility, and extent; throbbing and darting pain is felt in the part, the skin over it becomes hot and red, and at length presents that shining glazy look which but too surely indicates the formation of matter beneath, a circumstance which is still farther proved by the œdematous feel of the part, or by the presence of actual fluctuation.[73]

[Pg 192]Where the breast is capable of being drawn, whether by the child or by artificial means, the application of a cold evaporating lotion, and the frequent exhibition of saline laxatives, will generally suffice to check the determination of blood to the breast, and diminish the secretion of milk; but where these means fail to reduce its size and hardness, it should be frequently rubbed with volatile liniment, and then enveloped in a hot linseed-meal poultice: this may be advantageously made with Goulard, and changed every two or three hours, keeping up a brisk action upon the bowels, as before-mentioned.[74]

If there be much febrile excitement of the circulation, bleeding may be sometimes required: we have rarely, however, found it necessary, having been almost always able to exert a sufficient effect by means of nitre with small doses of Vin. Antimonii and Sp. Æth. Nitr. Leeches seldom give more that temporary relief, and that only when applied in large quantities; in which case so much irritation and inflammation is their bites as not unfrequently to counteract the benefit arising from the loss of blood. The patient should preserve the horizontal posture, or at least have the breast well supported by a soft handkerchief, as otherwise its weight will produce much painful dragging. It is not always easy to detect the fluctuation, particularly when it is seated deep beneath the fascia, which invests the mammary gland; but wherever it is tolerably distinct, especially in the upper parts of the gland, the abscess should be let out early, otherwise it will burrow through a large extent of the breast, and destroy a considerable portion of the gland; whereas, if it be felt below the nipple, it may be allowed to approach nearer to the surface and point, by which means it will not be necessary to make the incision so large or so deep, a point which is worthy of attention, as otherwise considerable-sized milk tubes and even blood-vessels may be divided. Dr. Burns has mentioned a case of fatal hæmorrhage from this cause. In either case, whether the opening has been made artificially or spontaneously, the breast should be constantly enveloped in a hot poultice of linseed meal: if this be made with boiling water it forms a gelatinous mass, which retains its heat for a very considerable time, and not only acts as a fomentation, but gives great relief by softening the indurated portions and diminishing the tension. If the patient can bear it, the breast ought to be drawn by a glass for that purpose: this is much better than the[Pg 193] breast-pump, being simple and easy of application. Where little or no milk comes, it is useless to persevere, as we should only expose the patient to much unnecessary pain, and the breast to a good deal of irritation.

It rarely happens that the breast recovers so far as to enable the mother to nurse with it, and she will therefore be obliged to nourish the child entirely from the other, which generally bears the double duty without inconvenience: in some cases, however, there has been so much fever, and the process of inflammation and its consequences has been so long, that it is neither possible nor advisable to keep up or recall the secretions. In succeeding labours great attention must be paid to a breast which has been thus injured, and every disposition to distension and accumulation of milk carefully watched.

By the time a mammary abscess has been fairly opened, the strength of the patient is considerably lowered, not only from the quantity of discharge, but also from the nature of the previous symptoms and treatment; her food should now be more nutritious, she should take a little wine or porter; and if the appetite be delicate, two pills, consisting of equal parts of Extr. Gentianæ and Extr. Hyoscyami should be given night and morning; she will thus be enabled to sleep better, and the general irritability arising from her state of weakness will be relieved. If, however, the appetite fail entirely, and she has a pale flabby tongue, or if it is brown and dry in the centre; if the bowels are deranged, and she has a disposition to profuse perspiration, with much pain in the front or summit of the head, and other signs of debility, the Hydr. c. Cretâ and Dover's powder should be given at night followed by a rhubarb and manna draught the next morning, and if these have acted sufficiently, she may be put upon the use of quinine and sulphuric acid with Tinct. of Hyoscyamus two or three times during the day.

Excoriated nipples. When the nipples are merely excoriated, or there are fissures in them, they should be bathed with tepid Lotio Plumbi or a solution of Zinci Sulph. in rose water, which must be carefully washed off before applying the child to them. If they are too tender to permit being drawn by the child, they should be covered by the shield, to which is attached a cow's udder or some form of artificial nipple, through which the child can draw the milk without pain to the mother; the udder should be kept very clean, and there should be one or two spare ones soaking in water, in order that they may be changed from time to time. Excoriation of the nipples frequently arise from the extreme thinness of the skin which covers them, and from their unnatural softness. Whatever renders the nipples soft and tender, makes the operation of sucking difficult, because the child can draw them out too easily: we should rather be careful to have them firm, and less sensitive of irritation, just as they[Pg 194] would be if they had not always been covered by the dress from the earliest childhood, and thus rendered perfectly unfit to perform the office designed them by nature. The best means of attaining this end is to expose them frequently to the air during the latter months of pregnancy, and by dabbing them occasionally with cold water mixed with a little lavender water or eau de Cologne. (Boer.)[75]

It is important that the child should be suckled at regular intervals of about three hours during the day; and if this be done the last thing at night, and the first thing in the morning, there will be no need of giving it the breast during the night. With a little[Pg 195] perseverance on the part of the mother, the child soon learns not to require the breast at this time, which ensures her a good night, and spares her much trouble and annoyance. Those mothers who are obliged to suckle their children at all hours of the night to pacify their screaming, have brought the trouble upon their own heads, for if, instead of dosing the children with castor oil, and feeding them for the first day or two after birth, they had put them to the breast at once, the derangement of stomach and bowels which is the cause of this restless-ness would have been avoided.

Diet during lactation. Attention should be also paid to the diet of the mother, for upon this subject much erroneous opinion prevails. If she be strong and healthy, her food should be entirely farinaceous for the first three or four days, using gruel, tapioca, farinaceous powder, arrow root, &c. with a due admixture of milk; if there are no symptoms to forbid it, an egg may now be taken in the morning, and she may gradually proceed from chicken, &c. to the stronger meats, as her general condition and appetite point out. Where she is naturally delicate, or has been weakened by a sickly pregnancy, &c. it will be advisable to allow her chicken broth, and weak beef-tea from an earlier period.

"Serious mischief is frequently done by the mother attempting to remedy every temporary diminution of milk, by increasing the quantity of her food, or by imagining that some stimulating drink will answer this valuable end. Owing to some trifling disturbance in the system of a temporary kind, the secretion of milk may be for the moment suspend-ed or diminished. An attempt is made to recall it by an increase of food, by which a slight inconvenience is converted into a permanent derangement of the system, or a fever of even a dangerous character may be generated; or owing to a false theory, or imperfect observation, it has been supposed that certain liquors have a control over the secre-tion of milk, and hence the too free use of certain combinations, into which ardent or fermented spirits too largely enter. We must not, however, be supposed to deny the influence of certain solid as well as fluid substances upon the secretion of milk, for we well know, that unless the body be properly supported, there must soon be a diminution of milk. We only mean to insist that it is the nutritious, and not the stimulating part of the diet, which is subservient to the plentiful and healthful formation of this fluid. In proof of this we need only observe, that we have often been consulted upon the subject of the failure of milk, where an anxious mother herself, or a hireling nurse, was con-cerned, and had been informed by them that they had tried every thing with a hope of improving it, such as rich food, porter, ale, beer, &c. without success, or it was followed, perhaps, by a diminution of it. In such cases we have often succeeded in producing a plentiful supply of milk, by[Pg 196] adopting the opposite plan of treatment, for it must be borne in mind, as an important truth, that this failure proceeds more frequently from an over, than from an under, quantity of food or of drink. It is a fact well-known to all who have paid attention to the consequences of arterial excitement, that when it amounts to even moderate fever, the milk almost immediately diminishes in quantity; and also when this action is diminished by suitable remedies (provided it has not continued too long,) that the secretion of milk again becomes more abundant. Upon this principle we have frequently prescribed evacuants and abstinence to promote the secretion of milk." (Dewees, on Children.)

Where the mother does not intend to nurse her child, a different plan of treatment must be adopted: the shoulders should be lightly covered, cold evaporating lotions applied to the breasts, and the bowels freely opened by saline laxatives, her diet must be abstemious until the fulness of the breasts subsides, and she ought not to take much fluid: where there is a disposition to febrile action, an antimonial may be advantageously combined with the salines. In most instances the milk is thus checked without any inconvenience, but every now and then much illness and suffering is produced before this can be effected. Wherever, therefore, it is possible for the patient to suckle, the practitioner should urge the importance of it in the strongest terms.

"A very serious evil from a woman neglecting this imperious duty is the probability of her becoming more frequently pregnant than the constitution of most females can sustain without permanent injury. A woman who suckles her children has generally an interval of a year and a half or two years between each confinement; but she who without an adequate cause for the omission does not nurse, must expect to bear a child every twelve months, and must reconcile her mind to a shattered constitution and early old age." (Conquest's Outlines.)

Management of the lochia. The management of the lochia constitutes also an important part of the treatment of a natural labour, for the patient's health will be materially affected by any alteration either in its quantity or quality. The lochia usually continues to be a sanguineous discharge for about three days, becoming paler, thin, watery, and of a brownish hue, and gradually disappears: a free lochial discharge for the first forty-eight hours, at least, is one of the greatest safeguards against the different forms of puerperal fever and inflammation which are so justly dreaded by the practitioner, and nothing tends to ensure this desirable object so much as the early application of the child to the breast. It may seem paradoxical to assert, that what prevents hæmorrhage after labour should promote the lochial discharge: we do not attempt to explain why such is the case, but merely mention it as a fact repeatedly observed. As the lochia is secreted from the internal surface of the uterus, it will [Pg 197]continue to accumulate in this cavity and that of the vagina so long as the patient remains in the horizontal posture, the direction of the vagina preventing its spontaneous escape: it will, therefore, be desirable to favour its discharge by occasionally altering the position of the patient, and thus prevent its becoming offensive, which it would readily do from the temperature at which it is kept by the surrounding parts, from being in contact with the external air, and from its muco-sanguineous character. In the same way it frequently happens that small coagula of blood lodge in the uterus and rapidly grow putrid. In either case much irritation and fever are their presence in the passages, and serious symptoms would soon result if they were allowed to continue there. Hence we make it a rule, that whenever the patient requires to evacuate the bladder, she should do it by kneeling: by this means the position of the vagina is altered, and the accumulated discharges and coagula readily drain away and produce the greatest relief. Wherever the patient complains of abdominal pain, and the lochia has become scanty and somewhat offensive, it will be advisable to wash out the vagina with a warm water injection: for the farther treatment of these symptoms, we must refer the reader to the chapter on Puerperal Fever.

After-pains. When coagula have remained or formed in the uterus after labour, these irritate it by their presence, and excite it to contract: pains therefore of a crampy spasmodic character are produced, which have received the name of after-pains. Women who have already borne children are more liable to them than primiparæ. They vary considerably in degree: in some cases they are scarcely sufficient to excite attention; in others they rise to great intensity, and may even be mistaken for inflammation; indeed, they occasionally pass into this condition. During these pains the uterus is evidently in a state of contraction, for the fundus feels hard, and for the moment it is more or less painful to the touch: the patient has also pain in the back like a labour pain.

After-pains do not only arise from coagula in the cavity of the uterus irritating it to contraction, but also from little plugs of coagulated blood, which fill the sinuses opening upon the internal surface of the uterus. After awhile they excite contractions, by which they are squeezed out and come away in the discharges: this fact was first pointed out by Dr. Burton in 1751. Having to introduce his hand into the uterus for the purpose of removing a portion of the placenta, he felt several of these little oblong fibrinous masses exuding from the orifices of the uterine sinuses, whenever he at all stretched the uterus by opening his hand; these proved to be so many fibrinous casts of the above vessels, the blood having been retained and coagulated in them, when the uterus contracted after the birth of the child. When the uterus[Pg 198] has been slowly emptied during labour, it contracts gradually and uniformly, and forces the blood from its numerous sinuses into the rest of the circulation; but where its contents have been suddenly removed, the contraction is unequal, and a portion of the blood is retained, which coagulates as described. This fact affords an additional argument in favour of putting the child early to the breast: the active contraction of the uterus, which is thereby induced, effectually expels the coagula from its sinuses: hence we see that where a patient suckles shortly after labour, she seldom (cæteris paribus) has severe after-pains; but where this has been delayed until the second or third day, the first application of the child to the breast is sure to induce a sharp attack; the truth of the old adage, that "the child brings after-pains," is thus verified.

After-pains must be looked upon as an important agent in preventing those attacks of inflammation and fever which arise from the retention of putrid coagula and lochia: they ought not therefore to be checked, unless their severity is such as really demands it: hence the custom of giving an opiate after every labour cannot be too strongly reprobated, for by this means those uterine contractions are suspended, by which nature would have rid herself of the offending cause: nor do we consider ourselves justified in giving an opiate where after-pains are severe, until by change of posture, &c. we are satisfied that no accumulation exists in the passages. "Wherefore," says Burton, "we must not be too forward in giving strong opiates and other internal medicines, which may take them off while this grumous blood is lodged within these sinuses. I doubt not but those patients who die from the eighth to the fourteenth day, whose uterus has been inflamed with the symptoms above-mentioned, have been injured by the too free use of opiates." (Essay towards a complete new System of Midwifery, by J. Burton, M. D. p. 342.) We do not deny that a mild sedative is frequently of great benefit after labour: it calms the irritability of the system and procures sleep: these effects will be much better obtained by a little extract of hyoscyamus, lettuce, or hop. Where an opiate is really necessary, twenty minims of Liq. Opii Sed. in any aromatic water will be as good a form as any.[76]

CHAPTER III.

MECHANISM OF PARTURITION.

Cranial presentations—first and second positions.—Face presentations—first and second positions.—Nates presentations.

If we were asked to point out the basis on which the principles of practical midwifery should be founded, we would answer, on an accurate knowledge of the manner in which the child presents, and passes through the pelvis and soft parts during labour. In confirmation of this remark, we may observe, that almost every great improvement in midwifery practice which has taken place during the last century, has resulted from farther investigation into this difficult field of inquiry, and from the gradual addition of new facts to our knowledge respecting this interesting process.

Unless a practitioner be thoroughly acquainted with every step in the mechanism of a natural labour, how can he be expected to understand and detect with certainty any deviation from its usual course, still less make use of those means which may be required under the particular circumstances of the case; and yet, strange to say, there are few subjects which, generally speaking, have excited so little attention, and upon which such incorrect opinions have prevailed even up to the present time. The investigation is confessedly one of considerable difficulty, and as it was more easy to calculate how the head ought to pass in this or that position through the pelvis than to ascertain how it really did pass, ingenuity has been taxed, and theories have been invented, and positions of the child without number have been described, which have never existed in nature, and which have only added to the difficulty and perplexity of the subject.

We consider that to form an accurate diagnosis in these cases, requires the highest perfection of the tactus eruditus, which can only be acquired by long practice and patient observation: and it is chiefly from this circumstance that we can explain why such gross errors and vague notions should have existed about a process of every day occurrence, and why, with but few exceptions, they should have been transmitted from one author to another even up to the present time. In the last century, when it was so much the fashion to resolve every physiological process into a[Pg 200] mathematical problem, it was scarcely deemed necessary to spend much time in actual observation and examination; the proportions between the head and pelvis were ascertained, their angles were measured, and their curves determined, and from these data it was inferred, what must be the course which nature would follow; few attempted the slow but surer method of ascertaining by patient research the real facts connected with the process of parturition.

When the long axis of the child's body corresponds with that of the uterus, the child (provided the passages are normal) can be born in that position: it matters little, as far as the labour is concerned, which extremity of the child presents, so long as this is the case; but where the long axis of its body does not correspond with that of the uterus, the child must evidently lie more or less across, and will present with the arm or shoulder, a position in which it cannot be born. In stating this, we wish it to be understood, that we merely refer to the full grown living fœtus, and not to one which is premature, or which has been some time dead in the uterus, as these follow no rule whatever, hence the positions of the child at the commencement of labour resolve themselves into two divisions, viz. where the median line of the child's body is parallel with that of the uterus, and where it is not; the first we shall call natural, the second faulty, presentations of the child. A description of the natural presentations will form the contents of the present chapter.

The reader will almost anticipate us when we state, that the natural presentations consist of two classes, those where the cephalic, and those where the pelvic end of the child presents; in the first case, it will be a presentation of the cranium or of the face; in the second, of the nates, knees, or feet.[77]

Cranial presentations. The presentation of the cranium, (or vertex, as it has been improperly called,) is of by far the most frequent occurrence; thus, for instance, of 4042 children which were born in the lying-in hospital, at Heidelberg, 3834 presented with the head; of these the 3795 with the cranium, and 39 with the face: in either case, whether it be a presentation of the cranium or of the face, it will be either with the right or the left side more or less foremost; the former, from its greater frequency, has been called the first position of the cranium or face, the latter the second position.

First cranial position. It will be recollected we have stated, that the os uteri at the end of pregnancy is turned obliquely backwards, corresponding to the upper part of the hollow of the sacrum. If we examine during the first stage of labour, when it is just dilated sufficiently to allow the finger to pass, we shall feel the sagittal suture of the head running across it, dividing[Pg 201] it into two unequal portions, the os uteri itself corresponding nearly to the middle of this suture. If the os uteri be sufficiently dilated to let us trace its course, we shall find that it corresponds more or less to the direction of the right oblique diameter, viz. that it runs from the right and backwards, obliquely forwards, and to the left. If we follow it with our finger in this last-mentioned direction, we come to a spot where it divides into or meets two other sutures; these are the right and left lambdoidal sutures, and beyond them is the hard convex occiput, the point where they meet being the posterior or occipital fontanelle. If we trace our finger along the suture in the other direction, viz. backwards and to the right, we shall come to a four cornered space, where four sutures meet at right angles to each other; these are the sagittal, the frontal, and right and left coronal sutures; the open space itself is the great or anterior fontanelle.

That part of the head which lies lowest or deepest in the pelvis, and which the finger first touches upon when introduced along the vagina, is the right parietal protuberance; and if the os uteri be sufficiently dilated, we distinguish it by its hard and conical feel. In primiparæ, where the head usually is deep in the pelvis at the commencement of labour, and where the anterior and inferior segment of the uterus is closely stretched over it, the parietal protuberance may be felt through this part. Hence, then, the first position of the cranium, (or more correctly speaking, parietal bone,) is marked by the following characters: the sagittal suture crosses the os uteri, and runs parallel with the right oblique diameter of the pelvis: the vertex is therefore turned towards the upper part of the hollow of the sacrum, the posterior fontanelle forwards and to the left: the right perietal protuberance, therefore, is necessarily that part which is deepest in the pelvis; and the perpendicular diameter of the head, instead of corresponding to the axis of the pelvic brim, runs in an oblique direction upwards and forwards.

If the head at this early stage of labour be high up in the pelvis, viz. has scarcely entered the brim, as is frequently the case in multiparæ, the sagittal suture approaches in its direction to that of the transverse diameter, or to one between the transverse and oblique diameters, the posterior fontanelle corresponding to about the left acetabulum. The higher the head is in the pelvis, the nearer does its greater diameter correspond to the transverse one of the pelvis: the more oblique also is its perpendicular diameter, from which reason the right ear at this time can usually be felt without difficulty behind the pubic bones. Sometimes both fontanelles can be reached with equal ease; most frequently the posterior one is lowest, but occasionally the reverse is the case, and it is the anterior fontanelle, without, however, at all influencing the progress of the labour.

As the head advances through the brim and begins to enter[Pg 202] the cavity of the pelvis, the sagittal suture corresponds more closely with the right oblique diameter, so that now the posterior fontanelle is turned towards the left foramen ovale, and as it approaches the outlet of the pelvis, the occiput advances still more forwards, although the head entirely quits its oblique position. At this stage of the labour, the fontanelles can usually be again reached with equal facility, and we find the anterior one corresponding to the right sacro-iliac synchondrosis, the occiput is completely behind the left descending ramus of the pubes, the right lambdoidal suture running parallel with it. Owing to this slight change in the position of the head, the occiput having advanced somewhat forwards, we no longer feel the right parietal protuberance to be lowest and in the centre of the pelvis, but the finger now touches upon the posterior and superior quarter of the right parietal bone, for this is the part of the head which first comes under the pubic arch, and first enters the external passages.

If there be but little liquor amnii, or the membranes have been ruptured prematurely: if the head be firmly pressed against the os uteri, and we examine when it is not more than two-thirds dilated, we feel a puffy œdematous swelling upon that part of the head which corresponds to the os uteri. This will therefore be found to be situated upon the sagittal suture, nearly equidistant from the anterior and posterior fontanelles; it arises from the circulation in the scalp being obstructed by the pressure of the os uteri upon the head. If the remaining portion of the labour be rapidly completed, this will be the situation of the swelling with which the cranium is born; if, however, it follows a more gradual course, and the head passes slowly through the os uteri into the vagina, as it thus advances deeper into the pelvis, and alters its position more or less, the swelling upon the sagittal suture disappears in part, and forms on that portion of the head which is advancing under the pubic arch, and is now tightly encircled by the external passage: we shall, therefore, find that this second swelling is situated upon the posterior and superior quarter of the right parietal bone, and this is precisely the situation of the swelling of the head, which the child is usually born with.

From these facts we may deduce the following simple law respecting the mechanism of parturition, where the head presents: viz. that the head enters, passes through, and emerges from, the pelvis obliquely; and this is the case not only as to its transverse diameter, but also as to the axis of its brim; the side of the head being always lowest or deepest in the pelvis. This shows the beautiful mechanism of the process, for, on account of its oblique position, there is no moment during the whole labour at which the greatest breadth (still less length) of the head is occupying any of the pelvic diameters; even at the last, when the head is passing under the pubic arch, the complete obliquity[Pg 203] of its position, in order that it should take up the least possible room, is very remarkable; for the ring of soft parts, by which the head is now encircled, passes obliquely across it, running close behind the left, and before the right parietal protuberance. The head never advances with the occiput, forwards, under the pubic arch, as is stated in works on midwifery, still less with the sagittal suture parallel to the antero-posterior diameter of the pelvis; for the direction of the right lambdoidal suture, as also of the posterior fontanelle, and the position of the cranial swelling, or caput succedaneum, as it has been called, completely prove the inaccuracy of such a theory, the sagittal suture crosses the left labium at an acute angle, the right lambdoidal suture being parallel with the left descending ramus of the ischium.

Not less incorrect is the theory (for we can call it nothing else) of the head presenting with the vertex, and turning with its long diameter, from the oblique, into the antero-posterior or conjugate diameter, and the face into the hollow of the sacrum, for it is disproved by all the above-mentioned facts, which careful examination during labour puts us in possession of. When the head is born, the face looks backwards and to the right, viz. to the back part of the mother's right thigh, for the shoulders are by this time passing through the pelvis in its left oblique diameter, the right shoulder being forwards and to the right, and lowest in the pelvis: it is also that which is first expelled.

Such is the manner in which the head presents in the first or most common position: a slight modification of it is occasionally observed during the early stages of labour, without influencing the favourable character of its progress: the head at first is in the left oblique diameter of the pelvis, the occiput towards the left sacro-iliac synchondrosis, the anterior fontanelle towards the right acetabulum; but as the labour advances, the head turns, so that the occiput corresponds to the left acetabulum, the anterior fontanelle being turned towards the right sacro-iliac synchondrosis, the sagittal suture running parallel with the right oblique diameter of the pelvis. This peculiar commencement of the labour is probably not detected so frequently as it really occurs, owing to its changing into the common position at so early a period.

Second position of the cranium. The other or second position of the cranium is, where the left side of the head presents. It is, in fact, merely the reverse of the one just described: the sagittal suture crosses the os uteri at the beginning of labour, as in the former case, only now the posterior fontanelle is turned to the right instead of to the left; it is the left parietal protuberance which is deepest in the pelvis, and which the finger first touches upon. As the labour advances, and the head approaches the pelvic outlet, it is the posterior and superior quarter of the left parietal bone which first enters the vagina and protrudes through[Pg 204] the os externum, and upon which the swelling of the scalp or caput succedaneum is situated.

The chief peculiarity is, that the change, which we noticed in the first position as an occasional occurrence at the beginning of labour, is in this case the regular commencement of it. In the second cranial position, the head at the beginning of labour, with very few exceptions, is always with its long diameter parallel with the right oblique diameter of the pelvis, the posterior fontanelle turned towards the right sacro-iliac synchondrosis, the anterior one towards the left foramen ovale. During the early periods of labour, when the head is passing through the brim, both fontanelles may be reached; and, generally speaking, the posterior one with greater ease, from its being usually somewhat the lower; but as labour advances, and the head has fairly engaged in the pelvic cavity, they may both be reached with equal ease, the anterior fontanelle still corresponding to the left foramen ovale, or rather to the descending ramus of the left pubic bone. "As soon as the head experiences the resistance which the inferior part of the pelvic cavity opposes to it, or, in other words, the oblique surface which is formed by the lower end of the sacrum, the os coccygis, the ischiadic ligaments, &c. by which it is compelled to move from its position backwards in a direction forward, it turns by degrees with its greater diameter into the left oblique diameter of the pelvic cavity, viz. the posterior fontanelle is directed to the right foramen ovale, and as the head approaches nearer and nearer to the inferior aperture, it is the posterior and superior quarter of the left parietal bone which is felt in the cavity of the pelvis opposite to the pubic arch, so that when the point of the finger is introduced under and almost perpendicular to the symphysis pubis, it touches nearly the middle of the posterior and superior quarter of the left parietal bone: and this is precisely the part, as the head advances farther, which first distends the labia, with which the head first enters the external passages, and the spot upon which the swelling of the integuments forms itself." (Naegelé, Mechanism of Parturition, transl.)

The manner in which this change in the position of the head takes place, varies a good deal in different labours: in primiparæ it usually takes place slowly, and requires several pains before it is completed; as the pain comes on, the posterior fontanelle, which was backwards and to the right, now advances more forward and comes more within reach; the anterior fontanelle, which was towards the left foramen ovale, retreats, so that when the pain has reached its maximum the head will for a moment be felt in the transverse diameter of the pelvis, and again resumes its former position as the pain goes off: with the recurrence of each pain there is a repetition of this screw-like motion, but by degrees the head not only passes from the right oblique into the[Pg 205] transverse diameter, but from the transverse into the left oblique, so that at length the anterior fontanelle corresponds to the left sacro-iliac synchondrosis, and the posterior one to the right foramen ovale.

In women who have already had children, the whole change is frequently effected during one pain, so that the head, which but a few minutes previously was presenting in what is called the third position of the German schools, will now be found to be in the second.

It is to the celebrated Naegelé of Heidelberg that we are indebted for having first pointed out the uniform occurrence of this change in the second position. From his extensive and accurate observations, confirmed since by ourselves, as well as by many others, the head presents with the occiput originally forwards and to the right very rarely, but passes into this position during the course of labour. No one has ever described the mechanism of parturition so minutely and correctly; and the value of his investigations is the more enhanced, when we recollect what erroneous notions have prevailed upon this important subject up to the present time. "In the former part of my practice," says this distinguished obstetrician, "not knowing that the head made this turn, I always concluded that my examinations in the early part of labour were incorrect, and was very uneasy that I did not find it all exactly as the books described, and attributed my want of success in ascertaining the position to my own awkwardness. At length in a private case, in which I was much interested, I again felt what I thought was the anterior fontanelle towards the left foramen ovale; and circumstances occurring which rendered it necessary to apply the forceps and terminate the labour, I found that the head had been actually in the position which I imagined I had felt. Since this time I have, in many cases, sat by the bed-side during the whole labour, with my finger upon the head, and thus come at the truth." (MS. Lectures.)

The very circumstance of this change in the position of the occiput from the sacro-iliac synchondrosis to the foramen ovale of the same side, is of itself quite sufficient to mislead; nor is it to be wondered at that it should have been so long unnoticed, when we recollect how difficult the examination is at this early stage of labour, and how few give themselves the trouble to attain that degree of dexterity and tact, which, even under the most favourable circumstances, is required for this species of investigation.

The diagnosis of the sutures and fontanelles may be rendered more difficult by other circumstances: when there is a large quantity of liquor amnii between the head and membranes, it renders the diagnosis exceedingly obscure in the early part of labour. In some cases the cranial bones are remarkably thin and yielding, and communicate a sensation to the finger as if it were touching a fontanelle; in others, the sutures run an irregular course, and[Pg 206] form ossa triquetra, &c. which may easily mislead. We may also notice the changes, already mentioned, which are the death of the child, and the various congenital anormalities of hydrocephalus, acephalus, &c. &c. In some cases the sagittal suture is continued backwards through the occipital bone, dividing it into two equal portions, and thus making the posterior fontanelle four cornered, and not to be distinguished from the anterior. Nor is it always easy to distinguish the posterior from the anterior fontanelle under more normal and favourable circumstances; for it would be hazardous to conclude that it is the posterior fontanelle merely because we feel three sutures meeting together, as it may possibly be the anterior one, and we are not able to reach the sagittal suture beyond. In this case we may ascertain which it is by the following rule: if it be the posterior fontanelle in the first position we shall feel a suture running more or less forwards (the right lambdoidal,) but none backwards; but if it be the anterior fontanelle forwards and to the left, we shall also feel a suture (the right coronal) running backwards. Lastly, in the second cranial position the face when born turns to the posterior surface of the mother's left thigh.

Such are the two positions in which the head presents during labour, and such is the manner in which it passes through the pelvis and external passages. Slight deviations do occasionally take place, the chief of which is, that the head in the second position does not always make the quarter of a turn as above described, but comes out with the anterior fontanelle forwards and to the left: this is by no means of common occurrence, and, as far as we have observed, increases the difficulty of labour very little.

Face presentations. The face, like the cranium, may present in two ways, either with its right or left side forwards. The former is the most frequent occurrence, and bears a striking analogy to the first cranial position; indeed, we cannot too strongly impress upon the minds of our readers the advantages of accurately knowing the different features of the two cranial positions just described; for by this means the positions of the face will be rendered much more simple and easy of comprehension. Whether the right or the left side of the face presents (first or second facial position,) the root of the nose crosses the os uteri exactly in the same manner as the sagittal suture does in the two cranial positions; the chin is turned to the right acetabulum, and as the face descends through the pelvis during the progress of the labour, the chin moves somewhat more forwards, as the occiput does in the cranial positions.

At an early stage of labour the right eye and zygoma is that part of the face which is lowest in the pelvis, and which the finger first touches upon during examination, precisely as it was the right parietal protuberance in the first cranial position; and as in this case the caput succedaneum was situated upon the[Pg 207] posterior and superior quarter of the right parietal bone, so here the livid bruise-like swelling, which the face brings with it into the world, is situated upon the right cheek, this part being the first which presses through the os externum; the chin passes under the right branch of the pubic arch, as the occiput in the first cranial position does under the left, the face during the whole process preserving a strictly oblique position, both as to the transverse diameter and axis of the pelvis.[78]

Second position of the face. The second position of the face is merely the reverse of the first: it is now the left side which is turned forwards, the left eye and zygomatic process being those parts which are lowest in the pelvis; the chin is turned to the left side and somewhat forward, and advances towards the left foramen ovale during the farther progress of the labour. As the face approaches the inferior aperture of the pelvis, it is the left cheek which first enters the os externum, and upon which the swelling is situated: likewise the chin passes beneath the left branch of the pubic arch.

It has been supposed by some authors, and we think correctly that the majority (if not all) of face presentations are originally cranial presentations: if this be the case, we can easily understand why the right side of the face presents more frequently than the left, for if the head in the first cranial position moves round upon its transverse diameter, and thus allows the face to turn downwards, we shall immediately have a first position of the face. We are the more inclined to adopt this opinion, not only from the greater number of cases where the right side of the face presents, but also from our having more than once met with cases where so long as the head of the child was moveable above the brim, the presentation was midway between one of the cranium, and of the face. On one side of the pelvis we could feel the anterior fontanelle; on the other we could, with some difficulty, reach the orbital process of the frontal bone: as the pains increased, and the head advanced lower, the side of the face came more within reach; so that by the time it had fairly entered the cavity of the pelvis, it had become a complete presentation of the face.[79]

We distinguish the face by the bridge of the nose, which from its crossing the os uteri may be detected at a very early period of labour: it is far better than the eye, for not only is this liable to mislead us in our examination, but it may also receive injury from the finger. Nor is the malar bone a guide, for this might easily be mistaken for the tuberosity of the ischium, or even for the shoulder. The nose not only tells us that the face is presenting[Pg 208] but also in which position, for at one end we shall feel the soft cushiony extremity of it, at the other we shall reach the broad hard expanse of the forehead.

It was not until nearly the end of the last century that presentations of the face ceased to be accounted unnatural, and impossible to be terminated by natural means. Although the fact had been pointed out by Portal so early as 1685, that these presentations were very little removed from the usual one, it seems to have excited but little attention until the time of Deleurye in 1770. "I have," says Portal, "delivered several women whose children came with the face foremost, and always without any great difficulty, it being only observed, that in such cases no violence must be used, but nature be left to its own course; which done, there is no danger either of mother or child." (Portal's Midwifery, transl. obs. 66:) La Motte in 1721, although so accurate an observer, could not divest himself of the general opinion that these were unfavourable positions, even although the face was usually expelled by the natural efforts, after he had fruitlessly endeavoured to rectify it, and although he himself confesses never to have "seen any that had not done well."

Giffard has recorded two cases of face presentation (Cases in Midwifery, 1734, p. 59, 443.,) both of which he delivered by his extractor, which was one of the early forms of midwifery forceps; and in both, although the labour had lasted some time, the child was alive. He describes the position of the face in the second case, the chin being turned towards the right side. The only practical observation which he makes is, that turning is very difficult where the "waters are gone off, and the uterus closely envelopes the child." This is probably given as an explanation for his deviating from the usual practice of turning in these cases. Deleurye in supporting Portal's views observes, "one daily sees similar labours terminate naturally: it is true they are somewhat longer, but they terminate without the aid of art." (Traité des Accouchemens, 1770, § 736.)

Lastly, the celebrated Boer of Vienna (1793) placed the matter in a still more decided point of view when he asserted, that "face presentations being merely a rare form of natural labour, should be left to be completed by the natural efforts, since neither the mothers nor their children were exposed to any more danger in this form of labour than they were in the most usual forms of all." Having charge of the great lying-in hospital of Vienna, Boer had ample means of ascertaining the most accurate results on all points of practical midwifery, and his observations on labours where the face presented, are, therefore, peculiarly interesting, and tend strongly to contradict the prevailing opinion respecting the difficulty and danger of these presentations.

"Of eighty cases of face presentations which have occurred during a period of some years, and which I have myself observed[Pg 209] and noted down, there were three, or at the most four, where the children were born dead. None of the patients suffered in the slightest degree from any of these labours; and, except one case, all were left entirely to nature: in one case only, on account of the weakness of the pains and doubtful character of the symptoms, I deemed it necessary to terminate the labour by the forceps." (Boer's Natürliche Geburtshülfe, erstes buch, p. 137.) In spite of this valuable practical fact, supported by experience on so great a scale, the opinion that face presentations were preternatural, continued to prevail upon the Continent, being supported by the authority of Baudelocque and Osiander. A similarly unfavourable opinion was entertained by Dr. Smellie in this country, although Dr. W. Hunter, in his lectures delivered prior to the publication of his plates on the gravid uterus (and, therefore, at an early date,) states, "in this case I do not turn the head round in order to deliver, but nineteen times in twenty leave it to itself to come as it will." (W. Hunter, MS. Lectures.)

Dr. R. W. Johnson, who dedicated his New System of Midwifery, &c. to Dr. W. Hunter and others, in 1769, and probably attended his lectures, expresses a similar opinion, and says, that in these cases "nature herself will do the work." (p. 267.) Dr. Alexander Hamilton, in 1784, also speaks favourably of these presentations. "The head will, however, in most cases, advance in that position by the force of the natural pains, though the delivery will be more slow or painful." (Outlines of the Theory and Practice of Midwifery.)

Farther experience has shown that, so long as the pelvis is of the natural size, the head can be born in this position without peculiar difficulty, the soft parts usually require a little more dilatation than where the cranium presents, and, therefore, this stage of the labour is generally somewhat slower. Although presentations of the face are not so favourable for the child as those of the cranium, they stand next to them in point of safety. Where the cranium presents, a slight misproportion between the head and pelvis produces little or no increase of difficulty to the passage of the child; but under similar circumstances, where the face presents, the difficulty may become very serious, for if the labour is prolonged, "the brain and vessels of the neck," observes Smellie, "will be so much compressed and obstructed as to destroy the child." (Explanation to table 25.) A similar view has been given by Dr. Denman, and still more recently by Professor Chaussier, of Paris, and Professor Naegelé; the two latter authorities examined the brain in several still-born children where the face had presented, and invariably found the cerebral vessels gorged with blood.

The presenting side of the face when born is frightfully distorted by the livid swelling above-mentioned; the mouth is pulled to one side and upwards; the angle of the eye is drawn [Pg 210]downwards, and the corresponding ala of the nose scarcely discernible amid the purple mass of tumefaction: the less this is meddled with the better, for in the course of a day or two the parts will have returned to their condition; whereas, if friction or hot poultices, &c., be used, ulceration may be the result, and produce considerable disfigurement.[80]

Nates presentations. "After the presentations of the cranium those of the nates are the most frequent in point of occurrence, and also the most natural," says the celebrated Boer, in the work already quoted. Under the term nates presentations, we include those of the knees and feet, as these latter presentations can only be looked upon as modifications of the former. Professor Naegelé, jun., in his new edition of the admirable essay upon the mechanism of labour, published by his father, in Meckel's Archiv. für die Physiologie, has very properly brought these different positions under one head, viz. "positions of the pelvic extremity of the child:" as, however, we possess no word in English to express this, we shall attain the same object by considering knee and footling births as mere modifications of breech presentations.

"As regards the relative situation of the limbs to the body of the child, the position is the same as in the two genera of head presentations above described, viz. the knees are usually drawn up to the abdomen, the feet close to the nates, so that not unfrequently they may both be felt together at the beginning of labour, and afterwards descend into the pelvis and are born together. Sometimes the feet (or perhaps only one foot) are felt higher above the brim than the nates; in which case, as the nates descend they rise, and are turned upon the abdomen and breast of the child, and descend with these parts as labour advances. Frequently it is the reverse: the feet are somewhat lower than the nates; they are felt in the os uteri at the beginning of labour, and descend before them as labour advances. It is rare that the knees come down before the nates during the farther progress of labour, and it is not probable that they are ever found alone in the os uteri at the commencement of it." (H. F. Naegelé, Mechanismus der Geburt, 1838, p. 57.)

The nates may present in two ways, either with the back of the child forwards, or with its abdomen forwards: of these the former occurs most frequently; thus of 161 cases which were accurately ascertained at the lying-in hospital of Heidelburg, 121 were observed with the back of the child forwards, and 40 with it backwards: in either of these positions the transverse[Pg 211] diameter of the child's pelvis always corresponds to one or other of the oblique diameters.

"Labours with the nates or feet presenting, follow certain laws quite as much as those where the head presents, only that one more frequently sees deviations from them, both with respect to the manner in which the child presents at the time of labour, and its passage through the pelvis; but where, under a proper state of the other requisites for healthy parturition, no prejudicial result occurs." (Naegelé, on the Mechanism of Parturition, transl. § 19. p. 128.) "In every case, whether the nates have at first a completely transverse or oblique direction, they will be always found, on pressing lower into the superior aperture of the pelvis, to have taken an oblique position; and that ischium, which is directed anteriorly, to stand lowest. They pass through the entrance cavity and outlet of the pelvis in this position, which is oblique, both as to its transverse diameter as well as to its axis."

Thus, if in the first species the left ischium were either originally directed more or less forward, (which is usually the case,) or had taken this direction in passing through the superior aperture, the nates descend in this direction into the pelvic cavity, with the left ischium during the whole time standing lowest; and this is the part, during the farther progress of the nates, which first passes between the labia as the os externum dilates. As they advance, and while the left ischium, which is directed forwards and always somewhat to the right, comes completely under the pubic arch and presses against it, the other ischium, which is situated in the opposite direction, and which has to make a much greater circuit, passes forwards over the strongly distended perineum, so that, when the pelvis is born, the abdomen of the child will be directed to the inner and posterior surface of the mother's right thigh.

"The rest of the trunk follows in this position, and as the breast approaches the inferior aperture of the pelvis, the shoulders press through its superior aperture in the direction of the left oblique diameter; and during its passage (viz. the breast) through the pelvic outlet, the arms and elbows which were pressed against it are born at the some moment. But whilst the shoulders are descending in the above-mentioned oblique position, the head, which during the whole progress of the labour rests with its chin upon the breast, presses into the superior aperture in the direction of the right oblique diameter, (viz. with the forehead corresponding to the right sacro-iliac synchondrosis,) and then into the cavity of the pelvis in the same direction, or one more approaching the conjugate diameter. After this, it presses through the external passage and the labia, in such a manner, that whilst the occiput rests against the os pubis, the point of the chin, [Pg 212]followed by the rest of the face, sweeps over the perineum as the head turns on its lateral axis from below upwards.

"But it is sometimes the right ischium, which, in this chief division, is either originally turned forwards, or in the process of time assumes this direction. In this case the child passes through the pelvis in the same manner as before, only with the difference, that the surface of the body takes of course a different position with respect to the pelvic parietes, viz. its anterior surface, which in the former case corresponded to the right side of the pelvis, will be directed to the left, and the head will press through the superior aperture of the pelvis, in the direction of the left oblique diameter (the forehead passing before the left sacro-iliac synchondrosis.)"

"As in positions of the cranium, the swelling of the integuments is chiefly met with on that parietal bone which during the passage of the head, is situated lowest, and on that spot with which it enters the external passage, so in this case the livid coloured swelling appears on that part which, directed forwards, was situated lowest during the passage of the nates, and with which the nates were born.

"In the second chief position, viz. with the anterior surface of the child corresponding to the anterior abdominal parietes of the mother, it is chiefly the left ischium which is either originally situated forwards, or takes this direction as the nates sink through the superior aperture of the pelvis, which latter preserve this oblique direction during the farther progress of the labour, both whilst pressing into the pelvic cavity, and when entering the external passages.

"If the ischia be already born, the anterior surface of the child turns itself to the right and backwards, either immediately, or as the rest of the trunk advances; but the manner in which the head in this case presses through the entrance cavity and outlet of the pelvis, is the same as has already been described." (Naegelé, op. cit. p. 128, 130.)

It appears to be a law in nates presentations, that whatever may be the direction of the child (first or second position) at the beginning of labour, it will always, if not interfered with, be found with its anterior surface turned towards one or other of the sacro-iliac synchondroses, when the thorax or the shoulders are beginning to pass through the outlet of the pelvis. When the nates have once passed the os externum, the position of the child frequently varies a good deal, the abdomen turning first to one side and then to the other. This is especially the case in the second position, where it is more or less forwards; nevertheless, as labour advances, it will almost invariably turn obliquely backwards, and be born in this position. Dr. Collins is, as far as we know, the only English author who has distinctly noticed this[Pg 213] fact. "It is very desirable," he observes, "the child should be delivered in this position (viz. the back of the child towards the mother's abdomen,) as it renders the getting away of the head much less difficult; yet where there has been no interference by the attendant in the previous part of the labour, he will rarely find it necessary to alter subsequently the child's position, the breech naturally making the turn above alluded to in its passage." (Practical Treatise on Midwifery, by Robert Collins, M. D. p. 41.)

It sometimes, although rarely, happens in these presentations, that the head does not rest with the chin upon the breast, but the occiput is pressed against the nape of the neck, as in presentations of the face. The passage of the trunk through the pelvis follows, as above-mentioned, as far as the head: this enters the brim with the occiput in advance, and vertex towards one or other ilium. As it advances through the brim into the cavity of the pelvis, it gradually turns more and more backwards, so that when the body is born, the vertex is turned towards the hollow of the sacrum, and the under surface of the lower jaw behind the symphysis pubis.

The diagnosis of nates presentations is not difficult. The pointed and more or less moveable coccyx, bounded at its broader end by the hard uneven sacrum, and in the contrary direction by the anus, will scarcely admit of a mistake. The tuberosities of the ischia may easily be mistaken, for the malar bone of a face presentation, or even a shoulder, can scarcely be distinguished from them, and the external organs of generation become too much swollen and pressed together to give any certain diagnosis; nor indeed can they be examined in this state without considerable risk of injury. The direction of the sacrum, like that of the forehead in face cases, points out the exact position of the child.

Presentations of the nates, although perfectly natural as far as labour is concerned, are far more dangerous for the child than those of the face, for when the head enters the pelvis, if every thing be not favourable for its passing rapidly through it, the cord is so long compressed that the child is almost certainly lost.

The natural position of the fœtus in utero is admirably adapted for its safe passage through the pelvis under these circumstances, and is what we ought to maintain, as far as possible, during labour. The legs are turned upon the abdomen, the arms are crossed upon the breast, the chin rests upon it, the head being bent forwards, so that the whole forms an oval mass. So long as the child advances gradually, the fundus presses firmly upon the head, and keeps the chin close upon the breast; the head therefore enters the pelvis in the most favourable position possible, and the uterus, not having been suddenly emptied of a part[Pg 214] of its contents, continues to act briskly, and presses the head so rapidly through the pelvis, that the child is born without having suffered from any serious pressure upon the cord. As however the body of the child diminishes from its pelvis up to the axillæ, it is very apt to be rapidly expelled as soon as the nates have passed the os externum; and if not, it is but too frequently assisted, as it is called, at the very moment when it ought rather to be supported and prevented from advancing too suddenly. When this is the case, the fundus ceases to press upon the head, the chin quits the breast, and as a space is thus left between them, the arms slip into it, and then turn upwards, so that the head not only enters the pelvis in a most unfavourable position, but, to make matters still worse, it has an arm on each side of it: at this critical moment the uterus, from having been suddenly emptied, ceases to contract, and the head remains so long in the pelvis that the child has no chance of escaping with its life.

Where the child has descended gradually, and the arms have advanced with the breast into the pelvis, if the cord be considerably upon the stretch, a portion should be pulled gently down in order to relax it, and we should endeavour as far as possible to guide that part of it which is within reach towards one of the sacro-iliac synchondroses, being less liable there to suffer from pressure. One or two fingers should be introduced to bring down the arms, which are

108

now coming into the lower part of the hollow of the sacrum: they should be hooked down by the bend of the arm, in order to prevent the humeri from sticking across the passage. When this has been effected, the shoulders follow as the head descends through the pelvis. The body of the child should now be wrapped in warm flannel, and two fingers passed up towards the face: the lower jaw must not be trusted to in bringing the head through the pelvic outlet and os externum, for it may easily be broken: the fingers should be applied one on each side the nose, and the chin depressed as much upon the breast as possible, by which means the head will come in a much more favourable direction, and pass readily.

In no case is so much mischief done by impatient interference as in presentations of the lower end of the child. This is still more so in footling cases, for here the soft parts are not so well dilated as in nates presentations, where the child comes double: hence the fact, that presentations of the feet are easier to the mother but more dangerous to the child. In either case, the passage of the head through the pelvis must ever be attended with considerable hazard, for if it be delayed beyond a short time, the child's death is certain. "The more gradually the nates and body of the child are expelled, the quicker will its head pass through the pelvis, and the better will be its chance of being born alive." (Obstet. Memorand. 2d ed.) Hence, therefore, if the pains are slow at this moment, it will be desirable to[Pg 215] rouse them with a dose of ergot; and if the child gives a convulsive twitch, the forceps ought instantly to be applied. The result of Professor Busch's practice in the lying-in hospital at Berlin shows, that by the timely use of the forceps a large majority of children may be saved. For the same purpose, the nurse should be instructed to have a warm bath in readiness, with some spirit, &c. for resuscitating the child the moment it is born.

The numbers which we subjoin are taken from the cases in the Dublin Lying-in-Hospital, under the late Dr. Joseph Clark and Dr. Collins, from the private practice quoted in Dr. Merriman's Synopsis, and from the General Lying-in-Hospital.

Of 71,578 labours, the nates presented once in every 78 cases, and the feet once in every 108½. Of the nates cases the child was born dead in the proportion of 1 to 3·8, and in the footling births 1 to 2·8.

[Pg 216]

PART IV.

MIDWIFERY OPERATIONS.

CHAPTER I.

THE FORCEPS.

Description of the straight and curved forceps.—Mode of action.—Indications.—Rules for applying the forceps.—History of the forceps.

Before describing the various species of dystocia, or faulty labour, it will be necessary to consider the different means with which the increasing experience of years has furnished us, of giving artificial assistance in such cases. These may be brought under two heads, first, where delivery can be effected with safety to the mother and her child; secondly, where this can only be effected at the expense of the infant's life. Under the first head come the forceps, turning, the Cæsarean operation, and artificial premature labour; under the second are craniotomy or perforation, and embryotomy.

Of these the forceps is by far the simplest and safest means of artificial delivery, and is therefore an operation which should always be had recourse to in preference to any of the others wherever it is possible.

The forceps is the simplest imitation of nature, for in fact it is nothing more than a pair of artificial hands introduced one on each side the head. It is impossible to define any precise limits of pelvic contraction, within which the forceps can, or beyond which it cannot, be safely applied, for the difference in the size and hardness of the child's head, and in the condition of the soft parts, will greatly modify the degree of resistance to the progress of the labour: hence the attempt to fix the exact degree of contraction beyond which the forceps becomes inapplicable is quite[Pg 217] impracticable, as in some cases we might be led to make a trial of it where it would be quite improper, and in others have recourse to the perforator where a cautious application of the forceps would have been attended with success. For the farther consideration of this subject we must refer to the chapter on Dystocia Pelvica.

The forceps consists of three parts—the blades, the lock, and the handles.

The blades of the present forceps are not solid, but are merely elongated bows of polished metal, by which they are not only rendered much lighter, but allow the most prominent parts of the head to project between them, and thereby take up no additional room when introduced into the pelvis. In the simplest form, viz. the straight forceps, the blades have only one curvature for adapting them to the convexity of the head. The degree of curve varies a good deal in different instruments: the greater the curve the more firmly will the blades hold, because they act more or less as blunt hooks, and do not require much pressure upon the head for the purpose, but on the other hand, they are more difficult to introduce; whereas, blades which are slightly curved can be applied with greater ease, but require much more pressure upon the head in order to hold fast.

It has been a general rule with almost every modification of forceps, that the greatest distance between their blades should not be less than two inches and a half, for as this is the breadth of the basis cranii in the fœtal head, it would be impossible to compress the head beyond this extent. The form of the head curvature will determine the situation of the point where the blades are most distant from each other: in some forceps it is about one-third the length of the blades from their extremities; in some it is nearly equidistant; whereas, in others it is nearer to the lock; the medium between these extremes is the best. The extremities of the blades ought to be at least half an inch apart: in this country they are usually somewhat more; on the Continent they are much less, being rarely more than one or two lines asunder. The fenestræ, or open spaces in the blades, should be wide and ample, for not only are the projecting parts of the head allowed to protrude between them, but the pressure of the blades is diffused over a larger extent of surface: this is remarkably seen in the forceps of the late Dr. Hopkins and that of Professor Davis, both of which are extensively used. It is also important that the edge at the extremities of the blades should be well rounded and not too thin; it is thus less liable to catch against corrugations either of the vagina or fœtal scalp. The greatest breadth of the fenestræ is generally towards the extremities of the blades; in some, their edges are parallel; whereas, in those of Drs. Orme and Lowder the greatest breadth is near the lock: upon the whole, an[Pg 218] oval shaped fenestra is the best, for it can be easily introduced, and has the advantages of a wide blade.

In 1751 and the following year another curve was given to the blades of the forceps by the celebrated M. Levret of Paris, and by the equally distinguished Dr. Smellie of London, by which the instrument was adapted to the curve formed by the axes of the brim, cavity, and outlet of the pelvis, and by which the head could be seized much higher in the pelvis than by the straight forceps. Each have an equal claim to the merit of having invented this "pelvic curvature," as it has been called: the priority of the invention is perhaps due to Levret; but as he made a secret of it for some years, it is impossible to ascertain the precise fact. The pelvic curve, as it is called,[81] is especially adapted to the long forceps, which thus becomes an instrument of very considerable power. Numerous modifications of these curved forceps have since been made, but they are merely varieties of the original ones invented by Smellie and Levret, which have become the national instruments of their respective countries.

Perhaps the greatest improvements in the blades of modern times is seen in the forceps of Dr. Hopkins, above alluded to: the head curvature forms an elongated oval, admirably adapted to the form of the fœtal head when considerably compressed during a difficult labour; and from the great breadth of the fenestræ, the pressure of the blades is applied over a large extent of surface; the pelvic curve is but slight, being greater on the posterior edge of fenestræ than on the anterior; the blades themselves are thin, their inner surface flat to ensure a firmer hold, their outer surface slightly rounded in order to be introduced with greater ease; and for a similar reason the edges of their extremities are somewhat thicker and carefully rounded in a peculiar manner.

Naegelé's forceps.
The lock of the modern English forceps consists of two deep grooves, into which the shank of each blade mutually fits, so that the two blades are fixed upon each other merely by the pressure exerted upon the handles. In former times the blades were united together by a pivot, which could screw and unscrew at pleasure. This was abandoned by Chapman, who published the first work in English on operative midwifery.[82] He found that the forceps held

better without the pivot than with it; and from what we have brought forward elsewhere (Med. Gaz. Jan. 8, 1831,) there can be little doubt that he invented the lock which is now generally used in this country. Chapman's forceps was adopted in France prior to this improvement in its lock, especially by Gregoire, and has retained the original pivot lock which now forms one of the most distinguishing marks between the French and English forceps.[Pg 219] Although the pivot forms by far the firmest lock, for the blades can never slip from each other, still the difficulty in locking, and also in separating, the blades at a moment's notice, render it much inferior to the English lock. An ingenious modification was invented by the late Professor Von Siebold of Berlin, but the most perfect lock is that of Professor Brüninghausen of Würzburg, first introduced by ourselves into this country, and commonly known among the instrument-makers under the name of Professor Naegelé's forceps. The shank of one blade has a semicircular indentation, which at the moment of locking fits into a fixed pivot in the other: this, therefore, combines the advantages of the French and English locks. We can safely affirm, from extensive experience for many years, that there is even less difficulty in locking it than with the English lock: the blades are capable of instant separation, and yet when locked, the firmness of their union is equal to that of a pivot joint.

The handles of the English forceps are pieces of wood or ivory fixed upon each shank below the lock, flat upon the inside, convex externally and furnished with a depression or groove at the lower end for fixing a ligature round them. These handles were probably first introduced by Dr. Smellie, who seems to have borrowed the idea from the forceps of M. Mesnard, for the earlier English forceps, viz. of Giffard and Chapman, terminated in blunt hooks, those of the former being curved inwards, those of the latter outwards, a form of handle which has been retained in the French forceps up to the present time.

There are two pieces of forceps, the long and the short forceps; the former for cases where the head is still high in the pelvis, the latter when it is at the pelvic outlet and approaching the os externum; the former with few exceptions being curved, the latter straight.[83]

The forceps act in three ways, 1. by mere pulling; 2. as a species of double lever, by moving the handles from side to side;[Pg 220] and 3. by compressing the head, thus still farther disposing it to elongate and adapt itself to the passage through which it has to be expelled.

The blades should always, if possible, be applied one on each side of the head, the position of which must be determined by the direction of the fontanelles and sutures, not by feeling for the ear, as is usually recommended in this country. The ear can seldom be reached without causing a good deal of pain, even under the most favourable circumstances; in cases, therefore, where the head is so impacted as to be incapable of advancing by the natural powers, it cannot surely be justifiable to force up the finger between the head and the pelvis to ascertain this point, the more so, as the soft parts soon become swollen and more or less inflamed, and, therefore, little able to bear such rude treatment. No operation requires such an intimate acquaintance with the mechanism of parturition as that for applying the forceps: it is simple and generally perfectly easy when the precise position of the head and its relations to the pelvis are accurately known; on the other hand, it is not less injurious and painful to the patient than difficult and unsatisfactory to the practitioner.

The most usual circumstances under which the forceps is applied, are where the head is already deep in the pelvis and approaching the os externum; in such cases it is generally required not so much for the purpose of overcoming an unusual degree of resistance, as for assisting the natural powers, which are becoming exhausted: the head is near the os externum, and therefore easily reached; and from there being little or no impaction present, the blades are applied without difficulty.

The application of the forceps when the head is at the upper part of the pelvis, and where the greater portion of it has not yet passed the brim, is rarely practised in this country, because as the necessity for performing the operation at this stage arises in most instances from contraction of the brim, the perforator has usually been preferred, wherever the expelling powers have proved incapable of overcoming the resistance to the passage of the head. The circumstance also of this condition requiring the long forceps has been another source of objection, from the much greater power which this instrument is capable of exerting, and from its being therefore more liable than the short forceps to prove mischievous in the hands of the inexperienced.

Cases however do occur where there is but a very slight want of proportion between the head and pelvis, where the obstacle is easily overcome, and where, but for the application of the forceps, the labour would either have been protracted to a dangerous degree, or have required the use of the perforator.[84] "On the whole," says Dr. Burns, "I would give it as my opinion that a well instructed practitioner, who has already had some [Pg 221]experience in the use of the short forceps, is warranted to make a cautious, steady, but gentle attempt to apply and act with the long forceps in a case where he is not quite decided that the perforator is indispensable, and where the head is higher than admits the application of the short forceps." (Principles of Midwifery, 9th ed. p. 493.)

In applying the forceps, whether short or long, there are two conditions which, cæteris paribus, are requisite in every case; first, that the os uteri shall be fully dilated; secondly, that the pains are within the bounds of what are commonly known as moderate pains. In the first case it will be very difficult and frequently quite impossible to pass the blades between the head and os uteri when only partly dilated; it will be difficult to avoid injuring its edge more or less, and if we do succeed in applying and locking the forceps, on making an extractive effort we shall find that the uterus descends with the head as we draw it down.

In the second place we ought never to apply the forceps whilst the pains are violent, for not only do they render its application difficult and even dangerous, but we are adding still farther to the force (already too great) with which the head is pressed against the pelvis. Where the head remains immoveable under violent exertions of the uterus, it is not a case for the forceps but for the perforator; nor does it admit of much delay, for it endangers much injury of the soft parts or even rupture of the uterus.

It is exceedingly difficult to assign any precise limits of pelvic contraction, within which the forceps can, and beyond which they cannot be applied, for the size and hardness of the fœtal head, the nature of the pains, and the condition of the patient must also be taken into account in every instance; hence, we frequently meet with cases where the pelvis is scarcely if at all contracted, and yet where the labour has been terminated with the greatest difficulty by means of the forceps; whereas, in others where we know the pelvis to be more or less deformed, the child has been delivered by the natural powers. This subject will be still farther considered under Dystocia Pelvica.

The general indications for the use of the forceps are two: 1. They are indicated in all labours which are difficult or impossible to complete, either from deficiency in the expelling powers, or from misproportion between the head and pelvis, or from the arm coming down with the head. 2. They are indicated by circumstances or accidental causes, which render labour dangerous for the mother or child, and where the danger can only be removed by hastening labour, as in cases of hæmorrhage, convulsions, syncope, alarming debility, faulty condition of the organs of respiration, danger of suffocation, obstinate vomiting, unusually severe pains in nervous irritable habits, hemorrhoids[Pg 222] which have burst, hernia, retention of urine, determination of blood to the head, prolapsus of the cord, (in certain cases,) inflammation of the uterus, &c. (Naegelé, MS. Lectures.)

We have already stated that an intimate acquaintance with the mechanism of parturition is of the greatest importance in applying the forceps. Knowing that the head always presents in one of the two oblique diameters of the pelvis, and that the blades are applied on each side of the head, it follows that the forceps must always be applied in the contrary oblique diameter of the pelvis to that in which the head is. Before speaking of the operation itself, we must first consider what position of the patient will be the most convenient. In this country no alteration is made in her position, beyond bringing her close to the side of the bed, with the nates projecting as much as possible over the edge, for the greater convenience of the operator; unless this be attended to, it will be difficult to depress the handle of the upper blade sufficiently when introducing it. Upon the continent, and also in America, where the long forceps is more generally used, the patient is usually delivered on her back; she is placed in a half-sitting posture upon the edge of the bed, her back supported by pillows, &c., her feet resting on two chairs, between which the operator stands or sits, and applies the forceps in this position. This, in many respects, is the most convenient posture for him, but the very preparation which it requires cannot but be alarming to the patient, who is obliged to be a witness of all his manipulations; whereas, when she lies upon her left side, she is aware of little or no preparation being made, and if any slight exposure happens to be necessary, viz. at the moment of locking, it can be done without her knowledge.[85]

The simplest case for applying the forceps is, where the head has already descended nearly to the os externum, and has begun to press upon the perineum: it is for this that the straight forceps is chiefly intended; and as this is the instrument which is generally used, we shall describe its application first.

Mode of applying the forceps. Having ascertained that the rectum and bladder are empty, examined the position of the head, and warmed and greased the blades, we proceed to introduce the upper or lower blade first, according as its lock is directed forwards: this precaution is for the purpose of preventing the locks being turned away from each other when brought together after the introduction of the second blade. The [Pg 223]trochanter major will guide us as to the precise position of the patient's pelvis, and is especially useful in pointing out the direction of the left oblique diameter, in which the forceps (on account of the first position of the head being in the right oblique diameter) should be most frequently applied: in this case, we pass the upper blade, as it were, beneath the trochanter, and the lower one in the opposite direction.[86]

Let us suppose that the head is in the first position, with its sagittal suture parallel with the right oblique diameter of the pelvis, and that in accordance with the above rule, the upper blade is to be introduced first. Having passed one or two fingers up to the head, we guide the blade along them, depressing the handle so as to make the extremity of the blade lie closely upon the head, neither allowing the point alone to impinge upon the head, nor vice versâ, to protrude against the vagina. The extremity of the blade, therefore, must be our guide for the direction in which we hold the handle: we must carefully insinuate this by a gentle vibratory motion between the head and passage which surrounds it: the convexity of the head will show the course which it has to take, nor is there any need of passing the finger farther; for when once the extremity of the blade is fairly engaged between the head and passage, it will almost guide itself, and needs little more than to be pushed on gently, the handle gradually rising according to the curve of the blade. The shank or handle should, therefore, be held lightly like a pen, by which means the operator will possess much more feeling with his instrument, than if he grasped it with his whole hand. As the blade advances, he should keep his eye on the general form of the pelvis, the curve of the loins, the situation of the trochanter and symphysis pubis, and thus gain a more accurate idea of the course which the instrument must take. This will, in great measure, depend upon the situation of the head: if it be quite down upon the perineum, the blade should be pointed towards the promontory of the sacrum, and the handle turned downwards and forwards; if it be still in the cavity of the pelvis, and only beginning to engage in the outlet, the blade must be directed upwards towards the centre of the brim, and the handle turned directly downwards. Having passed the blade to its full extent, we must press the handle backwards against the perineum, to allow sufficient room for the introduction of the second blade, and give it to an assistant or the nurse, with the caution to hold it steadily and firmly, especially during the pains, when it is apt to slip into the hollow of the sacrum if held carelessly.

[Pg 224]As we have passed the upper blade behind the right acetabulum or foramen ovale, so now we must introduce the other in the opposite direction, viz. before the left sacro-iliac synchondrosis: and, as the blades being exactly opposite to each other is essential to the easy locking of the instrument, it will be necessary to guide the course of the second blade, not so much by the form of the pelvis, as by the direction of the first blade. It must, therefore, pass up, so that when introduced to its full extent, the inner surface of its handle shall correspond precisely to that of the first blade. The easy or difficult locking of the blades is a proof of their having been correctly or incorrectly introduced. If, therefore, on bringing the locks together we find that they do not correspond, that the inner surfaces of the handles are not parallel, but form an angle with each other, we must endeavour to rectify this, by withdrawing, to a short extent, that blade which deviates most from the proper direction, and pass it up again more correctly. All attempts to twist the handles so as to correspond with each other, are bad and cannot fail to put the patient to much suffering.

When we are about to lock the blades, we cannot be too careful in preventing the soft parts from being pinched between them, for it causes most intolerable pain, and frequently makes the patient give such an involuntary start, as to run the risk of altering the position of the instrument.

The whole process of introducing and fixing the forceps should be conducted in as gentle and gradual a manner as possible: no attempt should be made to proceed with the operation during a pain; and in no case is force either necessary or justifiable.

Every thing being now prepared for the extraction, we must endeavour to make this resemble as far as possible the natural expulsion. When a pain, therefore, comes on, we should grasp the handle firmly, and pull gently, at the same time giving them a rotatory motion. The direction of the handles, as before said, will depend upon the situation of the head in the pelvis: if it be at the outlet, it will point downwards and forwards; if in the cavity, nearly directly downwards. If the head makes but little or no advance with one or two efforts, it will be advisable to tie the handles firmly together, and thus keep up a continued pressure upon it, and dispose it the more to elongate and adapt itself to the passages. As it advances and begins to press upon the perineum, we must be more than ever cautious not to hurry the expulsion, and give the soft parts time to dilate sufficiently. At this period it is desirable to make the extractive effort not so much forwards as the direction of the handles would seem to indicate: we thus avoid pressing too severely upon the urethra and neck of the bladder, which might otherwise suffer, and assist the dilatation of the perineum. When the head is on the point of passing the os externum, all farther extractive efforts should cease; the [Pg 225]perineum must be supported in the usual manner, and the head should be expelled if possible by the patient herself.[87]

113

In applying the curved forceps we must bear in mind another rule in addition to the one above-mentioned for selecting the first blade, viz. the pelvic curvature must correspond with that of the sacrum. As with the straight, so also with the curved forceps, the extremity of the blade will be our best guide as to the direction in which we should hold the handle at the moment of introduction; it must be directed more or less forwards in proportion to the degree of the pelvic curvature of the blade. If, for instance, it be the upper blade which is to be introduced first, we pass it obliquely over the lower thigh or nates of the mother, making it glide closely round the convexity of the head, between it and the pelvis, without impinging either on the one or the other. As the position of the head is still more distinctly oblique at this earlier period of its progress through the pelvis, so will the blades require a more oblique direction, and also (as in the former case) they must be introduced in the contrary oblique diameter to that in which the head is.

As the blade passes up between the head and pelvis, so does the handle gradually make a sweep backwards, until at length it approaches to the edge of the perineum. During the process of introduction, one or two fingers should press against the posterior edge of the blade to guide it up to the brim of the pelvis, and prevent its slipping too far backwards towards the hollow of the sacrum.

The second blade will be guided in its direction by that of the first: it must be introduced so that the inner surface of its handle corresponds exactly with that of the first. The locking must be performed under the same precautions as with the straight forceps: the more so, as in some cases it has to take place just within the os externum, and therefore requires the most careful attention to prevent the soft parts from being caught and pinched between the blades when they are brought together. In extracting the head we must bear in mind the part of the pelvis in which it is impacted, and make our effort in the direction of its axis; we must also recollect the curved form of the instrument, and that we must not pull in the direction in which the handles point, but rather hold them firmly with one hand, and, by pressing against the middle of the forceps with the other, guide the head downwards and backwards into the cavity of the pelvis. We shall thus make our extractive effort in the direction of the upper portion of the blades, or that part which has the chief hold upon the head: hence, therefore, as it descends, the handles are directed[Pg 226] more and more forwards, so that when it has reached the perineum, the handles will not only point forwards, but considerably upwards. Whilst extracting we should, as with the straight forceps, slowly move the handles from side to side, and even make them describe a circle: we thus not only use the forceps as a simple extracting instrument, but make it act as a lever in every direction, and greatly facilitate the advance of the head, even under circumstances of considerable impaction. It is in these cases where keeping up a continued pressure upon the head by tying the handles tightly together, and tightening it after every successive effort, has such excellent effects in diminishing the degree with which it is wedged against the pelvis and soft parts, and in disposing it by gradual elongation to assume a form which is better adapted for advancing through the passages.

The slow and gradual pressure of the forceps thus exerted upon the head of a living fœtus will have a very different result to that of the experiments by Baudelocque and others, in attempting to compress the head of a dead fœtus by the application of a sudden and powerful force. Even if we were capable of effecting no greater diminution of its lateral diameter than a quarter, or at the most, three-eighths of an inch, as stated by Dr. Burns, we should, in most cases of impacted head, where the forceps is justifiable, find it quite sufficient to remove the obstructing causes.

The forceps is also occasionally required in presentations of the face and nates. In the first case we must pass up the blades on each side of the face, and along the side of the head, having previously ascertained to which side of the pelvis the chin is turned. In nates cases, the blades should also be passed up along the sides of the child's pelvis, and here the advantages of a broad fenestra will be very evident, for otherwise our hold will not be firm enough without exerting an improper degree of pressure.

Cases every now and then occur, where from convulsions, &c., it is desirable to apply the forceps whilst the patient is lying upon her back, as is practised upon the continent. "The patient is placed across the bed, propped up in a half-sitting posture, by pillows, &c., her pelvis resting upon the edge, her feet on two chairs, the knees supported by assistants. Two, and generally three fingers are passed, if possible, up to the os uteri, on the side where the blade is to be introduced: the index finger, is held a little behind the middle finger, so that this last, by projecting somewhat, forms a species of ledge upon which the blade slides, and which acts as a fulcrum to it. The handle is held at first nearly perpendicular; but as the blade advances, it gradually approaches the horizontal direction, being guided by the pelvic curve of the instrument. The middle finger, along the ulnar surface of which the convex edge of the blade slides, prevents its extremity from passing too far backwards, and directs it in the axis of the pelvis. When introduced to the full[Pg 227] extent, the handle is inclined obliquely downwards, and is now grasped by an assistant passing his hand below the patient's thigh. The other blade is introduced in the same way on the opposite side of the pelvis; and the locking, extraction, &c., conducted much in the same manner as in England." (British and Foreign Med. Rev. vol. iii. April 1837, p. 419.)

History of the forceps. We have already mentioned some historical points connected with the improvements of the present French and English forceps; it will now be unnecessary to enter more fully into the history of this instrument. The earliest trace of the midwifery forceps which we possess is under the form of a secret in the hands of an English family, named Chamberlen. As to when and by whom it was first invented, this must probably remain for ever unknown; and at any rate there is no more reason to suppose that Dr. Hugh Chamberlen was the inventor than his father or brothers were. He was compelled to quit England on account of being involved in the political troubles of the time, and went to Paris in the beginning of the year 1770, and evidently had then been some time in possession of the secret. He returned to London, in August of the same year, having in vain attempted to sell it to the French government, after having entirely failed in a case of difficult labour which he had asserted he could deliver in a few minutes, although Mauriceau had stated that the Cæsarean operation would be required. Dr. H. Chamberlen published in 1772, a translation of Mauriceau's work, which had appeared four years previously, and in his preface he publicly alludes to this secret, and says, "My father, brothers, and myself (though none else in Europe, as I know) have, by God's blessing and our industry, attained to, and long practised a way to deliver women in this case without any prejudice to them or their infants: though all others (being obliged, for want of such an expedient, to use the common way) do or must endanger, if not destroy, one or both, with hooks." He thus apologizes for not having divulged this secret: "there being my father and two brothers living, that practice this art, I cannot esteem it my own to dispose of, nor publish it without injury to them."

Whether a work, entitled Midwife's Practice, by Hugh Chamberlen, 1665, was by the translator of Mauriceau's work, or by his father, must now remain a matter of doubt: it was, however, in all probability by the latter, from what the translator says in his preface, viz. "I designed a small manual to that purpose, but meeting some time after in France, with this treatise of Mauriceau, I changed my resolution into that of translating him." On account of his being attached to the party of James II. he was again obliged to quit England, in 1688, and crossed over to Amsterdam, where he settled, and in five years after succeeded in selling his secret to three Dutch practitioners, viz. Roger [Pg 228]Roonhuysen, Cornelius Bökelman, and Frederick Ruysch, the celebrated anatomist. In their hands, and in those of their successors, it remained a profound secret until 1753, when it was purchased by two Dutch physicians, Jacob de Visscher and Hugo van de Poll, for the purpose of making it generally known. It turned out to be a flat bar of iron, somewhat curved at each end: this lever was stated to have been received from Roonhuysen, one of the original purchasers of the Chamberlen secret; but there is no reason to suppose that any such instrument had been communicated by Chamberlen either to him or the others, as we have distinct evidence that both Ruysch and Bökelman possessed forceps, the blades of which united at their lower end by means of a hinge and pin. It is known also that Roonhuysen used a double instrument consisting of two blades. The above-mentioned flat bar of iron, commonly called Roonhuysen's lever, was, without doubt, invented after his time, by Plaatman, who received the Chamberlen secret from him. (Edin. Med. and Surg. Journal, Oct., 1833.)

Chamberlen's Forceps.
Not many years ago a collection of obstetric instruments were found at Woodham, Mortimer Hall, near Mildon, in Essex, which formerly belonged to Dr. Peter Chamberlen, who, having purchased this estate "some time previous to 1683," was, in all probability, one of the brothers alluded to by Dr. Hugh Chamberlen, in his preface to the translation of Mauriceau's work. This collection, (now in the possession of the Medico-Chirurgical Society, of London,) contains several forceps, two of which appear to have been used in actual practice: these differ from each other only in size, and present a great improvement upon the instrument possessed by Hugh Chamberlen, at Amsterdam. The blades are fenestrated and remarkably well formed: the locks are the same as of a common pair of scissors, except that in one case the pivot is riveted into one lock, which passes through a hole in the other when the blades are brought together. In the smaller forceps there is merely a hole in each lock through which a cord is passed, and then wound round the shanks of the blades to fasten them together, an improvement in which Dr. Peter Chamberlen had evidently anticipated Chapman, in making the first approach to the present English lock.

The earliest professors of the forceps, besides the Chamberlens, were Drinkwater, who commenced practice at Brentford, in 1668, and died in 1728; Giffard, who has given cases where he used his extractor as early as 1726; and Chapman, who [Pg 229]possessed a similar instrument about the same time. These forceps correspond very nearly with the above-mentioned ones of Dr. Peter Chamberlen; and as it is well known that from those of Giffard and Chapman, the forceps of the present day are descended, we cannot consider ourselves so much indebted to Dr.

Hugh Chamberlen for these instruments, to which his bear so distant a resemblance, as to his relations, who, from living together in England, had doubtless assisted each other by their mutual inventions, and thus brought the instrument to that state of improvement in which it was found as above-mentioned.

For more detailed information respecting the history of the forceps we may refer our readers to Mulder's Historia Forcipum, &c., particularly, the German translation by Schlegel, to a similar work brought down to the present time, by Professor Edward von Siebold, to our own lectures on this subject, published in the London Med. and Surg. Journal, for March 28, 1835, vol. vii., and to the two papers already alluded to in the London Med. Gazette, Jan. 8, 1831, and Edinburgh Med. and Surg. Journal, October, 1833. [Also, Researches on Operative Midwifery, &c. By Fleetwood Churchill, M. D., essay iv. on the Forceps. Dublin, 1841.—Ed.]

[Pg 230]

CHAPTER II.

TURNING.

Turning.—Indications.—Circumstances most favourable for this operation.—Rules for finding the feet.—Extraction with the feet foremost.—Turning with the nates foremost.—Turning with the head foremost.—History of turning.

Turning is that operation in midwifery where the feet, which had not presented at the time of labour, are artificially brought down into the os uteri and vagina, and in this manner the child delivered. (Naegelé, MS. Lectures.)

Besides turning with the feet foremost as now described it has also been proposed, as being safer for the child, to bring down the nates or the head, but these operations, especially the former, have scarcely ever been practised, and in most cases are impracticable.

Turning, in the strict sense of the word, is that operation, by which, without danger to the mother or her child, the position of the latter is changed, either for the purpose of rendering the labour more favourable, or for adapting the position of the child for delivering it artificially.

The delivery of the child with the feet foremost, by means of the hand alone, may be looked upon as a second stage of the operation; where, however, the turning has been undertaken on account of malposition of the child, it has been very properly recommended by Deleurye, (Traité des Accouchemens, 1770,) Boer, (Naturliche Geburtshülfe, 1810,) Wigand, (Geburt des Menschen, 1820,) and other high authorities in midwifery, that as the position is now converted into a natural one, (viz. of the feet,) it should be left as much as possible to the natural expelling powers; hence, therefore, under these circumstances, artificial extraction of the child with the feet foremost can scarcely be said to exist, the operation itself being confined to changing the position of the child.

Where, however, the circumstances of the case require that labour should be hastened in order to avert the impending danger, the extraction of the child with the feet foremost, by means of the hand alone, becomes a distinct operation.

[Pg 231]The artificially changing the child's position into a presentation of the feet is indicated in cases where, on account of malposition of the child, the labour cannot be completed, or at least without great difficulty.

Indications. The artificially delivering the child with the hand alone, or the extraction of it with the feet foremost (which of course presumes that it has presented with the feet, either originally or has been brought into that position by interference of art,) is indicated in all cases where the labour requires to be artificially terminated either on account of insufficiency of the expelling powers, or from the occurrence of dangerous symptoms. Under this head, on the part of the mother, are violent floodings, especially under certain circumstances, convulsions with total loss of consciousness, great debility, faintings, danger of suffocation from difficulty of breathing, violent and irrepressible vomiting, rupture of the uterus, death of the patient, &c.;—on the part of the child, prolapsus of the cord under certain circumstances. (Naegelé, Lehrbuch der Geburtshülfe, §§ 394, 395. 3d edit.) Hence, therefore, the general indications of turning are the same as those of the forceps, it being indicated in all those cases where nature is unable to expel the fœtus, or which demand a hasty delivery of the child, but which cannot be attained by the application of the forceps.

Turning is an operation which is far inferior to that of the forceps, both as regards the safety of the mother and her child, and also the ease with which it is performed. Whenever the circumstances under which it is undertaken are unfavourable, it not only becomes a very difficult operation, but also one of considerable danger: for the child especially is this the case, as the very circumstance of its being born with the feet foremost shows that it is necessarily exposed to the same dangers as those already mentioned in nates presentations, in addition to those of the first part of the operation, viz. the changing its position.

The most favourable moment for undertaking the operation of turning is when the os uteri is fully dilated and the membranes are still unruptured. In this state, the vagina and os uteri are most capable of admitting the hand, and the uterus, from being filled with liquor amnii, is prevented contracting upon the child, the position of which is changed with great ease and safety; but when the os uteri is only partially dilated, its edge thin and rigid, the membranes ruptured, and the liquor amnii drained off for some hours, it becomes a matter of great difficulty and danger either to introduce the hand into the uterus under such circumstances, or to attempt changing the child's position: the os uteri tightly encircles the presenting part, and the uterus contracts upon the child itself so as to render it nearly, if not altogether immoveable.

The os uteri ought always if possible to be fully dilated: this however is not so essential as with the forceps, for when once it[Pg 232] has reached the size of a crown piece, it mostly yields easily to the introduction of the hand. Where turning is indicated in malposition of the child we may safely await its full dilatation so long as the membranes remain unruptured. Where the membranes have been ruptured some hours and the os uteri hard, thin, and rigid, it will be impossible to turn until, either spontaneously or by proper treatment, it becomes soft, cushiony, and dilatable.

In cases which require turning as a means of hastening labour, as for instance in flooding from placenta prævia and other causes, the hæmorrhage is seldom so severe as to demand it without at the same time rendering the os uteri so relaxed as to present little or no obstruction to the hand. Where convulsions indicate turning, the bleeding and other depleting measures, which are necessary to control them, will have a similar effect in preparing the os uteri for this purpose.

In ordinary cases of turning there will be no need to change the patient's position, as it will be just as easy to perform it as she lies upon her left side, merely bringing her pelvis nearer to the side of the bed in order to reach her with greater facility. Where, however, from the position of the child or from the state of the uterus, the introduction of the hand and searching for the feet will probably be attended with considerable difficulty, it may be advisable to place her across the bed, sitting upon its edge, her back supported by pillows, her feet resting on two chairs, in the same way as it is used by the Continental practitioners for applying the forceps; or if it be really a case of very unusual difficulty, it will be better to put her upon her knees and elbows, for in this position we gain the upper and anterior parts of the uterus with greater ease.

In choosing which is the best hand for performing the operation, the practitioner must not only be guided by the position of the child, but also by the hand with which he possesses most strength and dexterity: many always use the left hand for turning when the patient lies upon her left side; for our own part we have always used the right, and have never failed except in one or two cases of great difficulty, where we judged it more prudent to put the patient on her knees and elbows than risk any injury by using too much force. In introducing the hand into the vagina as the patient lies on her left side, the right is moreover preferable, as we can pass it more completely in the axis of the vagina, than we can the left.[88]

The directions which are usually given to introduce one hand or the other according to the child's position, are not practical,[Pg 233] because cases occur where it is impossible to ascertain this point without passing the hand into the uterus, as in placenta prævia, and occasionally in shoulder presentations; and it would be by no means justifiable to make the patient undergo the suffering from a repetition of this operation, merely because the position of the child is such as is stated in books to require the left hand instead of the right.

Having evacuated the bladder and rectum, and greased the fore-arm and back of the hand, we should gently insinuate the four fingers, one after the other, into the os externum: the whole hand must be contracted into the form of a cone; the thumb will pass up easily along the palm; the passage of the knuckles is the most difficult, for as the os externum is the narrowest part of the vagina, and the hand is widest across the knuckles, it follows that this is the point of the greatest resistance and suffering, and that, when once this is overcome, our hand will advance with greater ease both to ourselves and to our patient. This part of the operation can scarcely be conducted too gradually or gently, for if we give the soft parts sufficient time to yield, it is scarcely credible what an extent of dilatation may be effected by a comparatively moderate degree of pain; the os externum is also the most sensitive part of the vagina, and serious nervous affections may even be provoked by the intolerable agony arising from a rude and hasty attempt to force the hand through it. We must not advance the hand merely by pushing it onwards, but endeavour to insinuate it by a writhing movement, alternately straightening and gently bending the knuckles, so as to make the vagina gradually ride over this projecting part as the hand advances.

In passing the os uteri the same precautions must be observed, particularly when the os uteri is not fully dilated; at the same time we must fix the uterus itself with the other hand, and rather press the fundus downwards against the hand which is now advancing through the os uteri. In every case of turning we should bear in mind the necessity of duly supporting the uterus with the other hand; for we thus not only enable the hand to pass the os uteri with greater ease, but we prevent in great measure the liability there must be to laceration of the vagina from the uterus, in all cases where the turning is at all difficult. "In those cases (says Professor Naegelé) where artificial dilatation of the os uteri is required to let the hand pass, it should be done in the following manner:—during an interval of the pains, we introduce, according to the degree of dilatation, first two, then three, and lastly four fingers; and by gently turning them and gradually expanding them we endeavour to dilate it sufficiently to let the hand pass. This must only be done under circumstances of absolute necessity and always with the greatest caution—in fact, only in those cases where the danger consequent upon artificial dilatation of the os uteri is evidently less than that, to avert, which we are compelled to turn before it is[Pg 234] sufficiently yielding or dilated." (Lehrbuch der Geburtshülfe, p. 212. 3tte ausgabe.) This observation from so high an authority evidently applies to those cases where the os uteri is not only soft and yielding, but also nearly dilated; the forcible dilatation of the os uteri is justly deprecated by Madame la Chapelle: "I never attempt to produce this forced dilatation, not even in cases of hæmorrhage. But we may frequent-ly promote the dilatation of the passages in a remarkable manner by moistening and relaxing them and diminishing their state of excitement, viz. by the steams of hot water, tepid injections, and more particularly by warm baths and bleeding." (p. 49.) Her diagnosis of the condition in which the os uteri will yield to the introduction of the hand is well worthy of attention. "If the inactive uterus be unable to expel the child, or to make the head clear its orifice although considerably dilated, if, in this state of affairs, the membranes give way, we can feel the os uteri retract, from being no longer pressed upon. How different is this state of passive contraction to the rigidity of an orifice which has not yet been dilated: in this case, although the os uteri is contracted and even thick, it is soft, supple, and easily dilat-able; there is no feeling of tightness or resistance; it is little else than a membranous sac, and the head has not descended sufficiently to press upon it; or if the head does not present, it is some part of the child, as for instance the shoulder, which is unable to advance and act upon the os uteri: in this case operate without fear—in the other wait." (Pratique des Accouchemens, p. 86.)

If the membranes be not yet ruptured we should use the greatest caution to preserve them uninjured: the hand must be gently insinuated between them and the uterus, and should be passed either until the feet are felt, or at least, until it has gained the upper half of the uterus. Now, and not till now, ought they to be ruptured. As this is done at the side of the uterus little or no liquor amnii escapes, for the torn membranes are pressed closely against the uterine parietes, and the vagina is completely closed by the presence of the arm in it acting as a plug; the uterus is unable to contract upon the child on account of the fluid which surrounds it, and the hand, therefore, passes up with great facility. The uterus is not diminished by the loss of its liquor amnii; its contractile power is, therefore, not increased. When the hand has broken the membranes it can move about in perfect freedom: if the feet have not as yet been reached they will now be easily found, and the position of the child will be changed without difficulty.

The importance of passing in the hand without rupturing the membranes was first shown by Peu in 1694.[89] But it excited[Pg 235] little or no notice at the time, not even by La Motte, who paid so much attention to improving the operation of turning. Dr. Smellie appears to have been the first after Peu who recommended this mode of practice, although he makes no mention of his name. "Then introducing one hand into the vagina we insinuate it in a flattened form within the os internum, and push up between the membranes and the uterus as far as the middle of the womb: having thus obtained admission, we break the membranes by grasping and squeezing them with our fingers, slide our hand within them without moving the arm lower down, then turn and deliver as formerly directed." (Treatise on the Theory and Practice of Midwifery, vol. i. p. 327. 4th edit.) In 1770, Deleurye again pointed out the value of this mode of introducing the hand, and expressly directs us "introduire la main dans la matrice sans percer la poche des eaux, détacher les membranes des parois de ce viscère, et les percer à l'endroit où l'on juge que les pieds peuvent le plus naturellement se trouver."[90] Dr. Hamilton, of Edinburgh, five years afterwards recommended the same method, and in nearly the same terms. Little notice, however, has been taken of it since, either in this country or upon the Continent, and the old objectionable mode of rupturing the membranes at the os uteri is still taught even by the most modern authors. The celebrated Boer also added his testimony in favour of Deleurye's mode of practice,[91] and it has still farther been confirmed by Professor Naegelé.

Turning under these circumstances is an easy operation, and a very different affair compared with its performance in cases in which the membranes have been some time previously ruptured, and the uterus drained of liquor amnii: the hand is passed up with difficulty, the feet are quickly found, and the child moved round with a degree of facility which is scarcely credible. Where, however, the uterus is irritable and closely contracted upon the child, the liquor amnii having long since escaped, where the os uteri is not more than two-thirds dilated, its edge thin, hard, and tight, as is especially seen in a neglected case of arm or shoulder presentation, every step of the operation is attended with the[Pg 236] greatest difficulty, and in fact is neither possible nor justifiable, until by bleeding to fainting, by the warm bath and opiates, we have succeeded in producing such a degree of relaxation as to enable us to introduce the hand. "Blood-letting is the only remedy with which we are acquainted that has any decided control over the contracted uterus. It is one almost certain of rendering turning practicable under such circumstances, if carried to the extent it should be. A small bleeding in such cases is of no possible advantage, for unless the practitioner means to carry the bleeding to its proper limits, which is a disposition to, or the actual state of syncope, he had better not employ it." (Dewees' Compendious System of Midwifery, § 629.) "The vagina is never so soft, so dilatable, and capable of admitting the hand as during the presence of an active hæmorrhage, and this is equally the case in primiparæ as in those who have had several children: and it is a mistaken kindness in the medical attendant, who in order to spare his patient's sufferings, under these circumstances delays to introduce his hand until the hæmorrhage shall have ceased. The moment this is the case, the vagina regains more vitality, sensibility and power of contraction, the hand now experiences much more opposition, and excites far greater pain than during the state of syncope." (Wigand, Geburt des Menschen, vol. ii. p. 428.)

When once a powerful impression has been made upon the system by an active bleeding, opiates, which before it, would have only tended to render the patient feverish, are now of great value: they relax the spasmodic action of the uterus, allay the general excitement and irritability, and induce sleep and perspiration. As with bleeding in these cases, they must be given in decided doses: a grain of hydrochlorate of morphia given at once, or in two doses quickly repeated, and at the same time from half a drachm to a drachm of Liquor Opii Sedativus thrown into the rectum with a little thin starch or gruel, will rarely or never fail to produce the desired effect. The opiate by the mouth may be advantageously combined with James's powder, and thus assist its diaphoretic action. The warm bath will also prove a valuable remedy.

"If the arm or funis of the child presents and is prolapsed into the vagina, we must not try to push back these parts into the uterus again, but we must endeavour to pass our hand along the inner surface of the presenting arm; or if it be the cord, we must guide it so as to press the cord as little as possible: if however a coil of it has passed out of the vagina and is still beating, we had better carry it upon the hand with which we are about to turn the child." (Boer, op. cit. vol. iii. p. 5. 1817.) For farther information on this head we must refer to the observations on Malposition of the Child.

If the head or nates be occupying the brim of the pelvis it will[Pg 237] be necessary to raise them gently and press them to one side: this however is usually effected by the very act of passing up the hand, and seldom produces any difficulty, unless these parts have already advanced deeper into the pelvis; in which case, as turning under these circumstances can only be undertaken with a view to hasten labour, it will become a matter of consideration whether we shall not be able to attain this object better by the aid of the forceps.

Although it ought ever to be considered as a rule that turning must not be attempted whilst the pains are violent, the introduction of the hand into the uterus always excites it more or less to contraction: the degree of pressure and impediment which it will produce to the progress of the hand will in a great measure depend upon the quantity of liquor amnii which it contains. Where the uterus has been drained of the fluid, every contraction will be felt in its full force by the operator: his hand is firmly jammed against the child, and if it happens to be caught in a constrained posture at the moment, is liable to be attacked with a severe fit of cramp, which benumbs and renders it powerless. Wherever we find that the hand is tightly squeezed during a pain, we should lay it flat with the palm upon the child, and hold it perfectly still: in this posture it will bear a powerful contraction without inconveniencing ourselves or injuring the uterus; and by letting it be quite flaccid and motionless we shall not provoke the uterus to farther exertions. Attempting to turn during the pain would not only be useless, but we should exhaust the strength of our hand which cannot be spared too much; we should torture the patient unnecessarily, and run no small risk of rupturing the uterus.

In letting the pressure of our hand be upon the child during a pain, instead of against the uterus, we must select any part rather than its abdomen, for pressure here seems to act as injuriously as pressure upon the umbilical cord.

Rules for finding the feet. In searching for the feet we must endeavour to gain the anterior surface of the child, for (unless its position be greatly distorted) they are usually turned upon the abdomen: in arm presentations the position of the hand will also guide us, the palm of it being mostly turned in the same direction as the abdomen, and therefore points to the situation of the feet; the rule also, as above given by Boer, of passing the hand along the inside of the presenting arm, is well worthy of recollection, for this can scarcely fail to guide us to the anterior part of the child. Where, either from the pressure of the uterus or other circumstances, it is difficult to distinguish the precise position of the child, it will be better to follow Dr. Denman's simple rule, that the hand "must be conducted into the uterus, on that side of the pelvis where it can be done with most convenience, because that will lead most easily to the feet of the child." The soft [Pg 238]abdomen, the curved position of the child, and its extremities crossed in front are so many reasons why there should be more room in this direction.

During all this time the other hand placed externally will be of great service, not only in supporting the uterus, but in fixing the child and rendering the different parts of it more attainable. Where the feet are at some distance, we frequently come first to an arm or thigh, which soon leads us to the elbow or knee; if the introduction of the hand has been attended with some difficulty, it will not be very easy to distinguish these joints from each other, without bearing in mind the following diagnostic points:—the knee present two rounded prominences (condyles of the femur) with a depression between them, whereas, the elbow presents also two rounded prominences, but with a sharp projection (olecranon) between.

If the foot is not easily reached, there will be no need of forcing up the hand farther to gain it: it will be much better and safer to hook the finger into the bend of the knee and hold by it for a pain or two: this will generally be sufficient to bring it within reach; or during an interval of the pains, the leg may be gently disengaged and brought down. Not unfrequently we can only feel the toes with the extremities of our fingers, and therefore cannot maintain a sufficient hold upon the foot so as to bring it down: here again the same rule will be applicable, for by keeping but a slight hold upon it during a pain, it will be found to have approached nearer when the pain has gone off; in fact our first attempt to move the child must be done in this cautious manner, and we shall effect our object with greater certainty by merely holding the feet still during the pain, not allowing them to recede from that position in which we had placed them during the intervals, than by using considerable efforts to bring them to the os uteri. By the time we have got one foot fairly within grasp, the other is seldom very distant and should always be brought down if possible: by bringing down both feet we cause the hips of the child to enter the brim of the pelvis more equally; whereas, if one leg only is brought down, the pelvis of the child comes more or less awry, and the ischium of the other side is apt to lodge against the brim of its mother's pelvis.[92] This practice has been recommended on the grounds that, by bring down only one leg, we make the presentation rather resemble a breech case, which is known to be more favourable for reasons already mentioned, and that by having the other leg turned upon the abdomen it will protect the cord from undue pressure. As far as the abdomen is concerned this may possibly be the case, but the pressure of the head upon the cord, which is the real source of danger to the child in turning, can in no wise be influenced by this position.

[Pg 239]In bringing down the feet it must be done with the articulation, that is, the child must be turned forwards; at the same time the hand upon the abdomen, externally, will be of great service in assisting us to move the child, and in preventing the change of its position from taking place in too sudden and violent a manner, a circumstance which is apt to paralyze the uterus considerably, and even produce alarming symptoms from the shock it occasions.

Extraction. When once we have brought the feet into the vagina, the first part of the operation, viz. the changing the position of the child, is completed: it has now become a presentation of the feet, and as such ought to be treated, unless some source of danger be present which requires that the delivery should be hastened. The value of this practice in footling cases was first pointed out by Deleurye,[93] and particularly applied to the second act of turning by Wigand. "I have made it," says he, "a strict rule in turning, from the moment that I have brought a foot of the child as far into the vagina as I can without force, to do nothing beyond patiently waiting for the return of the pains, even if this did not take place for many hours, and leaving the rest of the labour entirely to nature. I have found by doing so that when the pains at length began to expel the child, they did it with so much force and activity as was not even seen in the most natural case of head presentation." (Geburt des Menschen, vol. ii. p. 130.)

As the feet descend towards the os uteri, the presenting part, particularly if the arm has been prolapsed into the vagina, begins to recede, the hand externally will assist in moving the child round, and we should perform this step of the operation so gradually as to be assured that the presenting part has quitted the pelvis before the feet have entered. Without attention to this point, the child may easily be fixed across the upper part of the pelvis, or even the body brought down, while the head is wedged into the cavitas iliaca of the ilium, and produce a serious obstacle to its farther advance. This is a sort of mishap which can rarely happen except to young practitioners. If the process be slowly and carefully conducted, we doubt much if it be ever necessary to disengage the presenting part as has been so frequently recommended: the uterus in fact will move the child round with very little assistance on our part, and we shall find that after every pain the advance of the feet and recession of the part has increased considerably. From our own observations we would say that in all difficult cases, of turning especially, it is desirable for the patient to have several pains between the moment of gaining[Pg 240] the feet and bringing them fairly into the vagina: very little force is required to bring them down, and the uterus does not appear to suffer; but where the position of the child has been rapidly changed, its contractile power seems to be injured, and it is ill able to make those exertions during the last stage, which will be required of it in order to save the child's life.

Not less necessary is it that we should proceed with the second stage as cautiously as possible: the grand principle is the same, viz. to conduct the expulsion as gradually as possible: there is no use whatever in hurrying this part of the operation, for if the child be alive, we place it in imminent danger of its life; and if it be dead, as will easily be known by the cord not pulsating, we are putting the mother to a great deal of suffering for no reason. Now that it has become a footling case, it must be managed according to rules already given for this species of presentation: the uterus must be emptied as slowly as possible, the anterior part of the child must be directed more or less backward, and the funis guided into the vicinity of one or other sacro-iliac synchondroses. By retarding the advance of the child, we resist the action of the uterus somewhat, and thus excite it to contract more actively, the head enters the pelvis in the most favourable position, and as the pains are still brisk, it passes through so quickly as to subject the child to little or no danger by pressing upon the cord. Where however the passage of the head through the pelvis threatens to be delayed, we would strongly recommend the application of the forceps in order to terminate the delivery before the child has begun to suffer: it is to this mode of practice that Professor Busch, of Berlin, attributes the extraordinary success of turning in his hands; of forty-four cases where turning was deemed necessary only three children are stated to have lost their lives from the effects of the operation, a result which is by far the most favourable known.

Turning with the nates foremost. It has been proposed by several authors of the last century to turn the child with the breech foremost, as being a less dangerous operation for it than the common one of bringing down the feet. Levret has distinctly proposed this mode (L'Art des Accouchemens, § 767,) and Smellie on more than one occasion has alluded to bringing down the nates. Dr. W. Hunter has also recommended turning with the breech foremost: still more recently has this mode of practice been confirmed by W. J. Schmitt, of Vienna,[94] also by some other continental authors; but the difficulty in bringing down a part of the child's body, upon which we can exert so little hold, will always be very considerable, wherever the circumstances under which the operation is undertaken is at all unfavourable.[Pg 241] Schmitt recommends that as soon as we reach the nates we should apply the hand flat upon them; while in order to turn the child, active pressure is kept up from without by the other hand: when once we have succeeded in moving the breech somewhat downwards, its farther descent is very easy.

A still more recent modification of turning the child in arm and shoulder presentations has been proposed by Dr. v. Deutsch, of Dorpat: it consists in raising the presenting part, and at the same time turning the child upon its long axis, as the hand placed in the axilla carries the shoulder to the upper parts of the uterus, after which, as the hand descends, it brings the feet along with it into the vagina.

Turning with the head foremost. In former times, as the head was considered the only natural presentation of the child, every deviation of its position from this was looked upon as unnatural, and, therefore, the operation of turning only applied to bringing down the head, which had not presented: as, however, the difficulties already mentioned, in turning with the nates, would apply still more forcibly to bringing down the head, it is plain that this mode of turning would rarely be practicable. "Were it practicable at all times," says Dr. Smellie, vol. i. book iii. chap. iv. sect. iv. number v., "to bring the head into the right position, a great deal of fatigue would be saved to the operator, much pain to the woman, and imminent danger to the child: he, therefore, ought to attempt this method, and may succeed when he is called before the membranes are broke, and feels by the touch that the face, ear, or any of the upper parts present." Still, however, he confesses that the usual method of turning by the feet is the safest. In his first volume of cases, (collection 16, number 6, case 5,) he has given a description of this mode of turning. Dr. Spence also turned with the head foremost, as is shown by his thirty-second case, where the hand and cord were prolapsed into the vagina. "I introduced my hand into the vagina, and in the intervals between the pains reduced both the arm and the cord: but as I found they were like to return again upon my withdrawing my hand, I therefore continued to support them till such time as, by the strength of the pains, the child's head was so far forced down as to prevent any danger of their returning, the happy consequence of which, was, that she was delivered of a live child in about half an hour after: both mother and child did well." (Spence's System of Midwifery, p. 465.) Dr. Merriman has recorded a similar case in his own practice: "The arm was returned at two o'clock; there was afterwards no occurrence of pain till six, after which, they became very strong, and between eight and nine the child was born. This was the only infant that Mrs. R. has seen alive out of six." (Synopsis of Difficult Parturition, 1838, p. 250.) Still more recently turning with the head foremost has been tried by[Pg 242] Dr. Michaelis, of Kiel, (Neue Zeitschrift für Geburtskunde, vol. iv. 1836.) When once the faulty position has been altered, the liquor amnii is allowed to drain off, the uterus contracts and presses the head down into the pelvis, and the child is born without farther difficulty.

History of turning. Turning, as it is generally practised at the present day, viz. changing the position of a living child so that the feet are brought down foremost into the vagina, was unknown to the ancients. There is little doubt, however, that if they could have been induced to have looked upon presentations of the nates and feet as natural labours, they would have been in possession of this valuable means of effecting artificial delivery; as it is, we meet with detached allusions to it in their writings, although applying only to cases where the child is dead. In the writings of Aspasia and Philumenus, which, but for the quotations of Œtius, would have been entirely lost to us, we find directions for turning the child. Thus, Philumenus states, "Si caput fœtûs locum obstruxerit ita ut prodire nequeat infans in pedes vertatur atque educatur." At a still later period, Celsus gave similar directions, but to all appearance they also merely apply to a dead child. "Medici vero propositum est, ut infantem manu dirigat, vel in caput vel etiam in pedes si forte aliter compositus est;" and again he says, "Sed in pedes quoque conversus infans, non difficulter extrahitur. Quibus apprehensis per ipsas manus commode educitur." (Celsus, de Medicinâ, lib. vii. cap. 29.)

From this time the whole subject seemed to sink into oblivion, until Pierre Franco, in his work on surgery[95] proposed the extraction of the child with the feet foremost: this was put into practice by the celebrated French surgeon, Ambrose Paré, (Ambr. Paræus, Opera Chirurgia, 1594,) who, nevertheless, recommended turning with the head foremost, where it was possible. His work was afterwards translated into Latin by Guillemeau, who, although he still adhered to the old plan of bringing down the head, showed the value of Paré's mode of turning in hæmorrhages and convulsions. To Francis Mauriceau, a man of great learning and experience, we are indebted for this operation being greatly improved, by means of his valuable work, in 1668; but it is Philip Peu, in 1694, and William Manquest de la Motte, in 1721, to whom the merit is due of having pointed out the value of two great laws in turning—the one of not rupturing the membranes as already mentioned, the other of not attempting to push back the arm which presents.[96]

[Pg 243]

CHAPTER III.

CÆSAREAN OPERATION.

Indications.—Different modes of performing the operation.—History of the Cæsarean operation.

The next operation in Midwifery for delivering the full-grown fœtus alive is that of Hysterotomy, commonly called the Cæsarean operation, viz. where the fœtus is extracted through an artificial opening made through the parietes of the abdomen and uterus.

The indications for performing the operation are so different in this country to what they are elsewhere that they require especial mention: in England the operation is never performed upon the living subject except where the child cannot be delivered by the natural passage; under these circumstances it is scarcely undertaken in this country for the purpose of saving the child's life, but merely that of the mother, it being considered preferable to deliver the child by perforation or embryotomy, even when known to be alive, than to expose the mother to so much suffering and danger.

On the Continent and also in America, it has not been considered in so dangerous a light as in this country, still less as an operation almost certainly fatal to the mother: therefore, besides being indicated as a means for preserving the mother's life, it is performed for the purpose of saving the child's life in cases where, by using the perforator, the child might be brought through the natural passages. The results of the Cæsarean operation have been so unfavourable, and the character of the process so frightful, as to have rendered it a measure of peculiar dread to practitioners, and in different times and countries the strongest feelings have been excited against it. By many of the celebrated authors of former times, viz. Ambrose Paré, Guillemeau, Dionis, &c. it was looked upon as altogether unjustifiable, and a similar opinion was entertained by many of our own countrymen at a much more recent period, (Dr. W. Hunter, Dr. Osborn, &c.)

There is no doubt that in England it has been peculiarly unsuccessful. Dr. Merriman has collected the results of 26 cases of Cæsarean operation: of these only 2 mothers and 11 children survived; thus out of 52 lives only 13 were saved. On the Continent it has been far more successful. Klein has collected with the greatest care 116 well authenticated cases, of which 90 [Pg 244]terminated favourably; and Dr. Hull, in his Defence of the Cæsarean Operation, has recorded 112 cases, of which 69 were successful. M. Simon has not only collected a number of cases which were favourable, to the number of 70 or 72, but which were performed on a few women, "some of them having submitted to it three or four times, others five or six, and even as far as seven times, which if they were all true, would superabundantly prove that it is not essentially mortal." (Baudelocque, transl. by Heath, § 2095.)

During the last fifteen or twenty years the operation has become remarkably successful in the hands of the German practitioners, so that there has been scarcely a journal of late from that part of the Continent which has not contained favourable cases of it. One of the most interesting instances of later years is that recorded by Dr. Michaelis, of Kiel, where the patient, a diminutive and very deformed woman, was operated upon four times:[97] the second operation was performed by the celebrated Wiedemann, and is stated to have been completed in less than five minutes, and without any extraordinary suffering on the part of the patient, who complained most when sutures were made for bringing the lips of the wound together. The uterus became adherent to the anterior wall of the abdomen, so that in the fourth operation the abdominal cavity was not even opened, the incision being made through the common cicatrix into the uterus.

There is every reason to suppose that the chief cause of its want of success in this country has been the delay in performing it. "In France and some other nations upon the European Continent," says Dr. Hull, "the Cæsarean Operation has been and continues to be performed where British practitioners do not think it indicated; it is also had recourse to early, before the strength of the mother has been exhausted by the long continuance and frequent repetition of tormenting, though unavailing pains, and before her life is endangered by the accession of inflammation of the abdominal cavity. From this view of the matter we may reasonably expect that recoveries will be more frequent in France than in England and Scotland, where the reverse practice obtains. And it is from such cases as these, in which it is employed in France, that the value of the operation ought to be appreciated. Who could be sanguine in his expectation of a recovery under such circumstances as it has generally been resorted to in this country, namely, where the female has laboured for years under malacosteon (mollities ossium,) a disease hitherto in itself incurable; where she has been brought into imminent danger by previous inflammation of the intestines or other contents of the abdominal[Pg 245] cavity, or been exhausted by labour of a week's continuance or even longer." (Hull's Defence of the Cæsarean Operation.)[98]

The difficulty of deciding upon the operation according to the indications of the Continental practitioners, is much more perplexing than according to that which is followed in this country: the question here is, can the child under any circumstances be made to pass per vias naturales with safety to the mother? The impossibility of effecting this object is the sole guide for our decision. In using the operation as a means for preserving also the life of the child, we must not only feel certain that the child is alive, but that it is also capable of supporting life, before we can conscientiously undertake the operation upon such indications. This uncertainty as to the life or death of the child greatly increases the difficulty of deciding. Under circumstances where there is reason to believe that, although the child may be alive, it is nevertheless unable to prolong its existence for any time, and the pelvis so narrow that it can only be brought through the natural passage piecemeal, we are certainly not authorized in putting an adult and otherwise healthy mother into such imminent danger of her life for the sake of a child which is too weak to support existence. Circumstances may nevertheless occur where the pelvis is so narrow that the child cannot be brought even piecemeal through the natural passage: in this case, even if the child be dead, the operation becomes unavoidable.

Under the above-mentioned circumstances, it is the duty of the surgeon to perform the operation; and he can do it with the more confidence from the knowledge of many cases upon record where it has succeeded even under very unfavourable circumstances, and where it has been performed very awkwardly: moreover, it seems highly probable that the unfavourable results of this operation cannot often be attributed to the operation itself, but to other circumstances. Not unfrequently the uterus has been so bruised, irritated, and injured by the violent and repeated attempts to deliver by turning or the forceps, and the patient so exhausted, and brought into such a spasmodic and feverish state by the fruitless pains and vehement efforts, together with the anxiety and restlessness which must occur under such circumstances, that it is impossible for the operation to prove successful. Here it is[Pg 246] an important rule that we should decide as soon as possible, whether she can be delivered by the natural passages or not: we should allow of no useless or forcible attempts to deliver her; and if these have been made, we should carefully examine whether the passages, &c. have been injured, and proceed to the operation without delay. Moreover, the patient can the more easily make up her mind to the operation, as she will suffer far less than from the fruitless efforts and attempts to deliver her by the natural passages. (Richter, Anfangsgründe der Wundarztneikunst, band vii. chap. 5.)

Although it is so important that we should lose no time, still nevertheless it does not appear desirable to operate before labour has commenced to any extent; for unless the os uteri has undergone a certain degree of dilatation, it will not afford a sufficiently free exit for liquor amnii, blood, lochia, which, by stagnating in the uterus after the operation, would soon become irritating and putrid, in which case they would be apt to drain through the wound into the abdominal cavity and create much mischief.[99]

Different modes of operating. The incision has been recommended to be made in different ways by different authors; but the highest authorities, as also later experience, combine in favour of that in the linea alba. Richter states, that one great advantage from making it in this direction is, that when the uterus contracts and sinks down into the pelvis, the incision in it still corresponds with that through the abdominal parietes, and therefore admits of a free discharge of pus, &c. through the external wound; whereas, if it have been made to one side, viz. at the outer edge of the rectus abdominis muscle, as recommended by Levret for the purpose of avoiding the placenta, the wound in the uterus when contracted ceases to correspond with it, and the discharge escapes into the abdominal cavity. Besides this the abdomen is usually more distended at the linea alba; the uterus here lies immediately beneath the integuments; the intestines are usually pressed towards each side; and therefore when the incision is made on one side they frequently protrude, a circumstance which rarely happens when it is made in the linea alba, except perhaps towards the end of the operation. In the linea alba we have only to cut through the external integuments in order to reach the uterus, while at the side, we have to cut through considerable layers of muscle.

[Pg 247]Previous to operating, the rectum and the bladder should be emptied, particularly the latter, because it is desirable to carry the incision of the abdominal integuments, for reasons just given, as near as possible to the symphysis pubis (viz. an inch and a half,) which otherwise would endanger the safety of the bladder. The experience of later years proves decidedly that three intelligent assistants are necessary, "two to prevent the protrusion of the intestines, and a third to remove the placenta and fœtus." (Neue Zeitschrift für Geburtskunde, band iii. heft 1. 1835.) We are convinced, that the success of the operation depends more upon carefully preventing the slightest protrusion of any portion of the intestines, and excluding all access of the external air than upon any other cause, for by this means alone can we save the patient from the dangerous peritonitis which is so apt to follow. The two assistants, whose duty it is to support the abdominal parietes and keep the edges of the wound closely pressed against the uterus, should be furnished with napkins or sponges soaked in oil in order instantly to cover any coil of intestine which may protrude, and press it back as quickly as possible; it is to this that the great success of the Cæsarean operation in later years is chiefly owing.

The incision in point of length varies from five to six, seven, or more inches, beginning at about two to four inches below the navel, and terminating at rather less than that distance above the symphysis pubis. The peritoneum is usually divided with a bistoury and director, and the wound through the uterus made an inch or two shorter than that of the abdominal integuments. If, on dividing the uterine parietes, the placenta presents, it must be separated, and removed as quickly as possible to one side, the membranes ruptured, and the child extracted; after which the uterus rapidly contracts, and thus prevents all fear of hæmorrhage: for this reason the sooner the child is removed the better, as otherwise the uterus is apt to contract upon a portion of it when passing through the wound, and thus retain it. It is desirable to remove the membranes as far as possible, especially from the os uteri, to allow of a free discharge from the uterus per vaginam. No sutures are needed for the uterine incision: the contractions of the organ not only diminish its length, but generally bring its edges into sufficiently close contact.

Some discrepancy of opinion has existed respecting the treatment of the external wound: sutures are of course the most secure means of retaining the edges in apposition, but they produce great suffering, and, from taking up a good deal of time, delay the closing of the abdominal wound more or less; whereas, straps of sticking plaster are applied much quicker and without any suffering to the patient. To do this most effectually it will be advisable to arrange them under the loins previous to the operation: they should be from five to six feet long, and the ends[Pg 248] may be rolled up until wanted; the wound can thus be instantly closed and in the most secure manner. Where the operator finds it necessary to use sutures, he must avoid puncturing the peritoneum as far as possible: the lower inch of the wound should be left open to allow any matter to drain out, and the whole dressed according to the common rules of surgery. The patient should be placed upon her side with the knees bent to relax the abdominal parietes. A grain of the hydrochlorate of morphia has been given in these cases with the best effects, having procured sleep and allayed the disposition to spasmodic coughing and vomiting, which so frequently exists after the operation.

One of the greatest triumphs of modern surgery is the performance of this dangerous operation four times successively on the same patient. The first operation was performed in June 1826, the woman being then in her twenty-ninth year, the second in January 1830, the third in March 1832, and the fourth on the 27th June, 1836. The second operation was performed by Wiedemann, of Kiel, and scarcely lasted five minutes; nor does it appear that the patient's sufferings were very great, for the application of sutures on this occasion elicited more complaint than all the operations put together.[100]

History. Although the early records of the Cæsarean operation are not very distinct, still we possess sufficient data to pronounce it of very considerable antiquity. The earliest mention of it shows that it was at first used merely for the purpose of saving the child by extracting it from the womb of its dead mother, a law having been made by Numa Pompilius, the second king of Rome, forbidding the body of any female far advanced in pregnancy to be buried until the operation had been performed.

The mythology of the ancients refers to two cases of an exceedingly remote period where a living child was taken from the dead body of its mother: these were the birth of Bacchus and Æsculapius; but as these traditions are so enveloped in allegory and mystery, it is difficult to come to any other conclusion than a mere inference of the fact: one circumstance, however, connected with the birth of Bacchus is curious, viz. that his mother Semele died in the seventh month of her pregnancy.

The oldest authentic record is the case of Georgius, a celebrated orator born at Leontium in Sicily, b. c. 508. Scipio Africanus, who lived about 200 years later, is said to have been born in a similar manner. There is no reason to suppose that Julius Cæsar was born by this operation, or still less that it[Pg 249] derived its name from him, for at the age of thirty, he speaks of his mother Aurelia as being still alive, which is very improbable if she had undergone such a mode of delivery. We would rather prefer the explanation of Professor Naegelé, viz. that one of the Julian family at Rome had been delivered ex cæso matris utero, and had been named Cæsar from this circumstance, so that the name was derived from the operation, not the operation from the name.

"The earliest account of it in any medical work is that in the Chirurgia Guidonis de Cauliaco, published about the middle of the fourteenth century. Here, however, the practise is only spoken of as proper after the death of the mother." (Cooper's Surg. Dict.) Among the Jews, however, it appears to have been performed on the living mother at a very early period; a description of it is given in the Mischnejoth, "which is the oldest book of this people, and supposed to have been published 140 years before the birth of our Saviour, or, according to some, even antecedently to this period. In the Talmud of the Jews, also, their next book in point of antiquity, the Cæsarean operation is mentioned in such terms as to render it extremely probable that it was resorted to before the commencement of the Christian era. In the Mischnejoth there is the following passage, 'In the case of twins, neither the first child which shall be brought into the world by the cut in the abdomen, nor the second, can receive the rights of primogeniture, either as regards the office of priest or succession to property.' In a publication called the Nidda, an appendix to the Talmud, there is the following remarkable direction: 'It is not necessary for women to observe the days of purification after the removal of the child through the parietes of the abdomen.'" (Introduction to the Study and Practice of Midwifery, by W. Campbell, M. D. p. 260.)

The first authentic operation upon a living woman in later times was the celebrated one by Jacob Nufer, upon his own wife, in 1500, after which, owing to its fatal character and the strong feeling against it, it was performed but rarely: still, however, sufficient evidence existed to mark its occasional success and urge its repetition in similar cases; and from what we have already stated, the history of the last twenty years shows that its results have rapidly become more and more favourable, so that in the present day it can be no longer looked upon as an operation of such extreme danger and almost certain fatality, as it was in former times.[101]

CHAPTER IV.

ARTIFICIAL PREMATURE LABOUR.

History of the operation.—Period of pregnancy most favourable for performing it.—Description of the operation.

Perhaps the greatest improvement in operative midwifery since the invention and gradual improvement of the forceps is the induction of artificial premature labour for the purpose of delivering a woman of a living child, under circumstances of pelvic contraction, where either the one must have been exposed to the dangers and sufferings of the Cæsarean operation, or the other to the certainty of death by perforation, or at least where the labour must have been so severe and protracted as to have more or less endangered the lives of both. It consists in inducing labour artificially, at such a period of pregnancy that the child has attained a sufficient degree of development to support its existence after birth, and yet is still so small, and the bones of its head so soft, as to be capable of passing through the contracted pelvis of its mother.

History. Few improvements have met with more violent opposition, or have been more unjustly stigmatized or misrepresented, than artificial premature labour, and it redounds, not a little, to the credit of the English practitioners that they have not only had the merit of its first invention, but with very trifling exceptions, have been the great means of bringing it into general practice and repute.

To the late Dr. Denman we are under especial obligations in this respect; for, although himself not the inventor of this operation, he, nevertheless, was one of the first who widely recommended it to the profession, and actively promoted it by the powerful support of his name and writings. "A great number of instances," says he, "have occurred to my own observation of women so formed that it was not possible for them to bring forth a living child at the termination of nine months, who have been blessed with living children, by the accidental coming on of labour when they were only seven months advanced in their pregnancy. But the first account of any artificial method of bringing on premature labour was given me by Dr. C. Kelly.[Pg 251] He informed me that about the year 1756 there was a consultation of the most eminent men in London, at that time, to consider of the moral rectitude and advantages which might be expected from this practice, which met with their general approbation. The first case in which it was deemed necessary and proper, fell under the care of the late Dr. Macauley, and it terminated successfully.[102] Dr. Kelly informed me he himself had practised it, and among other instances mentioned that the operation had been performed three times on the same woman, and twice the children had been born living." (Denman's Introduction to the Practice of Midwifery, 2d ed. vol. ii. p. 174.) Since this the observations of Mr. Barlow, Dr. Merriman, Mr. Marshall, Drs. J. Clarke, Ramsbotham, &c. &c., have afforded an ample body of evidence in its favour, and have, we trust, tended not a little to diminish the frequency of perforation. On the Continent it experienced a very different reception, being regarded as immoral, barbarous, and unjustifiably endangering the life of the mother and her child. In France, although at first successfully adopted by a few practitioners, (Sue,) its farther progress was completely stopped by the powerful opposition of Baudelocque, and by the plausible though erroneous objections which he made against it. A similar course was pursued by Gardien and Capuron, and even by the celebrated Madame la Chapelle, all of whom have taken a singularly incorrect view of it and assign it a totally different object to that which is intended: the very name which they have given to it of Avortement artificiel, plainly shows how little they have understood of its real character.

Among his objections, Baudelocque states, that "the neck of the uterus at seven months has seldom begun to open; it is still very thick and firm. The pains, or the contractions of that viscus, cannot then be procured but by a mechanical irritation pretty strong and long continued; but those pains, being contrary to the intentions of nature, often cease the instant we leave off exciting them in that manner. If we break the membranes before the orifice of the uterus be sufficiently open for the passage of the child, and the action of that viscus strong enough to expel it, the pains will go off in the same manner for a time, and the labour afterwards will be very long and fatiguing; the child deprived of the waters which protected it from the action of the uterus, being then immediately pressed upon by that organ, will be a victim to its action before things be favourably disposed for its exit, and the fruit of so much labour and anxiety will be lost. Premature delivery obtained in this manner is always so unfavourable to the child, that I think it ought never to be permitted except in those cases of violent hæmorrhage which leave no[Pg 252] chance for the woman's life without delivery; the nature of the accident also disposes the parts properly for it." (Baudelocque, transl. by Heath, § 1986, 1987.) All this plainly shows that Baudelocque did not rightly understand the real objects and nature of artificial premature labour, to which, in fact, his objections do not apply, but to the accouchement forcé of the French practitioners, where, on account of the sudden accession of dangerous symptoms, such as hæmorrhage, convulsions, &c. &c., the os uteri was rapidly and violently dilated by the hand, which was then passed into the uterus, the feet seized, and the child forcibly delivered, an operation which is now rarely performed in Germany and never in this country.

The celebrated Carl Wenzel, of Frankfort, was the first in Germany who declared himself in favour of the operation. Kraus and Weidemann followed, the former two having performed it with complete success. The favourable results also in the hands of English practitioners and its increasing reputation quickly silenced the virulent abuse which was levelled at it by Stein, jun., and some other German authorities; the celebrated Elias von Siebold, of Berlin, who had first opposed it, candidly confessed his error and became one of its earliest supporters. Increasing experience showed that it could scarcely be looked upon as a dangerous operation for the mother, and that in by far the majority of instances it was also successful as regarded the child. Professor Kilian, in his work on operative midwifery, has collected the results of no less than 161 cases of artificial premature labour. (Operative Geburtshülfe, erster band, p. 298.) Of these, 72 occurred in England, 79 in Germany, 7 in Italy, and 3 in Holland: of these cases, 115 children were born alive and 46 dead; of the 115 living children, 73 continued alive and healthy; 8 of the mothers died after the operation, but of these, 5 were evidently from diseases which had nothing to do with the operation.

The most unfavourable circumstances under which the operation can be undertaken are, where the child presents with the arm or shoulder: here it will require turning, which, in many cases, owing to the faulty form and inclination of the pelvis, cannot be effected without considerable difficulty, and greatly diminishing the chances of the child being born alive. With this exception we cannot see why it should not be as favourable as labour at the full term of pregnancy; it is far less dangerous than other species of premature labour, for the hæmorrhages, which are so apt to attend them, are never known to occur here.

This mode of delivery has not only been proposed in cases of contracted pelvis: "There is another situation," says Dr. Denman, "in which I have proposed and tried with success the method of bringing on premature labour. Some women who readily conceive, proceed regularly in their pregnancy till they approach the full period, when, without any apparently adequate cause, they[Pg 253] have been repeatedly seized with rigour and the child has instantly died, though it may not have been expelled for some weeks afterwards. In two cases of this kind, I have proposed to bring on premature labour, when I was certain the child was living, and have succeeded in preserving the children without hazard to the mothers." (Introduction to the Practice of Midwifery, 2d ed. vol. ii. p. 180.)

Period for performing the operation. Although under the head of Premature Expulsion we have stated that a fœtus is capable of maintaining its existence if born after the twenty-eighth week of pregnancy, we must not be supposed to recommend the artificial induction of premature labour at so early a period as this. "Experience has shown that it was not necessary to induce labour at so early a period as was first imagined, on account of the very great difference which even one or two weeks are found to make in the hardness of the fœtal skull. Thus, for instance, in cases where the antero-posterior diameter was only three inches, six weeks before the full term of utero-gestation were found sufficient, and where it was three inches and a half, fourteen days made sufficient difference." (Naegelé, MS. Lectures.) Still, however, as it is so difficult to be quite sure of the data upon which we have made our reckoning, it will be safer to fix the operation a week or two earlier; and if we lose a little time by failing in our first endeavours to induce uterine action, it will be of so much the less consequence: hence, therefore, as a general rule, the most eligible time will be between the thirty-fourth and thirty-sixth week; and if the deformity be very considerable, we may commence operations as early as the thirty-second week or two months before the full term, short of which it will seldom either be justifiable or necessary. On the other hand, where the state of the cervix and the history of her pregnancy combine to make our reckoning nearly a matter of certainty, the later we can safely delay the operation the better, for by so doing the process resembles more a natural labour, and the chances in favour of the child are much increased.

Operation. The original mode of artificially inducing premature labour was merely by puncturing the membranes and allowing the liquor amnii to escape; the more gradually this is done the better, for by this means the uterus is not entirely drained of its fluid contents, and is, therefore, prevented contracting immediately upon the child; the value of this precaution was pointed out by the late Dr. Hugh Ley, and also by Wenzel. A considerable interval may elapse between puncturing the membranes and the first contractions of the uterus, generally varying from forty to eighty hours: it should be performed while the patient is in the horizontal posture, in order to prevent the escape of too much liquor amnii. A moderately curved male catheter, open at its point and carrying a strong stilet sharpened at the end, is the best[Pg 254] and simplest instrument for the purpose: on passing it up to the membranes, the stilet should be protruded, but to a short extent, to avoid injuring the child; and as soon as the liquor amnii runs from the other end, the instrument should be withdrawn, and the patient desired to remain quiet. A dose of opium has been usually given after the operation by the English practitioners, but its utility appears rather questionable: a brisk purge of calomel and jalap, some hours previously, is much more important; uterine action comes on much more regularly and effectively, and there will be much less chance of those rigours occurring which some practitioners, although erroneously, have supposed, were connected with the death of the child.

The practice of dilating the os uteri first, as recommended by Brüninghausen, Kluge, and others, has, as far as we know, never been attempted in this country, and resembles much too closely the accouchement forcé of the French authors ever to be permitted.

The simplicity of the operation of tapping the membranes has rather led practitioners to overlook a still greater improvement, viz. the inducing uterine action first: this was proposed by Dr. Hamilton to be effected by passing up a catheter, and separating the membranes from the uterus to a considerable distance above the os uteri. The operation certainly succeeds in some cases; but our own experience goes to prove, that in the majority it is not sufficient by itself to provoke uterine contraction, and in order to ensure success we must combine with it other means.

The plan of treatment which we have found most certain is first to clear out the bowels by a full dose of calomel and colocynth, then to give the patient a warm bath, in which she may remain twenty or more minutes, after which the abdomen should be well rubbed with stimulating liniment as she lies in bed, and the secale cornutum given in doses of a scruple of the powder in cold water, repeated every half hour for five or six times. Contractions of the uterus rarely fail to follow, and although they generally require the secale to be renewed after a few hours, they will be found to have effected several very important changes preparatory to actual labour;—the abdomen has sunk, the fundus is lower, the cervix is shorter or has disappeared, and not unfrequently we feel the head has already passed the brim and is now in the cavity of the pelvis; the vagina and os uteri are lubricated with a copious secretion of remarkably pure and albuminous mucus; and in these cases especially, we frequently meet with those little lumps of inspissated mucus which were formerly called the ovula Nabothi. All these precursory changes are so many preparations of nature for a natural labour, and contribute not a little to the successful termination of the case, advantages which cannot be enjoyed where the membranes have been previously ruptured. If, however, we do not succeed in producing more than a slight dilatation of the os uteri, if the repeated [Pg 255]exhibition of the ergot only produce vomiting, or constant pains which have no other effect beyond preventing rest and inducing exhaustion, the separation of the membranes from the uterus, as proposed by Dr. Hamilton, will now have the best effects: even if this fail and we are compelled to puncture the membranes, it will now be performed under so much more favourable circumstances, from labour having already commenced to a certain extent.

A warm bath and the other usual means for recovering the child should be in readiness. In most cases the secretion of milk follows as after labour at the full term, which is a great advantage; for the thin watery secretion of this early period is much better adapted to the weak digestive organs of the premature child. It is frequently a matter of some difficulty under these circumstances to make a child take the breast at first, and this is the chief reason why their digestive organs so soon become deranged. "In case no milk be present, a good substitute may be made by beating up fresh eggs and milk, boiling them over a gentle fire and straining off the thin fluid." (Reisinger, die künstliche Frühgeburt.)

One great encouragement in cases requiring this operation is the fact that in every successive pregnancy the uterus is more easily excited to premature action; and in some cases where it has been induced several times, it has at length, as it were, got so completely into the habit of retaining its contents only up to a certain period, that labour has come on spontaneously exactly at the time at which in the former pregnancies it had been artificially induced.[103] We have already alluded to this circumstance in the chapter on Premature Expulsion of the Fœtus.[104]

[Pg 256]

CHAPTER V.

PERFORATION.

Variety of perforators. — Indications. — Mode of operating. — Extraction. — Crotchet. — Embryulcia.

The perforation is that operation "where we make an opening into the cranial cavity, and, by allowing the brain to escape, thus diminish the bulk of the head." (Obstetric Memoranda.)

Perforation is one of the most ancient operations in midwifery, for in former times it was the only means of artificially delivering the child when the head presented: hence we find that from the age of Hippocrates down to the last century, midwifery instruments almost entirely consisted of knives or lancets for piercing the fœtal head, and blunt or sharp hooks for extracting or dismembering the child.

Thus Hippocrates, Celsus, and Albucasis, and others, have described a variety of such instruments and given full directions for their use.

Variety of perforators. No instrument has been so greatly modified or has appeared under such different forms as the perforator; but it is not our object to enter into any detailed account of its history, for it would not, like that of the forceps, lead to any useful information; we shall, therefore, content ourselves with mentioning those few which have been in general use during the last century. They are chiefly of the scissor kind; the two most commonly known are the perforators of Dr. Smellie and M. Levret: the former are merely strong long-handled scissors, the backs of the blade being neither exactly sharp nor blunt,[105] and furnished each with a projecting shoulder or rest to prevent them from entering too far. Levret's perforator, which is extensively used in this country under the name of Dr. Denman's perforator, and which was originally invented by Bing, of Copenhagen, is also formed like scissors,[Pg 257] but has its cutting edges outside; the blades are also furnished with rests or shoulders like the Smellie perforator.

Naegelé's perforator.
A useful modification has been invented by Professor Naegelé, which supplies a considerable defect in the two above-mentioned instruments, viz. the necessity of using both hands to open the blades, thereby requiring that the hand which guides the instrument in the vagina should be removed at this moment: for this purpose the blades do not cross at the lock as the others do, by which means the grasp of one hand is sufficient to squeeze the handles together, and thus make the blades diverge in order to dilate the opening. A similar one has been invented by the surgical instrument maker, Mr. Weiss, but it does not appear to be quite so safe.

The object of these instruments is not merely to bore through the skull, but to break down the parietal bone to a certain extent, in order to enlarge the opening: a slight curve of the blades is advantageous, because their points thus impinge more directly upon the skull, and enter it at once without running the risk of slipping along the surface.

Indications. "The perforation is indicated, first, in all cases where the labour is dangerous for the mother, and where the antero-posterior diameter, although more than two inches and a half, is so small that the head which presents, cannot be delivered by the forceps. Secondly, it is indicated where the head is much larger than natural, as in hydrocephalus." (Naegelé, MS. Lectures.) For a more detailed and special account of the precise circumstances under which it will be required, we must refer to those different forms of Dystocia, where it is occasionally required, particularly our fourth species, viz. Dystocia Pelvica.

Much discrepancy of opinion has existed as to how far the operation itself was justifiable, and has, therefore, given rise to very different results in the practice of different schools. The most obstinately prejudiced against perforation was the late celebrated Benjamin Osiander, of Göttingen, who asserted, that it was never necessary, for, where others were obliged to open the head, he would deliver the patient by means of his forceps, an instrument which, from its great length and the various hooks &c. for applying additional hands, was capable of exerting a degree of force which nothing could justify. In France, the predilection for using exceedingly powerful forceps to a degree, which in this country and the greater part of Germany would[Pg 258] be looked upon as very injurious, if not dangerous, has tended to render the perforation a comparatively rare operation: thus out of somewhat more than twenty thousand labours at the Maternité, of Paris, only sixteen were delivered by this means. Of the ninety-six cases in whom the forceps was applied, no mention is made as to the result with respect to the mothers; but, from the description of a forceps case at the Hôtel Dieu which we have received from an eye-witness, the force used must have been carried to a most unwarrantable extent.

The English practitioners have frequently been accused by their Continental brethren with being too ready in the use of the perforator; but, with one or two exceptions, the charge is not just, for, as already stated, we are not justified in subjecting an adult and otherwise healthy woman to so much suffering and danger for the sake of a child which, after all, will be probably sacrificed by the severity of the labour.[106]

Operation. In performing the operation we introduce two or three fingers along the vagina to the presenting part of the fœtal head, and carefully guide up the perforator against it: these fingers will not only protect the soft parts from injury, but steady the point so firmly upon the skull, as to enable the other hand to bore through it without difficulty. Having passed the blades up to the shoulders or rests, we dilate the opening, first one way and then the other, to form a crucial incision: we now insert the instrument up to the basis cranii, breaking down the attachments and structure of the brain, and thus enabling it to come away with greater facility. To favour this object still farther, and make the cranial bones collapse more readily, we must pass a long elastic tube through the opening, and by means of a syringe, throw up a powerful stream of water into the cavity of the skull: if this be introduced to the base of it, the water will necessarily drive out the brain before it, so that with every stroke of the piston, a quantity of brain will be expelled nearly equal to that of the water injected.

When the perforation has been made, it will be desirable to wait a few hours before making any attempt to extract: we thus give the mother an opportunity of getting a little rest; the attachments of the cranial bones after a short time become more yielding, the head collapses more readily, and adapts itself better to the form of the passages. "In all circumstances," says Dr.[Pg 259] Osborn, "which admit and require precision, I would recommend the delaying all attempts to extract the child till the head has been opened at least thirty hours: a period sufficient to complete the putrefaction of the child's body, and yet not sufficient to produce any danger to the mother. From such conduct, the beneficial effects of facilitating the extraction of the child, I am firmly convinced, by frequent experience, will much overbalance any possible injury which may reasonably be expected from the putrid state of the child and secundines in so short a time. The propriety, however, of this delay entirely depends upon the head being opened in the beginning of labour: for if we do not perform the first part of this operation till the labour has been protracted so long as that the woman's strength begins to fail, we must expedite the delivery as speedily as possible, otherwise, the danger which we wish to avoid, will infallibly be incurred: no woman can suffer continued labour beyond a certain period without fever, inflammation, and the most imminent danger, if not death ensuing." (Osborn's Essays on the Practice of Midwifery.)

It has been recommended to perforate the head at the sutures, on account of the greater facility in passing the instrument through them: but that part of the head which is lowest in the pelvis, or which, in other words, presents, must necessarily be the most convenient, not only for the introduction of an instrument, but also for the evacuation of the brain. When the perforation is made at a suture, the edges of the bones gradually overlap as the head diminishes in size, and thus close the opening, a circumstance which cannot occur when it is made through a bone. Splintering the bone in making a crucial opening has been objected to on the ground that the sharp edges and spiculæ are apt to wound the soft parts of the mother: of this, however, there will be but little danger so long as they are covered by the scalp, which we should be somewhat cautious of, and not tear or otherwise destroy the cranial integuments unnecessarily, for it has long since been remarked by the celebrated Peter Frank, that inflammation of the uterus wounds from spiculæ of bone or sharp instruments becoming blunt, &c., usually prove fatal: it is also desirable to disfigure the head as little as possible. Still, however, we are far from recommending the trepan-shaped perforators which have been used by Professors Assalini, Joerg, &c. as they cannot make a sufficiently free opening, nor break down the skull to the necessary extent.

Extraction. Where sufficient time has been allowed for the cranial bones to collapse, the finger inserted into the opening and acting as a blunt hook will, if assisted by the pains, be enabled to exert a sufficient degree of force to bring the head down to the pelvic outlet; by which time the action of the vagina and abdominal muscles in aid of the uterine efforts will soon succeed[Pg 260] in pressing it through the os externum. By using the finger in this way we pull by that part of the head which is already lowest in the pelvis, and, therefore, run no risk of altering the position of the head and bringing it down in an unfavourable direction; this objection (among others) applies to the hook, whether it be fixed internally or externally, and thus frequently renders the passage of the head through the outlet and os externum more tedious, difficult, and painful, than it otherwise would have been. The craniotomy forceps are still more objectionable in all ordinary cases of perforation, for they not only alter the position of the head, but by tearing away portions of bone from time to time are very liable to wound the soft parts.

From our own experience, we would recommend the application of the common curved forceps in all cases where the pelvic deformity is not of a very unusual degree, for by this means the hand is equally grasped and compressed, the soft parts to a considerable extent are protected by the blades, and the whole mass brought down exactly in the position in which it presented. On several occasions where the craniotomy forceps and crotchet have failed to move the head, the midwifery forceps has been applied, and the delivery easily and quickly accomplished. Dr. Smellie recommends the crotchet to be applied on the outside of the head, and was evidently aware that its position was liable to be altered by this means. He directs the practitioner to "introduce it along his right hand with the point towards the child's head, and fix it above the chin, in the mouth, back part of the neck, or above the ears, or in any place where it will take firm hold. Having fixed the instrument, let him withdraw his right hand, and with it take hold on the end or handle of the crotchet, then introduce his left to seize the bones at the opening of the skull (as above directed) that the head may be kept steady, and pull along with both hands." (vol. i. chap. 3. sect. 7. numb. 4.) Where there was considerable difficulty in bringing down the head, Dr. Smellie used to introduce a second crotchet opposite to the first, like the second blade of the forceps, and having locked them together was thus enabled to apply a greater degree of force.

Crotchet. The usual mode of applying the crotchet at the present day is to pass it into the cranial cavity, and endeavour to fix it upon some portion of the skull, which will afford a sufficiently firm hold for the purpose; the best spot is the petrous portion of one or other of the temporal bones. The plan of passing up the hook on the outside of the head is objectionable, for in most cases where there is much impaction of the head, it will be exceedingly difficult, if not impossible, to push the hook past it without much suffering and probable injury. Not wishing to differ from so great an authority as Dr. Smellie without reason, we have repeatedly tried this mode of using the crotchet, but [Pg 261]invariably found that its introduction on the outside of the head was attended with so much difficulty and pain as to make us relinquish the attempt. His objections to passing the hook into the cranial cavity are not valid, for we should never try to fix it upon the "thin bones," nor should we hold it in such a manner that, if it did slip or tear through, it would wound either our hand or the soft parts of the mother.

The common form of the crotchet in general use is but ill adapted for taking hold of any part within the skull: it is, in fact, the very instrument left us by Dr. Smellie for applying on the outside of the skull: and, therefore, that which was intended to take hold of a convex surface cannot possibly be also suited for one of the contrary form, viz. a concavity; for this reason, the shank of the hook requires to be straight, so that the point may project at a considerable angle, by which means it will take hold with much greater ease.

The point of the hook guarded by the finger should be cautiously introduced up the vagina, and passed into the cranial cavity; having fixed it, as above directed, the finger should be applied externally, so as to correspond with the hook inside: by so doing, if the point slips or tears through the bone, the finger is ready to protect the soft parts from it; the operator is equally safe from injury, for, by grasping the shank of the hook with his thumb and other fingers, his whole hand moves with it and gives him instant warning of its going to slip. Where the deformity of the pelvis is very great, it may be necessary to break down the bones of the head still farther, in order to produce greater comminution; but even here, so long as the bones collapse well together, it will be better not to displace them from their attachments, the whole mass will come down better and with less chance of injuring the soft parts. Where, however, this is admissible, we must give the head sufficient time to undergo that process of softening which is one of the early stages of putrefaction; the cranial parietes may be gradually removed, one after the other, until we have nothing remaining but the base of the skull and the face. Dr. Burns recommends us now to convert it into a face presentation with the root of the nose directed to the pubes: "I have carefully measured, (says he,) these parts placed in different ways, and entirely agree with Dr. Hull, a practitioner of great judgment and ability, that the smallest diameter offered, is that which extends from the root of the nose to the chin."

Embryulcia. This is merely a degree farther than the perforation: it consists in evacuating the chest and abdomen of their contents, and thus enabling their parietes to collapse. It is chiefly had recourse to in cases of deformed pelvis, where the arm or shoulder has presented, or where the distortion is so great as to prevent the trunk from passing without its bulk being [Pg 262]lessened. Dr. Smellie's perforator with its scissor edges is best suited for this object. Having made an opening into the most presenting part of the thorax, we enlarge it by cutting away portions of the ribs and thoracic parietes, and removing the contents of the chest. The abdominal viscera are brought away in a similar way through a perforation in the diaphragm; and if this be not sufficient to let the trunk pass, the crotchet must be inserted into the brim of the child's pelvis, which must be brought down doubled upon the spine, somewhat like the process of spontaneous expulsion.

The success of this operation, will, in a great measure, depend not only upon its being undertaken sufficiently early before the patient's strength is exhausted, but upon a sufficient length of time intervening between the removal of the thoracic and abdominal viscera and the extraction of the child. The excellent rule of Dr. Osborn, above quoted, is peculiarly applicable here; for when softened by the effects of incipient decomposition, the body will sometimes even be expelled by the unassisted efforts of the uterus.

In a case of this sort, the perforation of the head is the last part of the process to be performed. It will be by all means, desirable not to separate it from the body, but to pass up the curved perforator along the neck, and make an opening behind the ears: this is effected without much difficulty, and the head can be brought away whole, or in portions, according to the nature of the case.

[Pg 263]

PART V.

DYSTOCIA, OR ABNORMAL PARTURITION.

Divisions and species. By the term Dystocia, we understand those labours which either cannot be completed by the natural powers destined for that purpose, or at least, not without injury to the mother or her child.[107] These will, therefore, consist of the two following classes:—

1. Labours that are difficult or impossible to be completed by the natural powers.

2. Labours which are rendered faulty without obstruction to their progress.

The first division of dystocia may either arise from a faulty condition of the expelling powers, or, without any anormality in this respect, it may depend upon the faulty condition either of the child, or of the parts through which it has to pass.

As respects the child it may arise from,

1. Malposition.

2. Faulty form and size of the child.

3. Faulty condition of the parts which belong to the child.

On the part of the mother this division of dystocia may arise from a faulty condition.

4. Of the pelvis.

5. Of the soft passages.

6. Of the expelling powers.

The second condition where labour is rendered dangerous for the mother or her child, without any obstruction to its progress, may arise from,

1. Following too rapid a course.

2. Prolapsus, &c. of the umbilical cord.

3. From accidental circumstances, which render the labour dangerous, viz. convulsion, syncope, dyspnœa, severe and continued vomiting, hæmorrhage, &c.

We propose to consider the different species of dystocia in the order above enumerated.

CHAPTER I.

FIRST SPECIES OF DYSTOCIA.

Malposition of the child.—Arm or shoulder the only faulty position of a full-grown living fœtus.—Causes of malposition.—Diagnosis before and during labour.—Results where no assistance is rendered.—Spontaneous expulsion.—Malposition complicated with deformed pelvis or spasmodically contracted uterus.—Embryulcia.—The prolapsed arm not to be put back or amputated.—Presentation of the arm and head.—Presentation of the hand and feet.—Presentation of the head and feet.—Rupture of the uterus.—Usual seat of laceration.—Causes.—Premonitory symptoms.—Symptoms.—Treatment.—Gastrotomy.—Rupture in the early months of pregnancy.

We have already stated that the presentations of the full-grown living fœtus may be brought under three classes, viz. those of the head, of the nates or lower extremities, and of the arm or shoulder: the former two have already been considered under the head of eutocia or healthy parturition, and may be distinguished from the latter, by the great peculiarity that in them the long axis of the child's body is parallel with that of the uterus, whereas, in arm or shoulder presentations this cannot be the case, its body lying across the uterus.

Although malposition of the child, strictly speaking, refers to one species of presentation only, viz. to that of the arm or shoulder, yet it has been rendered a matter of great perplexity by the speculations and theoretical notions of authors. No one has propagated more serious errors upon this subject than the celebrated Baudelocque, the more so as the great authority of his name has tended to silence all doubts as to the accuracy of his views upon this subject. Almost every author since his time has contented himself with copying more or less from him, without ascertaining by personal observation how far they corresponded with the actual course of nature. By forcing a stuffed figure into a pelvis in every possible direction, he succeeded in making actually ninety-four presentations of the child, all of which he described as if they had really occurred in nature.

Few have taken so simple a view of this subject as the late Dr. Denman. "The presentations of children at the time of birth," says this distinguished accoucheur, "may be of three[Pg 265] kinds, viz. the head, the breech or inferior extremities, the shoulder or superior extremities; the back, belly, breast or sides, properly speaking, never constitute the presenting part."

The two greatest Continental authorities of modern times, viz. Madame La Chapelle and Professor Naegelé, confirm this opinion: the former points out one of the sources of error which has induced practitioners to suppose that they had met with other species of faulty presentation besides those of the arm or shoulder. "In the greater number of shoulder presentations," says this experienced authoress, "I have very distinctly touched the chest, in some positions of the nates I have been able to reach the loins, the hips, or lower part of the abdomen; but it would require no slight bias from prejudice and theoretical systems to find presentations of the chest, the back, the abdomen, or the loins, the neck or the ear."[108]

We would, therefore, limit the term malposition of the child merely to presentations of the arm or shoulder: other presentations, it is true, occur, but not of the full-grown living fœtus; they are only where the child is premature, or has been dead in utero some time. Under such circumstances it will follow no rule whatever; for in the first case it is too small, and therefore the passages can have no effect in directing its course through them; and, in the second, a child which has been dead some time becomes so softened by gradual decomposition, that it may be squeezed by the pressure of the uterus into almost any shape: it is by this cause that we occasionally see in still-born children parts in close contact, which in a living child could not have been brought together.

We do not deny that such presentations may be made by ignorant and awkward attempts to deliver, but it is to be hoped that such cases are daily becoming of rarer occurrence.

Malposition of the child is fortunately not of very frequent occurrence: as a general average we would say that it occurs once in 230 cases, as the following results will show:—At the Westminster General Dispensary (1781) it occurred to Dr. Bland once in 210 cases: at the Dublin Lying-in Hospital, to Dr. Joseph Clarke, once in 212: in private practice, to Dr. Merriman, once in 155: "calculated from a great number of cases," to Professor Naegelé, once in 180: at the Dublin Lying-in Hospital, to Dr. Collins, once in 416: at the Maternité, of Paris, to Madame La Chapelle, once in 230.

In arm and shoulder presentations the back of the child is turned towards the anterior part of the uterus more than twice as frequently as it is in the contrary direction, from which circumstance Professor Naegelé has called this the first position of[Pg 266] the shoulder to distinguish it from the other, which, as being rarer, he calls the second.

In investigating the nature of the causes which produce malposition of the child, which, from the above observations, is evidently a circumstance of rare occurrence, the question naturally suggests itself, by what means is the long diameter of the child in so large a majority of cases kept parallel with that of the uterus? This depends in great measure on the form and size of the uterus. Where the uterus is not unduly distended with the liquor amnii, and where it preserves its natural oval figure, it is scarcely possible that the child should present in any other way than with its cephalic or pelvic extremity foremost. There can be no doubt that the first early contractions of the uterus in the commencement of labour have a great effect in regulating the position of the child; for, by the gentle and equable pressure which they exert upon it, they not only maintain it in the proper direction, but tend materially to correct any slight deviations from the right position. Hence, therefore, we find that where any cause has existed to impair or derange the action of these precursory contractions of the uterus, the child is apt to lie across, or, in other words, to present with the arm or shoulder. Thus, for instance, if the uterus be much distended with liquor amnii, the contractions of its parietes can have little influence upon the child's position; this will be particularly the case where the accumulation is very considerable, for here the uterus becomes more or less globular, and presents but little variation as to the length of its diameter in any direction.

The form of the uterus is no less worthy of attention as a cause of malposition, and is also in a great measure influenced by the character of its early contractions. Thus in a uterus for the first time pregnant, they generally act equally on all sides: hence it is why in primiparæ the uterus is so exactly oval, and why we so rarely meet with faulty presentations. Sir Fielding Ould, of Dublin, was the first and almost the only practitioner in this country who noticed the influence which the early contractions of the uterus have in determining the position of the child. "The first labour pains, which are very short, continue their repetition for two or three hours, or perhaps for more, before there is the least effect produced upon the os tincæ, which time must certainly be employed in turning the head towards the orifice." (Treatise of Midwifery, p. 14.)

Wigand, in reasoning upon the physical impossibility of a child presenting wrong, where the uterus is of the natural configuration, says that "the chief cause of faulty position of the child does not depend so much upon the child itself, as upon the deviation of the uterus from its natural elliptical or pyriform shape." (Wigand, vol. ii. p. 107.)

The theory at one time so universally entertained, that the [Pg 267]obliquity of the uterus was the chief cause of malposition of the child, has long since been disproved, although it continues to find a few adherents to the present day: the uterus, in fact, towards the end of pregnancy, is scarcely ever quite straight; the upright posture of the human female rendering it almost necessary that the fundus should incline somewhat to one side or to the other, or forwards, and yet we find that it has no influence upon the position of the child when labour comes on. The moment a pain commences, the fundus moves towards the median line of the body, so that its axis corresponds nearly with that of the pelvic brim: as the pain goes off, so does it return towards its former oblique position. Even in those cases where it is strongly inclined forwards, and where the abdomen is quite pendulous, the position of the child is unaffected by it.

Where, however, the uterus has been altered in point of form, where from irregular contractions of its fibres it has been pulled down unequally to one side, while it is quite relaxed in the opposite direction, the position of the child may be seriously affected, for it will now present obliquely as regards its long axis, and become a case of malposition.

We may, therefore, state that the causes of arm or shoulder presentations are of two kinds, viz. where the uterus has been distended by an unusual quantity of liquor amnii; or where, from a faulty condition of the early pains of labour, its form has been altered, and with it the position of the child.

It is a well-known fact that cross births, as they have been called, are frequently preceded by severe spasmodic pains in the abdomen, from which the patient suffers for some days or even weeks before labour has commenced: the uterus is more or less the seat of these attacks, which usually come on towards night-time; and, in some instances, it is felt for the time hard and uneven from irregular contraction. It was the circumstance of this symptom having preceded five successive labours of a patient, in all of which the child had presented with the arm or shoulder, which induced Professor Naegelé, when attending her in her sixth pregnancy, to endeavour to allay these cramp-like pains, which had begun to show themselves as severely as on former occasions. Having tried opium by itself, and also in combination with ipecacuanha or valerian without effect, he ordered her a starch injection with twelve drops of Tinct. Opii every night as long as she continued to suffer from these attacks: the spasms soon ceased, nor did they appear again during the remainder of her pregnancy, and he had the satisfaction of delivering her at the proper time of a living child, which presented in the natural manner.

Many other causes of malposition have been enumerated by authors, which evidently exist only in theory and not in reality: thus, shortness of the umbilical cord, or its being twisted round[Pg 268] the child, insertion of the placenta to one side of the uterus, faulty form or inclination of the pelvis, obliquity of the uterus, as above-mentioned, violent exertions or concussions of the body, plurality of children; of all these, we do not believe that there is one which can exert the slightest influence in determining the position of the child. There is no doubt that several of them will render labour difficult or even dangerous, more especially deformed pelvis; but we constantly meet with it under every degree and variety without at all altering the child's position. Indeed, if malformation of the pelvis were to be a cause of malposition of the child during labour, what difficulties would it not add to the process of delivery under such circumstances? And yet we find, with very rare exceptions, that in every case requiring artificial assistance on account of contracted pelvis, the head is resting upon the brim which is too narrow to allow it to pass.

We may also mention another circumstance which has occasionally seemed to produce a faulty position of the child. It sometimes happens that the hand, which is frequently felt lying by the side of the face at the beginning of labour, instead of slipping up out of reach as the head descends, which is usually the case, advances more and more, until it not only prevents the head from engaging farther into the pelvis, but pushes it out, so that the head slips up to one side, and lodges in the cavitas iliaca, allowing the shoulder with the rest of the arm to descend.

Where, however, the pelvis is large or the head small, the arm will not always force it to one side, but the two will come down together and be born in this position. (See case in our Midwifery Reports, Med. Gaz. April 19, 1834.)

Sometimes the two hands present (La Motte, book iii. ch. 26.,) or a hand and foot: this, however, does not long continue so, for when the membranes have ruptured, the liquor amnii flowed away, and the uterus contracted upon the child, one shoulder and arm descend before the rest, and remain in this position.

The complication of two arms presenting with the head we disbelieve entirely, except where it has been made during some awkward and ignorant attempts at delivery.

Although the symptoms of malposition of the child during the last few days before, or at the commencement of labour, are far from being distinct, still, however, when taken collectively, they will be sufficient to excite our suspicion. The abdomen is irregularly distended, and marked with unequal prominences; anteriorly, it is more or less pointed. It is usually much increased in breadth, and this is generally in an oblique direction, forming a globular protuberance at the upper part on one side, and at the lower part on the other: the former is the pelvic extremity of the child; the other, from its size, form, and hardness, may easily be recognised as the head.

"The movements of the child feel differently to what they did[Pg 269] before; they are no longer exclusively confined either to one side or the other. Sometimes, as before-mentioned, cramp-like pains are felt in the abdomen, during which it is more or less distorted with violent movements, apparently of the child, as if it were trying to force its way through the abdominal parietes at this spot." (Naegelé, Lehrbuch, p. 223.)

Upon examination per vaginam, either no presentation is to be reached at all, or only small parts can be indistinctly felt, such as the hand, the arm, or the shoulder. The not being able to feel a presenting part in a primipara shortly before or at the commencement of labour, is an unfavourable symptom; for the head at this time ought to be deep in the cavity of the pelvis; still, however, it does not necessarily prove that the child is presenting wrong, for it may be a presentation of the nates, which, as we have before shown, do not descend so low into the pelvis just before labour, as the head does; or it may arise from the unusual size of the child's head, especially in cases of congenital hydrocephalus. It may arise from a large quantity of liquor amnii, and where the head is nevertheless presenting; it may be a case of twins, or lastly of dystocia pelvica, where the head is presenting, but unable to pass through the contracted brim.

In women who have had several children, it is frequently impossible to reach the presentation during the early part of the labour: this arises either from the abdomen in these cases being generally more or less pendulous, or from the circumstance of the uterus having been distended in so many previous pregnancies: its lower part does not become so fully developed as before, but continues more or less funnel-shaped, a considerable portion of the cervix still remaining. Where this is the case, the head will not descend so low as usual at first, but remains out of reach, or nearly so, until the os uteri is fully dilated and the membranes have given way.

"If, upon such an examination, it should be ascertained that the os uteri is considerably dilated, and the child cannot be felt, this affords reason to suspect that the presentation is preternatural. Should the liquor amnii be discharged and the child be out of reach of the finger, the probability of a preternatural position is greater. Should the membranes be found hanging down in the vagina not of the usual globular form, but rather conical and small in diameter, this likewise is a presumptive proof of a cross-birth; especially if there be any part presenting through the membranes which is smaller, feels lighter, or gives less resistance when touched than the bulky heavy head."[109]

[Pg 270]The diagnosis of the shoulder is by no means easy: it offers no distinctive marks, and may readily be mistaken for the nates, or even for the head. It feels round, but is smaller and softer than the head. The scapula and clavicle, the neck, the armpit, the arm itself, and the ribs, assist us in our diagnosis. From the direction of these parts, we shall be able to ascertain the position of the rest of the body, and which shoulder presents. If the hand has prolapsed, the direction of the palm and of the thumb will soon show the position of the child.

Labours with malposition are always dangerous; when left without assistance, they are almost always fatal to the child, and generally so to the mother.

When a full-grown child has presented with the arm or shoulder, and nothing has been done to assist the delivery of it, the results are usually as follow:—After the membranes have burst, and discharged more liquor amnii than in general where the head or nates presents, the uterus contracts tighter around the child, and the shoulder is gradually pressed deeper into the pelvis, while the pains increased considerably in violence, from the child being unable, from its faulty position, to yield to the expulsive efforts of nature. Drained of its liquor amnii, the uterus remains in a state of contraction even during the intervals of the pains; the consequence of this general and continued pressure is, that the child is destroyed from the circulation in the placenta being interrupted, the mother becomes exhausted, and inflammation or rupture of the uterus or vagina are almost the unavoidable results.

Another although much rarer consequence of malposition of the child, is that peculiar mode of expulsion which was first noticed by Dr. Denman in 1772. From the supposition that the shoulder receded and the nates came down into the pelvis, in which position the child was born, he called it "the spontaneous evolution of the fœtus;" but the term spontaneous expulsion, as proposed by Dr. Douglas in 1811, is much better adapted, it having been shown by that gentleman that the explanation of this process as given by Dr. Denman was not correct. (An Explanation of the real Process of the spontaneous Evolution of the Fœtus, by J. C. Douglas, M. D. 2nd ed. 1819, p. 28.,) but that whilst the shoulder rested against the pubes, the side of the thorax and abdomen, followed by the nates, passed in one enormous sweep over the perineum, leaving the head and other arm still to be extricated.

The shoulder and thorax thus low and impacted, instead of receding into the uterus, are at each successive pain forced still lower, until the ribs of that side, corresponding with the protruded arm, press on the perineum, and cause it to assume the same form as it would by the pressure of the forehead in a natural labour. At this period, not only the entire of the arm but the[Pg 271] shoulder can be perceived externally, with the clavicle lying under the arch of the pubes. By farther uterine contractions the ribs are forced more forwards, appearing at the os externum, as the vertex would in a natural labour, the clavicle having been by degrees forced round on the anterior part of the pubes with the acromion looking towards the mons Veneris. "The arm and shoulder are entirely protruded with one side of the thorax, not only appearing at the os externum, but partly without it: the lower part of the same side of the trunk presses on the perineum, with the breech either in the hollow of the sacrum or at the brim of the pelvis, ready to descend into it, and, by a few farther uterine efforts, the remainder of the trunk, with the lower extremities, is expelled." (Douglas, op. cit. p. 28. 2nd ed.)

Farther experience has confirmed the correctness of Dr. Douglas's views (Med. Trans. of the Royal Coll. of Physicians, vol. vi. 1820;) and, indeed, the original case as related by Dr. Denman himself tends to prove that nothing like an "evolution" of the fœtus takes place. I found the arm much swelled, and pushed through the external parts in such a manner that the shoulder nearly reached the perineum. The woman struggled vehemently with her pains, and during their continuance I perceived the shoulder of the child to descend.

Some years afterwards, the late Dr. Gooch had the opportunity of observing a case of spontaneous expulsion with great accuracy, and came to the same conclusion as Dr. Douglas had done. "Resolved to know what became of the arm, if this (the spontaneous expulsion) should happen, and thus fit myself for a witness on this disputed point, I laid hold of it with a napkin and watched its movements: so far from going up into the uterus when a pain came on, it advanced, as well as the shoulder, still forwarder under the arch of the pubes, the side of the thorax pressing more on the perineum and appearing still more externally; it advanced so rapidly that in two pains, with a good deal of muscular exertion on the part of the patient, but apparently with less suffering than attends the birth of the head in a common first labour, did the side of the chest, of the abdomen, and of the breech, pass one after the other in an enormous sweep over the perineum till the nates and legs were completely expelled." (Ibid.)

The celebrated Boer, has, however, detailed a case where the arm had prolapsed into the vagina, the hand appearing externally; and on introducing his hand for the purpose of turning, he felt the hand distinctly receding, and the breech beginning to occupy the cavity of the pelvis. This is very different to a case of spontaneous expulsion: "the child lay completely across, with its abdomen towards the back of the mother;"[110] it had, in fact, not yet[Pg 272] begun to press against the brim, or to assume any definite position, there having been as yet but little uterine contraction, and both rectum and bladder being considerably distended. When these were evacuated the pains increased: the breech being nearest to the brim, descended, and the arm in consequence receded. Dr. Gooch considers it most probable that "it was only a breech presentation, the hand having accidentally slipt down into the vagina."

Although in cases of malposition where turning has become excessively difficult and dangerous, the spontaneous expulsion must be looked upon as a most fortunate process by which nature effects delivery, still, however, we must never venture to wait for it without making such attempts to turn the child as the state of the patient may justify. It is always more or less dangerous to the mother, and almost certainly fatal to the child. Indeed, it is our opinion, that the spontaneous expulsion can rarely, if ever take place, except where the child has been already dead some time, or where it is premature. "Nor can any event," says Dr. Douglas, "ever be calculated upon than that of a still-born infant. If the arm of the fœtus should be almost entirely protruded with the shoulder pressing on the perineum, if a considerable portion of its thorax be in the hollow of the sacrum with the axilla low in the pelvis, if with this disposition the uterine efforts be still powerful, and if the thorax be forced sensibly lower, during the presence of each successive pain, the evolution may with great confidence be expected." (Op. cit. p. 42.)

On the other hand, if either from the rigidity, &c. of the child or of the passages, but little material advance is made in the manner above-mentioned, if the soft parts are become swollen and inflamed, and the powers of the patient are beginning to flag, and exhaustion coming on, if turning has been attempted as far as could be done with safety, and still without success, we have no choice left but that of embryotomy; the chest and abdomen must be evacuated of their contents as already directed under the head of Perforation, and in this manner the child delivered.

Malposition with deformed pelvis, or rigidity of the uterus.—Where the pelvis is deformed, or the uterus (from the early escape of the liquor amnii) spasmodically contracted upon the child, and the os uteri in a state of rigidity, the difficulties and danger of the case are greatly multiplied: in the former complication the embryotomy must be carried much farther, in the latter we must have recourse to bleeding, opium, warm-bath, &c. as recommended under the head of Turning.

The prolapsed arm is not to be put back or amputated.—Where the arm has been some time prolapsed, and, from the pressure of the soft parts, much swollen, it fills up the vagina so completely that it would seem almost impossible to introduce the hand, unless we push up the arm first: experience however confirms the[Pg 273] valuable rule of La Motte, viz. that we must slide our hand along the arm into the uterus; we shall rarely find, where the passages are in a proper state for undertaking the operation, that the prolapsed arm presents any serious obstruction to the passage of the hand. "An arm presenting," says Chapman, "and advanced as far as the armpit, is not to be returned, but the hand is to be introduced (which, as Deventer justly observes, is often found to penetrate with much more ease when the arm hangs down than when it is thrust back again) and the feet to be sought for, which, when found, the arm will prove no great hindrance in turning the child." (Chapman's Midwifery, p. 46. 2nd. ed., 1735.)

In no case is it necessary to separate the arm at the shoulder, "for I have found it," says Dr. Denman, "a great inconvenience, there being much difficulty in distinguishing between the lacerated skin of the child and the parts appertaining to the mother." (Essay on Preternat. Labours, p. 32.)

Dr. Meigs, of Philadelphia, has added another powerful argument against this practice, viz. that cases have occurred where the arm had been cut off and where the child was nevertheless born alive.

As to how far it is possible or advisable so to alter the position of the child as to make it present with the nates or head, this has already been considered in the chapter upon Turning.

The presentation of the arm with the head is of very rare occurrence, so much so that some have doubted if it really existed: two cases of this kind have come under our own notice, in both of which the child was born in this position, although with some difficulty.

"Independent of the awkwardness of position which the head may assume, from the circumstance of the hand or arm descending with it into the pelvis, there will be so much increase in the bulk of the part as to render its passage slow and difficult; yet if the case be not interrupted by mismanagement, it will terminate favourably, for this complication of presentation seldom happens but in a wide pelvis." (Merriman's Synopsis, p. 48, last ed.)

It is by no means uncommon to feel the hand lying upon the side of the head or on the cheek; but this produces no impediment to the labour, for as the head descends through the brim of the pelvis the hand usually slips up: in the other case we have felt the arm bent over the head, and pressing the ear on the opposite side.

Presentation of the hand and feet. We sometimes also meet with cases where the hand presents with one or two feet; but these complications merely exist at the commencement of labour, where the uterus has been greatly distended with liquor amnii, and where its contractions have not yet begun to press the child[Pg 274] into the brim. Cases of this nature sooner or later are sure to terminate in presentations of the nates or shoulder, unless the process of labour has been interfered with.

Presentation of the head and feet. Presentations of the head and one or both feet have also been described: these, however, have only occurred during the operation of turning, when the feet have been brought down into the pelvis before the head had left it, and, therefore, must be considered as having been made by unskilfulness on the part of the practitioner. Where this is the case it may be necessary to premise blood-letting, &c., on account of the inflamed condition of the parts from the previous unsuccessful attempts to turn: after this, a fillet should be passed round the feet in order to secure them, and then the head may be safely pushed out of the pelvis.

Rupture of the uterus. Of the injurious results arising from protracted or neglected cases of arm or shoulder presentation none can compare in point of danger with those where the uterus has given way or burst. This state may also be deformity of the pelvis, tumours, and other causes of obstruction to the passage of the child, by which the uterus is excited to unusually violent efforts in order to overcome the impediment during which the laceration is effected. It may also arise from injuries to the uterine tissue without undue exertions, as from exostosis of the pelvis, sharp projecting edges of the promontory or brim, and also from organic disease: thus, "when the rent speedily follows the accession of labour, before the pains have become severe, or the uterus has scarcely begun to dilate, its structures will probably be found diseased." (Facts and Cases in Obstetric Medicine, by I. T. Ingleby, p. 176.)

Usual seat of the laceration. The part of the uterus in which laceration is most frequently observed to occur is near to or at the junction of the uterus with the vagina: this happens rather more frequently behind than before, but the difference in this respect is very trifling. Thus in 36 cases which were collected by Mr. Roberton, of Manchester, "in 1 the cervix was separated from the vagina except by a thread: in 11 the laceration was posterior, in 8 it was anterior, in 5 lateral, in 3 anterior-lateral, and in 3 posterior-lateral." (Edin. Med. and Surg. Journal, vol. xlii. 1834, p. 60.) In 34 cases which occurred at the Dublin Lying-in Hospital, "in 13 the injury was at the posterior part; in 12 anteriorly; in 2 laterally; in 1 the mouth of the womb was torn, and in 6 the particular seat of the laceration was not described." (A Practical Treatise on Midwifery, &c., by Robert Collins, M. D., 1835, p. 244.)

The nature and extent of the laceration varies a good deal: in the worst cases the uterus is torn completely through, and the child escapes either partly or wholly into the abdominal cavity; whereas, in many, the peritoneum has not given way,[Pg 275] the laceration being confined entirely to the tissue of the uterus itself. Thus, in 9 of the 34 cases recorded by Dr. Collins, "the peritoneal coat of the uterus was uninjured, although the muscular substance of the cervix was extensively ruptured." In other instances the peritoneum has been cracked or torn in numerous places without any injury to the subjacent tissue.

From the greater degree of resistance to the passage of the child, in cases of first labour, we might naturally suppose that rupture of the uterus would be more frequently seen among primiparæ: this, however, is not the case, for of 29 cases mentioned by Mr. Roberton, only one of them was a primipara; a larger (and as an average probably more correct) proportion, viz. 7 in 34, has been given by Dr. Collins: of the multiparæ, 5 were in their sixth pregnancy, 2 in their tenth, and 2 also in their eleventh pregnancy.

Experience also shows that in a large proportion of these cases, the duration of the labour has been very far from being longer than usual; indeed, in a considerable majority, the mischief has taken place very few hours after the commencement of active labour. Thus, the average duration of it in the 36 cases recorded by Mr. Roberton, was 15 hours: in 24 of those by Dr. Collins, it was 17 hours: but if we take merely the majority of them we shall have a much smaller average: thus, in 20 of Mr. Roberton's cases it was 9 hours, and in 15 of Dr. Collins's it was only 6 hours.

Causes. A large proportion of cases where the uterus gives way during labour, are connected with more or less deformity of the pelvis, and where, from previous severe and difficult labours, its structure has been injured, and rendered incapable of bearing that degree of tension, which even the ordinary exertions of the uterine fibres would require. In many others, the impediment the contracted pelvis, or malposition of the child, has roused the uterus to those violent efforts which have produced the laceration. Organic diseases of the uterus, or cicatrisations of the soft passages from extensive injuries in former labours, either render its powers of resistance defective, or, by increasing the resistance, excite it to unusual violence. "The operation of turning is not unfrequently a cause of laceration of the vagina or mouth of the uterus, particularly, where it is performed previous to the soft parts being sufficiently dilated to admit the easy passage of the hand, or where great haste is employed. The same consequences may ensue from rash or violent attempts to remove a retained placenta. I have also known the mouth of the womb to be torn by the imprudent use of the forceps when not sufficiently dilated." (Dr. Collins, op. cit. p. 242.) "The sex of the infant, it would appear, may also have some share in occasioning this very distressing occurrence." (Practical Remarks on Lacerations of the Uterus and Vagina, by Thomas M'Keever,[Pg 276] M. D., p. 4.) Thus, of 20 cases reported by Dr. M'Keever, 15 were delivered of boys and 5 of girls; of the 34 cases described by Dr. Collins, "23 of the children were males. This is satisfactorily accounted for by the greater size of the male head, as proved by accurate measurement made by Dr. Joseph Clarke."

Another circumstance which influences to a certain extent the frequency of rupture of the uterus, is the rank of the patient: in private practice, especially among the better classes of society, it is an extremely rare occurrence; but in the lower grades of life several causes concur to render it more frequent. They are "much more exposed to falls, bruises, and other accidental injuries during pregnancy, in consequence of which the uterus may be either ruptured at the time they have sustained the violence, or may be so weakened in structure at some particular point, as readily to give way during its efforts to accomplish delivery. Lastly, they are more liable to fall into the hands of ignorant inexperienced midwives, who not unfrequently, with a view of expediting the process of delivery, rupture the membranes at an early period of the labour; in consequence of which, the firm unyielding head of the child is prematurely brought in contact with the passages, exciting by its pressure, swelling, inflammation, and an interrupted state of the circulation in the uterus and adjacent parts. In such a case should there unfortunately exist any disproportion between the parts of the mother and the head of the infant, or should proper measures not be employed to obviate distressing symptoms, and that the labour pains continue to recur with extreme violence, there is great risk of the uterus giving way, the laceration being of course most likely to occur at that part where the greatest pressure has been sustained." (M'Keever, op. cit. p. 3.)

The premonitory symptoms of rupture of the uterus are not always sufficient to warn us of the impending danger, for in many cases nothing unusual has occurred until the actual injury has been produced, and it has then been inferred by the alarming change observed in the patient's appearance. In many cases, especially where the muscular substance only of the uterus was torn, the pains have continued with a sufficient degree of power to expel the child; in others the mischief has been attended with so little suffering at the moment, and for the time with so little constitutional derangement, as to excite no suspicion, either on the part of the patient, or her attendant. "Farther, as on some occasions, the uterus has been known to give way during the very pain which effected the delivery of the child, instances of which may be found in the works of Crantz and Guillimeau." (Ibid. p. 15.)

Symptoms. "When a rupture of the uterus has really happened, it is generally marked by symptoms which are decisive; but it being a case which occurs so very rarely, they do not[Pg 277] immediately create suspicions. When labour has continued violent a considerable time, if a pain expressive of peculiar agony is followed by a discharge of blood, and an immediate cessation of the throes, there is reason to apprehend this mischief. If nausea and languor succeed, with a feeble and irregular pulse, cold sweat, retching, a difficulty of breathing, an inability to lie in a horizontal posture, faintness or convulsions, there is still more reason to suspect the nature of the case. But if the presenting part of the child, which was before plainly to be distinguished, has receded and can be no longer felt, and its form and members can be traced through the parietes of the abdomen, there is evidence sufficient, I believe, to determine that the uterus is ruptured. The labour pain, in consequence of which the rupture is supposed to have happened, is often described by the patient, as being similar to cramp, and as if something was tearing and giving way within them. It has been said likewise, to have produced a noise which could be heard by the people present." (Observations on an extraordinary Case of ruptured Uterus, by Andr. Douglas, M. D., 1785, p. 48.)

Where the peritoneal coat only has been torn, we may have many of the above-mentioned symptoms resulting from laceration of the uterus, without any impediment to the progress of labour. This peculiar species of partial rupture was first noticed by the late Dr. John Clarke, (Trans. for the Improvement of Med. and Surg. Knowledge, vol. iii.,) since which cases have been recorded by Mr. Partridge (Med. Chir. Trans. vol. xix. p. 72.,) Dr. Collins, Dr. Ramsbotham, &c. In Dr. Clarke's case the uterus and vagina "were found to have sustained no injury whatever; but on turning down the fundus uteri over the pubes, between forty and fifty transverse lacerations were discovered in the peritoneal covering of its posterior surface, none of which were in depth above the twentieth of an inch, and many were merely fissures in the membrane itself. The edges of the lacerations were thinly covered with flakes of coagulated blood; and about an ounce of this fluid was found in the fold of the peritoneum, which dips down between the uterus and the rectum."

Where the uterus has been torn quite through, a frequent result is, that the child passes either wholly, or in part, through the rent into the abdominal cavity: this occurrence will, in great measure, be influenced by the situation and extent of the laceration, and also by the degree of the uterine contractions. It is easily recognised by the presenting part having receded, and in all probability by the members of the child being felt with unusual distinctness through the abdominal parietes.

Treatment. Under such an unfortunate complication nothing remains but to effect the delivery in as speedy and gentle a manner as possible. Where the os uteri is fully dilated, the head[Pg 278] presenting and but little receded, and the pelvis only slightly contracted, the application of the forceps will be justifiable; but in many instances the circumstances of the case will not warrant it, and the attempt must be made to bring down the feet, which has been most usually had recourse to with success although it occasionally happens that even this is attended with no slight difficulties: the rigid and partially dilated os uteri may be a serious bar to the introduction of the hand; this has been successfully overcome by incisions into its edge;[111] but it is a remedy which no practitioner would use if by any means to be avoided.

Gastrotomy. Where the whole child has passed into the abdominal cavity, and the uterus has evidently contracted, so as to produce a serious, if not insurmountable obstacle to delivering it through the vagina, or at any rate without the risk of increasing the extent of the laceration, the question then remains as to whether we should perform gastrotomy, or leave the fœtus in the abdominal cavity to be gradually discharged, like an extra-uterine pregnancy, by abscess and sloughing. There can be no doubt that the former plan is preferable, nor are there wanting upon record successful cases of gastrotomy after rupture of the uterus; one of which is doubly interesting from the operation having been twice performed with a favourable result in consequence of a repetition of the injury in the patient's succeeding pregnancy.[112] Mr. Ingleby, of Birmingham, gives a similar opinion in favour of the operation: "The result of two cases of Cæsarean operation in which I have been engaged, leads me to view the mere abdominal incision with very different feelings. The operation is not half so dangerous as the Cæsarean, whilst the celerity with which it is done, the absence of hæmorrhage, and the facility with which the intestines are confined within the abdomen, tend to divest it of much of its terror." (Op. cit. p. 201.)

Rupture during the early months of pregnancy. Cases of rupture of the uterus have occasionally been observed at an early period of pregnancy; in many of these the fœtus has passed into the abdominal cavity, where it has been enclosed in a species of cyst, and afterwards expelled through the rectum or abdominal parietes by an abscess. It may be doubted whether some of these have not been cases of extra-uterine pregnancy. On the other hand, there is reason to believe that those extraordinary cases of ventral pregnancy, to which we have alluded, where[Pg 279] the fœtus has been found in a sac in the abdomen, which communicated with the uterus, and to which the placenta was attached, were the results of rupture at an early period of pregnancy, in all probability the result of ulceration or organic degeneration of the uterine parietes. In some instances it has been violence: and it is by no means impossible that it might take place during a miscarriage, when the uterine contractions are occasionally very violent. Mr.

Ingleby remarks that in a case of premature expulsion at the fifth month, the violence of the pains seemed quite equal to produce a breech of surface.

Dr. Collins has recorded a case of ruptured uterus in about the fifth month. The laceration appears to have taken place imperceptibly: the child was very putrid; and as the os uteri was sufficiently dilated, the head was perforated, and "was brought away almost without any assistance. It was nothing more than a soft mass, being so completely broken down by putrefaction."[113] There was no previous history to explain it; the muscular structure of the uterus at the anterior part of its cervix was torn, leaving the peritoneum entire.

Lastly, we may mention a very singular species of laceration of the uterus, of which we know of but two cases, the one recorded by Mr. P. N. Scott, of Norwich, (Med. Chir. Trans. vol. xi.) the other which occurred under our own notice, where the whole os uteri separated from the uterus during labour.[114] In both cases, the os uteri presented a degree of unnatural rigidity, which was quite peculiar, and which in one case, defied repeated and active bleeding, as well as opiates. In Mr. Scott's case, the laceration took place during a violent pain, when the patient "felt something snap, the noise of which one of the attendants declared she heard." In the other case, the patient was not aware of any thing peculiar having happened: it was a first labour in the eighth month of pregnancy; the os uteri had dilated to nearly the size of half a crown, but would dilate no farther; the child had evidently been some time dead; the cranial integuments gave way from putrefaction, the brain escaped, the bones of the skull collapsed, and the bag of scalp protruded so far that we could lay hold of it, although the basis cranii had not passed. We were thus enabled to use more extractive force than we could have ventured upon with the crotchet: after a little effort, but without even a complaint from the patient, the head descended and passed through the os externum. "On the bed lay[Pg 280] a disc of fibrous matter with a circular hole in the middle; in fact, the os uteri separated from the uterus to the extent of near half an inch, the edge of the laceration being as clean and smooth as if it had been carefully cut off by a knife." In both instances the patient recovered. Whether incisions into the os uteri for the purpose of effecting the necessary degree of dilatation would have been justifiable under circumstances of such unusual rigidity, does not belong to the present subject; for the consideration of this, we must refer to the Fifth Species of Dystocia.

[Pg 281]

CHAPTER II.

SECOND SPECIES OF DYSTOCIA.

Size and form of the child.—Hydrocephalus.—Cerebral tumours.—Accumulation of fluid and tumours in the chest or abdomen.—Monsters.—Anchylosis of the joints of the fœtus.

In this case the labour is rendered difficult or impossible to be completed by the natural powers on account of the faulty size, form, or condition of the child. In the first instance, it is merely a case of disproportion between the child and the passages, owing to the unusual size of the former. Where the child is well formed throughout, but larger than usual, it rarely happens that the head experiences any serious degree of difficulty in passing through a well-formed pelvis, the greatest resistance being observed during the dilatation of the external passages. Even when the head is born, the shoulders may produce a considerable obstruction to its farther passage, requiring a good deal of careful manipulation, in order to disengage the foremost shoulder from under the pubic arch, and thus diminish the pressure of the child against the parietes of the pelvic cavity. Where the shoulders have been severely impacted in this position, it has been in great measure owing to the practitioner having endeavoured to bring down the wrong shoulder first, viz. that which is directed more or less backwards.

Size of the child. We have already stated that the average weight of the full grown fœtus is between six and seven pounds, and its length about eighteen inches; but it is frequently found to exceed these proportions very considerably. Children are not uncommonly observed to weigh 10lbs. at birth. Dr. Merriman once delivered a still-born child, which weighed 14lbs., and the late Sir Richard Crofts is said to have delivered one alive which actually weighed 15lbs.; but by far the largest child which we have yet heard of is recorded by Mr. J. D. Owens, surgeon, at Haymoor near Ludlow; it was born dead, and the weight and admeasurements ten hours after birth were as follow:—

The long diameter from the occiput to the root of the nose   7¼   inches.
The occipito-mental   8½   —
From one parietal protuberance to the other 5   —
Circumference of the skull 15¼   —
Circumference of the thorax over the xiphoid cartilage 14½   —
Breadth of the shoulders   7¼   —
Extreme length of the child 24   —
Weight of the child   17 lbs. 12 oz.
(Lancet, Dec. 22. 1838.)

We have already pointed out the difficulty of determining the presence of twins merely from the appearance of the mother's abdomen; the same will necessarily hold good with regard to one large child. The size of the patient must rarely have any influence in forming our prognosis: in most cases she will have many symptoms, which arise either from pressure or weight in the pelvis, such as difficulty in passing water, œdema of the feet and legs, varicose veins of the thighs and labia, or from cramps, the result of pressure upon the absorbents, veins, or nerves; considerable expansion of the inferior segment of the uterus: all these will give us reason to suspect the presence of a large child even although the abdomen may not be remarkably distended.

Where the head is very large, the bones are seldom much ossified; they therefore yield easily, and the head accommodates itself to the shape of the passage: sometimes, however, it is unusually hard, the bones are well ossified and very unyielding, so that even if it be not larger than common, still, from its hardness, it meets with considerable difficulty in passing through the pelvis. Cases have been described where the cranial bones were completely ossified, and the sutures perfect; but this latter is very doubtful. Perfect mentions an instance where the head was "almost one entire ossification, and where it passed through the pelvis with great difficulty." (Perfect's Cases in Midwifery, vol. ii. p. 370.) We have also met with cases requiring perforation on account of deformed pelvis, and where the cranial bones had almost the feel of a hard nut or shell; still, however, as already observed, we seldom see any serious impediment to the passage of a large head, so long as it is naturally formed; and this applies also to the other parts of the child.

Form of the child. On the other hand, where there is an unnatural form of the child, either from a disproportionate size or anormal configuration of certain parts, labour may be rendered not only very difficult but dangerous: thus one of the three great cavities may be distended with an accumulation of fluid, the most common form of which, is the congenital hydrocephalus.

Hydrocephalus. In many cases it produces much less resistance than might be expected from the size of the head; this is, in great measure, owing to the unusual width of the sutures and[Pg 283] fontanelles, but chiefly to the almost entire want of ossification in the cranial parietes, which are little else than membranous, and so flexible as to allow the head to be squeezed into almost any shape. In some very rare cases the head has burst, a large quantity of fluid has come away suddenly, and this has been followed almost immediately by the birth of the child:[115] but in the majority the labour has been tedious and severe, and in some instances attended with dangerous results to the patient; thus, Dr. Merriman has "known one hydrocephalic fœtus pass entire, the circumference of whose head was 17 inches; another passed alive and lived nearly an hour, whose head measured in circumference nearly 22 inches; both the above labours were long and painful." Perfect relates a case of hydrocephalic head, of which he has given engraved delineations; the labour was attended with extreme difficulty, and the woman expired in less than two hours after delivery; the circumference of this head was 24 inches. (Cases in Midwifery, vol. ii. p. 525.) An interesting case of hydrocephalus, attended with convulsions and laceration of the vagina, has been recorded by Dr. Collins: "the perforator was used, upon the introduction of which into the head fully three half pints of water gushed out; the bones then collapsed, and the delivery was easily completed." (Practical Observations, p. 205.)

Cerebral tumours. The bulk of the head is sometimes increased by tumours or sacs of fluid, which arise from a suture or fontanelle: they are of the same nature as the spina bifida, being formed by a protrusion of the integuments and cerebral membranes from an accumulation of fluid beneath: these are of very rare occurrence, and appear to have retarded labour but little, even although of considerable size. The largest cases on record are those which have been described by Ruysch, where one was as big as the head itself, and another where it was nearly as large as the child's body.[116] A case of fluctuating tumour[Pg 284] upon a child's head has been described by Mauriceau, (Case 544,) but the precise nature of it is not very apparent.

Accumulations of fluid, and tumours in the chest or abdomen. It is very rare that the chest is distended by any accumulation of fluid or morbid growth, although this is not unfrequently met with in the abdomen. La Motte has given three cases of ascites which, by the distention of the abdomen, produced considerable obstruction to the delivery of the child. (Cases 331, 332, and 333.) In other cases the liver or the kidneys have been enormously enlarged. A case is described by Dr. Hemmer, where the child was born as far as the shoulders, and there stuck; finding it impossible to extract the child, he perforated the abdomen in two places, but could not extract it; in a few minutes after it came away of itself. The abdomen had been distended with small hydatids; these gradually escaped, and thus diminished the size of the abdomen. (Neue Zeitschrift für Geburtshülfe, band iv. heft 1, 1836.) Where the child has been dead some time in the uterus, the abdomen is frequently tympanic, and thus retards its expulsion.

Monsters. Certain cases of monstrous formation may produce very serious obstacles to the progress of labour: the most considerable is of twins united by the breast. It is difficult to conceive how so large a mass can be forced through the pelvis: we can only suppose it possible where the children have been dead some time before birth, or where they were premature: to this latter circumstance only we can attribute the fact of their having been born alive, as in the celebrated case of the Siamese twins. Where the children have been united by one pelvis, &c., the chances here of the fœtus being dead before birth would be even still greater. M. Rath, of Zetterfeld, has lately described a case of extremely difficult labour, in consequence of twins united by the breast. "The children (two girls) weighed 15lbs.; they were 17 inches long. The part by which they were united was 9 inches broad and 3 long, and extended from the upper extremity of the sternum to the navel, into which one umbilical cord, which was common to both, entered. The diameter of the two children when laid together was between 7 and 8 inches from one back to the other. One child had two thumbs on the right hand. The cord was 19 inches long, and unusually thick. After suffering some time from peritonitis, &c., the patient recovered." (Siebold's Journal, band xvii. heft 2. 1833.)

Anchylosis of the joints of the fœtus. Lastly, we may mention a very rare cause of this species of dystocia, which has been observed by Professor Busch, where the obstruction to the passage of the child arose from anchylosis of its joints. "The head had been delivered by the forceps, but the body would not follow. As no cause of obstruction could be discovered, a gentle and then more powerful traction was used: this[Pg 285] was followed by a cracking sound, and the upper part of the trunk passed through the os externum: here again it stopped, but still, as no cause of obstruction could be discovered, and as the child was dead, another traction was made, with a repetition of the cracking sound, and the child was delivered. On examination it was found that all the joints of the extremities were anchylosed in the usual position of the fœtus in utero, so that the ossa humeri and then the ossa femoris had given way. The child had been dead some time." (Neue Zeitschrift für Geburtskunde, vol. xv. 1837; and British and Foreign Med. Rev. April 1838, p. 579.)

No precise rules can be given for the treatment of these cases of malformation of the child; it must be modified according to the peculiarities of each individual case. Whenever a part has undergone considerable increase of size from accumulation of fluid, this can be in most cases removed without much difficulty by perforation, whether it be of the head or abdomen. With monstrous growths the accoucheur must depend upon his own resources, ingenuity and knowledge of the mechanism of parturition. The more careful and correct his diagnosis is, the more efficient will be the means he adopts for delivering the child. In such cases the examination can scarcely be made effectually by the finger alone, but the hand will be required for this purpose.

[Pg 286]

CHAPTER III.

THIRD SPECIES OF DYSTOCIA.

Difficult labour from faulty condition of the parts which belong to the child. —The membranes. —Premature rupture of the membranes. —Liquor amnii. —Umbilical cord. —Knots upon the cord. —Placenta.

In describing this species of dystocia, according to the arrangement of Professor Naegelé, which we have adopted, it will be necessary to observe that serious obstructions to the passage of the child is seldom it, although, at the same time, many slight derangements in the progress of labour are liable to result, which demand the care of the practitioner.

The membranes when too thick or tough (Merriman's Synopsis, p. 217,) may retard the labour occasionally, especially during the second stage, when instead of bursting and allowing the uterus to contract more powerfully upon the child by the evacuation of the liquor amnii, they are pushed down into the vagina, forming a large conical sac, which may even protrude externally. We doubt much, however, if the non-rupture of the membranes at the proper time during labour is of itself sufficient to retard its progress, for it is frequently observed that the head will, nevertheless, advance rapidly and even be born covered by the protruded membranes. Where labour is rendered tedious by the unusual strength of the membranes, it is generally connected with considerable distention of the uterus from liquor amnii; in which case the bag of waters is so spherical that it will not descend readily into the vagina, even although the os uteri is fully dilated, and, therefore, prevents the advance of the head: to this we shall recur immediately. So long as there is no undue accumulation of liquor amnii, we may safely allow the membranes to descend to the os externum before we rupture them. In former times a variety of instruments were employed for this purpose, many of which were dangerous, and all unnecessary, the finger being in most cases sufficient. The most effectual way of doing this is to press the thumb and middle finger upon the membranes during a pain and thus increase their tension, whilst the point of the fore-finger is pushed against them: scratching them with the[Pg 287] nail during a pain will be sufficient when they are higher up the vagina.

Premature rupture of the membranes. More frequently the membranes rupture too soon, that is, before the os uteri is fully dilated: this may arise from their being too thin, a condition, however, which it is not very easy to prove: in most instances, it is observed where the uterus is but moderately distended, and where it has that oval or pyriform shape which we have already pointed out as being best adapted for acting efficiently upon the os uteri. This, perhaps, is one reason, why too early rupture of the membranes so frequently occurs in primiparæ; and this may be one cause, among many others, why first labours are generally so much more tedious and severe. The membranes may also be prematurely ruptured by violent exertions, coughing, sneezing, vomiting, &c. by straining immoderately and too soon, by rough and awkward examination, &c. Where this is the case, the patient should preserve the horizontal posture, and keep as quiet as she can until the os uteri has dilated sufficiently and allowed the head to advance.

Liquor amnii. Where the uterus is distended by an unusual quantity of liquor amnii, its contractile power is necessarily much impaired; and until the quantity of its contents be somewhat diminished, the progress of the labour will be more or less retarded. The average quantity of liquor amnii at the full period of pregnancy is about eight ounces; but it frequently exceeds this very considerably, occasionally amounting to several pints or even quarts. The causes of this extraordinary accumulation are still but little known. "M. Mercier has, in some cases, attributed it to an inflammatory condition of the amnion, the fœtal surface of this membrane being stated to have been partially coated with false membrane, and the amnion itself crowded with blood-vessels of a rose colour:" in another case "about a quarter of the fœtal surface of the amnion was inflamed, being of a deep red colour and double the natural thickness."[117] The results of Dr. R. Lee's observations, after having paid a good deal of attention to the subject, do not tend to confirm this view: he has described six cases of unusual accumulation of the liquor amnii, in one amounting actually to sixteen pints. In five of them "there existed with dropsy of the amnion some malformed or diseased condition of the fœtus or its involucra, which rendered it incapable of supporting life subsequent to birth." In two only of the preceding cases was "the formation of an excessive quantity of liquor amnii accompanied with inflammatory and dropsical symptoms in the mother; and in none did the amnion, where an opportunity occurred for making an examination, exhibit those morbid[Pg 288] appearances inflammation, which M. Mercier has described, and which led him to infer that inflammation of the amnion is the essential cause of the disease." (Lee, op. cit.) Dr. Merriman has given a similar opinion, and states, that "when the embryo or fœtus is diseased, the liquor amnii is sometimes immense in quantity. I once saw at least two gallons evacuated from the uterus: the child was monstrously formed and much diseased."[118]

In these cases the size and globular form of the uterus, the tenseness of its parietes, the more or less distinct feel of fluctuation, the absence of the child's movements and of any prominences arising from the projecting portions of its body, the rapid increase which has been observed in the size of the abdomen, the pain in different parts of the uterus, especially in the groins and pelvis, the œdema or anasarca of the lower extremities, serve to mark this condition. On examination per vaginam we also feel the inferior segment of the uterus much expanded, the cervix probably shorter than might be expected for the period of pregnancy; the ballottement is unusually free and distinct. In some instances the patient has suffered so much, either from the effects of the retarded circulation in the lower extremities, or from the impeded respiration as to require the membranes to be punctured in order to reduce the size of the uterus. The child is usually born dead where the accumulation has gone to so great an extent: in the three cases recorded by La Motte, it was dead before birth in the first two, and died immediately after birth in the third. Many of these cases, which have been complicated with disease or malformation of the fœtus, have appeared to arise from a syphilitic taint; but in others, of more common occurrence, where there was merely an unusually large quantity of liquor amnii without any disease either of the mother or her child, the cause must still remain a matter of uncertainty. This latter condition is mostly seen in women who have been frequently pregnant; the os uteri in them is generally yielding, and when once it has attained its full degree of dilatation, we may safely rupture the membranes and thus expedite labour considerably.

There being an unusually small quantity of liquor amnii can scarcely operate as an obstruction to labour, except where the membranes have been prematurely ruptured.

The umbilical cord may obstruct labour, by either being too short, or rendered so from being twisted round some part of the[Pg 289] child. Its length varies very considerably. Although we have stated it to average about eighteen or twenty inches,[119] we have met with extreme deviations both within as well as beyond this medium length. The shortest cord which we know of occurred some years ago at the General Lying-in Hospital, "where, after two or three violent pains, the child was suddenly and forcibly expelled the cord was found ruptured at about two inches from the navel of the child, which cried stoutly. After removing the child the matron sought for the other end of the funis, but could not find it; she examined per vaginam but could not feel it; and on introducing her hand into the uterus, found the placenta with the remains of the cord ruptured at its very insertion; so that in this case the cord could not have been much more than two inches long." (Printed Lectures in Renshaw's Lond. Med. and Surg. Journ. May 1835, p. 426.)

We quite agree with Professor Naegelé, that unusual shortness of the cord can rarely if ever retard labour; and that where the cord really produces an impediment to its progress, it is from being twisted round the neck, or some other part of the child. (Lehrbuch, 2d ed. p. 289.) This generally arises from its unusual length, and from its having formed several coils around the child: we have met with it forty-eight inches long, and twisted four times round the child's neck; but Baudelocque mentions a case where it actually measured fifty-seven inches, "forming seven turns round the child's neck." (Heath's Transl. vol. i. § 516.) Mauriceau has given an instance (Obs. 401.,) where the cord had "longueur d'une aune et un tiers de notre mesure de Paris:" which, converted into English measure, amounts to somewhat more than sixty-one inches.

Although nothing is of more common occurrence than the cord being twisted once or twice round the child, it nevertheless, happens, but very rarely, that its advance is thereby obstructed. In a case of this sort, the labour usually commences quite favourably; the os uteri dilates, and the head advances to a certain extent, beyond which it makes no other farther progress; the uterine contractions are attended with much pain in the fundus, during which the head advances somewhat, but retires again during the intervals. Where the head is already near the os externum, this may be easily attributed to the elasticity of the soft parts, until the delay which takes place to the farther progress of the labour warns the practitioner that something more than ordinary is the cause. But where this takes place, and the head is still in the pelvic cavity; where at the same time, although it refuses to advance, it is quite moveable, and allows the finger to be passed freely round it; where any attempt to extract it with the forceps[Pg 290] has not only met with great opposition, but has greatly aggravated the sense of painful dragging in the upper parts of the uterus there will be pretty certain evidence of the cord being either too short, or, what is most probable, of its being twisted round the child. In each of the three cases recorded by La Motte, the head had descended to the os externum; whereas, in two others described by Burton, it was evidently much higher up: he ruptured the cord in both instances; La Motte succeeded in cutting the cord with a pair of scissors in one case, in another he appears to have separated the placenta, and in the other to have delivered by little else than force. Where upon introducing the hand we find it impossible to undo the coil of the funis, we should endeavour to slip it first over one and then the other shoulder, as we have recommended under the more ordinary circumstances: should this fail, we must try to cut it through either by a finger nail slightly notched for the purpose, or by the introduction of a Smellie perforator well guarded.

The cord being twisted round the child's neck may not only retard labour, it may destroy the child itself by preventing the free return of blood from the head: this may take place some little time before birth, or during the actual process of labour. That suffocation cannot possibly be the cause of death under these circumstances is sufficiently evident.

Knots upon the cord have been mentioned by some authors as a cause of danger to the child shortly before and especially during labour; for the circulation in the umbilical vessels being more or less compressed, the child would either be born dead or in a very weakly state. Experience has, however, shown that these effects have been much over-rated, and that these knots are seldom injurious to the child.[120] Baudelocque has not only met with single, but even triple and very complicated knots tied tightly upon the cord, and yet the child was not only born alive, but remarkably robust and healthy. Circumstances, however, may occur by which the knot is gradually drawn so tight as to destroy the child. Smellie has given a case of this kind; but it is to the late Matthew Saxtorph, of Copenhagen, that we are indebted for an admirable essay on this subject. The result of his observations coincides with those of Baudelocque, viz. that it rarely proves fatal to the child.[121] The manner in which these knots are formed[Pg 291] may be easily imagined; when by chance the cord lies in the form of a ring, and the fœtus happens to float through it, a noose is made, which, when drawn tight by accident, forms a knot.

The most favourable time for the formation of such knots is in the earlier months of pregnancy, when the quantity of liquor amnii, in proportion to the bulk of the fœtus, is so much greater than at an after period, and when its movements are consequently less impeded. The circulation in the knot will be obstructed in proportion as the knot is drawn closer: if it be merely somewhat impeded, the vessels on each side of the knot will be distended and varicose, and the cord itself, where it forms the knot, from the constant gradual pressure of one fold against the other, will become more or less flattened.[122] We believe that in every case the cord has been of unusual length.

The placenta cannot easily obstruct the birth of the child, although it may render the labour exceedingly dangerous in a great variety of ways: these circumstances will be considered under their respective heads.

[Pg 292]

CHAPTER IV.

FOURTH SPECIES OF DYSTOCIA.

Abnormal state of the pelvis.—Equally contracted pelvis.—Unequally contracted pelvis.—Rickets.—Malacosteon, or mollities ossium.—Symptoms of deformed pelvis.—Funnel-shaped pelvis.—Obliquely distorted pelvis.—Exostosis.—Diagnosis of contracted pelvis.—Effects of difficult labour from deformed pelvis.—Fracture of the parietal bone.—Treatment.—Prognosis.

This may arise from there being either too much or too little resistance to the passage of the child; where, in the one case, labour is rendered difficult or impossible to be completed by the natural powers; in the other, it is unnaturally rapid. The latter condition belongs to the second great division of dystocia, where the faulty character of the labour does not depend upon its progress being deranged, but upon other circumstances: we shall, therefore, delay speaking of precipitate or too rapid labour from unusually large pelvis, until then, and devote the present chapter to the consideration of those cases where the labour is more or less obstructed by the faulty condition of the mother's pelvis.

The pelvis may obstruct the passage of the child in a variety of ways.

1. It may be merely a diminutive or dwarfish pelvis, viz. well formed but smaller than usual in every direction—the pelvis simpliciter justo minor of Continental authors.

2. It may be distorted and deformed.

3. It may be of the natural form and size, but the passage through it more or less obstructed by exostosis.

Equally contracted pelvis. The first species of faulty pelvis (pelvis simpliciter justo minor,) is not of common occurrence, and has received but little notice in this country. It has been said to resemble the pelvis of a girl in its general appearance; but this only holds good in point of size; for, in the relative proportions of its diameter, it presents all the characters of a well formed adult pelvis. From this circumstance, it can scarcely be said to be an arrest of development, the necessary changes in the form of the pelvis having taken place at the time of puberty, as [Pg 293]completely as if it had been of the ordinary size. A pelvis of this sort may be not more than a quarter of an inch too small in every direction, or it may be as much as a whole inch: we do not know of any case where the diminution has exceeded this last degree.

The pelvis equaliter justo minor is not accompanied with a corresponding diminutiveness in the rest of the skeleton, most of the patients in whom it has been observed being well formed and of the usual stature. Fortunately, as before stated, it is of rare occurrence, for even a small diminution in the size of the bony passages, which is uniform in every direction, presents a most serious obstacle to the passage of the child. Thus, in three cases of the sort, which have been described by Professor Busch in his report of the Berlin Lying-in Hospital, the labour terminated fatally in two. "The first case was a presentation of the breech; the head was delivered by the forceps; the child was dead; the pelvis measured half an inch too small in every direction. In the second case, which was a head presentation, the delivery was effected by the forceps, but not without the greatest efforts; the child was still-born, and the mother died in a day or two after from peritoneal inflammation. The third case required perforation; this also terminated fatally, the forceps having been previously applied, and considerable efforts made without success. On examination after death, every diameter of the pelvis was three quarters of an inch smaller than usual: in appearance it resembled that of a child." (Neue Zeitschrift für Geburtskunde, vol. xv. 1837.)

Unequally contracted pelvis. The unequally contracted pelvis (pelvis inæqualiter justo minor) may exist under a variety of forms; the most common is where the antero-posterior diameter is defective, or, in other words, where the distance between its anterior and posterior parietes is less than usual. In a slight degree, it is frequently met with among the poorer classes, and arises from the patient having been compelled to carry heavy burdens in early childhood, or otherwise subjected to severe labour. The practice of entrusting a girl of eight or ten years of age with the care of a heavy infant, which she carries about in her arms for many hours every day, is a fruitful source of this species of pelvic deformity; the young and plastic pelvis is unable to bear the additional pressure which is thrown upon the sacrum by the overloaded trunk, without having the just proportions of its growth materially influenced and perverted, especially at a period of life when the whole form of the pelvis is undergoing considerable changes. The constant pressure and counter-pressure to which the pelvis is subjected by the undue weight which is applied to the sacrum above, and supported by the resistance of the femora against the acetabula below, must necessarily tend at this age, even in an ordinary state of health, to impair its [Pg 294]symmetry, more or less, and gradually to diminish the distance between its anterior and posterior parietes. Under no circumstances has this cause of pelvic deformity acted to such an extent as in the English manufactories, where young children are compelled to remain standing for twelve or more hours at the machines: the physical powers are unequal to the endurance of so much unceasing labour, the skeleton of the child soon suffers in its growth, and the pelvis almost certainly becomes contracted.

Similar effects may also be undue pressure on the other parts of the pelvis. Thus the outlet may become much contracted by sitting many hours a day on a hard seat, as is frequently the case in schools. The tubera ischii are pressed together, the pubic arch is thereby contracted, and the sacrum becomes strongly curved forwards. Much riding on horseback at an early age is said to be injurious; and it is stated that the females of those American nations who are constantly on horseback bear but few children, and are frequently three or four days in severe labour.

Rickets. Similar effects, only in a much more aggravated form, are rickets in early life; the pelvic bones having become soft from the loss of their earthy matter, gradually give way under the pressure of the superincumbent trunk, to the support of which they were unequal. In this way the sacrum is forced downwards and forwards towards the symphysis pubis, the acetabula are driven upwards and backwards, the pubic arch becomes distorted; and if the disease continues for a considerable period of time, the whole pelvis becomes so squeezed together as entirely to lose its original proportions.

The manner in which the distortion takes place varies exceedingly, and will be more or less influenced by the circumstances under which the child has been placed. The most constant change is the shortening of the antero-posterior diameter at the brim. In severe cases the base of the sacrum has, as it were, sunk down between the illia, so that its promontory occupies the cavity of the pelvis, the fourth, or third, or even the second, lumbar vertebræ occupying its former position. The gradual yielding of the bones seldom takes place with that degree of uniformity as to allow the sacrum to approach the symphysis pubis in a straight line: the more common result of rickets is, that the promontory is, at the same time, wrung more or less to one side.

"If the superior strait does not constantly present the same figure in deformed pelvis; if it is sometimes larger on one side than the other; if one of the acetabula is nearer to the sacrum, while the other approaches less; if the symphysis of the pubes is removed in many cases from a line which would divide the body into two equal parts, it is because the rickets has not equally affected all the bones of the pelvis, nor equally hurt all their [Pg 295]junctions; and because the attitude which the child takes in walking or sitting may change a little the direction of the compressing power, which I have just mentioned." (Baudelocque, translated by Heath, vol. i. p. 60.) Nor is it necessary that the degree with which the disease affects the different parts of the pelvis should vary in order to produce these inequalities of distortion, for there is no reason to suppose that the promontory of the sacrum would approach the symphysis pubis in a straight line, even where the softening of the bones was uniform throughout; the attitude of the child, as above-mentioned, and the manner in which it supports itself, will have no inconsiderable influence in determining the direction in which the distortion takes place.

In those instances where the promontory is forced low down into the pelvic cavity, the sacrum becomes bent upon itself, the upper part of it forming a sharp curve backwards, while its lower portion together with the coccyx being confined by their attachments, and more or less compressed by sitting, are directed forwards. This is not seen where the projection of the promontory is but slight; the curve of the sacrum so far from being increased is rather lessened; the sacrum is straighter and flatter than usual, so that, although the brim of the pelvis is contracted, we not unfrequently find the outlet even larger than natural: in other cases, where the softening of the bones has gone to a considerable extent, the outlet is diminished, from the tubera ischii having been forced inwards.

The degree to which the promontory projects, of course, varies considerably. The distortion is occasionally so great as not even to leave an inch of antero-posterior diameter. This excessive deformity, however, is more frequently the result of mollities ossium coming on after puberty, for we seldom find children live through this critical period where it has been the result of rickets. The brim of a deformed pelvis varies considerably in shape: "sometimes it has the form of a kidney, or that of the figure eight (∞); sometimes it is triangular or heart-shaped, the sides being curved inwards, from the acetabula having been pressed backwards or inwards, the ossa pubis are bent forwards and outwards, and form at their symphysis a sort of beak-like process, which is the apex of the heart: in this species of deformed pelvis, which is usually the result of mollities ossium, the outlet also is usually much distorted: this arises from the tubera ischii being forced nearer to each other, thus contracting the pubic arch." (Naegelé's Lehrbuch, 2te Ausgabe, p. 247.)

From Naegelé.
Malacosteon, or mollities ossium. An arthritic, rheumatic, or gouty diathesis is a morbid state, in which softening of the bones may take place at a much later period of life, and to a most extraordinary extent. In almost all the cases of extreme pelvic deformity which have been recorded, the distortion has been owing to this disease, and not to rickets in early life: in a [Pg 296]pathological point of view there is a considerable analogy between these two diseases. From a variety of causes there is a superabundant formation of acid in the system, which its excreting organs are unable to throw off. The effects of this condition will vary according to circumstances; among them the softened state of the bones from a deficiency of insoluble bone earth is not the least remarkable. Mollities ossium seldom attacks women who have had no children: sometimes it begins shortly after delivery, and very frequently during pregnancy, during the progress of which it continues to increase. Hence, it occasionally happens, that a woman has given birth to several healthy living children without any unusual difficulty in her labours, and where, after this, the pelvis has gradually become so deformed from mollities ossium, as to render delivery impossible by the natural passages, and, therefore, to require the Cæsarean operation. Pelves of this sort, may be easily distinguished from those which have been deformed in early life by rickets; they have evidently attained their full adult growth before the process of softening had commenced: the ilia, for instance, are of the natural size, but bent across, as if they had been folded like wet pasteboard; whereas, the bones of the ricketty pelvis have not attained their full development, they are stunted in growth as well as distorted in shape, the two processes, viz. of growth and distortion, having evidently, co-existed.

The form of the pelvis in mollities ossium necessarily varies with the peculiar circumstances under which the individual is placed: thus, if her strength allows her to sit up, or even to get about, as is generally the case more or less, the promontory and the pubic bones are gradually pressed towards each other, so that the antero-posterior diameter is greatly diminished:[123] if,[Pg 297] however, she is confined entirely to bed for a considerable period, the distortion takes a different and much rarer form. From her lying first on one side and then on the other, the pelvis is laterally compressed; the transverse diameter becomes even shorter than the antero-posterior; and if the disease continues long enough, the pelvis is at length so altered and mis-shapen, that nearly all its original configuration is obliterated. The weight of such a pelvis varies considerably: where the disease has ceased some time before death, and bone earth has been again deposited, there will be little difference in this respect from a natural healthy pelvis; but if the patient has died with the disease in full activity, its weight will be greatly diminished, amounting sometimes only to a few ounces.

Mollities ossium, to a slight extent, we believe, is not very uncommon, although cases of extreme deformity from this cause are of rare occurrence. Mr. Barlow states, that "eight cases of this species of progressive deformity have fallen under my notice, in one of which the projection of the last lumbar vertebra at its union with the angle of the sacrum was so much bent forwards into the cavity of the pelvis, that on the introduction of the fore-finger up the vagina, a protuberance was presented to the touch very much resembling the head of the fœtus pretty far advanced into its cavity. On carrying the finger a little anteriorly past the projection, I could with difficulty ascertain the head of the child: but on moving it around, the distortion appeared so great, that the whole circumference did not exceed that of a half-crown piece. This occurrence was on the 29th of April, 1792, at which time I delivered the woman with the crotchet, and the bones of the pelvis receded considerably to the impulsive efforts during the extraction of the head of the fœtus; yet, notwithstanding, the flexibility of the bones of the pelvis, and the debilitated state of her constitu-tion, she recovered[Pg 298] speedily and without interruption." On the 2d February, 1794, being in the neighbour-hood, and learning that she was still alive, Mr. Barlow visited her and requested an examination. "I found her unable to walk without assistance, and as she sat, her breast and knees were almost in contact with each other. The superior aperture was nearly in the same state as when I delivered her with the crotchet, but the outlet appeared more contracted, the rami of the pubes overreached, leaving a small opening under the symphysis barely sufficient to admit the finger to pass into the vagina by that passage, and another aperture below, but rather larger, and parallel with the junction of the tuberosities of the ossa ischii. From what I learned afterwards respecting this decrepit female, she survived this period about two years, at which time she was become still more distorted in the spine; and after her death it was with difficulty she could be put into her coffin; this woman bore nine children, and died in the thirty-ninth year of her age." (Barlow's Essays, p. 329.)

Mollities ossium may be feared when, in addition to the general breaking up of the health and strength, the patient suffers from arthritic pains and swellings of the limbs, the urine is generally loaded with lithic secretion: and most of all, where distinct shortening and gradual distortion of the skeleton is taking place. Where the deformity has been the result of rickets in early life, a little careful observation of the patient's external appearance will quickly lead the experienced eye to suspect the nature of the case.

Symptoms of deformed pelvis. Among the external appearances which would lead us to suspect a deformed pelvis, are "the lower jaw projecting beyond the upper; the chin very prominent; the teeth grooved transversely; unhealthy appearance; pale ashy colour of the face; diminutive statue; unsteady gait; when the woman walks the chest is held back, the abdomen projects, and the arms hang behind; there is deformity of the spine and breast, one hip higher than the other, the joints of the hands and feet are remarkably thick; curvature of the extremities, especially the inferior, even without distortion of the spine is a very important sign; wherever the lower extremities are curved, the pelvis is mostly deformed: it is well to ascertain also if, when a child, it was a long time before she could walk alone; whether she had any fall on the sacrum; whether as a girl she was made to carry heavy weights, or to work in manufactories." (Naegelé's Lehrbuch. § 444.)

Funnel-shaped pelvis. Besides the above-mentioned species of pelvic deformity, others are occasionally met with, the origin of which is but little understood. The funnel-shaped pelvis is of this character, where the brim is perfectly well formed, but where it gradually contracts towards the inferior aperture. There are no evidences of its having been any[Pg 299] disease; nor in fact can we assign any satisfactory cause for this peculiar configuration: it appears to have been a congenital formation.

Obliquely distorted pelvis. A still more remarkable species of pelvic deformity is the pelvis obliqué ovata, which, of late years, has been pointed out by Professor Naegelé. In this case the pelvis appears awry, the symphysis pubis being pushed over to one side; and the sacrum to the other; one side of the pelvis is more or less flattened, the other bulges out, so that one oblique diameter is shorter, the other longer than natural; and this applies not only to the brim, but to the cavity and outlet of the pelvis. In most cases the sacro-iliac symphysis on that side which is flat-tened, and to which the sacrum is inclined, is completely anchylosed, not a trace of the division between the ilium and sacrum to be detected, the two bones being completely united into one. In many, the sacrum on this side is smaller than on the other, as if a portion of it had been removed by absorption during the process of anchylosis, or at least not properly developed. When we consider the form of the pelvis, and the appearances which the sacro-iliac symphysis and the sacrum present, we are almost led to conclude that ulcerative absorption must at one time have existed between the sacrum and ilium at this point, probably at an earlier period, by which means more or less bone had been destroyed before the termination of the disease in anchylosis; indeed, we can to a certain extent imitate this peculiar species of pelvic deformity by sawing off the surfaces of the sacrum and ilium which had formed the symphysis, and then putting the bones together again. Still, however, in the various cases which have been collected by Professor Naegelé, no proofs could be obtained of disease having existed in the pelvis during early life.

"In none of the cases, the particulars of which have come to my knowledge, has there been any trace of rachitis; nor have any of the symptoms, appearances, and morbid changes been observed which characterize mollities ossium coming on after puberty. None of these cases have been traced to the effects of external violence, as falls, blows, &c.; nor has there been any complaint of pain in the region of the pelvis, inferior extremities, &c." (Das Schräg Verengte Becken, p. 12.) "With respect to[Pg 300] the strength, colour, structure, &c. of the bones of this species of deformed pelvis, no difference could be observed between them and the bones of young and perfectly healthy subjects; not a trace either in form or other respects could be detected of those changes which usually result from rachitis or mollities ossium; and but for this distortion and some other slight irregularities, which required close inspection to detect, these pelves would have been looked upon as well-shaped, and of sufficient capacity." (Naegelé, op. cit. p. 11.) In some specimens no trace of anchylosis at the sacro-iliac symphysis has been observed; but whether this was the case throughout the union of the two bones we cannot say. Professor Naegelé is inclined to look upon them as modifications of the pelvis obliqué ovata, and certainly in the majority of known cases anchylosis has been found present.

It is scarcely necessary to do more than enumerate other varieties in the form of the pelvis, which are occasionally met with: it is sometimes round, the transverse and antero-posterior diameters being of the same length; in other cases it possesses many of the characters which distinguish the male pelvis, being more or less triangular, deep, and with a contracted angular pubic arch.

Exostosis. Lastly, the pelvis may be perfectly well formed, but the passage through it more or less interrupted by the exostosis: this is, perhaps, the rarest species of dystocia pelvica. It may arise from wounds of the periosteum, from fracture of the bones, callus, &c. and may vary in size from a small protuberance to a large mass, which completely fills up the pelvis.

Diagnosis of contracted pelvis. The difficulty of detecting an abnormal configuration of the pelvis, will depend, in great measure, upon its extent: where it is but slight, it may easily be passed over unobserved by a young practitioner, although it may, nevertheless, be quite sufficient to render labour both difficult and dangerous. In the ordinary form of contracted pelvis, where the antero-posterior diameter is shorter than natural, the being able to reach the projecting promontory of the sacrum with the finger is of itself a sufficient evidence: but the converse of this is not true, for we frequently meet with cases of contracted pelvis, without being able to reach the promontory. The numerous instruments which have been invented at different times for measuring the pelvis are of such doubtful accuracy, as to be nearly useless; the experienced finger is the best pelvimeter; and the power of correctly estimating the dimensions of the pelvis during examination, can only be acquired by constant practice, based on a thorough knowledge of them in the healthy pelvis.

The manner in which labour commences is frequently sufficient to make us suspect the presence of a contracted pelvis. Besides, the general appearance of the patient, we frequently find that the uterine contractions are very irregular; that they have but little[Pg 301] effect in dilating the os uteri; the head does not descend against it, but remains high up; it shows no disposition to enter the pelvic cavity, and rests upon the symphysis pubis, against which it presses very forcibly, being pushed forwards by the promontory of the sacrum. It is probably from this circumstance that the os uteri, more especially its anterior lip, shows so little disposition to dilate in these cases, for the lower portion of the uterus being jammed between the head and symphysis pubis in front, and promontory behind, the contractions of the longitudinal fibres can have little effect upon the os uteri. Hence we find, that in cases of diminished antero-posterior diameter requiring perforation, and where the os uteri in spite of violent pains, bleeding, &c. has refused to dilate beyond a certain point, on lessening the head, and thus removing its pressure from the symphysis pubis, it has quickly attained its full degree of dilatation.

Where the pains have been active, and a portion of the head has forced itself through the brim, and now projects to a certain extent into the cavity of the pelvis, it will be still more difficult to reach the promontory before delivery; and if, as is frequently the case, the sacrum is bent strongly backwards, so as to render the cavity and outlet very spacious, the real cause of impediment to the progress of labour may be entirely overlooked. It is here that the position of the head upon the symphysis pubis will prove a valuable means of diagnosis. The straightness of the sacrum will also be a guide in other cases.

In that form of the pelvis which has been called the funnel-shaped pelvis, and where the brim and upper portion of the cavity are of the natural dimensions, but where it gradually diminishes towards the outlet, the appearances are frequently very deceptive, the head advances without impediment, and descends as far as the inferior aperture, with every promise of speedy delivery; but here its progress is arrested, and even in the very last stage may require perforation.

It occasionally happens, also, where the deformity is very considerable, that the promonotory projects to such an extent as to be even capable of being mistaken for the head itself; and cases have actually occurred where, under this impression, the bone has been perforated instead of the child's head. So gross an error as this may easily be avoided by care in making the examination; by ascertaining that the projecting mass is immoveable; that the patient is sensible to the pressure of our finger; and that the promontory can be traced to be continuous with the adjacent parts of the pelvis.

The effects which may result from labour protracted by pelvic deformity are very various, both as regards the mother and her child. The most common form of injury which is this cause, is the contusion and consequent inflammation and sloughing[Pg 302] of the soft tissues which line the pelvis from the long continued pressure of the head against the symphysis pubis in front, and against the promontory of the sacrum behind. Not only may sloughing of the vagina and lower part of the uterus be the result, but the mischief may extend through the posterior wall of the bladder, and thus render the patient incapable of retaining her urine, and an object of great, and, generally speaking, incurable suffering.

The danger from rupture of the uterus will chiefly depend on the degree of pressure with which the uterine contractions force the head against the brim. Where the pains are violent, and yet insufficient to overcome the obstacle which the contracted pelvis presents to the advance of the head, there is not safety for a minute, and perforation must be immediately had recourse to. Where the edge of the promontory is very projecting and sharp, the structure of the uterus may be seriously injured by the pressure and contusion. In some cases it has evidently been the cause of ruptures, the fibres having given way first at this spot.

The constant severe pressure upon the head will be not less injurious to the child's life; it must inevitably produce a considerable impediment to the cerebral circulation; and where the liquor amnii has escaped, the pressure of the uterus upon the body of the child will scarcely be less prejudicial. The cranial bones frequently become remarkably distorted, so that after a difficult labour a deep furrow is found on that part of the head which corresponded to the projecting promontory.

Fracture of the parietal bone may even be produced, a fact of which practitioners, till lately, have not been sufficiently aware; and cases have occurred where children have been born dead, with the head greatly distorted, and one of the bones fractured, from which circumstances the mothers have been suspected of infanticide. Dr. Michaelis, of Kiel, has lately reported an interesting case of this kind, where the fracture seems to have resulted from the great immobility of the coccyx. The head was much disfigured, and on examining it the frontal bones were uninjured, but so flattened that the frontal and parietal portions of the sagittal suture lay nearly in the same place; the fontanelle and anterior two-thirds of the sagittal suture projected high up, and the sagittal borders of the parietal bones were firm and well formed. In the posterior third of the sagittal suture, where the parietal bones were firm and well formed, and the suture only two lines in width, were seen small livid portions of the longitudinal sinus forced between the bones. The occipital bone was flattened and forced deep under the parietal bones, but not otherwise injured. The right parietal bone, which during birth had been turned towards the promontory of the sacrum, was covered anteriorly and superiorly with effused blood, and on[Pg 303] removing the periosteum, was found fractured in five places. (Neue Zeitschrift für Geburtskunde, vol. iv. part 3. 1836.[124])

Where the action of the uterus is not very violent, and the bones yielding, the head gradually adapts itself to the form of the passage without destroying the fœtus; it elongates itself more and more until it is enabled to pass, so that after a tedious labour of this sort, we sometimes find the configuration of the head remarkably altered. Baudelocque, has mentioned a case recorded by Solayres de Renhac, where the head was so elongated that the long diameter measured eight inches all but two lines, the transverse being only two inches and five or six lines.

Treatment. Where the pelvic deformity is very considerable, there can be little difficulty in deciding upon the line of conduct to be adopted. It is in those cases where the obstruction is but slight that the indications for treatment are less distinctly marked: nor must we be satisfied with merely ascertaining the relative proportions of the head and pelvis; for the hardness or softness of the cranial bones, the disposition which they manifest to yield to the pressure of the uterus and surrounding parts, the state of the cranial integuments, and though last not least, of the soft tissues which line the pelvis, must all be carefully ascertained before a correct opinion as to the precise mode of treatment can be formed. Nor, if the woman has already had children, can we altogether be guided by the history of her previous labours; for where the above-mentioned circumstances have been favourable, a slight diminution of the pelvis will scarcely be attended with any perceptible delay or increase of difficulty beyond the natural degree; whereas, if the head happens this time to be a little larger, its bones more ossified, the fontanelles smaller, the scalp and soft linings of the pelvis more swollen, &c. a serious obstruction to the progress of labour will be the result. Thus it is that we not unfrequently meet with patients in whom the first labour has been tolerably easy, the second has been attended with much difficulty and required the forceps, in the third, the difficulty was so much increased as to require perforation, and the fourth where the labour was, like the first, perfectly easy and natural.

It is impossible for the head to remain long in the pelvis (except under unusually favourable circumstances) without more or less obstruction to the circulation, both in the scalp itself and in the surrounding soft tissues. The necessary consequence of this is swelling, by which the head increases while the passage diminishes in size; and this must still be more remarkably the case where the pelvis is at all contracted. It is in these cases that we frequently see such relief venesection;[Pg 304] and it is also as a topical depletion to the overloaded vessels, that we can explain why a free secretion of mucus is so favourable a symptom.[125]

Prognosis. Where the pains are moderate and equable, the os uteri nearly or quite dilated, the head not large, its bones yielding and overlapping at the sutures; where the greater portion of it has evidently passed through the brim, and, although slowly, advances perceptibly with the pains; where the passages are cool and moist, the pulse good, and the patient not exhausted, we may safely wait awhile and trust to the efforts of nature. On the other hand, where the pains are violent, the os uteri thin and undilatable, the head forced forwards upon the symphysis pubis by the projecting serum, if the greater part of its bulk has not yet passed the brim, if the soft parts are much swelled, the vagina hot and dry, the pulse has become irritable, the abdomen tender, the patient exhausted and much depressed both in mind and body, the powers of nature are evidently incompetent to the struggle, and require the assistance of art.

Such cases seldom permit the application of the forceps; the head is already pressing too firmly against the brim, and its greatest bulk having not yet passed, a still farther increase of pressure will be required to effect this object, which therefore cannot be attained without producing serious mischief. Where, however, the head has fairly engaged in the cavity of the pelvis, and the case is rather becoming one of deficient power, the forceps will be justifiable, and generally quite sufficient to effect the delivery safely.

The young practitioner must be cautious not to mistake an increase in the swelling of the scalp for an actual advance of the head itself—an error which may very easily be committed if he merely touches the middle of the presenting portion: he must carefully examine the circumference of the presenting part, where the head is pressing against the pelvis, and where there is little or no swelling, and he will frequently find to his disappointment, that although the cranial swelling may have even nearly approached the perineum since his last examination, the head itself has remained unmoved.

Where the forceps has been determined upon, we should endeavour to render its action as favourable as possible, viz. by bleeding, by the warm bath, and by evacuating the bladder and rectum before proceeding to the operation: we thus improve the condition[Pg 305] of the soft parts, and diminish the chances of its acting injuriously.

From what has now been stated respecting the various circumstances which may tend to aggravate or alleviate the existing degree of pelvic deformity, it will be seen how incorrect and unpractical must be the attempt to classify the means of treatment merely according to the dimensions of the pelvis. To assert that within certain limits of pelvic contraction the child can be delivered by the natural powers, and that beyond these limits the forceps must be used; and that where it proceeds to a certain extent farther, it can only be delivered by perforation, &c. is evidently objectionable: for there are no two cases alike, even supposing that the degree of pelvic contraction is exactly similar; hence, on the one hand, we might (under such fallacious guidance) be induced to trust to the natural powers when they are wholly incompetent to the task, and on the other, to have recourse to art when the real condition of the case justified no such interference.[126]

With regard to the diagnosis and treatment in the case of obliquely distorted pelvis (pelvis obliqué ovata,) our data are still too scanty to enable us to give any decided rules: the immobility of the head, although the antero-posterior diameter appears of its full length, the shortness of one oblique diameter, and consequent undue pressure upon the head in this direction, and the unusual length of the other, are the characteristics which we have observed in the only case of the kind which has come under our notice during life. In all the cases of labour rendered difficult by this condition of the pelvis, which have been collected by Professor Naegelé, the perforation has been strongly indicated; and where the forceps has been used, it has either failed, as with us, or if the delivery has been effected by this means, it has been attended with fatal consequences.

In exostosis of the pelvis we must be guided by our knowledge of the healthy pelvis, and by our carefully ascertaining the form and size of the bony growth, and in what degree it is likely to impede the passage of the child. As in cases of simple projection of the promontory, the head may be capable of passing, but in doing so becomes more or less distorted: thus Dr. Burns quotes a case from Dr. Campbell, where from exostosis within the pelvis, the left frontal bone was so greatly sunk in, as to make the eye protrude. Professor Otto, of Breslau, mentions a woman who had pelvic exostosis being the mother of four children, in[Pg 306] each of whom a small portion of the cranium was depressed and not ossified.

An interesting case has been described by Dr. Kyll, of Cologne, where the patient was the mother of seven children; her former labours had been perfectly natural, except that in the last there had been preternatural adhesion of the placenta, which had required to be removed by the hand; in six days after she was seized with feverish symptoms and violent pain at the spot where the placenta had been attached. The attack yielded to proper treatment, but she continued feverish at night with perspirations, frequently deranged bowels, difficulty in passing water, and severe pain in the abdomen, especially when she tried to stand on the right leg. An abscess formed in the right groin, which was opened and discharged a large quantity of pus, from which her recovery was very slow, and in three years afterwards she became again pregnant. When labour came on, no presenting part could be reached; after a long time the feet came down one after the other, but the nates would not advance. Dr. Kyll found the child resting with the hips on the brim of the pelvis, and completely wedged fast by a hard immoveable tumour as large as a hen's egg, springing from the upper part of the right sacro-iliac symphysis, and apparently having been a result of the pelvic abscess; the child was delivered with great difficulty by embryotomy.

Exostosis of the pelvis.

Perhaps the most remarkable case of pelvic exostosis is that which has been described by Dr. Haber of Carlsruhe, and where also the cause was ascertained to have arisen from a violent fall on the ice when carrying a heavy load upon the head; on coming to herself the woman found that she was unable to move, and in this state was conveyed home; she recovered to all appearances in a few weeks, married, and soon became pregnant. When labour came on it was found impossible to deliver her, from the pelvis being entirely filled with a huge exostosis: the Cæsarean section was performed, but she died, and on examination after death an immense mass of bony growth was found springing from the sacrum, which had been apparently fractured, not only filling up the whole cavity of the pelvis, but arising to a considerable extent above the brim.

In those cases of funnel-shaped pelvis which we have had the opportunity of observing, perforation has been ultimately required, although the head had passed easily through the brim and[Pg 307] entered the cavity; in one of these we have subsequently used the artificial premature labour with success.

We have already stated the doubtful utility of arranging cases of deformed pelvis according to their degree of contraction, and of classifying the different modes of treatment by such a scale; still, however, there must be certain limits beyond which it will be impossible to make the child pass, even when diminished by embryotomy. To draw the precise line of demarcation, however, will be nearly if not quite impossible; and, as in cases of slighter deformity, we must take many other circumstances into consideration which we have already mentioned. An inch and a half from pubes to sacrum has been mentioned by many as the extreme degree of contraction through which a full grown child can be delivered by embryulcia; generally, however, in these cases of unusually deformed pelvis, there is much more space on each of the sacrum; and on this, in great measure, will depend the possibility of effecting the delivery. The celebrated case of Elizabeth Sherwood, which Dr. Osborn has recorded, and where he succeeded in delivering the child, although the antero-posterior diameter "could not exceed three-quarters of an inch," has been looked upon as being of doubtful accuracy, and that Dr. Osborn had unintentionally deceived himself. When, however, we learn that on the right side of the sacrum the antero-posterior diameter was an inch and three-quarters, the incredible nature of the case diminishes considerably, the more as the patient was examined by Dr. Denman and others who fully coincided with Dr. Osborn's statements. To assert that in this case the antero-posterior diameter was only three-quarters of an inch, as many have done, is evidently incorrect, and tends to throw doubt upon it: the case was evidently the closest possible approach to the limits requiring the Cæsarean operation; its success was mainly attributable to the gradual manner in which it was performed; the child had become completely soft and flaccid from putrefaction, and was thus more capable of being moulded to the contracted passage.

CHAPTER V.

FIRST SPECIES OF DYSTOCIA.

Obstructed Labour from a Faulty Condition of the soft Passages.

Pendulous abdomen.—Rigidity of the os uteri.—Belladonna.—Edges of the os uteri adherent.—Cicatrices and collosities.—Agglutination of the os uteri.—Contracted vagina.—Rigidity from age.—Cicatrices in the vagina.—Hymen.—Fibrous bands.—Perineum.—Varicose and œdematous swellings of the labia and nymphæ.—Tumours.—Distended or prolapsed bladder.—Stone in the bladder.

In speaking of the uterus itself as a cause of this species of dystocia, we only mention it here as one of the soft passages, not as the organ by the contractions of which the child is expelled; we merely refer to those faulty conditions of the uterus which produce an impediment to the child's progress, not to those which interfere with the natural condition of its expelling powers, as this will be considered under the next division of dystocia.

We have already stated our disbelief that an oblique position of the uterus can have any influence in producing malposition of the child. With the exception of extreme anterior obliquity, or pendulous belly, we equally doubt that it can have any effect in retarding the labour when the child presents naturally. The highest authorities in midwifery during the last hundred years unite in asserting that this celebrated opinion of Deventer, was a misconception.

Pendulous abdomen. Where, from great relaxation of the anterior abdominal wall, (a frequent result of repeated child-bearing,) the fundus is inclined so forwards as almost to hang over the symphysis pubis, the child's head does not readily enter the brim of the pelvis, nor can the uterine contractions act so favourably in dilating the mouth of the womb; and in this manner the first part of labour may be considerably retarded. Pendulous abdomen to this great extent is not very common; and in ordinary cases the horizontal posture, especially upon the back,[Pg 309] is quite sufficient to allow the head to engage in the pelvis. "We have found more than once," says Dr. Dewees, "in cases of extreme anterior obliquity, that it is not sufficient for the restoration of the fundus that the woman be placed simply upon the back; but we are also obliged to lift up and support by a properly adjusted towel or napkin, the pendulous belly until the head shall occupy the inferior strait. To illustrate this, we will relate one of a number of similar cases in which this plan was successfully employed. Mrs. O., pregnant with her seventh child, was much afflicted after the seventh month with pain and the other inconveniences which almost always accompany this hanging condition of the uterus; was taken with labour pains in the morning of the 10th of October, 1820. We were sent for about noon. The pains were frequent and distressing, and, upon examination per vaginam, the mouth of the uterus was found near the projection of the sacrum, dilated to about the size of a quarter dollar, but pliant and soft. During the pain, the membranes were found tense within the os uteri, but did not protrude beyond it.

As this was the first time we had attended this patient, and from the history she gave of her former labours, in which she represented her abdomen being in all equally pendulous, with the exception of the first, we waited several hours (she being placed upon her side) for the accomplishment of the labour. During the whole of this period the head did not advance a single line; nor could it, as the direction of the parturient efforts carried it against the projection of the sacrum. We had several times taken occasion to recommend her being placed upon her back, but to which she constantly objected, until we urged its being absolutely necessary. She at length reluctantly consented to the change of position; when upon her back it was found that it did not advance the os uteri sufficiently towards the centre of the superior strait. The abdomen was therefore raised, and a long towel placed against it, and kept in the position we had carried it by the hands, by its extremities being firmly held by two assistants; at the same time we introduced a finger within the edge of the os uteri, and drew it towards the symphysis pubis, and then waited for the effects of a pain. One soon showed itself, and with such decided efficacy, as to push the head completely into the inferior strait, and three more delivered it." (Compendious System of Midwifery, § 224.)

This peculiar displacement of the uterus, which has been called by some anteversion of the gravid womb, has occasionally given rise to the suspicion that there was no os uteri, from its being tilted upwards and backwards towards the promontory of the sacrum: it has been said, in some cases, to have even contracted adhesions with the posterior wall of the vagina, from[Pg 310] the firmness with which it was pressed against it, and thus tended still farther to increase the deception. "Within our knowledge," says Dr. Dewees in the paragraph preceding the one just quoted, "this case has been mistaken for an occlusion of the os uteri, and where upon consultation it was determined that the uterus should be cut to make an artificial opening for the fœtus to pass through. They thought themselves justified in this opinion, first, by no os uteri being discoverable by the most diligent search for it; and, secondly, by the head being about to engage under the arch of the pubes covered by the womb. Accordingly, the labia were separated, and the uterine tumour brought into view. An incision was now made by a scalpel through the whole length of the exposed tumour down to the head of the child, the liquor amnii was evacuated, and in due course of time the artificial opening was dilated sufficiently to give passage to the child. The woman recovered, and, to the disgrace of the accoucheurs who attended her, was delivered per vias naturales of several children afterwards, a damning proof that the operation was most wantonly performed." Where, in addition to the anteversion, strong adhesions have taken place between the os uteri and posterior wall of the vagina, no trace of os uteri will be felt, and the operation above-mentioned does become sometimes necessary.

Rigidity of the os uteri. The chief way in which the uterus can obstruct the passage of the child, is, by an undilatable state of its mouth: this may arise from a variety of causes, which may be chiefly brought under the two heads of functional and mechanical. Under the first head comes rigidity of the os uteri, either from a spasmodic contraction of its circular fibres, or from irregularity or deficiency in the contractions of the longitudinal fibres of the whole organ. In a slight degree this is frequently met with, especially in first labours, where the patient is young, delicate, and irritable, and where, in all probability, there is some source of irritation in the primæ viæ which tends to disturb and divert the proper and healthy action of the uterus. We see it also in robust plethoric primiparæ; the os uteri dilates to a certain degree, perhaps an inch in diameter, and remains tense and firm, with its edge thin; the contractions of the uterus produce much suffering, and to all appearances are very violent; but they are chiefly in front, and produce little or no effect upon its mouth; the vagina is hot and dry, the patient becomes exhausted with fruitless pains, and fever or inflammation would quickly follow, if nothing be done to relieve this state. As this subject, however, belongs rather to the next species of dystocia, viz. that arising from a faulty condition of the expelling powers, we shall delay the consideration of the treatment.

Belladonna. It has been recommended, and not very [Pg 311]judiciously, to apply belladonna to the os uteri in cases of great rigidity: it was repeatedly tried by the celebrated Chaussier in the Maternité, at Paris, and, according to his observations, it produced a considerable effect upon it. "The knowledge of the extraordinary powers which this drug possesses in causing dilatation of the iris, led to its employment for the object of enlarging the aperture of the uterus; but there is certainly no similarity in the structure and office of the two organs, and no analogy can be drawn between their functions. It is not likely that this means will produce the relaxation we require; and if no good results from its use, it must be injurious; not in consequence of the poisonous quality resident in the drug itself, but in the friction which is necessary for its efficient application. The mucus which naturally lubricates the part must be wiped away, and this irritation must predispose the tender organ to take upon itself inflammatory action." (Dr. F. H. Ramsbotham's Lectures, in Med. Gaz. May 3, 1834.)

For our own part we must confess, that, although we have seen this application tried repeatedly, it has never produced the desired effects, but has invariably brought on very troublesome and distressing symptoms, such as sickness, faintness, headach, vertigo, &c.

There is a condition of the os uteri which is occasionally met with, and which presents a degree of rigidity which we have never seen except where there have been adhesions and callous cicatrices from former injuries. It has nothing of the thin edge put strongly on the stretch during the pains; but it is thick and firm, presenting nothing of the elastic cushiony softness of the os uteri in a favourable state for dilatation; it dilates to about an inch across, tolerably regularly, and without much apparent difficulty, but no efforts of the uterus can dilate it farther. We have already alluded to two extreme cases of this when speaking of ruptured uterus, and where in each instance the os uteri entirely separated from the uterus and came away. Whether there is something peculiar in the structure of the part which renders it thus undilatable, or whether it required even still more powerful measures than those employed, is not very easy to decide.

Edges of the os uteri adherent.—Cicatrices, &c. A serious impediment to the passage of the child may be adhesions of the sides of the os uteri to each other; by hard callous cicatrices resulting from ulcerations, lacerations, &c. in former labours; by abnormal bands, or bridles, as they have been called; and by tumours and other morbid growths.

Where the structure of the os uteri has been much injured by previous injuries of this character, the resistance will probably be so great as to require artificial dilatation with the knife. Generally speaking, however, the whole circle of the uterine opening is not involved,[Pg 312] portions still remaining of natural structure, and, therefore, capable of dilatation. On examination, it feels irregular both in shape and hardness; a part being soft, cushiony, yielding, and forming the segment of a well-defined circle, the rest of it uneven, knobby, and hard, being evidently puckered up by cicatrisation.

In many cases, these callous contractions give way more or less when the head begins to press powerfully against them; but even where this is not the case, the healthy portion of the os uteri is so dilatable as to yield sufficiently. It would be difficult to estimate how far an os uteri in this state, with perhaps, not more than half, or even a third, of its circle in a healthy condition is capable of dilating. But from cases which have come under our own observation, and others which have been recorded by authors in whom we place the greatest reliance, we are quite confident that with proper treatment a sufficient degree of dilatation can be effected without resorting to artificial means.

Bleeding to fainting, the warm bath, laxatives, and enemata, will assist greatly in promoting our object. Where, however, the contracted portion shows no disposition to yield to this treatment, or to the pressure of powerful pains, but forms a hard resisting bridle or band, which effectually impedes the farther advance of the head, it must be divided by the knife in order to prevent dangerous laceration of the part on the one hand, or protraction of labour on the other. The mode of doing this will be described when these conditions as effecting the vagina are considered.

Artificial dilatation of the os uteri by incision has been practised very rarely, the chief of these operations having had reference to the vagina. F. Ould considered that mere contraction of the os uteri from former lacerations did not require this operation; but that where it was in a state of schirrus, there would be "no chance for saving either mother or child but by making an incision through the affected part."

We have quoted, on a former occasion, a case of cicatrised os uteri recorded by Moscati, and where, in consequence of injury in a former labour, the opening was nearly closed; fearing the laceration which had occurred in a similar case under his father's care, in consequence of making merely one incision, he made a number of small incisions round the whole of the orifice until a sufficient dilatation was produced.

Agglutination of the os uteri. Another condition of the os uteri which may produce very considerable impediment to the passage of the child, is that which has been called agglutination, where by some adhesive process, apparently that of inflammation, the lips of the opening adhere and completely close it. These species of imperforate os uteri may occur in primiparæ as well as in those who have borne children: the agglutination of its edges takes place during pregnancy, probably shortly after conception. Upon [Pg 313]examination we find no traces of hardness, rigidity, or any other morbid condition, either in the os uteri itself, or the parts immediately surrounding it; the os uteri is closed by a superficial cohesion of its edges, and which in some cases seem to adhere by means of an interstitial fibrous substance; this when of a firmer consistence forms a species of false membrane, which in some cases is capable of resisting the most powerful uterine contractions, and in others it appears to cover the os uteri so completely as to conceal it most effectually, and give rise to the erroneous conclusion that the os uteri is altogether wanting. Baudelocque describes this condition (Op. cit. § 1961;) but from the brief mention which he makes of it, as also from the treatment recommended, it is plain that he had no very distinct notions about it, for he advises that "in all cases the orifice must be restored to its original state, and be opened with a cutting instrument as soon as the labour shall be certainly begun."

In by far the majority of cases which have been recorded, the pains have after a time been sufficient to dilate the os uteri. Dr. Campbell has described two of these cases, where no os uteri could be traced for some time after the commencement of labour: both were first pregnancies: in the former, uterine action continued about twelve hours before the os uteri could be distinguished, when it felt like a minute cicatrix; the other patient had regular pains for two nights and a day before the os uteri could be perceived, and she suffered so much as to require three persons to keep her in bed; both these patients were largely bled, gave birth to living children, and had a good recovery.

We may suspect that the protraction of labour arises from agglutinated os uteri, when at an early period of it we can discover no vestige of the opening in the globular mass formed by the inferior segment of the uterus, which is forced down deeply into the pelvis, or at any rate, where we can only detect a small fold or fossa, or merely a concavity, at the bottom of which, is a slight indentation, and which is usually a considerable distance from the median line of the pelvis. The pains come on regularly and powerfully; the lower segment of the uterus is pushed deeper into the cavity of the pelvis, even to its outlet, and becomes so tense as to threaten rupture; at the same time it becomes so thin, that a practitioner who sees such a case for the first time would be induced to suppose the head was presenting merely covered by the membranes. After a time, by the increasing severity of the pains, the os uteri at length opens, or it becomes necessary that this should be effected by art: when once this is attained, the os uteri goes on to dilate, and the labour proceeds naturally, unless the patient is too much exhausted by the severity of her labour. Although the obstacle in some cases is capable of resisting the most powerful efforts of the uterus, a moderate degree of pressure[Pg 314] against it whilst in a state of strong distention, either by the tip of the finger, or a female catheter, is quite sufficient to overcome it; little or no pain is produced, and the appearance of a slight discharge of blood will show that the structure has given way. Two interesting cases of this kind have been described by the late W. J. Schmitt, of Vienna, under the title of two cases of closed os uteri which had resisted the efforts of labour, and where it was easily dilated by means of the finger.[127]

Contracted vagina. The vagina may be naturally very small, or unusually rigid and unyielding: in the first case serious obstruction to the progress of labour is rarely produced, the expelling powers being generally sufficient ultimately to effect the necessary degree of dilatation; the proper precautions must be taken to avoid every species of irritation and excitement of the circulation; the bowels must be duly evacuated; the circulation controlled either by sedatives, or, if necessary, bleeding, and where it is at hand, a warm bath; if this latter cannot be easily procured, a common hip bath, or sitting over the steam of warm water will be of great service; the great object will be to ensure a soft and cool state of the passage with a plentiful supply of that mucous secretion which is so essential to the favourable dilatation of the soft passages.

Nauseating remedies, and even tobacco injections, have been tried to a considerable extent for the purpose of relaxing the mouth of the uterus; but they produce little or no good effects, and cause much suffering to the patient. In Dr. Dewees' second case of obstructed labour from the above causes, a sufficient trial of this remedy was used to satisfy all doubts as to its effects. "It produced great sickness, vomiting, and fainting, but the desired relaxation did not take place: we waited some time longer and with no better success. In the course of an hour, or an hour and a half, the more distressing effects of the infusion wore off; and resolving to give the remedy every chance in our power, we prevailed on our patient with some difficulty to consent to another trial of it: its effects were the same as before,—great distress without the smallest benefit, the soft parts remaining as rigid as before its exhibition." Bleeding was now proposed; the patient became faint after losing ten ounces, and the most complete relaxation followed: the forceps were applied, and a living child delivered.

Rigidity from age. In women pregnant for the first time at an advanced period of life, the vagina and os externum are said to oppose considerable resistance to the passage of the child from[Pg 315] their rigid condition, the parts having lost the suppleness and elasticity of youth; the vessels also convey less blood to the mucous membrane and adjacent tissues: hence the secretion of mucus is more sparing; the cellular tissue is more condensed and firm; still nevertheless, although it is constantly mentioned by authors as a cause of this species of dystocia, we cannot help declaring that it exists to a much less degree than has been generally supposed, and that primiparæ at a very early age are much more liable to have tedious and difficult labours than those at an advanced age. Still, however, the circumstance is well worthy of notice; and in such cases we may produce much relief by the warm bath, or hip bath, by sitting over the steam of hot water, by warm water enemata, and great attention to the state of the intestinal canal and of the circulation. Mucilaginous or oleaginous injections into the vagina have been recommended; but we have no experience of their effects: we have frequently used lard, &c. to the edges of the os externum when the head was beginning to distend it, and we think with relief; at any rate it produces a feeling of comfort to the patient, being soft and cooling.

Cicatrices in the vagina. The most serious impediments to the progress of labour connected with the vagina are the contractions of this canal from callous cicatrices, the results of sloughing and other injuries in former labours. The vagina may be contracted throughout its whole length, its parietes hard, gristly, and uneven, and so small as not to admit even the tip of the little finger; the course of the canal from the irregularity of the contractions and adhesions is frequently much distorted; in other cases it is obstructed in different places by bands or septa, which have been similar causes.

Where the condition of the vagina has been ascertained before labour, much may be done to ameliorate the condition of the parts, not only by the treatment already mentioned for rigidity of the vagina under other circumstances, but also by the judicious application of tents, bougies, and other means for dilating the passage. A case of this kind came under our notice some years ago; the patient had been married many years without being pregnant, and was considerably beyond the age of forty. The deranged health and enlargement of the abdomen which took place excited no suspicions of pregnancy either in her mind or that of her medical attendant: the case was suspected to be ovarian dropsy, and a variety of medicines under this supposition were administered, both internally and externally: the commencement of actual labour appears to have been equally mistaken; nor was it until labour had advanced considerably that the real nature of the case was discovered; from its length and severity, violent inflammation and sloughing of the vagina was the result, the canal became much contracted, and was rendered still farther[Pg 316] impervious by the formation of strong bands or septa which were stretched across it, and which effectually prevented the os uteri from being reached; sponge tents, and oval gum elastic pessaries of different sizes were introduced, and by degrees such a state of dilatation was produced as not only permitted the os uteri to be reached, but restored the vagina in great measure to its natural size.

The action of labour forcing the head of the child against these contractions and adhesions is frequently sufficient ultimately, to effect the necessary degree of dilatation; where, however, this is not the case, they require to be divided by the knife. The proper moment for doing this is during a pain, when the parts are put strongly on the stretch: we can now feel exactly where there is the greatest resistance, and where an incision will produce the most effect. In this state also the incision can be effected with most ease, for the stricture being firmly distended, the knife will more readily divide it than where it is relaxed; the patient also at this moment is not sensible to the cutting of the knife. The lower part of the blade well armed with lint or tow should be cautiously introduced along the side of the finger during an interval of the pains: in this way the necessary number of incisions may be made: this is usually followed by a good deal of bleeding, which tends still farther to relax the parts; and when the head has advanced low enough, a cautious attempt may be made with the forceps to deliver it.

In recommending dilatation by means of the knife, it must be distinctly understood, that a sufficient time should be allowed in order to see how much can be effected by the uterine efforts, for in many of these cases the stricture has at length yielded after severe and protracted suffering.[128] In cases of this kind, also, the effects of bleeding are by no means inconsiderable, and must not be neglected.

The unruptured hymen has been said to be capable of impeding the progress of the head, but this can only be where the membrane is of unnatural strength and thickness. It has more than once occurred to us at the commencement of labour, to find the hymen uninjured; but it has broken down under the finger, even during examination, and we are convinced would have produced no obstacle whatever to the child. Where its structure is abnormal, and the advance of the labour is evidently retarded by it, division is the simplest and easiest remedy.

Bands of firm fibrous or almost ligamentous tissue are [Pg 317]sometimes found stretched across the vagina or os externum. We described a remarkable case of this sort in the Medical Gazette, Sep. 26, 1835, where it extended from the symphysis pubis backwards to the perineum; it had resisted the pressure of the child's head so powerfully as to produce a deep indentation along the cranial bones; it was divided by a bistouri, and the head was immediately expelled.

The perineum can rarely, if ever, prove a serious hindrance to the labour in primiparæ so long as its structure is healthy, even although it may be unusually broad. With patience and due management the necessary degree of dilatation may be obtained by the pressure of the head; and proposals to dilate it artificially, or even to make a slight incision into it, do not deserve a moment's consideration. Where, however, it has been extensively lacerated in a previous labour, and has healed again throughout its entire length (by no means a common occurrence) or when there has been much sloughing, the cicatrix thus formed may render it incapable of relaxation, and thus produce much resistance to the passage of the head. Even here we may do a great deal by warm hip baths, fomentations, and especially by bleeding; an incision through the callous portion is by no means desirable where it can be possibly avoided, as it only endangers a farther laceration during the expulsion of the head. Cases nevertheless, occur where the contracted ring of the os externum is so unyielding and gristly as to make this operation necessary.[129] In all these cases, where, either the adhesion and contractions have given away, or have been divided during labour, great care should be taken to prevent them forming again during the process of healing, by using sponge tents well greased, and other appropriate means.

Varicose and œdematous swellings of the labia and nymphæ also deserve mention, although they rarely interfere with the progress of labour to any great extent. Varicose labia seldom annoy the patient during her pregnancy; the veins of the part may have become somewhat dilated and the labium swollen; but it is generally not until the commencement of labour, that they become hard and knotty: at first they feel like a bunch of currants imbedded in the cellular tissue of the labium, and as labour advances, and the return of blood from the part is still more impeded, the swelling continues to increase in size, and frequently obstructs the os externum very considerably. The danger here is not so much from its acting as an obstacle to the passage of the child, as from its bursting during labour and causing loss of[Pg 318] blood and other serious consequences. The tumour seldom bursts directly externally, but first gives way beneath the skin, producing extravasation, after which, in consequence of still farther distention, the labium itself ruptures. In some cases the hæmorrhage is not very profuse externally, while the extravasation internally, amounts to some pounds, extending not only to the vagina and perineum, but also to the groin; and instances have occurred where it has spread to a great distance over the glutæus muscles.

"The extravasation," says Mr. Ingleby, "usually happens during the pain which expels the child; but sometimes at an early period of labour, as in the example of severe hæmorrhage here annexed. I had just left a patient to whom I had been called, in consequence of the difficult transmission of the child's head through a distorted pelvis, in connexion with an inordinate varicose enlargement of the labia pudendi (especially the left,) when a messenger overtook me urging my immediate return. It appeared that during the violence of the straining, the tumour on the left side had sud-denly burst at the edge of the vagina posteriorly. The patient lay in a little lake of blood; and as the bleeding recurred in gushes with the return of every pain, it became essential to complete delivery, and a child weighing fifteen pounds was extracted with the forceps. A large slough separated at the end of the third week." p. 109.

Where no laceration has taken place externally, it is seldom that an opening for the purpose of removing the effused blood will be of use; on the contrary, the access of external air cannot but be prejudicial in many cases. The action of the absorbents is generally sufficient for this purpose, and may be increased by friction with stimulating liniments, and most remarkably of all by the application of electricity. Where the extravasation extends beneath the lining membrane of the vagina, so much swelling may be produced as nearly to close the passage; this, however, gener-ally takes place after the birth of the child, the rupture of the varicose vessel having occurred whilst it was passing.

On perceiving, at the commencement of a labour, that there are varicose veins in the labium, which are beginning to increase in size and hardness as the head advances, it will be as well to compress them as much as possible during the intervals of the pains, when there is less impediment to the blood returning from them: we can, by thus squeez-ing out their contents to a certain degree, lessen the size of the swelling, and thus prevent it from gaining that extent which might endanger laceration. We may instantly know when this injury has taken place, by the livid tumefaction of the parts, and our being no longer able to feel the knotty portions of the varix. In order to check the effusion of blood as much as possible, we must apply cold, and thus favour[Pg 319] its speedy coagulation beneath the skin. Where the distention is very great, it may become necessary to evacuate the effused fluid; but, generally speaking, it is deeper beneath the surface than might, at first sight, be expected. "It has been proposed," says Mr. Ingleby, "that the swelling should be punctured, provided there has been no delay, and the puncture is made whilst the blood is still liquid. On one occasion I promptly carried this suggestion into effect, but without success; and, considering the structure of the labium, it is probable that the greater part of the blood will coagulate almost as rapidly as it is effused." (Ingleby, op. cit. p. 109.)

A considerable degree of suffering and annoyance to the patient may arise from œdematous swelling of the labia and nymphæ, both previous to and during her labour. The labia are occasionally so distended as not only to close the os externum, but to require that the legs should be kept as wide asunder as possible, to prevent the swollen parts being crushed: the patient is thus rendered very unwieldy and helpless, if she were not already so previously by an anasarcous state of the lower extremities, which frequently accompanies this condition.

Œdema of the labia is of less consequence where the patient has had several children than where she is a primipa-ra, and seldom either retards labour to any serious extent, or is attended with any troublesome consequences afterwards: where, however, it is her first labour, and the swelling is very considerable, laceration may be produced, the results of which may be sloughing and gangrene: a fatal case of this kind has been described by Burton.

Where the labia are much swollen, they not only render the patient incapable of moving, but are apt to become inflamed and excoriated, from being in such close contact, and constantly moistened by the trickling of the urine over them. By preserving the horizontal posture, and thus taking off the pressure of the child from the soft parts of the pelvis, by keeping the bowels open by saline laxatives, and by using saturnine and evaporating lotions to the part, a good deal may be done for the patient's relief. Where there is no disposition to inflammation, and the parts appear somewhat flabby, warm and gently stimulating applications will be preferable. Mr. Ingleby remarks that, "if the swollen parts are punctured (and a particularly fine curved needle answers best,) a load of serum is drained off, and relief is rapidly obtained. I have not observed any of the reported bad effects (sloughing and gangrene for instance) succeed this little operation; nor are they likely to occur in an unimpaired constitution." The celebrated Wigand of Hamburgh, who strongly opposed making incisions into the dropsical structure, does not appear to have tried the plan recommended above. He [Pg 320]considered that, as these swellings are the result of pressure, the less we do with them the better, merely taking care to keep up the action of the skin.

Œdema, or rather dropsy, of the nymphæ, is not of common occurrence, and, when it takes place to a considerable extent, produces a singular alteration in the appearance of the external organs. The nymphæ protrude beyond the labia, and depend so much as to rest upon the bed on which the patient lies, forming a soft membranous bag, fluctuating with the fluid which it contains. If labour has not actually commenced, we would prefer endeavouring to excite the absorbents of the part, and thus remove the effused fluid, to its evacuation by puncture: we have perfectly succeeded, by the use of warm aromatic stimulating fomentations. The "species aromaticæ" of the Continental pharmacopeiæ may be used with much advantage in these cases: the mode of its application is, to tie some up in a loose muslin bag, and soak it in hot wine; this forms an excellent warm stimulating application, and appears to excite the absorbents very briskly. A very good imitation of this, is to scald some chamomile flowers, and having squeezed them tolerably dry, to sprinkle some port wine over, and then apply them as a poultice. A swelling of this sort can offer but little obstruction to the passage of the head; and if labour commence before we have been able to reduce its size sufficiently, we may at the last let off the fluid by puncture, should the pressure of the head be such as to threaten laceration.

Tumours of different sorts may obstruct the passage of the child, and, in some cases, produce an impediment of the most serious character. Fibrous polypi and hard tubercles of the subcartilaginous character (commonly called the fleshy tubercle) are those which may present the greatest resistance, while fungoid growths of malignant disease, whether cephaloma (brain-like tumour,) hæmatoma (fungus hæmatodes,) or carcinoma, rarely oppose much obstruction. Their structure is soft and spongy, they therefore yield to the gradual pressure of the head, become more or less flattened, and thus allow it to pass. But fibrous or chondromatous tumours are of too firm a structure to admit of this, and are capable of rendering the labour not only difficult, but very dangerous. The mass being situated at the lower part of the uterus, or attached to it by means of a pedicle, is perhaps forced down into the cavity of the pelvis, beyond which its attachments do not allow it to advance; if it be a fleshy tubercle imbedded in the structure of the uterus, it will not be able to advance so far, but will obstruct the brim of the pelvis, and thus prevent the head descending into it. In many cases, these tumours are merely covered by the lining membrane of the uterus, which sometimes forms a species of pedicle. In either case, an early diagnosis is of great importance, as we may thus[Pg 321] have the opportunity of removing the mass either by the scissors or ligature.

Dr. Merriman has recorded an interesting case of this kind, where the polypus which arose from the inner surface of the right lip of the os uteri was tied, and removed rather more than three weeks before labour came on. A fatal case, communicated to him by the late Dr. Gooch, is equally valuable, inasmuch as it shows the results of a contrary practice.[130]

"The class of tumours which most frequently obstruct labour comprise follicular enlargements and the prolapsed ovarium. The former disease originates in the vagina, and has been shown by Mr. Heming to consist in a dilated state of one of the mucous follicles, which acquires a cyst, and secretes a fluid of varying colour and consistence, from a dark to a straw-coloured serum, or a deposition purely gelatinous. Owing to the density of its walls, and its general tension, the fluid contents of the tumour are[Pg 322] not easily distinguished; but the flaccidity which succeeds a free puncture is very striking."

"There are two forms of ovarian tumour which obstruct the passage of the child; in the one, a small cyst in connexion with a very bulky cyst; or else a portion of a large cyst passes into the recto-vaginal septum, and bulges through the posterior part of the vagina: in the other, and that which occurs by far the most frequently, the whole ovary, moderately enlarged, prolapses within the septum. The descent is peculiarly liable to happen at two periods; the first near the end of gestation, the second during labour, the prolapsus being promoted by the relaxation of the soft parts. The changes which the ovary undergoes when long detained in the septum, will chiefly depend upon the capacity and yielding state of the parts. If the woman has not previously borne children, it may remain small, and scarcely retard delivery; but under contrary circumstances, it acquires a large size, and nearly fills the vagina. In rare instances, the bulging is said to have appeared at the anterior part of the pelvis." (Ingleby, op. cit. p. 118.)

The contents of these tumours vary a good deal; the hard ones are usually lipomatous or fatty tumours, not unfrequently containing hair and rudiments of teeth. Numerous cases have been recorded where ovarian tumours, which had been pushed down before the child, have at length burst, discharging their contents, and thus ceasing to act as an obstacle to the labour. We quite agree with Mr. Ingleby in recommending puncture under such circumstances; for, independent of pregnancy, it is a well-known fact, that there is a much better chance of successfully tapping an ovarian dropsy per vaginam, than through the abdominal parietes. The same holds good in operating through the rectum; and he has described two highly interesting cases where this mode of treatment was completely successful; one in his own practice, the other in that of our friend Mr. W. Birch.

Distended or prolapsed bladder, &c. Lastly, the urinary bladder may obstruct the passage of the child, from being prolapsed and distended with water, or from containing a calculus which is forced down below the head. In the first case, a prolapsus of the distended bladder can scarcely take place without much inattention on the part of the practitioner, not having ascertained whether the bladder had been lately evacuated. In case we find, upon examination, that there is a disposition to this displacement, the elastic catheter will enable the tumour of the prolapsed bladder to collapse, and thus remove all farther trouble. The examination in these cases must be conducted with care; for an elastic fluctuating tumour of this kind may be mistaken for the distended membranes, or a hydrocephalic head; and Dr. Merriman[Pg 323] has given a melancholy case where, in consequence of such an error, the bladder was punctured.

A stone in the bladder is sometimes more difficult to manage. If the head is only just beginning to enter the brim, the stone may be pushed up above it; but if it has already engaged completely in the pelvic cavity, it becomes a question whether it will not be necessary to cut down upon it, and thus remove it. These cases are, however, of very rare occurrence, and we must be entirely guided by circumstances, it being impossible to lay down any precise rules for their treatment.

[Pg 324]

CHAPTER VI.

SIXTH SPECIES OF DYSTOCIA.

Faulty Labour from a faulty Condition of the expelling Powers.

I. Where the uterine activity is at fault—functionally or mechanically—from debility—derangement of the digestive organs—mental affections—the age and temperament of the patient—plethora—rheumatism of the uterus—inflammation of the uterus—stricture of the uterus.—Treatment. II. Where the action of the abdominal and other muscles is at fault.—Faulty state of the expelling powers after the birth of the child.—Hæmorrhage.—Treatment.

Although this species includes that condition of the expelling powers, where their action is excessive, we shall defer this portion of the subject until we treat of precipitate labour, with which it is essentially connected.

The agency by which the child is expelled during labour is of two kinds: 1st, involuntary action of the uterus, assisted, secondly, by the partly voluntary and partly involuntary action of the abdominal muscles.

On the approach of labour, the uterus, which hitherto had been merely performing the office of a receptacle and a means of conveying nourishment to the fœtus, now assumes a totally different character; from being in a nearly passive state, it assumes an entirely opposite condition, viz. of high irritability and powerful action. We might almost suppose that its connexion with the nervous system was become more close and intimate; for it is now sensible to the influence of impressions which had before produced no effect upon it. Thus, we see, that affections of the mind, even but of moderate intensity, and to which it was, before labour, nearly, if not quite, insensible, are now capable either of rousing its efforts to the utmost violence, or of arresting them in the midst of full activity; and, on the other hand, we[Pg 325] see that where its action has been deranged or interrupted, it gives rise to serious affections of the nervous system, or even convulsions.

With all this, it now displays peculiarities of function, which strikingly distinguish it from all other organs of the body; in some cases it appears to annihilate or to absorb, by its all-pervading influence, the functional energies of other organs; and, in spite of its increased nervous power and susceptibility to various impressions, it seems to possess the faculty of continuing its efforts uninfluenced by general disease, unimpaired by exhaustion, and, for a time, almost independent of the life itself of the mother. In convulsions and paralysis, in general fever and inflammation of vital organs, its powers appear to be undiminished: on the contrary, where the patient, from whatever cause, is rendered incapable of assisting its efforts by the abdominal muscles, the uterus will take upon itself the whole task of expelling the child, which will be born apparently without a single effort upon the part of the mother.

We also observe, that organs, the various conditions and derangements of which have exerted little or no influence upon the uterus in its state of quiescence during pregnancy, now affect it powerfully, and are capable of modifying its action very considerably. The stomach, the intestinal canal, and the skin, are remarkable instances of this, and seldom fail to disturb or pervert the natural efforts of the uterus, whenever these organs deviate from a healthy condition. It will be, therefore, of the highest importance to watch their functions narrowly, in order that we may form a correct estimate of their effects upon the uterus.

Derangements in the contractile power of the uterus may arise from a variety of causes, which may be chiefly brought under two heads, viz. functional and mechanical.

The functional derangements may arise from insufficient activity, the result of general or local debility; from a deranged condition of the digestive organs; from passions or affections of the mind; from hereditary temperament, constitution, or peculiarity; from the patient's age, being either very young or considerably advanced in years, and pregnant for the first time; from plethora, general or local; from rheumatic affection of the uterus; and from uterine inflammation.

The contractions of the uterus may be mechanically impeded, by tumours imbedded in its substance; by organic diseases, as schirrus, cephaloma, and hæmatoma; cicatrices from former ulcerations or rupture, or by any other circumstances which interrupt the action of the longitudinal fibres upon the os uteri.

From debility. Where uterine action is insufficient from debility, the pains are feeble, and do not appear to act in the right direction; they are frequently attended with much greater suffering[Pg 326] than might be expected from their inefficiency; the intervals between the pains are unusually long, the pains themselves are very short, or, after a while, cease altogether.

This condition, when depending on general debility, may be the result of previous disease, loss of blood, or other debilitating evacuations, poverty, with its attendant miseries, depressing passions of the mind, and health broken down by intemperance.

The contractile power of the uterus itself may be injured by previous leucorrhœa or menorrhagia, by abortions, or by attacks of hæmorrhage during the latter part of pregnancy; it may be weakened by over-distention of the uterus, either from plurality of children or too much liquor amnii, by the patient exerting herself improperly at the commencement of labour, straining violently, and endeavouring to bear down before she is involuntarily compelled to do so by the presence of the head in the vagina. It may also be the membranes giving way too soon, as is so frequently observed in first labours.

From derangement of the digestive organs. We have already described the change which takes place in the relation between the uterus and other organs, as soon as it passes into a state of action. The intestinal canal stands foremost in the influence which it exerts upon the uterus; whether it be from constipation or diarrhœa, irritation from acrid contents, &c., it will greatly modify, and even derange, its contractile power; the pains cease to be genuine uterine contractions, and assume a spasmodic character, producing much painful griping and pinching about the front and lower part of the abdomen, without any of that regularity of interval and duration, and gradual accession and recession, which mark the presence of real labour pains, and, we need scarcely add, with little or no effect upon the progress of the labour itself. These griping colicky pains appear to supersede the true process of parturition, and either to prevent the uterus acting with due regularity and effect so long as they last, or so to pervert its action as to produce a species of metastasis towards other organs. The pains lose their peculiar character as the expelling powers of the uterus; they cease entirely, and the patient is suddenly attacked with dyspnœa, cramps in the extremities, violent shivering, great restlessness, intense headach, delirium, convulsions, or even mania.

Wherever the action of the uterus is deranged by gastric or intestinal irritation, the abdomen is generally more or less tender in front, particularly over the symphysis pubis; the os uteri is thin, tense, and rigid; the vagina is hotter than natural; the secretion of mucus is sparing; and both os uteri and vagina are more than usually tender to the touch.

From mental affections. The mind is capable of influencing the action of the uterus during labour in a remarkable manner, not only where it is suffering from depressing emotions, as grief,[Pg 327] great anxiety, or painful anticipations as to the result, but from causes of a much slighter character, which are nevertheless well worthy the attention of the practitioner: his sudden appearance in the room, without the patient having been properly warned of his arrival: the dread of an examination; or annoyances of a much slighter character, as regards his manner, or that of the nurse, &c., will not unfrequently be quite sufficient to stop the progress of the pains.

The age and general temperament of the patient will also affect the character of the pains. When pregnancy occurs for the first time, either at a very early age, or considerably advanced in life, labour is apt to be protracted, from defective uterine contraction; in the first case, she has not yet attained that degree of adult strength which is requisite to undergo a process requiring so much exertion; the pains are weak, of short duration, and inefficient, but very exhausting to the patient. From the irritability both of the nervous and vascular systems, so peculiar to youth, arises a long train of troublesome symptoms, such as congestion of blood to the head, spasms, syncope, convulsions, &c. In the other case, the condition of the system is the reverse, the irritability is diminished, the uterus is sluggish in its action, the pains are weak and inefficient, follow each other very slowly, and the course of the labour is much protracted; besides this, the short passages through which the child advances are now less capable of dilatation, from having that elasticity and suppleness peculiar to youth, and therefore oppose a much greater resistance.

Where the patient is of a slothful phlegmatic habit, the uterus generally indicates a corresponding state, by the slowness of its action and want of excitability during labour. The same condition is manifested during the catamenial periods in the unimpregnated state, by the absence of pain, weight, throbbing, and other symptoms of local congestion, which are usually observed at these times; so that, but for the discharge, the patient has scarcely any guide to mark their recurrence. On the contrary, where the appearance of the menses is preceded and accompanied by severe pain in the back and loins, throbbing, heat, weight, &c., indicating considerable excitement in the uterine system, we usually observe a similar condition in the uterus during labour, the pains being quick, energetic, and efficient. It is probably from some peculiarity of temperament that we can explain the hereditary disposition which some women show in the unusually lingering or rapid character of their labours.

From plethora. A congested or overloaded state of the uterine circulation, whether from general plethora or from other causes, is not an uncommon cause of feeble contractions. The spongy tissue of the uterine parietes is so gorged with blood, as to prevent, in a great measure, the free action of the pains, and may thus seriously impede the progress of labour. We have already[Pg 328] pointed out, when speaking of the signs of pregnancy, the disposition which the system manifests for forming a larger quantity of blood than before; the pulse is stronger and more full, the animal heat is increased; this is especially observed in the uterus, and continues so during the whole process. Whilst in the state of inaction which belongs to pregnancy, but little inconvenience, comparatively, is felt; but when labour commences, and it contracts, the blood is driven from its engorged veins and sinuses into the general circulation; if, however, it cannot do this, from the general state of plethora, its contractions are rendered very imperfect and inefficient.

Besides the appearances of general plethora, we shall easily recognise this condition by the following symptoms: "the patient has much heat of surface and yet but little thirst; the face, eyes, and skin, are red and considerably swollen; we can feel vessels pulsating in every direction; she gets but little sleep, and finds the bed and the bedclothes uncomfortable to her; the uterus is large, thick, tense, and very warm: the os uteri swollen and cushiony, and the vagina also warm and spacious; the fœtus is very restless, and causes a good deal of pain by its movements. The pains are short and ineffective, and accompanied with a peculiar sensation of painful stretching or tension, without any symptoms of rheumatism, cramp, or other morbid conditions of the uterus being present." (Wigand, Geburt des Menschen, vol. i. p. 138.) This condition is not unfrequently accompanied with tendency to hæmorrhoids, inactivity, constipation, varicose veins of the lower extremities, &c.

Rheumatism of the gravid uterus is an affection which, although it has received but little or no notice in this country, has been long known and described by the continental authors. It appears to be a similar condition of the uterine fibres, when developed by pregnancy, to rheumatism in other muscular tissues, arising from the same causes, connected with the same conditions of the system, and producing similar effects; hence, therefore, it must interfere considerably with the healthy action of the uterus, and greatly diminish or entirely destroy, the efficiency of the pains.

The whole uterus is unusually tender to the touch; the contractions are excessively painful from their very commencement, the slightest excitement of the uterus producing a sensation of pain; they come on with a sudden twinge or dragging pain about the pelvis and loins, and where the contractions are still powerful, they sometimes rise to an intolerable degree of intensity. This condition is frequently observed to a slight extent at the commencement of labour; the mild precursory pains which, in a healthy state, are merely attended with a sensation of equable pressure and tightness round the abdomen, now produce much suffering and give rise to one form of spurious pains, to which we have already, under that head, alluded. Where the symptoms[Pg 329] are of considerable severity and have been aggravated by improper treatment, this state may easily pass into that of actual inflammation.

On examining into the history of the case, we shall frequently find that for several days, or even more than a week, the patient has remarked the uterus to be unusually tender to the touch, scarcely bearing the pressure of the clothes; and at night-time the uneasiness has increased to such a degree that she could scarcely remain in bed. There is a frequent desire to pass water, which is highly acid, and deposites much red sediment; and in all probability she complains of rheumatic pains in other parts of her body.

The causes of this condition are the same as those of rheumatism under ordinary circumstances: exposure to cold, and alternations of temperature, particularly when heated; derangement of the stomach, with much prevalence of acid, &c.: insufficient clothing, and, upon the Continent, especially in Holland, where it is said to be very frequent, by the use of chauffe-pieds.

Inflammation of the uterus is another condition which can not only greatly impair, but entirely suspend, the activity of the uterus. It is usually brought on by improper treatment during labour, where the real cause of the lingering ineffective pains at the commencement has been entirely overlooked, and a state of uterine irritation aggravated into one of actual inflammation by the abuse of stimuli and other heating drinks, given with the view to increase the pains; it may be external violence, improper attempts to dilate the os uteri, rough and too frequent examination, endeavouring to turn the child or to apply the forceps before the soft passages were in a fit condition for that purpose.

The whole abdomen becomes extremely tender, and even the slightest contractions of the uterus produce intense suffering; the vagina is hot and dry, and very tender to the touch—its mucous secretion suppressed; the os uteri is swollen, tense, and painful, and the anterior lip is sometimes so distended as to have been actually mistaken for the bladder of membranes; the bowels are confined; the urine is suppressed; the abdomen becomes distended from tympanitis; and general, and probably fatal, inflammation of its contents follows.

Treatment. The causes of insufficient uterine action are so numerous that the modifications to which they give rise are almost endless, and demand no little variety of treatment. A great deal may be done to avoid this state by attention to the patient's health shortly before labour; and by so carefully regulating it as to ensure a healthy condition of the whole system. Lingering labour from feeble uterine activity is seen most frequently in young primiparæ of delicate form and nervous irritable habit; the pains produce much fruitless suffering, and greatly exhaust the patient. If the cause continues, the case becomes much[Pg 330] protracted, and serious consequences may ensue; such as hysterical symptoms, or even convulsions, inflammation of some organ, general fever, or complete and dangerous exhaustion, hæmorrhage, retained placenta, or hour-glass contraction of the uterus. In a slight degree this condition is not of unfrequent occurrence, whether from an enfeebled uterus or general debility, and requires general, rather than special treatment for its removal. Change of posture, walking about the room, gentle friction of the abdomen, and occasionally taking some refreshing or mildly nutrient drink, as tea, wine and water, or beef-tea, &c., prove serviceable in such cases; friction of the abdomen, if well applied, frequently produces a great alteration in the character of the pains, and greatly assist the progress of labour: if it be still in the first stage (the os uteri not yet fully dilated,) an enema will not only clear the rectum of any fæcal matter which may be lodging there, but assist in rousing the uterus to greater activity.

Where we can satisfy ourselves that none of the above-mentioned causes are present to protract the labour, we may proceed to the use of those remedies which are considered to have the power of exciting the uterine contractions, such as secale cornutum, borax, cinnamon, and the several diffusible stimulants. This state of uterine inactivity is, however, rare; and we would earnestly warn young practitioners against too readily concluding that it is present. They will find that the more carefully they investigate such cases, the less frequently will they require these remedies. In using the secale cornutum, we give the preference to the powder: it should be carefully kept from moisture, air, or light: from twenty to thirty grains, mixed in cold water, will be the proper dose, and this may be repeated two or three times, at intervals of half an hour, or rather more. Borax is also another remedy which appears to possess a peculiar power in exciting the activity of the uterus: although it is scarcely ever used for such a purpose in this country, its effects upon the uterus have been long known in Germany; and in former times, both it and the secale cornutum entered largely into the composition of the different nostrums which were used for the purpose of assisting labour. We have combined these two medicines with the best effects, and generally give them in the following manner:—℞ Secalis Cornuti ℈ i—ij; Sodæ Subborat. gr x; Aq. Cinnamomi ℥ jss. M. Fiat haust. Cinnamon, which is a remedy of considerable antiquity, has also a similar action upon the uterus, although to a less degree.

Our own conviction with regard to the use of these remedies is, that they are seldom required during labour, except in nates, or footling presentations, or in cases of turning, where the head is about to enter the pelvis, and where, at this critical moment, the action of the uterus is apt to fail, when it is important to the[Pg 331] safety of the child that there should be brisk pains to force the head through the pelvis and internal parts with sufficient rapidity. The chief value of these remedies is for the purpose of exciting uterine contraction after labour, and thus to promote the safe expulsion of the placenta, where there is a disposition to inertia uteri, and ensure the patient against hæmorrhage.

Where the contractile power of the uterus is so enfeebled that it becomes nearly powerless, we deem it much safer and better to apply extractive force to the head by means of the forceps, and thus overcome the natural resistance of the soft parts, to using medicines which excite uterine action, and thus stimulate the exhausted organ to still farther efforts. The mere cessation of uterine action, however, where the labour has been tedious and fatiguing, is no proof that the uterus is exhausted, and incapable of farther efforts: so far from its sinking into a state of quiescence, being a symptom of exhaustion, experience shows that, in labours of this character, it indicates a very opposite condition, being nothing more than a state of temporary repose, during which nature affords it an opportunity of recruiting its own powers, as also those of the whole system. The interval of ease which is thus given to the patient is accompanied by refreshing sleep; the skin grows moist; a gentle diaphoresis creeps over her; the circulation becomes calm; and after a time, the uterus awakes again to renewed and astonishing exertions; thus, Wigand has remarked, "the pains during the same labour may cease once, twice, or even oftener, and yet after a little rest will return with renewed strength." (Geburt des Menschen, vol. ii. p. 242.) On the other hand, where the pains, in spite of their becoming more and more ineffective, continue to exhaust the patient with fruitless suffering, and prevent her from enjoying that repose which is so desirable under such circumstances; when the uterus, from increasing irritability, scarcely ceases to contract even for a moment, but continues tense and more or less tender during the intervals of the pains, we can have little or no reasonable expectation that such a labour can be terminated by the natural powers. If the head be not far advanced in the pelvis, or the passages fully dilated, if the bowels have been relieved before labour, and there is no febrile excitement of the circulation, a mild diaphoretic sedative, like Dover's powder, will be of great service: it calms the irritability of the system, and induces that state of quiet or actual repose to which we have just alluded. If, on the other hand, the labour be much farther advanced, the head approaching the pelvic outlet, and the soft parts well dilated, a little assistance, by means of the forceps, will quickly terminate the case, and free the mother and her child from farther suffering and danger.

Where the uterus is enfeebled by lesion or change of structure, it becomes very difficult to decide as to what course ought to be[Pg 332] pursued: in some cases, the soft passages partake in the loss of tone, and offer but little resistance to the advance of the child; in others, however, the uterus is so powerless as to give us no choice but of employing artificial delivery.

We have already pointed out the importance of paying the strictest attention to the bowels shortly before and during labour, and how frequently a neglect of this precaution acts as a means of perverting the due action of the pains, and giving them that character, already described under the head of False Pains. "After the labour has made much progress, the rectum, if loaded, should be emptied by clysters; indeed, the utility of clysters in almost every stage of labour is so apparent that it is to be lamented they are not more frequently employed." (Synopsis of difficult Parturition, p. 19.) We have seen cases where, although the bowels had been opened at the commencement of labour, after a time, the pains have gradually lost their dilating effect upon the os uteri, although they have increased in severity; the os uteri has remained tense and hard, and the labour has become very tedious and exhausting; the administration of an enema, and removal of a quantity of fæcal matter from the rectum, has been followed by an instantaneous change in all the symptoms; the pains have become powerful and effective, the os uteri has quickly dilated, and the whole labour has been completed in a very short space of time. In like manner, vomiting during the early part of labour produces the best effects; for it not only assists to relax the parts, by the nausea which usually precedes it, but, by emptying the stomach of unhealthy contents, it tends not a little to restore the uterus to its natural activity.

Where the bowels are distended with flatus, and loaded with acrid and unhealthy contents; we rarely see the pains become regular and effective until these sources of irritation are removed: the abdomen is painful with spasmodic colicky griping, and excites the uterus to partial and very painful contractions of a cramp-like character, which entirely supersede the regular pains, and thus exhaust the patient with protracted suffering without at all advancing the labour itself. If this condition be allowed to continue uninterfered with, the tenderness of the abdomen increases, the circulation becomes excited, and inflammation, and fever of a most serious kind will be the result.

In the management of primiparæ, who are pregnant either at a very early age or considerably advanced in life, our chief attention must be directed to the management of them for some little time before labour is expected, in order that we may place them in as favourable a state of health as possible, and thus enable them to meet the coming trial with safety.

Where the patient is very young, we should endeavour, by early hours, regular exercise, good air, and simple nourishing diet, &c., to increase her strength, and the general tone of health,[Pg 333] and thus diminish that irritability of the nervous system peculiar to females of this early age. She should lead a country life, be as much as possible in the open air, enjoy the absence of restraint and excitement, which are almost necessary consequences of a residence in town, and, by agreeable occupation and cheerful society, train herself, as it were, to that state of moral as well as bodily health best adapted to ensure a favourable result. It is in cases of this kind where the bodily powers have not yet ripened into adult womanhood, that so much good may be effected by using the tepid or (if the season permit) cold salt water bath; and we would beg to refer our readers to our observations on this subject in the chapter on Premature Expulsion. In a case which has recently come under our notice, we have had reason to attribute the remarkably healthy and favourable labour of a young and delicate primipara solely to the invigorating effects of regular exercise and the daily use of sea-bathing, which she continued to within a very few days of her confinement.

It is commonly supposed that women pregnant for the first time, and advanced in years, always have severe labours: this is not necessarily the case, although, at the same time, the greater rigidity of the soft parts considerably increases the resistance to the expelling powers. It will be equally important in this case, also, to improve her health and strength as far as possible, and, by exercise, warm hip baths, &c., to give the parts a greater degree of suppleness and elasticity.

Where the labour is protracted by a state of general plethora or local congestion, the expelling powers are not only enfeebled by the engorged state of the uterine circulation preventing effective pains, but the resistance to the passage of the child is increased by a similar condition of the soft passages, which are swollen and turgid with blood. It is in these cases that bleeding effects such a sudden and complete change; the pulse loses its oppressed character, and rises in point of strength, the uterus loses the thick solid feel which it had before; its contractions become active and powerful, the os uteri dilates, the passages become soft and yielding, and the whole process assumes a different character. By careful observation, this state can easily be discovered before labour has actually commenced; in which case much useless suffering may be prevented by previously reducing the circulation to a proper standard, and thus fitting the uterus for the exertions it has to undergo: besides bleeding, mild saline laxatives, with or without antimonials, will be of great service. The nitrate of potass in these cases has the best effects, either in farthering the effects of the bleeding, or removing the necessity of using so powerful a remedy.

In treating rheumatism of the gravid uterus, our practice will differ but little from that in cases of ordinary rheumatism in other parts: this condition, we believe, is rarely excited, until[Pg 334] the system had been already predisposed to it by deranged digestion, and that general prevalence of acid diathesis, which manifests itself in different individuals and under different circumstances so variously; hence, therefore, it will always be important to unload the primæ viæ effectually by an active dose of calomel or some other mercurial, before prescribing for the immediate symptoms of the complaint: beyond producing a little occasional nausea, five grains of calomel will act much more comfortably to the patient's feelings than a smaller dose; there will be less griping and intestinal irritation, but the effect will be more complete and general; not only will the bowels be thoroughly evacuated, but the liver relieved of a large quantity of unhealthy acrid bile, the removal of which cannot but be highly advantageous. We may now proceed to the use of diaphoretics and opiates: of these, Dover's powder stands foremost; and if given in doses of from ten to fifteen grains, accompanied with warm diluent drinks, rarely fails to induce sleep and a pretty active perspiration, which gives great relief. As the abdomen is usually more or less tender on pressure, it should be covered with a piece of soft flannel, or, still farther to ensure the full diaphoretic effect of the remedies, a warm bath may be had recourse to. Where calomel in the above dose has been premised, we seldom fail in procuring a free action of the skin, and, according to our own experience, with far greater relief to the system than where the perspiration has been induced merely by diaphoretics and external warmth.

If this condition of the uterus has been neglected, and the contractions are beginning to produce intense suffering; if the abdomen is rapidly becoming more tender to the touch, it should be covered with a hot poultice of linseed meal, made more stimulating by the addition of mustard flour, and this should be continued until the skin is considerably reddened. In the slighter cases of this affection, where the bowels have been opened, friction upon the abdomen frequently produces the happiest effects. We presume it is to these cases that Dr. Power alludes when he says, "in some, the improper action will be removed almost instantly, and, as it were, by a miracle; so that a case which has been protracted for the greater part of a week, under the most intense suffering, without the least progress, has been happily terminated in fifteen or twenty minutes from the first commencement of the friction." (Power's Midwifery, 1819.)

Where inflammation of the uterus takes place during labour, the case becomes one of the most serious character; for not only is the suffering, which is every contraction, of the most intense description, but the presence of the child aggravates the state of inflammatory action, and excites the uterus to still more violent efforts, while the swollen and unyielding state of the os uteri, &c., precludes the chance of speedy delivery.[Pg 335] Under such circumstances, we must trust almost entirely to the lancet in aiding this important object; for, until the circulation has received an effectual check by fainting, the dilatation of the parts cannot proceed, nor can any attempt be made to give artificial assistance. The abdomen should be covered with a hot linseed meal poultice, as above described, in the treatment of rheumatism of the uterus; warm decoction of poppies should be thrown up the vagina, or, if this cannot be procured at the moment, some thin gruel mixed with a little laudanum, or in which a few grains of Extr. Conii or Hyoscyami have been suspended; the bowels should be opened by a simple enema, after which a small opiate injection will be desirable, in order still farther to allay irritation.

Stricture of the uterus. We have already had occasion to allude more than once to that species of violent and continued contraction which we have denominated stricture of the uterus, but have chiefly considered it where it affects the os uteri; a somewhat similar condition of spastic rigidity is occasionally, though rarely, seen in other parts of this organ, and is capable of producing a most serious obstacle to delivery. The uniform and regular action of the uterus disappears; its contractions become partial, both in extent and effect, one part alone contracts whilst the rest of the uterus is relaxed; its shape thus becomes altered; for, by these partial contractions of its fibres, it may become elongated, shortened, flattened, &c.: the spasmodic action frequently varies its seat, and successively attacks different portions; thus, where it affects the body of the uterus, it becomes contracted almost like an hour-glass, having a transverse circular indentation, as if it had been tied with a cord. Where the contraction affects one side of the organ, it alters the shape of it materially; the fundus is pulled down equally, and the position of the child, as we have shown in the first species of dystocia, may be seriously affected. If the stricture has its seat in the os uteri, this becomes tightly contracted, hard, unyielding, and painful upon pressure: it does not dilate sufficiently, and the inferior segment of the uterus is generally pushed downwards, whilst the os uteri itself is drawn upwards. In cases of this kind, we find that although the uterus contracts, the child does not advance, but rather retracts, during a pain; the contractions are never general, but partial, and even where they are general, the fundus does not attain its due preponderance over the os uteri, so that the one contracts as much as the other does; in severe cases, also, the uterus continues in a state of spasmodic action during the intervals of the pains: this is frequently accompanied with a painful and harassing sensation of tension and stretching, very different to that the action of regular pains upon the os uteri; and in the worst cases we occasionally observe a peculiar state of the brain,[Pg 336] which manifests itself by attacks of insensibility, faintings, or even convulsions.

Although the head does not advance in spite of the strongest pains, yet, upon examination, we find no want of proportion between it and the pelvis; if the intervals of uterine action be of sufficient duration to allow it, we shall feel the head quite moveable in the pelvis, or, at any rate, with plenty of room for the finger to pass round it, and yet when a pain comes on, the head remains fixed, or if it does descend somewhat, it returns again to its former situation as soon as the pain is over. This state of things is usually seen where the body of the uterus is the seat of the stricture, and is contracted transversely upon that of the child, which it tightly encircles, and renders all farther advance impossible.

This state of spasmodic action is whatever tends to irritate the uterus and excite it to irregular action; thus, premature rupture of the membranes, especially when it has been suddenly drained of a large quantity of liquor amnii; the irritation arising from acrid matter in the intestines, or from their being loaded with accumulations of fæces; improper examination, and more especially, attempts to dilate the os uteri by the fingers or hand; endeavouring to strain and bear down during the early part of labour, and when the patient is not involuntarily compelled to do so; attempting to apply the forceps when the os uteri is not fully dilated, or whilst the instrument is very cold: malposition of the child, especially after rupture of the membranes; and lastly, anxiety, fear, and other affections of the mind. The circulation is generally in an irritable state, the patient is of a delicate excitable habit, and is apt to be nervous and hysterical.

The treatment in these cases will be precisely on the same general rules as we have above described; the bowels must be relieved by a laxative or by an enema; if necessary, the circulation must be reduced to the proper standard by bleeding, and the irregular uterine action controlled by opiates. Besides these means, the warm bath is of the utmost service, and seldom fails to produce a favourable change. Where the action of the uterus is impeded, or otherwise rendered faulty by organic disease, lesions of its structure, &c., we shall in all probability be compelled to use artificial assistance.

II. Where the action of the abdominal and other muscles is at fault. Where the faulty character of the labour arises from a faulty state of the partly voluntary, partly involuntary, action of the abdominal muscles which is destined to aid the uterus in expelling the child, this may equally be a result of general debility from previous disease, exhaustion from the long duration of the labour, from the abuse of spirituous liquors, &c. It may also arise from various causes which tend to impede the respiration;[Pg 337] such as excessive corpulence, great deformity of the spine, broncho-cele, spasmodic asthma, rheumatism of the diaphragm, ascites, hydrothorax, phthisis, pneumonia, aneurism of the aorta, dilatation of the heart, &c.

Where the size is such as renders the patient very unwieldy, or the spine is much deformed, we must place her in that position in which she can exert herself with greatest effect, and at the same time experience the least possible obstruction to her breathing: with deformed people, this is of great importance; she should be propped up with pillows, &c. into whatever posture she can lie with most comfort, and the practitioner must manage to deliver her in this position. Patients suffering from pluerisy or pneumonia are unable to bear the continued strong inflation of the lungs which is necessary during the second stage: under these circumstances, the pain and inflammation are greatly aggravated; venesection must be used with great promptness, but it does not always bring relief or remove the danger; for the disease is kept up by the presence of labour, which, therefore, in all probability, will require to be terminated by art. In some cases, however, as we have already mentioned, especially where the disease is of an acute character, the uterus appears to take upon itself the whole exertion of the labour, so that the child is born apparently without any effort on the part of the mother.

Faulty state of the expelling powers after the birth of the child. The last stage of labour, which comprehends the expulsion of the placenta, may also be retarded by a faulty state of the expelling powers. This not only arises from the causes which we have already mentioned, but from those connected with the labour itself; as from premature and immoderate straining during the pains, misuse of medicines given to increase the pains; also, where the uterus has been exhausted by the length and severity of the labour, or where it has been thrown into a state of inertia by the sudden evacuation of its contents, especially when previously much distended. This condition is frequently induced by not supporting the child sufficiently when the shoulders are about to pass through the os externum; the main bulk of the child is therefore suddenly expelled, and the uterus is at once thrown into irregular action by the sudden shock of so great a change, or falls into a state of inertia. The separation and expulsion of the placenta may be also retarded where the labour has required the forceps, turning, or perforation, especially the latter, on account of considerable pelvic deformity; the more so if there has been considerable delay in giving assistance. Irregular and partial action of the uterine fibres, after the expulsion of the child, may easily render the last stage of labour danger-ous; for, under such circumstances, the portion of the uterus to which the placenta is attached may be in a state of firm contraction in one part, while[Pg 338] the other is quite relaxed, so that incomplete separation of the placenta will be the result, and hæmorrhage follow: hence we cannot be too cautious in avoiding every cause which may at all influence the regular action of the uterus during the last stage of labour, which is far more dangerous than the two others put together.

In a case of this kind, we do not feel the uterus contracting into the firm globular mass above the symphysis pubis, as might have been expected; but if inertia uteri be present, it remains soft and large, the peculiar pains of the last stage which indicate the speedy separation and expulsion of the placenta do not make their appearance, or only in a very insufficient degree. If it be contracting irregularly and only in part, we shall feel this distinctly, from the unequal shape and hardness of the uterus, which in some cases will have almost a lobulated feel; in others, it presents a considerable depression either upon the fundus or anterior wall.

Hæmorrhage. The danger here, chiefly depends upon the occurrence of hæmorrhage: if the placenta be still attached by its whole surface to the uterus, no hæmorrhage can ensue; but if the contractions have been of suffi-cient power to detach more or less of it from the uterus, large trunks, which have hitherto conveyed maternal blood into the placental cells, are torn through, and a profuse discharge must be the result. The degree of the hæmorrhage will in most instances furnish us with a tolerable estimate of the extent to which the separation has taken place; but it is far from easy to ascertain correctly the quantity of blood which has been lost, and we must rather try to ascertain what are the effects produced upon the system of the patient. The pulse becomes smaller and quicker, the column of blood is evidently diminished, and the heart for a time drives on its contents more rapidly; but as the loss increases, so does it become enfeebled, and although beating with a very frequent stroke, it now becomes so weak as to be scarcely or no longer capable at the wrist of producing such a resistance to the finger as will give the sensation of a pulse; the necessary consequence of this is, that the patient at first complains of great weakness, the face becomes pale, the lips white, the breathing anxious; this is followed by a sense of great prostration, the perspiration breaks out upon the face and forehead, tinnitus aurium, confusion of ideas, and sense of darkness before the eyes succeed; the load at the præcordia, and the oppression of breathing, become more insupportable; she tosses her arms about, and in some instances has a sensation that the room is going round with her, or that she is sinking through the bed; in other cases, the breathing becomes gradually more feeble, until it is almost imperceptible; she every now and then takes a deep sobbing grasp, which seems to rouse her to consciousness for a moment, and then she relapses into a state verging upon[Pg 339] insensibility; the pulse is probably now no longer perceptible at the wrist, the face is undergoing a rapid change, the features are contracting, and there is a general expression of death-like collapse which shows too truly the urgency of the danger. The alterations which are taking place in the state of the brain and nervous system, vary in different individuals: in some, there is strabismus; in others, temporary mania, or at least, delirium; and in more unfavourable cases, even convulsions; these last are especially formidable, as they not only show that the system has been severely affected by the loss of blood, but are apt, from their violence, to extinguish the little spark of life which is left, or, in other words, to be followed by sudden death.

These are some of the many symptoms indicating a sudden and extensive loss of blood; others also occur, depending on the external or internal character of the hæmorrhage. The want of contraction and general flaccidity of the uterus, as felt through the abdominal parietes, have been already noticed; if the blood be prevented escaping by the contracted state of the os uteri, by coagula, or the detached placenta, it begins to collect in the cavity of the uterus, which therefore swells as the accumulation continues to increase, so that it may even equal the size which it had before labour, containing many quarts of blood, and the patient may be in the most imminent danger of dying from hæmorrhage, perhaps, without any blood having issued externally: this is the internal uterine hæmorrhage, a form which is justly looked upon as peculiarly to be dreaded, from the insidious character of its attack. In most cases, the uterus fills to a certain extent only, and then, as if excited to contraction by the distention of its parietes, or any slight concussion, coughing, &c. it expels a large quantity of coagula and half coagulated blood, and returning to its former state of atony, again begins to swell from fresh accumulation of blood in its cavity.

Treatment. So long as the inertia or atony of the uterus continues without any symptoms either of external or internal hæmorrhage, we are not justified in interfering directly, either for the purpose of exciting the uterus, or still less of removing the placenta. This condition chiefly occurs where the uterus has been previously much distended, or suddenly emptied of its contents, where it has been exhausted by long and difficult parturition, and also, as Leroux has observed, "in women of a phlegmatic temperament and lax fibre, who, during pregnancy, have suffered much ill-health, by which the tone of the solids has been weakened; who have very large pelves, and a soft dilatable os uteri." (Sur les Pertes de Sang, 1776.)

We must therefore give the uterus time to recover from the great and sudden change which it has undergone, to collect its strength, to remodel and arrange its forces, until it is at length able, not only to resume its efforts, but to contract to that extent[Pg 340] which shall both ensure the expulsion of the placenta and the safety of the patient. Whilst this state of inertia lasts, the patient should be kept as quiet as possible; she should be placed in a comfortable posture, take a little cool drink from time to time (as cold tea, toast and water, &c.,) in order to refresh her;[131] or, if she has been much exhausted by her labour, a glass of wine may be given with good effect. If, however, hæmorrhage appears, this shows that a separation of the placenta from the uterus must have taken place: our great object should now be to excite contraction of the uterus, for by this means alone can we stop the discharge.

In ordinary cases, a little circular friction with the tips of the fingers over the fundus will generally be sufficient. If the uterus begins to swell, we may grasp it with a sudden but moderate degree of force; or we may give the fundus every now and then a smart jog with our hand. Whilst these measures are pursuing, a dose of secale cornutum (see Dystocia, p. 330,) will be of great service; for even if it does not act soon enough to aid the expulsion of the placenta, it contributes greatly to ensure the contraction of the uterus afterwards. If the hæmorrhage nevertheless continues profuse, it will be necessary to introduce the hand into the uterus and remove the half-separated placenta: its contractions are too feeble for that purpose of itself, and the presence of the hand in its cavity, and the artificial separation of the placenta, act as a stimulus, and rouse it to greater activity. The opinion that we only increase the danger by thus increasing the bleeding surface does not hold good, when, from the profuseness of the hæmorrhage, it has become evident that the greater part of the placenta is already separated from the uterus; on the other hand, where there is but a slight discharge, the case is very different, and would not justify our having recourse to so strong a measure.

If the contraction which has been excited by the artificial removal of the placenta be but temporary, we must proceed to the use of other means for the purpose of rousing the activity of the uterus. The sudden application of cold is a most valuable means; it acts here solely by the shock which it produces at the moment, and not by lowering the circulation and favouring coagulation. Thus we find that a cold wet napkin suddenly flapped upon the abdomen has an immediate effect upon the uterus; but it ought not to remain on long, and the skin should be dried with a warm towel, in order that a fresh application of the cold may produce the greater effect. A series of such shocks may be using another wet napkin to the vulva, and[Pg 341] a third to the sacrum and loins; an assistant should remove them in the order in which they have been applied, and dry the skin, for a repetition of the remedy, if necessary.

A still more powerful mode of producing a sudden shock, and thus rousing the uterus to activity, is by a douche of cold water upon the abdomen. This may easily be effected by a teapot or kettle held at some height above, and slowly emptied upon the lower part of the abdomen; the uterus will seldom refuse to obey such a stimulus as this, however great may be the inertia into which it has fallen. The inefficiency of a prolonged application of cold to the abdomen, however severe, and the efficiency of the contrary practice, is admirably expressed by Dr. Gooch, in his description of a dangerous case of hæmorrhage:—"Finding the ice so inefficient, I swept it off, and taking an ewer of cold water, I let its contents fall from a height of several feet upon the belly: the effect was instantaneous; the uterus, which, the moment before, had been so soft and indistinct as not to be felt within the abdomen, became small and hard; the bleeding stopped, and the faintness ceased—a striking proof of the important principle that cold applied with a shock is a more powerful means of producing contraction of the uterus than a greater degree of cold without the shock." (An Account of some of the more important Diseases belonging to women, by Robert Gooch, M. D.)

Another mode of applying cold to induce uterine contraction, and little, if at all, inferior to that above-mentioned, is the injection of cold water into the uterus itself: this can only be effectually employed after the removal of the placenta and membranes, and frequently proves of the greatest assistance, being capable of rousing the uterus when many other means have failed. If, from the sultriness of the weather, water cannot be procured of sufficient coldness, or if the case be very urgent, vinegar and water in equal parts may be used; but the injections of spirit and water, which some have recommended, can scarcely be considered as a safe proceeding.

These various means frequently require to be repeated several times before the contraction of the uterus becomes permanent, nor must we be discouraged by finding the uterus becoming soft again in a minute or two after ceasing to use them; for we may feel assured, with few exceptions, that if we can only keep the uterus, by this means, in a state of tolerable contraction for half an hour, it will ultimately become permanent, and remain so of itself.[132]

It is, in these cases, where pressure is of so much importance, not for the purpose of producing uterine contraction, as of[Pg 342] maintaining it when once excited. By pressure applied at this moment, we may frequently keep the enfeebled uterus in a state of contraction, which, but for this support, would have yielded to the general force of the circulation, and have again expanded. For the same reason, whenever the uterus begins to swell again from internal hæmorrhage, and by the renewal of the above remedies, it becomes hard, but does not diminish in size: this shows that the contraction has not been powerful enough to expel the blood, which, in all probability, has already begun to coagulate in its cavity: where this is the case, the hand, or at least two fingers, should be passed, to dislodge the clots, and assist in their expulsion; after which, a cloth folded into a thick compress should be placed over the fundus, and firmly bandaged upon the abdomen by a broad towel.

Where every means has failed to induce a sufficient or permanent degree of contraction, we believe that the only certain means which remains, is putting the child to its mother's breast. Under no circumstances do we see the sympathy between the uterus and the breast so beautifully displayed as here, and we may most truly affirm that we have never known it fail where the mother was sufficiently conscious to know that it was her own child. To a by-stander, ignorant of what was taking place, the sudden gush of blood mixed with coagula, which follows the application of the child, would be nothing less than a sign of renewed danger, while, in fact, it is a proof that the uterus is beginning to contract and expel its contents.

If the pulse has been seriously reduced by the loss of blood which the patient has sustained, a glass of wine, or a spoonful or two of brandy, will be of great service in rousing the vital powers; and this must be repeated or increased, according to the urgency of the circumstances; a little weak beef-tea, given from time to time, frequently appears to rouse the system, even more than the brandy, and is more refreshing to the patient; it can also be taken in larger quantities, for when the exhaustion is very great, stimuli appear to excite vomiting, which is by all means to be avoided. Where, however, it occurs spontaneously, it need not be looked upon in so formidable a light: thus Dr. Denman observes, "when patients have suffered much from loss of blood, a vomiting is often brought on, and sometimes under circumstances of such extreme debility that I have shrunk with apprehension lest they should have been destroyed by a return or increase of the hæmorrhage, which I concluded was inevitable, after so violent an effort: but there is no reason for this apprehension; for, though vomiting may be considered as a proof of the injury which the constitution has suffered by the hæmorrhage, yet the action of vomiting contributes to its suppression, perhaps by some revulsion, and certainly by exciting a[Pg 343] more vigorous action of the remaining powers of the constitution, as is proved by the amendment of the pulse, and of all other appearances immediately after the vomiting."

When a slight trickling of blood continues, although the uterus is tolerably hard and contracted, it will be desirable to make an examination, for we shall frequently find a long slender coagulum hanging through the os uteri into the vagina, upon the removal of which, the discharge will cease.

The application of the child to the breast is not less valuable for preventing any return of the hæmorrhage than for stopping it in the first instance: we are never perfectly secure against hæmorrhage coming on during the first few hours after delivery, even where every thing has turned out as favourably as possible: the exhaustion from the length or severity of the labour, the warmth of the bed, and in some cases, it would even seem, the relaxing effects of deep sleep, are all liable to be followed by inertia uteri and hæmorrhage. In no way can we ensure our patient so completely against this kind of danger as by putting the child to the breast; the uterine contraction which it excites is not only powerful, but permanent; nor do we consider that a practitioner is justified in leaving a patient in whom the uterus has shown a disposition to inertia without having ensured her safety by this simple but effectual safeguard.

There is a form of hæmorrhage after the birth of the child, which seems to depend upon an over-distended state of the circulation, and where its activity appears too great for the contractile power of the uterus; so that, in spite of the uterus being tolerably firm and hard, a profuse hæmorrhage is almost sure to follow the separation of the placenta. This condition has been described by the late Dr. Gooch, and still more recently by Professor Michaelis, of Kiel; to the former, especially, we are indebted, not only for having first pointed out this important fact, but for having placed it before us in the simplest and clearest light. "I had now witnessed," says Dr. Gooch, "two labours in the same person, in which, though the uterus contracted in the ordinary degree, profuse hæmorrhage had nevertheless occurred: let me be understood—after the birth of the child, I laid my hand on the abdomen, and felt the uterus within, of that size and hardness, which is generally unattended by, and precludes hæmorrhage; in both instances, the labour had been attended by an excessively full and rapid circulation. I could easily understand that a contraction of the uterus, which would preclude hæmorrhage in the ordinary state of circulation, might be insufficient to prevent it, during this violent action of the blood-vessels; and the inference I drew was, that, in this case, the hæmorrhage depended not on a want of contraction of the uterus, but on a want of tranquillity of the circulation; and that if ever she[Pg 344] became pregnant again, a mode of treatment which would cause her to fall in labour with a cool skin and a quiet pulse, would be the best means of preventing a recurrence of the accident." This will be effected by an occasional venesection during the last weeks of pregnancy, by the use of saline laxatives; and if there be still much disposition to heat the surface, and excitement of circulation, by doses of nitre three times a day, and by strict antiphlogistic regimen.

[Pg 345]

CHAPTER VII.

INVERSION OF THE UTERUS.

Partial and complete.—Causes.—Diagnosis and symptoms.—Treatment.—Chronic inversion.—Extirpation of the uterus.

The uterus is liable, although rarely, to a peculiar displacement called inversion, where the fundus is forced down into the cavity of the uterus, and so through the os uteri into the vagina; or where the whole uterus is turned wrong side outwards, the fundus appearing at the os externum, the former being the partial, the latter the complete inversion: in the latter it is not only the entire uterus which is inverted, but it is also the vagina, so that the whole mass which the uterus forms at the os externum is attached to the inverted vagina as by a hollow pedicle, and is encircled by the os uteri close to the labia; the external surface of the mass is the inner surface of the uterus.

As it is impossible for the fundus to descend through the os uteri when this is not dilated and open, it is evident that, except in certain cases of polypus, inversion of the uterus can only take place immediately after delivery. If, at this moment, especially when the uterus has been too suddenly emptied of its contents, any force be applied to the fundus, it may be easily pushed down into the cavity, or, by the continued action of that force, the fundus may be carried through the os uteri or even through the os externum.

Causes. Where this force has been applied externally, it may be violent straining during the last pains, violent efforts, as coughing, vomiting, sneezing, &c., or by sudden attempts to rise in bed, by which the abdominal muscles are put into powerful action. Where, on the other hand, it has been applied from within, it may arise from improper attempts to extract the placenta before the uterus was sufficiently contracted; where the cord has been unusually short, or twisted round the child, or where the patient has been suddenly surprised with violent pains, and the child dashed upon the floor before she could reach her bed, by which means the cord has received a violent jerk, or has been even broken.

It has been very much the habit to attribute inversion almost solely to these latter causes, and that, except where it takes place[Pg 346] from the shortness of the cord, or the sudden expulsion of the child whilst the mother is in the erect posture, it must almost necessarily be a result of improper pulling at the cord on the part of the practitioner: the cases on record, however, go to prove that, in by far the majority of instances, no force of this sort had been applied to the fundus; and in those instances where the child has been dashed upon the floor and the cord broken (some six or seven of which have at different times occurred under our own notice,) the fundus has not once been pulled down, although the force applied to it must have been very considerable, since the very cord which had thus given way to the weight of the child resisted afterwards, on more than one occasion, a considerable effort which we made to break it. In by far the majority of these cases, the cord has given way nearly at the same spot, viz. about three inches distance from the umbilicus, apparently justifying the inference, that it was weaker here than elsewhere. Another reason why the fundus should not have been pulled down by the weight of the child might be stated, viz. that the placenta being at that moment above the brim of the pelvis, the direction in which the strain was made upon the cord (viz. in that of the outlet, or downwards and forwards,) was not much calculated to affect the fundus.

"The practice of pulling too early and violently at the cord," says Dr. Radford, "after the expulsion of the child, before the uterus has contracted, so as to detach and expel the placenta, has been generally considered as the cause of inversion; but we know that the accident happens before any force has been applied to the funis. In case fourth, the descent was so rapid and forcible through the os externum, that it would have been quite impossible to have resisted the unnatural action by which the organ was carried down. It has occurred when the patient was delivered of a dead child, the funis so putrid as to break with a slight effort. It has been found before the cord was separated, and the child given to the nurse. In the practice of Ruysch, this circumstance took place after he had extracted a dead child."[133]

Still, however, it is not the less important to recommend caution, especially to young beginners, against pulling at the cord with too much force, in their hurry to bring the placenta away; the condition of the uterus at this moment is highly favourable if in a state of inertia.

Diagnosis and Symptoms. In cases of partial inversion of the uterus, we distinguish the disease by the absence of the hard spherical tumour of the fundus above the pubes, and by the presence of a globular fleshy body in the os uteri, which is sensible to the touch. This tumour will be found broader at the base than[Pg 347] at its extremity; and surrounded by the os and cervix uteri, forming, as it were, a tight ring round it. The patient complains of a sense of dragging amounting to severe pain in the groins and lumbar region, and which compelling her to strain violently, often forces the uterus farther down, and sometimes induces complete inversion; hæmorrhage more or less consid-erable accompanies it; the pain is more acute in this than in the complete inversion, and the hæmorrhage more violent; the patient suffers under an oppressive sense of sinking, with nausea or vomiting, cold clammy sweats, feeble fluttering or nearly extinct pulse, faintings or even convulsions.

In the complete form we have neither the hæmorrhage nor that frightful train of symptoms the strangulated condition of the inverted uterus; for now that it is fairly turned inside out, it is just, or nearly as capable of contracting as in its natural state, which it is prevented from doing when only partially inverted: complete inversion, however, is not the less to be dreaded, for death may suddenly follow from the shock which the nervous system has sustained, or from dangerous fainting in consequence of the sudden evacuation of the abdominal cavity; this latter circumstance will be aggravated by the inversion of the vagina which is apt to accompany the complete form, and thus give rise to considerable displacement of the intestine.

Treatment. The sooner we endeavour to return the uterus the better, for we shall seldom experience much difficulty in effecting our object, if done immediately upon the occurrence of the accident; indeed, we know of a case where, under these circumstances, it was successfully returned by a midwife. If, on the other hand, some hours are permitted to elapse before the attempt at reduction is made, it will be attended with great difficulty, or even prove entirely abortive; the os uteri contracts powerfully, the uterus swells from the obstructed return of the circulation, inflammation rapidly follows, and diminishes still farther our chances of success. Dr. Denman says, "The impossibility of replacing it, if not done soon after the accident, has been proved in several instances, to which I have been called so early as within four hours, and the difficulty will be increased at the expiration of a longer time." Still, however, we must not despair of success, for numerous cases have been recorded by different authors where the reduction has been effected after a much longer period.

There has been a considerable discrepancy of opinion as to the management of those cases where the placenta is still adhering to the uterus, viz. whether it is not safer to reduce the fundus with the placenta, and excite the uterus to throw it off afterwards in the usual way, or whether we ought not to separate the placenta before making the attempt at reduction. Mr. Newnham, the author of almost the only monograph upon this subject, [Pg 348]recommends the former mode of practice. "It has been recommended by several respectable authorities to remove first the placenta, in order to diminish the bulk of the inverted fundus, and thus facilitate the reduction. But it is surely impossible that this proceeding can be attended with any beneficial consequences, whilst the irritation of the uterus will necessarily tend to bring on those bearing down efforts, which would present a material obstacle to its reduction; and would increase the hæmorrhage at a period when every ounce of blood is of infinite importance, besides returning the placenta while it remains attached to the uterus; and its subsequent judicious treatment as a simply retained placenta will have a good effect in bringing on that regular and natural uterine contraction, which is the hope of the practitioner and the safety of the patient." (Essay on the Symptoms, Causes, and Treatment of Inversion of the Uterus, by W. Newnham, Esq. p. 14.)

On the other hand, many authorities, especially of modern times, advocate a very opposite practice, and recommend that the placenta should be removed before attempting to reduce the fundus; as by so doing it will pass back much more easily than where the bulk of the placenta is added to it. There can be no doubt that this practice is correct in cases of complete inversion, where, as we have already observed, there is little or no danger from hæmorrhage, and where it is of the greatest importance to avail ourselves of every advantage by lessening the size of the inverted uterus as much as possible: where, however, it is a case of partial inversion, it is generally accompanied with hæmorrhage; and here, therefore, it becomes a question how far we are justified in detaching the placenta, and therefore increasing the flooding, either before we are certain that we are able to reduce the fundus, or before we have placed the uterus in a condition in which it is capable of contracting. In Mr. Mann's case, quoted by Dr. Radford (op. cit.,) the inversion was evidently complete, for the uterus was found to have "passed externally from the vagina, and the placenta attached to it." "I first peeled the placenta from the fundus uteri, and then grasping the extruded part with my hand, I did not find it very difficult to re-introduce it into the vagina, and to carry it through the os uteri. I followed with my hand, or rather pushed it forward, when I observed it suddenly start from me as a piece of India rubber would."

Dr. Merriman, who candidly owns that he has altered his opinion on this point, since the last edition of his work on difficult parturition, in favour of removing the placenta, distinctly proves that the presence of this mass was the chief cause of the difficulty. "I tried," says he, "to effect the reduction without removing the placenta, but could, by no possibility, accomplish it till I had first separated the placenta: this being effected, I succeeded to my[Pg 349] entire satisfaction in re-inverting the fundus." (Synopsis of Difficult Parturition.)

In reducing the fundus, we must not thrust our fingers collected into a cone against the tumour, as has been recommended by most authors; for, by so doing, we only produce a depression in it, and, as it were, re-invert or double the uterus upon itself, and thus add considerably to the bulk of the mass, and the difficulty of the reduction. We should grasp the tumour firmly, and push it bodily upwards in the direction of the pelvic outlet: at first little or no change is produced, until it has ascended so far, that the vagina which had been dragged down is returned again to its natural situation; the hand must follow the tumour, and now that the lower part of the uterus is fixed, by the vagina being put upon the stretch, the pressure which is applied to the fundus will act with so much greater effect. We should endeavour to "return, first, that portion of the uterus which was expelled last from the os uteri." (Newnham, op. cit. p. 616.) As the hand rises into the cavity of the pelvis, and is no longer able to grasp the tumour, so far from contracting the points of our fingers into a cone, it will be desirable to spread them at equal distances round it, and thus apply the pressure over a larger space: it was to attain this object that Leroux recommended the application of a cloth to the fundus, as by this means the force applied to it was more equally divided. (Sur les Pertes de Sang, § 218.) The hand, however, will be far preferable. We must gradually alter the direction in which we press up the tumour as it ascends, guiding our hand in the axis of the pelvic cavity, and lastly bringing it upwards and forwards in that of the superior aperture. When once the fundus has repassed the os uteri, it usually recedes suddenly from the hand, as already described in Mr. Mann's case: if we feel the uterus through the abdominal parietes well contracted, there will be no need of passing the hand into its cavity; but if it be still flaccid and soft, the hand should be introduced, not only for the purpose of guarding against any return of the inversion, but of exciting more active contractions by its presence. The patient should avoid making any sudden efforts to raise herself, or to cough, strain, or by any means excite the abdominal muscles to exert pressure upon the fundus, for it is occasionally observed, that the disposition to inversion continues some time after the reduction has been effected.

Where some little time has elapsed before any attempt is made to reduce the fundus, the inverted portion begins to swell from obstruction to the return of blood, especially where the inversion is partial, and, therefore, tightly girded by the os uteri; the passages grow hot and dry, and the chances of reducing the tumour diminish in proportion. "Is it not reasonable," as Mr. Newnham observes, "to suppose that the first effect of the accident will be to bring on inflammatory action and tension of the parts,[Pg 350] and this very state will in itself be a sufficient obstacle to success." (Op. cit. p. 18.) If, under these circumstances, we find that the attempts at reduction is attended with considerable difficulty, or is evidently impossible, it will be necessary to wait until the excitement of the circulation, and the congestion and swelling of the parts are reduced, and the passages duly relaxed by bleeding; besides this, the external parts should be well fomented, the patient should use the warm hip bath, or sit over the steam of hot water, and throw up emollient and sedative enemata as recommended in our treatment of inflammation of the uterus; the operation, which was during the state of inflammation and feverish excitement in which the patient was, strongly contra-indicated, now becomes practicable and safe, and the difficulties, which before would have rendered it nearly or quite impossible, are now in a great measure removed.

Wherever the uterus is completely inverted, and there is reason to expect considerable difficulty in reducing it, we shall find great benefit in adopting the mode of practice recommended by Mr. C. White, of Manchester, viz. of firmly grasping the tumour until we have succeeded in considerably diminishing its size, and thus removing the chief obstacle to its reduction. "I grasped the body of it in my hand," says Mr. W., "and held it there for some time, in order to lessen its bulk by compression. As I soon perceived that it began to diminish, I persevered, and soon after made another attempt to reduce it, by thrusting at its fundus; it began to give way. I continued the force till I had perfectly returned it, and had insinuated my hand into its body: it was no sooner reduced, than the pulse in her wrist began to beat: she recovered as fast as we could wish." (White, on Lying-in Women, case, 19. Appendix, p. 429, 2d edit.)

Where the fundus is partially inverted, and the os uteri girds it very tightly, so as not only to produce very frightful symptoms arising from the strangulated condition of the organ, but also to render its reduction a matter of great difficulty, or even impossibility, Dr. Dewees has advised that, so far from attempting to push up the fundus, we should rather try to bring it down, and thus render the inversion complete; by this means, the "pain, faintness, vomiting, delirium, cold sweats, convulsions, extinct pulse," &c. will not only be relieved, but the farther danger from hæmorrhage prevented.

"The propriety and safety of this plan is, it must be confessed, predicated upon the happy result of a solitary case, but, from its entire and speedy success in this instance, it is rendered more than probable that it will be of equal advantage if employed in others; "all reasoning upon the subject" is certainly in its favour; and experience, so far as a single case may be entitled such, is equally so. The patient is to be placed upon her back near the edge of the bed, and have her legs supported by proper assistants;[Pg 351] the hand is to be introduced along the interior part of the vagina, but sufficiently high to seize the uterus pretty firmly; it is then to be drawn gently and steadily downward and outward, until the inversion is completed: this will be known by a kind of jerk, announcing the passing of the confined part through the stricture. Traction should now cease, and the part be carefully examined; if the inversion be complete, the mouth of the uterus will no longer be felt, and there will be an immediate cessation of pain and other distressing sensations." (Dewees, Compendious System of Midwifery, § 1318.)

Chronic inversion. Where some time has already elapsed since the occurrence of the accident, and the more distressing symptoms have subsided, the inversion now passes into a chronic state, which, although not immediately dangerous to life, will ultimately be not less fatal. The form of the tumour gradually alters; it assumes a more polypoid shape, from the increasing contraction of its mouth narrowing the upper part of it; and now the diagnosis from polypus sometimes becomes exceedingly difficult, the more so as the pressure the os uteri diminishes the sensibility of the fundus. Hence, as Mr. Newnham observes, we may conclude, "that it is always difficult and sometimes impossible, with our present knowledge, to distinguish partial and chronic inversion of the uterus from polypus; since, in both diseases, the os uteri will be found encircling the summit of the tumour, and, in either case, the finger may be passed readily around it. And if, in order to remove this uncertainty, the entire hand be introduced into the vagina, so as to allow the finger to pass by the side of the tumour to the extremity of the space remaining between it and the os uteri; and if we find that the finger soon arrives at this point, it will be impossible to ascertain whether it rests against a portion of the uterus which has been inverted in the usual way, or by the long-continued dragging of the polypus upon its fundus. And if, under these embarrassing circumstances, we call to our assistance our ideas concerning the form of polypus, its enlarged base and narrow peduncle, we must also recollect the abundant evidence to prove that the neck of such a tumour is often as large, and sometimes larger, than its inferior extremity, and we shall still be left in inexplicable uncertainty."

The periodical hæmorrhages, with profuse leucorrhœa during the intervals are too common, both to chronic partial inversion and to polypus, to afford any certain means of diagnosis; and the gradually increasing debility, from the constant drain upon the system and ultimate breaking up of the general health, may be as much the result of the one as of the other. The rugged uneven surface of the inverted uterus, the smoothness of a polypus, are distinctions not of long continuance; for, after awhile, the uterus gradually becomes smoother, whereas, a polypus rarely continues[Pg 352] long in the vagina without its surface becoming irregular from ulceration.

It might be a question whether it would not be possible to detect the menstrual fluid at the catamenial periods oozing from the surface of the inverted uterus: that this is quite possible in cases of complete inversion, is a well-known fact, but how far it can be detected in the partial form is not so certain, as the position of the tumour pretty high up in the vagina would prevent our ascertaining it, especially when there is more or less hæmorrhage going on. In most cases, the history of the case, and our not being able to pass up a catheter far beyond the os uteri, which completely surrounds the neck of the tumour without adhering to it, are the chief points upon which we must found our diagnosis.

"Whilst the inverted uterus remains in the vagina, the discharge (excepting at the periods of menstruation) will be of a mucous kind; but if the uterus falls lower, so as to protrude beyond the external parts, the exposure of that surface, which in a natural state lined the cavity, to air, as well as to occasional injuries, may induce inflammation and ulceration over a part or the whole of its surface; and the mucous discharge may be changed to one of a purulent kind, so considerable in quantity as to debilitate the constitution, and to cause all the common symptoms of weakness." (Sir C. M. Clarke, on the Diseases of Females, part i. p. 155.)

Although such a length of time has elapsed since the inversion, that it has become of the chronic kind, still we are not justified in giving up all hopes as to the possibility of returning it. Dr. Churchill has given an interesting summary of cases where many days, and in one case even twelve weeks, had intervened, and yet, nevertheless, where the reduction was successfully effected. (On the Principal Diseases of Females, p. 331.) We may also add two very remarkable cases related by Boyer (quoted by Kilian,) viz. where the uterus had resisted every endeavour to reduce the inversion, which in one case had remained fourteen days, in the other more than eight years, and where, in consequence of a sudden and violent fall upon the nates, reduction followed spontaneously and permanently.

Extirpation of the uterus. Where, however, the powers of the system are rapidly breaking, from the profuse hæmorrhages at each menstrual period, and not less profuse discharge during the intervals, the only means of saving the patient is by treating the case as one of polypus, or in other words, removing the uterus by ligature. Numerous cases are on record where this has succeeded perfectly, although during the process the patient suffered from several attacks of pain and even inflammation, occasionally requiring the ligature to be loosened for awhile. In the case[Pg 353] recorded by Mr. Newnham, rather more than three weeks were required before the separation of the tumour was effected. When once this source of irritation is removed, the hæmorrhage and other discharges which had so greatly reduced the patient cease, and, as in cases of polypus, a most striking and favourable change is produced, the health and strength return, and the recovery of the patient is complete.

CHAPTER VIII.

ENCYSTED PLACENTA.

Situation in the uterus.—Adherent placenta.—Prognosis and treatment.—Placenta left in the uterus.—Absorption of retained placenta.

By the term encysted placenta, we mean that state of irregular uterine action after the expulsion of the child, where the lower portion of the uterus, particularly the os uteri internum, is closely contracted, while the fundus contains the placenta enclosed in a species of cyst or cavity formed by itself and the body of the uterus.

Upon examination externally, we find the fundus pretty firmly contracted, but probably somewhat higher up the abdomen than usual; the vagina and os uteri externum, or os tincæ, are usually found dilated, the passage gradually tapering like a funnel to the os uteri internum, or upper end of the canal of the cervix.

Situation in the uterus. This state has been very generally considered to arise from a spasmodic contraction in the circular fibres of the body of the uterus, by which it was as if tightly girded by a cord at its middle, and, from the form it was supposed to take, was called hour-glass contraction of the uterus.

From the observations of later years there is much reason to suppose that the true hour-glass contraction, as now described, is of very rare occurrence, even if it does take place at all; and that, in by far the majority of cases, the stricture is either the upper part of the cervix, as we have already mentioned, or resides in the os uteri externum or inferior portion of the cervix.

Baudelocque was the first who pointed out the neck of the uterus as the real seat of the stricture in these cases: "that circle (says he) of the uterus which is round the child's neck, according to the general laws of its contraction, must narrow itself much quicker after delivery than the other circles which compose that viscus, because it is already narrower, and its forced dilatation[Pg 355] at the instant of the expulsion of the child's trunk is only momentary, and because it has naturally more tendency to close than the other circles have, since it is that which constitutes the neck of the uterus in its natural state." (Baudelocque, Heath's Trans. vol. ii. § 969.)

Dr. Douglas, of Dublin, also investigated this subject, and came to a similar conclusion: he considered that encysted or incarcerated placenta from hour-glass contraction, resulted either from morbid adhesion of the placenta, or from inactivity of the uterus, and does not occur as a primary affection; his observations lead to the conclusion that the stricture in hour-glass contraction "does not form from the middle circumference of the uterus; it is formed by the lowest verge of its thickly muscular substance, at the line of demarcation of its body and cervix." "Thus, then, it would appear that the upper chamber comprises in its formation the entire of the body of the fundus; whilst the lower chamber engages only the cervix uteri and the vagina." (Medical Transactions of the Col. of Phys. vol. vi. p. 393.)

The late W. J. Schmitt of Vienna considered that the stricture was the os tincæ, or os uteri externum.

From our own experience we would say that the seat of the stricture varies considerably in different cases; that in the simplest form it is nothing more than a contracted state of the os uteri externum; that in others it is formed by the upper portion of the cervix uteri, or os uteri internum; but in other instances it appears to be formed by the inferior segment of the uterus itself. The contraction in this part of the uterus, which, according to the observations of Professor Michaelis, comes on when the os uteri is fully developed, and, by closely surrounding the head, is one chief means by which prolapsus of the cord is prevented, may easily produce a state of stricture after the birth of the child, and thus retain the placenta; it may, however, be questioned whether this portion of the uterus, when fully dilated by pregnancy, and which then forms its inferior segment, would not become the os uteri internum when the uterus is empty and contracted.

Hour-glass contraction of the uterus is liable to occur where the action of the uterus has been much deranged or exhausted, either by the unusual rapidity or excessive protraction of the labour. In all cases where the child has been rapidly expelled before the uterus has had time to contract regularly and uniformly, the disposition in the os uteri to contract, as pointed out by Baudelocque, will manifest itself. This state may also be induced by great previous distention, as from twins, or too much liquor amnii; by irritation, as by improperly pulling at the cord, by having used too much force in artificially delivering the child, by the introduction of the hand or instruments too cold, &c. The most frequent cause, however, is over anxiety to remove the [Pg 356]placenta; the cord is frequently pulled at, and at length the os uteri is excited to contract; in this case we generally find the stricture at the os tincæ, which yields without much difficulty, either by gentle friction with the hand over the fundus, and cautiously pulling the placenta in the axis of the superior aperture, or by introducing the hand and bringing it away.

Adherent placenta. When the placenta is still attached either wholly or in part, there are generally some preternatural adhesions to the uterus, which, by keeping its upper portion distended, give rise to partial contractions below. This condition of the placenta is observed to attend nearly every severe case of hour-glass contraction; in some instances its whole surface appears as if grown to the uterus, forming an adhesion so close and intimate as to be overcome with the greatest difficulty: we have met with cases where the placenta tore up into shreds which still adhered to the uterus as strongly as before; in others, however, the adhesions are of smaller extent, varying from the size of a shilling to that of a crown piece, sometimes there being only one, sometimes two or three in the same placenta.

The nature of these adhesions is but little understood; it is generally considered that they have been some inflammatory process taking place between the uterus and placenta; and certainly the firm feel and lighter colour of the part which has been adherent might, perhaps, justify such a conclusion. Cases have occurred where the inflammatory action has extended in the contrary direction (outwards,) producing mischief in the neighbouring parts, viz. abscess and injury of the pelvic periosteum with subsequent pelvic exostosis. (Neue Zeitschrift für Geburtskunde, band v. heft 1.) We may also observe, that these adhesions of the placenta usually occur several times in the same individual.

Prognosis and treatment. The danger in these cases depends chiefly on the presence or absence of hæmorrhage; in the latter case, we may wait safely, and give the uterus the opportunity of contracting upon the placenta, so as ultimately to dilate the stricture and expel it. In most instances, where the os tincæ is the seat of the contraction, and the placenta (as is usually the case here) already detached, a little patience, aided by gentle friction of the fundus, and carefully abstaining from all irritation of the os uteri, will be sufficient to attain this object; the os uteri will gradually relax and the placenta slowly exude into the vagina. Where, from the feel of the fundus, the uterus appears still unable to exert such a degree of contraction as shall overpower the os uteri, we may follow the plan of Dr. Dewees, in his section "On the enclosed and partially protruded Placenta," and rouse its activity by some doses of ergot: "should this not succeed within an hour, the uterus must be gently entered, by slowly dilating the[Pg 357] os uteri, and the placenta removed." One finger after the other must be passed through the os uteri, until it has yielded sufficiently: if the placenta be quite detached, two fingers will generally be sufficient for this purpose, by which means it may be gradually brought down into the palm of the hand, and then removed.

Where more or less of it is morbidly adherent, which may be presumed when it continues for some time at the upper part of the uterus without any disposition to descend, we must carefully introduce the whole hand, and endeavour to find the edge of the placenta at which we should begin the process of separation. Where, however, the edge is very thin, and the attachment firm, it is not easy to effect this without risk of injuring the structure of the uterus itself with the nails, nor can we always distinguish the thin and closely adherent edge of the placenta from the uterus itself: in these cases it will be safer to plunge the fingers into the central and thicker portions of the mass, and gradually separate it towards the circumference. Wherever this close adhesion prevails over a considerable extent, it becomes nearly impossible to prevent portions being left adhering to the uterus; thus it not unfrequently happens, where a placenta under these circumstances has been artificially removed, that there are one or more large irregular cavities on its uterine surface, from a portion of its mass having been torn from it, and left adhering. Cases have occurred to us,[134] where the whole central portion has thus remained, the amniotic surface of the placenta having come away entire with the larger umbilical vessels attached to it, and merely a narrow margin of parenchyma at its edge; in others, the whole mass has broken up, the cord, the larger branches of the umbilical vessels, and the membranes have come away, but the greater part of the placenta has remained closely adhering to the uterus. In such a case it becomes a question, whether it be safe to persist in our efforts to remove the remains of the placenta, or whether it will not be better to leave the case to nature: experience shows that the latter plan is the safer, and that a practitioner is not justified in running the risk of severely injuring the uterus by repeated and violent efforts to effect his object.

Placenta left in the uterus. Where a portion of placenta has been thus left in the uterus, the case may terminate in one of three ways: either it may be expelled in the course of from twelve to twenty-four hours, without any perceptible marks of putrefaction, and with but little or no disturbance to the system; or where, after a longer interval, the discharges have become very offensive, and the placenta has been expelled in a putrid state, with serious distur- bance of the health; or lastly, where the[Pg 358] lochia has been sparing but natural, and where no trace whatever of the placenta has appeared.

In the first mode of termination it may be presumed that the attachment of the placenta has yielded either to the continued contraction of the uterus, or from a slight degree of incipient putrefaction, by which its union with the uterus was weakened; in the second case, from contact with the external air, and being constantly kept at a consid- erable temperature by the heat of the surrounding parts, the lacerated placenta rapidly putrefies, putrid matter is carried into the system, producing all the effects of a deadly poison, and the patient is placed in a state of the greatest danger; the pulse becomes quick and small, the tongue red and dry, accompanied with great depression of the vital powers, the uterus frequently swells, grows hard, and excessively painful, followed by general peritonitis; it is not, however, the inflammation which necessarily destroys the patient, but the prostrating effects upon the nervous system, the introduction of an animal poison into the circulation.

Absorption of retained placenta. Where the placenta has not been much lacerated, or at any rate where every portion has been removed which could be separated without violence, where also the uterus has contracted firmly and closely, the part which is retained does not pass into putrefaction, little or no inconvenience is experienced by the patient; the lochia, as we before observed, is sparing but natural, and ceases after the usual time, but not a trace of the placenta comes away. This fact has been repeatedly noticed, especially in later years; but the attention of medical men was first called to the subject by Professor Naegelé, of Heidelberg, in 1828. In 1802, and again in 1811, cases of premature expulsion of the fœtus occurred to him where the membranes and placenta did not come away, and where no trace whatever of them appeared afterwards. In 1828[135] his assistance was required in a case of unusually firm adhesion of the placenta, and where, from this as well as other circumstances, the extraction was so difficult that he was compelled to leave considerably more than one-third in the uterus. (Med. Gaz. Jan. 10, 1829.) About the same time, a most interesting case was published by Professor Salomon, of Leyden, where the whole placenta of a child only three weeks short of the full time was retained by the firm contraction of the uterus, and, according to Dr. Salomon's view of it, removed by the process of absorption. About the end of the third week, the uterus, which had hitherto been larger than is natural under ordinary[Pg 359] circumstances after labour, and more globular, now diminished considerably, and began to assume the usual form as in the unimpregnated state. Besides the cases already alluded to, which we have described in our Midwifery Hospital Reports, we may again refer to one which was mentioned by Dr. Young, formerly professor of Midwifery at Edinburgh: "I could get my hand to the placenta, but no farther, the uterus having formed a kind of pouch for it, so that I at last was obliged to trust to nature; what was very remarkable, the placenta never came away, yet the woman recovered."

Cases have also occurred where the placenta, after having been retained many days in the uterus, has been expelled quite fresh, the edges worn or rather dissolved away by the process of absorption; thus Dr. Denman mentions one where the whole placenta was retained till the fifteenth day after labour, and was then expelled with little signs of putrefaction except upon the membranes, the whole surface which had adhered exhibiting fresh marks of separation. Cases of abortion have occasionally been observed where the embryo has escaped, but the se- cundines have never come away, although the discharges, &c., have been watched with the greatest attention; after a time the menses have returned, the patient has again become pregnant, and has passed through her labour at the full term without any thing unusual occurring.

The subject has recently been considered very fully, and much interesting knowledge added, by Dr. Villeneuve, of Marseilles. Besides putting the fact beyond all doubt, he shows that cases of total adhesion are rarely if ever fatal; and that, where cases have terminated fatally, the placenta has only partially adhered, and the patient has been either destroyed by hæmorrhage, or by the effects arising from the absorption of putrid matter, or from injury of the uterus in attempting to remove the placenta. He considers that a placenta which is not fixed to the uterus by organic and intimate adhesions cannot be absorbed, though it may perhaps be retained for several days without danger, if there is contraction of the uterus. (Gazette Médicale de Paris, July 8, 1840.) It may, however, be doubted whether this last observation be correct, as it is a well-established fact that cows which had been supposed with calf, and in which the symptoms of pregnancy had again subsided, have afterwards been killed and nothing but the bones of the calf found in the uterus, the soft parts having been removed by absorption. The same fact has been observed also in sheep and other animals; and knowing how abundantly the human uterus is supplied with absorbents, coupled with what has been already stated, there can be little or no doubt but that the placenta in these cases had been acted upon by a similar process. Although we strongly deprecate repeated attempts to remove the adherent portions of[Pg 360] placenta, especially where we have brought away a considerable quantity of its fœtal part, still we would warn our readers against leaving any loose ragged pieces in the uterus, for these rapidly pass into putrefaction, and produce the alarming symptoms above-mentioned. The safety of our patient mainly depends on the firm contraction of the uterus preventing the access of air, and on our constantly removing, by means of injections, any putrid discharge which may have collected. The sparing quantity of lochia which has generally been observed, especially where the whole surface of the placenta has adhered, can easily be accounted for, the greater portion of the vessels which ordinarily furnish this discharge being closed up by the adherent mass: from the same reason we can explain why cases of total attachment of the placenta are rarely or never attended with hæmorrhage.

Lastly, should any symptoms of fever or abdominal inflammation supervene, they must be treated according to the rules which we have given under these heads.[136]

[Pg 361]

CHAPTER IX.

PRECIPITATE LABOUR.

Violent uterine action.—Causes.—Deficient resistance.—Effects of precipitate labour.—Rupture of the cord.—Treatment.—Connexion of precipitate labour with mania.

The second division of Dystocia comprises those species of labour where it becomes dangerous for the mother or child, without obstruction to its progress. Of these we shall first consider precipitate or too rapid labour, not only because it is liable to be followed by a great variety of injurious results, but also because it has received little or no notice by the obstetric authors of this country.

Precipitate labour depends on one of two conditions; either the expelling powers exceed their ordinary degree of activity, or the resistance to the passage of the child is less than usual. "Every normal labour has a certain course, which is neither too slow nor too quick. The passages are thus dilated gradually and without excessive suffering; the uterus is felt alternately hard and soft; and the pains have certain and regular intervals, which become very gradually shorter, during which both mother and child are enabled to recover themselves." (Wigand, Geburt des Menschen, vol. i. p. 68.)

Violent uterine action. In the present case the pains are extremely violent from the very commencement of the labour; they produce great suffering; each pain lasts a considerable time, and the intervals between them are very short. During their presence, the patient is irresistibly compelled to bear down and strain with all her force; the whole body partakes of the general excitement: the patient is more restless and less manageable than usual, her manner is altered and becomes strange; the head is hot, the face flushed, and the pulse quick and full.

In some cases the intervals between the pains are scarcely perceptible, for one pain has scarcely left off before the next has already commenced; or the uterus falls into a state of continued violent contraction, which does not cease until the child is driven into the world. The abdomen is very hard during the pain, the whole body stiff and rigid; the patient expresses her sufferings very loudly, or actually raves with pain. From the constant[Pg 362] and irresistible effort to strain, it seems as if she has scarcely time to get her breath, for she continues to hold it so long that respiration might be almost supposed to have stopped altogether. "As long as consciousness remains, the impulse to lay hold of any object within reach and pull by it is extraordinarily strong, until at length, in the midst of a violent scream, or grinding of the teeth, covered with sweat and with simultaneous evacuation of the rectum and bladder, she is suddenly delivered." (Wigand, op. cit. vol. i. p. 71.)

Causes. This storm of uncontrollable uterine action "appears to depend upon an unusually powerful influence of the nervous system upon the contractile fibres of the uterus or upon a morbid degree of irritability." (Ibid.) In some cases it appears as an individual peculiarity, every successive labour of the patient being remarkable for its violence and rapidity. Precipitate labours of this kind are frequently observed to be hereditary, and like an opposite and equally faulty condition of the expelling powers, viz. slow and lingering uterine action, are sometimes peculiar to certain families, the mother and the sisters of the patient having had all their labours peculiarly rapid and violent.

The character of the catamenial periods before pregnancy is frequently observed to bear a considerable relation to that of the labours in the same individual; thus, if she has always suffered much pain and other symptoms of uterine excitement just before or during these times, so much so as even to require slight medical treatment to allay the periodical suffering, the uterus almost invariably manifests a similar degree of energy and irritability during labour. On the other hand, where the menstrual periods produce so little suffering or derangement that, but for the appearance of the discharge itself, the patient has scarcely any means of determining their recurrence, the uterus betrays a similar want of activity when labour comes on, which may therefore, cæteris paribus, be expected to be slow and lingering.

Mental affections, which we have already shown to be capable of retarding labour, occasionally have the opposite effect, and rouse the uterus to violent action. It is well known that the dread of the forceps, which the practitioner has declared would be required, has frequently been followed by so much activity of the uterus as to render its application unnecessary.

Where the patient is stout, robust, and plethoric, or of a nervous hysterical habit, this state of unruly uterine action is frequently attended with great cerebral excitement; during the pains she raves wildly, and for some time becomes quite unmanageable, or in other cases this state passes into actual convulsions.

In febrile diseases, especially of the eruptive kind, the labour is usually of this character; the exertions of the uterus in such cases, especially in scarlet fever, are sometimes quite extraordinary,[Pg 363] so that the child seems to be born without any effort on the part of the mother. This is of great importance in inflammation of the lungs, &c. where the patient would be unable to inflate the lungs to that extent which is necessary for any violent efforts.

Deficient resistance. Where the rapidity of the labour arises from want of that degree of resistance to the expelling powers which is natural, it may depend on circumstances connected with the mother or the child; thus, it may arise from too large a pelvis; the head, covered by the inferior portion of the uterus, is forced down deeper into the pelvis than usual, especially if, as is not unfrequently the case, this state be accompanied with violent and powerful pains; the head may thus be actually forced through the os externum before it has passed the os uteri: cases have been recorded where nearly the whole uterus, has been thus protruded. In an "extraordinary case," as Deventer justly terms it, "the head of the child had passed the os externum as far as the shoulders, and only the summit of it was visible, three-quarters at least of the head being still enclosed in the uterus, although the head and neck had already passed." (Novum Lumen, part. ii. chap. 3.)

In other cases the sudden expulsion of the child appears to depend merely upon the great dilatability of the soft parts, and may occur quite independently of any disease. We recollect a case of this sort where the patient, a healthy woman, had only two pains—the first awoke her out of a sound sleep and ruptured the membranes, the next drove the child with great violence into the bed. Where the patient is weakened by previous disease, and the soft parts are very relaxed and flaccid, they produce no resistance to the advance of the head: this condition is very unfavourable, "as it implies a greater state of relaxation, or want of tone, than is compatible with the welfare of the patient: hence it is seldom found to take place except when the unfortunate subject is sinking under the last stage of debility, as in phthisis," &c. (Power's Midwifery, p. 138.)

The want of due resistance to the expelling powers may depend upon the size and hardness of the head; it is either smaller than usual, from the child being premature, or, if of the full size, the cranial bones are imperfectly ossified, the sutures are wide, the fontanelles large, and the whole head very yielding and soft; or it may depend on some congenital defect, in which the brain and cranial coverings are more or less imperfect.

In the ordinary cases of precipitate labour the case depends generally on a complication of violent pains, wide pelvis, and small child.

Effects of precipitate labour. Besides the mischief which may result from the rapid expulsion of the child causing prolapsus uteri, laceration of the vagina, perineum, and hæmorrhage from inertia coming on in consequence of the uterus being so suddenly[Pg 364] emptied, dangerous syncope, or even asphyxia, may follow from the shock which the nervous system has sustained, or in consequence of the sudden removal of that degree of pressure which the gravid uterus had exerted upon the abdominal circulation during pregnancy. Where the patient has been very unruly, and has exerted herself with great violence, "emphysema of the face and neck (says Dr. Reid) may suddenly occur during labour, and cause great alarm to a young practitioner, as it alters and disfigures the countenance in an extraordinary manner. Great straining or screaming may produce it, and it probably depends on some partial rupture of the lining membrane of the larynx. I have seen two or three cases of this description, and one which occurred to a great extent in the case of an out-patient of the General Lying-in Hospital, in whom this tumefaction spread to the shoulders and chest." (Manual of Pract. Midwifery, by James Reid, M. D. p. 231.)

The child also may suffer from a precipitate labour, where the pains are excessively violent and run into each other, so that the whole labour is effected during one continued storm of uterine action. If the membranes have given way at an early period, so that the body of the child is exposed to the immediate pressure of the pains, the abdominal circulation suffers, and the child is destroyed in the same way as by pressure on the cord itself; or it may be suddenly dashed upon the floor before the mother has had time to reach her bed, or even put herself in a recumbent posture upon the floor: in this way it may receive a severe injury upon the head, or the cord may be lacerated, and the child die from hæmorrhage before assistance can arrive: such accidents, however, are not so dangerous to the child as have been supposed, a fact which has been proved by medico-legal investigations. The direction of the pelvic outlet and vagina is such as to expel the child obliquely downwards and forwards when the mother is in the upright posture, so that the force of the blow is in a great measure broken by this circumstance; the head also, as well as the other parts of the body, are soft and yielding, and nearly preclude the chances of injury taking place; the violence of the fall is generally diminished in some measure by the patient being almost always compelled to drop upon her knees at the moment of great suffering, whilst the child is passing; her clothes also surround it more or less, and thus shield it from any severe injury.

Rupture of the cord. The cord is liable to be torn in these cases, showing that a considerable jerk had been applied to it, but neither the child nor its mother have suffered from it. Ten or twelve cases of ruptured cord have come to our own immediate knowledge, and in none of them were any unfavourable effects produced. It can scarcely be imagined possible that so much force could be applied to the cord, at the moment when the[Pg 365] uterus is so suddenly evacuated, without inversion or prolapsus being the almost unavoidable result, the more so when we recollect that the cord at the moment of birth requires considerable force to break it. This circumstance may be partly attributed to the firmness with which the uterus contracts at the moment that the child is expelled, but chiefly to the fact that the axis of the brim is nearly at right angles with that of the outlet, more especially if the fundus, as is usually the case, is inclined somewhat forwards; the cord passes round the posterior part of the symphysis pubis as upon a pulley, so that a considerable portion of the force which is applied to it, is spent here before reaching the fundus uteri. It is however remarkable, that the umbilicus of the child should receive no injury from a jerk which breaks the cord, when, if we try afterwards to break the remaining pieces of the cord, we find that it will resist very powerful efforts: this fact, and the circumstance that the cord usually ruptures at about two or three inches from the umbilicus, as in some animals, seems to imply that this part is weaker than elsewhere, as if intended by nature to give way with a moderate degree of force.

Wigand considers that patients are particularly disposed to have quick labours, who are of a scrofulous, rheumatic, or arthritic diathesis; that such patients are very liable to have adhesion of the placenta after the birth of the child, with hour-glass contraction: the observation, however, has not been confirmed by the experience of others, and certainly not by the cases which have come under our own notice.

Treatment. Where, from the smallness of the child or unusual size of the pelvis, the pains are forcing the lower portion of the uterus down to, or through, the os externum, it will be necessary to support it carefully, until the os uteri is sufficiently dilated to let the head pass. A case of this kind occurred to Professor Naegelé, of Heidelberg, where, during the patient's former labour, the pains had been so violent, and the uterus had been detruded to such an extent, that actually the lower half of it appeared between the labia: to prevent a similar accident occurring this time, (as the pains were beginning to show the same disposition to violent action as before,) he applied a broad T bandage very firmly upon her, coming over the os externum, so as to prevent the uterus being prolapsed beyond the labia; he cut a hole in it corresponding to the vagina, and the child was born through this with perfect safety to the mother.

Where we have sufficient warning, opium in effective doses will probably assist in lulling the irritability of the uterus: if the bowels have been previously well opened, an opiate enema will be desirable; if not, a large emollient enema should be premised.

The patient should be made to lie upon her side, and not only[Pg 366] strictly forbidden to resist to her very utmost, the urgent impulse which she feels to strain and bear down, but must carefully avoid even holding by or pushing against any fixed body with her hands or feet. Still farther, to quiet the turbulence of the abdominal muscles, a broad bandage should be fastened firmly round the abdomen; it not only gives the patient a comfortable feeling of support, but tends greatly to calm the spasmodic irritability of these muscles. These precautions will be of so much more service if they can be used early, as in cases where we have been already warned by the character of her previous labours: we can thus avoid the premature rupture of the membranes, which is a thing by all means to be avoided; the uterus acts with increased power where its bulk has been diminished by the escape of the liquor amnii, and at the same time becomes still more irritable and unruly from contracting immediately upon the child; and not only is there imminent danger of its giving way in some part, but the child is almost inevitably destroyed by the violence of the pressure to which it is exposed.

In cases where the vehemence of the expelling powers appears to be quite beyond our control, Wigand has recommended a copious bleeding to complete syncope as the only means; in which suggestion, he has been followed by Froreip: neither of these authors, however, appear to have had any experience of this mode of treatment, and knowing how much more active the uterus becomes after a smart bleeding in ordinary cases, and how powerfully the state of syncope promotes the dilatability of the soft parts, we should hesitate exceedingly to employ so doubtful a remedy. Wigand also proposes, in cases of this desperate nature, to use effusion with ice-cold water to the abdomen and lower extremities, and by this powerful species of counter-irritation, produce a temporary calm for a few minutes—a measure we should fear of as doubtful a character as bleeding.

Connexion of precipitate labour with mania. Lastly, we may observe, that the subject of precipitate labour involves a medico-legal question of great importance and interest, which has as yet excited little or no notice in this country, viz. as regards acts of child-murder after labours of this character. The state of mental excitement and frenzy into which a patient is brought, by a labour of such violence and suffering, in many cases falls little short of actual mania. We now and then meet with instances, where, for the first half hour or so after a severe and rapid labour, the patient takes a most insurmountable antipathy to her child, and expresses herself towards it in so unnatural a manner, as to contrast strangely with the tender and affectionate feelings which she had a short time previously expressed for it. Cases have occurred where the patient has been without assistance, during labour, and where, in a state of temporary madness from mental excitement and pain at the moment of the child's birth, she has committed an act of[Pg 367] violence upon it, which has proved fatal; a circumstance, which, from obvious reasons, would be more liable to occur with single than with married women. These cases have been very carefully investigated in Germany of late, and in many of them the patient has been, we think, very properly acquitted, on the grounds of temporary insanity, having herself voluntarily confessed the act with the deepest remorse, at the same time declaring her utter incapacity to account for the wild and savage fury which seized her at the moment of delivery.

[Pg 368]

CHAPTER X.

PROLAPSUS OF THE UMBILICAL CORD.

Diagnosis.—Causes.—Treatment.—Reposition of the cord.

Although by no means a common occurrence, it every now and then happens that a portion of the umbilical cord falls down between the presenting part of the child and the mother's pelvis either just before or during labour; so that, as the child advances through the passages, its life is placed in imminent danger from the pressure to which the cord is exposed, obstructing the circulation in it.

There is probably no disappointment, which the accoucheur has to meet with more annoying than a case of this kind; every thing has seemed to promise a favourable labour; the presentation is natural, the pains are regular, the os uteri is dilating readily, the mother, and, as far as we can ascertain, her child, are in perfect health, and yet because a minute loop of the cord has fallen down by the side of its head, the labour, unless interfered with by art, will almost necessarily prove fatal to it.

Diagnosis. If the membranes be not yet ruptured, we shall probably be able to feel a small projecting mass like a finger, close to the presenting part, and possessing a distinct pulsation, which, from not being synchronous with the mother's pulse, instantly declares its real nature. When the membranes give way, more of the cord comes within reach, and probably forms a large coil, which passes through the os uteri into the vagina, or even appears at the os externum.

Causes. The earliest writer that we know of who has given a detailed account of cord presentation was Mauriceau; few, even in hospital practice, and certainly none in private practice, have exceeded him in the number of cases described, and very few have surpassed him in the success of his treatment. He mentions chiefly three conditions as being liable to produce prolapsus of the cord, viz. a large quantity of liquor amnii, an unusually long cord, and malposition of the child: later authors have enumerated several other causes, many of which are imaginary; of these, by far the most correct list has been given by Boer, of Vienna, who has justly ridiculed the theoretical views which were maintained by his cotemporaries.

[Pg 369]"If there be a large quantity of liquor amnii present, and especially, as is not unfrequently the case, the child is at the same time under the usual size; if the head be not firmly pressed against the brim, and does not enter it sufficiently, or when the child's position is faulty, especially if, at the same time, the cord is unusually long; if, under such circumstances, a large bag of membranes has formed, and the brim of the pelvis itself is very spacious; if perchance, the rupture of the membranes takes place at a moment when the patient is moving briskly on in some unfavourable posture, the cord will be very liable to prolapse. Nevertheless, cases are occasionally seen which arise without these predisposing circumstances." (Boer, von Geburten unter welchen die Nabelschnur vorfällt.)

The uterus is the chief means by which the cord is prevented from falling down between the presenting part of the child and the passages, from the closeness with which its inferior portion encircles it: without this, from the erect posture of the human female, there would be a liability to prolapsus of the arm or cord in every labour.

"The contraction of the uterus, which comes on with the rupture of the membranes, and sometimes, where they protrude very much, even before, is of great importance. This contraction takes place in the inferior segment of the uterus; it surrounds the head, and when fully developed extends over the whole head of the child. Thus, for instance, if we attempt to operate at an early stage, it feels more like a hard ring round the head, of about a finger's breadth, and it may be felt to extend itself higher up, in proportion as the stimulus of the hand excites the activity of the uterus." (Michaelis, Neue Zeiteschrift für Geburtskunde, band iii. heft. 1.)

Hence, therefore, whatever prevents the uterus from contracting with its inferior segment upon the presenting part of the child, deprives the cord of its natural support, and, therefore, renders it liable to prolapse. Many of the causes enumerated by Boer act in this way; thus, where the uterus is distended by an unusual accumulation of liquor amnii; where the contractions at the beginning of labour have been exceedingly irregular; where the arm, or shoulder, or feet present; or where a large bladder of membranes is formed, the lower part of the uterus will either not contract at all upon the head, or so imperfectly as to endanger the descent of the cord.

Malposition of the child has been mentioned by many authors as a cause of prolapsus of the cord, and in some cases it may possibly act thus from the inferior segment of the uterus being unable to surround sufficiently close so irregular a mass as the shoulder. In the majority of cases, however, the coincidence of these two circumstances depends upon their being the same causes; thus an unusually large quantity of liquor[Pg 370] amnii, or irregular contractions of the uterus, will just as much dispose to the one as the other.

The form or size of the pelvis can have, we think, but little effect upon the cord, so long as the uterine action is of the right character and the child alive. Most authors enumerate a large pelvis or small fœtal head as a cause, why should we not, therefore, have prolapsus of the cord in every case of precipitate labour which arises from such circumstances? Nor are we at all disposed to consider deformed pelvis as capable of producing it, so long as the uterus is not immoderately distended and acting naturally: we do not deny that the cord is occasionally found prolapsed in cases of dystocia pelvica, but this is chiefly where the child has died from the severity of the labour, and where the flaccid pulseless cord has gradually slipped down during the intervals of the pains.

So long as the uterus exerts but a moderate degree of pressure round the head, it is impossible for the cord of a living child to descend, particularly as, according to Dr. Michaelis, the circular contraction of the portio vaginalis commences from below upwards, and would rather push back the cord if a portion of it had descended during the moments of uterine relaxation. The pulsating turgor of the cord when the child is alive will also assist much in preventing its descent, even where the uterus does not surround the presenting part so closely as usual.

The unusual length of the cord is also a very doubtful cause of its prolapsus, and will evidently, in great measure, depend upon the causes we have already alluded to.

We may also allude to another cause of prolapsus of the cord, which, although noticed nearly a century ago by Levret, and also by two or three authors after him, had nearly fallen into oblivion until lately, when it excited the attention of Professor Naegelé, junior. Levret, from the result of numerous observations on the insertion of the cord into the placenta, was led to suppose that the lower the situation of the placenta in the uterus, the lower also was the insertion of the cord into the placenta, so that if the edge of the placenta touched upon the os uteri, the cord was usually inserted into that part of its edge which corresponded with the os uteri.

Although it is certain that the situation of the placenta close to the os uteri, is by no means necessarily attended by insertion of the cord into its edge, and, therefore, by prolapsus of it when the membranes give way, inasmuch, as under such circumstances we ought to have every case of partial placenta prævia accompanied with the cord presenting: still, however, there is no doubt that cases of the above-mentioned complication do every now and then occur, and must necessarily incur no inconsiderable danger of prolapsus.

"There is no doubt that the situation of the placenta in the[Pg 371] vicinity of the os uteri, may be looked upon as one of the predisposing causes of the cord presenting during labour; an accident which is the more to be feared, the nearer the cord is inserted into the inferior edge of the placenta. If its edge extends quite down to the os uteri, and the cord is inserted into it, or the umbilical vessels divide, as in the cases we have described, at some little distance from it, viz. in the membranes, the cord will present as a necessary result, and prolapse as soon as the membranes give way." (Die Geburtshülfliche Auscultation, von Dr. H. F. Naegelé, p. 114.) The two cases referred to by Professor Naegelé, jun., of prolapsus of the cord from this cause, occurred so near after each other, as to render the circum-stance the more remarkable. The fact was noticed by Giffard as early as in 1728, in a case of flooding from partial placenta prævia; but he does not appear then to have drawn any inferences from the position of the placenta, which he did not consider was attached, but was "in part, if not wholly, separated from the uterus."[137]

Prolapsus of the cord is fortunately not a circumstance of frequent occurrence. Dr. Churchill, of Dublin, in a valuable paper, (Edin. Med. and Surg. Journal, Oct., 1838,) has collected the results of no less than 90,983 deliveries, amongst which the cord presented in 322 cases, being in the proportion of one in 282¼.[138] That prolapsus of the cord occurs most frequently in foot presentations, as supposed by Professor Naegelé, senior, is disproved by the results of Mauriceau's large experience, as well as of many others since; thus, out of 33 cases which occurred in labour at the full term, (or nearly so,) 17 presented with the head, 1 with the face, 1 with the feet, 9 with the hand or arm, 3 with the hand or foot, 1 with the hand and breech, and 1 with the hand and head. In the 16,652 births which have been recorded by Dr. Collins, at the Dublin Lying-in Hospital, the cord prolapsed in 97 instances. "Twelve of the 97 occurred in twin cases, and in seven of the 12 it was the cord of the second child. Nine occurred where the feet presented, (not including two met with in twin children,) which was in the proportion of one in every fourteen of such presentations. Two only where the breech presented, which was in the proportion of one in every 121 of such presentations: this approaches nearly the proportional average in all deliveries, which is one in 171½. Four occurred where the shoulder or arm presented: this is in the proportion of one in nine of such presentations. Seven occurred[Pg 372] where the hand came down with the head. Seven of the children were born putrid; three of the 97 were premature, viz. two at the seventh and one at the eighth month." (Collins's Practical Treatise on Midwifery, p. 346.) We may, therefore, conclude with safety, that presentations of the head are by far the most common.

Treatment. Left to itself prolapsus of the cord is almost certain destruction to the child, for unless the labour comes on very briskly, and the head passes rapidly through the pelvis, the cord is pressed upon so long as to render it impossible for the child to be born alive. Still, however, where the passages are yielding, and the pains active; where the head is of a moderate size, the pelvis spacious, and the cord in a favourable part of it, viz. towards one of the sacro-iliac synchondroses; where also the membranes remain unruptured until the last moment, there will be a very fair chance of the child being born alive. Under no circumstances is it of such paramount importance to avoid rupturing the membranes as in these cases, for the bag of fluid which they form dilates the soft passages and protects the cord from pressure.

"Many methods of relief have been recommended, such as turning, delivering with the forceps, pushing up the funis through the os uteri with the hand, and endeavouring to suspend it on some limb of the child, collecting the pro-lapsed cord into a bag, and then pushing it up beyond the head, pushing up, the funis with instruments of various kinds, endeavouring to keep it secured above the head by means of a piece of sponge introduced; these and many other similar expedients have been resorted to." (Collins, op. cit. p. 344.)

The first two of these means have been chiefly used in cases of prolapsed funis, the others having, for the most part, been found entirely inefficient. Thus Mauriceau, in the 33 cases which he has recorded, turned 19 times: the children were all born alive, except one, which was dead, but required turning as it presented with the arm. In later times, turning or the forceps have been preferred, according to the period of labour at which the prolapsus was discovered or occurred. Thus Madame Boivin has recorded 38 cases, 25 of which occurred at the commencement of, and 13 during labour, the former were all turned; in the latter the forceps was used; 29 children were saved, seven were lost, and the two others were putrid.

Our practice must be in great measure guided by the circumstances of the case: where the os uteri is not fully dilated, where the head is still high and not much engaged in the pelvis, the liquor drained away, and the cord beginning to suffer pressure during the pains, we dare not wait until the case be sufficiently advanced to admit the application of the forceps, but must proceed as soon as possible to turn the child. The operation should[Pg 373] be performed with the greatest possible caution; the cord should be guided to one of the sacro-iliac symphyses; the expulsion of the trunk must be very gradual; a dose of secale should be given to ensure the requisite activity of the uterus when the head enters the pelvis, and the forceps kept in readiness to apply the instant that its advance is not sufficiently rapid. On the other hand, where the labour has made considerable progress before the membranes give way, and the head has fairly engaged in the cavity of the pelvis, if the os uteri is fully dilated, it will be no longer advisable to attempt turning; the head is within reach of the forceps, which should be immediately applied, taking care that the cord does not get squeezed between the blades and the head. Where the arm or shoulder presents, this will of itself require that the child should be turned.

Reposition of the cord. Although the reposition of the cord has been recommended from the time of Mauriceau, and by the majority of authors since, it has nevertheless met with so little success as to have fallen into complete disuse until the last few years; one of its strongest opposers was the celebrated La Motte. "The delivery ought to be attempted as soon as we find that the string presents before the head, it being to no purpose to try to reduce it behind the head, which at that time fills up the whole passage, and can only admit you to push it back into the vagina, and it will fall down again at every pain; and if you have done so much as to reduce it into the uterus, what hinders you from finishing the delivery at once, by seeking for the feet? the chief difficulty is then over." (La Motte, English translation, p. 304.) This mode of delivery (turning) has been more adopted by practitioners in such cases than any other, especially in former times, when the forceps was either not at all or imperfectly known; by none has it been so with more success than by Mauriceau himself, having saved every living child in which he attempted the operation. Still, however, he recommended that the attempt should be made to return the cord wherever it was possible, and has recorded four cases of this mode of treatment, all of which proved successful, although one of the children was born so feeble as to die shortly afterwards. Giffard seems to have attempted the reposition of the cord only once, and failed, apparently from the unusual size of the child. In later years Sir R. Croft, "has related two cases in which he succeeded, by carrying the prolapsed funis through the os uteri, and suspending it over one of the legs of the child. In both these cases the children were born alive." (Merriman's Synopsis, p. 99.) It is to Dr. Michaelis of Kiel that we are indebted for much recent and valuable information on the subject of replacing the prolapsed cord. Having pointed out the fact that it is the uterus alone which prevents the cord from prolapsing, he shows that, in order to replace the cord, we must carry it "above that circular portion[Pg 374] of the uterus which is contracted over the presenting part." The reposition of the cord may be effected by the hand, or by means of an elastic catheter and ligature. In replacing the cord by means of the hand alone, Dr. Michaelis remarks that we shall effect this more readily by merely insinuating the hand between the head and the uterus, and gradually passing it farther round the head, pushing the cord before it. In this manner we do not require to rupture the membranes when we have felt the cord before the liquor amnii has escaped; a point of considerable importance.

The reposition, by means of the catheter, is effected by passing a silk ligature, doubled, along a stout thick elastic catheter, from twelve to sixteen inches in length, so that the loop comes out at the upper extremity; the catheter is introduced into the vagina, and the ligature is passed through the coil of the umbilical cord, and again brought down to the os externum. A stilet with a wooden handle is introduced into the catheter, the point passed out at its upper orifice, and the loop of the ligature hung upon it; it is then drawn back into the catheter and pushed up to the end. The operator has now only to pull the ends of the ligature, so as to tighten it slightly, passing the catheter up to the cord, which now becomes securely fixed to its extremity. When the reposition has been effected, he has merely to withdraw the stilet; the cord is instantly disengaged.[139] To prevent any injury, the ligature should be brought away first, and then the catheter.

"Dr. Michaelis has recorded eleven cases of prolapsus of the cord, where it has been returned by the above means, in nine of which the child was born alive. In three cases the arm presented also, which was replaced, and the head brought down; in two of these the child was born alive." (British and Foreign Med. Review, vol. i. p. 588.) A similar plan of replacing the cord by means of an elastic catheter has been tried by Dr. Collins, but he had not tried it sufficiently often at the time of publishing his Practical Treatise to be able to give a decided opinion about it.

The plan of introducing a piece of sponge after replacing the cord, in order to prevent its coming down again, is of no use whatever. Dr. Collins tried it in several instances, and considers that "it is quite impossible, however, in the great majority of cases, to succeed in this way in protecting the funis from pressure, as it is no sooner returned, than we find it forced down in another direction." The plan has been recommended by several modern authors, but it is by no means a new invention, having[Pg 375] been proposed by Mauriceau; it does not appear, however, that he ever put it in practice.

Where no pulsation can be felt in the prolapsed funis, which is flabby and evidently empty, no interference will be required; the child is dead, and therefore the labour may be permitted to take its course. We should, however, be cautious in examining the cord where it is without pulsation, and yet feels tolerably full and turgid, for a slight degree of circulation may go on nevertheless, sufficient to keep life enough in the fœtus, even for it to recover if the labour be hastened. We should especially examine the cord during the intervals of the pains, and after we have guided it into a more favourable part of the pelvis, where it will not be exposed to so much pressure, for then the pulsation will become more sensible to our touch, and prove that the child is still alive.

The following case by Dr. Evory Kennedy is an excellent illustration of what we have now stated:—"The midwife informed me that there was no pulsation in the funis, which had been protruding for an hour; on examination made during a pain, a fold of the funis was found protruding from the vagina, at its lateral part, and devoid of pulsation. As the pain subsided, I drew the funis backwards towards the sacro-iliac symphysis, and thought I could observe a very indistinct and irregular pulsation; I now applied the stethoscope, and distinguished a slight fœtal pulsation over the pubes. Fortunately on learning the nature of the case, I had brought the forceps, which were now instantly applied, and the patient delivered of a still-born child, which, with perseverance, was brought to breathe, and is now a living and healthy boy, four years of age. Had I not in this case ascertained by the means mentioned, that the child still lived, I should not have felt justified in interfering; but, supposing the child dead, would have left the case to nature, and five minutes, in all likelihood, would have decided the child's fate." (Dr. Evory Kennedy, on Pregnancy and Auscultation, p. 241.)

[Pg 376]

CHAPTER XI.

PUERPERAL CONVULSIONS.

Epileptic convulsions with cerebral congestion.—Causes.—Symptoms.—Tetanic species.—Diagnosis of labour during convulsions.—Prophylactic treatment.—Treatment.—Bleeding.—Purgatives.—Apoplectic species.—Anæmic convulsions.—Symptoms.—Treatment.—Hysterical convulsions.—Symptoms.

Women are liable, both before, during, and after labour to attacks of convulsions, not only of variable intensity, but differing considerably in point of character. We shall consider them under three separate heads, viz. epileptic convulsions with cerebral congestion; epileptic convulsions from collapse or anæmia; and hysterical convulsions. Other species have been enumerated by authors, but they are either varieties of, or intimately connected with, those of the first species.

No author has more distinctly pointed out the fact that epilepsy may arise from diametrically opposite causes than Dr. Cullen; a circumstance which, in a practical point of view, is of the greatest importance. "The occasional causes," says he, "may, I think, be properly referred to two general heads; the first, being those which seem to act by directly stimulating and exciting the energies of the brain, and the second, of those which seem to act by weakening the same." "A certain fulness and tension of the vessels of the brain is necessary to the support of its ordinary and constant energy in the distribution of the nervous power" (Practice of Physic;) and hence it may be inferred that, on the one hand, an over-distention, and, on the other, a collapsed state of these vessels, will be liable to be attended with so much cerebral disturbance as to produce epilepsy.

Epileptic convulsions with cerebral congestion. Epileptic convulsions connected with pregnancy or parturition, and which are preceded and attended with cerebral congestion, alone deserve, strictly speaking, the name of Eclampsia parturientium (which, in fact, signifies nothing more than the epilepsy of parturient females,) being peculiar to this condition; whereas, the anæmic and hysterical convulsions may occur at any other time quite independent of the pregnant or parturient state.

[Pg 377]The term "puerperal convulsions" is employed in a much more vague and extended sense, and applies generally to every sort of convulsive affection which may occur at this period, and as such, it therefore, forms the title of the present chapter.

Causes. The exciting cause of eclampsia parturientium is the irritation arising from the presence of the child in the uterus or passages, or from a state of irritation thus produced, continuing to exist after labour. The predisposing causes are, general plethora, the pressure of the gravid uterus upon the abdominal aorta, the contractions of that organ during labour, by which a large quantity of the blood circulating in its spongy parietes is driven into the rest of the system, constipation, deranged bowels, retention of urine, previous injuries of the head or cerebral disease, and much mental excitement, early youth: also "in persons of hereditary predisposition, spare habit, irritable temperament, high mental refinement, and in whom the excitability of the nervous, and subsequently the sanguiferous system is called forth by causes apparently trivial." (Facts and cases in Obstetric Medicine, by I. T. Ingleby, p. 5.)

Symptoms. From the above-mentioned list of causes it will be evident, that these convulsions will be invariably attended and preceded by symptoms of strong determination of blood to the head. Previous to the attack the patient has "drowsiness, a sense of weight in the head, especially in stooping; beating and pain in the head; redness of the conjunctiva; numbness of the hands; flushing of the face, and twitching of its muscles; irregular and slow pulse; ringing in the ears, heat in the scalp, transient but frequent attacks of vertigo, with muscæ volitantes, or temporary blindness; derangement of the auditory nerve; embarrassment of mind and speech; an unsteady gait; constipation and œdematous swellings." (Ingleby, op. cit. p. 12.)

As the attack approaches, the patient frequently complains of a peculiar dragging pain and sense of oppression about the præcordia, which comes on and again abates at short intervals, and is attended with much restlessness and anxiety: this is followed by intense pain, which usually attacks the back of the head, and upon the accession of which the præcordial affection apparently ceases; the pulse now becomes smaller and more contracted. If the convulsions do not make their appearance by this time, and the headach continues one or more hours, a slight degree of coma supervenes, the patient loses her consciousness more and more, and wanders now and then; after a time she becomes restless and evidently uneasy, the eye becomes fixed and staring, the countenance changes, and the outbreak of convulsive movements follows.

Sometimes the premonitory symptoms are much less marked; indeed, in some cases, there is scarcely a sign to warn us of the impending danger; in the midst of a conversation the patient[Pg 378] becomes suddenly silent, and, on looking to see the cause, we find the expression altered, the muscles of the face are twitching, the features beginning to be distorted, and the next moment she falls down in general convulsions.

Wigand (Geburt des Menschen, vol. i. § 102,) considers that the two symptoms which usher in the attack are, the frightful staring followed by rolling of the eyes, with sudden starts from right to left, and twisting of the head to the same side by the same sudden movements; as soon as the convulsions have commenced, the head generally returns to its former position, or rather is pulled more or less backwards; "the eyes are wide open, staring, and very prominent, the eyelids twitch violently, the iris is rapidly convulsed with alternate contractions and dilatations; the face begins to swell and grow purple, the mouth is open and distorted, through which the tongue is protruded, brown, and covered with froth; the lips swell and become purple: in fact, it is the complete picture of one who is strangled." (Op. cit.)

These convulsions, as in common epilepsy under other circumstances, usually if not always commence about the head and face, gradually passing down to the chest and abdomen, and then attacking the extremities. After the above-mentioned changes, they pass into the throat and neck, by which a state of trismus is produced, and the protruded tongue is not unfrequently caught between the teeth and severely wounded. The neck is violently pulled on one side, and from the pressure to which the trachea is subjected, severe dyspnœa is produced. The respiration is nearly suspended, and from the violent rushing of the air as it is forced through the contracted rima glottidis, the breathing is performed with a peculiar hissing sound. The muscles of the chest now become affected, and the thorax is convulsively heaved and depressed with great vehemence; those of the abdomen succeed, and the convulsive efforts are here, if possible, still more violent: such are the contractions of the abdominal muscles, and so powerfully do they compress the contents of the abdomen, that a person who had not previously seen the patient would scarcely believe she was pregnant; the next moment the abdomen is as much protruded as it was before compressed. From the same cause, the contents of the rectum and bladder are expelled unconsciously, the extremities become violently convulsed, and the patient is bedewed with a cold clammy sweat. The duration of such a fit is variable; it seldom lasts more than five minutes, and frequently not more than two, and then a gradual subsidence of the convulsions and other symptoms follow; the swollen and livid face returns to its natural size and colour, the eyes become less prominent, the lips less turgid, the breathing is easier and more calm, the viscid saliva ceases to be blown into foam from the mouth, and the patient is left in a state of comatose insensibility[Pg 379] or deep stertorous sleep, from which, in the course of a quarter of an hour or twenty minutes, she suddenly awakes, quite unconscious of what has been the matter; she stares about with a vacant expression of surprise; she feels stiff and sore as if she were bruised: this will be especially the case if it has been attempted to hold her during the fit. The convulsive efforts of the muscles of the body and extremities are not easily resisted, and thus it is that we hear of a delicate woman under these circumstances requiring several strong men to hold her: the result of such treatment is, that her muscles and joints are severely strained, and continue painful for some time after. Patients, on recovering their senses, frequently complain of pain and soreness in the mouth, arising from the tongue having been bitten; in some cases where the tongue has been much protruded, the injury is very severe, the tongue being bitten completely across, and hanging only by a small portion.

The woman may suffer but one attack, and have no return of the fit, or in half an hour, an hour, or longer, the convulsions again appear as at first. If this happens several times, she does not recover her consciousness during the intervals, but remains in a continued state of coma from one fit to another. Although it rarely happens, that the patient dies during a fit, still nevertheless, one fit will in some cases be sufficient to throw her into a state of coma from which she does not recover; in others, the patient may lie for even twenty-four hours in strong convulsions and yet recover.

The character of these attacks appears to vary a good deal with the cause; thus, where plethora has been the predisposing cause, and the fits frequently repeated, they take on more or less of an apoplectic character, the coma is more profound and of longer duration, and is frequently attended with paralysis; the cerebral affection is more severe, the patient does not recover her senses even where the intervals between the attacks have been of considerable duration; and when the fits have ceased and the coma abated, she is occasionally left in a state of imbecility and blindness, which lasts for several hours or even days.

Where it is connected with constipation or deranged bowels, we think that we have seen it more frequently attended with delirium or even temporary mania; the fits are numerous, the convulsions as severe, but the cerebral congestion is not so intense, the coma less profound; instead of being left in a state of torpid stupor, the patient is very restless and at times unmanageable, and when we consider the identity of the causes which produce these convulsions and one form of puerperal mania, it will be easily understood why the symptoms should assume this character. The degree also of determination to the head, will in no slight measure influence the character of the symptoms which attend these attacks. "One circumstance,"[Pg 380] says Dr. Parry, "of increased impetus deserves to be noticed. The delirium is preceded by a pain in the head, but as the delirium comes on, the pain ceases, though the impetus remains as before, or perhaps increases. Diminish in a slight degree the impetus, and you remove the delirium and renew the pain; diminish the impetus in a greater degree, and the frown on the forehead is relaxed, the features seem to open, and the pain entirely ceases." (Posthumous Medical Writings, vol. i. p. 263.)

By far the majority of cases of eclampsia parturientium occur in primiparæ: thus in thirty cases which occurred to Dr. Collins, during his mastership at the Dublin Lying-in Hospital, "twenty-nine were in women with their first children, and the other single case was a second pregnancy, but in a woman who had suffered a similar attack with her first child." In two instances, under our own notice, where the disease occurred in multiparæ, the fits did not appear until after delivery; the patients were plethoric, and in one especially, the bowels were excessively deranged; in the other, the attack had much of the apoplectic character, and the coma did not at once abate until the fatal termination.

Convulsions usually make their appearance towards evening; and if pains are coming on, they return with every uterine contraction. The patient's danger will, in great measure, depend upon the severity, frequency, and duration of the fits; and although they must ever be looked upon as a disease of the most dangerous character, yet we are justified in saying that in the majority of instances the patient recovers: thus, of the forty-eight cases recorded by Dr.

Merriman, thirty-seven recovered; and of the thirty by Dr. Collins, only five died, "three of which were complicated with laceration of the vagina, one with twins, and one with peritoneal inflammation. It is thus evident that the fatal result in these cases, with the exception of the twin birth, was not immediately connected with the convulsions; and the danger in all twin deliveries, no matter what the attack may be, is in every instance greatly increased." (Practical Treatise, p. 210.)

Although puerperal convulsions usually occur at the commencement of labour, it not unfrequently happens that they do not come on until after the child is born; whereas, in other cases they occur several months before the full period: these varieties depend entirely upon the circumstances under which the attack has appeared. "With respect to their occurrence in the last month of gestation, although the paroxysm mostly appears during the actual dilatation of the os uteri, or on the first approach of labour, still when we recollect that in the last week or two of pregnancy the neck of the uterus is fully developed, the subsequent changes being confined to the os internum (the most sensitive part of the organ,) it cannot be surprising that, in[Pg 381] very irritable persons, a serious impression should be made upon the brain at those periods." (Ingleby, op. cit. p. 11.)

Dr. Merriman has called it dystocia epileptica: there is, in fact, no difference between this disease and common epilepsy, beyond that, under ordinary circumstances, epilepsy is a chronic affection, and, generally speaking, not attended with much danger, whereas, in the present case, it is an acute attack, and of a highly dangerous character.

Many phenomena connected with uterine irritation, both in the unimpregnated state and during pregnancy, prove the intimate nature of the consent existing between the brain and uterus. Thus it is well known that menstrual irritation is accompanied with a great variety of nervous and hysterical symptoms, which are merely a part of the same series of results to which epilepsy itself belongs: it is occasionally attended with delirium, spasms, and even coma, and preceded by the oppression at the pit of the stomach and pain of head, which we have already noticed among the immediate precursors of puerperal epilepsy; on the other hand, as Dr. Parry has well remarked, "the beginning and end of each epileptic fit, before total insensibility begins and after it ceases, is often delirium, screaming, false impressions, attempt to annoy others under these impressions," &c. (Op. cit. vol. i. p. 396. &c.) Thus also during labour, either at the termination of the first stage, when the os uteri has attained its full degree of dilatation, or immediately after the birth of the child, the patient is frequently seized with a sudden convulsive rigour so violent as to make her teeth chatter and agitate the whole bed, and which is nothing more than a harmless modification of convulsive action arising from uterine irritation; the surface is perfectly warm, and the patient frequently expresses her surprise to find herself shivering thus violently and yet not feel cold.

It has been a common opinion that epileptic puerperal convulsions are almost certainly fatal to the child, especially if they continue for any length of time: experience, however, proves the contrary, as cases continually occur where the mother has laid for many hours in a constant succession of severe convulsions, and yet has been ultimately delivered of a living child. Still, however, it must be owned, that barely an equal number of the children are born alive under these circumstances. Thus, in Dr. Merriman's 48 cases, as already mentioned, only 17 children were born alive (including the 6 born before the mothers were attacked with convulsions;) in the 30 cases recorded by Dr. Collins, 18 of the 32 children (two of the women having had twins) were born dead; of these, however, it must be observed, that 8 were delivered with the perforator, and two were born putrid.

Tetanic species. There is one modification of eclampsia parturientium, which, from the spastic rigidity of the uterus which accompanies it, is peculiarly dangerous to the child's life: it has[Pg 382] been called the tetanic form: the convulsions are incessant, without any apparent interval, and the uterus actively participates in the state of general spasms: under such circumstances, the pressure which it exerts upon the body of the fœtus will seriously obstruct the abdominal circulation, and produce the same effects as pressure on the cord.

In most cases, however, the convulsions have no effect upon the process of labour, which continues its course uninterrupted; so that, where there has been no return of consciousness during the intervals between the fits, and the patient has laid in a continued state of coma for some time, the child may actually be born before there has even been a suspicion that labour was present. It is, therefore, of great importance that the practitioner should be on the watch to detect any symptoms of its coming on, not only for the purpose of giving her the necessary support at the moment of expulsion, but also such assistance as may tend to shorten that process.

"By attentively observing what passes in cases of convulsions, we remark that they do not always interrupt the course of the labour pains, whether they had excited those pains, or the pains had preceded them. All authors relate examples of women who have been delivered without help after several fits of strong convulsions; and others while

189

they were actually convulsed, whether there were lucid intervals between, or that the loss of understanding was permanent. The progress of labour in most of these cases seems even more rapid than in others, since we have often found the child between its mother's thighs, though an instant before we could discover no disposition for delivery." (Baudelocque, trans. by Heath, § 1109.)

Diagnosis of labour during convulsions. Where the patient is in a state of insensibility, we may infer the presence of labour by a variety of symptoms; every now and then, from a state of torpor, she becomes restless, and evidently uneasy; she pushes the bed-clothes from the abdomen, and gropes about it as if trying to remove something that is heavy or uncomfortable; she writhes her body, and moans as if in pain; after awhile, she again relapses into her former state of coma. A little attention will soon show us that these exacerbations of restlessness are periodical; and if we examine the abdomen at the moment, we feel the uterus evidently contracting; the os uteri also will be found tense and more or less dilated: if the head has already advanced into the vagina, these contractions will be accompanied by a distinct effort to strain.

It is rare to find convulsions complicated with malposition of the child; indeed, so uncommon is the occurrence of it under these circumstances, that we may feel almost certain, on being summoned to a case of convulsions, that there will be little chance of this additional difficulty being superadded. "There[Pg 383] was but one case," says Dr. Collins, "of convulsions during my residence in the hospital, where the child presented preternaturally; there was not one case with a preternatural presentation during Dr. Clarke's residence; and Dr. Labatt has stated the same fact in his lectures while master of the hospital. In these three different periods there were 48,379 women delivered, so that from this we may infer, where the presentation is preternatural, there is little cause to dread the attack." (Practical Treatise, p. 200.)

Prophylactic treatment. Under no circumstances is the old saying of "Prevention is better than the cure," so well illustrated as in the prophylactic treatment of puerperal epilepsy: it is only by carefully watching for and recognising those symptoms which we have already enumerated as threatening an attack, that we are able to adopt such measures as shall either keep it off entirely, or at any rate considerably diminish its violence.

The treatment which we have recommended during the last weeks of pregnancy, is particularly valuable in keeping off any disposition to these attacks: regular, and for her condition even tolerably active, exercise and strict attention to the bowels, should be required, especially in primiparæ. If any distinct symptoms of cerebral congestion make their appearance, such as flushed face, headach, or slight wandering; if, moreover, the pulse be slow and labouring, we must at once relieve the circulation by bleeding; and by an active dose of calomel and James's powder at night with a warm pediluvium, and a brisk laxative the next morning, endeavour to ward off the dreaded attack. Not unfrequently, however, we have no warning of the danger until the fits burst out, and are thus debarred the opportunity of preparing against them.

Treatment. During the fit itself little can be done beyond placing the patient in such a situation that she should not injure herself by her exertions. If she happens to be upon a chair when the attack begins, it will be as well to let her sink gently upon the floor, and lie there until the fit is over; if she is in bed when it comes on, we have merely to watch that she does not roll off during her struggles; her movements should be restrained as little as possible, and by so doing we shall spare her the suffering after the fit from strained muscles and half-wrenched joints, which is so severe where the assistants, from mistaken kindness, have endeavoured to hold her.

It has been recommended by Dr. Denman to have the patient's face frequently dashed with cold water during the fit, a remedy which, as Dr. Merriman observes, is very effectual in ordinary hysterical paroxysms, and which possibly may have a slight effect in moderating the violence of the epileptic convulsions; but from what we have seen we are not inclined to consider it of much use.

[Pg 384]Bleeding. As soon as the fit is sufficiently over to render the operation possible, the patient ought to be placed in a half-sitting posture, and bled from a large orifice in the arm; the quantity of blood abstracted must be determined by the appearance of the patient, the severity of the cerebral symptoms, and the condition of the pulse; this latter will usually be found labouring, and even small, but will rise considerably in fulness and volume as we gradually relieve the circulation. Syncope is an effect which, under these circumstances, it would neither be easy nor safe to produce; but at the same time it will be highly desirable to produce a powerful effect upon the circulation by so large and speedy an abstraction of blood as shall be certain of alleviating the cerebral congestion: this is not often attained until after a loss of twenty, or five and twenty ounces. She should be supported in the half-sitting posture by means of a chair turned against the head of the bed, so that its back forms an inclined plane, which should be covered with pillows for her to lean upon.

Purgatives. An active dose of purgative medicine should be given the moment the patient is able to swallow; for in case of the fit returning, it will be sometimes very difficult to make her take any thing. Eight or ten grains of calomel, with fifteen or twenty of jalap, should be mixed into a paste with a little thin gruel and laid upon the back of the tongue, and a few spoonfuls more of gruel, &c. given to carry it down. If this cannot be taken, a few drops of croton oil will seldom fail to produce the necessary effect.

It is of the greatest importance to do this as early as possible, not only for the reason we have just assigned, but also because we find that purgative medicines frequently take a longer time to operate in these cases than they do under ordinary circumstances, and require the repetition of even a powerful dose before the bowels can be made to act. Where the convulsions appear to depend in great measure upon the deranged state of the bowels, the indications for the immediate employment of purgatives become still more urgent, for although we may control the cerebral congestion by means of the lancet, we shall not remove the source of irritation; but when once the bowels have been freely evacuated, the chain of morbid actions is broken, and the disease ceases: hence, in some cases, we observe much more striking relief purgatives than even by bleeding. In order, therefore, to ensure a certain and speedy effect upon the bowels, she should take, about two hours after the powder, repeated doses of salts and senna, and if necessary, have their action still farther assisted by a purgative injection.

In the mean time, the hair must be closely shaven from the crown and back of the head, leaving the front bands, that she may be disfigured as little as possible, and a large bullock's bladder half filled with pounded ice, applied to the bare scalp; in lieu[Pg 385] of which, an evaporating lotion of vinegar spirit and water, may be applied until the ice is procured. Sinapisms to the calves of the legs and soles of the feet will also be required, so that, on coming into a room where a patient is lying in puerperal convulsions, the practitioner may quickly find employment for the numerous friends or assistants, who generally crowd round her on such occasions, and convert their officiousness into real utility. The air of the room must be kept as fresh as possible, and no more people allowed to remain in it than are absolutely necessary.

If she be tolerably conscious during the interval, a hot foot bath, rendered still more stimulating by some mustard flour, will be of great service; flannels wrung out of a hot decoction of mustard, and wrapped round the feet and legs, are also useful, and tend still farther to diminish the cerebral congestion.

In all cases of convulsions, especially if the patient be near her full time, it will be necessary to ascertain the state of the bladder; for the pressure of the head frequently produces much difficulty in evacuating it, and sometimes causes so much distention and irritation as to be itself quite capable of exciting the convulsions. Lamotte has given two instances where the fits had been evidently brought on by retention of urine, and where relief was immediately given by evacuating the bladder.

Where the patient has still some time to go, and no appearance of uterine action has been excited, the probability is, that the above-mentioned treatment, will be sufficient to prevent a return of the attack; and, if we have succeeded in calming the circulation, we may combine a little henbane with her medicine to allay irritability. But if she be near her full time, and labour has distinctly commenced, there will be little chance of the convulsions permanently ceasing until she is delivered, as the contractions of the uterus frequently appear to excite a return of them.

The practice in former times of dilating the os uteri, introducing the hand and turning the child, has been long since justly discarded, for the irritation such improper violence would run great risk of aggravating the convulsions to a fatal degree.

"No cases require more prudence, attention, and sagacity, than the accident of convulsions in women, with their first children especially. The state of the os uteri is of immense importance, and when it will admit of your delivering the woman without violence, trouble, or irritation, no doubt it ought to be performed with all prudent expedition, as you never can be sure of her being restored without delivery." (M'Kenzie's Lectures, MS. 1764, quoted by Dr. Merriman.)

Where we are called to a patient, who has been some little time in convulsions, and where bleeding and other necessary[Pg 386] measures have been already had recourse to, we may, with a tolerable degree of certainty, expect to find the os uteri fully dilated, and the head in a favourable state for the application of the forceps. The practitioner should be able to apply the forceps whether the patient be lying upon her back or her side, as it is not always possible to choose her position; the former, will generally be the safest, as she will not only lie more quietly upon her back, but can be kept with most facility in this posture. Generally speaking the fits subside immediately after the child is delivered, although not unfrequently they recur during the first twelve or sixteen hours after labour, coming on at increasing intervals.

If, however, the state of the os uteri forbids our interfering with art, we must be content to follow out that plan of antiphlogistic treatment which has been just laid down, bearing in mind, that in proportion as we reduce the power of the circulation we increase the disposition of the os uteri to dilate, and, as Baudelocque justly observes, "while we wait the favourable moment for operating, we should only employ those means which we could use after delivery, if the convulsions should continue." (Op. cit. § 1110.)

By the time that the medicine has begun to operate, a considerable change will usually be observed in all the symptoms—the violence of the convulsions abates, the coma is less profound, and if the child be not yet born, the process of labour much more speedy and favourable; but if we find that the convulsions assume a tetanic character, and that the uterus actively participates in this state of spasmodic rigidity, we must not expect any very favourable change until delivery is effected; and there will be little chance for the child of its being born alive for reasons already mentioned. Under such circumstances, which are fortunately of rare occurrence, it will be our duty to perforate rather than run the risk of losing the mother as well as her child; but before proceeding to this extremity we must satisfy our minds that the state of the os uteri forbids the forceps, and that, from the tetanic action of the uterus, there is little chance of its farther dilatation.

"It does not always happen that the convulsions cease upon the termination of the labour; on the contrary, they often continue after the birth of the child, and sometimes increase in violence, and at length produce death. If, however, the intervals between the fits become longer, a more favourable prognosis may be formed, but it will be expedient to continue our exertions in relieving the symptoms." (Merriman's Synopsis.)

The after treatment will be little more than a continuation of that which has been described during the attack, only in a much milder form: the head must be kept cool by a proper lotion, and the bowels sufficiently open by gentle laxatives; a little gruel,[Pg 387] with or without milk, may be given occasionally; and if the child be alive, it should by all means be applied early to the breast, in order to establish a flow of milk as soon as possible. Where the breasts have been very flaccid, and there were little or no signs of milk, we have now and then applied a sinapism over them with very good effect, for the mammary excitement thus produced has been attended with a copious lochial discharge, which has evidently produced much relief.

Apoplectic species. Dr. Dewees has described a species of convulsions by the term "apoplectic," but it is perhaps questionable how far he is correct in calling them "puerperal convulsions;" for, from the cases which have come under our own notice, the disease has been nothing else than genuine apoplexy occurring in the pregnant, parturient, or puerperal state: he justly observes, that "it may be brought on by causes independent of pregnancy, though this process may with propriety be regarded as an exciting cause; for it sometimes takes place when this process is at its height, but is no otherwise accessary to this end, than increasing by its efforts the determination of blood to the head." (Op. cit. § 1238.)

The treatment will in no respect differ from that of the genuine puerperal convulsions, except that, as the danger is still greater, so, if possible, must the treatment be more prompt; indeed, it can scarcely be said that there is a convulsion, for there is merely loss of motion with insensibility. It is fortunately of rare occurrence, as the patient seldom recovers.

Anæmic convulsions. The next form of epiplectic puerperal convulsions is the anæmic form, where, in consequence of serious loss of blood or debility otherwise induced, the due balance of the nervous system has been disturbed, and irregular and convulsive actions have been the result.

We have already shown that cerebral congestion is favourable to that state of irritability, which, by the help of any exciting cause, may easily pass into a state of epilepsy; an opposite condition, viz. that of exhaustion, is capable of acting in a similar way, and thus confirms Dr. Cullen's assertion, "that there are certain powers of collapse, which, in effect, prove stimulants and produce epilepsy."

"That there are such powers which may be termed indirect stimulants, I conclude from hence, that several of the causes of epilepsy are such as frequently produce syncope, which, we suppose, always to depend upon causes weakening the energy of the brain." "The first to be mentioned, which I suppose to be of this kind, is hæmorrhage, whether spontaneous or artificial. That the same hæmorrhage which produces syncope, often at the same time produces epilepsy, is well known; and from many experiments and observations it appears, that hæmorrhages [Pg 388]occurring to such a degree as to prove mortal, seldom do so without first producing epilepsy." (Op. cit.) It is a well-known fact, that when once a state of exhaustion or collapse has been carried beyond a certain point, the irritability of the nervous system increases in proportion: the due balance of its various actions becomes more and more unsteady; their equilibrium is disturbed by the slightest impressions, and losing the state of well-adjusted repose which belongs to health, they continually vibrate between the extremes of excitement or collapse, which seldom fail to produce some serious derangement.

"The symptoms of reaction from loss of blood," says Dr. Marshall Hall, "accurately resemble those of power in the system, and of morbidly increased action of the encephalon; and, from these causes, the case is very apt to be mistaken and mistreated by the farther abstraction of blood. The result of this treatment is, in itself, again apt farther to mislead us; for all the previous symptoms are promptly and completely relieved, and this relief, in its turn, again suggests the renewed use of the lancet. In this manner the last blood-letting may prove suddenly and unexpectedly fatal."

Symptoms. A very little attention, however, will discover the real features of the disease; the pale face, the glazy eye, the shrunken features and colourless lip, the cold moist skin, the heaving chest, the quick, weak, small, and irritable pulse, all betoken a condition of exhaustion and collapse. The history of the case will also show that the patient has suffered from profuse hæmorrhage, or some other debilitating evacuation; and the intense pain on the summit of the head, verging into actual delirium, the rambling thoughts and confused mental associations, the restlessness or absolute insomnia, the tinnitus aurium, disposition to strabismus or other derangements of vision, indicate the defective condition of the cerebral circulation.

We have already mentioned, in the congestive form of epilepsy, that where the irritation from gastric derangement is conjoined to a state of body already predisposed to the disease, that this is frequently sufficient to excite it into action; still more will this be the case where the system is rendered irritable by exhaustion; and it will occur under more formidable circumstances, from our means of treatment being confined within still narrower limits. Dr. M. Hall justly observes, that "exhaustion is sooner induced under circumstances of intestinal irritation:" and again, "paralysis has occurred in a state of exhaustion from other causes, as undue lactation; and in various circumstances of debility, as in cases of disorder of the general health, with sallowness and pallor, and a loaded tongue and breath."

Treatment. Our treatment of these cases will not vary essentially from that of exhaustion from hæmorrhage under the[Pg 389] ordinary circumstances; the patient must be placed with her head low, and as soon as she is able to swallow, a little hot brandy and water, or ammonia, should be given to rouse the circulation to a sufficient degree of activity. If the uterus be still flaccid and disinclined to contract effectively, a dose of ergot will be advisable, and the abdomen should be tightly bandaged with a broad towel. When the powers of the circulation have rallied somewhat, a little plain beef-tea will frequently prove very grateful and appear to revive her more powerfully than even the stimulants above-mentioned; and now, as it is of the greatest importance to calm the irritability of the brain and nervous system, we must proceed to the use of sedatives. Of these, opium and hyoscyamus have the preference, the latter especially so, from its not being liable, like opium, to derange the stomach, or contract the bowels. Moreover, where the exhaustion is very alarming, it is not always easy to control the sedative action of opium within due bounds; and in such cases we are sometimes apt to produce so much sopor, as to render it even difficult to rouse the patient. For this reason, the combination with a diffusible stimulant is always desirable: five grains of camphor and of extr. hyosc. in two pills, form, perhaps, the best and safest sedative which can be given; these may be repeated every hour, and then at longer intervals of two or more hours, until sleep has been produced. Sleep, in cases of this kind, is of the greatest importance, and produces the most favourable change in the patient's condition; the intense headach and irritability of the mind, of the sight, and of the hearing, all abate; the circulation becomes calmer, the pulse more full and soft, the heat of the body more equable; in short, the whole nervous system is returning to a more natural and regular state of action, the stomach is more capable of receiving and digesting its food, the bowels are more manageable, and we may now venture to remove a state of constipation, if present, or any morbid intestinal contents without running the risk of bringing on diarrhœa and increasing the debility.

We rarely find that the convulsions return when once the patient has enjoyed the calm of a sound and refreshing sleep, and consider the victory as more than half gained when this favourable state has been produced. The laxative should be of the mildest form, such as will merely excite the peristaltic action of the intestines without increasing their secretions; for this purpose a warm draught of rhubarb manna with hyoscyamus, or castor oil guarded by a little liq. opii. sed., will be the safest. Food of the blandest and most nutritious quality should be given in small and frequently repeated doses; it is important not to load the stomach much or suddenly, for vomiting is easily produced, and when once excited, the stomach becomes so irritable as to be scarcely capable of retaining any food whatever.

[Pg 390]Where, on the other hand, several hours have passed, not only without sleep but without even a temporary state of quiet; where the headach alternates with restless delirium; where the medicines and nourishment have produced little or no effect, or have been rejected by vomiting; where the pulse becomes quicker, and the debility increases, we have not only to dread a return of the fits, but that the stage of actual sinking is at hand.

"It would perhaps," says Dr. Marshall Hall, "be difficult to offer any observations on the nature and cause of excessive reaction; but it is plain that the state of sinking involves a greatly impaired state of the functions of all the vital organs, and especially of the brain from defective stimulus. The tendency to dozing, the snoring and stertor, the imperfect respiration, the impaired action of the sphincters, the defective action of the lungs, and the accumulation of the secretions of the bronchia, the feeble and hurried beat of the heart and pulse, the disordered state of the secretions of the stomach and bowels, and the evolution of flatus, all denote an impaired condition of the nervous energy." (On the Morbid and Curative Effects of Loss of Blood, p. 54.)

Hysterical convulsions scarcely deserve the name of puerperal convulsions, being liable to occur under circumstances quite independent of the puerperal state; they rarely occur during the process of labour itself, but are chiefly observed during the last few weeks of pregnancy, and the first week or so after labour, especially when the milk is coming on.

Symptoms. The patient is of a nervous hysterical habit; "she is either still very young, or is of a slim and delicate make; the face is pale and interesting; she has full blue eyes and light hair, and was always of a highly sensitive constitution; the pulse is quick, small, and contracted; the temperature of the skin is rather cool than otherwise; her spirits are variable, fretful, and anxious; she starts at the slightest noise, cannot bear much or loud talking, and misunderstands or takes every thing amiss. During her slumbers, which are short, there are slight twitchings of the eyes and mouth, and in her sleep the eyes are in constant restless motion, and she frequently starts. She complains of sickness, and has frequent calls to pass water, which is very pale; slight rigours alternate every now and then with flushing, and she is easily tired, even by trifling pains, and dozes a good deal during the intervals. She is excessively sensitive, even to the most gentle and cautious examination; the os uteri remains thin, hard, tense, and painful to the touch longer than is usually the case. The ordinary tension and stretching of the os uteri at the termination of a regular contraction is attended with much more pain, and with a peculiar feeling of lassitude, although uncomplicated with any rheumatic affection. The pains follow no regular course, being sometimes stronger, at others weaker, and frequently cease[Pg 391] entirely for considerable periods. The uterus has a great disposition from the slightest irritation, to partial and spasmodic contractions." (Wigand, Geburt des Menschen, vol. i. p. 164.)

Before the fit the patient usually passes a large quantity of colourless and limpid urine; she has oppression at the stomach, anxiety, difficulty of breathing and palpitation, with globus, sobbing, and other hysterical symptoms. There are not those precursory symptoms of cerebral congestion as mark genuine epileptic puerperal convulsions; the headach is neither so severe, nor is it in the same place, being usually at the temples and across the forehead; the face is rather pale than flushed, and when the fit begins, we see little or none of the convulsive twitching among the small muscles, as is the case with an epileptic attack; the face is less distorted, but the large muscles of the trunk and extremities are much more violently affected; the patient struggles furiously, and in severe cases has more or less of opisthotonos; she screams, and never appears to lose her senses so entirely as in the epileptic form; her raving may generally be controlled to a certain extent by suddenly dashing cold water in her face, and speaking loudly and sharply to her; at any rate it instantly produces a deep and sudden inspiration, which is frequently attended with a prolonged hooping sound; this is followed by sobbing, gasping, choking, and the ordinary phenomena of an hysteric fit, but the convulsions themselves are usually arrested more or less by this application: we hold the effects of cold water to be one of the best diagnostics of the disease from epilepsy, in which the patient is entirely insensible to such impressions.

A similar fact is observed during vaginal examination; the patient seems aware of our intention, and resists in every possible way.

"The patient, after the fit, can for the most part be roused to attention or will frequently become coherent so soon as she recovers from the fatigue or exhaustion occasioned by her violent struggles; and though she may lie apparently stupid, she will nevertheless sometimes talk or indistinctly mutter. After the convulsion has passed over, she will often open her eyes and vacantly look about, and then, as if suddenly seized by a sense of shame, will sink lower in the bed, and attempt to hide her head in the clothes." (Dewees's Compend. Syst. of Midwifery, § 1240.)

When sufficiently recovered to be capable of swallowing, she should sip some cold water, or what is still better, take a dose of spiritus ammoniæ fœtidus in water; this soon produces copious eructations from the stomach, which are followed with much relief. Where there is a disposition to vomiting, and other evidences of a deranged stomach, it should be encouraged by some warm water, chamomile tea, &c. The bowels are almost always in an unhealthy state, which frequently produces much irritation, and in plethoric habits so much tendency to cerebral congestion as[Pg 392] to endanger even an attack of the epileptic convulsions. One or two doses of a pretty brisk purgative should, therefore, be given, and if there be still heat or pain of head, a bleeding may be required.

Under ordinary circumstances hysterical convulsions are by no means dangerous, and beyond a little fatigue and exhaustion, the patient recovers from them almost immediately.

[Pg 393]

CHAPTER XII.

PLACENTAL PRESENTATION, OR PLACENTA PRÆVIA.

History.—Dr. Rigby's division of hæmorrhages before labour into accidental and unavoidable.—Causes.—Symptoms.—Treatment.—Plug.—Turning.—Partial presentation of the placenta.—Treatment.

There are few dangers connected with the practice of midwifery which are more deservedly dreaded, and which are wont to come more unexpectedly, both to the patient as well as to the practitioner, than that species of hæmorrhage which occurs in cases where the placenta is implanted either centrally or partially over the os uteri. Well has a celebrated teacher observed, that "there is no error in nature to be compared with this, for the very action which she uses to bring the child into the world is that by which she destroys both it and its mother." (Naegelé, MS. Lectures.) In other words, where there is this peculiar situation of the placenta it becomes gradually detached, either in proportion as the cervix expands during the latter months of pregnancy, or as the os uteri dilates with commencing labour, and is thus unavoidably attended with a profuse discharge of blood, which generally increases as the dilatation proceeds.

The peculiar feature of this species of hæmorrhage, necessarily accompanying the commencement of every labour where the placenta is implanted over the os uteri, was first fully described in this country in 1775, by the late Dr. Rigby, in his classical Essay on the Uterine Hæmorrhage which precedes the Delivery of the full-grown Fœtus, a work which has been justly looked upon, both in England and the Continent, as the great source to which we are indebted for our practical knowledge in the management of these dangerous cases.

History. There is abundant evidence to prove the sudden attacks of hæmorrhage during pregnancy, attended with circumstances of great danger to the life of the mother and her child, were known from the earliest times, and especially noticed by Hippocrates where he says, "that the after-burden should come forth after the child, for if it come first, the child cannot live, because he takes his life from it, as a plant doth from the earth." (De Morbis Mulierum, lib. i. quoted by Guillemeau.)

Hippocrates, therefore, evidently supposed that this presentation[Pg 394] of the placenta at the os uteri was owing to its having been separated from its usual situation in the uterus, and fallen down to the lower part of it.

This view has been closely adopted by Guillemeau, to whom we are indebted for having called our attention to the above passage. He has devoted his fifteenth chapter[140] to the management of a case where the placenta presents, and shows that "the most certain and expedient method is to deliver the patient promptly, in order that she may not suffer from the hæmorrhage which issues from the uncovered mouths of the uterine veins, to which the placenta had been attached; that, on the other hand, the child being enclosed in the uterus, the orifice of which is plugged up by the placenta, and unable to breathe any more by the arteries of its mother, will be suffocated for want of assistance, and also enveloped in the blood which fills the uterus and escapes from the veins in it which are open."

The operation of turning, which had been newly practised by his teacher, Ambrose Paré, and still farther brought into notice by himself, at that time formed a great æra in midwifery, for it furnished practitioners with a new and successful means of delivering the child in cases where urgent danger could only be avoided by hastening labour; hence, therefore, in all cases of profuse hæmorrhage coming on before delivery, it was a general rule, if the case became at all dangerous, to turn the child.

Guillemeau's explanation of the nature of placental presentations was still more explicitly adopted by Mauriceau, La Motte, and many others. Mauriceau invariably speaks of the placenta, when at the os uteri, as "entirely detached;" and adds that "even a short delay will always cause the sudden death of the child if it be not quickly delivered; for it cannot remain any time without being suffocated, as it is now obliged to breathe by its mouth, for its blood is no longer vivified by the preparation which it undergoes in the placenta, the function and use of which cease the moment it is detached from the uterine vessels with which it was connected: the result of this is the profuse flooding which is so dangerous for the mother; for if it be not promptly remedied she will quickly loose her life by this unfortunate accident." (Vol. i. p. 332, 6th ed.) He also adds, "it must be observed that the placenta, which presents, is nothing more than a foreign body in the uterus when it is entirely separated," (p. 333,) "for when it comes into the passage before the infant, it is then totally divided from the womb." (Chamberlen's Transl. p. 221. 8th ed.) In the sixteen cases which he has detailed, he has distinctly mentioned the fact in thirteen that the placenta was entirely separated from the uterus, and presented at the os uteri. In two[Pg 395] of these he has expressly stated his conviction that the placenta had been detached from the uterus, by the mother having been exposed to a violent shock, when the cord was shortened from being twisted round the child.

These facts prove that Mauriceau, considered presentations of the placenta to arise solely from its having been separated by some accident from the fundus, and fallen down to the os uteri.

Dr. Robert Lee, in his "Historical Account of Uterine Hæmorrhage in the latter Months of Pregnancy," (Edin. Med. and Surg. Journal, April 1839,) has omitted all mention of this circumstance, and from the account which he has given of Mauriceau's observations, would infallibly lead his readers to suppose that Mauriceau was fully acquainted with the real nature of these peculiar cases. Thus, he commences with saying, "The symptoms and treatment of cases of placental presentation are here accurately described, and in all cases of hæmorrhage from this cause he recommends immediate delivery;" and again, he observes, "The rules for the treatment of these cases are laid down with the greatest precision. When the placenta was entirely separated, then only did he consider it as a foreign body, and recommend its extraction before the child." The student would be led by such a statement to suppose that Mauriceau did not consider the entire separation of the placenta as the most usual occurrence in these cases, and will therefore naturally infer that in the majority of cases of placental presentation, he recognised the implantation of the placenta upon the os uteri. That such was very far from the case, we have already shown by quotations from various editions of his work. Dr. Lee has collected sixteen, (not seventeen,) cases of placenta prævia from Mauriceau, and has given a short summary of them. Out of the thirteen cases in which Mauriceau has distinctly mentioned that the flooding had been caused by the entire separation of the placenta which presented, Dr. Lee has noticed it in only three; and in one of these he has reversed the expression by saying, "placenta presenting and entirely detached:" thus leading his reader to infer that the placenta had presented at the os uteri, but had become detached from it. Nor is the case (No. 423,) to which Dr. Lee has referred "as a proof that Mauriceau, was aware of the fact, that the placenta had not been wholly detached from the uterus," at all tend to show that he had any idea of the placenta being implanted upon the os uteri.

By stating that "Mauriceau has also recorded the histories of thirty-seven cases of uterine hæmorrhage in which the placenta did not present, but had adhered to the upper part of the uterus and been accidentally detached," Dr. Lee has confirmed the erroneous inference that the implantation of the placenta upon the os uteri was known to this valuable author; whereas, we have proved by numerous quotations, that Mauriceau distinctly[Pg 396] supposed that in all cases of hæmorrhage before labour, whether the placenta was found presenting or not, it had been originally attached "to the upper part of the uterus."

Paul Portal was the first, as far as we are acquainted, who describes the placenta as adhering to the os uteri. He has recorded eight cases, "in which," as Dr. Rigby observes, "he was under the necessity of delivering by art, on account of dangerous hæmorrhages, and in all of them he found the placenta at the mouth of the womb." (Essay on Uterine Hæmorrhage, p. 22, 6th ed.) In these he distinctly mentions the placenta adhering to the os uteri. In several of these he separated it from the os uteri and brought it away; and in seven he turned the child. In the other (Case

39,) the head burst its way through the placenta. In one case only (51,) does he attempt to make any practical inference whatever, having in all the others contented himself with merely stating the fact of the placenta adhering to the os uteri. In this instance, however, he has described the real nature of the case, and pointed out the cause of the hæmorrhage. On introducing his hand he "found the after-burden placed just before and quite across the whole inner orifice, which had actually been the occasion of the flux of blood; for by the opening of the orifice the said after-burden then being loosed from that part where it adhered to before, and the vessels containing the blood torn and opened, produced this flooding, which sometimes is so excessive as proves fatal to the woman unless it be speedily prevented." (Portal's Midwifery, transl. p. 167.)

There is no doubt, as Dr. Renton has very justly observed, "that Portal in 1672 (not 1683) knew as much on the subject of uterine hæmorrhage occasioned by the displacement of the placenta from the os uteri, and the practice necessary for its suppression, as we do at the present time." (Edin. Med. and Surg. Journ. July, 1837.) But we cannot coincide with him in the passage which follows, viz. "It is to him unquestionably that we are indebted for our knowledge on the subject," because, as Dr. Renton himself has shown, all the authors in midwifery up to the time of Rœderer and Levret (1753) were ignorant of Portal's explanation. We do not even except Giffard, as there is sufficient evidence to show that he, for some time, entertained the prevailing erroneous opinions of Mauriceau, until he at last discovered the real nature of the case himself. We attribute the omission solely to the above observation of Portal being so short and isolated, and to its having been entirely unaccompanied by any other practical remarks or inferences which might have been expected from so remarkable a fact. To this reason alone can we attribute the circumstance of its not having been expressly mentioned by Dr. Rigby when alluding to Portal's cases. In a similar way we can explain why Portal has not had the merit of a valuable improvement in the operation of turning which has[Pg 397] been attributed to Peu, viz. the passing the hand between the membranes and uterus up to the fundus before rupturing them, solely because he mentions it as a cursory observation, without any farther notice or practical inference.

The next author who has at all alluded to the real nature of placenta prævia is Giffard, whose posthumous work was published in 1734. The value of his evidence on this subject is considerably modified by his having made no allusion to the implantation of the placenta upon the os uteri in the first ten cases of flooding, where he found the placenta presenting, but repeatedly describes the placenta as being wholly separated and lying in the passage, and in some, he expressly mentions that the placenta had fallen down to the os uteri. In cases 115, 116. and 224. he gives a perfectly correct explanation of the cause of flooding, but the opinion is expressed with such a degree of hesitation, and so cursorily, that we doubt much if it attracted more notice than the observations of Portal, above alluded to, more especially as in the six cases of placenta prævia, which occur between the last two above-mentioned (viz. 120, 121. 158. 160. 185. and 209.,) he returns again to his former mode of describing them. We, therefore, regret that Dr. Renton has not mentioned this circumstance, and that in quoting from "two of the numerous cases which he relates," he has not stated that these were two out of the only three cases which Giffard had described correctly.[141]

It is, therefore, to the above-mentioned circumstances of Giffard having given what is now recognised as the correct explanation, in only three out of nineteen cases, that we can explain why so little notice was taken of the subject at that time; why Dr. Smellie, when speaking of it, makes no allusion to Giffard; and why Dr. Rigby, in his Essay on Uterine Hæmorrhage, was led to suppose that he was ignorant of the real nature of these cases:[Pg 398] certain it is that his opinion could scarcely be called a decided one.

Smellie mentions that "the edge or middle of the placenta sometimes adheres over the inside of the os internum, which frequently begins to open several weeks before the full time; and if this be the case, a flooding begins at the same time, and seldom ceases entirely until the woman is delivered; the discharge may, indeed, be intermitted by coagulums that stop up the passage, but when these are removed it returns with its former violence, and demands the same treatment that is recommended above." His cases contain no observation beyond the recital that a considerable hæmorrhage had occurred, the placenta had been found presenting, and that he had turned the child. In his sixth case (Collect. 33, No. 2.) which is dated 1752, it is evident that he was ignorant of what had been said on the same subject by Giffard and Portal; for he observes, "This case being uncommon, I was uncertain at first how to proceed; but at last considering with myself, if I broke the membranes to evacuate the contained waters, so as to allow the uterus to contract and restrain the flooding, the fœtus would be lost by the pressure of the head against the funis (which presented) in the time of delivery. I resolved in order to prevent this misfortune to turn the child, and bring it along in the preternatural way, which would give it a better chance to restrain the one, and save the other, if the operation could be performed in a slow cautious manner." This forms the amount of his observations on this important subject, and, therefore, justifies the observation which Dr. Rigby has made, viz. that there are no practical inferences drawn from the cases; nor in his directions about the management of floodings, are there any rules given relative to this situation of the placenta.

Rœderer decidedly stands pre-eminent, as being the first author who gave a distinct and complete description of this species of hæmorrhage; he points out the cause of it, and accurately describes its symptoms and mode of attack; he shows that the placenta may be entirely or partially attached to the os uteri; that in the one case the hæmorrhage will be very profuse, and artificial assistance will be required; in the other it will be slighter, and in many cases it may be left to nature.[142]

[Pg 399]Levret cotemporaneously with the first edition of Rœderer's work, published at Paris, a valuable paper on placental presentation, which, with the above-mentioned chapter of Rœderer, must be looked upon as the first observations in which this form of hæmorrhage was made a distinct subject of consideration. Although Levret has in no wise claimed the merit of being the first who had noticed the fact of the placenta being implanted upon the os uteri, still there can be no doubt that to him and Rœderer we are indebted for having first investigated the subject and called the attention of the profession to its peculiar characters.

Levret has reduced his observations under three heads, viz. that the placenta is occasionally implanted over the os uteri, that hæmorrhage under such circumstances is inevitable, and that the safest mode of remedying this accident is the accouchement forcé. He has also added a few valuable remarks, but by far the greater part of the essay is occupied with theoretical arguments to prove that it is impossible for the placenta, which had been attached to the fundus, to sink down to the os uteri. Indeed, beyond stating the three above-mentioned positions, which are undeniably of great practical value (although by no means original,) Levret has added but little which is not contained in Giffard, his chief merit being that of making it a subject of distinct consideration, and establishing it as a matter beyond doubt.

Levret cannot, however, be looked upon as the first who considered that the flooding, in cases of placenta prævia, was "inevitable," although, from his not having quoted Giffard, we willingly concede to him the merit of originality, as far as he himself was concerned: it was Giffard, however, as far as we know, who first pointed out that hæmorrhage was the necessary consequence of placental presentation, as is shown from what we have already quoted from him, although, to a certain extent, it was hinted at by Portal, in his fifty-first case. Levret's memoir was afterwards reprinted in his large work, entitled L'Art des Accouchemens: the third edition, which appeared in 1766, was quoted by Dr. Rigby in the first edition of his Essay on Uterine Hæmorrhage, 1775,[143] in farther proof of the placenta being implanted over the os uteri, and being the cause of hæmorrhage.

We are chiefly indebted to Dr. Rigby for a complete exposition of this important and interesting subject. His well-known essay on the uterine hæmorrhage which precedes the delivery of the full-grown fœtus has stood the test of time, and will ever remain, not less remarkable for its practical value, than "for the perspicuity and simplicity of its style." (Renton, op. cit.) To Dr. Rigby, without doubt, is due the merit of having first [Pg 400]distinguished hæmorrhages, which occur before delivery, into accidental and unavoidable, a division so truly practical and appropriate, as to have placed this subject in the clearest and simplest possible light. "He was," as Dr. Collins has justly observed, "the first English author who fully established this most important practical distinction in the treatment of uterine hæmorrhages, although Levret had many years before published a somewhat similar statement." Dr. Rigby's arrangement has been adopted by Dr. Merriman, Dewees, and every other modern author of any note; and the medical world have amply testified their sense of its value, as well as of the work itself in general, by the numerous editions which it has undergone in this, and translations and reprints in other countries.

We have entered into an historical detail of the literature of this subject, from its having been asserted that Dr. Rigby "published an abstract of the doctrines of Puzos and Levret with the addition of some cases from his own practice," (Burns, Principles of Midwifery, 9th ed., 1837, p. 364;) that he availed himself of the discoveries of Dr. Smellie and M. Levret, while he contrived to make the profession believe that his doctrines were original, (Hamilton, Practical Observations, &c., 1836, vol. ii. p. 238;) and that "no fact of the slightest importance has since (Smellie) been discovered relating to the causes and treatment of uterine hæmorrhage in the latter months of pregnancy." (Dr. R. Lee, Edin. Med. and Surg. Journ., 1839, vol. li. p. 389.) We, therefore, deem it only just to our readers, and also to the author, to lay before them his own account of what, at the time, he supposed to be a discovery, and how far he considered himself justified in laying claim to its originality.

"A case of hæmorrhage, in which I found the placenta attached to the os uteri, occurred at a very early period of my practice; but not finding such a circumstance recorded in the lectures which I had attended, or taken notice of in the common elementary treatises on midwifery, I considered it at first merely as a casual and rare deviation from nature.

In a few years, however, so many similar instances fell under my notice, as to convince me, that it was a circumstance necessary to be inquired after in every case of hæmorrhage: and this conviction was confirmed by the perusal of cases in midwifery; for I then found that the fact of the placenta being thus situated had been recorded by many writers, though in no instance which had then reached me, had any practical inferences been deduced from it. It appeared to me, indeed, most extraordinary that such a fact, known to so many celebrated practitioners, should not long before have led to its practical application, and in consequence to more fixed principles in the treatment of hæmorrhages from the gravid uterus; and I may, perhaps, be allowed to say, that I congratulated myself, young in years and practice as I was, in[Pg 401] being, probably, the first to suggest an important improvement in the treatment of one of the most perplexing and dangerous cases in midwifery; and that I committed my observations on the subject to paper, not only under a conviction of their practical utility, but certainly also under an impression that my suggestions were original.

"Not long after the first edition was at press, indeed before the first sheet was printed, Levret's dissertation on this subject fell into my hands, and in a note I referred to it as additional testimony in proof of the placenta, in these cases, being originally attached to the os uteri.

"I have been led into this little detail, because it has been suggested that I have borrowed my theory from Levret. After remarking the gross folly I should have been guilty of in quoting Levret, had I furtively adopted his opinions, it will, I trust, be sufficient for me unequivocally to declare that my original ideas on the subject were derived solely from my own personal observation and experience; and that having previously neither read nor heard of the placenta being ever fixed to the os uteri, the knowledge of such a circumstance, derived as before observed, came to me and impressed me as a discovery.

"I was, certainly, afterwards struck with the coincidence of the sentiments of Levret and myself on the subject, with the similarity of our practical deductions, and, allowing for the difference of language, even with the sameness of our expressions. I am farther not reluctant to acknowledge, that after reading Levret's dissertation, I felt less entitled to the claim of absolute originality on the subject; and I now rest perfectly satisfied to divide with him the credit arising from the mere circumstance of communicating a new physiological fact. But were I even denied all claim to originality, I should still not be without the satisfaction of having, at least, materially contributed to diffuse the knowledge of an important fact, and of having established its practical utility on the unequivocal testimony of experience; for, had I seen Levret's dissertation sooner, or had even my attention been first directed to the subject by its perusal, ought it to have superseded my publication? Was the practice in this country, at that time, at all influenced by Levret's dissertation? or has it even since been translated into the English language? Was it, at that time, generally known that the attachment of the placenta to the os uteri was a frequent cause of hæmorrhage? and were any directions for our conduct in these cases, founded on the knowledge of the fact, given by those who there lectured on the art of midwifery?

"Levret's facts, moreover, though they proved that the placenta might be originally attached to the os uteri, (and a single instance would establish this,) were scarcely sufficient to prove the frequency of its occurrence, from which alone arises the[Pg 402] necessity of practically attending to it in every case of hæmorrhage. His observations (perhaps even more creditable to him for being founded on such scanty materials) were derived from four cases only, and of these, but two were under his own immediate cognizance; whereas, in the first edition of this essay my opinions were supported by 36 detailed cases, in 13 of which the placenta was found at the os uteri; and in the fourth edition the number was increased to 106, 43 of which were this peculiar original situation of the placenta." (Preface to the 5th ed.)

The causes of this peculiar deviation from the usual situation of the placenta are little if at all known. The condition of the decidua shortly after the entrance of the ovum into the cavity of the uterus, will probably influence the situation of the placenta considerably. Under the ordinary circumstances, this effusion of plastic lymph has already attained such a degree of firmness and coherence as to prevent the ovum from passing beyond the uterine extremity of the Fallopian tube from which it has emerged; but in cases of placental presentation it may be presumed that at this period the decidua was still in a semi-fluid state, had formed little or no attachment to the walls of the uterus, and had, therefore, no effect in preventing the ovum gravitating to the lower part, or even to the mouth of the uterus itself. We state this, of course, as a mere matter of theory, since the difficulty of investigation at such early periods, and the comparative rarity of placental presentations, will probably ever prevent our ascertaining the real cause.

Symptoms. The first symptom which warns us that the placenta is presenting, is the sudden appearance of hæmorrhage, which is usually more copious than ordinary hæmorrhage, and apparently comes on without any assignable reason: it is usually the more profuse the nearer the patient is to the full term of pregnancy, for not only now are the ruptured vessels larger, but the separation of the placenta is generally greater. If she has still some time to go, the discharge will be probably slight, and with rest and quiet, &c., will cease, to return again in ten days or a fortnight with increased violence: this usually happens at what would have been a catamenial period. The suddenness of its attack, the profuseness of the discharge, and its coming on without any evident cause, are peculiarly suspicious.

It has been stated that the abdomen is less distended in these cases than usual, from the placenta not being in the upper parts of the uterus: it is an observation, however, which requires to be confirmed, and certainly our own experience, as yet, has not led us to such a conclusion.

On examination, the os uteri is found to be larger and thicker than ordinary: it has a loose spongy feel, for its vessels are now as immensely distended as those of the fundus, when the placenta[Pg 403] has its usual situation. If the placenta be partially attached over the os uteri, it is generally upon the anterior lip, which is much thicker. In this case we shall feel the edge of the placenta projecting at one side of the os uteri, and the bladder of membranes, and probably the presenting part of the child at the other. Whereas, if the placenta be centrally attached, we shall find it attached to the whole circumference, except perhaps where the separation is, from which the hæmorrhage proceeds. We shall distinguish the placenta by its spongy mass, by its soft irregular surface, and by the stringy feel which it communicates where it has been torn.

The character of the hæmorrhage is also different from that of common hæmorrhage, inasmuch as it increases during a pain, and diminishes or ceases during the intervals, whereas, in hæmorrhage under ordinary circumstances it is the reverse.

Where the hæmorrhage takes place at some distance of time from the full period of utero-gestation, it probably arises from the gradual development of the cervix during the latter months of pregnancy: where, on the other hand, it does not appear till just before labour, the separation of the placenta will have been the incipient dilatation of the os uteri itself. It might therefore be supposed, that the period of the attack would, in great measure, depend upon whether the placenta was centrally, or only partially, attached to the os uteri; that in the former case the placenta would be more liable to be separated by the gradual development of the inferior segment of the uterus; and that, therefore, hæmorrhage would come on several weeks before the full term; whereas, if only a portion of it cover the edge of the os uteri, the patient would probably go to the very end of pregnancy before any flooding appeared. Although this view is supported by the high authority of Professor Naegelé, still we can scarcely agree with it, since not only do a considerable majority of recorded cases show that a patient with central presentation of the placenta may go to the full time without an attack of flooding, but also several of those which have come under our own observation lead to a similar conclusion.

The most alarming attacks of hæmorrhage are doubtless at the full term, when the os uteri is beginning to dilate from commencing uterine contractions, and the placenta is centrally attached over it: in these cases the discharge experiences little or no abatement beyond an occasional short remission, but returns with the pains, increasing in profuseness as the gradually dilating os uteri produces a still farther separation of the placenta. Such cases, if left to themselves, would almost necessarily prove fatal. The first fainting fit or two would probably produce a temporary cessation of the discharge, and favour the formation of coagula in the upper part of the vagina; but with returning contractions of the uterus, the hæmorrhage would be renewed with increased[Pg 404] violence, and quickly reduce the vital powers. In such cases the patient will probably die undelivered, or soon after the birth of a dead child. In some rare instances, the pains have been sufficiently powerful to force the head through the placenta, and thus enable the mother to be delivered by the natural means, although with little chance of the child being born alive, from the injury which the fœtal vessels in the placenta have received. Portal's twenty-ninth case terminated in this way. A similar and very interesting case was lately communicated to us by Mr. W. White, of Heathfield, in Sussex, where the placenta appears to have been centrally attached to the os uteri, and where, in consequence of two or three powerful pains, the head was forced through, tearing it quite across. The child was born dead, but the mother did well.

In a few rare cases the placenta has been entirely separated and expelled before the child, but these have usually been attended with a most alarming loss of blood. In almost all the cases related by Mauriceau, and in the majority of those by Giffard, the placenta is stated to have been entirely detached from the uterus, but this was evidently under the mistaken supposition of the placenta having been originally separated from the fundus. "It is extremely rare to meet with a total separation of the placenta. Dr. Clarke informed me that he met with but one case of total separation; the patient dying before he reached the house." (Collin's Pract. Treatise, p. 92.) A still more remarkable instance is recorded by Dr. Collins, where the placenta had been expelled many hours (probably about 18) before the birth of the child. "The membranes had ruptured, and the waters been discharged a fortnight previous to admission, from which time, until the evening before she was brought to the hospital, she had more or less hæmorrhage. It was now ascertained that the placenta had been expelled the evening before her admission, and separated by the midwife in attendance. She left the hospital well on the thirteenth day."[144] (Op. cit. p. 103.) In all these cases the child has been born dead, and must ever be so, where any period of time has elapsed between the expulsion of the placenta and that of the child. The only case we know of where a living child was born after the expulsion of the placenta is recorded by F. Ould. "I found this woman in imminent danger, being seized with faintings and hiccough, having her face pale and Hippocratic. Upon examination, I found the placenta presented to the orifice of the womb, which I immediately extracted; and although the head was far advanced in the passage, I put it back into the womb, and taking hold of the feet brought a living[Pg 405] though very weakly child into the world. The mother also recovered, though with much difficulty." (Treatise on Midwifery, p. 77.) La Motte has described a similar case, but where the child died immediately after birth. (Obs. 238.)

The irregularity with which cases of placental presentation have appeared at different times, have more than once excited notice: thus it frequently happens to ourselves that several years have elapsed without our meeting with a single case, although connected with a large lying-in hospital; whereas, at other times two or three cases have followed each other at comparatively short intervals. In selecting ten successive years from the period during which Dr. Rigby observed the numerous cases recorded in his essay, we see this irregularity remarkably exemplified.

In 1779 three cases.
In 1780 four cases.
In 1781 none.
In 1782 five cases.
In 1783 one case.
In 1784 five cases.
In 1785 two cases.
In 1786 two cases.
In 1787 one case.
In 1788 two cases.

A still more remarkable variation has been described by the celebrated Matthias Saxtorph, of Copenhagen. Having stated that placental presentation had occurred only once in 3600 cases, he adds, "the reader will be astonished when I assure him that this case, which is so rare that I had only seen it twice in so many years, and that I had met with it but once out of so many thousand labours at our lying-in hospital, occurred to me in the last six months, eight times." (Collect. Soc. Med. Havn. 1774, vol. i. p. 310.) Professor Naegelé has made a similar remark in his lectures, and states, that in some years placental presentation was so frequent that it seemed as if it were almost epidemic.

Experience proves beyond doubt, that, of the serious floodings which occur during the last weeks of pregnancy, the majority arise from the attachment of the placenta to the os uteri. Dr. Rigby also states "that this attachment of the placenta to the os uteri is much oftener a cause of floodings than authors and practitioners are aware of, I am from experience fully satisfied; and so far am I convinced of its frequent occurrence, that I am ready to believe that most, if not all, of those cases which require turning the child, are this unfortunate situation of it."

The period of pregnancy at which hæmorrhage may come on from placental presentation, varies very considerably. Although, in by far the majority of these cases, it does not come on until the last four or six weeks, it now and then occurs at a much earlier period, viz. the sixth or even the fifth month, and sometimes even earlier. Where this is the case, it must rather be[Pg 406] looked upon as one of "accidental" hæmorrhage or abortion, for it can scarcely be supposed that any changes about the os or cervix uteri could have been sufficient to have produced an "unavoidable" separation of the placenta at this time. Thus, for instance, in Dr. Rigby's seventy-fifth case, the first attack of hæmorrhage had appeared when the patient "was about three months gone with child;" and at that early period could hardly have been attributed to the peculiar situation of the placenta, but to the more common causes of hæmorrhage connected with abortion. In his forty-third case, the hæmorrhage, which came on about the twenty-sixth week, appears at first to have been purely "accidental," although it was afterwards "unavoidable" attachment of the placenta. "We very seldom meet with unavoidable hæmorrhage before the sixth month of pregnancy; it is not until the cervix uteri begins to distend freely, and the changes that take place previous to the approach of labour commence, any suspicions are observed; consequently, it will be in the last three months of utero-gestation that hæmorrhage of this nature is found to occur." (Collins, op. cit. p. 93.)

The examination of a case where the placenta presents is not always easy; the natural position of the os uteri during the latter months of pregnancy in the upper part of the hollow of the sacrum makes it very difficult for the finger to reach so completely as to afford us the means of ascertaining satisfactorily whether the placenta be attached to it or not. "For this purpose, however, the usual method with one finger will not always suffice, but the hand must be introduced into the vagina, and one finger insinuated into the uterus; for in several of the following cases it will appear, that though the women were frequently examined in the usual way, the placenta was not discovered till the hand was admitted for the purpose of turning the child." (Essay, 6th ed. p. 35.)

Treatment. We have already stated that the earlier the period at which the flooding comes on, the less profuse it will be; the treatment, therefore, where the hæmorrhage is inconsiderable, differs but little from that in an ordinary case of abortion or miscarriage. The indications, in fact, are the same, viz. to stop the discharge, and allay any disposition to uterine contraction.

The patient must be placed upon a mattress, and covered as lightly as possible with safety and tolerable comfort to herself. If the circulation be active, the pulse strong, with more or less heat of surface, it may even be desirable to reduce this by means of the lancet. "Under any kind of active hæmorrhage, when the pulse is vigorous, the taking away blood from the arm has uniformly been found useful, by producing contraction by the mere unloading of the vessels, and more especially in diminishing the velocity of blood within them." (Dewees, Compend.[Pg 407] Syst. of Midw. p. 441.) Cold cloths must be applied to the vulva, loins, and over the symphisis pubis; gentle saline laxatives with nitrate of potass should be given if the bowels are confined; and if there be the slightest appearance of the pains, an injection of twenty or thirty drops of Liq. Opii Sedat. into the rectum will be necessary. This may be given immediately where the bowels are not confined, or, if they are, after the rectum has been washed out by a large domestic enema. If necessary, she should also take an opiate by the mouth. Her food must consist of little else than plain drinks, as tea, milk and water, &c., all of which must be taken cold; and she must preserve the most perfect quiet of body as well as mind. We cannot agree with Dr. Dewees in permitting "our patients, under treatment for uterine hæmorrhage, to be five or six days without a discharge from the bowels;" as a loaded state of the lower bowels cannot fail in our opinion to obstruct seriously the free return of the circulation from the pelvic viscera, and thus greatly increase the disposition to congestion and hæmorrhage.

The longer the patient has still to go, the more desirable is it that we should, if possible, control the symptoms, and prevent them from proceeding to such extent as to require artificial delivery. It is of the utmost consequence that we should take such measures as will enable the pregnancy to go on safely, if not to the full time, at least to a later period, for by this means the uterus will have attained such a degree of development as will enable the turning to be undertaken with ease to the practitioner and with safety to the mother; the child also will have so far advanced towards maturity as to give it a better chance of surviving the operation.

Wherever hæmorrhage has occurred during the last three months of pregnancy, which has come on suddenly and without any assignable reason, we should earnestly warn the patient and her friends to summon the practitioner the moment there are any symptoms of its return; for if it be a case of placental presentation, it assuredly will return, and as certainly much more profusely than at first.

Where the patient has gone nearly or quite to her full time, the first attack is much more alarming; the hæmorrhage frequently appears with a sudden gush, and in a few minutes a serious and even dangerous quantity of blood is lost; thus a patient whom we had seen but a few hours previously in perfect health, was suddenly seized with profuse flooding as she was standing at the door of her house speaking to a person, and before she could move, a large pool of blood had formed at her feet; in another case, the patient while standing at her tea-table was attacked in a similar manner, and in a moment the floor was deluged with the discharge.

Although artificial delivery by turning the child is required in[Pg 408] every case of central presentation of the placenta during the latter periods of pregnancy, it is evident that this will not apply during the earlier months, when the uterus from its size will preclude the possibility of such an operation. Dr. Rigby has established a valuable axiom on this point, viz. "that when the uterus is too small for the admission of the hand, the expulsion of the placenta and fœtus will happily be timely effected by nature. It is well known that in the early months, instances of fatal termination by floodings have been very rare, as abortion sooner or later puts a stop to the discharge. It has been likewise before observed, that in floodings at any period of pregnancy, women seldom die, at least not in the first instance, unless a considerable quantity of blood has been suddenly lost. Now, as the danger of a great and sudden loss must obviously depend upon the size of the uterine vessels, and as the enlargement of the vessels is in exact proportion to the increased size of the uterus, it becomes probable that when the vessels have acquired such a magnitude, that when detached from the placenta they would bleed largely and suddenly, the uterus itself must have attained to such a capacity as to admit the hand for artificial delivery." (Op. cit. p. 48, 6th ed.) He farther observes, "that as the most material increase of the uterus does not take place until the end of the sixth month of pregnancy, a hæmorrhage before that period will seldom require artificial delivery; and after that period, should it become necessary, that it is probable the hand may then be admitted for that purpose." (Ibid. p. 51.)

In almost every case where the patient is some time short of her full time, the os uteri will be found unyielding and but little dilated; it will, therefore, seldom be possible, and scarcely ever proper, to introduce the hand into the uterus under such circumstances; the os uteri either entirely resists our efforts, or if we do overcome it, the degree of force required to effect this has been so great, as will in all probability have been attended with serious injury to the part itself. In no case is it proper or safe to force delivery by artificially dilating the os uteri, when it is contracted and unyielding (see Turning;) but where the placenta is presenting, it is peculiarly dangerous, for even slight laceration of the os uteri will be followed by serious consequences. Where the placenta is situated in the upper part of the uterus, it is of very little consequence if the edge of the os uteri has been torn somewhat during labour; but in the present case it is very different; the os uteri now plays the part of the fundus, its vessels are immensely dilated, and large ones are ruptured, which cannot be closed by the firmest contraction of the uterus.

"In recommending early delivery, I think it right, however, to express a caution against the premature introduction of the hand, and the too forcible dilatation of the os uteri before it is sufficiently relaxed by pain or discharge; for it is undoubtedly very[Pg 409] certain that the turning may be performed too soon as well as too late, and that the consequences of the one may be as destructive to the patient as the other." (Rigby, op. cit. p. 37.) Cases have occurred where the os uteri has been artificially dilated, where the child was turned and delivered with perfect safety, and the uterus contracted into a hard ball; in fact, every thing seemed to have passed over favourably; a continued dribbling of blood has remained after labour, which resisted every attempt to check it; friction upon the abdomen and other means for stopping hæmorrhage by inducing firm contraction of the uterus were of no use, for the uterus was already hard and well contracted; the patient has gradually become exhausted, and at last died; on examination after death, Professor Naegelé has invariably found the os uteri more or less torn.

"It must be acknowledged, indeed," says Dr. Rigby, "that it may sometimes happen that at the very first coming on of the complaint, if the discharge be small, and more especially, if it be the patient's first child, and the parts be close and unyielding, the admission of the hand into the vagina, as I have directed, will be attended with the utmost difficulty, and, perhaps, be almost impracticable: in this case let us wait (but let it be with the patient) till the discharge increases, and has continued long enough to relax the parts; for certainly, if the woman be able to bear losing a little blood, which at first she may safely do, the examination will be thereby rendered more easy, and the turning of the child, if necessary, be more practicable and safe." (Op. cit. p. 36.)

We have already shown (see Turning, p. 236.) that there is no means of rendering a rigid os uteri yielding and capable of admitting the hand equal to the relaxation loss of blood: wherever the powers of the system have already suffered from the effects of hæmorrhage, we may feel almost certain that we shall find the os uteri capable of dilating, even if it be so little open as barely to admit the finger. Where the patient has become faint or fallen into actual syncope, the relaxation of the soft parts is very striking, and frequently to an extent which could scarcely be believed by those who have not felt it; all resistance seems to be at an end for the time, and the hand enters the flaccid passages with scarcely a sensation of pressure from them, but rather (as has been aptly compared, to that of some wet bladder wrapped around it.)

"It has been advised (observes Dr. Rigby) never to introduce the hand till nature has shown some disposition to relieve herself by the dilatation of the os uteri to the size of a shilling, or a half-crown; and this rule is certainly founded on a rational principle, for when it is so much dilated, there is no doubt but the turning may be easily and safely effected; but from some of the annexed cases it appears that a dilatation to this degree sometimes does not take place at all; and that even when the woman is dying from the[Pg 410] great loss of blood, the uterus is very little open; the reason for which, seems to be, that when the discharge has been considerable, and more particularly when much blood has been suddenly lost, such a faintness is brought on, that though the uterus be totally relaxed, and might, therefore, be opened by the most gentle efforts, yet nature is unable to make use of these efforts; and, moreover, if there be slight pains, the adhesion of the placenta to the internal surface of the mouth of the womb, counteracts their influence, and thereby hinders its giving way to a power, which would otherwise, probably, very easily open it." (Op. cit. p. 39.)

Plug. Where, however, the case is at that doubtful period of early pregnancy, when even under the most favourable circumstances, as above-mentioned, the hand must experience considerable difficulty in entering the os uteri, and yet the expulsion of the child cannot be safely trusted to the natural powers, it becomes necessary, as in certain cases of premature expulsion, to have recourse to such means as shall enable the os uteri to go on dilating without the danger of farther hæmorrhage; in other words, we must plug the vagina. "If, after the commencement of a flooding, we favour the formation of a coagulum by means of a plug, are we not aiding nature? It brings on labour much sooner, and the os uteri has time to dilate without farther loss of blood." (Leroux, Sur les Pertes de Sang. § 309.) By means of the plug, we enable the patient to go on with perfect security until the pains have produced a sufficient dilatation of the os uteri to admit the hand; after a time we may withdraw it, and if then not satisfied with the state of the os uteri, it must be again introduced until our object be effected. (For directions as to the use of the plug we must refer to p. 152.)

"This remedy should be early employed, as it will, by proper management, save a prodigious expenditure of blood. We gain by its application important time; time that is essential for the successful delivery of the fœtus; for, by it, the woman's strength is preserved; pain is permitted to increase; and, eventually, though tardily, the os uteri is dilated, the placenta and fœtus thrown off, and the flooding almost immediately controlled. The other means which we have constantly pointed out, should also be tried: they may aid the general intentions, and render the operation of the tampon more certain." (Dewees, Compend. Syst. of Midw. § 1142.)

Although Dr. Rigby has given a short account of Leroux's views respecting the use of the plug in these cases, we cannot but agree with Dr. Dewees, in regretting that he either did not "put his plan in execution," or that if he did, he has not given us the details of his experience upon it. From what Dr. Gooch, however, has stated in his Account of some of the more important Diseases peculiar to Women, there is every reason to suppose that Dr. Rigby was latterly in the frequent habit of using the plug,[Pg 411] and that he thought highly of it. The plug is not only useful in keeping the hæmorrhage under due control until the os uteri be sufficiently dilated, but may occasionally prove of the greatest value in cases of extreme exhaustion from loss of blood, where the patient is too much reduced to undergo the act of delivery, without running the risk of dying during the operation; the plug will enable us to wait with safety until the system has had time to rally its powers and be recruited by the administration of proper nourishment. "Mr. Grainger, of Birmingham, on visiting a poor woman with placenta prævia, and apparently in a moribund condition, immediately filled the vagina and os uteri with linen cloths, and waited two days before he durst hazard delivery, which he accomplished with an auspicious result." (Ingleby, on Uterine Hæmorrhage, p. 155.)

Turning. The operation of turning the child will, in no wise, differ from that under more ordinary circumstances, and will require to be conducted according to the rules which we have already given. In no case is it more important to preserve the membranes unruptured until the hand has fairly entered the uterus than here; the hand should be carefully insinuated between the os uteri and placenta; if possible, this should be done at the part where the separation which has caused the flooding has already taken place, in order to avoid all unnecessary detachment of the placenta; the pressure of the hand prevents any great discharge of blood; and as it gradually makes its way between the membranes and the uterus, the arm which now occupies the vagina will effectually act as a plug. Portal, was, probably the first who practised this mode of operation, viz. passing his hand between the os uteri and placenta, and then between the uterus and membranes before rupturing them: in this respect he anticipated Peu, whose work appeared nine years after, (see Turning, p. 234.) and would have undoubtedly been looked upon as the originator of this improvement in turning, had he given any reasons for this mode of practice, or deduced any inferences from it.

Some discrepancy of opinion has existed as to whether it is better to perforate the placenta, or to follow the plan we have just recommended. Dr. Rigby's authority has rather tended to confirm the former opinion, although he afterwards modifies it so much so as to make us almost suppose that he must have preferred the other method. He states, "that by this means, (perforating the placenta,) not more of the placenta may be separated than is necessary for the introduction of the hand, and, consequently, that as little increase of bleeding as possible may be the operation; but if it be impracticable, as I have more than once found it, and it must ever be when the middle of the placenta presents to the hand, from the thickness of it near the funis, it must be carefully separated from the uterus on one side,[Pg 412] and the hand passed till it gets to the membranes." (Op. cit. p. 61.)

To Dr. Dewees are we chiefly indebted for having put the inexpediency of perforating the placenta in the strongest possible light. "We are advised by some," says he, "to pierce the placenta with the hand; but this should never be done, especially as it is impossible to assign one single good reason for the practice, and there are several very strong ones against it.

"1. In attempting this, much time is lost that is highly important to the patient, as the flooding unabatingly, if not increasingly, goes on.

"2. In this attempt we are obliged to force against the membranes, so as to carry or urge the whole placentary mass towards the fundus of the uterus; by which means the separation of it from the neck is increased, and consequently, the flooding augmented.

"3. When the hand has even penetrated the cavity of the uterus, the hole which is made by it is no greater than itself, and consequently much too small for the fœtus to pass through without a forced enlargement, and this must be done by the child during its passage.

"4. As the hole made by the body of the child is not sufficiently large for the arms and head to pass through at the same time, they will consequently be arrested; and if force be applied to overcome this resistance, it will almost always separate the whole of the placenta from its connexion with the uterus.

"5. That when this is done, it never fails to increase the discharge, besides adding the bulk of the placenta to that of the arms and head of the child.

"6. When the placenta is pierced, we augment the risk of the child; for in making the opening, we may destroy some of the large umbilical veins, and thus permit the child to die from hæmorrhage.

"7. By this method we increase the chance of an atony of the uterus, as the discharge of the liquor amnii is not under due control.

"8. That it is sometimes impossible to penetrate the placenta, especially when its centre answers to the centre of the os uteri; in this instance much time is lost that may be very important to the woman." (Op. cit. § 1153.)

We have already stated why it is so particularly important not to use any force in passing the hand through the os uteri: the less we separate the placenta, the less also will be the hæmorrhage; and even this will be in great measure controlled by the presence and pressure of the hand itself. In no case of turning is it so important to have all the circumstances connected with the operation as favourable as possible, for the case[Pg 413] itself is sufficiently dangerous without being increased by other unfavourable causes. To hurry the delivery would be only to increase the danger: the operation must be performed slowly and with caution: every rule which we have given, (see Turning,) for ensuring its safe and successful termination, must now be adhered to with double vigilence. "Should the woman," says Dr. Dewees, "be very much exhausted before we commence our operations, we should use additional caution in the delivery. It should be very slowly performed, and we should have at each step of the progress assurances, if possible, that the uterus has not lost, or rather that it possesses, sufficient contractility to render the completion of the operation eventually safe, if performed with due and necessary care." (Op. cit. p. 463.)

When once the os uteri is sufficiently dilated to admit the hand, there will not be much fear of the patient losing much blood during the turning, for during the first part of the operation the hand and arm act both as a compress and plug; and afterwards, when the body of the child is advancing, this will act in a similar manner. There is little danger of hæmorrhage coming on after the child is delivered, for the contraction of that part of the uterus to which the placenta has been attached is much greater in these cases than it is where the placenta is situated in the upper parts of the uterus under ordinary circumstances. The placenta, which is already separated to a certain extent by the introduction of the hand, usually comes away without any trouble as soon as the child is delivered. We once met with a case where it was firmly adherent to the os uteri on one side, and required to be artificially removed, which was effected without difficulty. In this instance, hæmorrhage returned after the labour from uterine inertia, and was checked by the means already recommended. (Med. Gaz. Sep. 2, 1837.) The after treatment should be conducted upon the same principles as in other cases of hæmorrhage.

Partial presentation of the placenta. Where this is the case, the danger is rarely so alarming, nor is it always necessary to effect artificial delivery by turning. The edge of the placenta frequently projects but a very little over that of the os uteri, feeling, as it were, like a second lip; at other times it covers a third or more of the opening, and is usually attached upon the anterior portion of it. Our own observations have rather led to the conclusion, that where the placenta is but partially attached over the os uteri, the first attack of flooding is rarely delayed until the full term of pregnancy, but makes its appearance some weeks earlier. We are inclined to attribute this to the os uteri being only in part covered with placenta; that its other portion, being free, is more capable of dilatation from slight causes, than it would be were the placenta centrally attached: from a similar[Pg 414] reason we may understand why the hæmorrhage is seldom so profuse in these cases as to be dangerous, and why the os uteri usually dilates sufficiently soon to allow the head to descend and be born by the natural powers. We are confirmed in this view by what we have already quoted from Dr. Rigby respecting the os uteri being prevented dilating by the close adhesion of the placenta—an opinion which is, moreover, approved of by Dr. Dewees as being "both ingenious and probable." Hence, also, we may reverse our position, and say, that in a case of partial presentation of the placenta, we shall seldom find the hæmorrhage very profuse, until the os uteri has attained a considerable degree of dilatation. Besides the portion of placenta which presents, there will be also a bag of membranes occupying the remaining portion of the opening; we shall rarely, if ever, meet with those difficulties connected with a contracted and unyielding state of the os uteri, which we described in cases of central presentation; and if the hand requires to be introduced, which is not often the case, it will seldom experience much opposition.

Treatment. In our treatment of partial presentation of the placenta, we must be guided, in a great measure, by the strength of the pains and the degree of dilatation which the os uteri has attained; the extent to which it is covered by the edge of the placenta, must also be taken into consideration. Where the pains are strong and active, the pressure of the membranes distended by liquor amnii against the mouth of the womb will be sufficient to check the hæmorrhage; if not, by rupturing them we shall be enabled to let off the liquor amnii, and thus allow the head to press directly upon the os uteri, and act in the double capacity of a plug and compress. Where the pains are slow and inactive, the rupture of the membranes will diminish the size of the uterus, and thus excite it to more powerful contraction; if not, a dose of secale cornutum, repeated according to circumstances, will be of great assistance. If the patient has suffered a good deal by the loss of blood, a little beef-tea, in small quantities frequently repeated, will rouse the powers; wine or a little brandy, may also be given at intervals; but unless the prostration be very serious, we have not found stimulants so useful as beef-tea, which is usually, also, much more grateful.

[Pg 415]

CHAPTER XIII.

PUERPERAL FEVERS.

Nature and varieties of puerperal fever.—Vitiation of the blood.—Different species of puerperal fever.—Puerperal peritonitis.—Symptoms.—Appearances after death.—Treatment.—Uterine phlebitis.—Symptoms.—Appearances after death.—Treatment.—Indications.—False peritonitis.—Treatment.—Gastro-bilious puerperal fevers.—Symptoms.—Appearances after death.—Treatment.—Contagious, or adynamic, puerperal fevers.—Symptoms.—Appearances after death.—Treatment.

In enumerating the different species of Dystocia, we have mentioned a long list of causes, by which the process of labour might be rendered one of considerable danger either to the mother or her child; but, for the most part, they are not of very common occurrence, those only which are of trifling import being met with most frequently. Even under the most dangerous forms of dystocia, as for instance, convulsions, and the different forms of hæmorrhage, the danger, although great, is capable of being averted, from the mother at least, in the majority of instances by timely and skilful assistance; the means of treatment which art and experience have supplied us with, being generally capable of affording both certain and effective relief, if used according to the rules which we have given when treating of these subjects; but we now come to a source of danger which follows the most favourable as well as unfavourable labours—which is extremely varied in its nature, fatal in its effects, and (what renders it so peculiarly formidable) by no means uncommon in its occurrence.

Of all the dangers to which a lying-in woman is exposed, puerperal fever is by far the most to be dreaded: there are few or no difficulties during parturition which the practitioner has to contend with that can be compared to it; there are none in which he is frequently made to feel so helpless, and his various means of treatment so utterly inefficacious; certain it is that puerperal fever in its worst forms has occasionally committed such ravages among patients of this class as to rival in destructiveness the most malignant pestilences with which the human race has been afflicted.

[Pg 416]One of the greatest improvements in our knowledge of puerperal fever which has taken place in modern times, is the having ascertained that it is not one specific disease, but occurs under different forms, each of which is subject to a good deal of variety, depending upon individual peculiarity, season of the year, and numberless other circumstances. The chief error into which authors have fallen when treating of this difficult subject, is their having merely described the peculiar form of disease which had come under their own notice, and to which they have exclusively awarded the name of puerperal fever—an error in judgment which has led to still greater errors in practice, and which has certainly tended to prevent the subject being so clearly understood as it might have been. The mode also in which it has been investigated by modern authors has been but of little assistance in disclosing the true features of the disease; they have indeed rather tended to mislead than to guide us, they have directed our attention to certain effects of it, which they have considered to be the disease itself, and thus rather conceal than disclose the real natura morbi.

In our printed lectures on puerperal fever we have taken a similar view. "I am not sure if the present fashionable morbid anatomy of the day, misnamed pathology, has assisted so much in developing the real nature of the disease as has been supposed: it appears to me rather to have withdrawn the attention of practitioners from a close observation of the phenomena presented during life, to the inspection of those changes which are to be found after death. They have rather sought to examine the effects of the disease at a time when it had attained such an extent as to be incompatible with life, than to investigate upon correct and physiological grounds the series of changes which were taking place during the earlier periods." (London Med. and Surg. Journ. June 27, 1835.) Dr. Alison, of Edinburgh, in his dissertation on the state of medical science (Cyc. Prac. Med.) has taken a similar view of this prevailing mode of investigating the nature of disease; he considers that it is "an important practical error to fix the attention, particularly of students of the profession, too much on those characters of disease which are drawn from changes of structure already effected, and to trust too exclusively to these as the diagnostics of different diseases, because in many instances these characters are not clearly perceptible until the latest and least remediable stage of diseases—the very object of the most important practice is to prevent the occurrence of the changes on which they depend. Accordingly, when this department of pathology is too exclusively cultivated, the attention of students is often found to be fixed on the lesions to be expected after death, much more than on the power and application of remedies either to control the diseased actions, or relieve the symptoms during life."

[Pg 417]"Pathological anatomy (says Dr. Stevens) is but one of the many 'points of view in which we may consider the science of disease,' and notwithstanding all that has been said about 'la médicine eclarireé par les ouvertures des cadavres,' I have a firm belief that morbid anatomy has done little good, particularly in the hands of those who do not understand its real value; for those who are constantly mistaking the effect for the cause, or confounding the immediate cause of death with the cause of the disease, and forming theories on this foundation, not only deceive themselves, but unfortunately, particularly for the inhabitants of hot climates, they have deceived others." (Obs. on the Healthy and Diseased Properties of the Blood, p. 182.)

We have made our last quotation from one of the most valuable and original works of the present day upon the subject of fevers, and which has tended in great measure to unveil the mysterious nature of these diseases. Dr. Steven's researches have been conducted in the truest spirit of pathological inquiry, and form a striking contrast with the modern morbid anatomy of puerperal fevers.

We use the term puerperal fevers precisely with the same meaning as Dr. Locock has done in his valuable essay on this subject (Library of Pract. Med. vol i.,) requesting our readers to bear in mind his observation, "that they vary in their nature and treatment as much as other kinds of fevers;" that whether occurring sporadically or in epidemics, they rarely, appear twice alike, but vary with the season of the year and the type of the prevailing fevers of the place; they are influenced by the rank, habits, and constitution of the patient, as well as by the nature and locality of her residence.

Although we cannot quite coincide with the views of Dr. Ferguson to their fullest extent, respecting the exclusive cause of the various forms of puerperal fever, viz. the vitiation of the fluids, still, in great measure, we consider them as correct, having not only taught them for many years, but published them in our lectures on this subject in 1835. Much praise is due to the last two mentioned authors for the able manner in which they have handled this difficult subject, they have carefully sifted the mass of jarring opinions, and tested them by their own great experience; and have not only reduced the subject to a simpler form, but have succeeded, we trust, in removing the very erroneous views of some modern authors respecting the supposed identity of certain forms of local inflammation with this disease.

Having drawn our information upon puerperal fevers from the same ample source, we willingly bear testimony to the accuracy with which they have described the different forms; and trust that in giving a detail of our own opinions and observations, it will be found that so far from differing from them, we have tended to confirm, reconcile, and carry out their views.

[Pg 418]Nature and varieties of puerperal fever. The history of puerperal fevers at the General Lying-in Hospital, would of itself afford an excellent monograph on this class of diseases in all their varied forms. When we resided at the hospital in 1826, the cases were all of the inflammatory character; they appeared to occur sporadically, among the out as well as the in-patients; and were successfully relieved by bleeding, hot poultices, and a mercurial purge, and occasionally leeches. During the following years, an epidemic of a highly malignant character spread destruction rapidly among the patients, setting at defiance the treatment previously employed. Still more remarkable was the sudden change in the character of the disease noticed by Dr. Locock in 1822. "In the spring of 1822, puerperal fever existed in the lying-in hospital in two very different and well-marked forms, at an interval of about six weeks between the last case of the first epidemic and first case of the second. The early cases were of an active inflammatory character; the peritoneal covering of the uterus and intestines was chiefly affected; the albuminous and serous effusions in the fatal cases showed a sthenic state of the system, that is, the serum was clear, the coagulable lymph firm and white; the patients bore blood-letting, and other active treatment to a great extent, fairly, and with much advantage; the blood drawn was strongly cupped and highly buffed, and the fatal cases were few. Six weeks afterwards a very different epidemic was found to exist. The same remedies which had been so beneficial a few weeks before, were naturally at first tried, but their bad success confirmed the sagacious remark of Gooch, that 'the effects of remedies form not only an essential but an important part of their history.' (Gooch on Peritoneal Fevers, p. 35.) The fever was attended with marked oppression and debility; the local pain was comparatively slight; the pulse was extremely rapid from the first, with no force, and easily compressible. In many of the cases, purulent deposites took place in the joints and in the calves of the legs, and in one case there was destructive inflammation of the eye." (Locock, op. cit. p. 349.)

The various forms and modifications under which puerperal fevers have appeared at different times, have produced an equal variety of arrangement in the classifications of authors. Thus, some who have attributed the disease to inflammation, have merely distinguished its varieties according to the different organs which have exhibited after death appearances of congested or injected vessels, or have been covered and imbedded in effusions of coagulable lymph, &c., or have had their structure more or less broken down and disorganized. Thus, for instance, Dr. R. Lee is of opinion, that "inflammation of the uterus and its appendages must be considered as essentially the cause of all the destructive febrile affections which follow parturition; and that the various forms they assume, inflammatory, congestive,[Pg 419] and typhoid, will in great measure be found to depend on whether the serous, the muscular, or the venous, tissue of the organ has become affected." (Med. Chir. Trans. vol. xv. part ii. p. 405, 1829.) He accordingly arranges "the principal varieties of inflammation of the uterus in puerperal women under the following heads, viz. 1. Inflammation of the peritoneal covering of the uterus, and of the peritoneal sac; 2. Inflammation of the uterine appendages, ovaria, fallopian tubes, and broad ligaments; 3. Inflammation of the muscular and mucous tissues of the uterus; 4. Inflammation and suppuration of the absorbent vessels and veins of the uterine organs." (Cyc. Pract. Med. art. Puerperal Fever.) This arrangement is manifestly incorrect, and by giving so partial a view of puerperal fevers, must, if adopted, necessarily lead to serious errors in practice. "That these forms of inflammation are the proximate cause of the various febrile affections is most completely refuted by the detail of his own (Dr. Lee's) experience, as relates to the varieties occurring under similar circumstances." (Moore, on Puerp. Fever.) We may also add, that, according to our own experience, and that of our colleagues at the General Lying-in Hospital, in the worst forms of puerperal fever, the fewest traces of inflammation have been observed; and that in the severest and most rapidly fatal cases it has frequently happened, that not a single vestige of inflammation could be detected. In our review of Mr. Moore's able work in the Brit. and For. Med. Rev. Oct. 1836, p. 483, we have made a similar remark, and quoted a striking passage from Dr. Stevens, when speaking of contagious fevers, that "there is not one symptom of inflammation during the fatal progress of the disease, nor one inflammatory spot to be seen after death, to mark its existence, or to induce us to believe that any thing but functional disease had existed in any of the solids; yet these are the very cases of all others which are the most fatal." (On the blood, p. 179.)

In many of the worst cases which have come under our notice, there has neither been time nor power sufficient to produce either a symptom or a trace of inflammation; the powers of life have from the very commencement sunk under the deadly influence of the disease, without a single effort to establish even a temporary reaction in the system: hence, in most instances, we are led to the necessary conclusion, that inflammation, when it does appear, is the result of disease, not the disease of inflammation. "For," as Dr. Ferguson observes, "if any or more of these (phlebitis, peritonitis, &c.) be assumed as constituting the essence of puerperal fever, abundant examples may be found of puerperal fever, in which the cause fixed on is absent. Thus to believers in the identity of peritonitis and puerperal fever, we can show puerperal fever with a perfect healthy peritoneum. To those who insist on inflammation of the uterine veins, as constituting puerperal fever,[Pg 420] we can show the genuine disease without this condition." (Essays on the most important Diseases of Women, part i. Puerperal Fever, p. 81.)

The vitiation of the blood has long been a subject which has excited our deepest interest, and the admirable researches of Dr. Stevens upon the condition of this fluid under the effects of malignant fevers, have tended to disclose the real nature of the diseases under consideration. We have long been convinced that one of the causes of puerperal fever is the absorption of putrid matters furnished by the coagula and discharges which are apt to be retained in the uterus and passages after parturition,—a view which has been adopted by Kirkland, C. White, and other older authors. It is with sincere pleasure that we now find ourselves supported by the able author, from whom we have just quoted, in this opinion. Dr. Ferguson's three positions respecting "the source and nature of puerperal fever" are highly valuable, for they have been deduced from careful physiological experiments, and not less sound physiological reasoning; they are as follows:—

1. The phenomena of puerperal fever originate in a vitiation of the fluids.

2. The causes which are capable of vitiating the fluids are particularly rife after childbirth.

3. The various forms of puerperal fever depend on this one cause, and may readily be deduced from it.

We do not agree with him in supposing that every form of puerperal inflammation is vitiation of the circulating fluids, because in one species of uterine phlebitis, which occurred sporadically, and prevailed a good deal from 1829 to 1832, it was, in our opinion, evidently produced directly by the absorption of putrid matter into the uterine veins and lymphatics, exciting inflammation in these vessels: the same cause, when only carried to a certain extent, produces a local inflammation, which, when affecting the general circulation, is followed by fever. Thus, then, we may have in the same case uterine phlebitis followed by the typhoid malignant puerperal fever—the local and constitutional disturbance arising from the same cause, imbibition or absorption of putrid matter; the one being the local, the other the general effect, but not the one resulting from the other. The doctrine of the vitiation of the blood from its admixture with pus secreted by the lining membrane of an inflamed vein, though very plausible, still requires farther confirmation, for it is doubtful if the introduction of pure healthy pus into the circulation produces any of those dangerous effects which result from the absorption of putrid matters, whether purulent, sanious, mucous, &c. It is the introduction into the circulation of an animal poison generated by putrefaction, which destroys the vitality of the blood, and renders it unfit for maintaining the vital powers.

[Pg 421]Few have expressed this opinion more strikingly than Dr. Kirkland, although so long ago as 1774; and it has often created our surprise, that amid all the numerous writings on this subject, which have excited attention during later years, so little notice should have been taken of his observations. We consider that Dr. Kirkland is one of the earliest authors who has shown that puerperal fever is not the result of inflammation, but that it may be the introduction of an animal poison into the circulation. "There are other causes beside inflammation which bring on a puerperal fever; for it sometimes happens that coagulated blood lodges in the uterus after delivery, and putrefying from access of air, forms a most active poison, is in part absorbed, and brings on a putrid fever. In this case the discharge which should immediately follow delivery is not sufficiently large, making allowance for the difference which happens to different women in this respect: small clots of blood make part of the lochia, which are less in quantity than they ought to be; but the patient has not any other sort of complaint for three or four days till the retained blood begins to putrefy. A fever then first makes its appearance, followed by a quick weak pulse, thirst, pain in the head, want of sleep, sighing, load at the præcordia, restlessness, great weakness, dejection of spirits, either wildness or despair in the countenance, and the white of the eyes is often a little inflamed." (A Treatise on Childbed Fevers, by Thos. Kirkland, M. D. p. 70.)

The late Mr. Charles White, of Manchester, adopted a similar opinion, and in our published lectures we have quoted largely from these two authors in support of the opinions which we have there advanced.

Dr. Ferguson's opinion, that the different modes in which the poison infecting the circulation manifests itself, give rise to the different forms of puerperal fever, is highly interesting, and deserves great attention. He conceives that in some instances it spends its virulence upon the peritoneum, producing the inflammatory peritoneal form of puerperal fever. He considers that the gastro-enteric form arises "from the action of the poison being directed to the liver, the organ through which, as the experiments of Gaspard and Fontana, and the admission of all physiologists show, most poisons received into the system endeavour to escape." (Op. cit. p. 85.) These views have been proved by injecting putrilage, &c., into the veins of animals, and the effects of which, both as seen in the symptoms during life and the appearances after death, tend strongly to confirm these opinions; still we cannot feel justified in excluding inflammatory forms which have not been indirectly the vitiation of the circulation, but which are the more direct effects of labour itself, or, as we have before observed, from the immediate absorption of putrilage, &c., into the veins and lymphatics, and production of inflammation in[Pg 422] them. The production of inflammation in that part of a vein or absorbent, with which putrid matter has come in immediate contact, is an important fact, for it is by this means that nature prevents the poison being carried into the general system, and thus, instead of generating a malignant fever, she limits the injury to a local inflammation, by which farther mischief is confined by the effusion of coaguable lymph, tumefaction, and other means for rendering the vessels impervious. In making these remarks we wish it to be distinctly understood, that we by no means under-value the views brought forward by Dr. Ferguson, that "the introduction of a poison into the circulation is capable of producing local inflammation, varying according to the strength and qualities of the agent," &c.

The results of Professor Tiedemann's experiments, of which we have given an abstract in the Brit. and For. Med. Rev. vol. i. p. 241, contain some facts which throw much light as to the modus operandi of certain agents when mingled with the circulation, and tend still farther to prove the correctness of Dr. Ferguson's views. In the experiments where musk was injected into the femoral vein of a small bitch, the effects of the poison upon the abdominal viscera were remarkable; the veins of the abdomen were distended with dark coloured blood, the whole intestinal canal was very red, the mucous membrane of the stomach had a reddish tinge; that of the whole intestinal canal was of a dark red, it was swollen, turgid, and in the highest state of engorgement—the canal also contained a quantity of effused dark blood in its lower part; the vessels of the liver and spleen were gorged with dark blood.

We are anxious to impress upon the minds of our readers the physiological fact, that most, if not all, vegetable and animal poisons do not act primarily on the nervous system, but indirectly through the medium of the circulation. "The physiological researches (as we have observed elsewhere) especially during the last thirty years, both in this country and the continent, have satisfactorily proved that most, if not all, of the agents which exert such destructive energies on the nervous system, do it through the medium of the circulation: this has been shown by the experiments of Christison and Coindet, of Brodie, Emmert, Viborg, and many others. Those of Sir B. Brodie on the action of the Woorara poison are well known. Emmert showed this to be the case in a still more striking manner, by amputating the leg of an animal, and leaving it connected to the body only by means of the nerves; poisonous substances introduced into the foot produced no effects, not even when applied to the trunk of the nerve; and Viborg even applied one drachm of concentrated prussic acid to the brain of a horse, which had been exposed by trepanning, without producing any effect." (Brit. and For. Med. Rev. vol. i. p. 559.)

[Pg 423]We cannot agree with the opinion, "that the vitiated state of the blood is the secondary and not the primary link in the chain of phenomena," and "that the nervous system is the main instrument by which this change in the blood takes place." (Locock, op. cit. p. 353.) "We believe that is not the deficiency of nervous influence which primarily tends to deteriorate this fluid (although it may possibly react in this way afterwards,) but the deteriorated condition of this fluid, which renders it incapable of supplying the brain and nervous system with their due degree of energy." (Brit. and For. Med. Rev. vol. ii. p. 483, 1836.)

In considering the phenomena of fever, Dr. Stevens has well observed, that we must not look upon them "as the result of either a nervous impression, or local inflammation, for even in the beginning of fever its symptoms are universal and peculiar to itself. It is not, therefore, a local affection; and in all the idiopathic fevers, but particularly in those that are the aerial poisons, there is but one thing which is never absent, namely, the diseased condition of the whole circulating current, and, therefore, this alone can be fairly considered as essential to the disease. This morbid condition of the blood is decidedly the first link in the chain of those phenomena which constitute fever, for even before the attack every drop of the vital currant is changed in its properties; and wherever this deranged blood can circulate, there fever extends its empire: for the cause which produces this disease is not confined to a part, but acts on every fibre, and in every tissue of the living system; it disturbs every function in the body, and deranges every faculty of the mind. All the excretions are in a diseased state, and every one of the secreted fluids is changed both in its quantity and quality. The blood is the medium that conveys the poison, while the impression on the nerves is merely the effect of the diseased condition of its natural stimulus." (On the Blood, p. 273.)

These observations just quoted, apply strictly to the causes as well as to the phenomena of puerperal fever, more especially of the adynamic kind; and show that, particularly in this form, we must not merely refer the cause to the absorption of putrid matters by the uterine veins and lymphatics, or to the commixture of the blood with pus secreted from the coats of an inflamed vein, but to the still more pervading and truly epidemic and contagious action of miasmata, with which the air that surrounds the patient is charged. The lungs afford a ready and ample means by which effluvia may be conveyed into the circulating current, and enables us to account for the fact adduced by Dr. Stevens, that in situations favourable to the production of fevers, the blood is frequently found in a very unhealthy state, even before the outbreak of the disease itself. Dr. Kirkland has nearly anticipated the discoveries of later years upon this subject; and considering the time at which he wrote, we think that his observations are both interesting as well as valuable.

[Pg 424]"Seeing then that an absorption of putrid matter will bring on a puerperal fever, with common symptoms, may we not conclude that the putrid miasms of lying-in hospitals will produce the same effect? Is it not reasonable to suppose, that the puerperal fever which has been observed in hospitals, is owing to some cause peculiar to hospitals? otherwise, would it not be equally frequent in other places? Dr. Pringle informs us that the foul air occasioned by one mortified limb brought on a malignant fever in the military hospital. Peu also seems to have proved, that the putrid effluvia exhaling from wounded men brought on a fever which killed a great many child-bed women who lay in the same hospital; and are not the putrid effluvia arising from the lochial discharge in lying-in hospitals capable of producing the same disease? I have sometimes been called to women in child-bed, where the offensive effluvia arising from this kind of evacuation, pent up in a small close room, at once evinced to what cause their fever was owing; and though I have not any doubt, but in lying-in hospitals every attempt is made to preserve the air pure and the patient in a state of cleanliness, yet where many women lie in the same ward, it is perhaps impossible to obtain these advantages in the perfection to be wished." (Op. cit. p. 73.)

Van Swieten compared the state of the inner surface of the uterus with that of a large wound,—"Something of a like nature seems to be affected in the womb, but in a slighter manner, because the injury is here superficial, but on a broad surface." (Comment. on Boerhaave, § 1329.) He quotes also an interesting description from Moschion of the changes which are observed in the evacuations after delivery,—"Primo sanguis, secundo fæculentus et paucus, ultimo purulentus." "It hence appears," he observes, "that that fever in lying-in women, which is called the milk fever, does not spring solely from the milk brought into the breasts, but also from the purifying of the womb by that gentle and superficial suppuration. But, as even the best pus when retained too long becomes acrid and putrefies, the same thing will hold with regard to the purulent evacuations after delivery, if they should be kept back." "But if that purulent matter does not come out, but being sucked back should be mixed with the humours, it may, being brought to the viscera by a bad metastasis of the morbid matter, give occasion to dangerous disorders."

This comparison by Van Swieten and Dr. Kirkland, of the state of the uterus with that of an open wound, has been recently brought into notice by Cruveilhier, and quoted by Dr. Ferguson, in his work. "All the uterine veins and arteries have been torn from the placenta, and they form a part of a large wound, and are, therefore bathed in all the secretions which necessarily take place while this wound is healing. In this [Pg 425]respect the uterus presents an exact analogy to the surface of an amputated stump; and it is, therefore, not surprising, that the secondary evils of amputation should be so similar to those of the puerperal state." (Op. cit. p. 75.) Professor Schönlein also considers that the contagion of puerperal fever has the greatest similarity with hospital gangrene.

The causes of puerperal disease which have been enumerated by Cruveilhier, apply almost solely to those inflammatory affections of the puerperal state which do not depend upon a vitiated state of the circulation, but "are derived from the changes induced by parturition, and are dependent on,

"1. The organic changes induced by pregnancy.

"2. Those induced by the act of labour.

"3. Those consecutive of labour.

"1. Pregnancy:—the hyperthrophy of the uterus; the enlargement of the ligamenta lata; the traction on the peritoneum of the neighbouring organs; the extraordinary development of the arteries, veins, and lymphatics.

"2. Changes induced by labour:—bruising of all the soft parts—they appear raw.

"3. Changes after labour:—the woman presents the faithful picture of one who has undergone a serious surgical operation. The internal surface of the womb may be compared to a vast solution of continuity; the whole of the mucous membrane has been altered by the inflammation, of which it has been the seat; the gaping veins are like the open mouthed vessels of an amputated limb.

"Except just at the inner surface of the cervix uteri, there is no mucous membrane at all; but the muscular tissue of the uterus is every where exposed. This, therefore, like the stump, is to be covered by a new membrane.

"This process of reparation is accompanied by a traumatic fever, called milk fever. Like the fever from wounds, it has its period of incubation, varying in various individuals: it lasts about twenty-four hours, and vanishes on the third day.

"As in amputation, a false membrane covers the stump, and precedes cicatrisation, so the inner surface of the womb is first covered with a false membrane before it is cicatrised. If there be no lochial discharge, there is union by the first intention, as in the stump where there is no discharge: this is the rarest of all cases.

"Ordinarily, this false membrane is thrown off with a purulent discharge, which is the lochia. At first it is sanious, i. e. mixed with blood, and fetid; then less fetid and more purulent; then thin and serous. The quality and quantity of the discharge are, as in amputations, an index of the state of the wound." (Cruveilhier, quoted by Dr. Ferguson, p. 76.)

The comparison between the inner surface of the uterus shortly[Pg 426] after parturition and that of a stump, does not hold good in every respect: in the one, the open mouths of the vessels are pretty firmly compressed by the contracted state of the surrounding uterine tissue, whereas, in the other they are uncontracted beyond the mere effects of the traumatic inflammation upon their cut extremities, and they are surrounded by the flaccid surface of divided muscles: still, however, it is quite sufficient to show, that the inner surface of the uterus must be for some days bathed in mucous, sanious, and purulent fluids, highly prone to decomposition; and that, in this state, absorption is peculiarly liable to take place.

The vehement exertions of the uterus and abdominal muscles during labour, and the violent pressure to which the abdominal circulation has been subjected at this time, are sources of inflammation, which, although not noticed by Cruveilhier, are frequently met with quite independent of puerperal fever, although, from what we have already stated, it will be evident that the disposition to absorption and consequent vitiation of the blood will be still farther increased by the excited state of the circulation.

Where blood has been vitiated by the action of aerial poisons, or introduction of putrid matter into its current, changes are quickly produced in its condition, which not only unfit it for the varied functions which it has to perform, especially in maintaining the activity of the brain and nervous system, but which may be perceived, as already shown, before the disease itself appears. It is dark, and of an unhealthy tinge. In severer forms of typhus, "when first drawn, it has a peculiar smell, and coagulates almost invariably without any crust. There are black spots on the surface of the crassamentum; the coagulum is so soft that it can easily be separated with the fingers, and during its formation, a large quantity of the black colouring matter falls to the bottom of the cup. When the serum separates, it has generally a yellow, and in some cases even a deep orange colour." (Stevens, op. cit. p. 219.)

Dr. Tweedie has observed similar conditions of blood in the common typhus of the metropolis, and remarks, "that in this class of fevers, the crassamentum of the blood, instead of forming a firm coagulum, is loose, small in proportion to the quantity of serum, and so soft that it breaks readily on attempting to raise it, resembling in consistence half-boiled currant jelly, and that in some instances, when abstracted late in the disease, it is scarcely coagulated at all." (Tweedie, Clin. Illust. of Fever, quoted by Dr. Stephens.)

This accords closely with the appearances of blood drawn from patients under puerperal fever, especially of the adynamic form. The blood is of a dark muddy colour, in some cases resembling even thin treacle in consistence: in this state the coagulation is[Pg 427] very imperfect, so that after a time it merely forms a homogeneous semi-gelatinous mass, with little or no separation of serum from the crassamentum. After death the blood is found perfectly fluid, readily infiltrating and staining the coats of the vessels which contain it, and resembling thin watery claret, both in colour and consistence. In the other forms, which are of a more inflammatory character, it is highly buffed and cupped; the crassamentum is small, the albuminous layer upon it is of a muddy yellow colour; and the serum, which is frequently large in proportion, is of a similar colour, or even of a slight bilious tinge; in some, there has been occasionally observed a white cloudy appearance, as if from the admixture of milk.

The mortality of puerperal fevers depends in great measure upon the form they assume; and, as we have already stated, this will vary in great measure according to the period of the year, the nature of the season, and the type of the prevailing epidemic fevers in the neighbourhood, whether they assume the character of synochus, or low malignant typhus. It varies a good deal according to the class of patients attacked, being more frequently of the inflammatory character among the middling and higher classes, whereas, among the lower orders, who are exposed to the depressing effects of cold, damp, and ill-ventilated dwellings, of insufficient clothing and food, of an atmosphere poisoned with the noxious effluvia arising from a dirty and thickly inhabited suburb, and habitual intemperance, it generally assumes the adynamic or contagious form. This is the reason that puerperal fever is not only seen less frequently among the middling and upper ranks, but even when it does appear, from being usually of the inflammatory form, it is more tractable. It is in lying-in hospitals, where it appears in all its terrors, and occasionally assumes such a degree of malignity as almost to equal the plague or yellow fever, in the frightful rapidity of its course, and in the almost certain fatality of its termination. Few have witnessed it in a more destructive form than the late Dr. W. Hunter at the British Lying-in Hospital. He observes in his lectures that he had seen a great many cases of it in the hospital, "and particularly in one year, when it was so remarkably prevalent there. It was so bad, that not only every gentleman belonging to the hospital, but all our friends in town, had a consultation to think whether we should shut up the house. In two months thirty-two patients had the fever, and only one of them recovered." (MS. Lectures.)

Although puerperal fever has never yet attained the frightful degree of mortality at the General Lying-in Hospital, nevertheless, it has appeared repeatedly with such malignity, as to commit fearful ravages among the patients. In these epidemics, the first few cases are generally comparatively mild, being of the peritonitic or gastro-bilious form (Douglas:) but as it advances,[Pg 428] the malignant adynamic form, which is so destructive, prevails. In some epidemics, as is seen in common fevers, after a short time the disease has become more tractable, it has assumed a milder character, and ultimately has again disappeared. This corresponds with the admirable remarks of Dr. Gooch, to whose graphic pen we are indebted for much valuable information on the subject of puerperal fevers. "Another remarkable circumstance about this disease is, that, when it is most prevalent, it is most dangerous. Each case is more difficult of cure than when it occurs seldomer. The practitioner finds, that, although the group of symptoms resembles what he was formerly accustomed to, he has now to deal with a disease far more obstinate and destructive, and his usual remedies are not so successful as formerly; he loses case after case in spite of his best efforts. When it has been thus raging for a considerable time, it at length subsides; the case becomes less frequent and less severe; the practitioner finds his treatment becoming more successful, partly because experience has taught him to detect it earlier, and to treat it better, but probably also because the disease has itself become milder." (Gooch on Peritoneal Fevers, p. 3.)

The table of the cases at the General Lying-in Hospital and their mortality, which Dr. Ferguson has calculated during the twelve years, from March 1827, to April 1838, is highly important, and points out the period of the year in which puerperal fever, prevails most, and the contrary. The last two and the first seven months of the year are those in which the greatest mortality occurred; whereas, in the month of July, during this whole period, not a single patient died; in August only one; in September two; and again, none in October, although several were attacked. "Puerperal fever was epidemic in the years 1828, 1829, 1835, 1836. 1838; in the other years it was only sporadic. The greatest mortality was in the years 1835 and 1838, in the last of which 20 in 26 died. The malady commenced in January, in which month Dr. Rigby saved only 1 out of 9. The hospital was closed for a month, and opened again in March, when he succeeded in rescuing only 2 in 8. Thinking that another mode of treatment might be more successful, I determined to bleed largely, and to salivate. This plan was fairly tried under the constant attendance of Dr. Cape, and with my supervision, but 3 only in 9 lived. Seeing that no treatment was of avail, the hospital was closed from May till November." (Ferguson, op. cit. p. 277.)

Different species of puerperal fever. Having premised these general observations on puerperal fevers, we now proceed to consider them separately, according to the various forms which they exhibit; and in doing so, shall adopt the arrangement of the subject made by Dr. Douglas, viz. under the three heads of inflammatory gastro-bilious, and the contagious or adynamic form. It is not only one of the earliest, but in our opinion, one of the[Pg 429] most correct; nor do the arrangements adopted by Drs. Locock and Ferguson differ essentially from it. We hope by this means to combine the advantages which each affords, while we hold ourselves free to differ or coincide with either, as our opinions lead us, trusting that we shall thus be able to render this complex and difficult subject more complete.

Under the inflammatory form we shall not only consider the acute peritonitis, so ably described by Dr. Locock, which is chiefly the effects of labour, to which we have already alluded in the quotation from Cruveilhier, but also that form which, according to Dr. Ferguson, arises from vitiation of the blood, by the introduction of putrid matter into the circulation; a form which has not only a great disposition to assume a typhoid character, but also to become epidemic. Under this head we must also bring the uterine inflammation and phlebitis, which we have described, as resulting from a direct action of putrid matters contained in the uterus, a form which is very liable to pass into uterine, and afterwards general peritonitis; lastly, there remains that species of nervous abdominable pain, which has received the name of false peritonitis.

Puerperal Peritonitis.

Symptoms. The acute peritonitis, which has been the effects of labour, generally makes its appearance at an early period after. The labour has probably been either tedious or severe, the efforts of the uterus and abdominal muscles have been violent, especially during the last stage; and from the moment of the child's birth, the patient has complained of considerable soreness over the lower part of the abdomen, amounting to much pain and tenderness when touched. At first she is tolerably easy, so long as she lies still, and keeps the abdominal muscles in complete repose; but, by degrees, fits of pain come on, they become more frequent, and the intervals between them shorter and shorter, until the pain is constant; she now complains of much tension and fulness of the abdomen; the tenderness is greatly increased, both in severity and extent, and is often attended with the painful sense of twisting about the umbilicus, which is observed in ordinary forms of peritonitis. The pain and tension are now so severe that she is constrained to lie wholly upon her back, with the knees drawn up, in order to relax the abdominal muscles, and thus, if possible, alleviate her sufferings. The abdomen itself is evidently fuller to the feel, and is beginning to be tympanitic; the breathing is quick and anxious; the tongue has a thin coating of white fur, which is browner and thicker at the back; the pulse is quick and hard, sometimes small and wiry, occasionally full and strong; the lochia and[Pg 430] milk have either never appeared, or only in small quantities, to be quickly suppressed again. As the tympanitis increases, the breathing becomes more anxious and painful; for every effort of the diaphragm in inspiration is followed by severe pain, from the movement which it produces in the abdominal contents. After awhile, the flatulent distention of the intestines, particularly of the stomach, renders the diaphragm irritable, and provokes hiccough, which is excessively painful from the involuntary jerk which it gives to the abdomen; or, what is still worse, retching and efforts to vomit frequently come on, which greatly aggravate her sufferings. She now lies upon her back, perfectly helpless and immoveable, for the slightest attempt to touch her is insupportable; even the jar of a person walking heavily across the room excites pain. The abdomen is now even larger than it was before labour, her anxiety and restlessness increase, and she rapidly becomes exhausted from suffering and want of sleep. The face becomes sallow, the features fallen, the tongue dry and brown, and sordes collect upon the teeth; she falls into an uneasy slumber, during which, the eyelids remain partly open, or she mutters incoherently with low delirium. The abdomen is less painful, but not diminished in size; the pulse is small, hurried, and feeble; subsultus tendinum and picking of the bed-clothes follow, with all the other symptoms of approaching dissolution.

Where the attack has risen from the introduction of putrid matter into the circulating current, it usually appears somewhat later, seldom before the third day after labour: it is almost invariably preceded by a severe rigour, followed by intense headach, and darting pain about the lower part of the abdomen, which gradually becomes constant. There is a nearer approach to the adynamic form, or rather, it is frequently attended, or at least followed, by this disease; hence the inflammatory stage is shorter, the pulse is even more rapid, and loses its strength sooner than in the other form; the milk and lochia have usually not only been established, but continue, we think, longer afterwards than in the other case; the pain is perhaps less in many instances, but in other respects, the first part of the attack does not differ essentially from the form above described; but as the disease advances, it gradually assumes the adynamic form; the inflammatory symptoms of the early part of the attack are merged in the general collapse which now exists, the same cause which had produced the peritoneal inflammation now acting on the whole system.

Peritonitis occurring by itself, is, as Dr. Ferguson observes, of comparatively rare occurrence in puerperal women, the condition of the system during childbed, disposing it quickly to assume more or less of the adynamic character.

Appearances after death. On examining cases of fatal puerperal peritonitis, we shall find marks of inflammation, or its[Pg 431] consequences, over a large extent of the peritoneum; large portions of it are highly congested, and more or less thickened; considerable effusions of serum or sero-purulent fluid, mixed with flakes of coagulable lymph, into the abdominal cavity: the omentum adhering to the intestines, and also the intestines to each other, by means of coagulable lymph, in which they are occasionally completely imbedded; the broad ligaments and ovaries are frequently much inflamed, covered with lymph, and the latter more or less softened; the Fallopian tubes engorged and adhering to the neighbouring parts; the uterus is covered at its fundus with a coating of coagulable lymph, as if it had been smeared with a quantity of dirty white paint, and this extends more or less in patches over the various reflexions of the peritoneum, in the upper parts of the abdominal cavity.

Treatment. We may take it as a rule, that the earlier we see the patient in the disease, the less active will be the treatment required. At first, when the pain has not yet assumed its full intensity, and only occurs in paroxysms, when little or no traces of abdominal tension and fulness are to be perceived from incipient tympanitis, we may frequently succeed in cutting short the disease by a full dose of calomel and James's powder, with some morphia or Dover's powder, to allay irritation and assist in producing a general determination to the skin; this must be followed by some castor oil, and if the pain is no longer constant, with the addition of a few drops of Liquor Opii Sedativus. Where the pain has already become severe, a draught of sulphate and carbonate of magnesia in peppermint water, with a little antimonial wine and henbane, will be preferable. We have long since been convinced, that common black draught, or any form of purge which acts violently or gripes, is objectionable, having frequently seen a return of pain brought on by its action. A hot poultice of linseed-meal, large enough to cover the whole abdomen, and as hot as the patient can bear it, must be applied; this, if made properly, will prove a great relief, for it not only allays the pain, but quickly acts as a powerful diaphoretic: there is a little art in making this, and unless it be done properly, it is apt to produce much discomfort, and do more harm than good. The water should be poured boiling hot on the linseed-meal, and the mixture well beaten with a large spoon, until it forms a nearly gelatinous mass; it should then be spread upon a large piece of linen, so as to be between a quarter and half an inch in thickness; there is now only one layer of cloth between the poultice and the patient's abdomen, and it can be applied or removed with perfect facility: without these precautions it is apt to form a pudding-like mass, which greatly annoys the patient from its weight, and from being applied directly to the abdomen, smears about, and is not easily changed. A poultice made in the manner now described, will keep hot for three hours at least, and is by far the[Pg 432] most effective form of fomentation which can be employed. Common fomentations of sponges, or flannels wrung out of hot water, are by no means desirable, as from the constant exposure, which is required for their frequent repetition, the patient has little benefit from the temporary heat, and is very liable to catch cold.

If the symptoms do not yield to this treatment, but assume a more formidable aspect, or if the attack has not commenced in this gradual manner, but has come on much more suddenly and with greater violence, recourse must be had immediately to the lancet. Leeches are seldom proper as a substitute for bleeding, although they frequently prove of great value afterwards. A certain effect is required to be produced upon the general circulation, before leeches are capable of affording even a temporary relief; and so far from economizing the patient's powers by using leeches instead of the lancet, we shall find that in order to overcome the inflammation by this means, the patient will require to lose a far greater quantity of blood than if it had been suddenly removed from the circulation by bleeding. Upon the same principle, therefore, we must take care, that the blood shall be drawn pleno rivo from an ample orifice: we thus spare the patient an unnecessary loss of power, for the required effect upon the circulation is produced in a much shorter time and with less expenditure of blood, than if the blood had been slowly dribbled from a small opening.

"In the treatment of acute inflammation in the vital organs, the customary practice is to consider local bleeding as a milder means of effecting the same object as general bleeding, and to postpone it till the stage for the latter is over. To me it appears that they are calculated to effect two different objects, both of which are necessary at the beginning of the treatment; the one to reduce the violence of the general circulation, the other to empty the distended capillaries of the part. As long as the pulse is quick, full, and hard, it is in vain to take blood from the affected part; if we could completely empty its gorged capillary vessels, they would be instantly gorged again, whilst the heart and large arteries are injecting them with so much violence. On the other hand, after having reduced the force of the general circulation, the capillary vessels of the part often remain preternaturally injected: this, I conclude, from the fact that the patient is often not relieved till local blood-letting has been used, and then is relieved immediately. Hence, as soon as the patient has recovered from the faintness occasioned by bleeding from the arm, leeches ought to be applied without delay." (Gooch, on Peritoneal Fevers, p. 47.)

It is impossible to fix what quantity of blood is to be drawn; nor is it easy, either from the patient's appearance or the feel of her pulse, to foretell how much she will require to lose: a certain[Pg 433] effect is to be produced on the circulation in order to bring it under such control as will moderate the state of inflammation. No two patients are alike in this respect; and it frequently happens, that where, from external appearances, we might have expected to find most strength, faintness is quickly produced, and vice versâ: on the whole, we think that where the patient has a small, quick, and oppressed pulse, we may expect she will require to lose a large quantity of blood, for in these cases the pulse rises in volume and strength as the bleeding proceeds; hence, as before observed, we must "carry the bleeding to its proper limits, which is the approach to, or actual state of, syncope." So far from removing the pillows, and letting her lie with the head low, so as to recover from her faintness as quickly as possible, it will be much better to support her in a sitting posture, and thus prolong the state of faintness for some while; the dilated vessels have now time to contract, the heart returns to a more moderate and healthy action, the effects of the bleeding are much more permanent, and the chances of its repetition being required considerably diminished. From this state of relaxation and temporary collapse being prolonged, we find that the secretion of the skin, and particularly the intestinal canal, are more easily re-established, the operation of a purgative being now much quicker and more effective.

As soon after the bleeding as possible, a smart dose of calomel and James's powder, followed by an active saline laxative, must be given; and the combination of sulphate and carbonate of magnesia with antimonial wine and Tinct. Hyosc. already recommended, is preferred by us: it is better given in divided doses, as then the effects of the antimonial is prolonged. The action of the bowels may also be assisted by a domestic enema: and if there are no signs of action in the bowels after two hours, the purgative should be repeated. The results of the leeches, fomentation, and purging, will guide us as to the necessity of repeating the bleeding. Dr. Gooch's truly practical remarks on these points are well worthy of attention:—"I waited till the purgatives had operated fully, that I might know what impression the combined operation of general and local blood-letting had produced on the disease, before deliberating on the employment of a second blood-letting. The common effect, of these remedies was this, as long as the faintness lasted in the slightest degree, the pulse remained soft and often slower, and the pain was much less, or ceased altogether; but an hour or two after the bleeding, when the circulation had recovered, the pain returned more or less, and the pulse regained much of its hardness or incompressibility. This state continued till the leeches had bled freely, and the purgatives had acted repeatedly and copiously." (Op. cit. p. 48.)

If, however, the pain has experienced but little abatement, or[Pg 434] has returned as severely as before; if the pulse has quickly reassumed its former condition; if the action of the purgatives has not taken place, or has been at most unsatisfactory, even with a repetition of the saline, we are justified in having recourse to a second bleeding; the faintness this time will probably be more complete; the effect upon the disease more decided; and, in all probability, it will be quickly followed by free evacuations from the bowels, which produce great relief. In some cases the bleeding requires to be repeated again and again before the disease can be subdued: this, however, usually arises not so much from the obstinacy of the attack, as from the first bleedings not having been performed in an effective manner. "The pulse," says Dr. Locock, "is the best guide, for the pain after the first full relief from the bleeding is often of a mixed character, partly inflammatory, partly nervous, to be detected only by watching closely the other symptoms. The tenderness is a less certain guide, for few will bear pressure for a considerable time after the inflammatory symptoms have been entirely relieved. Many patients also from fear shrink from the pressure of the hand, although by drawing off the attention, it will be found that they bear firm and steady pressure very well." (Op. cit. p. 355.)

Throughout the whole process of treatment, the linseed-meal poultices must be continued, and, if not made too heavy, can be borne when there is a considerable degree of abdominal tenderness.

In all cases where the disease has not been completely checked in the very outset, but has shown a disposition to return, the treatment above-mentioned should now be followed by a mild mercurial course. The effects of mercury in allaying inflammation at a certain stage, which does not appear to be fully under the control of mere antiphlogistic remedies, have been amply proved by British practitioners: this applies particularly to inflammation of serous membranes: mercury not only tends to prevent the effusions of serum and coagulable lymph, but, where they have taken place, it is of great value in promoting their absorption. We agree with Dr. Locock, that calomel is by far the best form in which it can be used, where we wish to obtain its specific effects. The Hydrargyrum cum Cretâ, which we have occasionally found useful in the gastro-bilious or enteric form to restore a depraved state of intestinal secretions, has failed us in the other forms where we wished to produce salivation. The purgative dose of calomel, which we have advised to be given after the bleeding, ought not to be less than six to eight grains; but now, as the dose is to be repeated every two or three hours, a smaller quantity will be sufficient: in order to save time we usually begin with five grains of calomel, and an equal quantity of Dover's powder, and repeat this in an hour's time, after which, we proceed with doses of two or three grains every second or[Pg 435] third hour according to circumstances. The sooner the system can be brought under the influence of mercury the better, the pulse becomes softer and less frequent, the pain and tension of the abdomen diminish, the tongue becomes moist and natural at the edges, and general improvement follows. Throughout the whole attack the vagina should be occasionally washed out with warm water, more especially if we have reason to suspect that the disease has arisen from the imbibition or absorption of putrid matter. The smell of the patient will frequently guide us in this respect, and point out the condition of the passages and their contents; even if there be no putrid matter lodging there, the application of warm water will always act as a comfortable fomentation to the patient, and assists not a little in favouring a return of the lochia.

If the pain and swelling of the abdomen still continue, and the case is evidently becoming more unfavourable, we have occasionally sprinkled the abdomen with spirit of wine or oil of turpentine, and then covered it with a fresh poultice: this has acted as a powerful rubefacient, and has in some cases relieved the patient at a very advanced stage. We have also tried blistering the abdomen, and dressing the vesicated surface with strong mercurial ointment, as recommended by Dr. Locock; but we have not met with the success which he mentions, probably from the disease having already assumed the malignant characters of the adynamic form, and, in some instances, because the patient could not endure the intense smarting which it produced. We have occasionally covered the abdomen with camphorated mercurial ointment without previous blistering, and with good effect. The internal use of turpentine, circular friction upon the abdomen, and enemata of Mist. Assafœtidæ, &c., which we have sometimes found useful in removing the tympanites of the adynamic puerperal fever, and which does not depend on an acute form of inflammation, are scarcely applicable in the present case.

When the powers are beginning to fail, as a last hope we must have recourse to stimulants combined with nourishment: the Mist. Spiritus Vini Gallici of the last London pharmacopœia,—anglice, "egg and brandy,"—has for many years been used at the Lying-in Hospital to support the system at this last stage, and sometimes even under the most unfavourable circumstances with marked success; powerful doses of ammonia will be required at frequent intervals, and an occasional opiate, to procure the still farther refreshment of sleep. Even where the face is assuming a Hippocratic appearance, the pulse so feeble and rapid as scarcely to be counted, where the abdomen is immensely distended, with cessation of pain and cold clammy state of the skin, we ought not to despair; no case, however bad, is entirely hopeless; and although the majority of such cases perish in spite of the greatest care and activity, still we are justified in [Pg 436]persevering till the last, knowing from experience that we every now and then succeed even at this late hour in rescuing our patient.[145]

Uterine Phlebitis.

In describing the other species of inflammatory puerperal affection, which we have designated by the title of uterine inflammation or phlebitis, and which we conceive arises in most instances, from the presence and absorption of putrid matter in the uterus, we shall merely confine our description to the early part of the disease, because, as it invariably terminates in peritotinis if not stopped at an early period, it will be unnecessary to go over this part of our subject again.

Symptoms. This affection generally makes its appearance on the second, third, or fourth day after labour, and varies considerably in its mode of attack. In some cases it will be observed to come on suddenly, with scarcely any premonitory symptoms. The patient is suddenly seized with severe griping pain in the lower part of her abdomen, generally extending more or less to one side, and usually preceded by a smart shivering fit, which is followed by intense headach. On examining the abdomen, the uterus is hard, larger than natural, and excessively painful to the touch; the pulse quick and usually small; the tongue covered with a thin white fur, becoming brown and thicker towards the back part; the countenance anxious. With all this, the abdomen is neither hard nor painful upon moderate pressure; not even over the uterus itself do we produce pain, until we begin to press so hard, that the organ becomes plainly distinguishable to the hand through the soft integuments. The lochia has either not appeared at all, or has been suddenly suppressed; and in all probability, the secretion of milk has followed a similar course.

Or the disease may commence in a much more gradual manner. The after-pains are observed to increase in severity and duration, producing a considerable degree of pain over the whole abdomen, but especially the uterus, which, during the paroxysms, is harder than in the intervals. The pains are increased by the slightest pressure, if suddenly applied; but, if gradually increased, the patient will bear a considerable degree of pressure, not only without complaining, but will even remark that the pain is, as it were, benumbed by it; if the hand be now suddenly removed, very severe suffering is produced. The pains become more and more constant, until they assume the uniform character of inflammation of the uterus, as already described, when the disease makes its attack suddenly. If the disease be not checked in its[Pg 437] progress, the pain becomes more intense, and gradually extends over the whole surface of the peritoneum; the abdomen swells from tympanitis, and is followed by the other symptoms of acute peritonitis already described. The latter stages of the attack are almost invariably mingled with symptoms of the malignant form of puerperal fever,—a circumstance which, when we consider the probable source of the disease is not to be wondered at. Indeed, we may say, that by the time the peritonitis is fairly established, the introduction of putrid virus into the circulation has been of sufficient duration and extent to render the production of adynamic symptoms almost unavoidable.

Appearances after death. Examination after death shows that the uterus and its appendages have been the chief seat of the inflammation, its whole peritoneal surface thickly covered with exudations of coagulable lymph; the broad ligaments vascular; the Fallopian tubes livid, swollen, and softened; the ovaries greatly altered in appearance and structure, being generally more or less swollen and much softened,—at times the natural tissue of the gland completely broken down into a pulpy semi-purulent mass, at others the external surface only has been red or gorged with dark-coloured vessels; the whole uterine appendages thickly imbedded in cogulable lymph. The uterus is large and soft, deposites of pus have been found beneath its peritoneal covering, or in the proper muscular tissue of the organ; and in many cases, on cutting into its substance, pus has appeared in numerous little points, oozing from the veins or absorbents which have been divided. In those veins which are large enough to be traced by dissection, their coats have been found vascular, thickened, and in many places lined with lymph, so that the vessel has become completely impervious: in others, they have been filled for a space with pus, and their canal then obliterated, either by swelling, effusion of lymph, or by plugs of fibrine from coagulated blood. These changes in ordinary cases do not extend beyond the substance of the uterus; but where the disease has been of some duration, as well as severity, they become much more extensive, affecting the neighbouring veins to some distance. "Inflammation," says Dr. R. Lee, who has examined this subject with great care, "having once begun, it is liable, as I have before stated, to spread continuously to the veins of the whole uterine system, to those of the ovaria, of the Fallopian tubes, and broad ligaments. The vena cava itself does not always escape, the inflammation spreading to it from the iliac, or from the spermatic veins." (Researches on the Pathology and Treatment of some of the more important Diseases of Women, p. 54.)

The surrounding structures are generally implicated in the inflammation; the muscular tissue of the uterus becomes soft and of a dark red, or even dirty black colour, and, as before stated, the peritoneum which covers the organ is particularly affected.[Pg 438] The appearances after death in this species of puerperal fever are those most commonly observed, for puerperal peritonitis is rarely met with in its uncomplicated form, being usually more or less mixed up with it; on the other hand, the majority of cases which belong to the adynamic form of puerperal fever (except the most malignant) are generally preceded to a certain extent and attended by this disease.

Treatment. In the early stage of the disease, before inflammation (especially peritonitis) has been established, we do not consider that the lancet is required, merely because there is pain with a quick pulse. The uterus may be hard, swollen, and painful, and yet there is not actual inflammation present: we will not deny that inflammation will quickly follow, if nothing be done to remove this state of uterine irritation. The pulse is quick, but seldom hard; and even if it be at all sharp, it produces but little resistance to the pressure of the finger. In these cases we may bleed, but we seldom reduce the quickness of the pulse, although it sinks still farther in point of strength. There is seldom much buffy coat upon the blood when drawn at this stage; and if the pain be relieved for a short time, it returns again as soon as the system has recovered from the immediate effects of the syncope. We do not see that striking relief follows a copious venesection in cases of this sort, which is remarkable in inflammation of the abdominal viscera under other circumstances; and we are more than ever convinced, not only from the fact just mentioned, and from the results of our own experience, but from the unfavourable results of the practice in which bleeding has been uniformly and largely employed, that it is not a remedy which is always to be premised before the employment of other treatment, as in cases of simple inflammation of the viscera or serous membranes. The only circumstances we apprehend, under which venesection ought to be employed in this affection are, where the pain is constant, without intermission, and where, besides its rapidity, the pulse betrays a degree of wiry resistance to the finger, which can never be mistaken. In this case the blood drawn will show all the usual marks of inflammation, and the relief procured will be proportionally great. On the other hand, where the pain, although severe, is not constant, but the patient experiences every now and then a slight abatement in its severity, or a short intermission altogether; where the pulse, although rapid, is soft, and resists the finger but feebly, we shall seldom produce any permanent relief by bleeding; the pulse becomes weaker, but its rapidity, so far from being diminished, is rather increased. The pain may be relieved for a short time, but it almost always returns as severely as before the venesection.

Under these circumstances, the pure antiphlogistic treatment seems to have little or no control, either in removing the pain,[Pg 439] or diminishing the pulse, or in preventing the disease from running into that state of tympanitic peritonitis, which is so fatal in its effects; and we are not only losing time by employing an inefficacious mode of treatment, but are exhausting the powers of the system, already more or less depressed. "Large hæmorrhages," as Dr. Ferguson correctly observes, "favour absorption," (op. cit. p. 108;) and it would seem that by thus reducing the powers of the system, we diminish its capability of ridding itself by the natural outlets of the virus which has been carried into the circulation; nor do we see how this is to be assisted by bleeding. If a state of actual hæmorrhage has been induced, bleeding, of course, must be used with the greatest promptness; but in employing this remedy in the above-mentioned form of puerperal fever, although we relieve the inflammation for a time, the cause is not removed. It still continues to act, and the symptoms return under much more formidable circumstances, from the increased debility of the system confining our means of treatment within still narrower limits.

According, therefore, to the views which we have taken of this form of puerperal fever, the indications for treating it will be the following: first, to subdue any inflammatory symptoms, if they be present; but it must be remembered, that we have no positive proof of the existence of inflammation, merely from the presence of pain and a rapid pulse, although these two symptoms denote a state of irritation, advancing with rapid strides into actual inflammation. The character of each must be carefully ascertained before we are justified in deciding upon the necessity of bleeding. As this operation is generally performed in the erect posture, to favour a state of syncope, we are following a second indication at the same moment, and perhaps one of the most important, viz. placing the patient in such a posture as will promote the escape of any coagula and discharges which may have been stagnating in the uterus or vagina. To effect this still more completely, a stream of warm water should be thrown up briskly into the uterus, to dislodge any offensive irritating matter which may have collected: the relief thus produced is sometimes quite extraordinary, the pain abates, the uterus becomes less hard, the pulse more natural, and the patient expresses herself greatly relieved. The rule which we have made in our treatment of natural labour, viz. that if possible, the patient should sit up to take her food, and suckle her child, and especially that she should always kneel to pass water, should never be neglected, for in many of these cases it will be found that the patient has not stirred from the horizontal posture, and that the attack had evidently followed the accumulation of stagnant lochia, &c., which from the warmth of the adjacent parts, and free contact with the external air, has rapidly become offensive; and, moreover, from her position, has been prevented from being discharged. To ensure that the uterus has expelled any coagula which may[Pg 440] have lodged in it, is a powerful argument in favour of applying the child to the breast as soon as possible after labour; this refers particularly to those long slender coagula, which were first noticed in the uterine veins by Dr. Burton, in 1751, as one of the chief causes of after-pains; for by thus inducing firm uterine contraction, the greater part of these will be generally expelled, and access of air to the venous orifices prevented. "These coagula may be distinctly perceived for several weeks after delivery, and both in their form and colour they differ from those inflammation." (R. Lee, op. cit. p. 53.)

Our third indication is to increase the action of all the excretory functions, and thus, as far as possible, remove the virus, which may have already entered the system. There is no remedy with which we are acquainted that has such a power of producing a general erethism throughout the whole excretory system, as calomel in large doses. The secretions of the liver, the mucous membrane of the intestinal canal, of the skin, and kidneys, are all very remarkably increased by the action of a large dose of this medicine, and we cannot help attributing the return of healthy lochia, which so frequently follows such a dose of colomel, to a similar action on the vessels of the uterus and vagina. No effort of nature can be so well directed for the removal of any noxious principle from the circulating fluids as a general increased action of the excretory system, and we have seldom or never seen calomel act with such success in this form of puerperal fever, except where it had been given in a sufficient dose to produce this effect. Salivation is by no means a necessary object, nor have we seen it produced even by a scruple dose of calomel. It is, however, seldom necessary to exceed ten grains at a time, although this may occasionally be required to be repeated. It should always be combined with some medicine which will assist its diaphoretic action. For this purpose, in cases where the pain is constant, without any remission, showing that a state of inflammation has been already induced, it will be advisable to combine it with a little of James's or antimonial powder. Where, on the other hand, the patient experiences evident abatement or even remissions of pain, ten grains of calomel with an equal quantity of Dover's powder, made up into pills, will be preferable; the opium acts by relieving the pain, and contributing to induce a copious perspiration. To assist this, and also to relieve pain still more, a hot linseed-meal poultice, as above described, will be of great service; and in a few hours (or the next morning, if the calomel has been given over night,) a saline of sulphate and carbonate of magnesia should be given. The vagina should be well syringed with warm water, and repeated from time to time as occasion requires; in like manner, the poultice must be continued until the pain has entirely ceased.

The general result of this treatment is, that in twelve or eighteen hours the uterus loses its tenderness and hardness, the[Pg 441] pulse becomes fuller and softer, the tongue cleaner and more moist, the kidneys and bowels have acted copiously, and the lochia and milk have returned.

False Peritonitis.

Under this title, which we believe first originated at the General Lying-in Hospital, and which has been adopted by Dr. Locock in his article upon the subject, we propose to describe that peculiar species of abdominable pain, which Dr. Ferguson has called the transient form of peritonitis. Strictly speaking, neither of these terms are exactly appropriate, for the disease appears to depend upon a state of high nervous irritability, perfectly independent of inflammation, or any other affection of the peritoneum; still, however, as it has been most frequently known and described under the former of these appellations, we shall also continue to use it, merely warning our reader, that the appellation of false peritonitis is more conventional than correct. Properly speaking, it should be called nervous abdominal pain; for we have reason to think that its real seat is in the muscular coat of the intestines, and in the abdominal muscles themselves, much more than in any portion of the peritoneum.

The disease chiefly attacks women of a delicate frame, and irritable habit of body, with small features, fair complexion, and of a nervous hysterical disposition, whose powers have but ill sustained them through the processes of pregnancy and parturition, and are now beginning to fail under that of lactation. Her mind is anxious and depressed, the sleep is restless, the circulation irritable and feeble; she is pale, forebodes all sorts of evils, and is unusually sensitive; complains inordinately of her sufferings in trying to suckle the child, and of the severity of her after-pains; not unfrequently she has severe headach, of that species which affects the top of the head, and which is generally considered to arise from a state of debility and anæmia. In many cases the pain has evidently been the action of a griping purge. The pain is of the most intense character; indeed, in many cases, it is evidently too severe for the ordinary suffering from abdominal inflammation. So irritable are the abdominal muscles, that the slightest motion, even that of respiration, will throw them into cramp-like contractions to the great agony of the patient. The breathing is short and timid, like that of a person under a severe attack of pleurodyne: the slightest touch of the hand, or of a single finger, produces intolerable suffering, not so much from the pain which its pressure produces, but from the sudden and involuntary contraction to which the irritable muscles are thus excited. The quickened breathing, from a dread of the abdomen being touched, is frequently sufficient to bring on a paroxysm. If[Pg 442] by soothing words and promises of cautious proceeding we induce her to let us apply our hand upon the abdomen so gently that it does not even rest with its weight upon it, we shall find that we may now gradually increase the pressure, until by degrees it becomes considerable, not only without her feeling any increase of pain, but with complete relief—the pressure of the hand appearing as it were, to benumb the pain. If we withdraw the hand in the same gradual manner, no pain will be produced; but if we remove it suddenly, a spasm of the muscles, with intense pain, is instantly excited.

The pulse is in an equally irritable state; after a few beats it rises in rapidity as soon as the patient's mind is directed to it; in others it is permanently quick. The tongue is sometimes slightly covered with a thin fur; in others it is pale and flabby; and in others disposed to be glazed, red, and dry.

The disease rarely exists long uncomplicated with any other form of puerperal affection, but soon passes either into acute peritonitis, or into the typhoid state of the malignant form, the latter transition being almost certain, if the practitioner has considered it as an inflammatory affection, and treated it antiphlogistically.

It is to the late Dr. Gooch that we are indebted for having first called the attention of the profession to this disease, and pointed out its true characters by the nature of the remedies which proved successful in relieving it. "The effects of remedies on a disease, if accurately observed, form the most important part of its history; they are like chemical tests, frequently detecting important differences in objects which were previously exactly similar. How many diseases are there in which the symptoms are inadequate guides?" "The local pains and constitutional disturbance which occur in feeble and bloodless persons, and which are aggravated by bleeding and other evacuants, strikingly resemble the local pains and constitutional disturbance which occur in vigorous and plethoric persons, and which the lancet and other evacuants relieve and ultimately cure; yet how many years is it before the young practitioner learns that there are cases apparently so similar, yet really so different, and how to distinguish them; and how many practitioners are there who never learn it at all? Symptoms and dissections can never do more than suggest probabilities about the nature of the disease, and the effects of a remedy on it. A trial of the remedies themselves is the only conclusive proof." (Op. cit. p. 37.)

In those cases which proved fatal, the post mortem appearances only tended to confirm the nature of the disease. So far from marks of inflammation being found, there was not a single trace to be discovered; in fact, an entirely opposite condition existed; the peritoneum and viscera were pale and bloodless.

Treatment. It is of the highest importance to distinguish these[Pg 443] affections from a state of inflammation; the treatment of the one will be precisely the reverse of the other. The lancet is as little indicated in this case, as it is in puerperal convulsions from anæmia, and the effects produced will be scarcely less mischievous. The fatal cases which Dr. Gooch has recorded, show that it was not the disease so much as the treatment which destroyed the patients, and prove, as we have already stated, that the presence of pain and a quick pulse do not surely indicate a state of inflammation, without being confirmed by the general symptoms of the patient's condition. "These cases taught me a new view of the subject: they taught me that a lying-in woman might have permanent pain and tenderness of the abdomen, with a rapid pulse, independent of acute inflammation of the peritoneum or any other part; that these symptoms may depend on a state which blood-letting does not relieve, and which, if this remedy is carried as far as it requires to be carried in peritonitis, may terminate fatally; and that the most effectual remedies are opiates and fomentations. Most of the patients who were the subjects of these attacks, were women, who, in their ordinary health, were delicate and sensitive; the attack sometimes seems to originate in violent after-pains, gradually passing into permanent pain and tenderness, resembling inflammation, or in the painful operation of an active purgative; but it could sometimes be traced to no satisfactory cause—the patient had had a common labour, and had experienced no unusual cause of debility or irritation. The pulse in all these cases, although quick, was soft and feeble: this, together with the previous constitution of the patient, were my chief guides. When I could trace it to any irritating cause, such as a griping purge, and when blood had been already drawn without relief, and without being buffed, I saw my way still clearer. When I doubted, I applied leeches to the abdomen." (Op. cit. p. 72.)

In ordinary cases a dose of Liquor Opii Sedativus, or of Dover's powder, repeated according to circumstances, will be sufficient to stop the attack, taking care to clear the bowels of any irritating matter with castor oil in some aromatic water, guarded by a few drops of Battley's solution. In many of these cases, where the circulation is below the natural standard in point of power, and the disease is more or less complicated with hysteria, the opiates should be combined with a gentle stimulant, of which camphor is by far the best. Five grains of powdered camphor with half a grain of hydrochlorate of morphia and a sufficient quantity of extract of henbane, to form two pills, may be repeated at intervals, whenever the pain shows a disposition to return, and constipation prevented by castor oil and Liq. Opii Sedativus as before-mentioned, or a gentle draught of sulphate of potass, rhubarb, and manna. In most cases, when the stomach and bowels are in a proper condition, mild tonics will prove useful, as equal[Pg 444] parts of extract of gentian, henbane, with or without a grain or two of quinine or sulphate of iron, at night; and, if necessary, the infusion of some vegetable tonic during the day. The diet should be simple but nutritious, and a certain quantity of malt liquor or wine allowed daily, if the condition of the patient permit it. In some instances the low diet which is usually deemed requisite for the first few days after labour, has appeared to have been the cause of this highly irritable condition, especially in those who have habitually accustomed themselves to pamper the appetite, and to use fermented or spirituous liquors in excess: with spirit drinkers, the loss of their daily stimulus is almost sure to be followed by a low, feeble, irritable state of the system, much gastric and nervous derangement, and the paroxysms of pain just described. It is astonishing how quickly every symptom subsides, and the system returns to a natural condition, by the daily allowance of a small quantity of their favourite beverage.

Gastro-bilious Puerperal Fever.

This is the gastro-enteric species of Dr. Ferguson, and corresponds with the "puerperal intestinal irritation" described by Dr. Locock. In its simple uncomplicated form, this disease cannot be considered as a dangerous affection; it occasionally passes into inflammation, but more frequently it assumes after awhile the typhoid or malignant form, especially where its true characters have not been recognised, and the powers of the system have become much exhausted by its severity and long continuance.

Like the false peritonitis it is frequently met with in cases where, from unwholesome or intemperate living, the digestive organs are greatly deranged, or where the bowels have been much neglected for some weeks before labour. We cannot help thinking that the view which Dr. Ferguson has taken of its cause, viz., a vitiated state of the fluids, as with the case of puerperal peritonitis, is far too exclusive, inasmuch as it is evidently produced in many instances by the direct irritation of matters which are contained in the intestinal canal: in others, we fully agree with him, that it is produced indirectly by the introduction of an animal poison into the circulation, which spends its virulence upon the stomach, liver, or intestines, or which, in other words, nature endeavours to remove from the system by these outlets. In the early stage of uterine irritation, or of phlebitis, from the absorption of putrid fluids, we have shown that the cause at first, in most instances, acts directly, and not through the medium of the circulation, otherwise the symptoms would not be so instantly checked by washing out the uterus with warm water, and thus removing the source of mischief; so in the gastro-bilious or[Pg 445] enteric form, the symptoms at first are produced in most, if not all cases, by the direct irritation of the unhealthy intestinal contents, upon the removal of which they at once disappear; although at the same time, if the source of irritation be not removed, we have no doubt but absorption will take place sooner or later and vitiate the circulation. Thus, Dr. Kirkland considers that retained fæces during a lying-in are capable of bringing on symptoms which "may, properly enough, be called puerperal fever" (op. cit. p. 87;) and Dr. John Clarke, in enumerating the different causes entertained by "writers of good reputation," mentions, where fæces are detained in the intestines, "the thin putrid parts of which are supposed to be taken up into the blood." (Practical Essay on the Management of Pregnancy and Labour, by J. Clarke, M. D., 1806, p. 53.)

There is, however, no reason to confine the source of the putrilage, which infests the circulating current, in cases of gastro-bilious or intestinal irritation, to unhealthy fæcal matter in the intestines; for in the experiment made by Professor Tiedemann, to which we have already alluded, viz. of injecting musk into the femoral vein of an animal, the poison seemed to concentrate itself upon the mucous membrane of the intestinal canal; and from the diarrhœa which had commenced shortly before death, it is probable, if the dose had been smaller, that nature would have succeeded in ridding the system of it by this means; we may, therefore, conclude, in most of the cases of this affection, which are not the result of direct enteric irritation, but an effort of nature to purify the circulation by expelling the morbid matter, with which it had been vitiated, through the medium of the mucous membrane of the bowels, that the uterus had been the source of its origin, introduction, or absorption, into the system.

Symptoms. This form of puerperal fever seldom commences so soon after labour as any of the other species, and frequently the symptoms are so trifling, at first, as scarcely to excite attention. There is an indistinct uneasiness about the abdomen; the tongue is never quite natural, being either slightly furred with a few prominent papillæ, or pale and flabby; the appetite is irregular, or fails considerably; the patient complains of weariness and lassitude; there is, perhaps, slight headach across the eyes and forehead; the face has a sallow tinge, and if her complexion be dark, there is a leaden-coloured ring beneath her eyes; the sleep is unrefreshing; the spirits are unequal and anxious; she is chilly at times, and at others, has considerable flushings of heat, with increase of headach. The abdomen becomes full and doughy to the feel; it is somewhat tender to the touch, but not distinctly so, as in peritonitis; the motions are dark, sparing, and excessively offensive; sometimes hard and scybalous; but more usually they assume the character of an irritable diarrhœa, with much acrid slimy mucus, the evacuation of which, is attended[Pg 446] with much flatus, and for a time produces great relief, although, at the moment of passing, it is frequently attended with a good deal of forcing. The abdomen becomes more tender, with severe griping flatulent pains at intervals; the diarrhœa assumes somewhat of the characters of dysentery; the pulse becomes quick and irritable; the tongue red and glossy at the tip and edges, with a patch of thin white fur in the middle, or with a red centre between two parallel streaks of creamy fur—the back part yellow, verging into brown; the breath is of a faint disagreeable odour; the attacks of fever, from time to time, are more distinct; and frequently, during the sweating stage, the skin throws out a strong peculiar odour, which taints the air of the whole room. In some cases there is frequent vomiting, either of watery fluid mixed with ropy mucus, or of a greenish colour; the result probably of subacute inflammation of the stomach. As the irritation of the intestinal canal increases, she becomes more exhausted, and rapidly emaciates. The tongue now becomes preternaturally red, its surface glossy smooth, the centre is parched and brown, and sometimes traversed with fissures; the fever assumes a low typhoid character, with delirium at night, and gradual sinking. The appearance of the evacuations varies considerably; at times they appear to consist of minute membranous shreds, floating in dark brown water; in others, they are clay-coloured, slimy, adhesive, excessively offensive, and even pungent; whereas, in others, they seem to consist chiefly of dark unhealthy bile, mixed with water and mucus.

This form of disease is frequently met with in patients who have been weakened by hæmorrhage, and necessarily tends to aggravate the state of anæmia which is present. She has the intense pain at the summit of the head, which characterizes this condition; she gets but little sleep, and that is disturbed by restless and uneasy dreams; she lies with the eyelids half closed, and the occasional twitchings of the muscles betray the irritable condition of the system; exhaustion quickly supervenes, and is usually attended either with low delirium, or the anæmic form of puerperal mania.

Appearances after death. If the dysenteric affection has been very severe, we shall probably find softened or even ulcerated spots in the mucous membrane of the large intestine; but in other cases, there have been no lesions of the kind; the intestines have been found a good deal distended with gas, but pale and bloodless. Where the disease has passed into the typhoid species, other appearances belonging to this form will be observed: coagulable lymph will probably be effused, and those changes in the structure of the uterus, which we shall mention when we come to the consideration of this species.

Treatment. The treatment will, in great measure, depend upon whether the disease is the result of irritation from loaded[Pg 447] bowels, scybalous and unhealthy contents, &c., or from that engorgement of the circulation belonging to the chylopoietic viscera, with more or less fever, which indicates the efforts nature is making to rid the circulation, by this outlet, of any morbid principle with which it may have been infected.

In the first case it is simple enough, and, in most instances, the disease is prevented, or, at any rate, checked in its very outset, by the dose of castor oil which is customarily given on the second or third day after labour. If the pulse be quick, the headach severe, with much fulness and uneasiness of the abdomen, and more especially if the bowels have been constipated, or in an unhealthy state before labour, five grains of calomel and carbonate of soda, made up into two pills, with extract of henbane, and followed in a few hours by a dose of castor oil, guarded with some Liquor Opii Sedativus, as before recommended, will be required. We combine a little soda with the calomel, to prevent it griping and acting violently, which it is liable to do where there is much acidity of stomach, from its being converted into the bichloride. We also think that there will be less chance of vomiting, when the calomel is combined with the soda, than with an antimonial, as recommended by Dr. Locock; a common domestic enema of gruel and salt will assist the purgative, and bring away much unhealthy fæculent matter. The medicines will generally require to be repeated in twenty-four hours, to insure the removal of the irritating cause from the bowels; the abdomen becomes softer and more free from uneasiness; the pulse rises in strength and fulness, but diminishes in rapidity, and the patient experiences general relief in her symptoms. She may now take an ammoniated saline, with tincture of hop or henbane during the day; five grains of Hydrarg. cum Cretâ with carbonate of soda and henbane at night, instead of the calomel, and a draught of rhubarb and magnesia with some aromatic confection the next morning, or of rhubarb and manna with sulphate of potash, rendered warm by a little spirit of nutmeg.

If diarrhœa has come on spontaneously at an early period, the true nature of the case is more liable to be mistaken; still, however, the evidences of gastric and enteric irritation are quite sufficient to guide the cautious and observant practitioner. The calomel here is not so desirable as where there is constipation; eight or ten grains of Hydrarg. c. Cretâ will produce less irritation, and act as effectually: it will require to be followed by the same treatment as above-mentioned, and to be repeated according to circumstances.

The diet should be chiefly farinaceous with milk; rice-milk, when the bowels have been sufficiently cleared, is generally very useful; it is slightly constipating, and soothes the irritable mucous membrane with its bland consistence. Milk and soda-water, as mentioned by Dr. Locock, or with lime-water, is very beneficial,[Pg 448] especially where the tongue is disposed to remain red, with a smooth glossy surface; as convalescence proceeds, a teaspoonful of the concentrated essence or decoction of sarsaparilla may be added with advantage.

This form of puerperal affection is never epidemic; it is mere intestinal irritation after labour from scybalous and other unhealthy contents; but this is not the case with the "gastro-enteric form," described by Dr. Ferguson; in the former, the febrile excitement of the circulation is but trifling, and frequently can scarcely be said to exist; whereas, in the latter, the disease rarely appears sporadically, but in conjunction with numerous cases of the same character, or of the malignant adynamic form; it is also, invariably accompanied with much febrile disturbance, and usually of a low form, unless complicated with abdominal inflammation at an early period.

"This form of puerperal fever," as Dr. Ferguson observes, "assumes the general characters of a mild typhus, accompanied with intestinal irritation." (Op. cit. p. 22.) The object of our treatment here is very different to that of the other form just mentioned; it is to unload the gorged circulation of the stomach, liver, and bowels, of the noxious and excrementitious matters which nature has brought to these emunctories, in order that they may be discharged from the system. It is in these cases where, although little or no food has been taken for some time, and without any evidences of fæcal accumulation, we find the exhibition of certain purgatives, especially calomel, to be followed by such copious fæculent evacuations, which we have every reason to believe have been secreted by the liver and bowels under the action of this powerful remedy. The treatment recommended by Dr. Ferguson, is so in accordance with our own views, and so concisely expressed, that we may be allowed to quote it.

"The following," says he, "I have found the most suitable treatment. Get rid of all local inflammations as soon as possible by leeching or by moderate depletion, so as to reduce the malady into simple fever with gastro-enteric irritation. When the skin is early dusky, and there is nausea or vomiting, begin with an emetic. If there be no nausea nor vomiting, but intestinal flux, with a red tongue smeared with suburra, a large dose of calomel, from ten to fifteen grains should be given. Small doses create purging, pain, and irritation, while the full dose produces one to six large pultaceous stools, after which the tongue is cleaned, rendered less red and more moist, and the pulse usually falls. These stools, when examined, appear to contain the fæcal matter suspended in large quantities of mucus and greenish bile, as if the turgid capillaries of the irritated intestinal canal and liver had been freed from their load. In some instances, a repetition only of the same dose is required to efface the main features of the[Pg 449] malady, and to leave nothing but debility to support. In others, after a short respite, diarrhœa re-commences, and soon is apt to become colliquative." (Op. cit. p. 158, 159.)

We have already shown the effects which calomel possesses in large doses of rousing the different excretory organs into full action, and thus assisting to secrete or separate from the circulation any offending principle which may have been carried into it. We are also convinced that where calomel has been promptly given in this manner, the chances of the disease being prolonged or terminating in the adynamic form are considerably diminished. Dr. Hamilton, in speaking of the advantages derived from the use of purgative medicines in typhus fever states, "I am now thoroughly persuaded, that the full and regular evacuation of the bowels relieves the oppression of the stomach, cleans the loaded and parched tongue, and mitigates thirst, restlessness, and heat of surface; and that thus the later and more formidable impression on the nervous system is prevented, recovery more certainly and speedily promoted, and the danger of relapsing into the fever much diminished." (Observations on the Utility and Administration of Purgative Medicines in several Diseases, by James Hamilton, M. D. p. 35.)

As the gastro-enteric form of puerperal fever which we have just described, is frequently observed in epidemics of the adynamic form, particularly at their commencement and going off, and frequently complicated with it, we would rather consider those local inflammations and deposites of puriform fluid in the muscles, joints, &c., which are occasionally seen after severe cases, to the disease being complicated with, or assuming the nature of, the malignant form.

If the symptoms have not yielded to the treatment which we have recommended, the alvine discharge becomes excessively unwholesome and fetid, the skin exhales a strong and unpleasant odour, the strength fails, the tongue is either dry and brown, or smooth and red like raw meat, the fever sometimes assumes the remittent character as described many years ago by Dr. Butter, of Derby; in others, the febrile symptoms subside, leaving the case one of chronic or subacute inflammation of the lining membrane of the bowels, with occasional attacks of irritative fever arising from it. In these cases mercurials, except in mild and guarded doses, appear to aggravate the irritation of the mucous membrane, and increase the disposition of it to ulcerate: five grains of Hydrarg. cum Cretâ and Dover's powder may be given once, or at the utmost, twice, in the twenty-four hours; half a drachm of carbonate of ammonia neutralized by lemon juice, and rendered alkalescent by a little Spirit. Ammon. Arom., may be given in some aromatic water every three or four hours; injections of starch into the rectum with a few drops of Battley are also useful. In some cases, where there was continued[Pg 450] flatulence, a small quantity of turpentine in some castor oil has had an excellent effect. Others, where every means had seemed to fail, have yielded under the use of copavia. Dr. Locock has found advantage from the occasional use of very small doses (eight to ten grains) of epsom salts with a few drops of laudanum in some aromatic water. The after treatment, as also, the rules for diet, are the same as in the other form.

The Contagious, or Adynamic, Puerperal Fever.

Although we have classed under the head of "puerperal fevers" a variety of affections connected with, and arising more or less from, the same cause with the dreadful malady which we are now about to describe, and although every form and modification of them is liable to assume its characters, still we must confess that the term puerperal fever belongs par excellence to this form, the adynamic, malignant, and, as we have upon a former occasion called it, the genuine puerperal fever.

It is in this form of disease that the vitiated state of the blood is shown with most distinctness, not only from the condition of the blood both during life, and after death, but also from the close connexion which exists between it and the plague, African typhus or yellow fever, and the other malignant fevers, both of the temperate as well as the tropical climates.

The interesting and daring researches of M. Bulard upon the pathology of the plague, tend to throw great light upon the nature of this formidable disease, and to confirm the views which we have long entertained of this and other diseases of the same class, that the essence of the disease consists in the vitiated condition of the blood.

Symptoms. The onset of this disease is almost invariably accompanied with a smart rigour, followed by intense headach, and rapid but generally powerless pulse. It seldom begins before the third day, although in some cases it seems to have commenced from the time of her delivery; whereas, in others the patient has gone on to recover favourably until the tenth or even the fourteenth day before being seized, and had already felt sufficiently well to leave her bed and sit up. The powers of the system seem prostrated at once; the shrunken features and dusky hue of the skin, the leaden colour of the lids, and circumscribed crimson or almost purple patches upon the cheeks, the short imperfect breathing and occasional deep sighing to relieve it, indicate but too surely the nature of the disease, and its depressing effects upon the whole system.

"The sensorium," says Dr. Douglas in describing this form, "is seldom in any degree disturbed, whereas, in the others, it is so frequently, and even sometimes it is excited to high delirium.[Pg 451] The pulse here is usually from the moment of the attack, soft, weak, and yielding, and in quickness often exceeds 150; whereas, in the first species it is full, bounding, and often incompressible; and in the second, small, hard, and contracted, and in both, moderately quick. The eye, instead of being suffused with a reddish or yellow tint, as in the others, is here generally pellucid with a dilated pupil. The countenance, instead of being flushed, as in the others, is here pale and shrunk with an indescribable expression of anxiety; an expression altogether so peculiar, that the disease could on many occasions be pronounced or inferred from the countenance alone. The surface of the body instead of being, as in others, dry and of pyrexial high heat, is here usually soft and clammy, and the heat not above the natural temperature; and not only is the skin cool with clammy exudation, but the muscles to the impression of the finger feel soft and flaccid, as if deprived of their vis vitæ by the influence of contagion. Indeed, there is such prostration of muscular strength and depression of vital principle from the very outset of the attack, that I must suppose the contagion to act through the medium of the nervous system in a manner analogous to that of the contagion of plague." (Report on Puerperal Fever. Dub. Hosp. Rep. vol. iii.)

Where the powers of the system are not annihilated from the commencement of the attack by the depressing effects of the poison with which the circulation is impregnated, an effort at reaction is frequently made, and for some hours afterwards the surface of the body is hot and dry; but sooner or later, as the stage of collapse comes on, it then assumes the same cold death-like feel, as in the worst cases of malignant cholera. The character of the attack will be in great measure modified by the intensity of the poison, and the extent with which the circulation has been infected by it. The same effort to produce such a state of reaction as will raise the temperature of the skin, will probably assist nature in throwing it off under the form of peritonitic or gastro-enteric species of puerperal fever already described; whereas, where the circulation has been thoroughly impregnated with it in its concentrated form, the vital powers succumb at once, and a state of collapse exists from the very commencement of the disease. The course which the symptoms follow and the duration of the disease, will, therefore, depend not only on the severity of the attack, but also on the power of the particular constitution to resist the deadly effects of the morbid principle upon which the disease depends. When broken down by previous disease, intemperance, poverty, and depressing passions of the mind, the vital powers can make no stand against the powerful enemy by which they are attacked; "the blood is so much vitiated, even early in the disease, that it loses the power of stimulating the heart so as to keep up its healthy action; and, perhaps, also the vascular organs are early affected by the action[Pg 452] of the poison, and lose the power of either feeling the stimulus, or reacting with force on the impression, which is communicated to their internal surface by the vitiated blood. In such cases, in place of increased excitement, there is frequently a want of action in the whole system." (Stevens, op. cit. p. 188.) The patient sinks without pain or complaint, beyond that of debility, but in such cases with a rapidity which would almost claim for the disease the name of "plague." The tongue becomes dry, red, and brown at the back part, the pulse weaker and more rapid, the debility and exhaustion more overpowering; still, even in this state, her mind usually remains clear, unconscious of the fate which awaits her, and occasionally even cheerful: a peculiar sickly odour exhales from the skin, and in many cases so distinctly, as to warn us the moment we enter the room of the patient's condition. The dusky ashen hue of the skin becomes darker, the fingers are shrivelled, and the nails dark, or of a livid black as in cholera; diarrhœa frequently attends, the fæces are unhealthy, and of the same peculiar odour just noticed; during the first stage the lochia are generally present, although of an unhealthy character; the milk also continues in the milder cases, but as the stage of collapse approaches they both disappear, and the breasts become quite flaccid. In some cases there is vomiting from an early period, with more or less tympanitic distention; but these symptoms rather depend upon the disease being complicated with one of the other modifications. Livid purpurous blotches sometimes appear upon the legs, &c. and in some epidemics it is accompanied with dark or livid eruptions. The surface has now the cold wet feel in its greatest degree, and in some cases even the tongue feels cold to the finger; a drowsy state of insensibility generally follows and continues until death.

The symptoms here enumerated present the characteristics of fever under its different degrees of intensity. The peritonitic and gastro-enteric forms may be compared with the ordinary fevers of temperate climates, and which are attended with more or less inflammation of some organ. The malignant adynamic form corresponds closely with the malignant typhus of this, and the pestilential fevers of warm countries, more especially the plague and the African typhus or yellow fever. In all of these diseases, the vitiated state of the blood appears to be the essential condition of their existence, quite independent of any inflammatory action; in fact, in this form, so rapid and overpowering are the effects of the poison which pervades the circulation, and so completely does it paralyze the whole system, that there is neither time nor sufficient vis vitæ to make any effort at reaction. Hence, as Mr. Moore has correctly observed, "when the patient is rapidly destroyed by the violence of the disease, the morbid changes bear no proportion to the severity of the previous symptoms; a dubious trace of inflammation, a little serum, or a few feeble adhesions,[Pg 453] are all that dissection under such circumstances displays." (Inquiry into the Pathology, Causes, and Treatment, of Puerperal Fever, p. 63.) In many of the most rapidly fatal cases which we have witnessed, there have not been even these questionable evidences of inflammation. The tissues have been pale and bloodless, the uterus softened, its internal surface ragged, and with a dark gangrenous appearance, extending to the os uteri, and dark thin claret-like blood in all the larger vessels. The heart is flabby, soft, and filled with dark blood; the lungs, liver, spleen, and kidneys much softened; the spleen dark, sometimes enlarged and almost pulpy. If we compare these appearances with those observed by M. Bulard in cases of plague, we shall find a striking coincidence between the two diseases. This intrepid pathologist remarks, that "the state of general turgescence and dilatation of the venous system; the presence of inflammable gas in eight cases in the cellular tissue, in the veins of the head, feet, and abdomen; the presence of petechiæ, both internally and externally; the general softening of the tissues; the enlargement, softening, and breaking down of the spleen; the petechial state of the mucous membrane of the stomach; the effusions of blood on the inner surface of that organ; the passive hæmorrhages and boils, are symptoms which result from a change in the condition of the blood. The symptoms connected with the state of the nervous system, viz. the rigours, headach, and confusion of mind, the quick and small pulse, the hurried respiration and vomiting, and also the petechiæ, carbuncles, and buboes, are neither those of vascular nor nervous inflammation. The blood has never shown the buffy coat; it was found just as black in the arteries as in the veins, but in the former, in much smaller quantity; it always had the appearance of being dissolved." M. Bulard observes, that the decomposition of the blood is quite independent of putrefaction being present before death takes place; and he feels convinced that it is not only the sole cause of death, but must also be looked upon as the origin of the various morbid phenomena during the course of the disease. He considers "these phenomena to result from an actual poisoning of the blood, similar appearances being observed in all cases where putrid matter and morbid secretions have been introduced into the system." With regard to the supposed inflammatory nature of the plague, M. Bulard states, that in many cases not the slightest trace of inflammation could be found. The changes in the spleen are of by far the most invariable occurrence. In one hundred autopsies, this organ was found only five times in a healthy state.

Where, on the other hand, the powers of the constitution, or the diminished virulence of the disease, have enabled the system to withstand the depressing action of its immediate effects, we find it considerably modified, both in the symptoms which it [Pg 454]presents during life, and the appearances after death. Instead of being little else than a state of collapse from the very outset of the disease, under which, not a single attempt is made by the powers of the system to set up even the most feeble effort of reaction, a variety of symptoms attend its commencement and progress, indicating that the vis vitæ has not altogether succumbed beneath the deadly effects of the malady. The very rigour itself, when violent, the headach and flushing of the face, if severe, are rather favourable than otherwise, and show that the system still possesses some power of reaction. It is usually observed, that where the attack commences with these precursory symptoms well marked, it is generally accompanied with peritoneal pain, tympanitis, and other symptoms of inflammatory action; whereas, in the worst cases, we have already stated, that from the very commencement of the disease there is neither a symptom of inflammation during life, nor a trace of it to be found afterwards. Dr. Armstrong rightly observed, that inflammation is not an essential constituent of typhus; and the same holds good in the strictest sense of the word, with the typhoid or adynamic puerperal fever.

"Whatever the remote cause of fever may be, it is very evident that this cause must invariably exist, not only at the moment of attack, but even previous to that period. Now in the fevers from poison, the blood is invariably diseased previous to the commencement of the cold stage. During this period there are premonitory symptoms; but these are evidently the effect of the diseased state of the vital fluid: and that these precursors of fever are not the effect of any local inflammatory disease, is evident from the fact, that frequently during this period there is no pain in any of the organs, but a want of action, particularly in the extreme vessels, and consequently a decrease of heat in the whole system.

"If inflammation in any of the organs were, in reality, the cause of fever, then the disease ought to be fatal, exactly in proportion to the violence of the local affection; but the very reverse of this is the truth. Mere excitement can easily be reduced, and the inflammatory form of fever is decidedly the most easily cured, though in it the excitement is often so great that the organs are very liable to be injured; while the malignant form of fever is by far the most fatal, though in this the excitement is less, and the organs are seldom affected. This is particularly the case in the worst form of the African typhus, and probably other varieties of malignant fever, where the blood is under the influence of an active poison, and where its vitality is diminished, and its structure is injured even before the attack.

"Those who have seen most of the malignant diseases know well that excitement in fever is invariably a good symptom; for this is a sure sign that the blood has not yet undergone any fatal[Pg 455] change, and independent of this, mere increase of action is always at the mercy of the lancet. But neither the lancet nor leeches, gum water, vitriolic emetics, calomel, antimony, brandy, opium, or acids, can redden the colour of the black blood, which we invariably meet with in pestilential diseases, or remedy the diseased state of the vital current, so as to cure that fatal form of fever where the malignant symptoms are produced, not by excitement, but by the vitiated state of that mysterious fluid, which in health gives life and nourishment to every solid of the system, and which, when diseased to a certain extent, is by far the most frequent cause of death in all those fevers that are some deleterious poison acting, in the first place, on the vital current, and then on the brain and the whole system through the medium of the blood." (Stevens, on the Blood, p. 186.)

We have quoted thus largely from the observations of Dr. Stevens and M. Bulard, to whose admirable researches we are so greatly indebted for our present knowledge, respecting the nature of pestilential diseases both of the East and West, for they tend not only to show the true pathology of malignant puerperal fever, but also the class of diseases to which it belongs.

Appearances after death. Where more or less inflammatory action has accompanied the first part of the disease, the lesions observed after death differ considerably from those of acute peritonitis: the effusions of cogulable lymph, of serum, and sero-purulent fluid, are seldom met with to such an extent where the case has been one of inflammation uncomplicated with the adynamic form of puerperal fever, even although it may have been exceedingly violent; whereas, in the present case, although there has been scarcely sufficient power in the system to set up even a moderate degree of inflammatory action, the intestines and uterine appendages are found glued together, and thickly imbedded in immense effusions of lymph. The ovaries, Fallopian tubes, and broad ligaments are engorged with purple vascularity, softened, and, especially the ovaries, quite disorganized, with numerous effusions of sero-purulent matter beneath their peritoneal coverings, or into their parenchymatous tissue. In others, their whole substance has been softened and pulpy, with little cyst-like cavities filled with blood or pus, the remains of the Graafian capsules. During the fatal epidemic which prevailed at the General Lying-in Hospital, in the early part of 1838, we met with several cases where the ovaries had entirely disappeared, their site being only discoverable by an oval thickening of the broad ligament, something like an empty cyst of peritoneum; this contained a small quantity of livid pulpy débris of the ovary, and (on that side where conception had taken place) a remarkably well marked or rather exaggerated corpus luteum. The uterus is larger and its tissue much softer than under ordinary [Pg 456] peritonitis, so that, in many instances, the finger can be easily pushed through its whole substance.

Where the constitution has borne the brunt of the attack without immediate collapse, and the local mischief been controlled by appropriate means, we find that fresh efforts are made to rid the circulation of the morbid matter with which it is infected. The patient is suddenly seized with severe pain, with heat, redness, and swelling of one of the large joints, presenting all the appearances of arthritic or rheumatic inflammation, and also of certain muscles, especially the supinators of the arm, the glutæi, and gastrocnemii. The painful spot soon becomes hard, it is intensely tender, and in two or three days the feeling of fluctuation indicates the formation of an abscess, from which a large quantity of greenish coloured pus mixed with blood and serum is discharged. The cellular tissue beneath the skin and between the muscles is equally affected, and if examined when the abscess is just beginning to form, will be found of a dirty brown colour, softened, infiltrated, and here and there condensed with lymph or pus, precisely as in cases of gangrenous erysipelas: the muscular tissue has entirely lost its red colour, and closely resembles the appearance of boiled meat, its structure so softened as to tear easily under the fingers, and interspersed with deposites of immature lymph and purulent fluid, the commencement of what would have been an abscess. Like gangrenous erysipelas the extent of the abscess does not seem to be limited by a surrounding wall of healthy lymph, as seen in a common phlegmon, but if deep beneath the surface it continues to spread in all directions until nearly the whole limb appears to be implicated in one immense abscess: hence, in those patients who have recovered under these attacks, the limb has frequently been rendered useless, the muscles being atrophied and coherent.

Inflammation of a similarly arthritic or rheumatic nature occasionally also attacks the eye, and presents all the usual characters of arthritic iritis under ordinary circumstances: there is the same intolerance of light, pain of the eye, dimness of vision, contracted pupil, and peculiar white ring round the edge of the cornea, which distinguishes this affection; but in the present case, the disease runs a far more rapid course, and defies the remedies which in common cases would be sufficient to check it; the inflammation soon extends to the deeper seated structures of the eye, the pain is excrutiating, and, in two or three days, disorganization takes place, followed by suppuration, staphyloma, and bursting of the cornea. So rapid and destructive is its course, that, although five or six cases have come under our notice, in only one instance, with the greatest difficulty, was the eye saved, and, even then, not before it had been considerably injured.

These attacks are attended by severe pains of a similar [Pg 457]nature in different parts of the body, more especially the joints and limbs; and, from the arthritic character which they assume, tend, in our opinion, still farther to elucidate the real condition of the system. The analogy between gout or rheumatism, and those diseases which arise from a vitiated state of the blood, is exceedingly close, nay, even identical, for in both, a principal pervades the circulating fluids which requires to be removed; and if this be not effected by any of the excretory organs, nature endeavours to throw it off by some process of local inflammation. The connexion between puerperal fever and typhus is very close, for it not only assumes the characters of the typhus epidemics which may chance to be prevailing at the time, but we have distinct evidence that the contagion of typhus will, in a puerperal woman, manifest itself under the form of puerperal fever. Dr. Collins has recorded a very interesting case of this sort:—"A patient was admitted at a late hour at night into one of the wards, labouring under a bad form of typhus fever, with petechial spots over her body; when observed next morning, she was removed into a separate apartment, where she died shortly after. The two females who occupied the beds adjoining hers, while she remained in the large ward, were attacked with puerperal fever, and died." (Collins, op. cit. p. 381.) During a typhus epidemic which prevailed a few years ago in the poor districts of the metropolis, a prominent feature of which were petechiæ and a livid rubeoloid eruption, precisely the same appearances were observed among the cases of adynamic puerperal fever at the General Lying-in Hospital.

The same has been observed with erysipelas; and, in one short but severe epidemic, the child of every woman who had died of the disease perished also from erysipelas, so severe that it ran its course in a few hours. Dr. Gordon, of Aberdeen, remarks, that "with it and, at the same time, epidemic erysipelas began, progressed with equal pace, arrived at its acmé, and terminated together." He also says, that a very frequent crisis of the disease was an external erysipelas. Mr. Hey remarks, that infectious fevers were common at the time; and he does not recollect ever having seen such malignant cases of erysipelas as then. Dr. Clark also observes, that those inflammatory diseases which occurred were principally erysipelatous. Dr. Armstrong states, "that in 1813 (the year of its greatest prevalence throughout England) low fever, typhus, and acute rheumatism also prevailed to an uncommon degree." (Moore, on Puerp. Fever, p. 164.)

During the same epidemic, to which we just now alluded, the housemaid of the hospital, a healthy young woman, was suddenly seized with sore-throat and violent erysipelas of the head and face, from which she was saved with great difficulty; her sister came and attended her, as the nurses were too much occupied by[Pg 458] the number of patients who were ill; just at the time that she was pronounced out of danger, her sister, not feeling well, went home, sickened, and died, in less than three days, of typhus fever.

The contagious nature of puerperal fever has long since ceased to be a matter of doubt, and instances have repeatedly occurred of practitioners and nurses communicating the disease to several patients in succession. Dr. Gooch has recorded some striking instances of the kind, and we could enumerate many others if necessary. Where a practitioner has been engaged in the post mortem examination of a case of puerperal fever, we do not hesitate to declare it highly unsafe for him to attend a case of labour for some days afterwards. The peculiar smelling effluvia which arises from the body of a patient during life is quite, in our opinion, sufficient to infect the clothes; and every one who has made a minute dissection of the abdominal viscera, especially in fatal cases of puerperal fever, knows full well that it is almost impossible to remove the smell from the hands for many hours, even with the aid of repeated washing; it must be, therefore, self-evident, that, under such circumstances, it would be almost criminal to expose a lying-in patient to such a risk.

That the discharges from a patient under puerperal fever are in the highest degree contagious, we have abundant evidence in the history of lying-in hospitals. The puerperal abscesses are also contagious, and may be communicated to healthy lying-in women by washing with the same sponge: this fact has been repeatedly proved at the Vienna hospital; but they are equally communicable to women not pregnant; on more than one occasion the women engaged in washing the soiled bed linen of the General Lying-in Hospital have been attacked with abscesses in the fingers or hands, attended with rapidly spreading inflammation of the cellular tissue.

We have stated that puerperal fever may arise from the effluvia which exhales from the body of the patient, and from the various discharges; it may also be noxious exhalation from sewers, ditches, and other sources of miasmata, the effects of which in producing typhus have been long ascertained. "With regard to the General Lying-in Hospital, its locality rather below the level of the river, and surrounded by a mesh-work of open sewers fifteen hundred feet in extent, receiving the filth of Lambeth, and some not thirty feet from the wards of the institution, may account for its unhealthiness. It is only after repeated remonstrances, that these sources of pollution have in part now begun to be obliterated." (Dr. Ferguson, op. cit. p. 104.) The commissioners of sewers refused the application of the hospital, to have the nearest of these nuisances properly bricked over, and assigned this remarkable reason for so doing, viz. that the hospital had come to them, not they to the hospital. Consent was ultimately only obtained by the agreement, that a large portion of[Pg 459] the expense should be borne by the institution. On completing the work they afforded us a striking instance of the effects of effluvia on lying-in women; a large quantity of black pestilential mud had been thrown out in making the necessary excavations, this they refused to remove, and actually spread it upon the ground to a considerable extent; the consequence was, that the first two cases of puerperal fever after the re-opening of the hospital occurred within twenty-four hours of this unjustifiable act.

Treatment. The fatal character of this disease and the varied form of its epidemics will in part explain why so much discrepancy of opinion should have existed among authors and practitioners respecting its treatment. Where its remote cause has been but imperfectly known, it is not to be wondered that practitioners, finding their efforts unsuccessful, should lose their confidence in any one set of remedies or mode of treatment, and try a variety, in the vain hope of hitting upon the right one. But in a great measure this is to be attributed to the difference of the affections which have been described by various authors under the same head; each has described it as it occurred to himself; and in many instances it has been only the description of a single epidemic, and, therefore, has given to the world the treatment which his experience in that particular form has proved successful. Thus, the lancet has been looked upon as the only means of saving the patient by those who have witnessed the inflammatory modification of the disease; whereas, in the hands of those who had to treat it in its adynamic malignant form, bleeding (as but too frequently every thing else) proved utterly inefficacious.

A variety of plans have been tried in this last species, and their success described by Dr. W. Hunter in his lectures, gives a fearful view of the nature of the disease we have now to deal with. We continue the quotation which we have already made from him. "In two months thirty-two patients had the fever, and only one of them recovered. We tried various methods. One woman we took from the beginning and bled her, and she died; to another we gave cooling medicines, and she died: to a third we gave warm medicines, such as Confect. Cardiac., cordial julep, Mithridate, &c., and she died. In private practice it was the same, and at least three out of four would die." (MS. Lectures.)

There is no doubt that, wherever the state of the patient will permit it, the lancet should be tried. Where the pulse is quick and small, with little power, it is scarcely more than an experiment to ascertain how the system will bear the bleeding: in the worst cases of the adynamic form, uncomplicated by the slightest effort at reaction, the state of collapse at once forbids such an attempt: but in many instances the circulation is merely oppressed, the pulse rises in volume as the depletion proceeds; and where from its feel before the operation we had little hopes[Pg 460] of taking away more than five or six ounces, we are often enabled to continue it until a considerable quantity is lost. In other cases frightful exhaustion is the immediate effect, and warn us instantly to discontinue it. The capability of bearing bleeding may be always looked upon as a favourable prognostic, not only because the patient's strength is better than we had perhaps expected, and also because these are precisely the cases where mercury can be used with decided benefit. Whether it be the bleeding, which, in all probability, renders the system more easily brought under the influence of this medicine, we will not stop to consider; at any rate, its effects are not only more easily obtained, but they exert a more decided control over the progress of the disease, the pain abates, the tympanitic abdomen becomes less tense, the pulse slower, fuller, and softer, the tongue moister, and there is a sense of general improvement in the patient's feelings. But in the adynamic form, when present in its greatest intensity, either there is not sufficient time to impregnate the system, or it is less sensible to its effects; at any rate, even if we succeed in producing salivation, little or no improvement follows.

In those cases where the inflammatory symptoms assume a metastatic character, we must act according to the organ implicated. The attacks are frequently of a very sudden nature, the patient being seized, without the slightest warning, with severe pain and heat of head, throbbing of the temples, intolerance of light and sound, and occasionally violent delirium; the face is flushed, the carotids are seen strongly pulsating. These signs denote a dangerous attack of cerebral congestion, which requires the most prompt and active measures for its suppression. In these cases the aberration of mind frequently continues for some time, even after the symptoms of active inflammation have subsided, and form a species of puerperal mania of a very dangerous character, which we shall describe under its proper head. In other cases, effusion rapidly comes on, followed by fatal coma or convulsions.

In some instances, the inflammatory action seems to fix itself upon the chest: the patient is suddenly seized with great dyspnœa, oppression, and pain, which latter is much increased by every effort at respiration, and sometimes is so violent as to threaten suffocation, unless promptly relieved by the lancet. These attacks sometimes return two or three times, with the same degree of sudden violence, or change with equal rapidity from one part to another.

So long as there are symptoms of local inflammation present, leeches and hot poultices, &c., must be applied, as already mentioned; but it must ever be borne in mind, that the local affection is not the disease, but one of its effects. We must, therefore, direct our energies to ridding the system of the cause upon which it[Pg 461] depends. In all cases we think it desirable to begin the calomel in doses of five grains, at intervals of two hours; and if properly guarded with Dover's powder, no disposition to purging will be produced: by this means we not only gain time, but, which is also of great importance, we premise a general increase of the excretions, which tends not a little to relieve the system. After two such doses, the calomel may be given at the ordinary rate of two grains every two hours, with half a grain of opium, or, what is still better, a little Dover's powder, until slight marks of salivation begin to appear. The action should now be kept up by an occasional dose, but never allowed to become at all severe, as considerable exhaustion may be the result. The dark and offensive lochia should be constantly removed by the most scrupulous attention to cleanliness, and by frequently washing out the vagina and uterus with warm water.

If diarrhœa has set in to an exhausting degree, the opiates must be increased, and the Hydrarg. cum Cretâ substituted for the calomel. Saline draughts of citrate or acetate of ammonia, rendered alkaline in excess by Sp. Ammon. Arom. may be given from time to time; they appear not only to refresh the patient, but also to allay flatulence and vomiting, if present. For her common drink we recommend a solution of carbonate of soda in water, in the proportion of two drachms to a pint, slightly flavoured with orange peel; and whenever she has taken this freely, we have observed a considerable amelioration in her symptoms.

Although strongly inclined to advocate Dr. Stevens's views respecting the action of salines in diseases of this character, we must confess that we have been in great measure deterred from carrying them out to the full extent that we could have wished, by the repugnance of the patient to taking a draught so intensely salt as his celebrated mixture. On several occasions we have seen the most beneficial effects from the use of salines; and in two cases, during one of the most malignant epidemics, where every thing seemed to be equally fruitless in arresting the progress of the disease, the exhibition of repeated doses of soda, and encouraging the patient to drink largely of the above-mentioned solution, was followed by the happiest effects. We have again recently tried the common salt, disguised as far as possible in the form of an effervescing draught, and in two cases with very decided results.

The acid state of the mouth is a very constant symptom in this disease, and the contents of the stomach after vomiting are frequently intensely sour, so that in most instances the soda drink has been greedily longed for, and by some patients even called lemonade. We have also tried still more recently warm injections into the vagina, of a weak solution of salt and water, but at present, can give no opinion from merely a case or two.

Ice has been lately recommended by Professor Michaelis, of[Pg 462] Kiel, not only internally but externally, by means of a large bladder. According to his observations it diminished the pain and tympanitis, reduced the quickness of the pulse, and relieved the patient considerably; this was followed by a profuse diarrhœa of light coloured and offensive evacuations, under which the pulse rose in power, followed by general improvement. We tried it on one occasion; it was swallowed with avidity like barley-sugar; it relieved the sense of inward heat and thirst, stopped the hiccough and vomiting which had become very troublesome, and seemed to diminish the tympanitis, but collapse followed as rapidly as in other cases; nor have our subsequent observations been more favourable. It may be given with advantage with other medicines to relieve several distressing symptoms, but does not appear to us to exert any power in arresting the progress of the disease.

The patient's diet should be mild but nutritious, much more so than in the other forms of puerperal fever; and if there be symptoms of sinking, wine and ammonia, &c., must be given with a liberal hand.

In reviewing what we have said upon the treatment of adynamic puerperal fever, we repeat our conviction, that where the state of collapse has precluded all antiphlogistic measures, and given us but little cause to expect much relief from mercury, we know of no treatment which holds out such rational hopes of success as the saline, based as it is upon the same principles on which it has been employed by Dr. Stevens, in the malignant fevers of warm climates, and by British physicians in the epidemic typhus of this country.

CHAPTER XIV.

PHLEGMATIA DOLENS.

Nature of the disease.—Definition of phlegmatia dolens.—Symptoms.—Duration of the disease.—Connexion with crural phlebitis.—Causes.—Connexion between the phlegmatia dolens of lying-in women and puerperal fever.—Anatomical characters.—Treatment.—Phlegmatia dolens in the unimpregnated state.

Nature of the disease. Although we shall not be justified in stating that the disease is one of the sequelæ of puerperal fever, inasmuch, as it is occasionally met with, entirely independent of labour and the puerperal state, still we must recognise a very close relation between these two diseases, especially between it and the uterine phlebitis, since, in a majority of instances, they both arise from the same cause, viz. absorption or imbibition of a morbid poison. At the same time, we can by no means agree with Dr. R. Lee, that "the swelling of the affected limbs in phlegmatia dolens, and all the other local and constitutional symptoms of this affection, invariably depend on inflammation of the iliac and femoral veins;" and, therefore, do not consider his proposition justifiable, "to substitute the term crural phlebitis in place of phlegmatia dolens" (Researches on the Pathology and Treatment of some of the more important Diseases of Women, p. 116,) for cases occur where the disease has manifested itself to a very considerable extent without any inflammation of the veins whatever. On the other hand, we willingly allow that in many others it has been preceded by crural phlebitis, although we most distinctly deny that it is ever identical with that disease.

Definition of phlegmatia dolens. We may define phlegmatia dolens to be tumefaction of a limb from inflammation and obstruction of the main lymphatic trunks leading from it. It is most frequently seen in the puerperal state, attacking one or both extremities, and is then almost always a concomitant or a consequence of puerperal fever. In the unimpregnated state it is usually the result of some organic malignant disease. "Women of all descriptions are liable to be attacked by it during or soon after childbed; but those whose limbs have been pained and anasarcous during pregnancy, and who do not suckle their offspring, are more especially subject to it. It has rarely occurred oftener than once to the same female. It supervenes on easy and natural[Pg 464] as well as on difficult and preternatural births. It sometimes makes its appearance in twenty-four or forty-eight hours after delivery, and at other times not till a month or six weeks after; but in general the attack takes place from the tenth to the sixteenth day of the lying-in." (An Essay on Phlegmatia Dolens, by John Hull, M. D. p. 132.)

Symptoms. As the phlegmatia dolens of lying-in women is almost invariably preceded by symptoms of puerperal fever, many of its early symptoms will differ but little from that disease. The patient is usually attacked with rigours, followed by flushing, headach, and generally more or less abdominal pain, with a quick pulse, or the disease has come on when recovering from a severe attack of puerperal fever.

"The complaint generally takes place on one side at first, and the part where it commences is various: but it most commonly begins in the lumbar hypogastric or inguinal region on one side, or in the hip, or top of the thigh, or corresponding labium pudendi. In this case the patient first perceives a sense of pain, weight, and stiffness, in some of the above-mentioned parts, which are increased, by every attempt to move the pelvis or lower limb. If the part be carefully examined, it generally is found rather fuller or hotter than natural, and tender to the touch, but not discoloured. The pain increases, always becomes very severe, and in some cases is of the most excruciating kind. It extends along the thigh, and when it has subsisted for some time, longer or shorter in different patients, the top of the thigh and labium pudendi become greatly swelled, and the pain is then sometimes alleviated, but accompanied with a greater sense of distention," (Hull, op. cit. p. 184.) The pain next extends down to the knee, and if depending on a state of phlebitis is most severe in the course of the femoral vein, which is felt hard and swollen, and rolling distinctly under the finger when pressed upon: it is precisely in the direction of this vessel that the greatest pain is felt on pressing with the hand: if phlebitis be not present, the pain is diffused more equally over the limb, and is more connected with the state of tension, or otherwise, is confined chiefly to the groin or upper part of the thigh. "When it has continued for some time, the whole of the thigh becomes swelled, and the pain is somewhat relieved;" "the pain then extends down the leg to the foot; after some time the parts last attacked begin to swell, and the pain abates in violence, but is still very considerable, especially on any attempt to move the limb. The extremity being now swelled throughout its whole extent, appears perfectly or nearly uniform, and it is not perceptibly lessened by a horizontal position, as an œdematous limb. It is of the natural colour or even whiter, is hotter than natural, excessively tense, and exquisitely tender when touched; when pressed by the finger in different parts, it is found to be elastic, little if any impression[Pg 465] remaining, and that only for a very short time. If a puncture or incision be made into the limb, in some instances no fluid is discharged, in others a small quantity only issues out which coagulates soon after, and in others a larger quantity of fluid escapes which does not coagulate; but the whole of the effused matter cannot be drawn off in this way. The swelling of the limb varies both in degree and in the space of time requisite for its full formation. In most instances, it arrives at double the natural size, and in some cases at a much greater. In lax habits, and in patients whose legs have been very much affected with anasarca during pregnancy, the swelling takes place more rapidly than in those who are differently circumstanced; it sometimes arrives in the former class of patients at its greatest extent in twenty-four hours or less, from the first attack." (Hull, op. cit.)

Phlegmatia dolens rarely or never proves fatal of itself; the patient either dies in consequence of the puerperal fever which has preceded or attended the affection, or from the system gradually sinking under the injury which it has sustained. In those cases where the patient has struggled through, the limb remains for a long time afterwards swollen, stiff, and incapable of motion, from which it slowly and not always very perfectly recovers.

Duration of the disease. "The duration of the acute local symptoms has been very various in different cases. In the greater number, they have subsided in two or three weeks, and sometimes earlier, and the limb has then been left in a powerless and œdematous state. The swelling of the thigh has first disappeared, and the leg and foot have more slowly resumed their natural form. In one case, after the swelling had subsided several months, large clusters of dilated superficial veins were seen proceeding from the foot along the leg and thigh to the trunk, and numerous veins as large as a finger were observed over the lower part of the abdominal parietes. In some women, the extremity does not return to its natural state for many months, or years, or even during life." (Lee, op. cit. p. 119.)

Connexion with crural phlebitis. We have already stated, that in phlegmatia dolens the lymphatic circulation of the swollen limb has been obstructed by inflammation and obliteration of the main lymphatic trunks leading from it. To call this disease "crural phlebitis," because in a case where the crural vein has been inflamed, the inflammation has spread to the surrounding fascia, or cellular tissue, through which the larger lymphatics of the thigh pass in their way to the abdominal cavity, is manifestly incorrect, and tends to confound two diseases together, which are of a very different character. From the situation of the crural vein as it emerges upon the anterior and upper part of the thigh, and the cribriform appearance of the inner side of the femoral sheath, and of the cellular tissue which fills up the opening in the fascia lata at this part, owing to the numerous [Pg 466]lymphatic trunks by which it is perforated, it would be nearly impossible that these structures should escape being inflamed wherever the attack of crural phlebitis is at all severe; and shows that although, as we have stated, phlegmatia dolens may occur without crural phlebitis, it is very questionable if crural phlebitis can exist to any extent without phlegmatia dolens.

To MM. Bouillaud and Velpeau, and also to Dr. Davis, are we chiefly indebted for having first pointed out the fact, that the large venous trunks of the thigh and leg are frequently found inflamed in this disease. Great credit is also due to Dr. R. Lee for his indefatigable researches into the history and anatomy of crural phlebitis, for they have taught practitioners to be on the watch for the existence of the one disease whenever the presence of the other has been determined.

"The sense of pain, at first experienced in the uterine region, has afterwards been chiefly felt along the brim of the pelvis, in the direction of the iliac veins, and has been succeeded by tension and swelling of the part. After an interval of one or more days, the painful tumefaction of the iliac and inguinal regions has extended along the course of the crural vessels, under Poupart's ligament, to the upper part of the thigh, and has descended from thence in the direction of the great blood-vessels to the ham. Pressure along the course of the iliac and femoral vessels has never failed to aggravate the pain, and in no other part of the limb has pressure produced much uneasiness. There has generally been a sensible fulness perceptible above Poupart's ligament, before any tenderness has been experienced along the course of the femoral vessels; and in every case at the commencement of the attack, I have been able to trace the femoral vein proceeding down the thigh like a hard cord, which rolled under the fingers." (R. Lee, op. cit. p. 117.)

Causes. We consider that the causes of crural phlebitis in the puerperal state are of precisely the same nature as those of uterine phlebitis, already mentioned, viz., the absorption or imbibition of putrid matter contained in the uterus; and from reasons which are self-evident, it will be easily understood why the former affection is so frequently preceded by the latter, or at any rate, by some modification of puerperal fever. Mr. Tyre, of Glouscester, in an essay published 1792, and quoted by Dr. Hull, has taken a somewhat similar view of the subject, although he does not appear to have confirmed it by actual observation. He conceived that "the obstruction to the return of the lymph may commence in the primary inflammation of a trunk or trunks; and, probably, this may be the case more frequently than I have hitherto discovered, or suspected it to be." He considered also that "the remote cause may still be sought for in pressure, in the presence of absorbed acrimonious matter, or in inflammation continued from some absorbent to the trunk or trunks," (An Essay on the Swelling of the[Pg 467] Lower Extremities incident to Lying-in Women;) but he overlooked the fact, that this inflammation of the lymphatic trunks, when passing through the cribriform portion of the fascia lata, was a result of its having either extended from the inflamed crural vein, or from inflammation of the peritoneum in the pelvis, and of the subperitoneal tissues.

The connexion between the phlegmatia dolens of lying-in women and puerperal fever has been demonstrated even still more closely by Dr. Hull, a fact which later experience, and a more intimate knowledge of these two diseases has tended to confirm. "It is, perhaps, in every instance, accompanied by considerable marks of pyrexia, and is very frequently preceded by coldness and rigours, which are succeeded by a hot stage, and during this, the pain, stiffness, heat and other inflammatory symptoms invade the loins, hypogastrium, inguen, or some part of the lower extremity, just as they attack the peritoneum in puerperal fever." We may safely assert, that, whenever this disease attacks a lying-in woman, it is invariably preceded by some form of inflammatory puerperal fever, the inflammation having either been transmitted along the vein, or along the subperitoneal tissues, until it reached the above-mentioned cribriform portion of the fascia lata, so that every lymphatic trunk which passed through it would necessarily be implicated in the inflammatory process, and thus rendered impervious. The opinion, therefore, of the inflammation passing along an absorbent until it reaches the main trunks of the lymphatics, appears to be objectionable, as we find it to have been rather transmitted by communication of adjacent parts, although occasionally it attacks the neighbouring glands, producing enlargement and suppuration of them.

Anatomical characters. The details of a dissection which Dr. Lee has reported with great minuteness, show marks of severe inflammation to such an extent around the crural vein, that it is evident the greater part, if not all, of the large lymphatic trunks in that neighbourhood had been rendered impervious by it. "The common iliac, with its subdivisions and the upper part of the femoral veins so resembled a ligamentous cord, that on opening the sheath the vessel was not, until dissected out, distinguishable from the cellular substance surrounding it. On laying open the middle portion of the vein, a firm thin layer of ash-coloured lymph was found in some places adhering close to, and uniting its sides, and in others, clogging it up, but not distending it. On tracing upwards the obliterated vein, that portion which lies above Poupart's ligament, was observed to become gradually smaller, so that in the situation of the common iliac, it was lost in the surrounding cellular membrane, and no traces of its entrance into the vena cava were discernible. The vena cava itself was in its natural state. The entrance of the internal iliac was completely closed, and in the small portion of it, which I had an[Pg 468] opportunity of examining, the inner surface was coated with an adventitious membrane. The lower end of the removed vein was permeable, but its coats were much more dense than natural, and the inner surface was lined with a strong membrane, which diminished considerably its caliber, and here and there fine bands of the same substance ran from one side of the vessel to the other. The outer coat had formed strong adhesions with the artery and the common sheath: the inguinal glands adhered firmly to the veins, but were otherwise in a healthy condition." (Op. cit. p. 123.)

In the other case there is also inflammation of the cellular tissue which fills up the femoral ring, but instead of having been a consequence of crural phlebitis, it has extended to this part from puerperal inflammation of the peritoneum and cellular tissue beneath.

In our midwifery hospital reports (Med. Gaz. Oct. 24. 1835,) we have given the details of an interesting case of this sort which came under our notice during the former year, and which are rendered peculiarly valuable by a most elaborate dissection of the parts after death, by Mr. Nordbald, who was house-surgeon at the time. The patient was single, excessively deformed in her back, and with the peculiarly unhealthy appearance of persons thus afflicted; her labour had been perfectly natural, but on the following day she was seized with rigours, followed by flushings, a quick pulse, and abdominal pain: these symptoms were in great measure relieved, and she appeared to be slowly improving. On the ninth day after labour, she first complained of pain at the outside of the left thigh, extending from the ilium to the knee, very exactly in the course of the inguino-cutaneous nerve: it was tender to the touch, but there was no pain on pressing the femoral vein at the groin. On the following day, the pain and swelling of the thigh had increased, but still no pain was to be detected on pressing the femoral vessels: leeches were ordered, but she sunk immediately after their application, and died early the next morning. Upon examination after death, the body was found "much attenuated; the left thigh one third greater in circumference than the right; abdomen tympanitic, not tense; parietes very thin; the lower part of the ileum, caput coli, and arch of the colon contain air; a streak of inflammation is delineated along the anterior surface of the colon from the centre of the arch, throughout the descending portion of this intestine, to the left iliac region; it is marked by a transverse band of capillary vessels, minutely injected in the thickened peritoneum, along the whole of this course. A few convulsions of the small intestines were smeared with recent lymph, and one fold was found to adhere closely to the left side of the pelvic peritoneum at the point of reflexion of the ligamentum latum uteri. A few small portions of coagulable lymph were also found loose amongst the intestines. At the posterior [Pg 469]surface, and left side of the body of the uterus, soft lymph and pus were effused for the space of an inch beneath the peritoneal covering of this viscus, the membrane itself being highly vascular from inflammation, but still showing the effusion through its texture; the fundus of the uterus, where it has the Fallopian tube and round ligament attached, was similarly affected, though in a slighter degree; lymph and pus were effused here also. From these two points, the inflammation appears to have spread to the rest of the serous membrane: from the first indicated point it has progressed along the posterior fold of the broad ligament to the surface of the rectum and colon; from the second situation the round ligament and Fallopian tube have formed the continuous line of its progress. On raising the peritoneum from the iliac fossa, the cellular membrane which envelopes the round ligament, where this cord is about to pass under the epigastric vessels, after quitting the peritoneal cavity, was found infiltrated and condensed with lymph and pus. The whole of the cellular membrane (which it will be borne in mind is the fascia propria of Sir Astley Cooper, and which fills the femoral ring, and moreover forms the medium of transmission for the lymphatics of the thigh) was in the same condition, densely matted by lymph, and containing pus in the interstices.[146] The lymphatic glands in the groin were slightly enlarged, and some serous fluid was effused into the surrounding tissue; the femoral vein and artery were free from disease; the inner coat of the former vessels, as well as the internal and external iliac veins and vena cava, had not the slightest trace of increased vascularity or thickening. The chain of glands from the femoral ring along the course of the iliac vessels and aorta on the left side, were enlarged, soft, and vascular; several of these lymphatic bodies contained between the layers of the meso-colon were found enlarged, and to contain soft lymph. The uterus was of the size usually found at this period; its tissue dense; the section shows the sinuses still large; the openings on the internal surface plainly indicated by adherent coagula."

We had been led at that time to suppose that phlegmatia dolens and crural phlebitis were identical, and that, therefore, this was not a veritable case of the disease, because no traces of inflammation of the veins were to be found. The history of the disease; its connexion with the puerperal fever which had preceded it, the examination after death, and the inflamed state of the cellular tissue which was perforated by lymphatic trunks on their way from the thigh to the abdominal cavity, plainly show[Pg 470] that it was not only a case of phlegmatia dolens, but that the proximate cause of this affection is obliteration of the lymphatics, whether from inflammation of the adjoining vein, or of the layer of cellular tissue through which they pass.

Treatment. As the earlier part of the disease, when occurring in lying-in women, is invariably accompanied with some form of puerperal fever, the treatment of this stage will be according to the rules we have already laid down in the preceding chapter. It is especially towards the wane of the attack, that any sensation of pain, or even tension about the hip or groin should be regarded with suspicion, and a careful examination of the part immediately instituted. The painful spot should be immediately covered with leeches, and if any pain or swelling be perceptible in the course of the femoral vein, this must be similarly treated in order to allay the inflammation; after this, cold evaporating lotions must be applied; and although we have not yet given it a trial, we would recommend the application of ice over the femoral ring. If she has not taken calomel to such an extent as to affect the system, it may now be given for that purpose; and when the pain has ceased, the part may be covered with a plaster of camphorated mercurial ointment. As the disease, in most instances, is a local affection consequent upon a general one, which has been more or less subdued, by the time that this has appeared, it will frequently be necessary to combine the local depletion and exhibition of mercurials with mild tonics, in order to sustain the powers of the system already somewhat exhausted by the debilitating effects of the puerperal fever. The diet should if possible be nourishing, and we shall frequently find that the general symptoms improve under the use of beef-tea, meat, jellies, &c.

When the acute stage of the disease is past, more powerful tonics, as quinine, will be required; and now we may direct our attention to reduce the swelling of the limb; it may be gently rubbed with the compound camphor liniment for the purpose of stimulating the absorbents. Dr. Hull has given a useful formula for the same object:—"℞. Ung. Adipis Suillæ, ℥jss; Camphoræ, Ziij; quibus liquefactis admisceantur Ol. Essent. Lavend. gtt xij; Tinct. Opii, Zij. Fiat Linimentum, quotide ter quaterve utendum." (Op. cit. p. 161.)

Phlegmatia dolens occurring in the unimpregnated state, is generally in connexion with some malignant disease of the uterus: it has been chiefly observed in cases of carcinoma uteri, and has evidently been the absorption of the fetid discharges which attend this loathsome disease. In all the instances which have come under our knowledge, the swelling of the leg has been preceded by crural phlebitis; the veins have been felt through the emaciated integuments like a hard cord running along the inside of the leg, acutely painful to the touch. A fact connected[Pg 471] with these cases, and for which we are indebted to our late friend and colleague Dr. H. Ley, tends greatly to prove the manner in which the disease is produced. The symptoms of it have never been observed so long as the patient was able to keep up, for by this means a free escape was allowed to the acrid discharges, which are so profuse in the last stages of cancer: but when her strength has been so broken down by loss and suffering that she was obliged to keep her bed, the horizontal position of her body no longer allowed the vagina to drain itself of the fetid secretions with which it was filled, and absorption and venous inflammation have been the result.

In our published lectures, we have mentioned two cases of phlegmatia dolens, which had been under our care at St. Thomas's Hospital, and where, in both, the disease had been thus produced during the ulcerative stage of cancer uteri: the interest of them was somewhat increased by their having been admitted at the same time, and by their happening to lie next to each other in the same ward: in one, the attack of crural phlebitis was severe, and the swelling of the limb very considerable; in the other, the affection was less severe: we did not take any notes of the cases, and must, therefore, refer to a similar one which has been recorded by Mr. Lawrence, and in which, the appearances after death were accurately detailed. The patient came under his care, on account of shooting pains in the loins and hypogastric region, which was tender upon pressure; she had incontinence of urine, and a sanious discharge from the vagina.

On examination, instead of the os tincæ and cervix uteri, a large irregular ulcerated excavation was found at the posterior end of the vagina. Shortly afterwards, increased uneasiness was experienced in the lower part of the abdomen, the right lower extremity swelled in its whole extent, with pain in the course of the femoral and iliac vessels, and all the other symptoms of phlegmatia dolens. The disease was treated by leeches and other antiphlogistic means, and the pain abated considerably; it, however, returned, and in about three weeks after, she died from a violent attack of uterine hæmorrhage. On dissection, the fundus uteri was found somewhat enlarged and firm, the cervix had been destroyed by that kind of phagedenic ulceration, which is commonly called cancer of the uterus. The hypogastric vein was closed in consequence of previous inflammation of its coats, and the same change had taken place in the internal iliac, the common iliac, the external iliac, the femoral and profunda veins, as well as in the internal saphena, all of which were completely impervious. The affection terminated above at the junction of the common iliac with that of the opposite side, the latter vessel being quite natural. The saphena vein was closed for a length of about four or five inches, beyond which it was natural.[Pg 472] The right spermatic vein was closed in its lower half. The coats of the affected vessels, and the surrounding cellular substance were a little thickened, and their cavities were plugged by a closely adherent and tolerably firm substance of a light brown colour; at some parts, the vessels and their contents were of a dark livid hue. (Med. Chir. Trans.)[147]

[Pg 473]

CHAPTER XV.

PUERPERAL MANIA.

Inflammatory or phrenitic form.—Treatment.—Gastro-enteric form.—Treatment.—Adynamic form.—Causes and symptoms.—Treatment.

There are many points of similarity between puerperal convulsions, and the disease which we are now about to consider, so that an acquaintance with the nature of the one, will greatly assist the reader in his study of the other: the same causes which induce the one, will, with trifling modification, induce the other; the different species of puerperal mania, will, therefore, resemble more or less those of puerperal convulsions.

Disorder of the mind, which comes under the head of puerperal mania, is rarely met with before labour; for when it occurs during pregnancy it is usually referrible to causes unconnected with that state, as to hysteria; or is, a form of ordinary mania arising from hereditary predisposition, cerebral diseases, &c. It is true these are conditions which will render the patient exceedingly liable to an attack of derangement during labour, and especially during the puerperal state; but the identity of the affections cannot well be carried farther.

According to our own experience puerperal mania may occur under one of the three following conditions, viz.—

1. Where it is attended with, and probably depends upon, cerebral congestion or inflammation.

2. Where it arises from gastro-enteric irritation.

3. Where it is the result of general debility and anæmia.

The last two rather deserve the title of melancholia.

Inflammatory or phrenitic form. We shall divide the inflammatory form into two species: first, where it is wild and furious delirium with phrenitis; secondly, where it is connected with, and is the result of, puerperal fever. The first, usually comes on during labour: the patient is attacked with violent pain, heat, and throbbing of the head, which are greatly increased by her efforts during the throes; the pulse becomes quick and hard; the face flushed and crimson; the eyes wild, and the manner more and more unnatural: if this state be not promptly checked, the[Pg 474] cerebral excitement becomes more intense, furious delirium follows, which in its turn is succeeded by coma, effusion and paralysis.

On examination after death the ordinary appearances of fatal phrenitis manifest themselves, viz. preternatural fulness of the cerebral vessels, thickening and opacity of the different membranes, softening or even suppuration of the substance of the brain, extravasation of blood, or effusion of serum into the cavities or substance of the brain, or between its membranes.

The other form of inflammatory puerperal mania, is only seen after labour, and is invariably connected with, and preceded by, symptoms of puerperal fever. These are the cases of puerperal mania, where the disease comes on with a rigour, a quick pulse, violent headach, and abdominal pain. In some, the attack has appeared from the very commencement to concentrate itself upon the brain; but in others, it more frequently appears in a day or two afterwards, when, from the subsidence of the abdominal pain, we are beginning to hope that the disease has been more or less controlled. The patient is suddenly seized with intense headach, and other symptoms of cerebral congestion, accompanied by disordered mind; but there is not that degree of furious delirium which is seen in the acute phrenitis; there is less excitement, but there is also, less strength; the powers of the system are rapidly giving away, not so much under the effects of the local disease, as under those of the general affection by which the local disease has been produced. The patient is frequently both violent and obstreperous; but we seldom see that state of wild and furious raving which is observed in acute phrenitis. The former of these two species is of very rare occurrence, but from not being complicated with puerperal fever, it is perhaps not so dangerous, if promptly treated, as the other. Dr. Ferguson, has correctly observed, in puerperal fever, that "any cerebral disturbance diminishes the chances of recovery," and that "the presence of delirium in any case is almost always followed by a fatal result." (Op. cit. p. 49, 50.)

The patient in whom we have chiefly observed phrenitic symptoms during labour were stout, robust, short-necked women, with black oily hair, and a swarthy complexion: from an early stage they had exerted themselves during the pain in a most violent and unnecessary degree, and had gradually worked themselves into that state of excitement, which was followed by the symptoms above-mentioned: in two instances, it was ascertained that the patient had received a violent blow on the head, either during pregnancy, or on some previous occasion. In similar habits the same symptoms have been observed occasionally to accompany the first appearance of the milk, or to follow its sudden suppression when established, or a similar state of the lochia.

Treatment. The treatment differs but little from that of the[Pg 475] congestive epileptic convulsions, already described: she must be bled to fainting, leeches must be applied to the temples, the head shaved and cold applied to it, the feet should be put into hot water, and the bowels opened by an active purge of calomel. If the child be not delivered, and the passages are sufficiently dilated, the forceps should be applied to shorten the labour.

In the other case, which is accompanied with puerperal fever, the propriety of bleeding to any considerable extent will be more questionable; it has probably been already employed in the early part of the original disease, and her powers more or less reduced by it: we must here rather trust to leeches and cold to the head, and bringing the system as soon as possible under the influence of calomel and opium. Whether or not the improvement which follows in some cases of puerperal fever has resulted from the use of saline medicines, we will not pretend to determine; but as, on more than one occasion, we have seen calm and refreshing sleep succeed their exhibition, it is not improbable that they might prove useful in this form of the disease.

We presume that these are the cases to which Dr. Gooch has referred, when he described them as being "attended by fever, or at least, the most important part of it—a rapid pulse;" and that the majority of them prove fatal: their unfavourable result, however, is not so much from the local affection, as from the puerperal fever under which the patient sinks.

Pure phrenitis, which is a rare disease during labour or the puerperal state, is by no means difficult to control by active antiphlogistic treatment, if taken in sufficient time, before the brain has suffered any serious injury; nor is there much danger of her continuing deranged even after the inflammatory symptoms have been reduced. This appears to be also the case in that form which attends puerperal fever; but here the danger to life is so much greater, that we rarely have an opportunity of ascertaining the duration of the mental disorder after the symptoms of cerebral inflammation have been subdued, since most of these cases terminate fatally.

Gastro-enteric form. In the gastro-enteric form, the cerebral symptoms are of a much milder character: the head is perhaps warmer than natural, and it aches a good deal across the forehead and eyes; the face is seldom flushed, but it is sallow, the eye is yellow, the tongue is foul, the breath offensive, and if any evacuations have been passed, they are excessively unhealthy; the abdomen feels full and loaded, the pulse is irritable, but devoid of strength; the patient is seldom violent, and if so, can usually be restrained by the mildest measures. Her previous history will also assist us in our diagnosis; we shall, probably, find that she has for some time suffered from constipation and deranged bowels, or is known to have greatly neglected them before her confinement.

[Pg 476]Puerperal mania from this cause is a result of cerebral irritation, not inflammation, and is a state which will generally cease the moment the cause is removed. As is the case with puerperal convulsions from gastro-enteric irritation, so here the moment we break the chain of morbid sympathies, upon which the disease depends, the symptoms disappear, and are instantly followed by a clearing up of the mental disorder. It usually comes on during the first few days after labour, before the patient has taken the laxative medicine which is customary at this time, and seems to be excited to an outbreak by any little source of mental annoyance or irritation. At first, it appears to be little else than giving way to caprice and temper, but by degrees her manner becomes more changed; and ultimately she grows violent and unmanageable. The state of mind, however, is very different to that of the inflammatory form of puerperal mania; there is no raving delirium, and but a slight degree of incoherence; she understands what is said to her, but reasons erroneously under the influence of a false impression. This state rarely proves dangerous either to her life or her reason, if the proper treatment has been promptly had recourse to; but where it has been allowed to run on for some time, or she has been reduced by antiphlogistic treatment under an erroneous fear of cerebral congestion or inflammation, there may be reason to fear that she will ultimately sink, or at any rate, that the derangement will become permanent.

Treatment. As the pulse scarcely ever betrays a febrile or inflammatory condition of the system, for although quick, it is seldom observed to be full and hard, bleeding is rarely required in this form of puerperal mania, leeches and cold applications being almost sufficient to control any symptoms of determination to the head which may be present: it is upon purgatives that we must place our chief hope in this disease, for until the bowels have been thoroughly and effectively cleared, there will be little chance of the symptoms being alleviated. In some cases it is scarcely credible to what an extent this may be carried; day after day sees the patient relieved of copious, dark, and offensive evacuations, which are evidently not merely the result of enormous accumulations in the bowels, but of excrementitious matters, which are thrown off by the secreting vessels of the liver and alimentary canal. So far from producing debility, the pulse rises with each relief and becomes fuller and slower, the face resumes a healthier aspect, the tongue becomes cleaner, the headach subsides, reason regains its ascendancy, and this favourable change is followed by calm and refreshing sleep. We could quote several cases of our own, in illustration of this form of puerperal mania and its treatment, where the symptoms have quickly yielded, as soon as the source of irritation had been removed from the system; the patient has recovered favourably,[Pg 477] although in most instances she has retained a sufficient recollection of what had passed to feel much vexed and even shocked at, what she was aware had been, very strange and unruly conduct; but we prefer selecting Dr. Gooch's thirteenth case, of which the details are given so graphically, as not a little to enhance the value of it.

"A lady, twenty-two years of age, clever, susceptible, and given to books, was confined with her first child at ——, — miles from town: she was anxious to nurse it; but several days passing with little appearance of milk, doubts began to be entertained whether she would be able: she thought she would, her nurse and surgeon thought she would not: this led to irritating discussions; her manner became sharp, quick, and unnatural; and at the end of a few days she was decidedly maniacal. I and another physician were now sent for; we found her in a straight waistcoat, incessantly talking and reciting poetry; her skin was hot, her pulse full, and much above 100; her tongue covered with a dark thick fur; her bowels were confined, and her stools excessively dark and offensive; she took a dose of calomel and jalap, followed by small doses of sulphate of magnesia; these produced a few evacuations, but they were followed by no relief; she talked almost incessantly, scarcely ever slept, and was so violent that it was impossible to keep her in bed without the straight waistcoat. Thus three days passed from our first consultation. The physician who attended with me, thinking the case would be protracted, withdrew, and I was directed to take Dr. Sutherland down with me. As the purgative had operated very moderately, and the tongue and stools were as unnatural as at first, he proposed a more active purge. The next morning, therefore, she took a strong dose of senna and salts, made still more active by the addition of tincture of jalap; after this had been taken about three hours, it procured a very large evacuation, nearly black, and horribly offensive; this was as usual discharged into the bed without any notice on the part of the patient; it acted again an hour or two afterwards; but now the nurse, who was sitting by her bed-side, was surprised to see her turn round, and in a calm and natural manner request to be taken up, as her medicine was going to operate; her waistcoat was immediately loosened, and she was taken out of bed, when she voided a stool of prodigous size, as dark and offensive as the first, and then walked back to her bed calm and collected. We saw her not many hours afterwards; her waistcoat was off, she was lying on her sofa perfectly tranquil, answered questions correctly, manifested no vestige of her complaint, excepting some strangeness in the expression of her countenance, and a timidity and abstinence from conversation which was not natural to her: she recovered rapidly and uninterruptedly." (Account of some of the most important Diseases peculiar to Women, by Robert Gooch, M. D. p. 156.)

[Pg 478]The chances of recovery in puerperal mania, from, gastro-enteric irritation are as great as they are small in the inflammatory form connected with puerperal fever: the danger is more from erroneous practice on the part of the medical attendant, who either prostrates the powers of life by active depletion, under the supposition that he is treating a case of cerebral congestion, or aggravates the disorder of the mind into wild delirium, by the exhibition of opium, to procure sleep. It is in these cases that we occasionally see so much relief procured by the action of emetics, as at one time to have been considered nearly specific in this disease, by some of the French practitioners. If the powers be good, we cannot agree with Dr. Gooch, in objecting to the use of antimony; when in a sufficient dose, and combined with ipecacuanha, it is too speedy in its operation to depress the patient much by nausea, and has the additional advantage of acting as a rapid and effectual purge: when its action is over, she usually falls into a sound sleep, perspires freely, and wakes greatly refreshed.

The indiscriminate use of emetics in puerperal mania, is not less mischievous than that of bleeding; they are chiefly indicated in those cases, where, in addition to the symptoms above-mentioned, there are signs of a foul and oppressed stomach, and where the patient either complains of nausea, or has already made several attempts to vomit. As soon as the offending cause is removed, the bowels should be kept open by mild alterative and laxative medicine, as equal parts of blue pill, compound extract of colocynth, and extract of henbane, in two pills at night, and a mineral acid in some bitter infusion during the day. The food should be bland but nutritious, the mind quietly but agreeably occupied, and all excitement carefully avoided. In this form of puerperal mania, it is not only a rare occurrence to find that the disordered state of the mind continues, when the cause which had produced it no longer exists, but it is scarcely ever known to return in the patient's subsequent confinements. In the case which has been so ably recorded by Dr. Gooch, the patient has since had a very large family, her labours have all been perfectly favourable, and without the slightest symptom of her former disease.

The adynamic form of puerperal mania is by far the most common species of the disease, and like the adynamic puerperal convulsions, arises from causes which produce exhaustion and collapse in the general powers of the system. It is to Dr. Gooch that we are indebted for a masterly exposition of this disease, and for having been one of the first to point out its real character.

Causes and symptoms. This form of disordered mind is a disease of true debility, and is closely allied to delirium tremens, and convulsions anæmia. It can scarcely be said[Pg 479] to deserve either the terms "puerperal," or "mania," for we frequently see a very near approach to it in females who are much weakened by hæmorrhage, either from menorrhagia, malignant disease of the uterus, or abortion; and from being a disease which arises from great exhaustion, it rather deserves the name of melancholia, than of mania. In lying-in women, "there are two periods at which this is chiefly liable to occur; the one soon after delivery, when the body is sustaining the effects of labour, the other several months afterwards, when the body is sustaining the effects of nursing." (Gooch, op. cit. p. 109.) In the one case, it is usually the result of profuse hæmorrhage, in the other, it is suckling her child when she is not strong enough for this purpose. "I have repeatedly seen the commencement of mental derangement in women who had recovered from their confinement and had been suckling several months. Nearly all these cases were instances, not of mania but of melancholia. They occurred in women who had been debilitated by nursing. The disease at this period has been attributed to weaning; but, in all cases, I have seen, the disease has begun before the weaning, and this measure has been resorted to, because the patient had neither milk nor strength to fit her for a nurse. There was a peculiarity about the commencement of the disease which I have seldom or never noticed at the commencement of mania; there was an incipient stage in which the mind was wrong, yet right enough to recognise that it was wrong." (Gooch, op. cit. p. 114.)

This half-way state of mind between reason and derangement is frequently seen in women who have been exhausted by menorrhagia, leucorrhœa, &c., or who have been drained by nursing. We confess that we can see but little difference in the effects of anæmia upon the brain and nervous system, whether it be in the unimpregnated or puerperal state, beyond that, on account of the great changes which have taken place in the system by the process of labour, by the secretion of milk, &c., the system is probably more irritable, and susceptible than it would otherwise be. Nothing is more common than to see, in cases of menorrhagia, the mind becoming enfeebled, the memory impaired; the patient begins to find that she can no longer control her thoughts in the ordinary manner, but that strange trains of ideas will pass through her mind, the source of which she cannot explain, and frequently so unaccountably, as to cause her serious uneasiness: "If this goes on so, I shall lose my senses," is almost a never failing observation; and the dread that this will be the case, tends to depress the system still more. The sleep is disturbed by frightful dreams, or she passes night after night in wakeful restlessness; she worries herself about trifles, her manner changes, and the mind at length is quite disordered. The same train of symptoms is a frequent result of over-suckling, and as Dr. Gooch[Pg 480] has justly observed, is not the result of weaning. "In all the cases which I have seen, months after delivery, the weaning has been the consequence of the disease, not the disease the consequence of the weaning. The patients had been reduced in health by nursing, their memories had become enfeebled, their spirits depressed, and their minds ultimately disordered; they were directed to wean their children, because they had neither milk nor strength to enable them to nurse." (Op. cit. p. 130.)

A similar state of mind may be induced at an earlier period and more suddenly, by the effects of a profuse hæmorrhage, by serious discharges, which occasionally take place shortly after labour, or even by mental depression; in fact, by whatever lowers the vital powers to a considerable extent. In these cases, the very history and appearance of the patient are sufficient to explain the nature of the disease: her hollow eyes, pale face, and blanched lip, show distinctly how her strength has been reduced. The source and extent of her debilitated state will in great measure determine the degree of danger, and the chances of her recovery. In ordinary cases of this form there is not much to fear, as far as the life of the patient is concerned; and the cases which have come under our own notice confirm the excellent remark of Dr. Gooch, "that mania is a less durable disease than melancholia; it is more dangerous to life, but less dangerous to reason." But if the disordered mind has come on shortly after labour, in consequence of profuse flooding; if the powers of the system have rallied but imperfectly, and from the tinnitus aurium, strabismus, half vision, &c., it is evident that the cerebral functions are greatly impaired; if the nights are passed without sleep, and the days in continued and exhausting excitement; if the pulse be feeble and rapid, the skin cold and clammy, the face covered with perspiration, and there is a disposition to colliquative diarrhœa, we shall have but too much reason to fear an unfavourable issue; every symptom denotes that the powers of the system have received a fatal blow, and she either sinks exhausted, or dies in a state of coma, probably from serous effusion upon the brain. On the contrary, if in addition to a general improvement, she has enjoyed some hours of refreshing sleep, there is every prospect, not only of returning health, but also of reason. A mere gleam of returning reason without a corresponding improvement of health, will afford but little satisfaction to the mind of a discerning practitioner, for it gives no assurance that the danger of fatal sinking is at all diminished.

Disordered mind coming on some weeks after delivery from the effects of over-nursing, when the patient has been unable to afford the necessary supply to her child, is seldom attended with so much danger to life, as where suddenly induced immediately after labour by hæmorrhage: the intermediate stage between[Pg 481] reason and derangement is more distinctly marked, and is of considerable duration; and the gradually increasing affection of the mind frequently warns even the patient herself to seek medical advice before the symptoms become more serious.

We believe that the proportion of patients in whom the mind continues deranged after their health has been restored, is very small, and feel convinced that the results afforded by the practice of lunatic hospitals are far from giving a correct estimate. A large majority of the cases of derangement in lying-in women are of such short duration that they never come even under the notice of those members of the profession whose attention is particularly devoted to this branch of medical practice, still less do they require to be removed into asylums for lunatics. "The records of hospitals contain an account of cases which have been admitted only because they were unusually permanent; they are the picked obstinate cases, and can afford no notion of the average duration of all kinds; the cases of short duration, which last only a few days or a few weeks, which form a large proportion, are totally lost in the estimate of a lunatic hospital." (Gooch, op. cit. p. 125.) The results of Dr. Gooch's practice, which is known to have been very extensive, and especially in consultation, shows that out of a considerable number of cases only two of his patients remained disordered in mind, "and of these, one had already been so before her marriage." There are two classes of patients in whom disordered mind is not only much to be apprehended during their lying-in, but in whom there will be some reason to fear that it may become permanent; first, in those who have already been deranged, independent of the puerperal state, or who inherit a strong predisposition to mental disease; and secondly, in those where hysteria has existed in an unusual degree during the latter part of pregnancy. These circumstances justify us in using every precaution in their lying-in to avoid any thing which may excite the disease; but, as already stated, not only is the disorder of the mind rarely of any duration, but it is seldom known to recur on any subsequent occasion.

Treatment. Our indications of treatment are two-fold, viz., to rouse and support the powers of the patient, and to allay as far as possible the irritability of the brain and nervous system.

If the patient has been prostrated by hæmorrhage, not only a nutritious, but even a cordial and stimulant diet will be necessary: the emulsion of egg and brandy, which we have before recommended in anæmic puerperal convulsions, will here prove very useful; and it must be given in small but frequently repeated doses, until an improvement is observed in the pulse and in her general appearance. Under all circumstances, it will scarcely ever be proper or even safe to confine her to low diet: beaf-tea, veal-broth, &c. should be given in considerable quantities during the twenty-four hours; and it is surprising what improvement will even[Pg 482] take place merely from the administration of this bland nutriment. If the face be pale and the pulse low, wine may be given according to the circumstances of the case.

To calm the cerebral excitement and procure sleep, sedatives will prove of the greatest value, and require to be repeated until the nervous system is fairly under their influence. The intense pain at the vertex, which of itself is sometimes quite sufficient to produce delirium, the tinnitus aurium, &c., all cease; the pulse becomes softer, fuller, and slower; and, even if sleep be not immediately induced, a state of calm tranquillity follows, in which the mind becomes more composed. The Liquor Opii Sedativus may be given in a dose of twenty-five minims, and repeated in an hour or so according to circumstances. The combination of camphor with morphia, or extract of henbane, is an excellent form, and may be given with perfect safety to a considerable extent.

The bowels should be opened by the mildest laxatives, such as castor oil, rhubarb and manna, &c., medicines which will neither act violently, nor weaken by producing watery evacuations; and, once in every few days, it will be desirable to rouse the action of the liver by Hydrarg. c. Cretâ, with extract of hop or gentian. To assist still farther in restoring her health and strength, she should take an infusion of a vegetable bitter with a mineral acid. As soon as her strength will permit, a change of residence may be recommended, and she should remove to some quiet watering-place, where invigorating air and agreeable scenery and occupations will assist in completing her recovery.

"The constant attendants on the patient ought to be those who will control her effectually but mildly, who will not irritate her, and will protect her from self-injury. These tasks are seldom well performed by her own servants and relatives.

"If the disease lasts more than a few days, and threatens to be of considerable duration, her monthly nurse and own servants ought to be removed, and a nurse accustomed to the care of deranged persons placed in their stead. Such an attendant will have more control over the patient, and be more likely to protect her from self-injury." "With regard to the removal of her husband and relations, this also will be a question; if the disease threatens to be lasting, it is generally right. Interviews with relations and friends are commonly passed in increased emotion, remonstrance, altercation, and obviously do harm: large experience also is decidedly favourable to separation as a general rule; yet there may be exceptions, which the intelligent practitioner will detect by observing the effect of intercourse." (Gooch, op. cit. p. 158.)

INDEX.

243

Presentation of the, 273. See Presentation.

Ventral Pregnancy, 119. See Extra-uterine Pregnancy.

Vesicle, germinal, of the egg, 65. See Egg.

Violent uterine action, precipitate labour from, 361.

Wigand's views as to the duration of labour, 178.

Womb, 30. See Uterus.

Yelk-bag, 65. See Egg.

THE END.

MEDICAL AND SURGICAL BOOKS.

PUBLISHED

BY

LEA & BLANCHARD,

PHILADELPHIA.

THE
AMERICAN
JOURNAL OF THE MEDICAL SCIENCES,
EDITED BY ISAAC HAYS, M. D.
SURGEON TO WILLS HOSPITAL, &c. &c.

TERMS.

Each number contains 260 pages, or upwards, and is frequently illustrated by coloured engravings. It is published on the first of November, February, May and August. Price Five Dollars per annum, payable in advance.

Orders, enclosing the amount of one year's subscription, addressed to the publishers, or any of the agents, will receive prompt attention. The year of this work commences with the November number.

Persons sending Twenty Dollars will be entitled to five copies of the work, to be forwarded as they may direct. All persons desirous of advancing the interest of medical science, are requested to use their efforts to increase its circulation.

The postage per number is, within 100 miles, about 16 cents; over 100 miles, about 28 cents.

A few complete sets may be had at a large discount from the subscription price. Odd numbers can be furnished to complete sets.

The following Extracts show the estimation in which the Journal is held.

"Several of the American Journals are before us. * * * Of these, the American Journal of the Medical Sciences is by far the better periodical; it is, indeed, the best of the trans-atlantic medical publications; and, to make a comparison nearer home, is in most respects superior to the great majority of European works of the same description."—The London Lancet.

"We need scarcely refer our esteemed and highly eminent contempory, [The American Journal of Medical Sciences,] from whom we quote, to our critical remarks of the opinions of our own countrymen, or to the principles which influence us in the discharge of our editorial duties."—"Our copious extracts from his unequalled publication, unnoticing multitudes of others which come before us, are the best proof of the esteem which we entertain for his talents and abilities."—London Medical and Surgical Journal.

"The Medical Journal of Medical Sciences is one of the most complete and best edited of the numerous periodical publications of the United States."—Bulletan des Sciences Medicales, tome xiv.

"The Medical Journal of Medical Sciences is conducted with distinguished ability. Published in one of the most literary cities in our country, and supported by a number of her most gifted and best educated physicians, its reputation is deservedly high as well abroad as at home."—Transylvania Journal.

MANUAL of MATERIA MEDICA and PHARMACY, By H. M. Edwards, M. D. and P. Vavasseur, M. D.

CHEMICAL MANIPULATION. Instruction to Students on the Methods of performing Experiments of Demonstration or Research, with accuracy and success. By Michael Farriday, F. R. S. First American, from the second London edition, with additions by J. K. Mitchell, M. D.

A FLORA of NORTH AMERICA, with 108 coloured Plates. By W. P. C. Barton, M. D. In 3 vols. 4to.

A MEDICAL ACCOUNT OF THE MINERAL SPRINGS OF VIRGINIA. By Professor Gibson. (In preparation.)

A MANUAL OF MEDICAL JURISPRUDENCE. By Professor R. E. Griffith. In one volume. (Now preparing.)

THE PRINCIPLES AND PRACTICE OF MEDICINE. By professor Dunglison. In two volumes, octavo. (In preparation.)

A NEW DICTIONARY,
OF
MEDICAL SCIENCE AND LITERATURE.

A NEW EDITION,
Completely Revised, with Numerous Additions and Improvements,
OF
DUNGLISON'S DICTIONARY
OF
MEDICAL SCIENCE AND LITERATURE:
CONTAINING

A concise account of the various Subjects and Terms, with a vocabulary of Synonymes in different languages, and formulæ for various officinal and empirical preparations, &c.

IN ONE ROYAL 8vo. VOLUME.

"The present undertaking was suggested by the frequent complaints, made by the author's pupils, that they were unable to meet with information on numerous topics of professional inquiry,—especially of recent introduction,—in the medical dictionaries accessible to them.

It may, indeed, be correctly affirmed, that we have no dictionary of medical subjects and terms which can be looked upon as adapted to the state of the science. In proof of this the author need but to remark, that he has found occasion to add several thousand medical terms, which are not to be met with in the only medical lexicon at this time in circulation in the country.

The present edition will be found to contain many hundred terms more than the first, and to have experienced numerous additions and modifications.

The author's object has not been to make the work a mere lexicon or dictionary of terms, but to afford, under each, a condensed view of its various medical relations, and thus to render the work an epitome of the existing condition of medical science."

"To execute such a work requires great erudition, unwearied industry, and extensive research, and we know no one who could bring to the task higher qualifications of this description than Professor Dunglison."—American Medical Journal.

"This is an excellent compilation, and one that cannot fail to be very much referred to. It is the best medical lexicon in the English language that has yet appeared. We do not know any volume which contains so much information in a small compass. The Bibliographical notices, though so short, are very important and useful; and altogether we can recommend to every medical man to have this work by him, as the cheapest and best dictionary of reference he can have."—London Medical and Surgical Journal.

"So far as we have been able to examine this Dictionary, it is exceedingly thorough and correct, not only in matters purely medical, but in whatever can fairly be arranged in the various branches of science, collateral or contributary to Medicine and Surgery."—Medical Magazine.

"So well known are the merits of this valuable work, that, in noticing a second edition of it, it will suffice to extract the remark of the author in the preface, 'that it will be found to contain many hundred terms more than the first, and to have experienced numerous additions and modifications.' It has been got up by the publishers in very handsome style, and must command, as it deserves, an extended circulation."—Medical Examiner.

"It is wholly unnecessary, we apprehend, to enter into a long or formal statement of the fact, that Dr. Dunglison's Dictionary, from the first day of its appearance, has been regarded with peculiar favour. And we have now a revised edition, constructed under the immediate eye of the author, who is most favourably circumstanced for adding to the previous edition whatever could give it additional claims on the score of accuracy. Here are eight hundred and twenty-one pages, large octavo, in double colums, distinct type, of which no one ought to complain. Finally, although most of our readers may be owners of the first edition, we cordially and conscientiously recommend to all future purchasers to procure this in preference to any medical lexicon extant. Its true and sterling value as a key to medical science, and its moderate price, are so many common-sense recommendations which should not be forgotten."—Boston Medical and Surgical Journal.

A NEW AND VALUABLE WORK
FOR
PHYSICIANS, APOTHECARIES, AND STUDENTS.

NEW REMEDIES,
The Method of Preparing & Administering them;
THEIR EFFECTS
UPON THE

HEALTHY AND DISEASED ECONOMY,
&c. &c.

BY ROBLEY DUNGLISON, M. D.

Professor of the Institutes of Medicine and Materia Medica in Jefferson Medical College of Philadelphia; Attending Physician to the Philadelphia Hospital, &c.

IN ONE VOLUME, OCTAVO.

"The value of this book is hardly to be estimated; to be without it, would be very much like obstinacy, and amount to the same thing as saying, like the Austrians in regard to their government, nothing can be improved, for we already live in a state of perfection. Dr. Dunglison, the author, has done an essential service to all classes of practitioners. It is creditable to the industry and wise discrimination of the author, and quite necessary to the libraries of those who feel the necessity of keeping pace with the improvements and discoveries in the broad but imperfectly exploded domain of medicine."—Boston Medical and Surgical Journal.

A Third Edition, Improved and Modified, of
DUNGLISON'S
HUMAN PHYSIOLOGY:
Illustrated With Numerous Engravings.
IN TWO VOLUMES, OCTAVO.

"We are happy to believe that the rapid sale of the last edition of this valuable work may be regarded as an indication of the extending taste for sound physiological knowledge in the American schools: and what we then said of its merits, will show that we regarded it as deserving the reception it has experienced. Dr. Dunglison has, we are glad to perceive, anticipated the recommendation which we gave in regard to the addition of references, and has thereby not only added very considerably to the value of his work, but has shown an extent of reading which, we confess, we were not prepared by his former edition to expect. He has also availed himself of the additional materials supplied by the works that have been published in the interval, especially those of Müller and Burdach. So that as a collection of details on human physiology alone, we do not think that it is surpassed by any work in our language: and we can recommend it to students in this country (England) as containing much with which they will not be likely to meet elsewhere."—British and Foreign Medical Review.

"This work exhibits another admirable specimen of American industry and talent, and contains an account of every discovery in Europe up to the period of a few months prior to its publication. Many of the author's views are original and important."—Dublin Journal of Medical Sciences.

GENERAL THERAPEUTICS;
OR,
PRINCIPLES OF MEDICAL PRACTICE.

With Tables of the Chief Remedial Agents and their Preparations, and of the
Different Poisons and their Antidotes.

By Robert Dunglison, M. D., &c., &c.

One Volume, large 8vo.

"There being at, present before the public several American works on Therapeutics, written by physicians and teachers of distinction, it might be deemed unjust in us, and would certainly be invidious, to pronounce any of them superior to the others. We shall not, therefore, do so. If there be, however, in the English language, any work of the kind more valuable than that we have been examining, its title is unknown to us.

"We hope to be able to give such an account of the work as will strengthen the desire and determination of our readers to seek for a farther acquaintance with it, by a candid perusal of the volume itself. And, in so doing, we offer them an assurance that they will be amply rewarded for their time and labour."—Transylvania Journal, Vol. IX, No. 3.

THE MEDICAL STUDENT; or, Aids to the Study of Medicine. Including a Glossary of the Terms of the Science, and of the Mode of Prescribing; Bibliographical Notices of Medical Works; the Regulations of the Different Medical Colleges of the Union, &c. By Robley Dunglison, M. D., &c., &c. In one volume, 8vo.

ELEMENTS OF HYGIENE; on the Influence of Atmosphere and Locality; Change of Air and Climate, Seasons, Food, Clothing, Bathing, Sleep, Corporeal and Intellectual Pursuits, &c., on Human Health, Constituting Elements of Hygiene. By Robley Dunglison, M. D. &c., &c. In 1 vol. 8vo.

MEDICAL ESSAYS.

THE CYCLOPEDIA OF
PRACTICAL MEDICINE AND SURGERY,

Or Essays on ASTHMA, APHTHÆ, ASPHYXIA, APOPLEXY, ARSENIC, ATROPA, AIR, ABORTION, ANGINA-PEC-TORIS, and other Subjects Embraced in the Articles from A to Azote, prepared for the Cyclopedia of Practical Medicine by

Dr. Chapman,
Dr. Jackson,
Dr. Horner,
Dr. Hodge,
Dr. Wood,   Dr. Dewees,
Dr. Hays,
Dr. Dunglison,
Dr. Mitchell,   Dr. Bache,
Dr. Coates,
Dr. Condie,
Dr. Emerson,
Dr. Geddings,   Dr. Griffith,
Dr. Harris,
Dr. Warren,
Dr. Patterson,
Each article is complete within itself, and embraces the practical experience of its author, and as they are only to be had in this collection will be found of great value to the profession.

⁂ The two volumes are now offered at a price so low, as to place them within the reach of every practitioner and student.

GIBSON'S SURGERY.
A NEW EDITION OF GIBSON'S SURGERY.

THE INSTITUTES AND PRACTICE OF SURGERY; being the Outlines of a Course of Lectures. By William Gibson, M. D., Professor of Surgery in the University of Pennsylvania, &c. &c. Fifth edition, greatly enlarged. In 2 vols. 8vo. With thirty plates, several of which are coloured.

"The author has endeavoured to make this edition as complete as possible, by adapting it to the present condition of surgery, and to supply the deficiencies of former editions by adding chapters and sections on subjects not hitherto treated of. And, moreover, the arrangement of the work has been altered by transposing parts of the second volume to the first, and by changing entirely the order of the subject in the second volume. This has been done for the purpose of making the surgical course in the university correspond with the anatomical lectures, so that the account of surgical diseases may follow immediately the anatomy of the parts."

DEWEES'S WORKS.

A PRACTICE OF PHYSIC, comprising most of the diseases not treated of in Diseases of Females and Diseases of Children. By W. P. Dewees, M. D., formerly adjunct professor in the University of Pennsylvania. In one volume, octavo.

A COMPENDIOUS SYSTEM OF MIDWIFERY.

By Dr. Dewees.

Chiefly designed to facilitate the Inquiries of those who may be pursuing this branch of Study. Illustrated by occasional cases and with many plates. The ninth edition, with additions and improvements. In one vol. 8vo.

DEWEES ON THE DISEASES OF FEMALES.

The seventh edition. Revised and Corrected. With additions, and Numerous plates. In one vol. 8vo.

DEWEES ON THE PHYSICAL AND MEDICAL TREATMENT OF CHILDREN.

With Corrections and Improvements. The seventh ed. In one volume, 8vo.

The objects of this work are, 1st, to teach those who have the charge of children, either as parent or guardian, the most approved methods of securing and improving their physical powers. This is attempted by pointing out the duties which the parent or the guardian owes for this purpose, to this interesting but helpless class of beings, and the manner by which their duties shall be fulfilled. And 2d, to render available a long experience to these objects of our affection when they become diseased. In attempting this, the author has avoided as much as possible, "technicality;" and has given, if he does not flatter himself too much, to each disease of which he treats, its appropriate and designating characters, with a fidelity that will prevent any two being confounded together, with the best mode of treating them, that either his own experience or that of others has suggested.

HORNER'S SPECIAL ANATOMY.

A Treatise on Special and General Anatomy. By W. E. Horner, M. D., Professor of Anatomy in the University of Pennsylvania, &c. &c. Fifth edition, Revised, and much improved. In two volumes, 8vo.

ELLIS' MEDICAL FORMULARY.

The Medical Formulary, being a collection of prescriptions derived from the writings and practice of many of the most eminent Physicians in America and Europe. To which is added an appendix, containing the usual Dietetic preparations and Antidotes for Poisons, the whole accompanied with a few brief Pharmacuetic and Medical observations. By Benjamin Ellis, M. D., Fifth edition, with additions. In one vol.

Broussais on Inflammation, 2 vols. 8vo.
Broussais' Pathology, 1 vol. 8vo.
Colles' Surgical Anatomy, 1 vol. 8vo.
Costers' Physiological Practice, 1 vol. 8vo.
Greys' Chemistry applied to the Arts, 2 vols. with numerous plates.

ELEMENTS of PHYSICS, or NATURAL PHILOSOPHY, GENERAL and MEDICAL, explained independently of TECHNICAL MATHEMATICS, and containing New Disquisitions and Practical Suggestions. By Neil Arnott, M. D. In two volumes, octavo.

"Dr. Arnott's work has done for Physics as much as Locke's Essays did for the science of mind."—London University Magazine.

"We may venture to predict that it will not be surpassed."—Times.

"Dr. A. has not done less for Physics than Blackstone did for the Law."—Morning Herald.

"Dr. A. has made Natural Philosophy as attractive as Buffon made Natural History."—French Critic.

"A work of the highest class among the productions of mind."—Courier.

ROGET'S PHYSIOLOGY AND PHRENOLOGY.

OUTLINES OF PHYSIOLOGY;
WITH AN
APPENDIX ON PHRENOLOGY;
BY P. M. ROGET., M. D.
Professor of Physiology in the Royal Institute of Great Britain, &c. &c.
FIRST AMERICAN EDITION,
Revised, with numerous notes,
In one volume, 8vo.

From the American Preface.—"Of the Author's qualifications as a physiological writer it is scarcely requisite to speak. The fact of his having been selected to compose the Bridgewater Treatise on Animal and Vegetable Physiology, is sufficient evidence of the reputation which he then enjoyed; and the mode in which he executed the task amply evinces that his reputation rested on a solid basis.

"The present volume contains a concise, well-written epitome of the present state of Physiology—human and comparative—not, as a matter to be expected, the copious details and developments to be met with in the larger treatises on the subject; but enough to serve as an accompaniment and guide to the physiological student.

"The attention of the American Editor has been directed to the revision and correction of the text; to the supplying, in the form of notes, of omissions; to the rectification of some of the points that appeared to him erroneous or doubtful, and to the furnishing of references to works in which the physiological inquirer might meet with more ample information.

"In Phrenology, the Author is a well-known unbeliever, and his published objections to the doctrine have been regarded as too cogent to be permitted to pass unheeded. It will be seen on farther examination in the interval of many years, which has elapsed since the publication of the sixth edition of the Encyclopædia, has not induced him to modify his sentiments on this head. On the contrary, he appears to be as satisfied at this time, of the fallacy of the positions of the Phrenologist, as he was at any former period."

☐ This work will be introduced into many of the Medical Colleges of the union as a Text Book, it being a cheap volume, and well fitted as an introduction to the larger works on Physiology.

COATES POPULAR MEDICINE:

POPULAR MEDICINE;
OR, FAMILY ADVISER.

Consisting of outlines of Anatomy, Physiology, and Hygiene, with such Hints on the Practice of Physic, Surgery, and the Diseases of Women and Children, as may prove useful in families when regular Physicians cannot be procured: Being a Companion and Guide for intelligent Principals of Manufactories, Plantations, and Boarding Schools: Heads of Families, Masters of Vessels, Missionaries, or Travellers, and a useful Sketch for Young Men about commencing the Study of Medicine.

BY REYNELL COATES, M. D.

Fellow of the College of Physicians of Philadelphia—Honorary Member of the Philadelphia Medical Society—Correspondent of the Lyceum of Natural History of New York—Member of the Academy of Natural Sciences of Philadelphia—Formerly Resident Surgeon of the Pennsylvania Hospital, &c.

Assisted by several Medical friends. In One Volume.

"It is with great satisfaction that we announce this truly valuable compilation, as the most complete and interesting treatise on Popular Medicine ever presented to the public. Simple and unambitious in its language, free from the technicalities, and embracing the most important facts on Anatomy, Physiology and Hygiene, or the art of preserving health; and the treatment of those affections which require immediate attention, or are of an acute character, this should be in the hands of every one, more particularly of those who, by their situations are prevented from resorting to the advice of a physician, nor would the careful perusal of its pages fail to profit the inhabitants of our cities, by giving them a more accurate knowledge of the structure of the human frame, and the laws that govern its various functions; whose perfect integrity is absolutely essential to health, and even to existence; the various systems of medical charlatanry, daily imagined to take advantage of the credulity and ignorance of mankind, would be rendered far less prejudicial to the community than they now are. We would particularly direct attention to the Chapter on Hygiene, a science in itself of the utmost importance, and ably treated in the small space allowed to it in this volume."—New York American.

DR. CLARK ON CONSUMPTION.

A Treatise on Pulmonary Consumption, comprehending an inquiry into the Nature, Causes, Prevention, and Treatment of Tuberculous and Scrofulous Diseases in General. By James Clark, M. D., F. R. S.

"As a text-book and guide to the inexperienced practitioner we know none equal to it in general soundness and practical utility—to the general as well as to the professional reader, the work will prove of the deepest interest, and its perusal of unequivocal advantage."—British and Foreign Medical Review.

"The work of Dr. Clark may be regarded as the most complete and instructive Treatise on Consumption in the English Language."—Edinburgh Medical and Surgical Journal.

CHITTY'S JURISPRUDENCE.

A Practical Treatise on Medical Jurisprudence, with so much of Anatomy, Physiology, Pathology, and the Practice of Medicine and Surgery, as are essential to be known by Members of the Bar and Private Gentlemen; and all the laws relating to Medical Practitioners; with explanatory plates. By J. Chitty, Esq. Second American edition: with Notes and Additions, adapted to American works and Judicial Decisions. 8vo.

A TREATISE ON THE PRACTICE OF MEDICINE, or a Systematic Digest of the Principles of General and Special Pathology and Theraputics. By E. Geddings, (now preparing.)

SMITH ON FEVER.

A Treatise on Fever. By Southwood Smith, M. D., Physician to the London Fever Hospital. Fourth American edition. In 1 volume 8vo.

FITCH'S DENTAL SURGERY.

A Treatise on Dental Surgery. Second edition, revised, corrected, and improved, with new plates. By S. S. Fitch, M. D. 1 vol. 8vo.

ABERCROMBIE ON THE BRAIN.

Pathological and Practical Researches on Diseases of the Brain and Spinal Cord. Second American, from the third Edinburgh edition, enlarged. By John Abercrombie, M. D. In 1 volume 8vo.

ABERCROMBIE ON STOMACH.

Pathological and Practical Researches on Diseases of the Stomach, the Intestinal Canal, the Liver, and other Viscera of the Abdomen. By John Abercrombie M. D., third American from the second London edition enlarged. In 1 vol. 8vo.

EWELL'S MEDICAL COMPANION.

The Medical Companion or Family Physician: treating of the Diseases of the United States, with their symptoms, causes, cure, and means of prevention.

BERTIEN ON THE HEART.

A Treatise on Diseases of the Heart and Great Vessels. By J. R. Bertien. Edited by G. Bouillaud. Translated from the French. 8vo.

BOISSEAU ON FEVER.

Physiological Pyretology; or a Treatise on Fevers, according to the Principles of the New Medical Doctrine. By F. G. Boisseau, Doctor in Medicine of the Faculty of Paris, &c. &c. From the fourth French edition. Translated by J. R. Knox, M. D. 1 vol. 8vo.

HUTIN'S MANUAL.

Manual of the Physiology of Man; or a concise Description of the Phenomena of his Organization. By P. Hutin. Translated from the French, with notes, by J. Togno. In 12mo.

BELL ON THE TEETH.

The Anatomy, Physiology, and Diseases of the Teeth. By Thomas Bell, F. R. S., F. L. S. &c., third American edition. In 1 vol. 8vo. With numerous plates.

WILLIAMS ON THE LUNGS.

A Rational Exposition of the Physical Signs of Diseases of the Lungs and Pleura; Illustrating their Pathology and facilitating their Diagnosis. By Charles J. Williams, M. D. In 8vo. with plates.

THE BRIDGE WATER TREATISES, COMPLETE IN SEVEN VOLUMES, OCTAVO. Embracing.

I. The Adaptation of External Nature to the Moral and Intellectual Constitution of Man. By the Rev. Thomas Chalmers.

II. The Adaptation of External Nature to the Physical Condition of Man. By John Kidd, M. D., F. R. S.

III. Astronomy and General Physics, Considered with References to Natural Theology. By the Rev. Wm. Whewell.

IV. The Hand: Its Mechanism and Vital Endowments as Evincing Design. By Sir Charles Bell, K. H., F. R. S. With numerous wood cuts.

V. Chemistry, Meteorology, and the Function of Digestion. By Wm. Prout, M. D., F. R. S.

VI. The History, Habits and Instincts of Animals. By the Rev. Wm. Kirby, M. A., F. R. S. Illustrated by numerous

Engravings on Copper.

VII. Anatomy and Vegetable Physiology Considered with Reference to Natural Theology. By Peter Mark Roget, M. D. Illustrated with nearly Five Hundred Wood Cuts.

VIII. Geology and Mineralogy, Considered with Reference to Natural Theology. By the Rev. Wm. Buckland, D. D. with numerous engravings on copper, and a large coloured map.

∴ The work of Buckland, Kirby and Rojet may be had separate.

Footnotes:

[1] On the Ova of Man and Mamiferous Animals, &c.: by T. Wharton Jones. (Med. Gaz.)

[2] "Inde vero cum viderum viviparorum testes ova in se continere, cum eorundem uterum itidem in abdomen, oviductus instar apertum notarim, non amplius dubito quin mulierum testes ovario analogi sint, quocunque demum modo ex testibus in uterum, sive ipsa ova, sive ovis contenta materia transmittatur, ut alibi ex professo ostendam, si quando dabitur partium genitalium analogiam exponere, et errorem illum tollere quo mulierum genitalia genitalibus virorum analoga creduntur." (Nicolai Stenonis Elementorum Myologiæ Specimen, &c. Amst. 8vo. p. 145.)

[3] "Ova in omni animalium genere reperiri confidenter asserimus, quandoquidem ea non tantum in avibus, piscibus tam oviparis quam viviparis, sed etiam quadrupedibus ac homini ipso evidentissime conspiciantur." (Regner de Graaf de Virorum et Mulierum Organis Generationi Inservientibus. Lugd. B. and Roterod. 1668. 8vo. p. 299.)

[4] Anat. Descript. of the Human Gravid Uterus: by W. Hunter, M. D.

[5] An Exposition of the Signs and Symptoms of Pregnancy, &c.: by W. F. Montgomery, M. D. p. 226.

[6] Phil. Trans. 1797.

[7] Purkinje and Valentin, de Phœnomeno generali Motus vibratorii. Wratisl. 1825.

[8] W. Hunter, Anatomical Description of the Human Gravid Uterus, &c. p. 13.

[9] Vesalius, Malpighi, Morgagni, Diemerbroeck, Vieussens, Ruysch, Monro, Heister, Haller, Rœderer, Meckel, Hunter, Wrisberg, Lobstein, C. Bell. (Meckel's Anat. vol. iv.)

[10] C. Bell, On the Muscularity of the Uterus. (Med. Chir. Trans., vol. iv.)

[11] Leroux, Sur les Pertes de Sang.

[12] The tortuous serpentine course which the arteries of the uterus take, is not, as has been generally supposed, a provision of nature against the increase of size which the uterus has to undergo during pregnancy, but is the result of the structure in which they ramify, having already undergone these changes during a previous pregnancy.

[13] Anatomical Description of the Human Gravid Uterus, &c.: by W. Hunter, M. D.

[14] The axis of the brim of the pelvis runs in such a direction, that if a line were drawn from its centre, it would pass upwards and forwards through the umbilicus: the gravid uterus has its axis rarely or never inclined less than this, and usually much more, especially in multiparæ in whom the fundus is occasionally inclined so strongly forwards as to receive the name of pendulous belly.

[15] We are inclined to think that the soft feel of the portio vaginalis is one of the earliest signs of pregnancy which can be detected by examination. Our attention was first drawn to it in an obscure case of early pregnancy, complicated with extensive disease, which we examined with Mr. Ingleby of Birmingham, and where we gave a wrong diagnosis, not considering the patient to be pregnant. If we had placed as much confidence in this symptom as we are now inclined to do, we should probably have formed a more correct view of the case. Since this we have, on several occasions, found that attending to this circumstance has considerably assisted us in determining cases of doubtful pregnancy at an early period.

[16] This description is given according to the lunar not calendar months, of which there are necessarily ten during the forty weeks of pregnancy.

[17] We are aware that the plan which we follow, in considering the development of the ovum, is very different to that usually adopted, and will probably be open to some objections on the score of defective arrangement; but it must be remembered that this is a work intended for students, where complete and perfect arrangement must, to a certain extent, be sacrificed in order to place an acknowledged difficult and complicated subject in the clearest and most intelligible light. We have, therefore, preferred describing first the coverings of the ovum during those periods of pregnancy at which they are most frequently seen, and shall delay its minute consideration until we come to the description of the fœtus itself, the development of the one being so essentially connected with that of the other, as to render a separate description of them impossible. By this means the reader, by having the general details first brought under his notice, will be enabled to enter with more ease and advantage upon the consideration of those which are obscure and difficult.

[18] Siebold's Journal für Geburtshülfe, vol. xiv. heft. 3. 1835.

[19] On the Signs and Symptoms of Pregnancy, p. 133.: by W. F. Montgomery, M. D. In a note to the above quotation, the learned author very properly calls them decidual cotyledons, "for to that name their form, as well as their situation, appears strictly to entitle them: but from having, on more than one occasion, observed within their cavity a milky or chylous fluid, I am disposed to consider them reservoirs for nutrient fluids, separated from the maternal blood, to be thence absorbed for the support and development of the ovum. This view seems strengthened when we consider that, at the early periods of gestation, the ovum derives its support by imbibition, through the connexion existing between the decidua and the villous processes covering the outer surface of the chorion."

[20] Observations by Dr. Baillie, in the posthumous work of Dr. W. Hunter, on the Anatomy of the Gravid Uterus.

[21] Observations on Certain Parts of the Animal Economy, p. 134.

[22] It has lately been supposed that the irregular nodules of wax in the Hunterian preparations were merely the result of extravasation, a rather hazardous conclusion against the authority of such men as the Hunters. Mr. J. Hunter has, however, expressly met this objection in the following observation:—"this substance of the placenta, now filled with injection, had nothing of a vascular appearance, or that of extravasation; but had a regularity in its form which showed it to be a natural cellular structure, fitted to be a reservoir for blood." (Observations on Certain Parts of the Animal Economy, p. 129.)

[23] In offering these observations on the placenta, we have purposely quoted, wherever it was possible, from the admirable essays of the Hunter's, on this subject. These works, more especially that of Dr. W. Hunter, are becoming too scarce to be easily attained by the student; and yet it is more peculiarly important to this class of our readers, that they should not only be aware how much we are indebted to these illustrious men for what we know upon the subject; but also that they should be as familiar as possible with their very words and expressions. The essays in question are master-pieces of original observation and correct description, and we may safely assert, that the one by Dr. Hunter is so complete, as to leave us little or nothing more to be wished for on this subject. With such feelings we cannot conceal our surprise, to find that an author like Dr. Burns should have passed over the whole subject of the placenta without once alluding to the name of Hunter; this omission is the more marked in the last editions of his work, where he has furnished the reader with copious references, &c. in the notes. One would have thought that Dr. Burns would have felt pride in acknowledging the merits of his distinguished countrymen.

[24] We said, "one of the earliest changes." Mr. Jones considers that "the breaking up of the surface of the yelk into crystalline forms," is the first change which he has observed.

[25] Allen Thomson on the Development of the Vascular System in the Fœtus of Vertebrated Animal. (Edin. New Philosop. Journ. Oct. 1830.)

[26] Pander. Beiträge zur Entwickelungs-geschichte des Hünchens im Eie. Würzburg, 1817.

[27] In making these observations upon the formation of the ductus arteriosus, we must request our readers to consider this as still an unsettled question.

[28] The vernix caseosa is a viscid fatty matter of a yellowish white colour, adhering to different parts of the child's body, and in some cases in such quantity as to cover the whole surface; it seems to be a substance intermediate between fibrine and fat, having a considerable resemblance to spermaceti. From the known activity of the sebaceous glands in the fœtal state, and from this smegma being found in the greatest quantity about the head, arm-pits, and groins, where these glands are most abundant, there is every reason to consider it as the secretion of the sebaceous glands of the skin during the latter months of pregnancy.

[29] Fourcroy, it is true, has shown that the fœtal blood is not only of a darker colour, but incapable of becoming reddened by the contact of atmospheric air, and that it coagulates very imperfectly. Others have shown that there is no perceptible difference in the colour of the blood of the umbilical arteries from that of the umbilical vein. Still, however, this by no means disproves what we have now stated, and which is now generally allowed to be the office of the placenta during the latter periods of pregnancy.

[30] "A gentleman," says Dr. Montgomery, "lately informed me that, being afflicted with a stepmother naturally more disposed to practise the fortiter in re than to adopt the suaviter in modo, he and all the household had learned from experience to hail with joyful anticipations the lady's pregnancy, as a period when clouds and storms were immediately changed for sunshine and quietness." (Exposition of the Signs and Symptoms of Pregnancy, p. 9.)

[31] Dionis says, that "women of a sanguine complexion, who form more blood every month than is necessary for the nourishment of the fœtus whilst it is small, discharge the overplus by the vessels which open into the vagina during the first months."

[32] The menstrual blood is more pale and sparing: it usually comes from the hæmorrhoidal vessels of the vagina, or at most, from those of the cervix uteri. (Levret, Art des Accouchemens, § 233.)

[33] Should the vessels of the cervix uteri take upon them the secretion of the menses, this discharge can thus continue through pregnancy. (Carus, Lehrbuch der Gynakologie, bd. ii. p. 67.)

[34] L'Art d'Accouchemens, § 369. (note;) also Deventer, Novum Lumen Obstet. chap. xv.; Perfect's Cases of Midwifery, vol. ii. p. 71. [Meurer, American Journ. Med. Sc., April 1841, p. 494.]

[35] This fact was observed so long ago as by Aristotle, also by Schenk, as quoted by Mauriceau, lib. i. chap. 1. Mauriceau himself mentions having seen several cases, one of which forms the subject of his 393d observation. "Le 8 Juin, 1685. J'ai vu une jeune femme agée seulement de seize ans et demi, marié depuis un an qui était grosse de cinq mois ou environ, quoiqu'elle n'eut jamais eu ses menstrues, à ce qu'elle me dit aussi bien que son marie, qui ne pouvait pas se persuader qu'elle cût pû devenir grosse, n'ayant pas encore eu ce premier signe de fécondité; m'alleguant, pour soutenir son opinion, qu'on ne voyait jamais de fruit d'un arbre qui n'eut été précédé de sa fleur. Mais je lui dis qu'il était certain, comme il reconnut bien par sa propre expérience en voyant accoucher sa femme d'un enfant vivant quatre mois ensuite, que les jeunes femmes pouvaient bien quelquefois devenir grosses, ainsi qu'il était arrivé à sa femme, sans avoir jamais eu leur menstrues, si elles usaint du coit dans le temps même quelles étaient sur le point d'avoir effectivement cette evacuation naturelle pour le premier fois."

[36] Rœderer, Elm. Art. Obst. p. 46. The original is a masterly specimen of description, not less remarkable for its singular comprehensiveness than the beauty of the style. "Menstruorum suppressionem mammarum tumour insequitur, quocirca mammæ crescunt, replentur, dolent interdum, indurescunt; venæ earum cœruleo colore conspicuæ redduntur; crassescit papilla, inflata videtur, color ejusdem fit obscurior; simili colore distinguitur discus ambiens qui in latitudinem majorem expanditur, parvisque eminentiis quasi totidem papillulis tegitur."

[37] "In women with dark eyes and hair, this discolouration is very distinct; in women with light hair and eyes, it is often so slight that it is difficult to tell whether it exists or no."... "In brunettes who have already borne children, the

areola remains dark ever afterwards, so that this ceases to be a guide in all subsequent pregnancies." (Gooch, on some of the more important Diseases of Women, p. 201 and 203.)

[38] We had, at the moment of writing the above, a patient just recovered from her first labour, in whom the discolouration extended nearly over the whole breast: it was darker in some spots than in others, and presented a variety of shades not unlike a large bruise of some days' standing. Dr. Montgomery mentions a case where the areola was almost black, and upwards of three inches in diameter. A similar case occurred not long since.

[39] Bibliothèque Universalle, t. ix. p. 248; also in the Isis for 1819, part iv. p. 542.

[40] "Mémoir sur l'Auscultation appliquée à l'étude de la Grossesse, ou Recherches sur deux nouveaux Signes propres à faire reconnaître plusieurs Circonstances de l'Etat de Gestation; lu à l'Academie Royale de Médecine dans la Séance Générale du 26 December, 1821. Par J. A. Lejumeau de Kergaradec."

[41] Dr. Evory Kennedy, Observations on Obstetric Auscultation, &c. 1833.

[42] H. F. Naegelé, Die Geburtshülfliche Auscultation, 1838; also Dr. Corrigan, Lancet.

[43] Die Geburtshülfliche Exploration, von Dr. A. P. Hohl.

[44] This sign of pregnancy has very recently excited some attention, and the researches of M. Tanchou of Paris, (see American Journ. Med. Sc. Feb. 1840, p. 483,) Golding Bird, (Ibid., Aug. 1840, p. 501,) and Drs. McPheeters and Perry, (American Medical Intelligencer, March 15th, 1841, p. 350,) conclusively establish, that taken in connexion with other symptoms, it forms a very valuable aid to diagnosis.

The following is the description given by M. Tanchou of the changes which the urine during pregnancy exhibits, and of the characters by which its peculiar ingredient, named by M. Nauche Kiesteine, may be recognised.

The urine of a pregnant woman, collected in the morning, is usually of a pale yellow colour and slightly milky in appearance; it is not coagulable by heat, or by any of the tests which indicate the presence of albumen. Left to itself and exposed to the air after the first day, there begins to appear suspended in it a cottony-looking cloud, and, at the same time, a flocculent whitish matter is deposited at the bottom of the fluid. These phenomena are not of constant occurrence, and, moreover, healthy urine sometimes exhibits analogous phenomena.

From the second to the sixth day, we perceive small opaque bodies rise from the bottom to the top of the fluid; these gradually collect together so as to form a layer which covers the surface: this is the kiesteine. It is of a whitish or opaline colour, and may be very aptly compared to the layer of greasy matter which covers the surface of fat broth, when it has been allowed to cool. Examined by the microscope, it exhibits the appearance of a gelatinous mass, which has no determinate form. Sometimes small cubical crystals can be perceived in it, when it has become stale.

The kiesteine continues in the state we have now described, for three or four days; the urine then becomes muddy, and minute opaque bodies detach themselves from the surface and settle at the bottom of the vessel: the pellicle thus becomes soon destroyed.

The characteristic feature, therefore, of the urine during pregnancy consists in the presence of kiesteine. It deserves, however, to be noticed, that the urine, in some cases of extreme phthisis pulmonalis, and also of vesical catarrh, will be found to exhibit on its surface a layer or stratum which is not unlike to that now described as peculiar to the state of pregnancy. But with proper attention we may easily avoid this mistake. The stratum, in the cases alluded to, does not appear so quickly on the surface of the urine as the kiesteine does; and also, instead of disappearing, as it is found to do, in the course of a few days, it (the former) goes on increasing in thickness, and ultimately becomes converted into a mass of mouldiness.

Of twenty-five cases, in which M. Tanchou detected the presence of kiesteine in the urine, seventeen occurred in women who were pregnant from four to nine months, four in women who had not quickened, and who considered themselves as labouring under disease of the womb, and the remaining four in patients who had been under treatment for casual complaints—one for sciatica at the Hôtel Dieu, another for ascites in the city, a third for an ulcer in the neck at La Pitié, and the last had been cauterized twice a week for a pretended disease of the uterus. In none of these cases had the existence of pregnancy been suspected, although in every one of them the fact was soon placed beyond doubt.—Editor.

[45] Baudelocque wrote an account of it to Professor Naegelé of Heidelberg, from whom we received the particulars.

[46] See Treatise on the Diseases of Females, 6th ed. p. 46. Ed.

[47] Ovum deforme, in quo partes embryonis et secundarum distingui vix possunt, molam vocabimus. (Rœderer, Elementa Artis Obstetricæ, § 738.)

[48] Dr. J. Y. Simpson on the Diseases of the Placenta. (Edin. Med. and Surg. Journal, April 1, 1836.)

[49] "One must be careful not to mistake these clots of blood, which being washed by the reddish serosities which flow from the womb, harden in the vagina, or womb itself, and look exactly like false conceptions." (La Motte.)

"Every mole is a blighted ovum which has been the product of conception. We are not justified in classing under the head of moles every mass which is produced and lodged within the uterus." (Froriep's Handbuch der Geburtshülfe, § 180.)

[50] Our friend, Dr. Nebel, of Heidelberg, has a preparation of a fœtus which was retained for fifty-four years in the abdomen. This is the longest period on record of a fœtus being retained in the cyst of a ventral pregnancy. Many other cases have been described. (See Burns, 9th edition, where the notes contain very ample references.)

[51] We had lately a case of this kind. The patient had been under our care for inflammation of the cervix uteri. There was that general enlargement of the uterus which attends this condition; and, on endeavouring to lift a heavy weight, she was seized with violent pain in the pelvis, great difficulty in passing fæces and urine, and, on examination, the uterus was found retroverted. The bowels were well opened with castor oil, and in a day or two it recovered its natural position.

[52] Dr. W. Hunter has evidently taken the same view of the case, and invariably considers retention of urine as an effect, not the cause, of this displacement. (Med. Observ. and Inq. vol. iv.)

[53] We were once misled in a case of this description. The os uteri lay close behind the symphysis pubis, and its opening, as well as so much of the neck as we could feel, looked straight downwards. We were unable to pass the finger sufficiently high to trace the continuity between the neck of the uterus and tumour in the hollow of the sacrum formed by the fundus; and the haggard aged appearance of the woman put all suspicion of pregnancy out of our mind.

[54] Dr. Burns makes a similar observation. "In most cases the cervix will be found more or less curved; so that the os uteri is not directed so much upwards as it otherwise should be." (Principles of Midwifery, p. 281. 9th edit.)

[55] "Sometimes it is perhaps better to introduce the fingers into the vagina only, and not into the rectum, not merely because, we can act better and more directly upon the uterus here, but also because if we press the posterior wall of the vagina upward towards the sacrum, and thus stretch the upper part of it which is between the fingers and the os uteri, it will act upon the uterus like a cord upon a pulley, and greatly favour its rotation." (Richter, op. cit. vol. vii. sect. 57.)

[56] Among others, we may mention an exceedingly interesting case recorded by Mr. Baynham, in the Edin. Med. and Surg. Journ. April, 1830. The real nature of the case was not ascertained for six weeks, the catheter only being used night and morning. Even when the bladder was empty, the fundus resisted every attempt to return it. The most prominent part of the tumour in the rectum was punctured with a trocar, and about twelve ounces of liquor amnii, without blood, were drawn off: the reduction followed in about a quarter of an hour. A full opiate was given, and the patient passed a better night than she had done before. Twenty-five hours after the operation, the fœtus, was expelled; it was fresh, and about the size of a six months' child. The patient recovered.

[57] Dr. Cheston's case, where the child was afterwards carried the full time, and born alive. (Med. Communications, vol. ii. p. 6.)

[58] Merriman, Med. Chir. Trans. Vol. xiii. p. 338.

[59] Exposition of the Signs and Symptoms of Pregnancy: by W. F. Montgomery M. D. p. 253.

[60] Dewees, Compendious System of Midwifery, sect. 408. A similar case is recorded by Dr. Montgomery.

[61] "Qui inter septimi et noni mensis, à prima conceptione, finem contingit partus, præmaturus vocatur: abortus vero quando ante dictum tempus embryo excidit; id quod circa tertium graviditatis mensem ut plurimum accidit. Vitalem esse præmaturum fœtum observatio nos docet, embryonem autem non manere superstitem constat." (Rœderer, Elem. Artis Obst. cap. xxiii. § 716.)

[62] During the great influenza epidemic, abortions were remarkably frequent.

[63] This is nearly the same arrangement which has been followed by Dr. Copland, in the article Abortion, in the Dict. Pract. Med.

[64] This crotchet consists of a piece of steel of the thickness of a small quill at its handle, and gradually tapered off to its other extremity which is bent to a hook of small size. (See accompanying figure which represents the instrument one third the natural size.)

This instrument is highly useful in cases in which the flooding continues after the ovum has been broken and its contents expelled. A portion of the involucrum sometimes insinuates itself into the neck of the uterus, and prevents the degree of contraction necessary to interrupt farther bleeding. This accident most frequently attends the earlier abortions. As hæmorrhage is maintained by the cause just named it suggests the propriety of never breaking the ovum; especially before the fourth month. When the flooding is maintained by this cause, it will not cease but upon the event of its removal. This condition of the placenta and neck of the uterus is easily ascertained by an examination; it will readily be felt to be embraced by the neck of the uterus; and though a portion may protrude a little distance below the os tincæ, it cannot be extracted by the fingers; for the os uteri or cavity of the uterus will not be sufficiently large to permit the fingers to pass into it, that this mass may be removed; the crotchet should then be substituted; the mode of using it is as follows:—The fore-finger of the right hand is placed within or at the edge of the os tincæ; with the left we conduct the hooked extremity along this finger, until it is within the uterus; it is gently carried up to the fundus, and then slowly drawn downwards, which makes its curved point fix in the placenta; when thus engaged, it is gradually withdrawn, and the placenta with it.

Dr. Dewees says, that in every case in which he has used this crotchet, the discharge instantly ceased. See Art. "Abortion," by Dr. Dewees, in American Cyclopedia of Pract. Med. and Surg. Dr. Dewees "from some late experience is induced to believe" that "in cases in which we cannot command the removal of the placenta by the fingers—that is, when this mass continues to occupy the uterine cavity, or but very little protruded through the os tincæ," the administration of ergot, will often supercede the necessity of the crotchet. Treatise on the Diseases of Females. Sixth Edition, p. 351.—Ed.

[65] Dr. Dewees recommends the crotchet only where the flooding continues after the ovum has been broken. See preceding note. Ed.

[66] "Clysteres injiciantur, quorum irritatione expultrix uteri facultas excitatur, et depleta intestina ampliorem locum utero relinquat." (Riverius, Prax. Med. de Partu difficili.)

[67] [Dr. Dewees recommends the woman to be placed for labour on her left side at the foot of the bed, in such a manner as will enable her to fix her feet firmly against one of the bed-posts; her hips within ten or twelve inches of the edge of the bed; her knees bent, her body well flexed upon her thighs; her head and shoulders will then be near the centre of the bed, where pillows should be placed to raise them to a comfortable height. This is the position we believe in which the patient is very generally placed in the United States.—Ed.]

[68] [See an interesting paper "on Laceration of the Perineum during Labour; by Wm. M. Fahnestock, M. D.," in American Journal of the Med. Sc. for Jan. 1841. Editor.]

[69] See a case of central perforation of the perineum, Med. Gaz. p. 782. Aug. 19, 1837.

[70] "The practice of using force to hurry the shoulders and body of the child through the os externum as soon as the head was born, is very generally laid aside. There can be no doubt that this imprudent conduct often brought on a retention of the placenta." (See White, on Lying-in Women.)

[71] "A ligature upon the navel string is absolutely necessary, otherwise the child will bleed to death; and when tied slovenly, or not properly, it will sometimes bleed to an alarming quantity. As we take such vast care to secure the navel string, you will naturally ask how brutes manage in this particular? I will give you an idea of their method of procedure, by describing what I saw in a little bitch of Dr. Douglas. The pains coming on, the membranes were protruded; in a pain or two more they burst, and the puppy followed. You cannot imagine with what eagerness the mother lapped up the waters, and then, taking hold of the membranes with her teeth, drew out the secundines; these she devoured also, licking the little puppy as dry as she could. As soon as she had done I took it up, and saw the navel string much bruised and lacerated. However, a second labour coming on, I watched more narrowly, and as soon as the little creature was come into the world I cut the navel string, and the arteries immediately spouted out profusely; fearing the poor thing would die, I held it to its mother, who, drawing it several times through her mouth, bruised and lacerated it, after which it bled no more. This, I make no doubt is the practice with other animals." (Dr. W. Hunter's Lectures, MS. 1752; from Dr. Merriman's Synopsis, p. 21. note.)

[72] Carus's Gynakologie, vol. ii. p. 138. This assertion, however, must be qualified, somewhat, as we know of several cases where flooding has come on after labour during sleep.

[73] "I have observed," says Dr. Hunter, "in women who do not give suck, and in nurses after they leave off suckling, that the axillary glands become painful, swell, and sometimes suppurate. Is not this owing to the acrimony which the milk has acquired by long stagnation in the breast, and affecting the gland through which it must pass in absorption? I have observed that they are at the same time liable to little fevers of the intermitting kind, which come on with a rigour, and go off with a sweat. Are not such fevers raised by absorption of acrid milk?" (Hunter's Commentaries, p. 59.)

[74] [The best application we have ever tried, is the vinegar and water as is commended by Dr. Dewees. See his admirable chapter on Milk Abscess. Treatise on the Principal Diseases of Females.—Am. Ed.]

[75] [Sore nipples is an affection, of so very frequent occurrence, often so exceedingly obstinate, and sometimes productive of such extreme torture to the patient, that some additional remarks relative to its treatment may be acceptable to the practitioner.

The solution of nitrate of silver, two grains to the ounce of water, is highly extolled by Mr. Allard (American Journ. Med. Sc. Feb. 1837,) and Dr. Churchill says that he has found it the most effectual application. (Diseases of Pregnancy and Child-bed.) This solution should be applied every time the child is taken from the breast, care being taken to wash the nipple previous to the next application of the child. We have frequently found this treatment very efficacious, but in some cases it entirely fails. Dr. Hannay says, that the solution is inferior to the solid nitrate of silver, and asserts that the latter never fails to afford relief and ultimately effect a cure. He uses it as follows. The nipple is to be gently and carefully dried, then freely touched with a sharp pencil of nitrate of silver, care being taken to insinuate the pencil into the chaps or chinks. The nipple is then to be washed with a little warm milk and water. The pain though smart soon subsides, and all that is necessary, according to Mr. H. to heal the sore, is a little simple ointment, or one made with the flowers of zinc. When the pain from the application is very severe, relief should be given by the administration of thirty drops of the solution of morphium. In some cases it is necessary to apply the caustic more than once. (Am. Journ. Med. Sc. Feb. 1835, p. 527.)

Dr. Chopin recommends repeated lotions with the solution of Chloride of Soda, which he says will often cure in one or two days. (Am. Journ. Med. Sc. May, 1836.)

Dr. Bard says that simply keeping a linen cloth constantly wet with rum over the nipple is frequently very useful, and as it is one of the easiest remedies, it should be first tried. (Compendium of the Theory and Practice of Midwifery.)

Stimulating ointments, such as ung. hydrarg. rub. diluted with lard, is, according to Burns, sometimes of service, as is also touching the parts with burnt alum, or dusting them with some mild dry powder. Solutions of sulphate of alumine and of sulphate of copper, of such strength as just to smart a little, are also recommended as occasionally of service by the last named practitioner. (Principles of Midwifery, 7th Ed. p. 543.)

We have found Kreosote, three to six drops in an ounce of water, very efficacious; in some cases affording more speedy relief than any other application. The mucilage of the slippery elm applied cold is often a most comfortable application, and its efficacy is sometimes increased by dissolving in it some borax.

When all these means fail, the mother must give up suckling for a time, when the parts heal rapidly. This last resource will not be often necessary.

The great number of remedies which have been employed for the cure of this complaint sufficiently attest its obstinacy. This obstinacy is owing, in some cases, we conceive, to an irritable condition of the patient's system, a fact overlooked so far as we know, by most practitioners. In such cases a mild and nutritious diet, fresh air, keeping the bowels free, &c. will do more towards effecting a cure than local applications; though the latter even here are not to be neglected. Editor.]

[76] [Dr. Dewees regards after-pains as an evil of magnitude, and always endeavours to prevent them as quickly as possible. For this purpose he recommends camphor or some preparation of opium. (See his System of Midwifery.) We have always adopted this practice to the great relief of the patient, and have never had cause to regret it. Dr. Dewees's observations on this subject should be attentively perused.—Ed.]

[77] See observations on Malposition of the Child.

[78] We have no words in the English language like the schrag and schief of the German to express these different species of obliquity.

[79] On the other hand, Dr. Merriman observes, that he has "twice known the presentation of the face converted by the pains alone into a natural presentation." (Synopsis, p. 48.)

[80] According to the results of Dr. Collins's experience at the Dublin Lying-in Hospital, the face presented once in about every 504 cases; but as, in several labours, the presentation was not noted on account of their rapidity, the proportion is probably larger.

[81] Madame La Chapelle calls this the courboure des bords, to distinguish it from the head curvature, courboure des faces (p. 61.)

[82] A Treatise on the Improvement of Midwifery, chiefly with regard to the Operation: by Edmund Chapman, 2d edit. 1735.

[83] [Dr. Dewees, prefers, in all cases, the long forceps. See the chapters on the Forceps in his System of Midwifery. Ed.]

[84] See Midwifery Hospital Reports, case of Mrs. Worsley, May 3, 1834, p. 187.

[85] Another circumstance is humanely insisted on by Madame la Chapelle with much propriety: "Je ne manque jamais de fair voir le forceps à la femme, et de lui expliquer à-peu près son usage, et sa façon d'agir. Il n'en est aucune que cette démonstration ne tranquillise, et j'en rencontre souvent qui à leur deuxieme accouchement sollicitent l'application du forceps qu'elles ont vu mettre en usage pour les débarasser du premier." (Pratique des Accouhemens, p. 64.)

[86] Madame la Chapelle confirms this mode of introducing the forceps: "Pour moi, je l'introduis constamment sur le ligament sacro-sciatique." (Pratique des Accouchemens, p. 66.)

[87] "Quand une fois la tête est hors les parties osseuses, elle ne retrograde plus, je les désarticule (the blades) avec la clef placée entre elles en forme de lévier; je les extrais en les inclinant graduellement, car souvent l'extraction un peu brusquée d'une branche produit l'expulsion de la tête." (La Chapelle.)

[88] "Mon avis est que la choix n'est point nécessaire quand l'uterus est encore rempli d'eau, et que la position est douteuse. En pareil cas je conseillerais même plutôt de faire usage de la main droite, quoique, pour mon compte, l'habitude m'ait rendu l'usage aussi familier que celui de l'autre." (Mad. la Chapelle, Prat. des Accouch. p. 88.)

[89] "Une chose très importante à observer quand on se trouve contraint par la perte de sang à en venir à l'opération, et que les eaux ne sont point encore ouvertes, c'est de couler la main tantôt à droit, tantôt à gauche le plus haut et le plus doucement qu'il est possible de long les membranes qui contiennent les eaux sans les rompre, jusqu' à ce qu' on ait trouvé les pieds de l'enfant pour s'en saisir. Car s'il arrive qu'elles se rompent avant qu'on ait pris cette précaution, pendant qu'on les cherche, les eaux s'écoulent, les sang se perd, a la matrice se referme en partie, et l'opération devient par-là plus difficile et plus dangereuse." (Pratique des Accouchemens, p. 277.)

[90] Traité des Accouchemens, 1770. § 691. "Pour moi, j'ai toujours au contraire trouvé un grand advantage à insinuer la main jusqu'aux pieds de l'enfant, et à n'ouvrir les membranes qu'en saisissant ces derniers." (La Chapelle p. 90.)

[91] "We must by no means burst the bag of liquor amnii until the hand has passed up between the membranes and the uterus. Every movement is easy whilst there is fluid in the uterus: hence, therefore, we must not withdraw the hand until we have fairly gained the feet and brought them down; for otherwise the waters escape, the uterus contracts, and the rest of the operation is more difficult." (Boer, vol. iii. p. 17. note.)

[92] "Je suis loin de prétendre, avec Puzos, que la traction sur un seul pied ait les avantages récis." (La Chapelle, p. 93.)

[93] "Dans tous ces accouchemens je laisse le plus souvent agir la nature, et je le fais avec bien plus de sécurité quand je sçais que la femme a accouché précédemment et fort aisément d'enfans volumineux, quand je reconnois son bassin pour avoir toutes les dimensions requises, quand les contractions de la matrice sont bonnes." &c. (Traité des Accouchemens, § 674.)

[94] Ueber die künstliche Wendung auf den Steiss, in the Heidelberg Klin. Annalen, vol. ii. part i. p. 142.

[95] Traité des Hernies, contenant une ample Déclaration, &c., par Pierre Franco de Turriers en Provence, de-meurant à présént à Orange: à Lyon, 1561.

[96] See Dystocia from Malposition of the Child. [The student who desires to investigate this subject farther, may consult Dr. Churchill's Researches on Operative Midwifery. Essay ii. on Version. —Am. Ed.]

[97] [Prof. Gibson has operated twice on the same patient, and both times successfully, for mother and children. See American Journal, for May 1838. —Ed.]

[98] [Dr. Churchill has collected the statistics of 409 cases of Cæsarean section, of which number, 228 mothers were saved; and 181 lost, or about 1 in 2¼: and out of 224 children, 160 were saved, and 64 lost—or about 1 in 3½.

Of the above cases, 40 occurred in the practice of British practitioners, of which, 11 mothers recovered, and 29 died; or nearly three fourths—and 37 cases, in which the result to the child is mentioned, 22 were saved, and 15 lost—or 1 in 2½.

Of 369 cases in the practice of Continental practitioners, 217 mothers recovered, and 152 died, or 1 in 2□—and out of 187 cases, where the result to the child is given, 138 were saved, and 49 lost; or nearly 1 in 4. Researches on Operative Midwifery. By F. Churchill, M. D., Dublin, 1841. Editor.]

[99] [The propriety of an early resort to the Cæsarean section, in cases where it is necessary, has been very properly insisted upon; but the circumstances which render it necessary, are not always readily determined. M. Castel states, that in a case at the hospice de perfectionnement, in which the operation was determined on, some delay became necessary in order to find accommodation for the crowd of students who collected to witness it, and before this could be effected the woman was delivered naturally. M. Gimelle says, that at the hospital of M. Dubois, a small woman, who had five times submitted to the Cæsarean section, was delivered naturally the sixth time. Am. Journ. Med. Sc. Aug. 1838. Ed.]

[100] For the particulars of this interesting case we must refer our readers to the British and Foreign Med. Review, vol. ii. p. 270; and also to vol. iv. p. 521. [Also to American Journal Med. Sc., August, 1838, p. 526, and Nov. 1837, p. 244. —Ed.]

[101] [Those who desire farther information on this subject, may consult, with advantage, Dr. Churchill's Researches, already quoted.—Ed.]

[102] Dr. Macauley was physician to the British Lying-in Hospital, in Brownlow Street, and colleague of Dr. W. Hunter.

[103] Barlow, Medical Facts and Observations, vol. viii. Although we are in great measure indebted to Dr. Denman for having brought this operation into general notice, it is to the late Professor May, the father-in-law of Professor Naegelé, that the merit is due for having first pointed out the advantage of exciting uterine contraction before rupturing the membranes. (Programma de Necessitate Partûs quandoque præmature, vel solo Instrumentorum adjutorio promovendi. Heidelberg, 1799.)

[104] [The student who desires to investigate this subject farther, is referred to Dr. Churchill's Researches on Operative Midwifery, and a copious analysis of his Essay on Premature Labour, in the American Journ. Med. Sc. for Nov. 1838, p. 172, also to the Nos. of the Journal just named, for Feb. 1838, p. 516, November 1839, p. 237, and July 1841, p. 226. Editor.]

[105] "The scissors ought to be so sharp at the points as to penetrate the integuments and bones when pushed with moderate force, but not so keen as to cut the operator's fingers or the vagina in introducing them." (Smellie, vol. i. chap. 3. sect. 7. numb. 2.)

[106] [Dr. Churchill who has collected the statistics of this operation, states, that in 334,258 cases of labour, the crotchet has been used in 343, or 1 in 974½.

Of this number, 41,434 cases of labour occurred to British practitioners; in which, there were 181 crotchet cases, or about 1 in 228.

Among the French, 36,169 cases of labour; of which there were 30 crotchet cases, or 1 in 1,205□.

And among the Germans, 132 crotchet cases, in 256,655 labours, or 1 in 1,944□. Of 251 cases, in which the result to the mother is given, the mortality was 52, or about 1 in 5. (Op. Cit.) Editor.]

[107] The above arrangement is that which is given by Professor Naegelé, in his Lehrbuch der Geburtschülfe.

[108] Pratique des Accouchemens, p. 21. "Je puis assurer n'avoir jamais rencontré aucune position du col, ni du tronc proprement dit." (p. 19.)

[109] Merriman's Synopsis of difficult Parturition, last edition, p. 69. The elongated form of the protruded bag of membranes is, however, by no means a constant occurrence, as cases frequently occur where nothing of the kind has appeared.

[110] Boer's Naturliche Geburtshülfe, b. iii. p. 64. A case of actual evolution has also been described by Mr. Barlow, p. 399.

[111] Med. Chir. Trans., case by Dr. Smith, of Maidstone. See also an interesting case by Professor Naegelé, in the British and Foreign Medical Review, where the uterus was ruptured by sudden violence, part of the child was delivered per vaginam, the rest by an abscess through the abdominal parietes. No. x. April, 1838.

[112] Lassus, Pathologie Chirurgicale, tom. ii. p. 237, quoted by Dr. M'Keever, op. cit. p. 27.

[113] Collins, op. cit. p. 277. An interesting case of rupture at the sixth month, is recorded by Mr. Ilot, of Bromley, in the seventh volume of the Medical Repository, and quoted by Dr. Merriman, who has also given another at the eighth month by Mr. Glen, p. 268. See also an interesting case in the Brit. and For. Med. Rev. for October, 1838, p. 539.

[114] [Another case is recorded by Dr. Carmichael, of Dublin. See Amer. Journ. Med. Sc., May 1840, p. 236.—Ed.]

[115] The late Professor Young, of Edinburg, has described a case of this sort in his lectures: he distinctly "heard the

head crack, and a large quantity of fluid came away."

[116] Observationes Anatomicæ, 52. A similar case has been recorded by Dr. Wrangel, in the Archiv. der Gesells-chaft der Correspondirenden Aerzte zu St. Petersburg.

When called to the case, the forceps had been already applied by a colleague, but could not be locked, owing to the enormous tumour of the head. A doughty swelling was felt between the blades of the forceps, of such a size that he could only just reach the cranial bones. He made pretty strong traction twice, when unluckily the instrument slipped off; it seemed, however, to have brought the head so much lower, that the child was delivered in ten minutes afterwards by the natural efforts: it was dead. A sac filled with serous fluid, and as large as the head itself, was attached to the occiput; it was covered by the cranial integuments, and in ten hours afterwards, as the fluid had found its way through the open sutures into the cranial cavity, the tumour had the appearance of a hydrocephalus.

[117] Quoted by Dr. Lee in the Med. Gazette, Dec. 25, 1830, from the Journ. Gén. de Méd. tom. xliii. xlv.

[118] Merriman's Synopsis, p. 216.; also Dr. J. Y. Simpson's fifth case of fatal peritonitis, in Edin. Med. and Surg. Journ. No. cxxxvii. The patient had suffered under four different attacks of venereal disease. Some interesting cases have been published in the Neue Zeitschrift für Geburtskunde, band vii. heft 1. by Dr. Bunsen of Frankfort and Dr. Kyll of Cologne. In almost every case of great accumulation of liquor amnii, the child was dead, hydrocephalic, or with ascites and in many the placenta was diseased.

[119] [Dr. Churchill has given a table of the length of the umbilical cord in 500 cases. In 127 of these, the cord was 18 inches long, in 77 cases 24 inches, and in 45 cases 20 inches long. The extremes were 12 and 54 inches. Op. Cit.—Ed.]

[120] In a case of this sort Mauriceau says, "Ce nœud étoit extrémement serré: mais cela ne s'etoit fait seulement que dans la sortie de l'enfant; car s'il eût été long-temps serré de la sorte dans le ventre de la mère, l'enfant auroit certainement peri; à cause que le mouvement du sang que lui étoit nécessaire, auroit été entièrement intercepté dans ce cordon. J'ai encore accouché depuis ce temps la, sept autres femmes, dont les enfans qui étoient tous vivans, avoient pareillement le cordon noüé d'un semblable nœud qui s'étoit fait de la même manière, par l'extraordinaire longueur de leur cordon." (Obs. 133.)

[121] [Dr. Zollickoffer, of Middleburg, Md., relates two cases, in each of which there was a knot upon the cord without any injury to the children. American Journal, Med. Sc. July 1841, p. 109.—Ed.]

[122] Van Swieten, in his Commentaries on Boerhaave, gives a remarkable instance of its occurring twice in the same patient, so as to destroy the child. "I had occasion to see two instances of the birth of a dead child in one lady of distinction, where every thing was exactly and rightly formed; only the navel string was, towards the middle, twisted into a firm knot, so that all communication between the mother and fœtus had been intercepted. The umbilical rope seems to have formed by chance a link, through which the whole body of the fœtus passed, and after-wards, by its motion and weight, had drawn the knot, already formed, into such a degree of tightness, that the umbili-cal vessels were entirely compressed; for when the knot was loosened out, all that part of the navel string which was taken into the knot was quite flattened." (Vol. xiii. § 1306.)

[123] One of the most remarkable cases of extreme pelvic deformity from mollities ossium is described by Professor Naegelé in his Erfahrungen und Abhandlungen. The patient was the mother of six living children when she was attacked with the disease: the seventh, after great difficulty, was born dead, and the eighth was delivered by the Cæsarean operation, which proved fatal. The spine was pressed so downwards, that the third lumbar vertebra was opposite to the superior edge of the symphysis pubis; the distance of the left ramus of the pubes from the fourth lum-bar vertebra was only 2½ lines; the transverse diameter of the inferior aperture only 1 inch 9 lines. For the farther details of this interesting case we may refer to our published lectures on this subject. A similar and highly interesting case has been recorded by Mr. Cooper, and communicated by Dr. Hunter in the Medical Observations and Inquiries, vol. v. The patient's first three labours were rather easy; in the beginning of her fourth pregnancy she had a violent rheumatic fever, which continued about six weeks; from this time she never enjoyed good health and suffered constantly from rheumatic pains over her whole body: these were followed by laborious respiration, and gradual distortion of spine: her fourth labour was accomplished with much difficulty. During her fifth pregnancy the distortion continued to increase. In her sixth and seventh labours the pelvis was found much contracted, so much so in the last as to require perforation. In her eighth labour the pelvis then appeared to be somewhat less than 2½ inches from the

symphysis of the ossa pubis to the superior and projecting part of the os sacrum, and otherwise badly formed. Embryotomy was again performed. She had become much more deformed and helpless, but in three years afterwards she was again pregnant. "She now appeared to be little more than an unwieldy lump of living flesh." The antero-posterior diameter was now only 1¼ inch, becoming gradually narrower at each side. The Cæsarean operation was performed with a fatal result. On examination after death, the rami of the ischium were found "little more than half an inch asunder."

[124] [A second case has been recorded by Dr. Schultzen, see American Jour. Med. Sc. July 1841, p. 238.—Ed.]

[125] "Mechanical obstruction to the progress of labour, is sometimes thus fatiguing the woman with continual walking. I have known the whole of the cellular substance lining the pelvis so much distended by œdematous tumefaction, as to make the pelvis greatly narrowed in its capacity, which repose for some hours has diminished, or entirely removed." (Merriman's Synopsis, p. 18. last edit.)

[126] Mr. Barlow has attempted to form a synoptical table of pelvic distortion. Thus, he says, where the antero-posterior diameter of the brim is from 5 to 4 inches, delivery can be effected by the efforts of nature alone; where from 4 to 3 or 2¾ inches, delivery may take place by the efforts of nature, or assisted by the crotchet, or lever; from 2¾ to 2½ inches, it requires artificial premature delivery; from 2½ to 1½ inches, embryulcia; and from 1½ inch to the lowest possible degree of distortion, the Cæsarean operation.

[127] For many of the above observations we are indebted to an admirable article upon the subject by our friend, Professor Naegelé, jun., in the Medicenischen Annalen, band ii. heft 2.

[128] Dr. Merriman has detailed two interesting cases, which were terminated by the natural powers. In the first (p. 59,) the patient died afterwards, a small laceration having taken place in the vagina; the other appears to have arisen from an unruptured state of the hymen, which was of unusual thickness; (see Appendix II.) The case did well.

[129] For much valuable information on this subject, as also for several interesting cases, we gladly refer to Facts and Cases in Obstetric Medicine, by our friend Mr. Ingleby, of Birmingham; a practical work of great value.

[130] [The following very singular case of tumour of the pelvis is recorded by Professor D'Outrepont, of Würtzburg.

A woman, twenty-six years old and well made, gave birth when twenty-five years of age to her first child without difficulty. Towards the end of her second pregnancy she again applied at the hospital in consequence of experiencing pain in the pelvic region. Vaginal examination discovered a hard and painful tumour, extending from the inner surface of the left ischium nearly to the corresponding point on the opposite side. It was hard, globular, even on its surface, and occupied the ascending ramus of the ischium and the descending ramus of the pubis, and extended over the obturator foramen. It was impossible to reach the lower segment of the uterus, or to feel any part of the child.

The size and hardness of the tumour seemed to leave no chance of the birth of a living child, even by the induction of premature labour. Professor D'Outrepont, who doubted whether the tumour was fibro-cartilaginous, or a true bony exostosis, asked the opinion of many eminent men who saw the case. They did not express themselves with certainty as to its nature, and the patient refused to allow an experimental incision to be made into the tumour.

A short time before labour began, the tumour was thought to have become slightly compressible. When labour commenced, the professor called a consultation in which it was determined that unless a great change had taken place in the character of the tumour, an attempt should be made to remove it, or to cut away the bone if that should be found to be implicated, and as a last resource, to perform the Cæsarean section.

On an examination being made, the right foot of the child was found to present, the cord was prolapsed, and did not pulsate. The tumour, however, was found to be so much softened that it was possible to pass three fingers through the outlet of the pelvis. Professor D'Outrepont brought down the foot, in doing which, he found that the hips had compressed the tumour still more. The chief difficulty was experienced in extracting the head by means of the forceps, which gave the patient considerable pain. The child was still-born, but was speedily recovered. After the birth of the child, the tumour regained its former size, so that the placenta could not be expelled by the natural efforts, and it was necessary to introduce the hand in order to remove it.

The patient recovered rapidly, and returned ten weeks after her delivery, in order to have the tumour removed, which operation was performed by Professor Textor. The growth was found to be fibro-cartilaginous, and was connected neither with the bone nor the periosteum. It weighed 11½ ounces, and was so hard that none but they who were present at the patient's delivery, could have believed its previous softening possible. The patient was completely cured.—Ed.]

[131] A sudden drink of cold fluid will generally excite contractions of the uterus, owing to the close sympathy which exists between it and the stomach. A couple of ounces, at most, will be sufficient for this purpose, if swallowed quickly; a larger quantity not only fails of its effect, by oppressing the stomach, but, by filling it with fluid, renders almost inert any stimuli or medicines which may afterwards be required.

[132] "Cold injections," says Dr. Young, "should be thrown into the uterus, and repeated ten or twelve times; as on this the success depends." (MS. Lectures.)

[133] Essay on Inversion of the Uterus. Dublin Journal for September and November, 1837, quoted by Dr. Churchill on Diseases of Females, p. 317.

[134] Midwifery Hospital Reports. Med. Gazette, May 31, 1834; also Aug. 26, 1837.

[135] "I have reason to believe that a placenta which is entire and uninjured, which is enclosed in the uterus, adherent to it, and shut out from access of air, never becomes putrid." (Matthias Saxtorph, Gesamm. Schriften.)

[136] [An interesting memoir on retained placenta, by Dr. Edward Warren, of Boston, will be found in the American Journal of Med. Sc. May, 1840, p. 71.—Ed.]

[137] Dr. Churchill observes, "I have found, in several cases of prolapse, that the placenta was situated low down on the side of the uterus, and in some few others that the funis was inserted into the lower edge of the placenta." (Edin. Med. and Surg. Journal, Oct., 1838.)

[138] [Dr. Churchill in his Researches on Operative Midwifery, subsequently published, has collected the results of 92,017 deliveries, in which there was prolapse of the cord, in 333 cases, or 1 in every 276□.—Ed.]

[139] [A figure of this instrument is given in Dewees' Midwifery, Pl. XVIII. and the method of using it fully described.—Ed.]

[140] In the edition which has been translated into English, a. d. 1612, it is the twelfth chapter.

[141] We subjoin the passages to which we have referred in the three above mentioned cases:—

Case 115. "I cannot implicitly accede to the opinion of roost writers in midwifery, which is, that the placenta always adheres to the fundus uteri; for in this, as well as many former instances, I have good reason to believe that it sometimes adheres to or near the os internum, and that the opening of it occasions a separation, and consequently a flooding."

Case 116. "The first thing I met with was the placenta, which I found closely adhering round the os internum of the uterus, which, among other things, is a proof that the placenta is not always fixed to the bottom of the uterus, according to the opinion of some writers in midwifery. Its adhering to the os internum was, in my opinion, the occasion of the flooding; for as the os internum was gradually dilated, the placenta at the same time was separated, from whence proceeded the effusion of blood."

Case 224. "It is generally believed that the ovum, after its impregnation and separation from the ovarium, and its passing through the tuba Fallopiana, always adheres, and is fixed, after some time, to the fundus uteri; in this case the placenta adhered, and was fixed close to and round about the cervix uteri, as I have found it in many other cases, so that upon a dilatation of the os uteri a separation has always followed, and hence a flooding naturally ensues."

[142] The second edition of Rœderer's admirable Elementa Artis Obstetriciæ, which was published by his distinguished successor, Wrisberg, in 1766, three years after his death, is that which is chiefly known, although it never

had an extensive circulation in this country. The means of communication with the Continent at that time were very different to what they are at present; and although none can regret more than ourselves that Rœderer's work should have passed unnoticed in Dr. Rigby's Essay on Uterine Hæmorrhage, still we feel assured that the liberal portion of the medical world, whether in this or other countries, will not attribute this omission to a disingenuous suppression of his name, but rather to the more probable circumstances that, residing in a provincial town, and actively engaged in the arduous duties of an extensive country practice, Dr. Rigby had not enjoyed an opportunity of consulting the work; at any rate, we have good reasons to know that he never possessed it.

[143] Not 1776, as stated by Dr. R. Lee.

[144] Dr. Merriman has also recorded three cases of this kind, one of which occurred to himself; in this case "the placenta was expelled many hours before the child was born;" the mother died from puerperal fever.

[145] [A very interesting account of puerperal peritonitis, as it prevailed in the Pennsylvania Hospital in 1833, is given by Professor H. L. Hodge, in the American Journal Med. Sc., for August, 1833, p. 325, et seq.—Ed.]

[146] This condition of parts bore the closest analogy to the state of the cellular membrane, so constantly observed in fatal cases of phlegmonoid erysipelas, or diffuse cellular inflammation.

[147] [The student may consult, with advantage, Dr. Dewees's chapter on Phlegmasia Dolens, in his "Treatise on the Diseases of Females," also the observations of Dr. Mann, in the "Massachusetts Medical Communications," vol. ii., and the interesting paper, by Professor Walter Channing, in the same work, vol. v. p. 46.—Editor.]

Lightning Source UK Ltd.
Milton Keynes UK
UKOW011830160513

210805UK00007B/391/P

9 781486 438273